BAL A LA FRANCOISE

MENUET DE L'EXILIBOURG

ALMANACH ROYAL POUR L'ANNEE M DC LXXXII

Portraits

around

Marc-Antoine

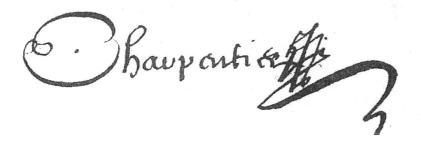

Patricia M. Ranum

Dux Femina Facti
2004

The text of this book is composed in
Goudy Old Style. Composition by the
author. Manufacturing by Sheridan
Books, Inc.
Printed on acid-free paper.

ISBN 0-9660997-3-7

Distributed by the author:
Patricia M. Ranum
208 Ridgewood Road
Baltimore MD., 21210
        U.S.A.
        or:
www.ranum.com/pmr

CONTENTS

ILLUSTRATIONS

PREFACE

Marc-Antoine Charpentier knew, or knew about, all the sitters in this imaginary portrait gallery. During my long pursuit of the composer in European archives and libraries, these same individuals have become my friends—although I confess to feeling less sympathy for some than for others. I never succeeded in unveiling Charpentier the Man, whom I consider my very closest seventeenth-century friend. Yet I could not leave my research papers to yellow in file drawers and force other scholars to retrace my steps and go down the blind alleys along which I made my frustrated way.

For close to two decades I have been making categorical statements about Charpentier and the Guises; but although I backed up these assertions with elaborate footnotes, no coherent picture emerged of the complex social relations of protection within which the composer worked. Hence this book.

For lack of space, I do not cite even the most basic books and articles here. Nor do I take current scholarship about the composer and his works into account. Rather, I have constructed my portraits from historical evidence alone—complemented here and there, in the endnotes, with articles that provide additional factual information. I consciously avoided repeating materials in the original edition of Catherine Cessac's indispensable *Marc-Antoine Charpentier*. Indeed, my portrait gallery is intended as a complement to her book, over whose forthcoming revised edition I rejoice.

I am refraining from naming the many people who helped me during those two decades. Over time some of the little slips with names and addresses have been misfiled; mentioning the generous individuals whose names I remember would be patently unfair to those whose names escape me. Thus I extend here a thank-you to everyone who came to my assistance—in Paris, in Baltimore, in Washington D.C., in Versailles, in Rodez, in Aix, in Rome, in Florence, in Mantua, in Turin, in Stockholm, in London, and in Munich.

Patricia M. Ranum
Baltimore, Maryland
January 1, 2004

Monsieur Charpentier.

In the foreground of Landry's large Almanac for 1682, entitled *Bal a la Françoise*, "French-style ball," Monsieur Charpentier presents a signed copy of the *Menuet de Strasbourg* to Madame de Guise, one of the few women in the realm whose rank permitted her to occupy a side chair in the King's presence. The young woman standing behind Her Royal Highness is probably Marguerite Pièche, a soprano, *dessus*, in the Dauphin's Music.

Introduction

THE PORTRAIT GALLERY

"No man is an island unto himself...." John Donne

A ray of sun penetrates the darkest corner of the gallery, illuminating panels of portraits from the seventeenth century. There are two abbesses with jeweled crosiers, ladies and gentlemen in rich court dress, Jesuits with their distinctive birettas, an actor with a flour-daubed face, a bewigged gentleman with sparkling eyes, a dancing master holding a violin, several modestly dressed women wearing white coifs, a group portrait of black-garbed officials, an elderly man sitting at his writing table . . . .

These portraits surround an empty frame. In the place of the missing portrait, someone has tacked part of Pierre Landy's engraved Almanac for 1682, where "Monsieur Charpentier" offers a signed composition to a seated noblewoman, as members of the royal court dance in the background. This schematic portrait surely represents the same "Monsieur Charpentier" who was mentioned in the *Mercure galant* during the 1670s and 1680s, composing for the Dauphin, for the Jesuits, or for the lofty princess known as "Mademoiselle de Guise."

Visitors strolling through this gallery usually keep their eyes glued to the portraits that line the wall. When they reach the fragment cut from the Almanac, they tend to pause, frown, and then move on, often wondering aloud: "What is *that* doing in the midst of so many fine paintings? There must a better portrait of Monsieur Charpentier!"

They do not realize it, but another, far more revealing portrait of Marc-Antoine Charpentier has survived. Beneath these portraits stands a gilded console piled high with twenty-eight blue-green folio volumes containing autograph copies of the composer's works, plus several smaller volumes and bundles of papers in the same hand. In a sense, these volumes are the portrait of Charpentier. They are his biography too, for they are arranged chronologically and are relatively complete for the period 1670–1698.

The contents of these manuscripts and the few known facts about the composer's life have not yet been assembled into a coherent whole. But it is not for want of trying. As with a jig-saw puzzle for which the illustration on the box has been lost, twentieth-century scholars began by connecting the border pieces that form the frame of Charpentier's portrait, of Charpentier's life. Early on they knew, for example, that the composer's career took him from Mademoiselle de Guise, to the theater, to the Dauphin, to the Jesuits, and finally to the Sainte-Chapelle. Inner pieces of the puzzle were subsequently joined together into large or small clusters, but it is not always clear where those clusters fit into the puzzle as a whole. For example, where do Charpentier's family and close friends, or the Guises, or the fathers of the Mercy, or Monsieur de Riants, or the Duke of Richelieu fit into the broader picture? And why did he write so many pieces for devotions to the Virgin and the Infant Jesus?

For there is a broader picture and more precise picture. A picture that suggests why Charpentier was singled out by the Guises; why the Jesuits, Molière, Riants, and members of the royal family approached him with commissions; and why he composed what he did.

By now it is unlikely that the answers to the questions that scholars are asking will turn up in correspondence hidden away in someone's attic. To know why Charpentier composed what he did, we must scrutinize the lives of the people whose portraits surround the engraving of "Monsieur Charpentier." In the France of Louis XIV, no composer could be an island unto himself. His livelihood depended upon the friends and protectors who surrounded him, supported him in time of trouble, and were ready to recommend him to a friend—as long as that friend was not likely to make off with their treasured protégé. Each portrait hanging in this gallery depicts an individual or a group that was part of the exceedingly complex network that shaped the career of Marc-Antoine Charpentier.

Network—rather, "web," as in a spider's web. When a ray of sun breaks through and illuminates the portrait gallery, shimmering gossamer threads can be seen reaching from one portrait to another. From the portrait of an abbess a thread stretches to the engraving of Monsieur Charpentier. The group portrait of four Jesuits is connected by a thin but resilient strand to the portraits of Marie Talon, Françoise Ferrand, and Mademoiselle de Guise. Threads run from the portrait of Riants to the paintings of Marie Talon and Mademoiselle Marie de Guise. And on and on, forming a vast web of shared experiences and memories.

Should the sun go behind a cloud, these threads can be recognized and followed, for each has left a mark on the portrait, has changed the type in which one or more names are set. That is to say, SMALL CAPITAL LETTERS refer the reader to another portrait in the gallery, where he will find additional information or will view a given event from that individual's point of view. SMALL CAPITALS also suggest, visually, the extent to which the people or the families in this gallery were interlocked over years, decades, generations. The greater the number of SMALL CAPITALS in a portrait, the greater the number of shimmering threads leading out from that portrait to others.

The manuscripts piled on the gilded console are not linked to the portraits by threads. Just as the autograph manuscripts stand *beneath* the portraits, footnotes beneath the text suggest a link between a piece in one of the composer's notebooks and an event in the life of that individual. The distinction between the arabic-numbered manuscript notebooks and the roman-numbered ones is crucial; for, as I have long argued, the former clearly represent the composer's "ordinary" musical creations, and the latter contain his "extraordinary" musical commissions.

Portraits

around

Marc-Antoine Charpentier

Panel 1

THE CHARPENTIERS OF MEAUX

The Point of Departure

Seven faded family portraits hang in this panel. Most of them date from the late sixteenth century. Seven paintings of men in black, some working in their shops, some seated at writing tables, some proudly carrying the staff of a bailiff-sergeant in the judicial administration of Meaux.

In one portrait a priest peers out from the background. In another, a woman in somber dress can be glimpsed through a door, measuring out linen cloth for a customer.

These are Marc-Antoine Charpentier's industrious, hopeful, but not always fortunate provincial ancestors—his grandparents, his great-uncles, his cousins. These are the upward-striving roots from which the Charpentiers of Paris budded.

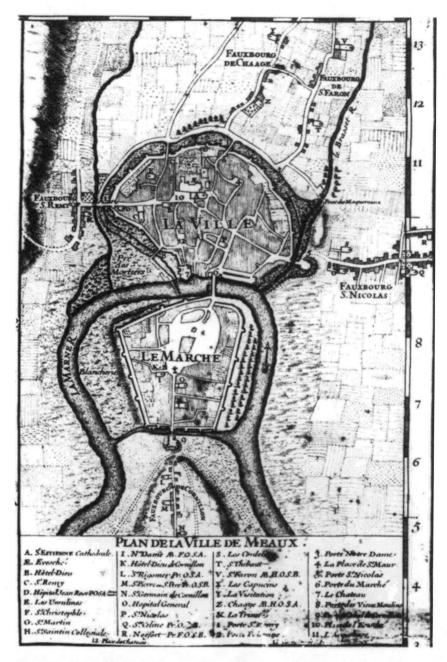

PLAN DE LA VILLE DE MEAUX.

The city of Meaux in the seventeenth century.
The walled city, *ville*, is situated upon a hill. In its very center are the cathedral and the bishop's palace. Pasquier Charpentier the Measurer and his family resided in the parish of Saint-Rémy, to the left of the cathedral close. Louis the Bailiff and his family lived at Châge, outside the walls, at the top of the map. The Great Market, *marché*, was reached by a bridge lined with mills that spanned the Marne.

I

The pater familias: Taught to live as a Catholic

DENIS THE TAWER

Denis Charpentier, *maître mégissier* of Meaux
the composer's great-grandfather

By 1500 the Charpentier family had left the land and had moved to the cathedral city of Meaux in Brie. There they earned their livelihood tanning leather and making gloves or shoes. In 1560 Nicolas Charpentier, a glove-maker, apprenticed his fatherless grandson, Denis Charpentier, to a *mégissier*, that is, a tawer of leather, a skin-dresser.[1] The elderly glove-maker was accompanied that day by Denis' stepfather, Nicolas Pasquier. It is significant that during these years when Protestantism was taking root at Meaux, the youth's master promised to "teach him to live as a Catholic."

If the Charpentiers had owned property in the surrounding countryside, it had long since been sold. Nor, it seems, were they affluent enough to acquire much real estate in Meaux. Over the years Denis signed acts involving land, essentially vineyards located at Coulommes, due south of Meaux; but they were his wife's property, not his.[2]

When Denis Charpentier the Tawer wed Geneviève Soudain, a young widow, circa 1571, he apparently brought little to the household beyond the thirty livres due him from the sale of a house that his glove-making grandfather had sold to Denis' saddle-maker uncle a decade earlier. His contribution to the household economy would be his ability to run the business of Geneviève Soudain's late husband, Antoine Esmerault, also a tawer, and his willingness to raise the two little girls born during her brief marriage.

Denis Charpentier's wife came from a family that was turning its back on trade, in favor of record-keeping. Geneviève's late father had been a royal notary at Meaux until his premature death in 1556; and her brother, a practitioner or legal clerk, *praticien*, was being prepared for that profession or for a related one. Despite the notary's early death, the Soudains had been able to retain their inheritances in the countryside, especially the vines and other land at Coulommes.

The events of August 1572 can scarcely have left Denis the Tawer and his bride unmoved. On August 23 news of the Saint Bartholomew's Day Massacre in Paris reached Meaux.[3] The next day the city gates were locked, the principal Huguenots arrested. Then, one after another, the prisoners were freed; and as they emerged from the building, they were dispatched by daggers, swords, and halberds wielded by the Catholic faction. Among those massacred were Guy Blondel, Geneviève Soudain's maternal uncle, and Quentin Croyer, whose son, DAVID CROYER, would one day marry into the Charpentier family. Although Denis Charpentier had presumably been raised as a Catholic, the sources reveal nothing about whether Geneviève Soudain was a Protestant or a Catholic.

In 1578 Meaux declared for the Catholic League and the Guises. By the early 1580s, the so-called "white processions" had begun. Chanting partisans of the League, garbed in white and carrying crosses and torches, would thread their way through the streets of the city and move out into nearby villages. The fervor of these processions intensified after the assassination of the Guise brothers in December 1588. A few months later, Denis the Tawer came down strongly on the Catholic side. On March 22, 1589, he swore to support the Holy Union, thereby avoiding the fines and confiscations to which "heretics" and non-Leaguers were being subjected. Not until December 24, 1593, did the Leaguers of Meaux offer their obedience to Henri IV.

During this turmoil, in 1588, a marriage was celebrated in the Catholic church of Saint-Nicolas. One of Denis Charpentier's stepdaughters, Magdaleine Esmerault (she signed her name "Emeraude"), wed PASQUIER CHARPENTIER, whose family had moved to Meaux from Chambry, a village north of the city. Like his father, Pasquier was a charcoal-measurer. This marriage created a family tree with two branches named *Charpentier* or *Charpentyer*, Pasquier's branch having been grafted, by marriage, upon the trunk from which Denis the Tawer had sprung. In notarial documents Pasquier described himself as the *beau-frère*[4] of Denis' three children, a term that could denote either a stepbrother or a brother-in-law. Both translations accurately describe Pasquier's relationship to Denis the Tawer's offspring: he was perceived as a brother, and his children were affectively as close to Denis' descendants as any blood relative could be.

By 1603 Denis the Tawer's two sons had reached majority and were seeking brides. With his father's help the older son, LOUIS CHARPENTIER THE BAILIFF, acquired the office of royal bailiff and sergeant, that is, he became a staff-carrying police officer in the bailliage of Meaux. When Denis' younger son, NICOLAS CHARPENTIER THE SERGEANT, wed in 1606, Denis purchased the same sort of office for him. (Since marriage and the acquisition of an office generally coincided with a young man's twenty-fifth birthday, the age of majority, it is likely that Louis was born circa 1577 and Nicolas in about 1581.)

These purchases apparently emptied Denis the Tawer's purse. His daughter, Agnès Charpentier, worked as a domestic and eventually married a widowed shoe-repairer. Her employer gave her 100 livres for her dowry, to compensate for the wages not paid during her years of service to him.[5] Denis the Tawer died at the Hôtel-Dieu of Meaux in 1611. No inventory of his possessions was drawn up, apparently because they were so minimal.

If NICOLAS THE SERGEANT, his son, dreamed of upward social mobility for his children, his hopes were dashed. His son Robert would become a grand chaplain at the cathedral of Meaux, but his other sons would become shoemakers, and one of his daughters would wed a tawer. LOUIS THE BAILIFF, the other son, did not fare much better. He survived his father by only a year or so; and, as was so often the case, his death appears to have left his widow in diminished circumstances.

II

The grandfather: He left her a widow with three young sons

LOUIS THE BAILIFF

Louis Charpentier, *huissier sergent royal* at Meaux,
and Anne Broquoys, *lingère*, his wife,
the composer's grandparents

On October 6, 1590, Louis ("Loys") Charpentier, the adolescent son of DENIS CHARPENTIER THE TAWER, stood as one of the two godfathers of a child born to PASQUIER CHARPENTIER THE MEASURER and Magdeleine Esmerault, Denis' stepdaughter. The infant being baptized was Louis' nephew, Jacques Charpentier, known in this portrait gallery as JACQUES THE NOTARY. Although Louis and his godson were both named *Charpentier* or *Charpentyer*, none of DENIS THE TAWER'S blood flowed in the child's veins. Jacques was Louis' nephew, through the Soudain– Esmerault bloodline, not the Charpentiers.

Evidence from notarial acts and parish records[1] suggests that Louis Charpentier was born between early 1573 and late 1579. Within those six years, a birth date between 1573 and 1575 seems likely. In short, at the time of the baptism, he was approximately fifteen years old.

This baptismal record is the oldest known document naming Marc-Antoine Charpentier's paternal grandfather. No record of Louis' marriage has been found in the archives for Meaux, although a few documents signed by him have survived.[2] He is mentioned in the marriage contract of his younger brother, NICOLAS THE SERGEANT. On that day in 1606, DENIS THE TAWER and his wife promised to "pay, furnish and deliver to the aforesaid Nicolas, their son, a comparable and similar marriage to the one they had paid, or had promised to pay, to Louis Charpentier, their son, upon his marriage with Anne Broquoys, his wife, and to make the two sons equal and each receiving the same advantages as the other."

6

In other words, Louis had married before 1606, probably in 1603 or 1604 when he became major; and to assure his betterment, the parents had purchased for him the office of bailiff and royal sergeant in the presidial and bailliage of Meaux—or were perhaps were negotiating such a purchase. Louis the Bailiff, now a lower-level member of the judicial system, could be dispatched by his superiors to give notification of a decision, bring in a wanted person, or confiscate property and keep a record of the items seized. A bailiff's functions were similar to those of a sergeant, hence the fusion of the two functions in a single purchased office.

Anne Broquoys was not a native of Meaux. The Broquoys came from Neuilly-en-Thelle, a village situated south of Beauvais, just a short walk from the hamlet where the grandfather of royal painter CHARLES LE BRUN had been born. Her brother, Jean Broquoys, had initially been a tailor in Paris; but by 1598 he and his wife had moved to Meaux, where Jean became concierge of the cathedral close.[3]

A Parisienne who was a linener[4] and settled in Meaux. How did Anne Broquoys' and Louis Charpentier's paths cross? Three scenarios can be constructed to account for their marriage. The first two are simple; the third one, considerably more complex, is suggested by the conduct and aspirations of Louis Charpentier's close relatives. (For each scenario, it is assumed that the couple wed in about 1599 or 1600, when the groom was approximately twenty-five years old.)

The simpler scenarios go as follows. Scenario 1: The marriage was arranged by the Charpentiers' Parisian cousins, Monsieur and Madame DAVID CROYER, and Anne and Louis did not set eyes on one another until the bride arrived in Meaux. Scenario 2: Shortly after her brother Jean's move to Meaux, Anne Broquoys paid him a visit, met Louis Charpentier, and married him.

Scenario 3 is suggested by the family politics that shaped the professional training that PASQUIER THE MEASURER arranged for his son Jean, and the analogous training given Pasquier's grandson, GILLES CHARPENTIER THE SECRETARY. In 1628 twenty-three-year-old Jean Charpentier became a *huissier sergent à cheval* at the CHÂTELET of Paris, that is, a mounted bailiff-sergeant, an office that permitted him to exercise his functions anywhere in the realm. Jean therefore presumably spent some months or years in Paris, where his paternal aunt, Suzanne Charpentier, the wife of DAVID CROYER, was living. This conjecture is strengthened by the fact that Madame Croyer advanced a large share of the purchase price of the office. Then, in 1639, Pasquier's son, JACQUES THE NOTARY, arranged to have his son study in Paris with a procurator, that is, a venal official who guided litigants through the legal system and acted on their behalf. The young man would be watched over by one of the Croyers' sons-in-law and would be "treated like a brother."

In sum, it is conceivable that Pasquier Charpentier's half-brother, Louis the Bailiff, likewise spent some time training in Paris, where he met (and perhaps married) Anne Broquoys. Hence the absence of a marriage contract in the notarial archives of Meaux. This period of study could have taken place at any time after the Croyers' move to Paris in 1594. Since Louis can scarcely have been born before 1573, he would have been in his early twenties in about 1595, just the age when finding a bride and purchasing an office were looming on the horizon.

The differences between the first two scenarios, and the third one, are the differences between the experiences and viewpoint of a person who never left Meaux and its environs, and those of an individual who had some familiarity with Paris. In other words, did Louis Charpentier visit the capital and become acquainted with his Parisian cousins and their friends in the CHÂTELET? Or did he spend his entire life in Meaux, exchanging occasional polite letters with cousins he barely knew, and struggling to imagine the amazing buildings and the busy streets that his wife described to him before the fire on a winter evening?

Whichever scenario should prove correct, by 1601 or 1602 Louis and his wife had set up housekeeping in Meaux, where Louis was now a royal bailiff. Oddly enough, he did not sign his brother Nicolas' wedding contract in 1606, although the document bears the signature of PASQUIER THE MEASURER, the groom's "brother-in-law."

The surviving parish records for Meaux mention the baptisms of several children born to Louis the Bailiff and Anne Broquoys. These records suggest that the couple initially lived within the city walls, then moved to the suburbs in about 1610. It is, of course, possible that they were residing in the suburban parish of Châge all the while, but that— owing to the lack of a parish priest at Notre-Dame de Châge between April 19, 1603, and May 17, 1609—their infants were baptized within the city walls, perhaps at Saint-Rémy, the parish of Pasquier the Measurer and his family.

One of Louis' sons, PIERRE THE CHAPLAIN, was in fact baptized at Saint-Rémy on June 13, 1604, as was his daughter Perrette on November 6, 1608. By contrast, another son, ÉTIENNE THE PRACTITIONER, was christened in the church of Châge on October 9, 1611, which now had a resident priest. Although the records of Saint-Rémy are almost intact for 1601–1610, they do not mention of the birth of LOUIS THE SCRIVENER, Marc-Antoine Charpentier's father. This suggests that Louis was the couple's oldest surviving child, born between November 10, 1600, and

August 9, 1601, a nine-month period for which the records of Saint-Rémy have been lost.

Louis Charpentier died in his late thirties, probably between October 1611 and June 1613, leaving Anne Broquoys with at least three minor children to raise. During the months that followed her husband's death, Anne clearly needed money. On June 17, 1613, the "widow of Louys Charpantier [sic], during his lifetime baillif in the bailliage of Meaux," sold to her Parisian relatives some land at Neuilly-en-Thelle that she had inherited from her father, in return for seventy-eight livres.[5] (In 1624 she was able to buy back this property for that exact sum, in what amounted to repayment of an interest-free loan that her relatives had made to the young widow a decade earlier, with the property as collateral.) Anne Broquoys sold linens from a shop on the rue de la Halle,[6] near the cathedral, but it is not clear whether she opened her business immediately after her arrival in Meaux, or during the straitened times that followed her husband's death.

By the 1630s Anne Broquoys' name had disappeared from the surviving notarial files and parish records for Meaux. She was not mentioned in the will of her grandmother, who had moved to Meaux to be near Jean Broquoys and his family.[7]

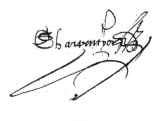

III

The great-uncle: His children returned to leather

NICOLAS THE SERGEANT

Nicolas Charpentier, *sergent royal* at Meaux,
the brother of Louis the Bailiff

D ENIS THE TAWER's marriage to Geneviève Soudain produced three
children who survived to adulthood and whom the sources
describe as the "brothers" and the "sister" of PASQUIER CHARPEN-
TIER THE MEASURER and his wife. Two of the children were boys: LOUIS
CHARPENTIER THE BAILIFF and Nicolas Charpentier, born circa 1580.

By 1597 Nicolas had become a clerk[1]; but he was a "preceptor,"
précepteur, in 1606, when he wed Françoise Dubois, a tawer's widow.[2] In
other words, as a late adolescent Nicolas was copying records for a notary
or a municipal official, and he subsequently taught reading, writing, and
arithmetic to the sons of one of the notables of Meaux, biding his time
until an office of bailiff or sergeant came on the market. Although
evidence is lacking about the education of his brother, Louis the Bailiff,
it is likely that Nicolas was more or less following in his elder's steps, as
he prepared to leave commerce for the world of offices and recordkeeping. Indeed, at the time of Nicolas' marriage to Françoise Dubois, his
parents promised to give him the exact amount of money they had given
LOUIS THE BAILIFF when he wed Anne Broquoys.

Nicolas evidently used the money to acquire the office of royal
sergeant, as his older brother had, winning for him the sobriquet in this
portrait gallery: "Nicolas the Sergeant." His parents' attempt to ensure his
betterment was to no avail. In 1660 the late Sergeant's daughter Jeanne
married a tawer,[3] not an office holder. Two of Nicolas' four sons were
earning their living as shoemakers, while a second daughter, Marie, had
remained a spinster, surely for lack of a dowry. Another son, Robert, had
been ordained as a priest and would become sacristan and churchwarden
at the cathedral. The latter position gave him considerable power: he set

the rates for pew rental; supervised burials; accepted legacies from benefactors; named the chanter, beadles, and bell-ringers; and selected the preachers for Advent and Lent. Robert eventually became a grand chaplain. Yet another son, Jean, seems to have been preparing for the same vocation, for he was "living at the Seminary" in 1660.

Jeanne Charpentier's wedding contract of June 1660 reveals that—a mere six months before the death of Marc-Antoine Charpentier's father, LOUIS CHARPENTIER THE SCRIVENER—the members of the two branches of the Charpentier family tree were still very close. In addition to the bride's brothers and sisters, the witnesses included Louis the Bailiff's son, PIERRE CHARPENTIER THE CHAPLAIN, "priest and grand chaplain" of the cathedral. Also present was Pasquier the Measurer's grandson, GILLES CHARPENTIER THE SECRETARY. He described himself as the bride's "cousin born of first cousins," a term that implies a closer blood relation than actually existed. Gilles' use of this term suggests the strong affective ties that continued to bind the offspring of the two sixteenth-century Charpentiers, DENIS THE TAWER and PASQUIER THE MEASURER.

At first glance, the Charpentiers who assembled to sign this and other notarial contracts form a modest, hard-working, yet rather impecunious clan who attempted to enter the social stratum of officeholders, but failed for reasons that are not understood, although the premature deaths of Louis the Bailiff and Nicolas the Sergeant surely were a factor.

Two figures standing in the shadowy background of this family portrait belie this first impression. Their names are Perrette Cosset (she was the wife of François Musnier, a provincial comptroller for war) and Jean Cosset, her brother. By her will of June 1641, Perrette Cosset made bequests to two of Nicolas the Sergeant's sons: thirty-six livres went to Jean, "in consideration of the services he has rendered," and twenty-four to Charles, "to help him became a master shoemaker."[4] On the surface, these modest gifts, sandwiched between a bequest to Perrette's godson and another to the paupers of Meaux, appear to be an old woman's charity toward needy young people who have done chores for her.

That clearly was not the case. Perrette and Jean Cosset (the children of Nicolas Cosset) were very old friends of PASQUIER THE MEASURER. In 1609, Jean Cosset and François Musnier, "friends" of the bride, signed the wedding contract of Nicolas Brion and Marie Charpentier, the Measurer's daughter.[5] (The document was also signed by LOUIS THE BAILIFF and Nicolas the Sergeant.) A few years later, Jean Cosset witnessed the transactions by which a notary's cabinet was acquired by Pasquier's son, JACQUES THE NOTARY[6]; and later still, he signed the wedding contract of

Pasquier's niece.[7] François Musnier's presence at the Brion wedding seems to be explained by the fact that his wife was Perrette Cosset.

Is there an explanation for this longtime link between the Cossets and the two apparently unrelated Charpentier families that fused to form the Charpentier family tree in the 1580s? An explanation that goes beyond a master–servant relationship or solidarity within a parish? There is indeed. The records for the parish of Saint-Rémy reveal just how old this link was. In the 1580s, various Croyers, Le Roys, Cossets, and Cousinets—all of them officers in the presidial or councillors in the election of Meaux—were standing as godparents for one another's children.[8]

The Cossets' strong affection for the Charpentiers may have had effects that went far beyond a notarial act, an engagement ceremony, a testament. Indeed, Perrette's testament is suggestive of crucial links between Meaux and Paris. Among her heirs were Roland Cosset, a judge at Meaux. It so happens that in 1656, some fifteen years after Perrette's death, Roland Cosset asked Marie Séguier de Boisdauphin de Laval to be the godmother of his child. This eminent woman was Chancellor Pierre Séguier's elder daughter; and at the time of the baptism, Pasquier the Measurer's great-nephew, CHARLES SEVIN, happened to be one of the principal aides to the Chancellor's other daughter, Charlotte. In other words, it is quite possible that the Charpentiers of Meaux, and their Parisian cousins as well, benefitted from the Cossets' affective ties to the circle around the Chancellor of France. In fact, not long after the baptism of 1656, Chancellor Pierre Séguier would protect GILLES CHARPENTIER THE SECRETARY from prosecution.

The closeness of the blood ties has not been determined between Marie Chalmot, the wife of ÉTIENNE THE PRACTITIONER (Marc-Antoine's paternal uncle) and the Chalmot girl who, in 1616, wed Nicolas Charpentier, a royal councillor in the election of Meaux and a member of a prestigious office-holding family.[9] It does however appear that Étienne Charpentier wed the humbler relative of one of the most notable families of Meaux. The prestigious Chalmots not only belonged to the same circle as the Cossets, they had married into the same families as the Cossets. For example, among their in-laws were Louis Royer (a close relative of Gilles Royer, the godfather of GILLES CHARPENTIER THE SECRETARY), Roland Cosset, Isaac Le Ber, and Pierre Musnier. (These same individuals were selected as godparents by the above official named Nicolas Charpentier whose relationship to the composer's ancestors has not been proved but cannot be ruled out.)

Collective memories of reciprocal gestures of support and friendship across the decades may explain why, in 1642, a member of this elite, Isaac

Le Ber, royal councillor and lieutenant general of the bailliage and presidial of Meaux, witnessed the wedding contract of PASQUIER THE MEASURER's great-niece, describing himself as a "friend" of the groom (who, like the bride's father, was a pie-maker and roaster). Le Ber even arranged to have the signing ceremony take place in his residence.

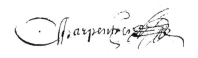

IV

The uncles: In the Church and in the law

PIERRE THE CHAPLAIN AND ÉTIENNE THE PRACTITIONER

Pierre Charpentier, *grand chapelain* at the cathedral of Meaux,
and Étienne Charpentier, *praticien* at Meaux,
the brothers of Louis the Scrivener and
the uncles of the composer

The parish records of Notre-Dame de Châge reveal that three sons
were born to LOUIS CHARPENTIER THE BAILIFF and Anne Broquoys.
One of them, LOUIS THE SCRIVENER, moved to Paris. The other
two remained in Meaux.

Pierre Charpentier

One of these sons was Pierre Charpentier, baptized in the parish
church of Saint-Rémy in 1604. He became a priest and moved up in the
hierarchy of the diocese of Meaux. By 1642 he was described as "venera-
ble and discrete person, Messire Pierre Charpentyer, priest and grand
chaplain of the Chapel of Saints Peter and Paul," at the Cathedral of
Saint-Étienne, a prestigious position that brought with it a sizeable living
and a little house and garden adjacent to the cloister. His unadorned
signature (not reproduced here) is found in the notarial archives of
Meaux, generally as one of the cathedral officials administering houses
owned by the diocese.[1]

As one of six grand chaplains, Pierre worked closely with the bishop
—who, from 1637 to 1659, was Dominique Séguier, Chancellor Pierre
Séguier's brother. Bishop Séguier's successor was his nephew, Dominique
de Ligny, whose sister was Superior at the ABBEY OF PORT-ROYAL and, in
1661, Abbess. These are additional meshes in the broad protective
network involving the Séguier family to which the Charpentiers of Paris
and the Charpentiers who remained in Meaux could turn. That is to say,
CHARLES SEVIN worked for the Chancellor from the mid-1630s into the

1660s; Pierre the Chaplain worked with the Chancellor's brother and nephew from the mid-1630s until 1662; MARIE CHARPENTIER THE CONVERSE, the composer's sister, was admitted to Port-Royal in about 1660 by Mother Ligny, probably without a pension or dowry; and in 1664 Gilles CHARPENTIER THE SECRETARY would be saved from prosecution by Chancellor Séguier himself.

In June 1660 Pierre Charpentier was present when the wedding contract of his first cousin, Jeanne Charpentier, the daughter of the late NICOLAS THE SERGEANT, was signed. Although listed among the witnesses, the Chaplain did not sign the document, in all likelihood prevented from doing so by the failing health that would bring his death a few months later. The bride's brother—Messire Robert Charpentier, "priest and churchwarden" in the cathedral church of Meaux—did however sign the document, as did another brother, Jean Charpentier, "living at the Seminary." A Parisian cousin, GILLES CHARPENTIER THE SECRETARY, came to Meaux for the event.

It is this wedding contract that made it possible to link, with absolute certainty, the Charpentiers of Paris and the Charpentiers of Meaux. One year later, Robert Charpentier would inform ÉTIENNETTE CHARPENTIER that she and her siblings would be receiving approximately one hundred livres from the estate of his late brother Jean, heir of their late uncle, Pierre Charpentier: "... according to a letter written to her by her cousin Sieur Charpentier, priest sacristan of Saint-Étienne of Meaux, since the death of Sieur Charpentier, his brother, there may be due from the late Messire Pierre Charpentier, her late father's brother, whose heir he was, the sum of at least forty écus and some change."[2]

Étienne Charpentier

For lack of evidence, the portrait of Louis the Bailiff's third son, Étienne Charpentier, remains a rough sketch. Aside from the record of his christening in October 1611 at Notre-Dame de Châge, the most meaningful document involving Étienne is the "marriage articles" he signed in February 1648.[3]

When he wed Marie Chalmot, Étienne was a practitioner at Meaux, that is, he knew the practices of the law courts, the formulae they used, and the laws they observed. His elaborate signature, with its paraph, calls to mind the signatures of his father and his uncle Nicolas. Because he was already major, no family member was asked to approve the union and to vouch that the groom would meet his financial obligations. The contract nonetheless bears the signatures of several Charpentiers, all of whom spelled their name *Charpentyer*. There is the signature of the groom himself; there is the signature of NICOLAS THE SERGEANT, the groom's uncle; and at the bottom of the page can be found the signature of Étienne's cousin, JACQUES THE NOTARY, who had drawn up the act.

Eight months later a son, Philippe, was born to Étienne the Practitioner and his wife. The infant's godmother, whose signature was preserved in the baptismal records for Châge, was Marie Charpentier, Nicolas the Sergeant's spinster daughter. (Marie's signature has also survived on the wedding contract of Nicolas' granddaughter, dated 1682.)[4]

V

The granduncle: He provided a link to Paris

PASQUIER THE MEASURER

Pasquier Charpentier, *marchand juré et mesureur de charbon* of Meaux,
Denis the Tawer's son-in-law

Pasquier Charpentier descended from a line of charcoal merchants who had purchased the office of charcoal-measurer. That was the stated activity of his paternal grandfather, Jean Charpentier, in a document dated 1579.[1] The transaction involved a vineyard owned by Jean's wife, Nicole Couppert, located at Chambry, a village due north of Meaux.[2] It is not clear that Jean Charpentier had been brought up at Chambry, but his ancestors clearly came from there. In fact, he descended from another Pasquier Charpentier, a plowman at Chambry, and his wife, Françoise Oudot. The property at Chambry was passed on to the Charpentier offspring, and allusions to it recur in notarial documents well into the 1640s.

Jean Charpentier fathered three children who survived to adulthood. One was Jeanne Charpentier, who married DAVID CROYER in 1587 at Notre-Dame de Châge, just outside the city walls of Meaux, and moved to Paris once the troubles of the League had subsided. Another was Marguerite Charpentier, who that same year, in the parish church of Saint-Rémy, wed Abraham Blanchet, a cloth-seller. And there was Pasquier, who succeeded his father as charcoal-measurer and in 1588 married Magdaleine Esmerault (or "Emeraude"), DENIS THE TAWER's step-daughter, in the parish church of Saint-Nicolas. Marrying in Catholic churches as they did—this despite David Croyer's Protestant origins—the Charpentiers presumably were solidly Catholic during these peak years of the League.

Son of a merchant and owner of the rights to supervise the measuring of his commodity, Pasquier the Measurer was literate and wielded a pen with ease. He had friends in high places, principally Jean Cosset, a councillor in the bailliage and presidial of Meaux, and his sister Perrette, the wife of Nicolas Musnier, a provincial comptroller for war. (Jean Cosset would sign the wedding contracts of Pasquier's daughter and niece, and he would vouch for Pasquier's son, JACQUES THE NOTARY, when he purchased his notarial study in 1614.[3])

Pasquier and his wife, who produced six living children, were quite conventional in the way they prepared them to earn a livelihood. The oldest surviving child, Marie, wed Nicolas Brion, a tawer, in January 1610, thereby consolidating a link to the associates and clients of old DENIS THE TAWER. For his eldest son, Jacques, Pasquier began accumulating the money that would permit the young man to purchase the office of royal notary at Meaux. The next son, Guillaume, went to Paris and kept an inn, Le Mouton blanc, "The White Sheep," on the rue Saint-Martin in the parish of Saint-Laurent.[4]

Over the years Pasquier stayed in touch with his Parisian sister, Jeanne Charpentier, and her husband, DAVID CROYER. It was thanks to the Croyers' financial help that Pasquier's third son, Jean, was able to purchase the position of mounted bailiff-sergeant in the CHÂTELET of Paris.[5] This office permitted him to supervise the sale or confiscation of personal property anywhere in the realm—and therefore in Meaux, where he continued to reside. (If he exercised this office for ten years, Jean would become a "noble"; and longer service would transmit that nobility to his offspring.) As was often the case, the family business was passed to the youngest son, Nicolas, who became a sworn charcoal-measurer. There was another son, Claude, who died in December 1643 and about whom little is known.

Of the six Charpentier children, JACQUES THE NOTARY occupied a crucial position in the family. He was party to many of the business and personal transactions of the inhabitants of Meaux, and at the same time he remained in touch with the relatives in Paris.

Pasquier Charpentier died in June 1627. Magdelaine Esmerault lived on until November 1643. Around 1614, the Measurer and his wife had promised each child 1,200 livres, the amount Jacques had been given when he became a notary. Since some of the heirs had not received full payment, the five surviving Charpentier children took these discrepancies into account when they divided their parents' estate in 1645.[6]

VI

The cousin: He acted with his accustomed wisdom

JACQUES THE NOTARY

Jacques Charpentier, *notaire royal* at Meaux,
the son of Pasquier the Measurer

Born in 1590, Jacques Charpentier was the oldest son of PASQUIER THE MEASURER and Magdaleine Esmerault. His godfather was his youthful "uncle," LOUIS THE BAILIFF, Magdelaine's stepbrother. Jacques considered himself to be the first cousin of Marc-Antoine Charpentier's father, LOUIS THE SCRIVENER, despite the fact that the only blood they shared came from their grandmother, Geneviève Soudain. Their shared family name, *Charpentier* or *Charpentyer*, doubtlessly helped blur the meaning of these terms of relationship.

In 1614 Jacques became engaged to Barbe Chabouillé, the daughter of Nicolas Chabouillé and Marguerite Delavoste. The Chabouillés, who belonged to the cream of the local notables, were related to the Cossets; and they were also linked to the SEVIN family, as a result of the marriage of Marie Delavoste and Gabriel Sevin.[1] Having acquired a notarial cabinet in August 1614, for 1,200 livres,[2] Jacques Charpentier and his bride set up housekeeping in the parish of Saint-Rémy. His position as notary, combined with the social status of his wife, permitted him to aspire to be a local notable.

The identities of the godparents whom the Notary and his wife selected for their children leave no doubt that Jacques was developing close ties to the office-holding circles of Meaux. In addition to Barbe's widowed mother, godparents included a canon of the cathedral, a collector of the gabelle, and the widow of a tax collector. Godparents of special interest included that old friend of the Charpentiers, François Musnier (the husband of Perrette Cosset, friend and benefactress of NICOLAS CHARPENTIER THE SERGENT and his family), and Gilles Royer, a councillor at the royal presidial of Meaux. These contacts with notables did not prompt Jacques Charpentier to turn his back on his shopkeeper relatives who worked in leather. To the contrary. During these very years, he agreed to stand godfather to the children of his sister Marie, wife of Nicolas Brion, a tawer.

In 1623 one of Jacques Charpentier's friends, Gilles Royer (he had agreed to be the godfather of Jacques' son, GILLES THE SECRETARY, born in 1620), witnessed the signing of the wedding contract[3] of his niece, a Chabouillé girl, and Jacques de la Garde, one of Cardinal RICHELIEU's household officers. The contract bears the Cardinal's signature, as well as that of Jacques the Notary, who had drawn up the document. With Royer as one of the witnesses, the Notary drew up several acts for Richelieu himself. Does the Chabouillé link to Cardinal Richelieu (and through him to ARMAND-JEAN DE RIANTS, presumably one of the Cardinal's godsons) explain why Marc-Antoine Charpentier's younger brother was christened ARMAND-JEAN CHARPENTIER in 1645, three years after the Cardinal's death?

The Notary and his wife had high aspirations for Gilles, who was being trained to follow in his father's footsteps. Jacques' Parisian cousin, DAVID CROYER, and his children, helped too. In 1639 eighteen-year-old Gilles was sent to Paris for a year's training with a procurator at the CHÂTELET. In a personal letter to the Notary, Hubert Ginet (David Croyer's son-in-law, who was handling a financial matter for the relatives in Meaux), included the following lines:

> The cousin your son began working yesterday with Monsieur d'Esponty, procurator at the Châtelet, at a fee of fifty écus a year; and if you hadn't been unwilling to talk about more than one year, it would have been possible to pay only eighty écus for two years. I saw him today, very busy. The said Sieur d'Esponty promised me that he would take good care of him, and I think that he will do so without fail, since we are close neighbors, and friends as well; and I personally will see him daily to convince him not to fail to do so, and for the said cousin your son, to wake his spirits so that he will rapidly learn the practice; and I said to him that if he needs something, he should tell me so freely. The cousin your wife should not be troubled, as I have been told she is, because he is close to my house and to that of his uncle [Guillaume, the innkeeper], and is being watched over by him. I will do things for him as if he were my brother; and if I can serve you in any other way, I will do so with quite good will, for I am and will be throughout my life ....[4]

This letter provides a rare glimpse into the affective and protective links between Jacques Charpentier's family and their Parisian cousins, the offspring of his Aunt Jeanne and her husband, DAVID CROYER. These ties between Paris and Meaux were no less strong in December 1643, when another Croyer son-in-law, HAVÉ DE SAINT-AUBIN, wrote the Notary a business letter:

> I received your last letter dated the 20th of this month. I am very unhappy at the news of the death of Madame [Pasquier] Charpentier, our aunt. My wife was very moved and had prayers to God said for her. She could only have had a good death, having always lived so well. That is an end that must come to us all.[5]

As a postscript he added: "My wife kisses your hands, and those of my cousin your wife, and of the grown female cousin too." Below these words, Marthe Croyer added her own signature. Two years later, in a similar hand-kissing postscript, Havé noted that Marthe was "overjoyed at the news that you are planning the marriage [of the grown female cousin]. We will have the honor of seeing her here, ... and we will receive her as best we possibly can."[6] (The cousin in question was the Notary's daughter Jeanne, born in 1626; but no reference to her marriage in 1644 or 1645 has been found, nor to a visit to Paris.)

In other words, across the decades there was continuous written and personal contact between the Charpentiers of Meaux and their cousins in the capital, each helping the other with financial matters so that trips between the two cities could be avoided. That is, in fact, the gist of an almost courtly business letter that a third Croyer son-in-law, CHARLES SEVIN, sent the Notary in February 1646:

> Monsieur, I am too obliged to you for the kindness you show me. I henceforth accept you as my guardian, for when you get involved in business matters, they work out so advantageously. ... Act then, please, with your accustomed wisdom. ... Without doubt you will be very obliging to us, by being willing to take this trouble. I kiss your hands and I am, Monsieur My Cousin, your very affectionate servant, *Sevin*, who kisses the hands of the mother and the daughter.[7]

Jacques the Notary, former alderman[8] and royal notary at Meaux for forty years, died in 1655. His sole heir was his son, GILLES CHARPENTIER THE SECRETARY.

VII

The distant cousin: He was a link to Molière

SAMUEL THE WEAVER

Samuel Charpentier, *maître tisserand en bays* and
merchant at the Great Market of Meaux

Samuel Charpentier the Weaver lurks unmentioned in the background of several portaits in this panel, ready to witness documents being signed by Marc-Antoine Charpentier's relatives in Meaux. Does this mean that Samuel was a relative? The sources do not permit an answer, although two of the documents discussed in this, his own portrait, provide strong evidence that he was PASQUIER THE MEASURER's cousin. Other acts suggest that he was, in addition, a cousin of DENIS THE TAWER's wife. Be that as it may, there can be no doubt that this particular Charpentier of Meaux knew the other Charpentiers quite well.

An early appearance of Samuel the Weaver in the notarial archives for Meaux dates from 1595, an act involving Macette Bienvenu, the widow of a man named Louis Charpentier.[1] Also present was Marie Charpentier, the widow of Théophile Pasquier. A year later, Samuel signed the wedding contract of his cousin, Nicole Soudain,[2] daughter of the late Thomas Soudain and Agnetz Charpentier, his wife. Soudain is, of course, the family name of DENIS CHARPENTIER THE TAWER's wife; Agnetz (that is, Agnès) is the first name of Denis' daughter; and the surname of Denis' stepfather was Pasquier. These coincidences do not, of course, prove that Samuel the Weaver was related to Denis the Tawer. Still, if he was not a relative, why, in 1611, was Samuel asked to witness the redemption of a loan that Geneviève Soudain's mother had taken out back in 1555?[3]

The wedding contract drawn up that same year, 1611—when Samuel's daughter, Nicole Charpentier, wed Jean Boudet, the son of a merchant at Meaux[4]—reveals that one of the witnesses for the groom was

22

Abraham Blanchet, the groom's "cousin." Abraham Blanchet happened to be PASQUIER THE MEASURER's son-in-law. These links of friendship or cousinship between the Boudets and the different Charpentiers of Meaux remained strong into the 1650s. In fact, when Jean Boudet's Paris-based brother, André, wed MOLIÈRE's sister in 1651, he did so in the presence of GILLES CHARPENTIER THE SECRETARY, the son of JACQUES THE NOTARY. In short, these two wedding contracts, one signed in 1611 and the other in 1651, suggest that when Molière selected Marc-Antoine Charpentier as a composer in 1672, he was turning to a family connection.

In 1619 Samuel, whose shop was situated at the Great Market, apprenticed his fourteen-year-old son Louis to a tower.[5] Louis subsequently made his living as a "merchant" in the Great Market; but by the 1640s he had added luster to his name by purchasing the office of archer of the provostship of the marshals of France.

Samuel Charpentier died circa 1634. That year, his children—Louis and his sister Marie, the wife of Nicolas Le Roy—exchanged some land with DAVID CROYER's brother Louis.[6] Most of Samuel the Weaver's land was situated at Neufmontiers, a village just northwest of Meaux where JACQUES CHARPENTIER THE NOTARY likewise owned property.[7] In short, not only does Samuel the Weaver appear to have been a cousin of DENIS THE TAWER, he seems to have been related to PASQUIER CHARPENTIER THE MEASURER. A document signed in 1649 strengthens the probability of a cousinship. That year Samuel's granddaughter, Geneviève Charpentier, sold her share in a house called the *Pot d'Étain*, "The Pewter Mug," which "belonged in its totality to Jacques Charpentier, notary."[8]

Panel 2

THE PARISIAN COUSINS

A World of Opportunity

The portraits in this panel depict descendants of Pasquier Charpentier the Measurer, born at Meaux in the sixteenth century. Most of these individuals have moved to the capital to take advantage of the opportunities it offers. And most of them are flourishing.

They are elegantly dressed, although their clothes are more somber and less ornamented than those of courtiers. One man, portrayed in a double portrait, stands out from the rest of the panel: he holds a bishop's crosier.

In several portraits, women hover in the background, but they are scarcely noticeable in the male world of these well-dressed men.

I

He made his fortune in Paris

MONSIEUR AND MADAME DAVID CROYER

David Croyer and Jeanne Charpentier,
the brother-in-law and sister of Pasquier the Measurer

In August 1576 news of the Saint Bartholomew's Day Massacre reached Meaux via a courier dispatched by Catherine de Médicis to Louis Cosset, royal procurator. Cosset promptly ordered the arrest of the principal Protestants of the city. With his overt approval, indeed with his active participation, these Huguenots were stabbed and hacked to death with swords and halberds. Among the dead was Quentin Croyer, "who loudly prayed God to forgive his murderers, which only made [Cosset] laugh." An account of the bloody events of that day described Cosset's house as being "so full of booty that one could scarcely enter."[1]

Quentin Croyer, a merchant, measurer, and broker of woolen cloth, had married Marie de Franqueville in about 1550.[2] Several children were born to the couple: Quentin, who became a master fuller of woolen cloth in the Great Market of Meaux; Louis, who became a merchant at Meaux; Marie; and David, described in 1587 as a "fuller of woolen cloth in the Great Market," and as a "merchant" in 1588.

In February 1587, at Notre-Dame de Châge, David, born into a Protestant family but now a convert to Catholicism, wed Jeanne Charpentier, the sister of PASQUIER THE MEASURER. The couple set up housekeeping in the parish of Saint-Rémy, where the Measurer and his wife lived. Two Croyer children were baptized there, one in November 1587, the other in February 1589. Neither survived into adulthood.

In March 1589, just one month after this second christening, Faron Croyer, councillor in the presidial of Meaux (he seems to have been a cousin of the massacred Quentin) received the oaths of fidelity to the League in conformity with a decree recently wrenched from the Parlement by the House of Lorraine. Among the signers were DENIS

27

CHARPENTIER THE TAWER and PASQUIER CHARPENTIER THE MEASURER. David's name is not on the list.

Baptismal records attest to the presence of David and his wife in Meaux until early 1594, but by October of that year they had moved to Paris and were living in the Guise parish of Saint-Jean-en-Grève, whose parishioners included David's cousins, Claude Croyer and Roland Croyer, the latter a councillor at the CHÂTELET. There, after what appear to have been five childless years, two more children were born to David Croyer and his wife: Michelle and Nicolas. Again, neither lived to adulthood. A transcription of Michelle's baptism record[3] states that her father was "honorable man David Croyer, cutler." ("Cutler," *coûtellier*, was doubtlessly a copyist's error.) The child's godmothers were Michelle Favier, wife of Roland Croyer, and Anne De Nielle, whose father was a barrister in the royal council and whose mother, born at Meaux, was Louise Cosset. (Louise presumably was a relative of Perrette and Jean Cosset of Meaux, the family friends of NICOLAS CHARPENTIER THE SERGEANT. In other words, any bitterness the Croyers felt over Louis Cosset's role in Quentin Croyer's death had long since dissipated.)

Little Nicolas Croyer's godfather was the son of Pierre Chabouillé, the criminal lieutenant of Meaux.[4] Nicolas Chabouillé's presence at Saint-Jean-en-Grève is but one more indication of how close the Charpentiers were to the notables of Meaux. That is, almost two decades before JACQUES THE NOTARY wed Barbe Chabouillé, this Chabouillé nephew of Gilles Royer of Meaux gave his Christian name to a Croyer infant. (In 1620 Gilles Royer would agree to stand as godfather for GILLES CHARPENTIER THE SECRETARY, Jacques' son.)

Soon after Nicolas' birth, David and his wife left the parish of Saint-Jean-en-Grève. By August 1606 they were living on the rue Saint-Martin, in the parish of Saint-Laurent, and David Croyer was now a "merchant" and a "bourgeois of Paris." By 1608 this "honorable man" was residing on the rue de la Mortellerie, near the Hôtel de Ville. He signed various notarized acts on behalf of his relatives in Meaux and its environs; and he was lending money, often with houses in Paris as collateral.[5] By the time of David's death in November 1614,[6] the Croyers had moved across the Seine to the rue des Fossoyeurs, near the Luxembourg Palace.

A cousin, Louis Le Roy, procurator at the CHÂTELET, was appointed as guardian to the couple's four minor daughters. Jeanne Charpentier promptly moved back across the river to the rue Saint-Martin. There she loaned money and exchanged real estate, consulting her late husband's notary. She stayed in close contact with her family in Meaux, contributing three hundred livres to the dowry of a Blanchet niece. She returned to Meaux several times. For example, in November 1620 she stood as godmother for her grandnephew, GILLES CHARPENTIER THE SECRETARY, baptized at Saint-Rémy; and in 1628 she was present (but did not sign the act) when ownership of jointly-held land at Chambry was transferred to her sister Marguerite Charpentier–Blanchet, who wanted to retire there.[7]

As was often the case, their father's death was quickly followed by a search for husbands for the Croyer girls. The first to wed was Étiennette, who contracted marriage with her guardian, Louis Le Roy, on January 11, 1615.[8] The groom was the son of Louis Le Roy, councillor in the bailliage of Meaux, and Marie Croyer (she appears to have been David's sister). In other words, the bride and the groom were very close cousins. Indeed, Roland Croyer, councillor at the CHÂTELET, signed the contract as the groom's "uncle," while Louis Croyer, merchant of Meaux, signed as the bride's "paternal uncle." PASQUIER CHARPENTIER THE MEASURER, Abraham Blanchet, and Nicolas Brion (Pasquier's tawer son-in-law) came from Meaux for the event. The bride received 15,000 livres from her late father's estate, 11,000 of them in real estate and furniture, the rest in cash. In addition, Faron Croyer, a merchant living at Sedan, promised to turn over to Étiennette 680 Spanish doubloons lent him by David Croyer. (Although he bore the same first and last names as the fervent Catholic who had received the Leaguers' oaths in 1589, Faron Croyer was carrying on business in a Protestant state.)

The wealth accumulated by David Croyer during his twenty years in Paris is quite astonishing. Étiennette's dowry was some three thousand livres greater than what a suitor would normally expect when wedding the daughter of a prosperous merchant. In fact, it was more appropriate for the daughter of a procurator in the Parlement, or a bailiff, or a notary.[9]

A year later, on January 20, 1616, in the house on the rue Saint-Martin, another Croyer daughter, Marthe, signed her wedding contract.[10] The groom was JACQUES HAVÉ, a barrister at the CHÂTELET who would eventually add "de Saint-Aubin" to his name. Havé was the son of a royal councillor and élu at Senlis, but his mother was a Le Roy from Meaux. Signing for the bride were her brother-in-law and guardian, Louis Le Roy; her paternal cousin, Roland Croyer, councillor at the CHÂTELET; her uncle, Louis Croyer, merchant at Meaux; and PASQUIER CHARPENTIER THE MEASURER and his sister, Madame Blanchet. Like her sister, Marthe Croyer received 15,000 livres.

In other words, within the space of a year, Widow Croyer had parted with the really quite enormous sum of 30,000 livres. In addition, at an unspecified date—and doubtlessly bringing with her a dowry just as large —another daughter, Catherine Croyer, wed Louis Cousin, a commissioner and examiner at the CHÂTELET. (Widowed by 1634, Catherine

remarried.[11] Her second husband was Hubert Ginet, likewise a commissioner and examiner at the CHÂTELET. Aside from the bride's maternal
cousin, Guillaume Charpentier (JACQUES THE NOTARY's Parisian innkeeper brother), no close relatives signed this second contract.)

What could the late David Croyer have been doing to accumulate so
much money? He clearly was moving in lofty circles, for on August 17,
1625, a decade after her father's death, his youngest daughter, Suzanne,
contracted marriage[12] with CHARLES SEVIN, a barrister. It was a prestigious
match. Among the witnesses for the groom were Charles' father, Eléazer
Sevin, barrister before the Parlement of Paris and civil and criminal
lieutenant for the barony of Silly. A host of illustrious paternal cousins
had also assembled: Henri Sevin, president in a parlementary chamber
of the Inquests; Thierry Sevin, councillor in the Great Chamber of the
Parlement of Paris; Pierre Sevin, royal councillor and first substitute for
the procurator general of the Cour des Aides; Barthélemy Sevin, royal
secretary; Samuel Sevin, maître d'hôtel to the Duke of Sully; Claude
Sevin, procurator at the Parlement of Paris; and Gabriel Sevin, secretary
to the Duke of Brissac. The bride was represented by only three people,
other than her mother. There was her brother-in-law, Louis Le Roy,
Étiennette Croyer's husband; there was another brother-in-law, Louis
Cousin, Catherine Croyer's husband; and there was her "paternal
cousin," Roland Croyer. The bride received two houses, one of them the
house on the rue Saint-Martin.

As a concluding touch to this portrait of the Croyers, it can be
pointed out that, like his brother David, Louis Croyer metamorphosed
over the years. By the time he died in September 1636, the "merchant"
of Meaux had became a "noble man" and had added "Sieur of Bercy" to
his name. He now resided in Paris, on the rue Saint-Martin.[13] By that
date, Widow Croyer, née Jeanne Charpentier, was dead. Her daughter
Étiennette appears to have predeceased her.

Cartissimo (handwritten)

II

In the good graces of Chancellor Séguier

SEVIN THE AIDE, SEVIN THE BISHOP

Charles Sevin de Troigny, aide to Charlotte Séguier,
and Suzanne Croyer, his wife;
and Nicolas Sevin, Bishop of Sarlat and Cahors, his brother

With Suzanne Croyer's marriage to a young Parisian barrister in the late 1620s, the Charpentiers of Meaux and of Paris entered the protective network around Pierre Séguier, the chancellor of France.

Charles Sevin de Troigny

On August 17, 1627, Charles Sevin, a barrister living on the Île de la Cité, site of the Palace of Justice and Notre-Dame Cathedral, signed his wedding contract with Suzanne Croyer, the daughter of the late DAVID CROYER, "bourgeois of Paris." Nine Sevins were present—among them the groom's father, Eléazer, a barrister before the Parlement of Paris and the civil and criminal lieutenant for the barony of Silly.

The Sevin family tree had many branches,[1] and although it is difficult to situate on that tree all the Sevins who signed the contract that day, most branches seem to have been represented. Among them were two officeholders in the Parlement of Paris. The first was Thierry Sevin, a councillor in the Great Chamber. (Since most Sevins named *Thierry* belong to the branch that had added "de Quincy" to its name, the Thierry Sevin of 1627 presumably descended from the groom's grand-uncle, Thierry Sevin de Quincy, councillor in the Parlement of Paris and president in a chamber of Inquests.) The other parlementaire was Pierre Sevin, royal councillor and first substitute for the general procurator in the Cour des Aides. (He was the son of Michel Sevin, a first cousin of the groom's grandfather.)

Many of the Sevins present that day do not appear on the family tree drawn up by the royal genealogists. Some of them had probably come to the capital relatively recently from Orléans, where the Sevin clan originated. For example, among the guests were Samuel and Gabriel Sevin, both in the employ of the Duke of Sully—who happened to be the son-in-law of Chancellor Pierre Séguier, for whom Charles Sevin would himself be working by the mid-1630s.

The Christian name *Gabriel* suggests that Gabriel Sevin, the Duke's secretary, was a close relative of another Gabriel Sevin[2] who is of special interest owing to his ties to Meaux. A member of the Miramion branch of the family, this Gabriel had left Orléans in his youth and by 1607 had acquired the office of provincial treasurer for the *extraordinaire des guerres* in Brie. In 1595, doubtlessly at Meaux, Gabriel Sevin married Marie Delavoste, the daughter of Jean Delavoste, a tax collector. The new Madame Gabriel Sevin was a close relative of both the Cossets and the Chabouillés, whose names appear in documents involving the Charpentiers of Meaux. By 1607 Gabriel Sevin and his wife had settled in Paris, in the parish of Saint-Médard. Within a decade they had drifted into the orbit of the Séguier family[3]—specifically Marie Séguier, widow of Antoine Duprat, baron de Nantouillet. (The Baroness was the paternal aunt of Pierre Séguier, future chancellor of France.) Gabriel Sevin died in 1625.

Eléazer Sevin, the father of Suzanne Croyer's fiancé, was a close enough relative of Gabriel's for both men to appear on a family tree drawn up by the royal genealogists. Eléazer too had come to Paris from Orléans. He had added "de Champgasté" to his name. Several testimonials dated October 1, 1632, but recopied by notaries in September 1648, reveal more about Eléazer Sevin than do the titles affixed to his name on his son's wedding contract. The testimonial contributed by an elderly servant of the Prince of Condé recounts Sevin's career at the time of the League. The witness attested that:

> Ever since the beginning of the League, since early 1589, he knew the late Eléazer Sevin, during his lifetime Squire and Sieur of Champgasté, having seen him often, sought him out, and frequented him. He knew that Sevin was using most of his money to serve the King [Henri IV], and had on several occasions heard people tell Marshal de la Chastre [governor of Orléans for the League] that the said Champgasté had not done a minor service for the King in causing the city of Orléans to capitulate; that to achieve this he found a way to enter the city two or three times with the complicity of several relatives he had there, whom he brought over to the royal side, along with several others; that the said late Champgasté notified the King of this, ... and the King sent him to La Chastre

with credentials; that the said Champgasté was a very daring, adroit, and a keeper of secrets; and he also knows that Champgasté was ... badly wounded and had his horse killed under him; and he knows this because he himself was present.[4]

Three other witnesses gave similar testimonies under oath, one of them adding that because Sevin "had been unwilling to adhere to the party of the League, he had lost his office as royal procurator at Orléans." Among these testimonials were two letters by the Duke of Brissac, both dated 1625 but, like the other documents, recopied and notarized in July and September of 1648. These statements reveal that Sevin had "on several occasions raised troops, both infantry and cavalry, for the service of the King" (or to be exact, for the service of Marie de Médicis, who with her new head of council, Cardinal Richelieu, wanted to protect Port-Saint-Louis from the Protestants). At the time of his son's marriage, Eléazer Sevin was the civil and criminal lieutenant for the barony of Silly, a position that could conceivably have put him in a position to raise troops for the royal army. (There are several Sillys in France, so the region where he might have raised these troops is difficult to determine.)

Why this inquiry into Eléazar's fidelity? Was his son seeking a pension? Is this investigation of the Sevin family's loyalty to the Crown somehow related to the duchy and city of Orléans? And to the fact that Louis XIII's conspirator brother, GASTON DUKE OF ORLÉANS, was in full rebellion during the summer of 1632? And why were these documents recopied and notarized in 1648, during the early days of the Fronde? No answer to these questions has yet been found.

A possible reason for the recopying of 1648 involves Charles Sevin's employer, Pierre Séguier. On June 13, 1661, in a letter of condolence after the death of Maximilien de Béthune, Duke of Sully, Sevin stated that for "twenty years" he had been in the employment of Bethune's widow, Charlotte Séguier, Pierre's daughter:

> After the crowd of so many people of condition who have come to
> express their regrets about the death of Monsieur the Duke of Sully,
> and about how they share the pain that it has caused you, I dare
> present myself to you here, Monseigneur, in the affliction I feel over
> this loss, and to give you renewed assurances about the services that
> I claim to have the honor of continuing in his household for the rest
> of my days, with the affection that can and ought to be produced by
> the command it pleased you to give me almost twenty years ago, and
> by the benevolence that [Sully] was kind enough to show, I who am,
> Monseigneur, your very humble and very obliged servant, *Sevin de
> Troigny*[5]

(Charles Sevin had been granted letters of nobility in 1633 and could in good faith add "de Troigny" to his name.)

Judging from this letter, when Charlotte Séguier wed the Duke of Sully in February 1639, Sevin was already serving Pierre Séguier. Soon after the wedding he was "ordered" to serve the Duchess. During his years of service to the Sullys—a period when he was able to profit from the power and influence of the Duchess and her father—Charles Sevin remained in close touch with his wife's relatives in Meaux, entrusting his business there to JACQUES CHARPENTIER THE NOTARY: "Monsieur," Sevin wrote the Notary, "I am too obliged to you for the kindness you show me. I henceforth accept you as my guardian."

Nicolas Sevin

By the late 1630s Charles' brother Nicolas had likewise gravitated into the Séguier orbit. Educated by the Jesuits at the College of Clermont, one of the THREE JESUIT HOUSES in Paris. Nicolas went on to study theology and was ordained a priest in 1640. Named bishop of Sarlat in 1647, he remained there until 1657, when he became coadjutor at Cahors and, in 1659, bishop.[6] A highly laudatory letter that Bishop Sevin sent Chancellor Séguier in April 1651 may be pure politeness; but another letter, dated May 5, 1654, is more personal, albeit courtly:

> You are too aware that I belong totally to you, for it to be difficult for me to persuade you of it, considering that even if I did not have a very special affection for your person, I could not in fairness refuse you the applause that everyone owes to virtue when it is being honored. But, Monsieur, allow me also, if you please, to complain a bit to you. You could advance my joy for some time by giving me some news that I was supposed to receive. This has caused me to have some scruples about not being so high in your good graces as I once thought I was. That would be extremely displeasing to me, since I have never had a stronger passion than to be esteemed by you; for I truly am, Monsieur, your very humble and obedient servant, *Nicolas, Bishop of Sarlat*[7]

By the early 1660s Nicolas Sevin could count on Séguier's protection.[8] For example, in 1665, grateful for a kindness Séguier had shown him and about which he had just been informed by his brother Charles, the Bishop told of "a heart that has long been totally devoted to you."[9] In January 1667 he referred to a decree that "it had pleased you to grant me five or six years ago, giving me power to confer livings without having them considered as vacant *en régale*."[10]

It doubtlessly was owing in large part to Pierre Séguier's protection that Nicolas Sevin was translated from Sarlat to Cahors, and that by

1662 Charles Sevin had become the "lord of great and little Troigny" and was a "royal councillor in the Council of State and the Privy Council." He lived in a fine house on the rue du Coq-Héron.

In this elegant residence the wedding contract[11] of Charles Sevin's son, François-Marie Sevin, lord of Cheries and captain in the cavalry, was signed in September 1662, in the presence of Louis de Bourbon, Prince of Condé; Henri de Lorraine, Count of Harcourt; and Pierre Séguier, chancellor and keeper of the seals. Also present was the groom's brother, Charles Sevin, priest, royal almoner, protonotary of the Holy See, abbot of Saint-Jean-de-Genève, count of Merin, archdeacon of the church of Cahors, and archpriest of Peirac in Quercy. (He was representing his uncle the Bishop.) Another brother of the groom also signed: Charles Sevin, lord of Fosses, a royal musketeer. As was customary with the Sevin clan, each branch of the family tree was represented, among them two judges in the Parlement of Paris (one of them a royal councillor and master of accounts, the other a royal councillor in the Great Chamber).

Tucked into this list of illustrious guests are three quite modest relatives of the bride, both of them the late DAVID CROYER's sons-in-law: Louis Cousin, now a royal councillor and president in the *Cour des monnaies* (the husband of the late Catherine Croyer); and "Emé de Saint-Aubin" (a miscopying of HAVÉ DE SAINT-AUBIN), gentleman in ordinary to the late GASTON D'ORLÉANS. Havé was accompanied by his wife, Marthe Croyer.

Two years after this ceremony witnessed by Chancellor Séguier, a disgraced GILLES CHARPENTIER THE SECRETARY would benefit from the Sevins' link to Séguier. Gilles convinced the Chancellor to save him from prosecution by his employer and to ensure his acceptance as notary at Meaux, despite the reprehensible behavior of which he was being accused.

III

From barrister to gentleman in ordinary

HAVÉ DE SAINT-AUBIN THE GENTLEMAN

Jacques Havé de Saint-Aubin,
gentleman in ordinary to Gaston d'Orléans,
and his wife, Marthe Croyer

On June 28, 1615, a wedding contract was signed at Meaux between François Havé, a royal councillor who resided in the city and election of Senlis, and Jeanne Le Roy, the widow of Olivier Clarcelier, an official in the salt warehouse at Meaux.[1] The bride came from an office-holding family. Her brother David ("Davit") was a councillor and *élu* at Meaux; another brother, Nicolas, was a royal procurator at the salt warehouse; and a third brother, Pierre, was a barrister before the Parlement of Paris.

A scant year later, on January 20, 1616, François Havé and his new wife journeyed to Paris to sign the wedding contract of his son by his first wife. Jacques Havé,[2] the groom, was a barrister at the CHÂTELET. The bride was Marthe Croyer, daughter of the late DAVID CROYER. Most of the groom's witnesses came from Senlis, where they were either merchants or local officials.

The contract was signed in the Croyer house on the rue Saint-Martin. In addition to her widowed mother, Jeanne Charpentier (PASQUIER THE MEASURER's sister), Marthe Croyer was represented by Louis Croyer, procurator at the CHÂTELET, her brother-in-law; noble Roland Croyer, royal councillor at the CHÂTELET, her paternal cousin (and his wife Michelle Favier); Louis Croyer, merchant and bourgeois of Meaux, her uncle[3]; and Marguerite Charpentier, wife of Abraham Blanchet, merchant of Meaux, her maternal aunt. The dowry totaled fifteen thousand livres.

Notarial documents reveal that by 1636 Jacques Havé had not only become a "squire," he was also "Sieur of Saint-Aubin." At the time, he

36

and his wife were living between the Louvre and the Halles, on the rue Saint-Honoré in the parish of Saint-Germain-l'Auxerrois. By 1639 the couple had moved to the rue des Mauvaises-paroles,[4] not far from the Halles and the Cemetery of the Innocents. There they remained for over two decades, keeping in touch with the family back in Meaux through their cousin, JACQUES CHARPENTIER THE NOTARY.

In the 1630s Marthe Croyer had obtained a decree of separation of property from her husband (but not a physical separation), a legal precaution that suggests that there was reason to fear that her husband's creditors might lay claim to the fifteen thousand livres she had brought to the marriage. Then, in an act dated 1645, Havé (who still resided on the rue des Mauvaises-paroles) was identified as a "gentleman in ordinary to Monseigneur the Duke of Orléans," that is, GASTON D'ORLÉANS, Louis XIV's uncle. Havé continued to add this title to his name after Gaston's death in 1660. The couple seems to have been childless, for in 1665 they gave gifts to their six Sevin nieces and nephews.[5]

By the early 1660s, and perhaps earlier, Marthe Croyer had been worshiping at the convent of the MERCY on the rue du Chaume, just across the street from the entry gate of the Hôtel de Guise. "For several years," she declared to the notary in March 1664,[6] she had been having the reverend fathers say a low mass every Wednesday. Now, in return for a gift of seven hundred livres, she wanted to make the mass perpetual. After her death, it would become a De Profundis mass.

In other words, shortly before orphaned Marc-Antoine Charpentier set off for Italy, his cousin Marthe was attending services in a church that was a de facto Guise chapel. The church owed many of its fine furnishings to the generosity of the princesses and princes of the House of Guise, who had been worshiping there since the 1620s. Still more significant is the fact that President Louis de Bailleul, a powerful friend of Marc-Antoine's sister, ÉLISABETH CHARPENTIER, and her dancing-master husband, was also worshiping at the Mercy in the early 1660s.

Jacques Havé de Saint-Aubin, by then in his mid-seventies, and his wife were still alive in August 1665; but after that date no notarial acts involving them have been found. However, in the mid-1660s, a "Madame de Saint-Aubin" who was a good friend of MONSIEUR DU BOIS and DOCTOR VALLANT, moved into lodgings at the ABBAYE-AUX-BOIS. Whether the boarder was Marthe Croyer is a matter for speculation.

IV

Enough time to obtain a fraudulent decree

GILLES THE SECRETARY

Gilles Charpentier,
secretary to the Marquis of Saint-Luc,
the son of Jacques the Notary

Gilles Charpentier was baptized at Meaux on November 14, 1620, in the church of Saint-Rémy. The infant's godmother was his widowed grandaunt, Madame DAVID CROYER (the sister of PAS-QUIER THE MEASURER), who had made the journey from Paris to Meaux for the occasion. His godfather was Gilles Royer,[1] royal councillor for the bailliage and presidial of Meaux. Royer moved in powerful circles—witness his presence, a few years later, at the signature of the wedding contract of Jacques de la Garde (a household officer of Marie de Médicis) and Magdelaine Chabouillé (who was not only Royer's niece but, it would seem, a relative of JACQUES THE NOTARY's wife). Among the other witnesses were Cardinal RICHELIEU and Claude Bouthillier, one of the Cardinal's "creatures." When Jacques the Notary asked Royer to be godfather for his infant son, Royer's links to power surely were a consideration.

In January 1639, when Gilles was eighteen, his father placed him with a procurator at the CHÂTELET of Paris, to learn how to draw up legal documents and see cases through the courts. His Parisian cousin, Hubert Ginet, made the arrangements and promised Gilles' weeping mother that he would keep an eye on the youth.[2] (Ginet, an examiner at the Châtelet, was the husband of one of DAVID CROYER's daughters.) JACQUES THE NOTARY expected the training to last for one year and to cost fifty écus (150 livres), although Ginet pointed out that a reduced rate of eighty écus for two years could be worked out. Gilles Charpentier did not become a procurator. Instead, at some point prior to 1651, he became secretary to François d'Espinay, Marquis of Saint-Luc, named lieutenant general for the King in the southwestern province of Guyenne in 1647.

On January 4, 1651, Gilles the Secretary, who had moved to Paris to be near his master, attended the engagement festivities of a young man from Meaux who was working in Paris and was about to wed a Parisienne. (Among the "friends" listed by the notary was "H. Charpentier, secretary of Monsieur de Saint-Luc."[3]) The bride was Magdelaine Pocquelin, MOLIÈRE's sister, and the groom was André Boudet. It is not quite clear why Gilles considered himself a "friend" of the Boudets. Perhaps it was because his granduncle, Abraham Blanchet, was Jean Boudet's "cousin."[4] Or perhaps the "friendship" was that of one distant cousin to another. That is to say, the groom's brother, André Boudet, had wed Nicole Charpentier, the daughter of SAMUEL CHARPENTIER THE WEAVER of Meaux—who appears to have been related to both PASQUIER CHARPENTIER THE MEASURER and DENIS CHARPENTIER THE TAWER.

A few years later, Gilles himself took a wife. She brought her husband 12,600 livres. On February 10, 1654, Gilles—described as a "noble man" residing in his master's hôtel on the rue Pastourelle, in the parish of Saint-Nicolas-des-Champs—contracted marriage with Justine Liger, the orphaned daughter of a surgeon to the queen and to the artillery of France. The bride had three brothers. The first was a *commissaire* in the artillery, the second was the equerry to the Marquis de Monteclair, and the third was prior of Sainte-Eutrope-de-Ternay. Her guardian was her brother-in-law, Robert Le Cointre, who had acquired several offices. (He was a "serving gentleman" to the king, a "councillor of His Majesty," and the receiver and payer of the wages for all the officeholders in the election of Rheims.) The Charpentiers were represented by JACQUES THE NOTARY's innkeeper brother, Guillaume Charpentier, and by CHARLES SEVIN, royal councillor in the Council of State and the Privy Council. The document exaggerates the closeness of Sevin's kinship: he is described as the groom's "first cousin," but his relationship to Gilles was one degree more distant.

Among the "friends" present that day were Procurator d'Esponty, with whom Gilles had studied in 1639 and 1640, and René Mignon, intendant of the household and affairs of the late Keeper of the Seals Châteauneuf. (Four years later, Mignon[5] would wed the daughter of Louis Le Vau, the royal architect. Among the witnesses at Mignon's marriage was Henri Guichard, who only a few days earlier had contracted marriage with Le Vau's other daughter. Does this link to Guichard, via Mignon, suggest yet another tie to the Orléans household? Perhaps, because Henri Guichard was the child of one of GASTON D'ORLÉANS' servants and would become the gentleman-impresario of PHILIPPE II D'ORLÉANS.[6])

After his wedding, Gilles the Secretary remained in Saint-Luc's service, but he and his bride moved to the parish of Saint-Gervais, to a house at the river end of the rue du Temple. From time to time the Secretary would sell, exchange, or rent out pieces of land at Coulommes, Varredes, and Chambry that he had inherited from his parents. He would sometimes journey to Meaux. For example, along with five other Charpentier males, the "Secretary of Monsieur de Saint-Luc" signed the wedding contract of NICOLAS THE SERGEANT's daughter in June 1660.

Not long after this wedding, the Secretary was fired.[7] On June 14, 1663, Gilles Charpentier had given a written "release" to a notary for safekeeping. The document, signed by Saint-Luc, read:

> We recognize that Charpentier, our secretary, has returned to us and placed in our hands each and every one of our titles, papers, accounts, receipts, documents, and procedures concerning our affairs and lands in Normandy, which [Charpentier] had in his possession and from which we release him. Written in Paris on the sixth day of June, 1661, *Saint-Luc*[8]

When Charpentier went to the notary's study in 1663, he no longer was in Saint-Luc's employ. In fact, the notary stated that Gilles Charpentier, who now lived on the rue Sainte-Avoie in the parish of Saint-Merry, was the Marquis' "former" secretary, and that he had asked the notary to keep this document among his minutes and make copies as needed. In other words, a dispute about the Marquis' papers was brewing, and Gilles the Secretary was trying to demonstrate his innocence.

A letter to Chancellor Pierre Séguier, sent from the Southwest by Saint-Luc in May 1665, suggests that Gilles Charpentier had become so mired in the contestation over these papers that he had appealed to his cousin, CHARLES SEVIN, and had been granted access to the Chancellor:

> Monseigneur, I learned that a certain Charpentier, who in the past was entrusted with my affairs in Paris, was so daring as to go and throw himself at your feet, although I am suing him to return the titles and papers he stole from me, and which has had such ruinous consequences for me that I do not know how to repair the disorder he created in my household affairs. ... That you thought you should create difficulties in getting a signature for the decree that it had pleased the King to grant me, in order to prevent a settlement of the lawsuit, gave [Charpentier] enough time to obtain a fraudulent decree from the Parlement, which has put the finishing touches on this embarrassing situation. If the King had not refused to grant me leave, and if the current state of affairs in this province had not

made my presence here absolutely necessary, I would have gone to tend to this disorder. I humbly beg you, Monseigneur, to grant me the honor of your protection in this situation, to prevent the consequences of this fraudulent decree, with all the more reason because I have to explain in person, to the judges, the faithlessness of this domestic. I expect this of your kindness, *Saint-Luc*[9]

No trace of the "fraudulent" decree has been found among the summaries of the decrees issued during Council hearings between January and July 1665.[10] It is, however, interesting to note that most of these records are signed *De Bailleul*. In other words, the magistrate in charge of the case was Louis de Bailleul, whose mother and daughter had signed the wedding contract of ÉLISABETH CHARPENTIER, Marc-Antoine's sister, only three years earlier.

The outcome of the lawsuit is not known, but the scandal clearly put an end to Gilles Charpentier's secretarial career. He therefore decided to claim his "hereditary" right to succeed his late father, JACQUES THE NOTARY. In June 1664 he petitioned the *bailli* of the bailliage of Meaux to grant him this office. In this autograph document Gilles alluded to a very important paper in his possession:

Request of Gilles Charpentier, son and sole heir of the late Jacques Charpentier, hereditary royal notary and note-keeper in the city and bailliage of Meaux, stating that he has obtained letters of provision from His Majesty for the said office ..., dated June 8, 1664, signed by the King ... [and] double-sealed with the great seal of yellow wax, and counter-sealed, into which office the petitioner has in addition been received by you [the *bailli*]: this considered, Monsieur, and since he [Charpentier] is preparing letters of provision for the said office, may it please you to receive the petitioner for this office, to exercise it in conformity with the said letters, offering to this end to take the required and accustomed oath.[11]

Before granting his request, the officials in Meaux conducted the usual investigation of the "life and morals" of Gilles Charpentier, "practitioner of the office." The procedure, which involved a series of interviews, was conducted by Isaac Le Ber, the lieutenant general of Meaux. (Le Ber was an old friend of the Charpentier family, especially NICOLAS THE SERGEANT's children.) One witness, Procurator Brayer, stated that he had known the father well and could state that he had "faithfully, diligently, and honorably carried out his duties as notary"; and that he also knew the son very well, "who is well-informed about the practice, capable, and living without reproach, and is a Catholic." Procurator Mondolot's testimony was similar. The content of these testimonials is extremely routine. These perfunctory statements differ little from the ones appended to the contract by which JACQUES THE NOTARY had acquired his office back in 1614.

There is, however, one significant difference between the report about the father and the report about the son. The official who drew up the committee report on June 29, 1664, inserted an expression of regret that is absent from the report of 1614: "I cannot prevent ... the aforesaid Charpentier from being received as notary." In other words, the officials in the bailliage were aware of the conflict with Saint-Luc but were helpless to prevent Charpentier's nomination.

Although pressure from protectors such as Le Ber in Meaux appears to have played a role in the favorable outcome of the investigation, several phrases in the royal letter suggest that the local officials had been faced with a *fait accompli* arranged by a protector so powerful that opposition was impossible. The royal letter states that "in our Council" Charpentier showed the contracts by which his late father had acquired the office; and that if the King was granting him the office, it was because his chancellor, Pierre Séguier, had asserted that Charpentier showed the requisite "capacity, probity, and experience."

In the end, Gilles Charpentier gave up the idea of being a notary. He remained in Paris, living as a "bourgeois." By 1672 he and his wife were residing in a house on the rue des Mathurins, in the parish of Saint-Benoît—the very street where the guardians of LOUIS THE SCRIVENER's orphaned sons were living in 1662. He seems to have lived on the income from his properties in and around Meaux. At one point he increased his revenues by serving as the paid "director of the rights of creditors" for a lengthy lawsuit.[12] Another time, he joined his wife's family in a suit against the Le Cointres, accusing them of having deprived Justine and her brothers of funds that were rightfully theirs.[13] By the early 1690s Gilles' hand was trembling. He died at seventy-five, on April 26, 1696.

The inventory of the furnishings in his house[14] makes it possible to recreate the living standards and the lodgings to which a pen-wielding Charpentier might aspire. The kitchen was in the basement. The family occupied two ground-floor rooms. One room contained a daybed, while the other was furnished with a walnut table, chairs, and stools, and with several walnut side tables. Food could be reheated in this room, whose fireplace boasted andirons with gilded globes. The walls of both rooms were decorated with devotional prints in gilded frames and mirrors in wooden or silver-trimmed frames. White linen curtains hung at each window. It appears that another family occupied the second, third, and fourth floors of the house, for the Charpentiers' sleeping quarters were situated on the fifth floor. A bedroom that opened onto the courtyard held a camp bed and a table covered with a piece of green cloth, and it was hung with the woven fabric known as "Rouen tapestry."

The decor in the bedroom facing the street was somewhat more sumptuous. The oak poster bed was hung with grey curtains with multicolored silk fringe, and the upholstery of the seven walnut chairs matched the fabric of the bed. The table was covered with a needlepoint cloth worked in flame stitch, and the walls were hung with so-called "Bergamo tapestry." A little tapestry-covered chest and a mirror completed the decoration. There were also two storerooms. One of them contained a Flemish tapestry, a large bed, and some Bergamo hangings. In the other room the notary found a solid oak chest, two pistols, a few pieces of silverware, two saltcellars, two tables, an armchair, and some tapestries and cushions. Once the sums stipulated by her wedding contract had been turned over to widowed Justine, and the costs of the inventory and the funeral had been paid, little or nothing was left. Although his wife retained over nineteen thousand livres, Gilles Charpentier technically died penniless.

The inventory had been requested by the widow and her three adult sons. Like his late father, the elder son, Jacques, was a "bourgeois of Paris." He lived in the parish of Saint-Nicolas-des-Champs, where his father had resided when he first came to Paris. René, the second son, was a bachelor of theology. In addition to being a canon in the royal collegiate church of Étampes, he was an almoner to PHILIPPE II, DUKE OF ORLEANS. The third son, Jean-Baptiste, was likewise an officer in PHILIPPE II D'ORLÉANS' household. He lived in the parish of Saint-André-des-Arts, where Curate Mathieu was organizing concerts at which Marc-Antoine Charpentier's music was played.[15]

Did René and Jean-Baptiste Charpentier owe their positions in the Duke's household to their cousin Marc-Antoine? That sort of protection would help explain how René's nephew, Jean-Baptiste-Thomas Charpentier, a tonsured religious, became almoner to PHILIPPE III D'ORLÉANS, the musically gifted prince who as "Duke of Chartres" had studied composition with Marc-Antoine Charpentier.[16]

Panel 3

THE COMPOSER'S FAMILY

Industrious but Impecunious

This panel consists of seven portraits clustered around the cutting from the Almanac that depicts "Monsieur Charpentier." These portraits show Marc-Antoine Charpentier's father, his three sisters, his brother, his niece, and his nephew.

The men wear the broad black hats and the somber black or gray clothes that mark the bourgeois of Paris and that also serve as a uniform of sorts for secretaries, scriveners, and shopkeepers.

The women too are garbed in grays and blacks, for they are *bourgeoises*, and sometimes shopkeepers as well. Their heads are covered with modest white coifs.

One picture depicts a nun wearing the habit of a Cistercian converse: a gray robe, a gray scapular marked with a red cross, and a black veil.

E. S! SÉVERIN.

The Church of Saint-Séverin and its cemetery.
This was the Charpentier family's parish church. Louis the Scrivener and Étiennette the Linener were buried there. In the background are medieval houses similar to the one where the Scrivener died in 1662.

I

The letters and charters in the expedition cabinet

LOUIS THE SCRIVENER

Louis Charpentier, *maître écrivain juré* of Paris,
the composer's father

L ouis Charpentier, the son of LOUIS THE BAILIFF and Anne Broquoys, was born in Meaux, probably in late 1600 or early 1601.
Thus he reached the age of majority in approximately 1625. No
allusion to this particular Louis Charpentier appears in the parish records
of Meaux for the 1610s and 1620s, for example as the godfather for one
of the children of NICOLAS THE SERGEANT. Nor is Louis named in notarial
acts involving the different Charpentiers of that city. It is as if he left
Meaux while a teenager and, instead of being apprenticed in Meaux,
spent the requisite three years with a Parisian *maître écrivain juré*, a sworn
master scrivener.

The family politics behind this choice of craft are easily inferred.
Under favorable circumstances, the family would have tried to ensure
that at least one son could purchase an office in the local administration;
but LOUIS THE BAILIFF's premature death circa 1613 almost certainly
dashed these hopes. PIERRE THE CHAPLAIN was therefore given to the
Church, and ÉTIENNE THE PRACTITIONER remained without an office.

As for Louis, rather than see him become an artisan, his mother
prepared him for a livelihood on the margins of the royal administration.
For example, an apprenticeship to a scrivener would teach him all the
official scripts employed at the CHÂTELET of Paris and in the Parlement.
His training would also consist of drawing up documents in proper form,
verifying the authenticity of contracts, keeping exact inventories of
documents received and dispatched, and doing arithmetic. Although
developing a clientele could be difficult for a newcomer to the corporation, Louis' relatives at the CHÂTELET would send clients his way. If
fortune smiled on him, he might become the secretary of a powerful man

47

or woman; and in the best of scenarios, a benefactor might reward him with an office.[1]

It was possible to become a master scrivener without completing an apprenticeship. The Parisian corporation would occasionally accept someone who had learned the requisite scripts on his own; but that individual could not add *sworn* to his title. The Charpentiers of Meaux clearly did not take that route, for Louis Charpentier's death inventory calls him a "sworn master scrivener of Paris."

In short, teenage Louis apparently was apprenticed to one of the masters in the capital between approximately 1618 and 1620. If he followed the usual patterns for his social group, it was in the late 1620s that he married Anne Toutré, about whom nothing is known beyond the fact that she predeceased her husband. Even her family name is not totally certain, the notary's rendition of it on her husband's death inventory being open to more than one reading.[2]

Five of the couple's children survived to adulthood: MARIE THE CONVERSE, who prior to 1660 took the vows of a converse nun at the Abbey of PORT-ROYAL; ÉTIENNETTE THE LINENER, born in the early 1630s, who became a shopkeeper and remained a spinster; ÉLISABETH THE WIFE AND MOTHER, born in about 1635, wife of Jean Édouard, a dancing master; MARC-ANTOINE THE COMPOSER, born in 1643 "in the diocese of Paris"; and ARMAND-JEAN THE ENGINEER (who tended to go by the name *Jean*), born in 1645 and apprenticed to a scrivener-engraver before becoming a royal engineer.

The inventory[3] drawn up in January 1662, after Louis the Scrivener's death, sheds minimal light on his career. At the end of the document the notary added a few words about a letter that Étiennette Charpentier had received from "Sieur Charpentier, priest and sacristan of Saint-Étienne of Meaux, her cousin," concerning money due the late Scrivener from the estate of his brother, PIERRE THE CHAPLAIN. This addendum made it possible to trace the Charpentiers back to Meaux. Sacristan Charpentier proved to be NICOLAS THE SERGEANT's son, Robert.

The enumeration of the deceased's papers proves less helpful than intriguing. The only document summarized by the notary was a contract signed in the Duchy of Nevers in May 1649, by which Louis Charpentier sold to an almoner to the Prince of Condé a "*corps de logis*" (a house, or perhaps the wing of a large structure) and "other inheritable property" at Dirol. Had Anne Toutré inherited this property? Or did the couple acquire the house while living in the election of Clamecy during the 1630s, then sell it after returning to the Paris region, where Marc-Antoine was born in 1643? If the latter was the case, why would a master scrivener with affective ties to Meaux settle in the vicinity of Clamecy?

There is a possible explanation that links Brie and the Duchy of Nevers.[4] Early in the seventeenth century King Henri IV not only gave Charles de Gonzague de Cleves, Duke of Nevers, substantial rights over the salt warehouses at Clamecy, he also gave him the right to name the comptroller for various taxes in that election. In addition to the power he wielded in Nevers, the Duke was governor of the region of Brie and owned a country estate at Coulommiers, due south of Meaux. He also maintained a residence in Paris, the Hôtel de Nevers, which housed the offices of his household staff. After Nevers' death in September 1637, the rights and income from Clamecy passed to his daughters, who by 1640 were replacing their father's appointees with their own. Would research in the archives for that region reveal that Louis Charpentier was among the staff dismissed in the late 1630s or early 1640s?

Be that as it may, by the early 1640s the Charpentiers were living somewhere in the "diocese of Paris,"[5] probably in Paris proper. ÉTIEN-NETTE THE LINENER later thanked the Jesuits of the Noviciate, one of the THREE JESUIT HOUSES in the capital, for the "fine instruction," *les bonnes instructions*, she had received from them—an apparent allusion to catechisms for girls. This "instruction" probably began around 1640, when she was approximately seven or eight years old.

It was also by the early 1640s that the Charpentiers could count among their friends or close associates an unidentified individual who had been christened *Armand-Jean* and who can therefore be presumed to have been the godson of either Cardinal Richelieu or his grandnephew, the future DUKE OF RICHELIEU. In 1645—some three years after the Cardinal's death—this unidentified Armand-Jean (was it ARMAND-JEAN DE RIANTS?) stood as godfather for the Charpentiers' youngest son, ARMAND-JEAN THE ENGINEER.

It probably also was during the 1640s, and perhaps into the 1650s, that Louis the Scrivener came into professional contact with the powerful families who would gather around his orphaned children in the 1660s. One of these protective links involved the CHÂTELET, specifically Lieutenant FERRAND and his family. Over the years, the Ferrands would watch over ÉTIENNETTE THE LINENER and make it possible for her to set up a shop. As she expressed it in her will, they "contributed to make me earn my living."

During these same years, Louis the Scrivener became acquainted with MARIE TALON, the wife of Daniel Voisin. A close friend of one of the FERRAND women, through her highly respected father, Advocate General Omer Talon, Marie had links to the families that made up the Parlement of Paris. And through her husband she was part of an extended family that had been serving the House of Guise since the Holy League of the 1580s.

By 1661 Anne Toutré had died, and Louis the Scrivener was living in the Latin Quarter on the rue du Foin, situated mid-way between the Sorbonne and his parish church, Saint-Séverin. The description of his lodging makes it clear that he did not teach school, as some master scriveners did; nor is there any evidence that he rented a tiny ground-floor shop, as many scriveners did, where he would wait for customers to come and dictate messages. Rather, his principal activity seems to have consisted of copying and classifying documents, more or less in solitude. His single room was situated on the fourth floor, to increase the intensity of the daylight that was so essential to his craft.

The Scrivener is known to have been in contact with two women. One of them, Madame Guyot, had borrowed fifteen livres from him. (Was she the future mother of Jeanne Guyot, born in 1666, who would join the GUISE MUSIC in the early 1680s? Since Jeanne Guyot's mother was née Jeanne Dupin, she may have been related to Nicolas Dupin, who would soon be appointed guardian to the Charpentier boys.) The Scrivener had also loaned a certain Madame Chevalier fourteen livres. The lady in question presumably was "Dame Cheron, wife of Pierre Chevalier, procurator at the Parlement," who would sign ÉLISABETH CHARPENTIER's wedding contract several months later.

In this fourth-floor lodging the Scrivener died on December 18, 1661. Étiennette had advanced the money for some of his medical expenses: there were "thirty-three livres due her for expenditures made at the end of her late father's illness and since his death." [6]

Since Louis Charpentier was probably just entering his sixties, he presumably was still active in his craft during the final months of his life. And indeed, that is the impression created by the preamble to the inventory of his possessions, which mentions not only the "usual registers" but also "letters and charters" shut up in "the expedition cabi-net," all of which his daughters swore to leave untouched. In other words, unspecified clients had entrusted important legal documents, deeds, and correspondence to Louis Charpentier, much as the Marquis of Saint-Luc had given GILLES CHARPENTIER THE SECRETARY all the papers involving the ownership and administration of his lands in Normandy.

Prior to their father's death, Étiennette and Élisabeth Charpentier had left home and were living on the rue de la Harpe, on the Left Bank. The papers of their father's estate do not say whether their brothers were staying with them, or whether the youths shared their father's bed and the "little mattress" in his lodging.

It took almost a month to select a guardian for the Scrivener's minor sons, eighteen-year-old Marc-Antoine and sixteen-year-old Armand-Jean. So lengthy a delay is atypical. Was it related to the arrest of Superintendant of Finance Nicolas Foucquet in August 1661? More specifically, was the delay connected to the arrests of the financiers in Foucquet's circle that began in December 1661 and continued into March 1662? The possibility cannot be ruled out, for the husbands of several friends of the Charpentier family—and of some of the "friends" of young Jean Édouard, who would marry Élisabeth Charpentier during the summer of 1662— were being placed under arrest that December and January: Macé Bertrand de La Bazinière (the stepbrother of Marie Talon's husband), Bénigne Le Ragois de Bretonvilliers (the brother of Madame Louis de Bailleul), Olivier Picques (whose daughter would soon marry Charles Sevin's cousin Claude)—and the mysterious war commissioner named Jacques Charpentier who acted as a strawman for Louis de Bailleul.[7] This raises a question for which no answer has yet been found: Did Louis the Scrivener's expedition cabinet contain the papers of one or more of these wealthy friends of the Charpentiers who had been caught up in Foucquet's disgrace?

The Châtelet eventually appointed people outside the family to be the legal guardians of Marc-Antoine and Armand-Jean. The principal guardian was Nicolas Dupin, a procurator at the Parlement who lived one street away, on the rue des Mathurins. (In another document Dupin described himself as a "friend" of the family.[8]) He would be assisted by Étienne Jacques, a bourgeois of Paris who likewise resided on the rue des Mathurins. (Jacques' name was not mentioned again in acts involving the Charpentier family.) The decree naming the guardians, dated January 13, 1662, does not appear to have survived,[9] so it is impossible to say whether the orphans' Parisian cousins—Charles Sevin, Jacques Havé de Saint-Aubin, and Gilles Charpentier the Secretary—were consulted during the selection process.

On the day their father's inventory was drawn up, Étiennette and Élisabeth Charpentier, assisted by Messieurs Dupin and Jacques, showed each item to the clerk who was enumerating the contents of the room. The clerk focused first on a little leather box that held just over four hundred livres in cash. Next he listed the cooking equipment and the principal furnishings: a walnut poster bed with green serge hangings, an armchair and several side chairs and stools, six pieces of shabby wall hangings woven at Rouen, a matching table cover, two trunks (one of them full of clothes and linens, among them a little packet containing some of Anne Toutré's undergarments), and a walnut cabinet with four locked doors. This doubtlessly was the "expedition cabinet" mentioned by the notary. Several decorative objects brightened the otherwise quite simply furnished room: a porcelain cup (that is, Chinese export ware), a little mirror with a tortoise-shell frame, a pax in an embroidered velvet box, a small copper "ball," *boule* (probably a hand-warmer), an ebony cross, a painting of a crucifix with a Magdalene, and a small gilded statue of the Virgin.

The description of the Scrivener's clothes reveals that he wore black, and that he had indulged himself by purchasing several pairs of morocco-leather shoes. He also owned a sword and a harquebus—the latter, and perhaps the former, surely the remnants of participation in the militia of the quarter.

Including the cash in the little box, the dead man's possessions were estimated as worth just over 515 livres, not counting eight silver spoons, two bowls, one cup, and a sewing needle, whose values were not specified. This meager total was augmented by the 120 livres still unpaid more than a decade after the sale of the property at Dirol, and by an additional 100 livres or so due the Charpentier children from the estate of their late uncle, PIERRE CHARPENTIER THE CHAPLAIN.

An estate of some 725 livres, to be divided four ways! In other words, each child would receive approximately 180 livres, considerably less than the annual wages (250 livres) of a country schoolmaster. Nicolas Dupin had his work cut out for him during the nine years his guardianship was scheduled to last. It was his duty to ensure that his two wards had been provided with the tools for a trade by the time they celebrated their twenty-fifth birthdays.

Étiennette Charpentier

II

At the Sign of the Carpenter

ÉTIENNETTE THE LINENER

Étiennette Charpentier, *maîtresse lingère* of Paris,
the composer's sister

Étiennette Charpentier appears to have been the oldest surviving child of LOUIS THE SCRIVENER. At the latest, her birth took place in 1635. Although it is not certain that she was born in the diocese of Paris like her brother Marc-Antoine, by the time Étiennette was eight or nine she lived in Paris—almost certainly in the Latin Quarter. In her will she made a bequest to the Jesuits of the Noviciate, "in recognition of the fine instruction I received from childhood and ever since."

When her father died in December 1661, Étiennette was on her own and living on the rue de la Harpe, at the sign of *La Barbe d'Or,* "The Golden Beard." Her sister, ÉLISABETH CHARPENTIER, resided on the same street, perhaps in the same house. By that date Étiennette had completed her apprenticeship as a linener, training that began when a girl was approximately sixteen and that could take as long as five years, although the minimum training stipulated by the corporation was three years.[1] She doubtlessly was already a shopkeeper when her father died, for her estate mentions some cloth she sold on April 29, 1663. In short, her shop appears to have been located at the *Barbe d'Or,* where she was still occupying in a second-floor room as late as 1676.[2]

As the financial woes of her niece, MARIE-ANNE ÉDOUARD, reveal, setting up a linen shop required a considerable financial investment. Rent alone could total 400 livres a year, and at least another 2,300 livres had to be spent to stock the shop. To that, add a minimum of 1,000 livres for the apprenticeship (400 livres per year was the average fee) and the obligatory reception fees paid to the lineners' corporation. In all, almost 4,000 livres had to be disbursed in the space of some five years. Louis the

The Jesuit Noviciate near the Luxembourg Palace.
Here Étiennette Charpentier was "given fine instruction in childhood and ever since."

Scrivener and his wife clearly had been unable to save that much, and they had four other children to care for and educate.

In the late 1650s some wealthy "friends" took Étiennette under their wing and, as she later expressed it, "contributed to make me earn my living." She named these benefactors in her will of 1707: "Madame Gouffé; ... [and] Monsieur Ferrand the father, and Madame his wife, and all his family; Monsieur Guyet, the master of accounts, and Madame his wife." In other words, if she had a shop and the merchandise to fill it, it was thanks to the Lieutenant of the CHÂTELET and his extended family: Antoine III FERRAND and Isabelle Le Gauffre, his wife; his son Antoine, who succeeded his father as lieutenant at the Châtelet, and their daughter FRANÇOISE FERRAND, wife of René Lefèvre de la Faluère; plus Antoine III's two aunts: Marie Ferrand, the wife of Jean Guyet, and Madeleine Ferrand, the wife of Germain Gouffé.

When did the Ferrands begin playing this crucial role in Étiennette's life? The death date of one of these benefactors reveals that the friendship between the Ferrands and the Charpentiers almost certainly predates Louis the Scrivener's death, for Jean Guyet died in 1661. The friendship between the Ferrands and the Linener continued until the latter's death in 1709, when Françoise Ferrand served as executrix for her will.

Étiennette's spelling was phonetic. She employed a quite learned vocabulary that her education had not prepared her to set down on paper. This does not mean that she lacked business acumen. Her testament of 1707 would prove a model of calculation and perspicacity. In January 1662 it was principally she who helped the notary and his clerk draw up the inventory of her late father's possessions. She did not, however, sign the wedding contract of her sister, ÉLISABETH CHARPENTIER, a few months later. Did she have doubts about the advisability of the marriage? Perhaps.

There may be another explanation for the absence of her signature. In several documents involving Louis the Scrivener's children, the only family members signing a document tend to be the ones who are materially guaranteeing the conditions set forth in the act. Other quite close relatives do not sign. It is as if they wanted to create a barrier between themselves and potential creditors. Although Étiennette was major when her sister married in 1662, she had a shop to worry about. Her minor brothers, on the other hand, were too young to be legally responsible: both of them signed Élisabeth's contract. And in 1689 neither Étiennette nor Armand-Jean nor Marc-Antoine signed the wedding contract of their niece, MARIE-ANNE ÉDOUARD, where the principal clauses hinged upon the linen shop she was bringing to the household. Nor did Marc-Antoine participate in taking the inventory of the possessions of ÉLISABETH CHARPENTIER's late husband, Jean Édouard. Yet only hours earlier he had attended a family council where he was not named guardian, probably because his financial situation was deemed too uncertain. Étiennette, who had her own shop to think about in 1685, did not attend that particular family meeting.

Over the years, Étiennette watched out for her sisters and brothers. A will drawn up in January 1676, when she fell quite ill, reveals the thought she had given to allocating the money she had earned. She proposed a pension of fifty livres a year to her sister, MARIE THE CONVERSE at the Abbey of PORT-ROYAL of Paris. When the nun died, the pension would go to her goddaughter and niece, Marie-Anne Édouard, "for the love that [I] bear her." To "each of her brothers," and to her sister Élisabeth, she bequeathed "what each of them may owe [me] and for which there is a receipt in their name, not wanting one of them to ask anything of the other." In addition, she named as her heirs "the children born or to be born of the marriage of Élisabeth Charpentier, wife of Sieur Jean Édouard, dancing master," or born to "Marc-Antoine and Jean Charpentier, her brothers." Until such a time as these children might require the money, her siblings could use the proceeds from the sale of her possessions.

The Linener recovered from her illness and went about her business.[3] She stayed in close touch with her widowed sister, and on three occasions "Mesdemoiselles Charpentier" went together to the theater for which their brother had written so much music, charging their tickets.[4] At some point Étiennette vacated the shop on the rue de la Harpe, to which she had added "improvements and adjustments in wood and other [materials] that she had ordered built for her convenience," and she moved to a house at the corner of the rue des Noyers and the rue des Anglais, near the Church of Saint-Séverin.[5] There, for three hundred livres a year, she rented an entire wing of the house, consisting of a shop on the ground floor, a cellar, three floors of living quarters with fireplaces in virtually every room, and an attic. To call attention to the shop, which was reached through the courtyard rather than directly from the street, she hung out a sign painted on linen depicting a carpenter, *un Charpentier*.

The Linener's death inventory, drawn up in 1709, is revealing of her taste. Like the inventories taken decades earlier for LOUIS THE SCRIVENER, and for ÉLISABETH CHARPENTIER's dancing-master husband, this inventory suggests continuities in the way the Charpentiers decorated their lodgings. There were, however, clear individual predilections. For example, in addition to the basic equipment found in most kitchens, in Étiennette's lodging the notary listed a coffee mill, two tin coffeepots, and a

La Marchande Lingere

Mon brave Cavalier tout remply de franchise
Si vous voulez de moy quelque chose acheter
Voyez, et si cela ne peut vous contenter
Je vous deployeray une autre Marchandise

A Paris chez la veue le Camu rue St jaque a la teste d'Or

Auec priuil du Roy

A mistress merchant linener.
The decor in this print resembles the one in Étiennette Charpentier's linen shop:
an oak counter, shelves on which merchandise is displayed, and side chairs
for customers. Mademoiselle Charpentier would have been disturbed by the
sexual innuendo in the poem that denigrates her profession: *Mon brave Cavalier
tout remply de franchise, Si vous voulez de moy quelque chose acheter, Voyez, et si cela
ne peut vous contenter, Je vous déployeray une autre Marchandise.*

box full of coffee beans. In other words, elderly though she was, the Linener had been caught up in the latest culinary fad.

The bedroom above the kitchen contained items described as "old." It appears to have been occupied by her shop assistant. A spare room contained several leather-covered chests full of slipcovers, embroidered table covers, curtains, and bed hangings—apparently used items or things passed down by the family, rather than new merchandise to be offered for sale.

Étiennette's own room opened onto the courtyard and was quite grand. The andirons had brass globes, the walls were hung with the fabric known as "Bergamo tapestry," its repetitive patterns broken by a small mirror in a black frame, a statuette of Christ on a black base, a small crucifix on velvet in a curved gold frame, twenty-four framed prints, and four little reliquaries in gold frames. Two "family portraits" also hung here. She owned a considerable amount of silver: tall candlesticks described as "antique" (that is, old-fashioned), a goblet, a sauceboat, "little coffee spoons," porringers, a saltcellar, a candle-snuffer and its tray, a holy-water font and its cross, and 234 tokens she had received for attending meetings of the lineners' corporation. She liked jewelry and owned a ring with seven diamonds, plus a gold ornament set with a half-dozen small diamonds. Most of the furniture was made of walnut, and some of it was described as "antique," probably because it had the turned legs that had been popular early in the previous century. The bed hangings were red with silk fringe; the upholstery was either gray cloth or needlepoint. At the window hung a white linen curtain. A cabinet with grilled doors held her library, which consisted of thirty-odd devotional books, among them an old two-volume folio edition of the lives of the saints, a translation of the *Meditations* of Luis de Ponte, S.J., and a small red-morocco copy of Pierre Corneille's verse rendition of Thomas à Kempis' *Imitation of Jesus*.

Most of the other rooms housed wardrobe closets full of merchandise, for Étiennette was one of those pioneers who were selling ready-made items: bonnets, lace-trimmed cuffs, coifs, scarves, aprons, pockets, peignoirs, and so forth. She also sold pillowcases, sheets, and pocket handkerchiefs. Like the clothes she wore in the shop, her house-robes were relatively somber: solid black, solid gray, black-and-purple-striped, and so forth. The shop was furnished with an oak counter, five needle-pointed side chairs, and a large walnut wardrobe filled with napkins, collars, and shirts. Most of the walls were lined with shelves to display the merchandise, but one wall was decorated with Bergamo tapestry. At the window hung a white linen curtain. The shop contained several items appropriate to a public space: a small copper pendulum clock in an oak case (she had willed it to her executor in 1676, as an expression of gratitude), a small mirror, a copper brazier, a spittoon, and two unidentified plaster busts.

Thanks to Étiennette's two surviving testaments—the first dictated to a notary in 1676, the other an autograph will dated 1707[6]—it is possible to discern some continuities in her devotions as well as certain transfers of loyalty from one religious house to another. An evolution in her understanding of Christianity also can be noted.

The continuities involve her burial (the later testament reduces the pomp), her modest gift to her shop girl, her pious bequests so typical of devout Catholics (money to free prisoners from the Châtelet, to help the poor at the Hôtel-Dieu hospital, to aid the poor and sick of the parish, and so forth). Between 1676 and 1707 the Linener did, however, shift her loyalties from the Mathurins (in whose church the confraternity of master scriveners met) to the Cordeliers; from one JESUIT HOUSE to another (specifically, from the Church of Saint-Louis to the Noviciate); and from the Petits-Augustins (while her siblings were still alive she wanted prayers said there for the lost souls in Purgatory) to the Capuchins (the church founded by MADEMOISELLE DE GUISE's maternal grandfather, where Étiennette now founded prayers for her deceased parents and siblings). In her will of 1707 she added a foundation for masses to be said at PORT-ROYAL of Paris in "remembrance of me."

In the course of the thirty years that separate these wills, Étiennette Charpentier's devotional outlook changed in a telling way. In 1676 she had implored the Virgin, her guardian angel, and her "protecting saints" to "help her with their intercession at the moment of her death, and to defend her from the temptations of the Evil Spirit." By 1707 she no longer talked of the Evil Spirit. Rather, she "stated, in the presence of all-powerful God and of the Holy Virgin Mary, my holy guardian angel, my protecting men and women saints, and all the celestial court, that I want to live and die in the Catholic faith."

When Marc-Antoine Charpentier was named to the SAINTE-CHAPELLE in 1698, Étiennette began to loan him money. The first loan, 2,700 livres, was dated January 12, 1699. It was followed by two smaller ones: 122 livres on January 12, 1700, and 70 livres the following April 24. All three loans appear related to the composer's mastership at the chapel. Each successive music master was expected to pay his predecessor (or his predecessor's estate) a lump sum of 3,000 livres, ostensibly to reimburse him for money advanced for the first year's food and upkeep for the choirboys and the housekeeper. In other words, for all intents and purposes the new master had to buy the office from his predecessor's family. Since Étiennette made it clear in her will that she had not expected repayment of any loans to one or another member of the immediate family, she in effect purchased her brother's position for him.

After Marc-Antoine's death in 1704, Étiennette handled the succession without the help of a notary. This suggests that the composer did not have much to leave to his niece and nephew, beyond the manuscripts that would come to be known as the *Mélanges*. The Linener's death inventory alludes to "a bundle of five documents concerning the estate of Messire Marcq-Antoine Charpentier, music master of the choirboys of the Sainte-Chapelle of the King in Paris, the said dead woman's brother," who died owing his sister 2,892 livres. This debt permitted her to claim his manuscripts as compensation. As his surviving sibling and de facto executrix, it would have been Étiennette who sat down with representatives of the Chamber of Accounts, surrendering the notebooks that contained works written for the Sainte-Chapelle because they belonged to the King, but insisting on keeping all notebooks filled with outside commissions. It would also have been Étiennette—not her apprentice nephew, JACQUES ÉDOUARD, nor her indebted niece, MARIE-ANNE ÉDOUARD, and her rapacious husband, Jacques-François Mathas —who refused to sell the manuscripts: "The heirs of Monsieur Charpentier refused four thousand livres for the entirety of his works."[7]

In the fall of 1708, Étiennette Charpentier, by now in her mid-to-late seventies, was being harassed by Mathas, who no longer concealed the fact that he had married MARIE-ANNE ÉDOUARD for her aunt's money. The situation had deteriorated by mid-January 1709, when Étiennette had to call the police. When a commissioner from the Châtelet came to interview her, she described Mathas as a "violent and very dangerous man" who on several occasions had come to her lodgings and "insulted" her and the people who were with her. A year earlier, when she happened to be ill, Mathas had asked her to "legally donate her property to him," adding that "if she did not do it, he would hit her so hard on the head that she would never recover, and that he would set fire to the house." Not only had this abusive behavior continued, it was now directed at the shop girl, whom Mathas called a "hussy."

Shortly before Christmas 1708, Mathas stood in front of her shop, spewing forth insults and "impertinent remarks" and asking: "Who will compensate [me] for having married her penniless niece?" Then, on January 16, he knocked on the door; and when the Linener refused to open it, saying that she was unwell, he said he would force her to open it, even if he had to come six times a day. The police report concludes with a summary of Mademoiselle Charpentier's position: she has nothing to work out with Mathas, "not having wished to become involved in her niece's marriage." With a trembling hand, Étiennette signed her name.[8]

It is not as if Étiennette Charpentier had been stingy toward her niece and nephew. Her will refers to gifts she had made to Jacques and Marie-Anne Édouard, gifts that were to play no part in the equal division of her estate between them. In addition, her death inventory alludes to several loans that had never been repaid: "A bundle of twelve documents that are acknowledgments of debts and I O U's for sums given and loaned by the said deceased, ... both to the late Élisabeth Charpentier, her sister, and to the said Sieurs Jacques Édouard, Mathas, and his wife."

On the afternoon of March 22, 1709, two months after filing her complaint about Mathas, Étiennette Charpentier died, one of the victims of that bitter winter. Two hours later, FRANÇOISE FERRAND DE LA FALUÈRE summoned a notary, who quickly put seals on the doors.[9] Scarcely had their aunt been buried in the cemetery behind the Church of Saint-Séverin, than the Mathases began voicing their opposition. Day after day they continued to protest, as they watched the notary list her possessions and summarize her business transactions. Their aunt's will dated April 20, 1707, was not found until April 11.

When the Civil Lieutenant read the will aloud two days later at the Châtelet, Mathas learned that JACQUES ÉDOUARD and MARIE-ANNE ÉDOUARD would share the estate equally, but with one crucial restriction: Marie-Anne would receive no money until her debts were paid. The Linener had also forseen trouble among her heirs and had taken steps to ward it off:

> My wish is that, for the share and portion of my said property that goes to Marie-Anne Édouard, my niece, the debts hereafter listed will be paid before she can be paid, the creditors only having given her time because I begged them and, out of respect for me, asking the said creditors named below not to seize or sue, and to consult the executors of my testament. ...

> I request that my said niece, Marie-Anne Édouard, and Jacques Édouard, her brother and my nephew, observe perpetually the above decisions, ... that they live in good union and friendship. I want and understand that he or she who refuses the conditions of this my testament, or disputes any of its dispositions, or troubles the other in the above dividing-up, using as a pretext and asking for the refund, one against the other, of what I may have given to the one or the other during my life, about which I request and forbid them ever to make a demand on one another, these having been given as a gift according to their need, with no obligations to render account for all these payments, ... on penalty that the infringer pay the one who acquiesces two thousand livres, which will be deducted from the share and portion due him for his or her share of my property,

before he or she can receive anything, begging my executors ... to keep control and use all their authority, this being my intention and last will.

Rather than risk losing two thousand livres, and obviously intimidated by Madame de la Faluère, the heirs stopped protesting. Two weeks later, the executrix presided over a final accounting of the Linener's estate. Jacques Édouard's share totaled 2,301 livres, while Marie-Anne's was 2,440 livres. Her outstanding debts totaled 2,328 livres. In other words, if Mathas did in fact wed Marie-Anne with her inheritance in mind, he did so for 112 livres!

III

To be housed, fed, and clothed for the rest of her days

ÉLISABETH THE WIFE AND MOTHER

Élisabeth Charpentier, wife of Jean Édouard,
maître joueur d'instruments and *maître à danser,*
the composer's sister

É lisabeth Charpentier was one of three surviving daughters born to
LOUIS THE SCRIVENER. Major at the time of her father's death in
1662, she was born in about 1637.

There is no evidence that Élisabeth learned a trade. She could
however sign her name quite skillfully, which may indicate that she
copied documents for her father. Yet she did not live with him during
the final months of his life. Instead, she resided on the rue de la Harpe,
probably in ÉTIENNETTE THE LINENER's lodgings in the house where hung
the sign, *La Barbe d'Or.*

Six months after the Scrivener's death, Élisabeth married Jean Édouard, a master instrumentalist who lived on the Île Saint-Louis. Although
it is impossible to determine the extent to which the marriage was
arranged by the wealthy and influential "friends" who would sign their
wedding contract, the considerations being weighed by the families
concerned, that spring in 1662, surely differed only in magnitude from
those enumerated by a somewhat more prestigious father with ties to
Port-Royal. He had to inform his son that marriage negotiations had
been broken off:

> Seconded by the opinion of all my best friends, I finally broke off the
> marriage that had been proposed for you. You would have been
> given a girl with twenty-eight thousand francs [livres], and with as
> much, or approximately as much, when her father and mother die.
> But they are both still young and can live another twenty years, and

one or the other could even remarry. And so you would run the risk of having, for a long time, only four thousand livres a year from annuities, and you would perhaps be burdened by eight or ten children before you are thirty. You could not have had either horse or carriage, because you would have spent everything for food and clothing. ... Add to that the humor of the girl, who is said to love luxury, society, and all the entertainments that society provides, and who perhaps would have made you despair. ... All I can say is that some very reasonable people who are fond of us embraced my wife and me very cordially, when they learned that I had pushed aside this affair. ... I will not name the persons who made the proposal: you scarcely know them other than by name. I beg you not even to try to guess. I must always be grateful for the good will they showed me on this occasion.[1]

Most of these considerations were beyond Jean Édouard's wildest imaginings. He would be taking a girl with a modest dowry and no hope of inheriting more from her parents or close relatives. Neither he nor the girl would bring an annuity to the union: they would have to live on his music-making and his dancing lessons. Édouard therefore could only hope that Élisabeth was as modest and thrifty as she was being portrayed. As for the burden of numerous children, that depended upon God.

On the afternoon of August 24, 1662, five friends and relatives of the bride came to the "house" where she lived, to witness the signing of the wedding contract.[2] The bride brought as a dowry seven hundred livres in furniture, linens, silver dishes, and "other togs." The first person to sign for her—first, because the most illustrious—was Dame MARIE TALON, wife of Daniel Voisin, master of requests. The bride's two brothers, "Marcq-Anthoine" and "Jehan," that is, ARMAND-JEAN THE ENGINEER, signed next. (No mention was made of Étiennette.) Then came two "friends": "Dame Cheron, the wife of Messire Pierre Chevalier, procurator in the Parlement," and Claude Chevalier, a barrister in the Parlement. (This presumably was the Madame Chevalier who had borrowed a small sum from LOUIS THE SCRIVENER.)

The groom was, by contrast, represented by fourteen friends and relatives. Some of the friends were quite illustrious. There was Dame ÉLISABETH-MARIE MALIER,, widow of Nicolas de Bailleul, royal councillor and president in the Parlement of Paris. She was accompanied by her granddaughter, Marie de Bailleul. There was also "noble man Lhuillier, councillor and royal secretary," and his wife, ÉLISABETH GRIMAUDET (who signed "Grymaudet"). Also present was Pierre Marlin, doctor of theology and curate of Saint-Eustache, who would officiate at the nuptial mass. These illustrious friends were joined by the groom's three aunts, née

Morlot, and their spouses, two of them bourgeois of Paris and the third an archer in the police; and by his two sisters, one the wife of a bourgeois of Paris, the other a spinster.

As the eye moves down the two lists of guests, it is not readily apparent that this marriage of a young woman from the rue de la Harpe and a young musician from the Île Saint-Louis was for all intents and purposes a union between the protégée of some faithful servants of the House of Guise and the protégé of a group of faithful servants of the House of Orléans. In a sense, this modest marriage parallels a far more prestigious union celebrated five years earlier, when LOUIS-JOSEPH DE LORRAINE, DUKE OF GUISE, wed Her Royal Highness ISABELLE D'ORLÉANS OF ALENÇON, the daughter of the King's late uncle, GASTON D'ORLÉANS. In short, years before Marc-Antoine Charpentier returned from Rome and began to compose for the Guises, a protective network was in place, ready to recommend young Charpentier to MADEMOISELLE MARIE DE GUISE THE REGENT, the Duke's aunt and guardian.

It is not clear how Jean Édouard came to have these "friends" who were benefitting from the benevolence of the House of Orléans. The young man was the son of a wine merchant (also named Jean Édouard) who in 1637 was living with his aunt in the Orléans' parish of Saint-Sulpice.[3] Morlot, the wine merchant's father-in-law, had been a bailiff-sergeant at the CHÂTELET, so it is not surprising that the wine merchant himself, having been widowed and left with a small daughter, would take as a second wife the daughter of a fellow bailiff-sergeant. Before his death, which occurred prior to 1662, the wine merchant had become an élu at Rozay-en-Brie.

Bits and pieces of information reveal that Élisabeth Charpentier and Jean Édouard settled in the parish of Saint-André-des-Arts, where several children were born to them. Some died in childhood, among them the godchild of Adrien de Roanne, organist of the churches of Saint-Hilaire and Saint-Étienne-des-Grès.[4] Jean Édouard's name appears among the guests at the wedding of a fellow dancing master in 1672,[5] at which time he described himself as a "dancing master." (Thirty years later, apparently embroidering upon the truth, his children would describe their late father as "one of the twenty-four violins of the King's chamber."[6])

As parishioners of Saint-André-des-Arts, the Édouards were by-standers to the squabble that followed the death of the curate in March 1678, and the selection of Nicolas Mathieu, son of a physician on the Faculty of Medicine, to be his replacement. (Owing to a dispute, Mathieu was not officially declared curate until June 1681.) Until his death in 1706, Mathieu not only filled the parish church with music, he also organized concerts at which Italian and Italianate works were performed,

Fille de qualité aprenant a danser

Elle entend fort bien la cadence   Mais toute son intelligence
Son air est Noble et tout charmant   C'est de faire au bal un Amant.

Se vend chez N. Arnoult rue de la fromagerie a jmage S.t Claude aux Galler avec privilege du Roy. 1687.

A noble girl learns to dance.
A dancing master plays his distinctive "pocket" violin, *pochette*, as he
teaches girls to dance. One girl hopes that her efforts will be rewarded
by attracting a lover: *Elle entend fort bien la cadence, Son air est noble et tout
charmant, Mais toute son intelligence C'est de faire au bal un Amant.*

including motets by Marc-Antoine Charpentier.[7] Were the Édouards—
and ARMAND-JEAN CHARPENTIER THE ENGINEER, who also resided in the
parish of Saint-André-des-Arts—the conduit by which some of Marc-
Antoine Charpentier's motets found its way into Mathieu's musical
library?

Jean Édouard died in 1683 and was buried at Saint-André-des-Arts
on May 19, in the presence of his brother-in-law, "Jean Charpentier,
royal engineer," that is, ARMAND-JEAN THE ENGINEER.[8] Marc-Antoine's
absence is explained by the fact that late in April he had become "very
ill," so ill that he had to withdraw from a competition for a sub-mastership in the royal chapel.

Despite having several minor children to care for—seven-year-old
Jacques, seventeen-year-old Marie-Anne, and Jean, whose birth date is
unknown—the widow appears to have done nothing to settle her
husband's estate. She served as the children's de facto guardian until
early 1685, when the end of Marie-Anne's apprenticeship as a linener
approached. In February 1685 ARMAND-JEAN THE ENGINEER, rather than
Marc-Antoine, was chosen to be the assistant guardian for the three
minor children of the late Jean Édouard, "bourgeois of Paris and master
instrumentalist."[9]

On February 20, 1685, the notary was summoned to the fourth-floor
lodging on the rue Saint-André-des-Arts occupied by the widow and
children of the late "dancing master and instrument player." The contents of only one room were listed.[10] Were the Édouards so poor that all
five of them had lived in a single room?

Poor, perhaps. But they liked nice things. In addition to the usual
cooking equipment, the notary listed a copper water-container on its
stand, pewter estimated as weighing forty pounds, and several dozen
napkins. The walls of the room were covered with so-called "Bergamo
tapestries" on which hung a small mirror in a black frame, two other
mirrors with Venetian glass in gilded copper frames, a print of the Holy
Sacrament in a gilded wooden frame, and a Christ of gilded wood on a
black velvet background. The Édouards owned a set of faience pots,
probably the sort commonly used to decorate chimneypieces. At the
windows hung white linen curtains. The furniture included two small
walnut tables with turned legs; ten walnut chairs with green linen
upholstery, plus a matching armchair, all with green wool slipcovers; two
small tapestried chairs; a poster bed with green serge hangings and the
usual bedding; a small wardrobe cabinet; two black leather-covered
chests; and a folding camp bed with its bedding. No musical instruments,
nor any musical scores or teaching methods, are mentioned. That the
only document summarized by the notary was the couple's wedding

contract suggests that they did not have enough spare cash to purchase interest-bearing annuities or to lend money at interest.

Left with three minor children to raise and prepare for a livelihood, Élisabeth leaned upon her younger brother. In 1688 ARMAND-JEAN THE ENGINEER was at his sister's side when MARIE-ANNE ÉDOUARD completed preparations for opening a linen shop. He watched Élisabeth as she paid three hundred livres here and three hundred livres there, in order to "please" and "establish" her daughter. (Had some of the money come from Armand-Jean's own purse?) The Engineer did not, however, sign his niece's wedding contract in 1689, nor does his signature appear on any Édouard documents after 1688. For example, when JACQUES ÉDOUARD was apprenticed to a printer in 1697, no mention was made of his guardian-uncle. This suggests that the Engineer may have died in around 1690, leaving his sister to arrange for her younger son's ill-advised apprenticeship on her own.

Élisabeth Charpentier's final years were not easy, financially. This does not mean that she turned her back on amusements such as the theater. On three occasions, between December 1687 and February 1688, "Mesdemoiselles Charpentier" charged tickets at the theater for which their brother had composed so much music.[11] For several years Élisabeth remained in her lodging near Saint-André-des-Arts, but by 1697 she had moved a few streets away, to the rue du Jardinet. It is unlikely that MARIE-ANNE ÉDOUARD was able to keep her commitment to house, feed, and clothe her mother for the rest of her days. Her business had failed by the early 1690s. ÉTIENNETTE THE LINENER made sure that her sister would not want, loaning her money that she did not expect to be repaid.[12] By 1697 Madame Édouard's handwriting was shaky. She probably died not long after arranging her son's apprenticeship, for her sister spoke of her in the past tense in a testament dated 1707.

IV

MARIE THE CONVERSE

Marie Charpentier, known in religion as Sister Sainte-Blandine,
converse nun at Port-Royal of Paris,
the composer's sister

M arie Charpentier, one of three daughters born to LOUIS THE
SCRIVENER, left the family circle to become a converse sister at
the Cistercian ABBEY OF PORT-ROYAL before the troubles over
Jansenism broke out there in 1661.[1] Since she had, so to speak, been
"established" in a prestigious convent, thereby assuring her future needs,
no mention was made of her when the inventory of her late father's
possessions was drawn up in January 1662. Marie de Sainte-Blandine
Charpentier was still alive when ÉTIENNETTE THE LINENER, her sister, wrote
a last will and testament in April 1707:

> I give and will to the Dames of Port-Royal, in the Faubourg Saint-
> Jacques, the lump sum of one hundred livres, on condition that they
> say, in their church, one hundred requiem masses for me; and in the
> event that my sister, Marie Charpentier, known as Sister Sainte-
> Blandine, has died, I beg them that fifty of the hundred masses be
> said on her behalf, begging the aforesaid Dames to remember me in
> their other holy prayers. *Estiennette Charpentier*[2]

An earlier will of Étiennette's, dictated when she was quite ill in January
1676, shows that Marie was living in the Paris house on the rue Saint-Jacques that was being purged of its Jansenist leanings, not at the fervent
Jansenist stronghold of Port-Royal-des-Champs, the house "in the fields"
southwest of the city. Together, these clues make it possible to sketch
Marie Charpentier's life from the late 1650s until her death in the early
eighteenth century.

Marie postulated to be a converse sister, not a more prestigious
"choir" nun. She and her parents did not make that decision on purely

Prosp. de l'Eglise du Monastere du S.t Sacrement
Des Religieuses de Port Royal, Ordre de Cisteaux.

The Church and Convent of Port-Royal.

In this Parisian convent situated in the Faubourg Saint-Jacques, Marie Charpentier, known in religion as Sister Sainte-Blandine, was a converse nun. In the 1680s Marc-Antoine Charpentier composed several works for devotions here.

financial grounds. True, at many abbeys becoming a choir nun would have required a sizeable dowry; but Port-Royal had long prided itself on admitting poor girls to its choir.[3] In fact, since Marie's admission to Port-Royal coincides chronologically with the election of Superior Magdelaine de Ligny as abbess in December 1661 (she and her brother, the new bishop of Meaux, were Chancellor Pierre Séguier's niece and nephew), the relative poverty of this cousin of CHARLES SEVIN, this niece of PIERRE CHARPENTIER THE CHAPLAIN of Meaux, presumably was overlooked. In sum, money can be ruled out as the compelling factor in Marie's decision to become a humble converse sister.

This decision may have been based on Marie talents, or lack of them. Perhaps she could not sing; and perhaps she lacked other skills that might compensate for this "defect."[4] Or was she intent upon humiliating her pride by spending the rest of her life as a domestic? Whatever her and her family's reasons, she committed herself to a life of service, glorying in the fact that God had given her the "talent" to serve. To be a converse, Marie had to be "solid" and healthy in body and mind:

> The converse sisters will be chosen [from those who are] healthy in body and gentle and docile in spirit, accompanied by solidity, so that their outside occupations will not rob them of their inner spirit. ... One takes great care that they delight in their condition, and that it is not solely the incapacity to be a choir nun, but a true love for lowliness and humiliation, that makes them embrace this state, being relieved that God has made the choice for them in not giving them the necessary talents to aspire to something else. If some girl who is capable of being a choir nun asks to be a converse, and if this can be done with discretion, let this be granted to her. ... Let the converse sisters therefore be glorified in their loftiness, to use Saint James's expression, which consists of their smallness and their abasement.[5]

In sum, if one assumes that the Charpentiers' and Marie's decisions were shaped by these considerations, one can conjecture that the girl was not pushed to enter Port-Royal as a converse because she had an intellectual or physical handicap that would have made it difficult for her to marry and/or conduct a business. Rather, her life of service can be seen as a devotional act, not only for the young woman herself but for the entire family. Louis Charpentier and his wife presumably felt mixed emotions about this vocation—emotions akin to those of another father whose devotion had been shaped by Port-Royal and whose beloved daughter would have taken her vows at Port-Royal-des-Champs had the religious dispute not led to the suppression of all noviciates there:

I don't know if I told you that my dear older daughter has entered the Carmelites: I have wept a lot over it, but she was absolutely determined to carry out the resolution she had made. ... I have gone to see her several times. She is charmed by the life she is living in the monastery, although that life is very austere; and the whole house is charmed by her. She is infinitely more gay than she has ever been. I have to believe that God wants her in that house, since He has caused her to be so happy there.[6]

At Port-Royal, girls usually began their noviciate at sixteen or seventeen years of age. They donned "a gray robe, a toque and a white veil, and a scapulary that [novice converses wore] only for Holy Communion, the procession of the Holy Sacrament, and the ceremonies they attend, which are Candlemas, Ash Wednesday, and Palm Sunday, and when they go to the parlor." A year later, the time came for Marie to take the habit of a novice: "The robing ceremony takes place in the chapter room or in the choir, with the grill closed. The Mother [Superior] will say all the prayers said for choir nuns, except the blessing of the habit and the veil, which will be done by the priest prior to the ceremony." At the end of her year-long noviciate, the new converse was questioned by the choir nuns, who voted either to admit her or reject her. If admitted, she immediately made her profession "in the hands of the Abbess," and she put on the habit of a professed converse, that is, "the gray scapulary with the red cross, and the black veil" that had been blessed prior to the vote. Sister Sainte-Blandine presumably was a full-fledged professed converse nun by the time she was twenty.[7]

On that day both the new nun and her family must have followed what had become a ritual: at the appropriate moment, each would burst into tears. The parents were expected to break down during the ceremony, but the stalwart young nun would master her emotions until she had left the church. Evoking his daughter's "courage," a Jansenist father—who "could not stop sobbing"—recounted the family's emotions:

She avoided looking at me and her mother during the ceremony, for fear of being moved by our emotions. When the time came for her to kiss all the other nuns, as was customary, ... an elderly nun had her kiss her mother and her sister, who were standing by, dissolving in tears. ... She nonetheless finished the ceremony with the same modest and tranquil air she had displayed since the beginning. But when it was over, she withdrew from the nuns' choir into a little room, where she let her tears flow in a torrent upon recollecting those of her mother.[8]

A few minutes later, "laughing at her own weakness," the new nun entered the parlor to take leave of her parents, "as if nothing had happened."

As a converse, Marie Charpentier had "no active or passive voice" in how the abbey was run. She and the other converses were expected to "show great respect for the choir nuns, who will treat them charitably and cordially, like their sisters." Their basic needs were to be met; but owing to the fact that most of them had lived simply and frugally since "their first nourishing," it was assumed that they could get by on less than the nuns of higher social rank. Indeed, they could not expect a more comfortable life in the convent than they would have lived in the world. The choir nuns were entitled to give orders to the converses, who under the cellarer's supervision did the "heaviest work, such as cooking, baking, washing, caring for the cows and chickens, shoemaking, and similar things." Under no circumstances, however, could a converse be asked to become the personal servant of the choir nuns or their nurse in the infirmary. Nor could a converse be assigned to serve the children who boarded at the abbey, nor any benefactresses (such as DOCTOR VALLANT's former patroness, Madame de Sablé) who visited or resided at the abbey. Owing to the physical labor the converses did each day, they were dispensed from most fasts and could eat their regular fare on the day of a "major laundry," whenever this arduous task was done on a Friday. Although she was not entitled to sing, Marie was expected to listen devoutly to the "angelic psalmody" of the choir nuns, whispering the words as sincerely as the choir nuns sang them. Like the choir nuns, she watched before the Holy Sacrament; and, like them, she went to bed at eight in the evening, rising at four for morning prayers.[9]

At Port-Royal there was nonetheless a special class of converses: nuns with a special skill that would facilitate the abbey's contact with the outside world. For example, after paying a lump sum to the abbey, a certain Mademoiselle Sevin (it has not been determined whether she was a relative of Marie Charpentier's cousin, CHARLES SEVIN) was admitted as a converse, to "continue her care and service to the Abbess, and other occupations suitable for a *demoiselle*, as the Abbess might deem appropriate." She could do this work "either inside the abbey, where she sleeps, or outside the monastery, where she inspects all the domestics to be sure that everything they do is in order."[10] A converse who knew how to copy documents and do sums—skills the daughter of a master scrivener was likely to have acquired—would be precious, for she could bridge an administrative gap between the world and the cloister.

When Marie Charpentier took her vows, there were just over thirty converses divided between both houses of the abbey, with most of them residing at Port-Royal-des-Champs. Then, in April 1661, all boarders, all postulants, and all novices were expelled from that fervently Jansenist house.[11] After the nuns in the Parisian convent refused to sign the Formulary denouncing Jansenius, the Archbishop of Paris took control of that house in July 1664, placing guards there and sending the recalcitrant nuns to Port-Royal-des-Champs—including at least thirteen converses who were "protesting about everything that was going on." Was Marie one of the "two or three" weeping converses whom the Archbishop encountered in the cloister on August 27, 1664? Addressing them "with great scorn," he said: "Be quiet, do not cry, you have no reason to. Your mothers were taken from you because they were disobedient and rebellious. You will be given others in their place who will be worth as much as they are."[12] During the year that followed, still more nuns and converses were sent to Port-Royal-des-Champs, during a battle of wills that ended in a withdrawal of the sacraments from any sister who refused to sign the Formulary. When the two houses were separated financially and administratively in 1668, there were only ten nuns in the Paris house, including three converses, while sixty-nine choir nuns and close to thirty converses were living at Port-Royal-des-Champs on reduced revenues.[13]

On June 30, 1665, Mother Agnès Arnauld had addressed a letter to the converses concerning "the plan the Archbishop had, ... to leave them all in the Paris house with the rest of the community that he was claiming to win over." "My dear sisters," she began, "I am so touched by the pain you feel at the separation that is being prepared, that I would do anything to sweeten this bitterness for you." It was a "time of sacrifice," she continued, urging the converses to remain calm and do what God leads them to do, and to remember that she would always be close to them.

Marie Charpentier spent the decade of the so-called "Peace of the Church," 1668–1679, in the Parisian house on the rue Saint-Jacques. In other words, there can be no doubt that she signed the Formulary. By a royal order, this house had not only been given the lion's share of the abbey's possessions, it could also accept the novices and boarders who would permit it to grow and prosper. By contrast, with no novices or pensioners permitted, and with a sharply reduced income, the house in the fields was doomed to a slow death. The will dictated by Marie's sister, ÉTIENNETTE THE LINENER, places Sister Sainte-Blandine at Port-Royal of Paris in January 1676; and other sources show that she was still in the Paris house during the tenure of Abbess Marguerite de HARLAY, 1685–1695. She remained there until her death.

Sister Sainte-Blandine probably helped prepare the "magnificent" food served after the mass[A] performed at Port-Royal of Paris on July 20, 1687. The music had been composed by her brother at the request of the Cordeliers of the Great Convent, to honor ARCHBISHOP HARLAY and his sister the Abbess. But was Sister Sainte-Blandine permitted to attend that glorious service or partake of the splendid repast?

It is not known whether the Charpentier family shared the Jansenist views being espoused by the Arnaulds during the late 1650s, when Marie began her noviciate at Port-Royal. Family documents do, by contrast, reveal that by the mid-1670s ÉTIENNETTE THE LINENER was very close to the Jesuits, those unconcealed adversaries of the Jansenists. That Port-Royal had abandoned some of its austerity by the late 1680s does not appear to have disturbed Étiennette unduly. Nor is it likely that Marc-Antoine Charpentier was a closet Jansenist. To the contrary. Owing, it would seem, to the family's JESUIT FRIENDS, he appears to have been composing for one or another of the THREE JESUIT HOUSES of the capital from the early 1670s on, and he became their music master in mid-1687.

As for Marie de Sainte-Blandine Charpentier, if any Jansenist coals glowed in her heart, for the rest of her life she was expected to struggle each day to extinguish them. As she heeded the orders of a succession of anti-Jansenist abbesses, was she guided by the memory of Mother Agnès' admonition? Did she always seek to do what God led her to do, remembering all the while that Agnès Arnauld would always be close? If so, that closeness had to be spiritual rather than physical, for Mother Agnès had died in 1671.

[A] Cahier LI, H. 5.

1662   1685

V

... to serve the King

ARMAND-JEAN THE ENGINEER

Armand-Jean Charpentier, *écrivain*,
engraver, and *ingénieur du Roi*,
the composer's brother

Armand-Jean Charpentier, some two years younger than his brother Marc-Antoine, was born in 1645. His father, LOUIS THE SCRIVENER, clearly was preparing him to be a scrivener. By 1662 the youth had settled upon the formal signature and ornamental paraph that he would use in his planned profession. Although this signature changed slightly over the years, he continued to use it as an adult. Armand-Jean was somewhat less consistent about his Christian name. He clearly preferred *Jean* to the *Armand-Jean* that proclaimed a link between the Charpentiers and the RICHELIEUS and their circle.

Shortly after his father's death in December 1661, sixteen-year-old Armand-Jean was apprenticed for three years, for a fee of two hundred livres,[1] although he could technically have been granted a mastership at twenty without completing an apprenticeship. That is to say, a son born during his late father's mastership did not have to pass an exam or pay an entry fee to the guild. He simply gave the syndic a sample of his handwriting and signature, and then he "completed a simple practical test." But on that winter day of 1662, Armand-Jean's guardian decided against this option, preferring a formal apprenticeship that would teach his ward not only the art of calligraphy but the art of engraving as well.[2]

Armand-Jean Charpentier presumably completed his apprenticeship and become a master scrivener, like his late father; but this must remain a presumption, for the surviving register of admissions to the corporation does not begin until December 1673. This source reveals, however, that if Armand-Jean did in fact earn his mastership, he did not play an active role in the guild.

Not until May 19, 1683, does his name reappear in the sources. Remnants of the parish records for Saint-André-des-Arts show him at the burial of his brother-in-law, Jean Édouard, the dancing-master husband of ÉLISABETH CHARPENTIER. He was described as being a "royal engineer"[3]; yet his name does not appear on the list of "engineers paid by His Majesty in the department headed by Monsieur de Louvois," drawn up in 1683.[4] Other documents in the military archives reveal that the lowest-level royal engineers (who were paid forty or fifty livres a year) were often badly wounded at sieges along the northern frontier, where they had been sent to draw up plans and compute distances. Those engineers who could not draw hired their own artists and secretaries.

A notarized agreement sheds light on what Engineer Charpentier was doing during these years. In April 1685 he and an "equerry to the king" named Antoine de Vandeuil signed an agreement about a portable flour mill they were developing "to serve the King." "Armand-Jean" Charpentier stated that he lived on the rue de Seine, in an "academy run by Vandeuil," that is, a school where young nobles learned riding and dancing. (Was he by any chance teaching these boys the art of fortification, so valuable for nobles who planned a military career, as well as draftsmanship and penmanship?) If the project failed, Charpentier agreed to reimburse Vandeuil for his costs and would keep the mill and its paraphernalia; but if it succeeded, the two men would share equally any reward that Louis XIV might give them.[5]

A few months earlier, on February 20, 1685, a family council had been held at the Châtelet to selected an assistant guardian for the Édouard children.[6] "Marc-Antoine Charpentier, bourgeois of Paris," dwelling in the "Great Hôtel of Guise," attended the meeting, as did several Édouard relatives and friends—who included a priest, a tailor, a clerk in the Parlement, and a bourgeois of Paris. The assembly concluded that ÉLISABETH CHARPENTIER, Widow Édouard, should be the children's guardian, and that she would be assisted by "Messire Jean Charpentier, bourgeois of Paris." Later that day, the Royal Engineer—who this time said his name was "Jean" and described himself as a "bourgeois of Paris" living on the rue de la Vieille-Bouclerie, just off the rue Saint-André-des-Arts—was present when an inventory was made of his late brother-in-law's possessions. None of the relatives and friends who had assembled at the Châtelet were at his side.

Three years later, in January and February 1688, "Armand-Jean Charpentier, royal engineer" was present when his niece, MARIE-ANNE ÉDOUARD, completed the formalities that would permit her to earn her living as a mistress linener. Charpentier gave his address as the rue de l'Éperon, in the parish of Saint-André-des-Arts; but by October of that year—when Marie-Anne chose her mother as her business partner—he had moved to the rue Dauphine, in the same parish. In other words, Armand-Jean may have moved into the lodging of Marc-Antoine, who is known to have been living that street in 1692,[7] having perhaps settled down in that parish when he left the Hôtel de Guise.

A year later, when family and friends assembled to sign the wedding contract of Marie-Anne, who was now major, Armand-Jean was not present.[8] Had he been advised to refrain from signing a contract where so much hinged on the success or failure of his niece's shop? (Neither Marc-Antoine nor ÉTIENNETTE THE LINENER signed this document, perhaps for the same reason.) Was he perhaps at the front, preparing fortifications for the following summer? Was he dead? Whatever the explanation for the absence of the various Charpentier signatures on this wedding contract, no allusion to Armand-Jean Charpentier has been found after October 1688. In 1707 his sister Étiennette referred to her late "brothers," in the plural. There is no indication that Armand-Jean the Engineer ever married.

Mathas   *Marie-anne Édouard*

VI

Left with a shay and a horse, which was taken

MARIE-ANNE THE UNFORTUNATE

Marie-Anne Édouard, *maîtresse lingère* of Paris,
successively the wife of François Moreau and Jacques-François Mathas,
the composer's niece

By February 1688, twenty-three-year-old Marie-Anne Edouard had completed her training as a linener. Once her widowed mother, ÉLISABETH CHARPENTIER, had paid the requisite three hundred livres to the lineners' corporation, Marie-Anne would officially become a "merchant linener." In order to "please and totally establish" the young woman, her mother and her uncle, ARMAND-JEAN THE ENGINEER—who at the time lived on the rue de l'Éperon, not far from his sister's lodgings on the rue Saint-André-des-Arts—worked out an arrangement by which Marie-Anne would become the associate of a linener who ran a shop on the rue Saint-Honoré, just opposite the rue de la Lingerie.

By early October the arrangement had been canceled in favor of a joint venture with her mother, who agreed to contribute an additional three hundred livres so that her daughter could set up a shop of her own. (To supplement the cash she had set aside, ÉLISABETH CHARPENTIER used the totality of her personal property as collateral for a loan of 112 livres.) In return, Marie-Anne would be a half-partner with her mother; and once she married, she promised to "nourish, lodge, and keep her mother, as befits her social status, for the rest of her days." Any marriage must meet her mother's approval: if not, Marie-Anne would have to repay the six hundred livres. Marie-Anne's new store was situated on the rue de l'Arbre-sec, near the Halles.[1]

A year later, Marie-Anne Édouard, now major, married François Moreau, the son of a sworn grain-carrier.[2] The groom, a bourgeois of Paris, apparently did tailoring, and his brother Louis was an engraver. (This raises the possibility that the marriage was promoted, if not arranged, by her uncle and guardian, ARMAND-JEAN THE ENGINEER, who had studied with an engraver in the 1660s.)

The bride's dowry consisted of 2,300 livres in merchandise (linen cloth, shirts, cravats, and "other sorts of lingerie") and 1,000 livres in household goods (a bed and kitchen utensils). Moreau's parents made the couple a gift of 6,000 livres. The bride's mother clearly approved of the union, for her name appears on the wedding contract, along with that of the bride's brother, Jean Édouard, the older of the two Édouard sons. (Jean disappeared from the family records after this event.) Marie-Anne's younger brother, JACQUES ÉDOUARD, did not sign. Neither did her uncles, Armand-Jean the Engineer and Marc-Antoine the Composer; yet their former guardian, elderly Nicolas Dupin, "former procurator in the Parlement," signed that day.

Marie-Anne's business did not flourish. In July 1690 François Moreau obtained a separation of property, having been forced to pay three thousand livres to his wife's creditors for business debts incurred prior to her marriage. By June 1691 she had lost her shop and its contents.[3] For eighteen years her creditors remained at bay, for ÉTIENNETTE THE LINENER had assured the wholesalers that they would be paid in full if they were willing to wait until her own death.

After François Moreau's death in 1693, in distant Toulouse, Marie-Anne declared to a notary that "the only property her husband had left her was a shay and a horse, which was taken by his father." On a legal technicality she sued the Moreaus for François' share of his mother's estate, asserting that the inventory had intentionally concealed the family's wealth, and that the Moreaus had threatened her. Her appeal to the judges ended with these words: "She hopes that the court will show some consideration for her, after her husband dissipated and spent everything she had brought as a dowry." If not, she will be "without any possessions and overwhelmed with debts," while the Moreaus will have everything.[4]

Marie-Anne remarried. Her second husband was Jacques-François Mathas, a bourgeois of Paris. He had been lured by the prosperous business being run by the young widow's spinster aunt, ÉTIENNETTE THE LINENER, who by then was well into her sixties. After years of waiting for the aunt's demise—and of frustration at watching her go about her business in good health—Mathas lost his head. He stood shouting in the street before her shop, asking "Who will reward [me] for having married her penniless niece?" When Étiennette died during the horrible winter of 1709, Marie-Anne received 2,440 livres. Her creditors were paid directly from her aunt's estate: 2,328 livres in all. In the end Mathas and his wife received only 112 livres.[5]

VII

A poor wretch who sells junk books

JACQUES THE BOOKSELLER-PRINTER

Jacques Édouard, master bookseller and printer,
the composer's nephew

J acques Édouard appears to have been the last child born to ÉLISABETH CHARPENTIER and Jean Édouard. According to one document, he was baptized on January 27, 1670, presumably as an infant. This would make him just over thirteen when his father died. (A different document suggests that he was only eight at the time of Jean Édouard's demise.)

No evidence has yet been uncovered to suggest that Jacques was a musician, like his dancing-master father or his composer uncle. If he showed interest in Marc-Antoine Charpentier's manuscripts later in life, it was primarily for monetary rather than esthetic reasons. Indeed, the fact that the family did not apprentice Jacques to a dancing master, thereby benefitting from financial exonerations the corporation granted to the children of deceased members, suggests that the youth had little talent for either music or dance.

Instead, in 1697 his mother—doubtlessly without the advice of her brother, ARMAND-JEAN THE ENGINEER, who may have died in around 1690 —made what proved to be an unfortunate decision: she would set her son up as a bookseller and printer.

Did she realize how difficult it now was to obtain a mastership as a printer? In 1686 the government had decreed that the number of print shops in Paris would henceforth be limited to thirty-six, and that no printers would be admitted to the guild until that goal had been reached through the closure of existing shops. A few posts fell vacant in 1694, but in principle only one new journeyman printer was admitted to the guild each year. These difficulties were exacerbated by the near impossibility of acquiring a shop. A would-be printer who did not belong to a printing dynasty either had to accumulate a large sum of money with which to buy a shop and equipment, or else he had to marry the daughter or widow of an established printer.

These obstacles apparently did not frighten Élisabeth Charpentier. In June 1697 Jacques was apprenticed[1] for five years to a printer and bookseller on the rue de la Huchette. The contract bears Élisabeth's shaky signature. By 1704 Jacques had completed his apprenticeship and had fulfilled the obligation imposed by the edict of 1687, to work at least three additional years with one or more master printers. Actually, Jacques was then working in his fourth print shop; and although he had completed his apprenticeship, he was, in the words of the royal officials who supervised the printing trade, still "only an apprentice," having not yet been received as a master.

In the spring of 1704 four positions as master printer opened, and Jacques Édouard was among the candidates. Selection depended on making one's intentions clear by June 1; but when the role was called that day, none of the four candidates replied. The positions therefore went unassigned until August 1705, when Édouard presented the requisite proofs of his apprenticeship, his subsequent work with printers, and his language skills. To be specific, he submitted a statement from the rector of the University attesting that he was "adequate" in Latin and "that he can read Greek," obligations imposed on all new masters by the edict of 1686.

In March 1706 Édouard was received as a master bookseller.[2] He immediately paid the entry fee of twelve livres to join the printers' and stationers' Confraternity of the Evangelist, which met at the Church of the Mathurins; but although he paid his annual membership fee in 1707, he never become a leader in the guild.[3]

Master Bookseller Édouard was not entitled to print books in a shop of his own, for no mastership as a printer was available. He nonetheless left the print shop where he was working and opened a bookshop in the square in front of Notre-Dame Cathedral. There he bided his time until he could wed a printer's widow or daughter. He waited for seven years. Not until October 1713, having married Marie-Anne Le Page, the widow of Pierre Lesclapart,[4] did Jacques Édouard ask the guild to list his name among the master printers of the city.

That does not mean that Édouard's name does not appear on the title pages of books published in Paris prior to 1713. In 1705 he obtained a three-year privilege to publish a commentary upon a recent printing of Louis Moréri's dictionary.[5] Since he could not print the book himself, the privilege states that he could "have it printed by whatever bookseller or printer he might choose," and with "fine paper and handsome type, according to royal rulings," after which he was entitled to "sell and distribute it throughout the realm."

A few years later, on March 23, 1709—just one day after the death of ÉTIENNETTE CHARPENTIER THE LINENER, his aunt—Jacques Édouard was granted a royal privilege to publish some of his late uncle's motets. The plates for the book already existed at the time of Aunt Étiennette's death. At the end of the volume of *Motets melez de symphonie composez par Monsieur Charpentier*, the engraver wrote: "Finished on March 9, 1709. Engraved by Roussel." In other words, some or all of the late composer's manuscripts were in Édouard's possession by early 1709, when MARIE-ANNE ÉDOUARD's husband, Jacques-François Mathas, was tormenting the elderly Linener and trying to extort money from her. (Étiennette Charpentier appears to have kept the manuscripts from 1704 until late 1708, at which point she passed them to her nephew, as a sort of ante-mortem legacy.)

Someone had delved into the bundles of music and had culled out a dozen works likely to appeal to chapel masters and entice them to buy the book. Most of the pieces were solos, duos, and trios, although a more ambitious *Domine salvum fac Regem* closed the volume. That same someone—the handwriting is not Édouard's—then marked the scores with a red pencil and added comments: "Mark it 'Fourth Motet'," and so forth. For the engraver's convenience, this anonymous individual either made a clean version of each work or delegated someone to do so. These clean copies were eventually returned to Édouard, who tucked them into the "fat notebook," *gros cahier*, that contained things his late uncle had written for PORT-ROYAL and for his own self—including his Latin "Epitaph." The copies used by the engraver were still there in 1726, but they were subsequently discarded by staff at the Royal Library.[6]

The papers listed in Étiennette Charpentier's death inventory show that she had loaned Édouard and Mathas money, but the date and amount are not specified. Did she subsidize the printing of this volume, partly as a memorial to her late brother and partly in hopes that the project would be lucrative enough to dissipate Mathas' growing resentment over her longevity?

By his privilege Édouard was authorized to "cause [these motets] to be engraved ... in such form, margins, characters, and as many times as he deems appropriate, as long as they are in conformity with Christianity"; and he was permitted to "sell the books or cause them to be sold throughout the kingdom for six consecutive years, starting today," March 23, 1709; and "no one in the city of Paris can print or counterfeit or sell a version, even if it is printed abroad."[7]

l'Eglize de NOSTRE DAME.

The square, *parvis*, in front of Notre-Dame Cathedral.
The people in the right foreground are emerging from the rue Neuve-Notre-Dame. If they walk to the right of the little domed fountain, and go past the gothic door of the Hôtel-Dieu hospital, they reach Jacques Édouard's tiny bookshop, *Les Trois Rois*, visible just to the left of the gothic door and leaning against the hospital wall.

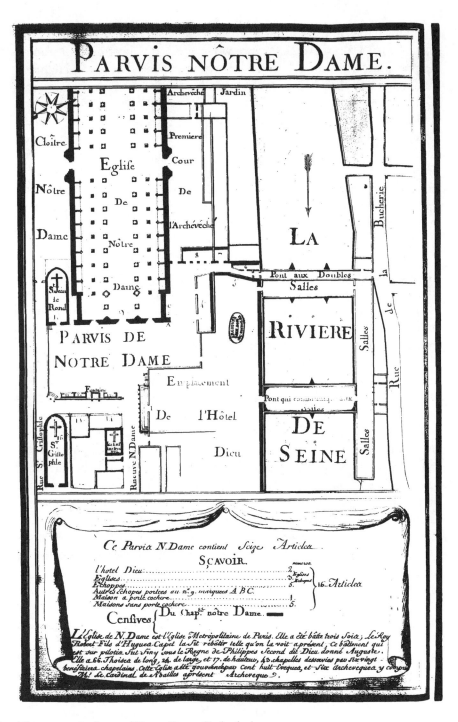

The square in front of Notre-Dame Cathedral.
Jacques Édouard's tiny shop can be seen just below the A in NOTRE DAME.

This publishing venture was an overt solicitation for protection from PHILIPPE III, DUKE OF ORLÉANS who, when Duke of Chartres, had studied composition with Marc-Antoine Charpentier. Once His Royal Highness had agreed to allow the book to be dedicated to him, Édouard wrote a dedicatory letter alluding to "the special protection" the Duke had "the kindness" to show the late composer; the "protection" the Duke surely will give to "works that sometimes were the subject of his entertainment"; and the "memory of a man who, during his life, received so many benefits from you." This past generosity, Édouard continued, was a "worthy recompense for the troubles we have taken to make these works public." He closed by suggesting that the "honor" of being two of the Duke's "servants" was sufficient reward for him and Mathas.

That this "first" volume of a planned series remained the only book of Charpentier's compositions published by his nephews, suggests that the customary gratification sent by His Royal Highness did not meet their expectations. Revealing a profound ignorance of his late uncle's activities during the 1690s, had Jacques Édouard unwittingly made himself ridiculous by assuming that the Duke remembered works that had been written and performed when he was a small child?[8]

In 1714 Jacques Édouard published a treatise on obstetrics.[9] Its title page bears the address of his shop near Notre-Dame, at the sign of "The Three Kings," *Les Trois Rois*. (The shop was located "near the Hôtel-Dieu," just where the rue Neuve Notre-Dame entered the open space before the cathedral.) This octavo volume, which cost three livres, sold so well that a second edition was printed in 1715. The final pages of the book shed light on Édouard's clientele. For sixteen livres he sold Chomel's economic dictionary in two folio volumes; and for five more livres his customers could obtain a folio-sized supplement to the dictionary. He also sold "several books on medicine and surgery by the best authors." His wares included a few volumes of music: for three livres one could still purchase the quarto, paper-bound volume of Charpentier's motets, and for five livres he sold a similar volume called *Les fragments en musique de M. de Lully* that Ballard had printed back in 1702. For one livre and fifteen sous one could acquire a little book of comedies, *Le Nouveau Théâtre italien* by "Monsieur Dominique" (Pierre-François Biancolelli). The final book on the list was *Réflexion sur le luxe des femmes*, a paper-bound brochure about women and luxury that cost only eight sous. In addition, Édouard "sells all sorts of books about devotion and about customs, both wholesale and retail." In other words, his principal clientele consisted of worshipers at the cathedral, physicians at the nearby Hôtel-Dieu, and barristers from the Palace of Justice who sought information about customary law.

By 1712 Édouard had more or less abandoned the Charpentier project. With the exception of Lully's operas, the royal court clearly wanted new music, not revivals of works first performed in the 1670s, 1680s, and 1690s. Casting about for other ways to make money from his uncle's manuscripts, Édouard put them up for sale. He inserted an advertisement in a literary journal whose primary readership was the international republic of letters, and he stated that, in addition to the engraved book of motets, his shop offered

> all the works [of the late Monsieur Charpentier] in the original scores; there are masses, vespers, and motets that were sung in the Royal Chapel, all in manuscript, in Charpentier's own hand. He proposes passing them on to some chapel master, to whom these sorts of works can be suitable.[10]

Were some of the missing notebooks sold during the months that followed?

In 1716 Jacques Édouard tried another tack. He petitioned PHILIPPE III D'ORLÉANS and was granted a special privilege by Louis XV—"on the advice" of the Duke himself, Charpentier's former pupil. "Our beloved Jacques Édouard having made known to us that he inherited the works of the late Sieur Charpentier, his uncle, one of the music masters of the late King [Louis XIV] of glorious memory," Édouard would be permitted, for thirty years, to offer three-act plays "in the Italian taste" but in the French language, at a new theater that would combine decorations, machines, singers, dancers, and symphonies. He had the right to choose the actors, who would form what would be known as "the Parisian Troop." He would, however, be obliged to turn over one-fourth of his profits to the Paris Opera. On March 19, 1716, Édouard sold these rights to Louis Gauthier de Saint-Edme, royal councillor, and his wife. Once the transfer of the privilege to Saint-Edme became official, Édouard would be paid the huge sum of twenty-six thousand livres; and when performances began, he would receive ten thousand livres a year, payable monthly.[11] The theater appears to have been stillborn; and if Jacques Édouard received any money from Saint-Edme, he squandered it.

In 1726 Édouard tried yet again to turn a profit on the music he had inherited. That February an anonymous appraiser went to his shop and made an inventory of the Charpentier manuscripts.[12] Édouard's latest idea differed little from the advertisement of 1712. He hoped that a Parisian music master, or perhaps a provincial one, would buy the manuscripts "cheaply"—that is, for a price far inferior to the four thousand livres the family had purportedly refused in 1704—and without breaking them up. With the proceeds, Édouard (ever a dreamer, for he apparently had not printed a book for over a decade) planned to produce "some fine printing job of a new book."

At that point Titon du Tillet, who was preparing his *Parnasse François*, got wind of the inventory and the projected sale. He went to Édouard's shop to learn more about the late composer's career. While there, he consulted either the memorandum or the actual manuscripts, jotting down the titles of a few works for his book, which was published the following year.[13] In the end, the inventory drawn up in 1726 served as the requisite "catalog" when Charpentier's manuscripts were sold to the Royal Library in 1727, for the modest sum of three hundred livres.[14]

In January 1753 Jacques Édouard, by then in his early eighties, was still running his little shop in front of Notre-Dame. *Les Trois Rois* had, however, seen better days. The police officials who supervised the book trade noted in their register that Édouard "lives in Paris, Notre-Dame. He is a poor wretch who sells nothing but junk books."[15] Jacques Édouard apparently died in 1761, because his name did not appear on the list of Parisian booksellers for 1762, which alludes instead to "Widow Édouard."[16] She kept the shop open until 1768, when she too disappeared from the police lists.

Panel 4

FAMILY FRIENDS

Doors on Which to Knock

Six portraits hang in this panel. In seventeenth-century documents, the individuals portrayed here describe themselves as "friends" of one or another Charpentier. That is, they are linked to the composer and his family by reciprocal services or protective gestures.

The first painting is a group portrait. Black-garbed royal officials at the Châtelet of Paris cluster around their presiding officer, the civil lieutenant.

Several of the portraits depict elegantly dressed women. Their husbands, who belong to the upper layers of the royal administration, can be seen in the background, poring over documents. On the walls behind these ladies hang portraits of the departed ancestors whose connection to either the House of Guise or the House of Orléans brought prosperity to their families as a whole.

A final portrait shows four Jesuit fathers.

Taken as a whole, these friends are doors upon which to knock and request the recommendations without which it was virtually impossible for an honestly born but impecunious young person to become "established."

Le Grand Chastelet de Paris.

The Châtelet of Paris.

The fortress known as the Great Châtelet was located across the Seine from the Palace of Justice. In addition to handling different types of litigation, the officials appointed guardians for minors. Numerous friends and relatives of the Charpentier family held positions at the Châtelet in the late sixteenth century and on into the 1680s.

I

The first and principal jurisdiction of the realm

THE CHÂTELET

A group portrait of the civil lieutenant and his associates

Adozen or so councillors, barristers, clerks, recorders, bailiffs, and sergeants—each wearing distinctive garb that sets him apart from his colleagues—cluster about their superior, the civil lieutenant, in this group portrait. In the background stands the fortress known as the Great Châtelet,[1] a vast, irregular rectangle that runs down to the Seine, just opposite the Palace of Justice on the island known as the *Cité*. Adjacent to it stand the prisons of the Châtelet, against which lean the shops of fishmongers and tripe-sellers.

Each tending to his specific tasks, these black-garbed officials carry out such a gamut of judicial functions that they have been likened to a parlement. For example, they have jurisdiction over all lawsuits involving acts passed before one of the notaries of the Châtelet or by the viscounty of Paris. The notaries and the mounted bailiffs of the Châtelet—among the latter is Jean Charpentier of Meaux, PASQUIER CHARPENTIER THE MEASURER's son—are entitled to conduct their business anywhere in the realm. The Châtelet is considered to be the "first and principal" jurisdiction of the realm, owing to the social rank of the potential litigators and the importance and diversity of the subjects being handled by the judges.

The civil lieutenant

For decades, nay, for generations, the civil lieutenant had been a FERRAND. First there was Michel Ferrand, who became civil lieutenant in 1596. His son, Antoine II Ferrand, became the "private" lieutenant, *lieutenant particulier*, at the Châtelet in 1594; but he died a few years after succeeding his father as civil lieutenant in 1618, leaving a son too young to shoulder these responsibilities. Nicolas de Bailleul therefore stepped into the breach, serving as civil lieutenant for several years before resuming his career in the Parlement. In 1638 Antoine II's grandson, Antoine III Ferrand, became civil lieutenant. Antoine III lived on until 1689, having served as civil lieutenant for a half century. In short, for nine decades a Ferrand (and, during a brief interregnum, a Bailleul) had administered the Châtelet; and during those ninety years, one or another of these civil lieutenants had an opportunity to get to know and appreciate the different Charpentier relatives who appear below in this group portrait.

Within a network whose contours are blurred and whose meshes are little understood, two generations of FERRANDS watched out for ÉTIEN- NETTE CHARPENTIER, Marc-Antoine Charpentier's sister. Why, and how, did this link form between the daughter of LOUIS CHARPENTIER THE SCRIVENER and the rich and influential Ferrands? Is this friendship ex- plained by the fact that both families lived in the parish of Saint- Séverin?[2] Or by mutual respect and affection among colleagues at the Châtelet that developed over the decades, and that eventually spilled over to the cousins and in-laws of these colleagues? Neither question can be answered; but by identifying some of individuals working at the Châtelet prior to 1670, a working hypothesis may one day begin to emerge.

Councillors at the Châtelet

By 1602 Roland Croyer, the son of Jean Croyer, an *élu* at Meaux, had acquired an office of royal councillor at the Châtelet. He was still active in this position in 1621.[3] Although Roland had held an office at Meaux, he married at Paris in 1587. His bride was Michelle Favier, the daughter of a royal councillor in the Parlement of Paris. Roland and his wife were very close to DAVID CROYER and his wife Jeanne, the sister of PASQUIER CHARPENTIER THE MEASURER. In fact, in October 1594 Michelle stood as godmother for one of the couple's children, baptized at the Church of Saint-Jean-en-Grève.[4]

Procurators at the Châtelet

Louis Le Roy, the son of Louis Le Roy of Meaux and Marie Croyer, was a procurator at the Châtelet. He was appointed guardian for DAVID CROYER's minor daughters in November 1614. A few months later he wed David's daughter Étiennette, in the presence of his paternal uncle and aunt, Roland Croyer, royal councillor at the Châtelet, and Michelle Favier.[5]

In 1639 and 1640 a procurator at the Châtelet named D'Esponty or Desponty (no first name is available) supervised the training of GILLES

CHARPENTIER THE SECRETARY. The two men were in touch as late as 1654, when D'Esponty signed the Secretary's wedding contract and said that he was a "friend."

Of the procurators, the "royal" procurator was the most prestigious. In the 1620s and 1630s, Germain Gouffé, the husband of one of the FERRANDS who had befriended ÉTIENNETTE CHARPENTIER, served as his "substitute."

After November 1657 the "substitute" was ARMAND-JEAN DE RIANTS, who in 1659 acquired the office of royal procurator. He continued to work at the Châtelet in this function until his retirement in August 1684. One of Marc-Antoine Charpentier's operas was performed at Riants' fine residence in 1678.

Louis de Pâris, procurator at the Châtelet, was selected as testamentary executor for a will dictated by ÉTIENNETTE CHARPENTIER THE LINENER in 1676. The friendship, clearly an old one, was apparently linked to another Charpentier friend, ÉLISABETH GRIMAUDET. At any rate, a decade before Étiennette asked this favor of Pâris, the latter had loaned money to Grimaudet.

Barristers at the Châtelet

JACQUES HAVÉ (who later added "de Saint-Aubin" to his name) was a barrister at the Châtelet when he married DAVID CROYER's daughter Marthe in 1616, in the presence of her brother-in-law and guardian, Louis Le Roy, procurator at the Châtelet, and her cousin Roland Croyer, royal councillor at the Châtelet.

Denis Talon, the brother of MARIE TALON (she witnessed ÉLISABETH CHARPENTIER's wedding contract in 1662) was a barrister at the Châtelet until 1652, when he succeeded his late father, Omer Talon, in the Parlement.

Bailiffs in the Châtelet

Jean Charpentier, PASQUIER THE MEASURER's son, became a mounted bailiff-sergeant at the Châtelet in 1628. The position permitted him to supervise the sale or confiscation of personal property anywhere in the kingdom. He chose to exert this prerogative from his native city, Meaux, thereby forming a link between the Charpentiers in Brie and their friends and relations in Paris—especially those at the Châtelet.

Étienne Morlot was a baillif-sergent at the Châtelet in 1637 when his daughter married a wine merchant named Jean Édouard.[6] In 1662 their dancing-master son, Jean Édouard, wed ÉLISABETH CHARPENTIER, the composer's sister.

Commissioners and examiners at the Châtelet

Louis Cousin, the first husband of DAVID CROYER's daughter Catherine, was a commissioner and examiner at the Châtelet, according to an act dated 1625. Hubert Ginet, who married Catherine in 1634 after Cousin's death, was also a commissioner and examiner at the Châtelet. It was Ginet who arranged the training of GILLES CHARPENTIER THE SECRETARY in 1639, and who watched over the young man while he was living in Paris. It is therefore certain that Ginet was well acquainted with Procurator D'Esponty, with whom Gilles was training. Indeed, Hubert's brother, Jacques Ginet, was D'Esponty's colleague, for he too was a procurator at the Châtelet, as was Hubert's maternal cousin, Louis Lizard. Another cousin, Jean Quinot, was a mounted bailiff-sergeant there.

II

Impassioned about the House of Guise

MARIE TALON

Marie Talon, wife of Daniel Voisin, *maître des requêtes*,
Élisabeth Charpentier's "friend";
and her Voisin, Verthamon, and Versoris in-laws

When ÉLISABETH CHARPENTIER and Jean Édouard signed their wedding contract in August 1662, the fiancée was assisted by "Dame Marie Talon, wife of Monsieur de Voysin, master of requests." (The gentleman in question, Daniel Voisin, was also provost of merchants for Paris, the highest office in the municipal government.) In her early thirties at the time, Madame Voisin was just a few years older than the bride. All but one of the prestigious "friends" of the bride and groom who signed this document were women, and these women were linked to either the House of Guise or the House of Orléans.

The underpinnings of the link between the Charpentiers and the Talons have not yet been discerned. True, Marie Talon's wedding contract[1] of May 1650 bears the signature of her "friend," Madame Guyet, a member of the FERRAND FAMILY to whom ÉTIENNETTE CHARPENTIER would later express gratitude. Still, this link to a Ferrand woman is too tenuous to explain why Marie Talon signed the Charpentier-Édouard contract. Whatever her reasons for being there that day, Madame Voisin stated that she was a "friend" of the bride, and she must be taken at her word.

Marie Talon belonged to a highly respected parlementaire family with links to the House of Orléans. Her late father was Omer Talon, advocate general in the Parlement of Paris. Her mother, Françoise Doujat, was the daughter of Denis Doujat, advocate general to GASTON D'ORLÉANS. Her brother, Denis Talon, began his career as a barrister at the CHÂTELET but moved on to the Parlement in 1652, when he succeeded his father as advocate general. During the 1650s, Denis had "worked wonders" for MADEMOISELLE DE MONTPENSIER and GASTON D'ORLÉANS in a suit against the Richelieus over some land. (Montpensier wrote Talon "unceasingly" as the suit made its way through the courts.)[2] When Élisabeth Charpentier wed Jean Édouard, Denis Talon had only just completed his successful defense of members of the House of Orléans. By the 1670s Denis would become a pillar in the charitable organizations in the parish of Saint-Sulpice, where he would work closely with MADAME DE GUISE; but on this summer day of 1662, this particular link to the princess had not yet been forged.

Through her husband, Marie Talon had the potential to open the great doors of the Hôtel de Guise to Élisabeth Charpentier's brother, Marc-Antoine. She embodied the Voisin family's longstanding fidelity to the House of Guise. At first glance, Daniel Voisin's services to MARIE DE GUISE THE REGENT appear to be routine financial dealings. For example, in 1657 he loaned Her Highness some of the money she needed to pay MADEMOISELLE DE MONTPENSIER's share of the late Duchess of Guise's estate; and in 1665 he loaned her an additional twenty-four thousand livres. Much of the latter loan was still unpaid when Mademoiselle de Guise died in 1688.[3]

If Daniel Voisin was, to use a seventeenth-century term, "serving" the princess in this way, it was not purely to earn interest. Everyone knew that the Guises could not be counted on to pay interest due. Rather, it was because his family had, to use another seventeenth-century term, "belonged" to the House of Guise for several generations. To be specific, Daniel Voisin was the great-grandson of Pierre Versoris, one of the Guises' most trusted confidants at the time of the League.

Pierre Versoris descended from Guillaume Versoris, a Norman who had come to Paris early in the sixteenth century and had become a barrister at the Châtelet of Paris. Three of Guillaume's sons likewise became barristers at the Châtelet during the 1540s; the fourth, Pierre, was a barrister at the Parlement of Paris. As religious divisions deepened during the 1570s and 1580s, Pierre not only supported the Jesuits, he became "very impassioned about the House of Guise, of which he was the principal councillor." Having learned, "while supping on Christmas Eve of 1588, that Henri de Lorraine, Duke of Guise, had died at Blois," Versoris

> remained totally calm. He went to bed determined to take
> communion at the Midnight Mass, for he had already been to
> confession; but feeling ill and not being able to go to church, he was
> found dead in his bed at five o'clock on Christmas morning by his
> daughters and his son-in-law, Monsieur de Verthamont.[4]

A legend would develop that Versoris had dropped dead upon learning of the scar-faced Duke of Guise's assassination.

One of the daughters who discovered the body that Christmas morning was Marie Versoris, who a year earlier had wed François de Verthamon, a fervent Catholic from Limoges who, like his father-in-law, was a barrister before the Parlement of Paris. In the course of his professional duties, Verthamon became close to Antoine Séguier, a president in the Parlement. Séguier treated him like a son. Upon Séguier's death in 1624, Verthamon learned that he had not only been named executor of the will, he had been elevated to the level of the deceased's "five illustrious nephews" and would therefore receive one-sixth of the estate.[5]

Antoine Séguier was the paternal uncle of Pierre Séguier, whose career he was busily promoting. Although Verthamont could not know it, Pierre Séguier would one day be the chancellor and keeper of the seals of the kingdom of France. Into this circle the Charpentiers' barrister cousin, CHARLES SEVIN, was just then finding his way; but no document makes it possible to assert that François de Verthamon, by then a mature and established barrister, was close to young Sevin.

In 1612 François de Verthamon's daughter, Marguerite, married Daniel Voisin. Several children were born to the couple, among them Daniel, who would wed Marie Talon in 1650, and Louis, who would become a Jesuit. (Louis stands beside his Jesuit uncle, Pierre de Verthamon, in the group portrait of FOUR JESUIT FATHERS that hangs in this panel.) Widowed in 1621, Marguerite de Verthamon married Macé Bertrand de La Bazinière, a wealthy treasurer of the Royal Receipts who left an estate of four million livres when he died twenty years later.[6] La Bazinière was so close to Cardinal RICHELIEU that he was among the few to receive an invitation to construct a house in the Cardinal's new city, Richelieu.[7] Among the guests witnessing Marguerite de Verthamon's wedding contract in 1623[8] was her father's old friend, Antoine Séguier, who had been present when she wed Daniel Voisin a decade earlier. In other words, the benevolence of the Séguier family extended to the children of François de Verthamon and Marie de Versoris.

During this same decade, the Guises were keeping alive some links of fidelity dating back to the late sixteenth century. For example, in 1627 François de Lorraine, Prince of Joinville, and "his sister Marie de Lorraine, called *Mademoiselle de Guise*," agreed to be the godparents of little François de Vanel, old Pierre Versoris' great-grandson. The child's mother was the second cousin of a certain François d'Alesso,[9] whose son, Jean d'Alesso, would first serve GASTON D'ORLÉANS and then, in the late 1660s, become one of LOUIS-JOSEPH DE LORRAINE OF GUISE's householders: "[Alesso] was a man of quality who had been cornet in the light horse of

the late Monsieur [Gaston]."[10] It was likewise during the late 1660s that
PHILIPPE GOIBAUT DU BOIS would be invited to join Mademoiselle de
Guise's household, along with his wife, Françoise Blacvod—whose
paternal aunt and uncle were Jean d'Alesso's grandparents.[11] In other
words, at least two of the Versoris' cousins or in-laws were being taken
under the Guises' wing during the very decades when Daniel Voisin was
lending money to Mademoiselle de Guise.

Tantalizing evidence of other cousinships and acquaintances crops up
in the archives, to suggest that longstanding loyalties underlie not only
Marc-Antoine Charpentier's selection as composer to the Guises but also
some commissions extended to him by other patrons. For example,
Madame Du Bois' cousins, the Alessos, were the cousins of ARMAND-JEAN
DE RIANTS, in whose mansion one of Marc-Antoine Charpentier's operas
would be performed in 1678. More surprising still, during the 1660s the
Versoris–Vanels were renting a house to the saddle-maker cousin of
ÉTIENNE LOULIÉ, a future member of the GUISE MUSIC.[12] This sort of
financial arrangement generally indicates a certain degree of familiarity
and trust between owner and tenant.

Over the decades, the Verthamon–Versoris–Voisin family remained
as faithful to the House of Guise as it had been in the 1580s. In January
1665, when Mademoiselle de Guise needed some forty thousand livres,
she borrowed the money from François de Verthamon, Daniel Voisin's
maternal uncle.[13] In short, only a year or so before Marc-Antoine
Charpentier set off for Rome, Marie Talon's Verthamon in-law was
literally "being of service" to Her Highness of Guise.

In view of the multiple documented contacts during the mid- and
late-1660s, between the Voisin–Verthamons and the Guises and their
householders, it is difficult to imagine that Marie Talon did not play a
crucial role in Marc-Antoine Charpentier's being chosen as composer to
the House of Guise.

III

Loyal to the Houses of Orléans and Guise, and to the Church of the Mercy too

ÉLISABETH-MARIE MALIER

Élisabeth-Marie Malier, the widow of President Nicolas de Bailleul;
Louis de Bailleul, president in the Parlement of Paris, her son;
and Marie de Bailleul, his daughter by Marie Le Ragois de Bretonvilliers

Among the "friends" of the groom signing the wedding contract of Jean Édouard and ÉLISABETH CHARPENTIER on August 24, 1662, were "Dame Ysabel Marie Malier, widow of Nicolas de Bailleul, knight, lord of Soisy, royal councillor and president *à mortier* in the Parlement of Paris." She was accompanied by her granddaughter, Marie de Bailleul. How had the young dancing master and instrument player made such illustrious friends?

The answer appears to involve loyalties within the household of GASTON D'ORLÉANS and his widow, the DOWAGER DUCHESS OF ORLÉANS. Élisabeth-Marie Malier was the sister of an important figure in the Duke's household in Paris, and the next signatory of the contract, ÉLISABETH GRIMAUDET, was the sister of Gaston's principal officer at Blois.

Who was Élisabeth-Marie Malier? She was the daughter of Claude Malier du Houssay and Marie Melissant. Like the ancestors of CHARLES SEVIN, the Maliers began their rise to prominence in the city of Orléans, where Claude's father was a treasurer of France. His mother came from Blois. In other words, owing to their places of birth, these people were perceived of—and perceived of themselves—as "belonging" to Gaston d'Orléans, who had been given the Duchy of Orléans as his appanage, and the chateau and lands in and around Blois as well.

Claude Malier, a comptroller general of finances, was living with his wife in the *Marais* section of Paris when he died in 1642. His death inventory reveals that—like MARIE TALON's father-in-law—Malier had been so close to Cardinal RICHELIEU that he had been invited to build a house in the prelate's new city.[1]

Claude's son (he too was named Claude Malier) became a councillor in the Parlement of Paris in 1624, married in 1631, and was named ambassador to Venice in 1633. His wife died there in 1640, leaving him with a young son, christened Claude Malier but known as *Marc* because he was a godchild of the Republic of Venice. The Ambassador entered the priesthood after his wife's death and was named to the bishopric of Tarbes in 1649. He soon was appointed first almoner to the wife of GASTON D'ORLÉANS; and when he retired in 1668, his son succeeded him at Tarbes and in the DOWAGER OF ORLÉANS' household.[2])

Claude's sister—Élisabeth-Marie Malier, the Charpentier-Édouards' future "friend"—married a widower named Nicolas de Bailleul in 1621.[3] The first member of his family to have chosen the robe as a profession, Nicolas began his career as a councillor in the Parlement of Paris and eventually was rewarded for his services by Louis XIII, who made him president of the Grand Council. The year of his marriage to Mademoiselle Malier, Bailleul resigned his office in the Parlement in order to become civil lieutenant at the CHÂTELET. There he almost certainly worked closely with several of Marc-Antoine Charpentier's cousins. A few years later, Bailleul was elected provost of merchants, the highest administrative position in the municipal government. Within six years he was back in the Parlement, this time as a president *à mortier*. He subsequently was honored by being appointed chancellor to Queen Anne of Austria; and in 1643 he was made royal superintendant of finance.

Élisabeth-Marie Malier produced several children, among them a son, Louis de Bailleul. In 1643—the year his father became royal superintendent of finances—Louis bought the office of councillor in the Parlement of Paris. Upon his father's death in 1652, he succeeded him as president. At his country house, situated along the principal road by which one entered Paris from the royal chateau of Fontainebleau, Louis gave lavish receptions whenever young Louis XIV or a foreign dignitary passed by.

His expenditures for these entertainments did not overly threaten Louis de Bailleul's budget, for in 1644 he had married wealthy Marie Le Ragois de Bretonvilliers,[4] whose family, like the Maliers, had come to Paris from the Duchy of Orléans. (The couple's fourth child, Marie de Bailleul, would sign the Charpentier-Édouard wedding contract in 1662, just below her grandmother.) So many illustrious signatures were affixed to the Bailleul-Le Ragois wedding contract of 1644! First to sign was young Louis XIV, followed by his mother the Queen Regent, the Prince of Condé, Cardinal Mazarin, and Chancellor Pierre Séguier. Although the Chancellor's presence may seem pro forma, it clearly was not, for the groom's witnesses include two Béthunes of Sully, specifically, the aunt and uncle of the Duke of Sully—whose wife was Charlotte Séguier, the

Chancellor's daughter. Still more revealing is the fact that, when Bailleul wed Mademoiselle Le Ragois, the Charpentier's Parisian cousin, CHARLES SEVIN, had been serving Madame de Sully for approximately five years. In other words, Louis de Bailleul's wedding contract suggests deeper links between the Bailleuls and the Séguiers than are readily apparent. Although contacts between the Bailleuls and the Sevins during the 1640s and 1650s cannot be proved, they cannot be ruled out.

Among the witnesses for Mademoiselle Le Ragois was her brother, Alexandre Le Ragois de Bretonvilliers, who, as curate of Saint-Sulpice, would use his influence and vast wealth in 1675 to found an educational institution honoring MADAME DE GUISE's young son and dedicated to the INFANT JESUS. Present also was the bride's uncle, Séraphim Le Ragois, the intendant of MADEMOISELLE MARIE DE GUISE's mother, who had entrusted him with her financial affairs during the family's exile in Italy.[5] The bride's aunt was also there: Philippes Le Ragois, whose husband was the household treasurer for MADEMOISELLE DE MONTPENSIER (GASTON D'OR-LÉANS' daughter by his first marriage to Mademoiselle de Guise's half-sister). In short, the bride came from a family that was serving both the House of Guise and the House of Orléans. She consequently was just the sort of person with whom a Guise or an Orléans might consult con-cerning a potential householder. That is to say, MADEMOISELLE MARIE THE REGENT would begin by finding a candidate whose family already "belonged" to her House; and then she would seek recommendations from individuals who were linked to her family and who knew the candidate personally.

Louis de Bailleul was linked to the Guises by geographic proximity as well as through services that his wife's family had rendered to that House. During the 1650s his father, Nicolas, had resided on the rue de Braque, only a few steps from the entrance door of the Hôtel de Guise. Nicolas had been one of benefactors of the convent church of the MERCY, which was also benefitting from Guise largesse.[6] Louis and his wife likewise lived near the Hôtel de Guise, on the rue du Grand Chantier. Louis' longtime attentiveness to the dynastic milestones of that princely House has been preserved in the jottings he added year after year to a succession of almanacs.[7]

Proximity to the Hôtel de Guise; a manifest fascination for the princes and princesses of that House; and, after 1657, a rented chapel and pew[8] at the Church of Saint-Jean-en-Grève, the Guise parish church. Taken together, these apparently disparate facts suggest that, over the years, Louis de Bailleul did not lack opportunities to talk with Guise householders and to pay his respects to Their Highnesses.

The Church of Saint-Jean was not President de Bailleul's only place of worship. Like his late father, he was an active participant in worship services at Notre-Dame de la MERCY. For example, in April 1674 he gave the church a new processional banner for the week-long canonization service of Saint Peter Pascual.[9] (To another of the services held that week, MADEMOISELLE DE GUISE contributed candles and, it would seem, a mass for instruments "instead of an organ.") Louis de Bailleul probably was acquainted with another worshiper at the Mercy, Marc-Antoine Charpentier's cousin, Marthe Croyer, the wife of HAVÉ DE SAINT-AUBIN.

In sum, President Louis de Bailleul and his family were a link in a chain that, during the late 1660s, stretched from Élisabeth Charpentier's lodging, to the Mercy where the Bailleuls and the Havés worshiped, to the Luxembourg Palace, and on to the Guise parish church. The President and his mother were therefore in a position to evaluate for the Guises the morals and dutifulness of Marc-Antoine Charpentier.

Late in 1677 the investigators of the so-called POISON AFFAIR briefly focused their attention on Madame Louis de Bailleul, who was "given a personal summons," instead of being arrested like the other suspects. The records of the investigation do not specify the grounds for suspicion, nor do they summarize any interview to which she may have been subjected. (The silence of the documents is perhaps explained by her death in January 1678.) It is therefore not clear whether the investigators thought that Madame de Bailleul herself might be implicated in a plot, or whether they hoped that, as a Le Ragois, she could shed light on the suspicious activities of a certain Marguerite Charpentier, the widow of Le Ragois de Bretonvilliers' secretary.

After his wife's death, Louis de Bailleul withdrew to the Abbey of Saint-Victor. Having passed his office in the Parlement to his son in 1689, he resided at the abbey until his death in 1701, delving into the books in his sizeable library, which included Latin classics, books of poetry, the principal Jansenist treatises, a variety of devotional books, and the "memoirs of Guise."[10]

Élisabeth-Marie Malier survived her son, expiring in 1690 in a room decorated with eleven paintings, most of them devotional. There were several paintings of the Virgin, one of the Holy Family, and an *Ecce Homo*—plus a Saint Charles Borromeo and a Saint Cecilia, saints to whom the two Guise princesses were so attached that Marc-Antoine Charpentier had been asked to write oratorios in their honor. It cannot be determined whether the presence of these paintings in her apartment was in any way linked to the devotions sponsored by MADEMOISELLE DE GUISE and MADAME DE GUISE.

IV

Officers of Gaston d'Orléans at Blois

ÉLISABETH GRIMAUDET

Élisabeth Grimaudet, wife of César Lhuillier,
royal councillor and comptroller general of the *rentes*
of the Hôtel de Ville, "friend" of Jean Édouard

On August 24, 1662, when Élisabeth Charpentier and Jean Édouard signed their wedding contract, among the friends of the groom were "noble homme Lhuillier, councillor and secretary of the king for his finances, and Dame Eizable Grimaudet, his spouse."[1]

The woman standing at Monsieur Lhuillier's side in this portrait "belonged" to GASTON D'ORLÉANS. Élisabeth Grimaudet (she signed "Grymaudet") and her brothers—Michel II Grimaudet de Moteux and René Grimaudet de la Croiserie—were the children of Michel-Ange Grimaudet and Marie Petit, a couple from Vendôme.

Michel II's wedding contract, signed in 1648, reveals that the Grimaudets were members of Gaston d'Orléans' household. Not the household at the Luxembourg Palace of Paris, but the household that cared for His Royal Highness's properties at Blois. Indeed, René Grimaudet was the lieutenant general for the bailliage and government of Blois. In another document signed that same year, he stated that he was also a "royal councillor and councillor of His Royal Highness [Gaston] in his council," a detail that makes it possible to assert that Michel's functions in Blois were far from perfunctory, and that he was one of the Duke's principal advisors. His uncle, the late Jean Grimaudet, had been a councillor at the presidial of Blois; another uncle, Jacques Grimaudet, was a magistrate at the presidial of Blois; and a woman cousin whose husband had less prestigious titles likewise lived in Blois.[2]

In 1648, when the Fronde broke out, Michel's sister, Élisabeth Grimaudet, was living in Paris with her husband, Squire César Lhuillier. (He did not belong to the prestigious Parisian patrician family by that name.)

By 1652, as the Fronde wound down and Gaston was forced to withdraw to Blois, Lhuillier had purchased the office of comptroller general of the annuities, *rentes*, being sold by the city of Paris.[3] Until 1665 and perhaps even later, the Lhuilliers lived on the rue de Braque, the short street that led directly to the medieval entry gate of the Hôtel de Guise. During the first few years of their residence there, one of their neighbors was President Nicolas de Bailleul, whose widow, ÉLISABETH-MARIE MALIER, and granddaughter would sign the Charpentier–Édouard wedding con-tract in August 1662, alongside Élisabeth Grimaudet and César Lhuillier.

A document dated 1665 reveals that five years after GASTON D'OR-LÉANS' death, the Lhuilliers were still in close contact with the late Duke's former householders, not only in Blois (where René Grimaudet had been kept on as lieutenant general) but also at the Luxembourg Palace. At the Lhuillier house on the rue de Braque, Gaston's former financial secretary joined the Lhuillers and their two daughters to celebrate the engagement of a niece who had been raised in Blois. (She was the daughter of Jacques Grimaudet, Élisabeth Grimaudet's brother.[4])

Should the fact that the Lhuillers described themselves as "friends" of the groom when they signed the Charpentier–Édouard contract of 1662, be read as an indication that they were primarily concerned with the well-being of Jean Édouard and scarcely knew Élisabeth Charpentier? Should one assume that the children of LOUIS CHARPENTIER THE SCRIV-ENER had at best a tenuous link to GASTON D'ORLÉANS' household, through their cousin, HAVÉ DE SAINT-AUBIN, the Duke's gentleman in ordinary?

The sources provide an unequivocal answer to these questions. The link was far from tenuous. In 1665, shortly before Marc-Antoine Charpentier set off for Rome, the Lhuilliers were in contact with Louis de Pâris, procurator at the CHÂTELET of Paris, who lived near the Sorbonne.[5] To be specific, they were borrowing seventy-two hundred livres from him, a transaction that tended to be done between trusted acquaintances, not strangers.

This seemingly insignificant fact is actually quite meaningful, al-though its full implications cannot be discerned. Louis de Pâris happened to be a very close and trusted friend of ÉTIENNETTE CHARPENTIER's—so close that when she became very ill in 1676, she named him executor for a testament that never had to be carried out.[6]

V

A long time in Rome as secretary to the General

FOUR JESUITS

Pierre de Verthamon, Louis Voisin, François de la Faluère,
and François de la Chaise,
Jesuits at the profess house of Saint-Louis

This group portrait depicts four Jesuits. Three of them can be presumed to have known the Charpentier family very well, for they are the close relatives of some of the "friends" portrayed elsewhere in this panel. On the other hand, it is not at all certain that the fourth reverend father had much to do with Marc-Antoine Charpentier. He was however a compelling force at the Hôtel de Guise during the composer's final months there.

Pierre de Verthamon

In 1631 Pierre de Verthamon took his final vows as a Jesuit. The maternal uncle of Daniel Voisin, MARIE TALON's husband, he would be one of the principal movers and doers for the Society of Jesus. Among other missions, he "spent a long time in Rome as secretary to the General." (His actual title was "substitute secretary for the Society in Rome."[1]) The Jesuit triennial records reveal that Father Verthamon was still in Rome in 1669.[2] In other words he was living in one of the Jesuit residences in Rome throughout Marc-Antoine Charpentier's stay there. As secretary to the General, Verthamon was in constant contact with the Jesuits in Paris. He also had access to the rectors of all the Jesuit houses of Rome, among them the German College where CARISSIMI was teaching music and composing. In short, Verthamon did not lack the means to facilitate Marc-Antoine Charpentier's contacts with the famed chapel master, and he can be presumed to have done so.

Father Verthamon was back in Paris by 1671.[3] For the next two decades, he administered two of the THREE JESUIT HOUSES in the capital, principally the profess house of Saint-Louis, on the rue Saint-Antoine. In about 1672 he did, however, move across the river to the College of Louis-le-Grand, for a three-year stint as rector; but by 1675 he was back at Saint-Louis, where he was successively superior, provincial, and again superior.[4] Pierre de Verthamon died in Paris on July 26, 1686, seven months before the performance of Marc-Antoine Charpentier's first devotional opera for Louis-le-Grand.

From early 1671 until 1686, that is, while Verthamon was in residence at Saint-Louis, special religious services were held there that were not part of the ordinary duties of the chapel master for the profess house.[5] Among the quite lavish services mentioned in the *Gazette de France* are several that correspond to works in Marc-Antoine Charpentier's roman-numbered notebooks: vespers "sung by the Music" (that is, the King's Music) for the annual Feast of the Circumcision, January 1, 1671[A]; a week-long canonization of Saint Francis Borgia in January 1672, with its daily vespers and its pontifical mass of January 17 at which BISHOP ROQUETTE OF AUTUN officiated[B]; a memorial service for the late Pierre Séguier in March 1672, "with excellent music"[C] by an unnamed composer; a "ceremony" held in July 1676 to commemorate the anniversary of the consecration of the Church of Saint-Louis, which took the form of a pontifical mass and a Latin homily by Father Verthamon in honor of Louis XIII[D]; the conversion of a Huguenot woman at the Noviciate on November 22, 1676, in the presence of MADAME DE GUISE, who had worked actively on the conversion[E]; and so forth.

François de la Faluère

During much of his career, Father Verthamon was in contact with another powerful French Jesuit, François de la Faluère, who took his vows in Paris in 1637. A native of Tours, La Faluère was either the brother or the cousin of René Lefevre de la Faluère,[6] the husband of FRANÇOISE FERRAND, ÉTIENNETTE CHARPENTIER's trusted friend. A renowned teacher, Father La Faluère moved from college to college: Bordeaux, the Spanish Netherlands (where he taught the son of the exiled Prince of Condé), Paris (1661), Tours, Moulins.

Like Verthamon, La Faluère had the honor of serving as secretary to the General in Rome, a mission that lasted for three or four years, from

[A] Cahier VI, H. 158.
[B] Cahiers VI–VIII, H. 3, H. 236, H. 283, H. 514, H. 73, apparently recopied on Jesuit paper post-1687.
[C] Cahier 3, H 2 , funeral music the Guises permitted to be reused for Séguier?
[D] Notebook lost.
[E] Cahier 13, H. 394.

approximately the fall of 1667 until late in 1671.[7] This means that the first part of La Faluère's sojourn in Rome coincided with Marc-Antoine Charpentier's adventures there, which were well underway in 1667 and ended by the fall of 1669. In other words, although La Faluère probably did not know Marc-Antoine Charpentier as well as Father Verthamon presumably did, he was in a position to facilitate his young compatriot's visits to CARISSIMI.

Immediately upon his return to France, La Faluère spent three years as rector at Rouen; but by 1673 he and Verthamon were at the profess house in Paris. There Father La Faluère died on November 19, 1678.[8] It is noteworthy that his period of residence at Saint-Louis, 1673–1678, coincided with Verthamon's tenure there as superior. As a result, Father Verthamon could more or less count that La Faluère would come down in favor of Marc-Antoine Charpentier, during deliberations among the assembled Jesuits about accepting a Guise offer to lend them their composer for an extraordinary service, or about extending a commission to him themselves.

Louis Voisin

For much of this time, Father Louis Voisin (Verthamon's nephew and MARIE TALON's brother-in-law) was assigned to the Parisian profess house. The triennial records of the Society of Jesus show him at Saint-Louis from 1669 to 1678. In 1679 he became rector at Rouen and superior of the seminary there, where he represented MADEMOISELLE DE GUISE in a dispute over the implementation of her granduncle's legacy to the college.[9] By 1685 Father Voisin had been transferred to the renowned college at La Flèche.

François de la Chaise

Another influential Jesuit had moved into the profess house of Saint-Louis by 1675. It is unlikely that this Jesuit knew Marc-Antoine Charpentier personally. If he did, he could scarcely be described as the Guise composer's "friend." This individual was Father François de la Chaize d'Aix, Louis XIV's new confessor.[10] (Since sources of the period commonly spelled his family name La Chaise, that is the spelling used throughout this portrait gallery.) Preoccupied as La Chaise was with national and international policies involving the Church, he does not appear to have played much of a role in the administration of the THREE JESUIT HOUSES in the capital, although any opinions he might express doubtlessly carried a great deal of weight.

Allusions to La Chaise began to be made in 1677, in correspondence between ROGER DE GAIGNIÈRES, the Guise equerry, and Roger de Bussy Rabutin, concerning a living for the latter's cleric son. Gaignières was politely badgering ARCHBISHOP HARLAY (with whom he clearly was quite familiar) to talk with La Chaise, of whom Harlay "was a good friend" and with whom he had allied to destroy the Jansenist "*parti.*"

Harlay's and La Chaise's quite dissimilar personalities and skills complemented one another, as they worked together on religious issues that interested the King, especially Jansenism and the conversion of Protestants. Harlay "loved to shine and took great pleasure in upstaging, when he could, the most able royal councillors of state. It was not hard for him to upstage the King's Confessor. Father La Chaise was not a superior man. His only talent involved what is called 'courtly conduct.'"[11] Stated more bluntly, Harlay possessed wit and verbal brilliance, while La Chaise knew how to ingratiate himself by courtly flattery.

La Chaise's political skills were not to be underestimated. In fact, during the late 1670s he was more or less snatching the nomination rights for the archdiocese of Paris away from Harlay, under the prelat's very nose. Without Royal Confessor La Chaise's support, aspiring to a benefice was now hopeless, for he controlled the distribution of livings and abbeys:

> This privilege attracted a crowd of clients to Father La Chaise, not only among ecclesiastics of every religious order, but also their parents and friends who were involved in their advancement. As a result he holds audiences twice a week in the profess house of the Jesuits of Paris, where he lodges; and his antechamber is usually filled on those days by a large number of prelates and others of the aforesaid claimants, especially when the advowson of vacant livings takes place.[12]

As of the early 1680s La Chaise had gained a solid footing in the Guise circle. By the fall of 1682 he was sufficiently sure of MADAME DE GUISE to ask her to lend her name to a book (that is, allow it to be dedicated to her), so that the author could be granted a printing privilege.[13] By 1687 he had become quite close to PHILIPPE GOIBAUT DU BOIS and BISHOP GABRIEL DE ROQUETTE.

During the final weeks of MADEMOISELLE DE GUISE's life, La Chaise joined these two Guise protégés in what was seen as a "plot" to wrench legacies from the dying princess. Her Highness initially willed the Jesuit an annual pension of one thousand livres; but in the final codicil of her will, signed only hours before her death, she gave the profess house of Saint-Louis ten thousand livres—specifying that the money was not to be seized by her creditors and could be used in any way La Chaise ordered. The Jesuit himself received "the paintings, porcelains, and property not attached to the walls of her little Apartment of the Hermits," in return for which Her Highness asked him to "remember her in his prayers."[14] The artworks and precious objects included a dozen paintings of various saints framed in Mediterranean cherry wood, bas-reliefs and furniture made of this exotic wood, Chinese export porcelains, and precious objects carved from agate and mounted in silver.

While this purported plot was taking shape and the princess was, some asserted, being manipulated by avaricious men, Marc-Antoine Charpentier was chosen as music master to the Jesuits. Although the post was not technically a benefice, one can conjecture that La Chaise had a say in the selection, accustomed as he was to controlling nominations of all sorts, and enjoying as he did the court being paid him. Was La Chaise's last-minute legacy prompted, to some degree, by Mademoiselle de Guise's gratitude for his having obtained a permanent position for her faithful composer? The question is less frivolous than it might seem. As a great noble, she was duty-bound to ensure that her faithful servants would not be jobless after her death; and it was clear that Charpentier could no longer hope for an appointment at court, nor for long-term protection from MADAME DE GUISE, who had more or less withdrawn from the world and was spending an increasing amount of time at Alençon.

Ferrand de la Faluere (handwritten)

VI

They contributed to making me earn my living

THE FERRAND FAMILY

Françoise Ferrand, wife of René Lefèvre de la Faluère,
first president in the Parlement of Brittany,
and her paternal aunts and uncles,
"friends" of Étiennette Charpentier

In 1709 "Dame Françoise Ferrand, widow of Messire René Lefèvre de la Faluëre, knight, councillor of the king in his councils, former first president of the Parlement of Brittany, dwelling in her hôtel on the rue de Seine, parish of Saint-Sulpice," was named executrix of the last will and testament of ÉTIENNETTE CHARPENTIER, mistress linener. The nomination probably came as no surprise, for Mademoiselle Charpentier had entrusted the document to Madame de la Faluère's late husband two years earlier. The Linener's choice proved perspicacious. Without Françoise Ferrand, the testament would have provoked a family dispute. But the President's widow knew how to stave off creditors and money-hungry heirs. She had been raised in a family that had produced several generations of civil lieutenants for the CHÂTELET of Paris.

Françoise Ferrand's husband came from Tours, but he had close relatives in Brittany, specifically at Rennes, where several members of the family had acquired offices in the Parlement of Brittany. The President was not, however, the only La Faluère to settle in Paris: one of his close relatives, Father La Faluère, one of the FOUR JESUITS portrayed elsewhere in this panel, had been residing at one or another of the THREE JESUIT HOUSES during the 1670s. (These were the very years when Marc-Antoine Charpentier appears to have been given special commissions by the reverend fathers of the Jesuit Church of Saint-Louis.)

Françoise Ferrand herself was merely the capstone of a pyramid of Ferrands who had not only befriended the Charpentier family prior to the 1660s but had also known and worked with their cousins earlier in

110

the century. At the base of this pyramid were two brothers, Michel I Ferrand and Antoine I Ferrand. Both brothers were "private," *particulier*, lieutenants at the Châtelet in the 1590s, and they had financial dealings with some of DAVID CROYER's relatives who were officials there.[1]

The next generation of Ferrands included Michel II (the son of Michel I) and his first cousin, Antoine II (the son of Antoine I). Antoine II became private lieutenant at the Châtelet in 1594. On the other hand, Michel II had purchased a position as a councillor in the Parlement of Paris by 1607 and continued his functions there for some five decades. In 1657 MARIE DE GUISE THE REGENT called upon Michel II to help her determine MADEMOISELLE DE MONTPENSIER's share of the Duchess of Guise's estate.[2] The choice was perhaps governed by the fact that Michel Ferrand had not only acquired legal expertise as a judge in the Parlement, but also had an entrée to the officials at the Châtelet who handled litigation about estates. There may, however, be a still more telling reason for Mademoiselle de Guise's choice of Michel Ferrand. He knew a great deal about the properties owned by the House of Montpensier, for his ancestors had handled the Duke and Duchess of Montpensier's financial affairs during the sixteenth century.[3] (Household officers and financial managers customarily retained copies of correspondence and legal documents, which they preserved in their family archives for the convenience of subsequent generations.)

Antoine II Ferrand had several sisters, among them Magdeleine Ferrand,[4] who married Germain Gouffé, substitute for the royal procurator at the CHÂTELET, and Marie Ferrand, who wed Jean Guyet, a royal secretary at the Parlement of Paris. Madame Guyet was MARIE TALON's close friend—so close that she was the only non-cousin to sign for the bride when Marie Talon wed Daniel Voisin in 1650.[5]

Not long after that wedding, ÉTIENNETTE CHARPENTIER THE LINENER would become another of Madame Guyet's friends, and a friend of Madame Gouffé as well. More than forty years later, Mademoiselle Charpentier would refer to the "silver money-box given to me by the late Madame Gouffé," who had died in 1673. She requested that it be sold to pay for masses for the "other persons who contributed to making me earn my living, particularly Monsieur Ferrand, the father [Antoine III, d. 1689], and Madame his wife [Isabelle Le Gauffre, d. 1684], and all his family; Monsieur Guyet, the master of accounts [*sic*], and Madame his wife."[6]

Antoine II died in 1622 and was succeeded by his son Antoine, who died prematurely. The office of lieutenant therefore leaped a generation, to Antoine II's grandson, Antoine III, who carried on the family's traditional role at the Châtelet from 1638 until his death in 1689. He is the "father" to whom Étiennette Charpentier referred. His "family" included

Antoine-François Ferrand, who became private lieutenant at the Châtelet in 1683, and Françoise Ferrand, who would serve as Étiennette the Linener's executrix.

As wife of the First President of the Parlement of Brittany, Françoise Ferrand spent a great deal of time in the Breton city of Rennes during the 1670s, 1680s, and early 1690s. There she became rather close to Madame de Sévigné, whom she saw whenever the epistolary writer vacationed in that province.[7] And prior to the abrupt dismissal of the DUKE OF CHAULNES, royal governor for Brittany, in 1695, the La Faluères were in continual contact with the former ambassador to Rome. Any part that Lefèvre de la Faluère or his wife may have played in commissioning Marc-Antoine Charpentier's lost *Apothéose de Laodomas*, performed at the Jesuit college of Rennes in memory of the Duke of Luxembourg in March 1695, must remain a conjecture.

Panel 5

ROMAN CONTACTS

Opening Roman Doors

Four men who lived in Rome during the late 1660s are depicted in this panel. Each holds an emblem signifying his passion for music, sometimes music in the distinctive style of his native land, but sometimes the blend of French and Italian genres that would characterize the *Goût Réunis* of the 1720s.

Two of the men are elderly, verging on seventy. One, a cleric dressed in black, is sitting at a desk, copying out oratorios with Latin texts. A model of a small chapel sits on a nearby table, and through a window can be seen the Riario Palace, residence of Queen Christina of Sweden. The other elderly man is depicted in the streets, glancing about, in search of an employer. He wears shabby, rather theatrical clothes, and he holds a theorbo.

The third portrait depicts a powerfully-built, middle-aged gentleman dressed in expensive French-style court clothes and wig. On a table, beside some dispatch cases marked with the lilies of France, lies a handwritten piece of music labeled, in a bold hand, *comédie en musique*, a term more or less synonymous with the Italian word *opera*. Through a window a float with ride a dozen or so musicians and costumed figures can be seen in the square before the Farnese Palace, which is emblazoned with lights.

The fourth portrait shows a man who cannot be much more than thirty and who is dressed in Italian-style court dress. Standing in a sumptuously decorated galery, he holds the plans for a theater. His gaze is directed toward an adjacent room, where an assembly of applauding cardinals surrounds a queen seated beneath a gilded canopy of state.

I

Having resolved to take him into Our service

CARISSIMI OF THE GERMAN COLLEGE

Iacomo Carissimi,
chapel master of the Jesuit *Germanicum* in Rome

The *Germanicum*, that is, the German College run by the Jesuits in
Rome, was renowned throughout Europe for its composers and
for the skilled musicians who performed their works. The school
was housed in the Palazzo di San Apollinare, not far from the Piazza
Navona. In the adjacent Church of San Apollinare the musicians of the
College performed throughout the year, the more lavish musical services
coinciding with the major feast days of the Catholic Church and those
of the Society of Jesus.[1]

In about 1629 the Jesuits at the College appointed as chapel master
young Iacomo Carissimi, a tonsured cleric. It was his duty to teach the
students, compose all necessary music, and conduct the requisite
rehearsals and performances. Carissimi's fame spread throughout the
Peninsula and even beyond the Alps, for he had

> many students who considered it an honor to come and sing his
> music, even without payment. Moreover, through great work, and
> by training the musicians in his room, he created the best music,
> even with ordinary voices. For this reason, less was spent, ... and
> there was good music.[2]

Carissimi was criticized for hiring secular players to reinforce the
student performers—much as that famed JESUIT HOUSE in Paris, the
College of Louis-le-Grand, was criticized for hiring outsiders to perform
with the pupils during the assemblies that marked the end of the school
year. To quash such criticisms, Carissimi managed to transform some of
these paid musicians into boarders at the German College. For example,
from 1666 to 1669 (the years when Marc-Antoine Charpentier is pre-

sumed to have been in Rome), in addition to the Jesuit fathers, the pupils, and the domestics residing and working at San Apollinare, the annual list of "souls" taking Easter communion showed four, five, or even six boarders, *convittori*.[3] Carissimi also drew fire for concentrating on music and performance, to the detriment of his teaching.

The composer's fame stemmed in part from the high quality of the performances, but Athanasius Kircher, a Jesuit, praised him for his expressiveness. This praise went beyond the supportive statement one would expect from a Jesuit writing about a Jesuit-sponsored event:

> Iacomo Carissimi, most excellent, and a musician of celebrated fame,
> ... in talent and felicity of composition is stronger than others, for
> transforming the souls of listeners into any affections whatever; for
> his compositions are full of energy and vivacity of spirit.[4]

(Kircher's praise of Carissimi would find an echo in remarks about Marc-Antoine Charpentier published in 1709 in the *Journal de Trévoux*, which was primarily authored by Parisian Jesuits: "He was Carissimi's pupil. It is under this great master that he acquired the talent, so rare, of expressing by musical tones the meaning of the words, and of moving" his audience.[5] One of the tools that permitted Charpentier to be so expressive was his familiarity with the "energies" of each key, *mode*.)

As long as he did not shirk his duties, Carissimi was allowed to compose and conduct Lenten oratorios for the Archconfraternity of the Crucifix that met in the Oratorio del SS. Crocifisso, a chapel situated just behind the Church of San Marcello, with which it was associated.

He was also permitted to enter the service of Queen Christina of Sweden. In July 18, 1656, on the eve of the Queen's departure for Paris, Carissimi—whom she called "Our actual servant"—was appointed to be her "chapel master for chamber concerts":

> Having resolved to take him into Our Service as *Maestro di Cappella
> del concerto di camera*, and having already had him enrolled among
> Our actual domestics and servants, with the effect that he ought to
> enjoy in every place the due advantages, honors, and prerogatives
> which all Our servants and domestics ought to enjoy, and wishing
> that, in every necessity, it be known to everyone that with this
> character and quality, the aforesaid Iacomo enjoys Our royal
> protection.[6]

Why would Christina issue so strong a statement when she was about to leave Rome for an extended period?

For two reasons. As the decree states, it would "protect" Carissimi during her absence; but Christina was also proclaiming that the composer belonged to her, was "Ours." This official letter more or less made Carissimi her property, until she saw fit to dismiss him. (Her secretary, JACQUES II DALIBERT, would learn to his chagrin just how difficult it was to be released from serving her.) The Queen treated her domestics like so many objects. She traded a singer for a rare manuscript; she threatened to throw Secretary Dalibert out a window whenever he displeased her; she had Monaldesco, her grand equerry, assassinated for duplicity; and she told one of her prized castrati that if he did not immediately return to her palace and sing for her, he would not long sing for anyone.[7] In short, Christina's letter of appointment should be viewed as proof that Carissimi was already composing for her in 1655, and that he continued to do so over the years. As chapel master to the Queen, Carissimi was more or less obliged to work with Dalibert, a Parisian who, starting in 1662, played an increasingly important role as the Queen's impresario.

Somehow, probably in 1666, Carissimi came into contact with another young Parisian, Marc-Antoine Charpentier. If he did, it was because Charpentier had obtained a letter of introduction to him—perhaps through his JESUIT FRIENDS, perhaps through Dalibert. Politeness ruled out simply knocking at the great man's door and introducing oneself. And politeness required Carissimi to reply that he must ask his superiors for permission to meet with the young man, especially in view of the recurrent criticisms about shirking his duties.

Carissimi's request would have gone first to the Rector of the College, who as a precaution perhaps consulted the head of the Society, General Oliva. After all, Oliva had first-hand experience with such issues, having been rector at San Apollinare in 1657, when three cardinals had issued a ruling chastising Carissimi for giving too many outsiders an entrée to the College.[8] When Marc-Antoine Charpentier reached Rome, one of Oliva's secretaries was the French JESUIT, Pierre de Verthamon, the uncle of MARIE TALON, ÉLISABETH CHARPENTIER's friend. Under these circumstances, it is difficult to imagine Oliva refusing Charpentier's request for access to the German College and its chapel master.

Irrespective of the identity of the person who authorized these visits, as DONNEAU DE VISÉ and Corneille, Charpentier's collaborators in the theater would later assert in the *Mercure galant*, the young Frenchman was able to "see Carissimi often" during the "three years he lived in Rome."[9] This assertion should be interpreted in the seventeenth-century sense of the expression "to see." That is, Charpentier often visited Carissimi, talked with him face to face (as we "see" physicians today).

Marc-Antoine Charpentier is alleged to have returned to France with some of Carissimi's compositions preserved in his memory. This,

BROSSARD would later assert, "is how ... several of Carissimi's oratorios, which were not printed, reached France. At least that is what is claimed." Making copies of the chapel master's compositions was doubtlessly being discouraged during his lifetime, for immediately after Iacomo Carissimi's demise at the German College in 1674, the superiors of the college obtained a papal brief prohibiting the dissemination of the late composer's music, which was their property. "Since the late Iacomo Carissimi ... composed many musical works ... for use in the church, [and] not without great expense on the part of the said college,"

> wishing to do a special favor for the rector, ... [We] prohibit and
> forbid, ... any and every person, now or in the future enjoying
> whatever authority, superiority, preeminence, and powers ... ever to
> dare or presume in any way to remove or take away from the same
> college and church the above-mentioned musical works (or part of
> them) by the said Iacomo, ... or to lend them to any church, person,
> or pious place, or allow them to be removed, taken away, or lent.[10]

What firmer and more eloquent statement can one find to explain why, in France, 1670–1704, so few of Marc-Antoine Charpentier's compositions would become available to the public? Like the Jesuits of the *Germanicum*, the THREE JESUIT HOUSES for which he composed would insist upon retaining the exclusivity of the works that Charpentier had produced for them. For the same reason, PHILIPPE III, DUKE OF CHARTRES, would forbid the publication of the opera he had composed under Charpentier's tutelage. For the same reason the SAINTE-CHAPELLE routinely confiscated a deceased chapel master's manuscripts. And for the same reason the two Guise princesses expected the works that Monsieur Charpentier composed for them and their friends to remain exclusive.

The Queen has ordered me to continue to serve Her

DALIBERT OF THE RIARIO PALACE

Jacques II Dalibert, Parisian,
secretary and impresario to Queen Christina of Sweden

Born in about 1640, Jacques II Dalibert was the son of Jacques I Dalibert, superintendent and comptroller general of the household of GASTON D'ORLÉANS from the 1640s until the prince's death in 1660. (The Daliberts eventually gave luster to their name by spelling it "d'Alibert.") In 1629 Jacques I—"knight, royal councillor, treasurer of France in the generality of Béziers, and intendant of the salt taxes in Languedoc"—wed a girl named Étiennette Charpentier.[1] She was not the composer's sister, she was the daughter of Jean Charpentier, a war commissioner who appears to have had an entrée to Cardinal RICHELIEU's circle. A handful of family acts involving Jean Charpentier contain no suggestions that he was related to Denis Charpentier, the Cardinal's faithful secretary, although the possibility should not be ruled out.[2] Nor is there evidence that Étiennette Charpentier–Dalibert was related to ÉTIENNETTE CHARPENTIER THE LINENER, the daughter of LOUIS THE SCRIVENER. The bride's dowry consisted of a large tract of land just outside the city walls, worth sixty-six thousand livres.

Over the next twenty years, Jacques I Dalibert became extremely wealthy. His name appeared on the list of fiscal contractors reproached by the Frondeurs of the late 1640s. The family prided itself on being related to the Le Telliers, but the connection was quite distant, if in fact it existed. The Daliberts officially resided at the Luxembourg Palace, but they also maintained a stately residence along the quai des Grands-Augustins. When GASTON D'ORLÉANS was disgraced after the Fronde and retired to Blois in 1652, Jacques I Dalibert remained in Paris to manage the prince's finances—a task that included paying the wages or stipends of the Duke's householders, among them ÉLISABETH-MARIE MALIER's brother, and Marc-Antoine Charpentier's own cousin, HAVÉ DE SAINT-AUBIN.

By the late 1650s, Jacques I's son, Jacques II, had became his father's assistant and potential successor and was laying claim to his share of the sizeable sums that Gaston owed the elder Dalibert.[3] Having recently completed his studies in one of the Parisian colleges, Jacques II—who was about to set off on the customary tour of Italy in 1657—began bragging that he was being sent to Rome to deliver a letter from Gaston to another disgraced plotter, Cardinal de Retz, and to communicate still more information to the prelate verbally. When Cardinal Mazarin, the prime minister, got wind of these assertions, young Jacques was arrested; but he was released when Gaston asserted that he would scarcely have entrusted secrets to a seventeen-year-old. The youth promptly set off for Rome.[4]

As it turned out, Jacques II had indeed been entrusted with secret negotiations, but they were not the ones he had been bragging about. Gaston had ordered him to begin discussions about a marriage between one of his daughters and his nephew, the Duke of Savoy.[5] By the summer of 1658 Jacques II was in Turin, where his compatriot DASSOUCY, a poet, composer, and musician, had been living since the summer of 1657. Tactless and overly brash, Dalibert did not impress Madame Royale, the Duke's mother. "Everything I observe about that man, is that he is very diligent. What is he to my brother [Gaston]?" she wondered. Dalibert's mission nonetheless went quite well, and he returned to France to report to Gaston.

In July 1659 Dalibert was back in Turin, pushing the marriage negotiations ahead. Once again his loose tongue got him into trouble, and he was recalled to France, where he accompanied his father to Blois, to be at the bedside of the dying Duke of Orléans in February 1660.

Casting about for a new protector, the young man promptly dispatched a letter to Madame Royale in Turin, painting a very black picture and hinting that, by inviting him into her household, she could make amends for the hardships her late brother's indebtedness was causing the Daliberts:

> I have just returned from Blois, where I witnessed the death of His Royal Highness, my master. … One might say that his late Royal Highness carried off to the tomb the fortunes of all those who had followed his fortunes. As for me, I am the one in his household who loses the most, since in addition to the loss of the principal position in the household, my father had advanced him an infinitely large sum of money, in order to help Monseigneur in his affairs.[6]

Louis XIV promptly paid his late uncle's debts, including the money loaned by Jacques I Dalibert.

Meanwhile, Madame Royale had responded to Dalibert's not too subtle plea. By July 1661 Jacques II's name had found its way to her pension list. A bid to be named secretary to Prince Pamphili failed, however. In addition to negotiating with Turin, Dalibert was now involved in promoting a marriage between another of Gaston's daughters and a Medici prince. On April 9, 1661, Mademoiselle d'Orléans (who appears in this portrait gallery as "MADAME DE TOSCANE") wed Cosimo III de' Medici by proxy. In June she reached Florence, where Jacques II had been since May. DASSOUCY too was in the city; and as was his wont with potential protectors, he offered the bride a poem.

Jacques II had made a side trip to Rome in January 1661 and decided to settle there in July, although his negotiations with Turin were still going on. He was living near the Piazza di Spagna[7] when he learned that his father, one of the financiers implicated in the Foucquet Affair,[8] had been sent to the Bastille on January 30, 1662, and was being held incommunicado.[9] (The elder Dalibert was arrested only days after the inventory of Louis CHARPENTIER THE SCRIVENER's property was made, during the course of which the notary mysteriously neglected to enumerate the letters and charters locked up in the Scrivener's "expedition cabinet.")

By August 1663, the disgraced financier was dead. His son wrote to a friend in Turin, stating that he was "all ready to sacrifice the property I still have" in order to serve Madame Royale. His prospects were indeed gloomy, for the tribunal judging the financiers around Foucquet had forced the elder Dalibert to turn over 498,878 livres to the royal coffers, and had confiscated all the family's houses as well as its lands and quarries around the Butte of Montmartre.[10] Jacques II also sent off an appeal to Louis XIV's foreign minister, Hugues de Lionne, who in April 1662 recommended him to Cardinal Decio Azzolino, who was close to Queen Christina of Sweden.[11] Not long afterward, Dalibert entered the Queen's service, as "secretary of her embassy."

In the end, Dalibert was able to spirit fifty thousand livres out of France, when Christina sent him on a mission to Paris in late 1662, only a few weeks before the prosecution of Foucquet's collaborators was scheduled to begin. Thanks to this scheme, Jacques II could congratulate himself that "my business affairs are in a rather good state, and if Fate robbed me of the better part of my property, she left me what I need to pay for as large a household as is proper for a man who is neither a cardinal nor an ambassador."[12]

Having acquired "magnificent trappings" and "a coach, four lackeys, and a valet," Dalibert began working across the Tiber, in the Riario

Palace where Christina resided with what was known as her "family," that is, her domestics and her courtiers.[13] His lively chatter and pleasant manners charmed at first, but those who had to deal with Dalibert soon realized that the young Frenchman's tongue wagged a bit too much and that he did not always fulfill his promises: "He is a great talker and says nothing, he is quite dazzling but there is nothing solid; scheming and curious, but a bit timid, but still very supple. He is prey to a lot of impulses that often lead to nothing."[14]

In May 1663, in the Church of Santo Spirito in Sassia, "Count d'Alibert" wed Maria Vittoria Cenci, whom he had been led to believe was very wealthy.[15] In his wedding contract[16] Dalibert was described as being the "Count of Clignancourt and Beauregard" (his late father had owned several quarries at Clignancourt!), "councillor in ordinary in the supreme councils of the Most Christian King" (a distortion, and perhaps an outright appropriation, of his father's venal office of "royal councillor in the king's councils, secretary of His Majesty and for his finances") and "secretary for the embassy and commandments" of the Queen of Sweden (clearly the only accurate title of the three).

Since his wife was a parishioner of Santo Spirito, Impresario-Secretary Dalibert almost certainly talked music with the church's chapel master, Francesco Beretta.[17] (In other words, Jacques II Dalibert is an extremely likely conduit through which Marc-Antoine Charpentier gained access to a copy of Beretta's mass, *Missa mirabiles elationes maris*, and copied and annotated it in 1680 or 1682.)

Dalibert's responsibilities at the Riario involved paying frequent visits on the Queen's behalf to the French embassy at the Farnese Palace, writing poorly-spelled letters in his schoolboy hand, and entertaining Her Majesty:

> When he wants to write a letter, he sometimes succeeds, but only after having stolen from [writers such as] Balzac and Voiture. When talking, he declaims and gesticulates like an actor, and with all these fine qualities he talked with the Queen every day for two full hours, after her meal. She often straightened him out, but he bore it very patiently, especially when he brought her news from the Papal Palace or from the city, news that more often than not was invented, since he sometimes did not know what to talk about.[18]

If the Queen found it necessary to "straighten out" Dalibert, it was because he could not hold his tongue. On several occasions she almost dismissed him; but she inevitably relented, because he was so amusing: "The Queen knows full well that everything he says is nonsense, but she purposely makes him chatter on, to amuse her, and it is impossible for a man who talks every day for two full hours on no specific subject to keep from mixing a lot of his own inventions into it."[19]

Jacques II Dalibert was not merely the Queen's jester, he was her impresario. During the 1660s he prepared Mardi Gras floats bearing musicians[20]; he corresponded with Foreign Minister Lionne about obtaining a copy of Molière's Le Tartuffe, so that it could be performed for Christina; he negotiated the return of the Queen's favorite castrato, Ciccolino, from Turin; he organized a succession of operas, comédies en musique, that were performed at the Riario, including the one that provoked the Mardi Gras riot of 1666 to which DASSOUCY alluded in a petition to be admitted to the Queen's "comédie en musique."[21] Considering Dalibert's pivotal role in preparing Christina's entertainments, it is likely that he was among the "several people" who had "assured" Dassoucy that the Queen would welcome him into her household.

The Queen's close friendship with Cardinal Azzolino put Dalibert in touch with many of the religious composers of Rome, among them CARISSIMI, whom the Queen had appointed to her household in 1656. In addition, and somewhat surreptitiously, Dalibert corresponded with the secretaries to the House of Savoy, trying not to burn his bridges with Turin should Christina make good on her threats to dismiss him. For example, he sent the secretaries and the gentlemen of the court at Turin "all the most gallant things being written in prose and in verse in Paris." From proffering small gifts he progressed to offering paintings for sale.[22]

On May 22, 1666, having dismissed all but her most essential servants, Queen Christina set out for Hamburg, taking her ready cash. The members of her "family" would have to cope as best they could, for the Sacred Royal Majesty had no intention of paying her householders' wages. Dalibert and his wife therefore took temporary lodgings in the via della Croce, in the parish of San Lorenzo in Lucina. For Dalibert, the Queen's departure meant tightened purse strings. Only a few days before leaving, she had been pressuring the French to grant him a pension, as a reward for his services to the Crown; but her departure dashed that hope.[23] In addition, his stipend from the Queen was not being paid. She did not return to Rome until November 1668.

The vacuum created in Dalibert's duties by Christina's departure did not last long. A few months later the DUKE OF CHAULNES, Louis XIV's new ambassador, made his official entry into Rome. For at least one of the festivities at the Farnese Palace, the Ambassador engaged DASSOUCY; and it must have been with Jacques Dalibert's help that Chaulnes hired the musicians who had performed in Christina's opera the previous March. Throughout the Duke's stay, August 1666 to September 1668, Dalibert was in permanent liaison with the Farnese. He became very close to Chaulnes, who "was very fond of Monsieur d'Alibert" and who obtained for him a position as secretary for the French embassy. The friendship lasted for several decades: "He is a former friend of the Duke of Chaulnes, they still correspond with one another," noted a French cleric living in Rome in 1698.[24]

In addition to his obligations to the Queen, Dalibert developed several other entertainment ventures aimed at increasing his revenues. Shortly after his marriage he was granted a papal concession to build a tennis court near the Piazza di Spagna. By 1666 the establishment had opened and was being run by two Frenchmen.[25] Dalibert also operated what amounted to a used-clothing business. Foreigners—among them Abbé Le Tellier or his agent, "Carpentier," who in late 1667 and early 1668 was doing odd jobs for the DUKE OF CHAULNES at the Farnese Palace—could come to him when they needed makeshift livery or furniture:

> When he wanted to dress his servants in livery, he had a thousand inventive ways to do it with the Jews, without ever spending cash; sometimes he traded one thing, and sometimes another. In a word, swindlers were not better at it than he.[26]

With the Queen's connivance, Dalibert eventually created a marionette theater in his house, even though such activities were forbidden in Rome. Performances were accompanied by vocal and instrumental music.[27]

After Christina's return to Rome on November 22, 1668, Dalibert was put in charge of preparing an annual opera to be hosted by the Queen. Frustrated by the inadequacies of the theater in the Riario, Christina borrowed the Colonna Palace for Mardi Gras of 1669. There Dalibert organized performances of Filippo Acciaioli's L'Empio punita for an all-male audience. Meanwhile, at the Queen's instigation he was creating a public theater, the Tordinona, on which work began late in 1669.[28] (Marc-Antoine Charpentier did not remain in Rome long enough to see this dream become a reality, but he can scarcely have been unaware of the contribution that his compatriot was making to operatic theater.)

Jacques II Dalibert's career in Rome continued for four more decades, decades too full of projects and frustrations to be discussed in detail here. The Tordinona was soon closed by papal order and was eventually dismantled, leaving Dalibert deeply in debt. When Christina again left Rome for an extended period, he traveled to Turin and prepared operas for that court. His hopes of becoming an impresario there were dashed, however, for Christina refused to release him. The Queen, Dalibert informed his contact in Turin in May 1678, "has expressly ordered me to continue to serve her, refusing me the favor I hope to obtain from her, to go in person to contribute to entertaining M[adame] R[oyale] at the next Mardi Gras season." But, he continued, if the House of Savoy were to give him a "positive commitment that would serve as a legitimate excuse" to leave the Queen's household, he was resolved to prepare "one or two operas" for Madame Royale and to "direct everything very well." The "excuse," he pointed out, must however include an "honorific title," for he could not "appear in Turin as an opera-maker, after having handled rather important affairs there."[29] The project was stillborn.

Corresponding with his relatives back in Paris (and with the Duke of Chaulnes as well); transmitting Christina's messages to her French agent in Paris, poet and playwright Gabriel Gilbert; busily hawking the latest French poems to the elite of the Peninsula; and never taking his finger off the musical pulses of Rome, Florence, Venice, and Turin, Jacques II Dalibert emerges as a likely conduit through which Marc-Antoine Charpentier gained access to several Italian works, perhaps in the form of manuscripts that he was allowed to copy before passing them on to someone else: a recit from a Venetian opera, *Marcello in Siracusa*, which was not performed until 1670 ; and, of course, Beretta's polychoral mass.

Dalibert remained in the Queen's service until her death in 1689, but nearly three decades of faithful service to Christina did not make him wealthy. Her will contained no bequests to servants. Always short of money and rarely turning a profit, Dalibert "nonetheless, as usual, [went] on undertaking new things, without succeeding at any of them."[30]

III

Having needed my bread and my pity

DASSOUCY THE POET-COMPOSER

Charles Coypeaux Dassoucy,
author, musician, and adventurer

Charles Coypeau—the son of Grégoire Coypeau, Sieur d'Assoucy, an eloquent barrister with friends in the Parlement—was born in Paris in 1605. Raised in the Latin Quarter, Charles was educated by the Jesuits; but he would sneak away to the Pont-Neuf, so fascinated was he by street musicians and puppeteers. By his late teens he had made his way to southern France, where he taught the lute; and then he pressed on to Italy, learning to play the theorbo and steeping himself in Italian music.

By the mid-1630s Charles was back in Paris, performing at court and composing music for the theater. For example, in 1647 he not only played theorbo in Luigi Rossi's *Orfeo*, he was also commissioned by Pierre Corneille to write music for *Andromède*, his new "machine play," *pièce à machines*. It was at this time that Coypeau, who now went by the name "Dassoucy," became associated with a group of mildly non-conformists known as the *libertins*. One of the members of this circle was a young actor and playwright who had adopted the sobriquet "Molière."[1]

During the summer of 1650, Dassoucy set off for Turin, bearing a letter of introduction to the Dowager Duchess of Savoy, known as "Madame Royale." He spent approximately a year and a half at the court of Turin. On the return trip to France in late December 1651, his path crossed that of MOLIÈRE and his troop, who were performing for the delegates to the Estates of Languedoc. Back in Paris, Dassoucy renewed his contacts with the libertine circle. He performed at court, gave music lessons, and published some of his poetry and a volume of airs.

In 1655 (perhaps to escape the Company of the Holy Sacrament, which was aggressively rooting out various types of "immorality") he hastily left Paris with a talented young pupil, Pierre Valentin, whom he called "Pierrotin." During their slow journey to Savoy, Dassoucy and his singing "page" encountered MOLIÈRE's troop at Lyons and joined them in a trek across southern France.

Dassoucy and Pierrotin then pushed on to Turin, where they were performing for Madame Royale by June 1657. Although Dassoucy's name appears on the list of court musicians for 1657–1658,[2] he did not receive the permanent position he had hoped for, owing in large part to his penchant for off-color satire and to Pierrotin's debauchery.

His experiences in Turin dampened some of Dassoucy's enthusiasm for service in the household of so pious a lady. It involved too much kneeling!

> Although I already had too much work to do for this princess's chamber, ... I wanted ... to play for her chapel as well. Irrespective of whether she heard mass in her room, at the Cathedral of the Holy Shroud, or in some other church, I followed her everywhere like a poodle. Everywhere my lute and Pierrotin could be seen following her about. By this means, in a short time I became the most devout person in the world, for one should not believe that this pious princess, who usually wept before altars, thought she was satisfying her piety by attending only one mass; every day she needed at least two of them, and more often than not three, during which I played very long and very devout music, and always on my knees.[3]

He admitted to being torn by the conflict between his egotistic, libertine thoughts and the prayers to which he was paying lip service:

> Judge, reader, whether I should have been entirely given over to God. However, I assure you that the thing I was thinking about the least was to bother Him with my prayers. Apollo, who was constantly leading me around by the collar, was even less willing to pardon me in this holy place. My imagination was continually filled with the idea of some fine motet; and although all the words I muttered between my teeth were holy and sacred, it was not so much to glorify God that I wanted to unite them to my melodies as to satisfy this mortal divinity, which I, a wretch, would have preferred to the Divinity Himself. But in my ardent passion to please him, it was not only in church that I felt transported by the ardor of this uncontrolled zeal.[4]

Dassoucy left Turin in 1658. It is not clear whether he was still there in the summer of that year, when a young Parisian, JACQUES II DALIBERT, stopped in Turin on his way to Rome, on a semi-official diplomatic mission to promote the marriage of the Duke of Savoy and one GASTON D'ORLÉANS' daughters. (Among the candidates were ISABELLE D'ORLÉANS

OF ALENÇON, the future "Madame de Guise," and her older sister, "Mademoiselle d'Orléans, portrayed in this gallery as MADAME DE TOSCANE.) Although Dassoucy had once offered a poem to Gaston's wife, Marguerite de Lorraine, and although his own mother lived in Lorraine, there is no firm evidence that he and Dalibert met in Turin.

From Turin, Dassoucy and his "page" journeyed to Mantua—an unfortunate decision, for Pierrotin was kidnapped by henchmen of the Duke of Mantua, who seems to have had the boy castrated in order to preserve his lovely high voice, and who kept him a virtual prisoner, the better to maintain control over this vocal treasure. For over a year Dassoucy tried to get Pierrotin back.

By December 1659 Dassoucy was in Florence, teaching music. There he witnessed the festivities accompanying the wedding of MADAME DE TOSCANE (Marguerite-Louise d'Orléans, the daughter of Gaston d'Orléans) to the son of the Grand Duke of Tuscany in 1661. Even if Dassoucy did not meet JACQUES II DALIBERT at Turin, he probably got to know him in Florence that summer. Dalibert, who had been active in the wedding negotiations, arrived in the city in May and remained there until at least mid-July, when the French delegation that had brought the bride to Tuscany returned to France.[5]

Later that year Dassoucy moved to Rome, henceforth earning his livelihood by gambling, entertaining the wealthy, teaching music, and performing. Although most Frenchmen and women fled the city in September 1662, as a result of the international crisis provoked when the Pope's Corsican guards harassed French Ambassador Créquy, Dassoucy remained in Rome. So did JACQUES II DALIBERT, who earlier that year had entered the service of Queen Christina of Sweden. As her ambassadorial secretary, Dalibert went from one palace to another, doing errands for the Queen.

It is virtually certain that Dassoucy promptly got in touch with Dalibert, who in addition to being Christina's secretary was also her impresario. At some point between July 1662 (when the Queen returned from a trip abroad) and May 1666 (when she set off for Hamburg), Dassoucy borrowed money in order to look "glorious, superb, and triumphant, arriving at the court of the great Christina, who can pay him handsomely for his lute and his song."[6] The idea of serving the Queen was very appealing to a libertine; for, in marked contrast to Madame Royale of Savoy, Christina was attracted by the bawdy, the burlesque, the obscene.

Although Dassoucy apparently performed for the Queen, he was not appointed to her household. During the spring of 1666 he therefore sent her a poem entitled "To the Queen of Sweden, to gain entrance to her *comédie en musique"*—the term the French in Rome used to denote an opera. Alluding to a riot quelled by the Queen's Swiss guards during a recent Mardi Gras performance of *Amore e Fede*, Dassoucy expressed his hope that these same guards would, "without lesion or risk of a contusion, to your fine comedy [grant me] an introduction." The "entrance" he was hoping for was, of course, admission to the Queen's Music. The poem includes one revealing detail: "several people," he asserts, have "come to assure me" that my "entrance" depends on the Queen. If Dassoucy had been urged into action by "several" members of the royal household, it surely was with the support of Christina's young impresario, JACQUES II DALIBERT. The poem bore no fruit, for Christina was preparing her departure for Hamburg and was about to dismiss most of her servants, retaining only her secretarial staff and a skeleton household to care for the palace.

Dassoucy next directed his steps to the Farnese Palace, the official residence of the DUKE OF CHAULNES, the new French ambassador to Rome who had arrived in that city in July 1666. By the following January Dassoucy was working for the Ambassador, who was planning a *"comédie en musique,"* an *"opéra,"* for Mardi Gras, and who had hired the "troop" that had recently "performed for the Queen of Sweden."[7] Things went so well that a second troop of musicians was assembled. The entertainments included a "public comedy" performed for anyone who wanted to attend; an "opera" with music by Ercole Bernabei, plus ballets (it apparently was given the hybrid title *Les Accidents d'Amore*); a "comedy"; and a *"comédie en musique"* organized by Flavio Orsini, Duke of Bracciano, who was acting as the Ambassador's impresario. One of these events was preceded by a prologue in honor of Louis XIV's newborn daughter. In all, some twelve hundred people attended these entertainments. The "opera" pleased "not only the Italians but also the French."[8]

It is likely that Dassoucy wrote the prologue celebrating the royal birth; and he perhaps participated in readying the *comédie en musique*. At any rate, in February 1667, working closely with Ugo Maffei, an Italian employee at the Embassy, the poet wrote some "French verses"[9] to be recited by the Farnese staff as they rode about on a Mardi Gras float, disguised as sibyls.

Then, in November 1667, Abbé Le Tellier, the son of the powerful minister of war, Michel Le Tellier, came to Rome to seek papal bulls for his coadjutorship to the archibishopric of Reims. He was received, cared for, and entertained by CHAULNES and his staff. Le Tellier himself entertained frequently, so he asked Dassoucy to "come to see him every day." When the cleric did not remunerate him, Dassoucy sent him a "burlesque request" asking the "Grand Tellier" to "put a little something into my money-box."[10] (To procure a makeshift livery for the temporary domestics whom he had hired, Le Tellier turned to another Frenchman who either worked at the Farnese or had been recommended by the embassy staff: "Carpentier"[11]—perhaps the actual spelling of his family name, but perhaps the Italian pronunciation of *Charpentier*.)

By then Dassoucy was in desperate financial straits. Late in 1664 Pierrotin had joined him in Rome, and the poet had begun showering money and clothes on the dissolute young man. At some point prior to the fall of 1667, Dassoucy also helped out Marc-Antoine Charpentier, when his purse was empty: "having needed, in Rome, my bread and my pity," as he put it.[12] Dassoucy also implied that he had taught Charpentier in Rome—that is, had "nourished him at his breast" artistically, just as he had taught Pierrotin.

By mid-1667 Dassoucy was finding it increasingly difficult to keep his creditors at bay. Then, in November, Pierrotin attempted to poison him. The poet alerted the police, who hauled Pierrotin off to prison. Later in the month, or during the first days of December 1667, the burlesque poet was himself arrested, owing perhaps to the Italian clergy's opposition to his overtly dissolute behavior. Despite verse appeals to CHAULNES and his staff,[13] Dassoucy remained in prison until the fall of 1668. Immediately after his release, he hastened north.

Back in Paris by the summer of 1669, he began writing about his adventures in *Les Rimes redoublées*, printed in 1671. Meanwhile, his old acquaintance from Rome, Marc-Antoine Charpentier, who had returned to France in late 1669, had been invited to collaborate with MOLIÈRE on a revival of *Le Mariage forcé* and *La Comtesse Escarbagnas*. The shows opened on July 8, 1672, and continued until August 7, when Molière fell ill and the theater had to close for a week, ending the run. Dassoucy promptly went to call upon the ailing playwright, who "promised" to let him write the music for the new "machine play" he was preparing—that is, *Le Malade imaginaire*.[14]

Shortly after September 20, 1672, when a royal decree granted Lully the publication rights for every play to which he had contributed during his collaboration with MOLIÈRE, Dassoucy learned that the playwright had broken his promise and had asked Charpentier to compose incidental music for *Le Malade*: "Today, having lost M. de Lully," wrote Dassoucy in an open letter to Molière, "I learned yesterday ...." Then he got to the point: "They assured me that you were about to give your machine play to the incomparable Monsieur X–, to write the music."[15] Although Dassoucy had agreed to work for nothing, the playwright had bowed to pressure exerted by some "virgins," some "heroines and goddesses before whom he must burn incense."[16] (In the parlance of the day, the terms *vierges*, *héroïnes*, and *déesses* were reserved for a handful of unmarried or widowed princesses, either royal, like MADAME DE GUISE, or "foreign" but residing in France, like MADEMOISELLE DE GUISE.[17])

Dassoucy did not conceal his hurt. Nor did he mince words about Charpentier, whom he painted as quite incompetent when it came to fitting the melody to the words, and who, he asserted, needed a pair of stilts in order to be great. Perhaps motivated by sour grapes, but perhaps giving vent to an animosity dating back to Rome, Dassoucy painted Charpentier as harmlessly mad:

> [Charpentier is] a lad who, despite the fact that the ventricles of his brain are very damaged, is not, however, a madman to be constrained, but a madman to be pitied, and who, having needed in Rome my bread and my pity, is scarcely more sensitive to those boons than so many other vipers I have nourished in my breast; ... and this man, who without any doubt is an original, is not however so original that one can't find a copy at the Incurables [madhouse].[18]

Depicting his relations with Molière, the septuagenarian poet unwittingly declared himself outmoded, compared with the innovations that Marc-Antoine Charpentier, not yet thirty, could bring to the theater:

> [Molière] was once, however, my friend. ... He knows that it was I who gave a soul to Monsieur Corneille's verse for *Andromède* [in 1647]; that I had the reputation for writing beautiful airs before all these illustrious Amphions of our time ever thought about it. ... I can be proud of being, today, the dean of all the musicians of France. ... That is why [Molière] was not taking a very big risk in begging me to write the music for his machine plays.[19]

Having spoken his mind, Dassoucy remained Molière's faithful friend. He was among the mourners at the playwright's secret burial in February 1673. In a tribute to Molière, Dassoucy reiterated his attachment to him: "He was, however, always my friend. And if at the end of his life he ceased being so, I want everyone to know that I have never ceased to esteem him."[20]

In March 1673 Dassoucy was arrested and imprisoned for several months on unspecified charges. He was not disgraced, however, for he was a pensioned royal musician when he died in October 1677.

IV

I declare in favor of Italian music

CHAULNES OF THE FARNESE PALACE

Charles d'Albert d'Ailly, Duke of Chaulnes and peer of the realm,
French ambassador to Rome, 1666–1668

In May 1666, after successive delays, Charles d'Albert d'Ailly, Duke of Chaulnes, and his wife set off for Rome and the Farnese Palace, seat of the French embassy. Since August 1662, when the Pope's Corsican guards fired at coaches bearing Ambassador Créquy and his entourage, many Frenchmen had been avoiding Rome. Diplomatic relations had more or less broken off; and after an initial show of bellicosity, Créquy had left the city and put the Farnese in the hands of a skeleton staff

For four years Abbé Louis de Bourlemont, who had remained in Rome to fulfill his obligations as an auditor of the Rota, was France's chargé d'affaires for Rome. Bourlemont had worked to settle the Corsican crisis; and he often sounded out Queen Christina of Sweden's diplomatic secretary, JACQUES II DALIBERT, who would bring him messages the Queen wished transmitted to Louis XIV. Along with the messages came bits of gossip from Dalibert about what was going on in the Queen's household across the river, at the Riario Palace.[1]

In the spring of 1666, as Chaulnes was preparing his departure from Paris, Bourlemont was representing France's position to the Rota concerning the late Duke Henri of Guise's marriage to Madame de Bossut, which the French considered invalid. He corresponded regularly with the staff of Foreign Minister Hugues de Lionne about how the case was progressing, and Lionne relayed the latest developments to MARIE DE GUISE THE REGENT. In April 1666 the Rota declared in favor of Bossut, but France refused to accept the decision, thereby preventing her from laying claim to any of the property that LOUIS-JOSEPH DE LORRAINE, DUKE OF GUISE, had recently inherited from his spendthrift uncle.[2]

Ambassador Chaulnes did not have the honor of paying his respects to Queen Christina. She left Rome in May, and he did not enter the city until late June, in a procession that included approximately one hundred pages and one hundred thirty-two coaches. The Frenchman's appearance shocked the Italians, for Chaulnes had the "corpulence, the ponderousness, and the physiognomy of an ox." But he proved to be witty, dignified, cultivated.[3] If he had a shortcoming, it was his inability to speak or write Italian.

In addition to working with Bourlemont, the Ambassador had as an assistant a Frenchman named La Bussière, who had been serving as Bourlemont's secretary and was listed on the official payroll. The payroll also included an Italian cleric, Abbé Santis, Chaulnes' secretary. The Ambassador relied on two other Italians, the Duke of Bracciano and Ugo Maffei, both of whom received regular wages. Several other Frenchmen either lived at the Farnese or stopped by there regularly. Some of them wrote letters back to the Foreign Office, but in an unofficial capacity, for their names do not appear on the payroll. Among them were several clerics: Abbé Machault, Father Noillan, and Father Donat, a Jesuit. There were also "four French gentlemen," not named.[4] To them must be added the guests whose stays could last a month or two and for whom the Ambassador provided lodgings in or near the Farnese: Cardinal Retz, Abbé Hugues Servien (Lionne's godson) and Abbé Maurice Le Tellier (Louvois' brother).

On the margins of this circle an undetermined number of Frenchmen helped out, receiving gifts or tips for their service. One of them was DASSOUCY, rewarded with a silver candlestick by Madame de Chaulnes. Another hanger-on was called "Carpentier." (Was that the correct spelling of his surname and therefore its pronunciation in France? Or was this individual's name actually *Charpentier*, pronounced Italian-style, where *cha* becomes "ka"? Will a source one day make it possible to assert that Marc-Antoine Charpentier was "Carpentier"?) No sooner had Chaulnes arrived in Rome than Dassoucy sent him a poem.[5] The gift bore fruit, and the poet-musician was soon working for the Ambassador. February 1667 found him writing French entertainments to be performed at the Farnese.

For better or worse, the Ambassador soon got to know more of his countrymen. There were the numerous "loafers" who "ask for alms and shame the nation"; there were the drunkards he had to expel from the city; and there were the hundreds of Frenchmen who came to the Farnese for passports: "During the four summer months, when few people come to Rome, I issued almost nine hundred passports: which means that, in one year, more than three thousand have to be issued."[6]

Ambassador Chaulnes promptly set about preparing the lavish religious services and secular entertainments expected of an ambassador of the Most Christian King. The planning and implementation were shouldered by the Farnese staff, assisted by some of the hangers-on, among them DASSOUCY.

The first important event was a mass at the French church of San Luigi dei Francesi on the Feast of Saint Louis, August 25, 1666. Thanks to Bourlemont's efforts, the façade of the church was hung with tapestries, and "trumpets made known to the cardinals, when they arrived, the joy being experienced at receiving them." The entire church, up to the vaults, was hung with gold-laced damask, and the choir was draped with red velvet fringed with gold. The music was performed by "six choirs consisting of the best voices in Rome." After the mass came a banquet and a nocturnal concert by singers and instrumentalists who rode two floats around the square in front of the Farnese. The music was, Chaulnes informed Paris, "very beautiful; the musicians were satisfied by the applause and by the treats they were given."[7]

All was not play, however. The Ambassador was promptly bombarded with appeals from GABRIEL DE ROQUETTE and his brother, CHRISTOPHLE DE ROQUETTE—seconded by the House of Condé—to pressure the papacy to deliver the bulls for Roquette's recent nomination as bishop of Autun. To a missive from Condé, Chaulnes replied: "I beg you to be persuaded that I will employ ... all the more care for Abbé Roquette's affair, because I claim to have a share in his friendship."[8]

A few months later, preparations for Mardi Gras of 1667 got under way. It doubtlessly was with JACQUES II DALIBERT's help that Chaulnes managed to engage "a Roman troop that will perform exclusively in my palace." The performers were "the same ones who had performed before Christina of Sweden."[9] In other words, Chaulnes had snapped up the Queen's unemployed musicians who, exactly a year earlier at the Riario Palace, had "recited during Mardi Gras a *comédie en musique*" (an opera) for the Queen and the College of Cardinals—to the "great scandal" of the Jesuits, who judged the libretto to be "lascivious and ill-bred."[10]

Chaulnes was not content with performing the same work over and over. Plays alternated with operas, all of them performed in the vast vaulted gallery of the palace, with its superb acoustics and its famous frescos by Caracci. "On Sunday," wrote the Ambassador,

> I entertained all of Rome, having ... allowed everyone to attend the comedy I was sponsoring in this palace. I had a stage built at the end of the upper gallery, thanks to whose vaulted ceiling the people in the back row hear as well as those in the front row, and over five or

six hundred people attended. Something is performed almost daily, sometimes an operatic troop, sometimes a comedy; and as a concluding touch, the Duke of Bracciano has prepared a comedy in music, which will also be recited here.[11]

The "more serious" of the entertainments, noted Chaulnes, would continue throughout Mardi Gras, "being performed alternately with Italian comedies, which are played on those other days by two different troops." Once the festivities had ended, the Ambassador rectified his calculations: he had received more than twelve hundred guests, with none of the riots that had marked the Queen's theatricals of the previous year.[12] Maffei praised the opera: "This *comedià in musicha* had truly been a success." Indeed, it had pleased not only the Italians, but the French as well. There was "lovely recitative," the actors performed to perfection, their costumes were lavish and charming, the stage glittered with silver and crystal candlesticks, and the ballets were universally praised. The music was by a "great virtuoso," the chapel master of Saint John Lateran—that is, Ercole Bernabei, who was eager to enhance his reputation in hopes of being named chapel master at San Luigi dei Francesi.

The prologue to this "comedy," this "opera," appears to have been in French, for Chaulnes not only sent a copy of the lyrics back to Paris, he expressed his preference for Italian music: "I declare in favor of Italian music over French."[13] That he made this comparison between the two styles suggests that both national styles were woven into these entertainments at the Farnese. In short, for some two years the best of each nation was being blended into a *Goûts réunis* before the letter.

The Mardi Gras festivities ended with another musical procession around the Piazza Farnese. A dozen sibyls—one of them was Maffei—not only rode about in a triumphal chariot predicting the defeat of the Turks, they performed a "mascarade in French and Italian verse." Abbé Santis had written the Italian text, and DASSOUCY the French one. Trumpets, oboes, fifes, and bagpipes performed martial music as the float moved through the streets. The parade was followed by an "Italian comedy."[14]

A few months later, in August 1667, the embassy staff prepared yet another float, to celebrate Clement IX's coronation. The Ambassador invited the new pope's nephews to supper. "Curiosity having driven over two hundred people to come and see the novelty of how the French entertain, I did everything to satisfy them," he wrote, "and after the supper [they were treated to] the best concerts in Rome." The music was performed by violins playing alternately with trumpets.[15]

When Abbé Le Tellier arrived in Rome in November 1667, he became the center of attention for the entire staff at the Farnese, from

Ambassador Chaulnes down to "Carpentier," whose task it was to make the rounds of the tailors and used-clothes dealers of the city, in order to assemble a livery for the domestics the Abbé had hired.[16] For the next two months, Le Tellier entertained frequently. In fact, he hired DASSOU-CY to provide music in his apartment "every day."[17]

January 1668 brought preparations for yet another Mardi Gras season. When he learned that Le Tellier planned to leave Rome before the end of the month, the Ambassador urged his staff to work overtime on their preparations for a new opera: "We even gave the order to speed up the performance of a *comédie en musique*, so that he can see it before he leaves," wrote Chaulnes. Abbé Machault referred to more than one opera: "During Mardi Gras season we hoped to entertain him with some *comédies en musique*."[18] His use of the past tense suggests that the staff had more or less given up hope. By January 13 they nonetheless managed to treat Le Tellier to a "little comedy"; and on January 28, shortly before his departure, there was a grand fête and a "comedy."

There appears to have been a logistical problem at the Farnese in December 1667, a problem that temporarily put the opera on hold. The uncertainty and delay that marked the first weeks of January 1668 must be connected to DASSOUCY's arrest during the final days of November or the first week of December.[19] It is as if the poet-musician had agreed to work on an opera for Mardi Gras; and then, after a brief period of disarray provoked by Dassoucy's incarceration, someone stepped in to replace him. Was it Marc-Antoine Charpentier? Was it at the Farnese, in 1667, that Dassoucy had "nourished at his breast" his young compatriot? Were Charpentier's lost Italian operas, *La Dori e Oronte* and *Artaxerse*, performed at the Farnese in January 1668?[20] (Remember, Abbé Machault referred to "operas," in the plural.)

In the end, the "operas" performed for Abbé Le Tellier apparently were not offered to the public during Mardi Gras of 1668. Although Chaulnes was claiming that his purse was almost empty, sufficient money remained for other lavish events, many of them with music. If the operas were canceled, it must have been for political reasons. The new pope's relatives were hosting performances of the *Comica del Cielo*, a devotional opera; so the French at the Farnese appear to have given up the worldly entertainments they had planned, lest they offend the papal family.

In July 1668, the Ambassador ordered a *Te Deum* sung at San Luigi, "with all possible pomp" and in the presence of select cardinals, for news had arrived that a son had been born to Louis XIV. Just as Bourlemont had done for the Feast of Saint Louis in 1666, Maffei had the exterior of the church hung with tapestries provided by Chaulnes. The mass was followed by a sumptuous banquet at the Farnese and by splendid fire-works designed by Bernini in the square.[21]

A few days later, Chaulnes and his wife set off for France, leaving the Farnese in the hands of Bourlemont and Machault, who, in the name of France, welcomed Christina of Sweden when she returned to Rome in early December. It was to them that JACQUES II DALIBERT henceforth relayed messages from the Queen. With no ambassador in residence, Mardi Gras ceased to be a subject in the diplomatic correspondence.

During the weeks that followed his return to Paris, Chaulnes basked in the glory accrued from his Roman experience. He prepared a "magnifi-cent" repast for the papal nuncio, the Tuscan agent, and the ambassadors from Venice and Turin. He presided over the delivery, in great pomp, of a relic he had brought back for his sister at the ABBAYE-AUX-BOIS.[22]

After being rewarded with the royal governorship of Brittany in July 1669, he spent part of each year at Rennes. There he and his wife often saw FRANÇOISE FERRAND and her husband, the First President of the Parlement of Brittany. Chaulnes and his wife also spent time in Paris. They presumably attended services at the ABBAYE-AUX-BOIS, where his sister was coadjutrix, and then abbess until her death in 1687. Madame de Chaulnes would also go to visit MADEMOISELLE DE GUISE,[23] but it is not clear whether their friendship predates or postdates the Duke's mission to Italy. In 1684, SÉBASTIEN DE BROSSARD made an unsuccessful attempt be appointed almoner to the Duke,[24] but the young Norman did not identify the individuals who were recommending him.

It has not been determined whether Chaulnes was instrumental in the commission given Marc-Antoine Charpentier in 1695, to compose the lost *Apothéose de Laodomas* to honor the memory of the Duke of Luxembourg. Despite Chaulnes' dispute with Luxembourg in 1694, and despite the humiliation it provoked,[25] politeness obliged a provincial governor to demonstrate his respect for so illustrious a figure. Ironically, the performance of this "apotheosis" in March 1695 coincided with Chaulnes being relieved of his duties at Rennes and being transferred to Bordeaux, to serve the King as Governor of Aquitaine.

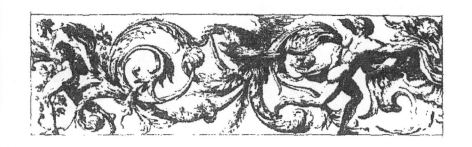

Panel 6

CHARPENTIER'S COLLABORATORS

One Does What One is Permitted to Do,
One Does What One Must Do

F ive portraits are grouped in this panel. Three of the sitters are
gentlemen wearing elegant clothes and laces. They all hold pens,
but the attributes surrounding each man differ slightly.

The first man ostentatiously shows a paper traced with a few staves
of handwritten plainsong. The table beside him is heaped with a disarray
of handwritten sheets and Latin tomes. An open songbook lies on a table
in the background, beside a pile of closed volumes labeled *Motets*. A viol
is propped against the table. Through an open window the garden façade
of the Hôtel de Guise can be glimpsed.

In the other two portraits of gentlemen, each sitter stares out from
behind a table strewn with crossed-out and scribbled pages. These two
portraits form a pair, for the background in each painting depicts the
same theater interior, although different combinations of dancers,
singers, instrumentalists, and props occupy the stage.

A fourth portrait also evokes the theater. The subject wears a
ridiculous hat, and his face is whitened. In the background is a worktable
covered with papers. Theatrical costumes hang from hooks on the walls.

The final portrait shows a group of attractive, modestly-dressed
young men and women, some singing, some playing instruments.

Together these portraits depict the artistic constraints and opportunities that confronted Marc-Antoine Charpentier during the 1670s and

1680s. He could not change the words that someone else put on his worktable. His role in the collaborative effort was to set those words to music. The final product had to match the skills and the vocal ranges of the performers at his disposal.

No portrait of Jean-Baptiste Lully is included in this panel, for there is little need to summarize here the constraints that the Florentine imposed upon Charpentier and his collaborators.

I

Censing heroines and goddesses

MOLIÈRE

Jean-Baptiste Pocquelin,
actor and playwright

The life of actor-playwright Jean-Baptiste Pocquelin, better known by his stage name, *Molière*, is familiar to all the visitors who pass through this portrait gallery. Familiar also is the story of his collaboration with Lully, his break with the Florentine, and his collapse and subsequent death in March 1673 during a performance of *Le Malade imaginaire*, for which Marc-Antoine Charpentier had written the music. Rather than repeat these facts, this portrait takes the form of a caricature. It focuses solely on those aspects of Molière's life that suggest constraints affecting Charpentier's career and his music.

So schematic is this portrait that the rather apocryphal tale of Molière's early fascination with the theater—a tale based primarily on Grimarest's not always trustworthy life of the great man—has been selected as a point of departure. For readers of the seventeenth-century, the tale in question embodied the stereotypical yet quite realistic quandary faced by many an artistically talented individual during the reign of Louis XIV. More specifically, it paints a picture that readers understood as representing the difficulties encountered by a man of talent or curiosity who had the misfortune to be born into a modest family. In that respect it resembles the tale of the modest origins of PHILIPPE GOIBAUT DU BOIS, and the tale of DOCTOR VALLANT's refusal to follow his father's trade.

As the story goes, Molière (born in 1622) was the son of

a seller of used clothes who was also a valet and upholsterer of the king's chamber. ... [His parents] gave him an education that conformed to their social status. He learned to read a little and to write, and until the age of fourteen he knew nothing but his father's shop. He was granted the right to succeed his father as valet and

141

upholsterer of the king's chamber; but his aversion for this
profession and his penchant for study prompted him to ask his
grandfather, who sometimes took him to the theater at the Hôtel de
Bourgogne, to convince his father to give him an education. He
finally won out: they sent him to a boarding school, and he studied
as an extern at the Jesuits [of the College of Clermont].[1]

Almost as an aside, this narrative of Molière's school days (1635–
1640) points out that he had the good fortune to be a classmate of
Armand, Prince of Conti, of the royal House of Bourbon. That this was
chronologically impossible does not affect the tale, for the purpose of this
aside is to prepare a future event: the "protection" offered Molière in the
1650s by his purported classmate.

Sharing a classroom with the rich and powerful did not mean that
Jean-Baptiste Pocquelin would be free to do what he wished, once he had
completed his studies. The tale recounts how, when his father became ill,
the youth was "obliged to exercise the function of his post" in the king's
household. (If this happened, it was in 1642.) It was not long, however,
before "his passion for the theater re-awoke, and he resolved to satisfy it
by becoming both an actor and an author." He linked up (in 1643) with
"several young people who had a talent for declaiming," and this little
troop soon was traveling through the southern provinces, performing
Jean-Baptiste's plays.[2]

In what could only be viewed by the Pocquelins as a downward social
move, their son chose a way of life that relegated him to the margins of
society. He rejected his father's craft, which offered the chance of rising
higher in the office-holding hierarchy, in favor of an art that put him
lower than a musician or a ballad-singer. Actors were excommunicated
by the Church, but musicians were not.

Back in Paris, the tale continues, the young man's father became
increasingly agitated: "Having vainly had several people talk to his son
about abandoning the actor's profession," old Pocquelin dispatched the
schoolmaster with whom his son had once boarded, to talk with him.
The master failed to persuade Molière to quit this trade; instead (so goes
the myth) the master joined the troop.

The biography continues by telling how Molière encountered his
former classmate, Conti, now Governor of Languedoc, who promptly
became the troop's "protector." This happens to be an accurate statement. (It was during their stay in Montpellier and vicinity, November
1655 to June 1656, that DASSOUCY performed with Molière's "Illustrious
Theater," as he had at Carcassonne from December 1651 to January
1652, and at Lyons in July to October 1655.)

Here the biography omits an important fact: unfortunately for the troop, Conti underwent a religious conversion and withdrew his patronage by 1658. It is not clear to what extent this conversion was brought about by GABRIEL DE ROQUETTE, a young abbé who had worked his way first into the good graces of Conti's mother, the Dowager Duchess of Bourbon-Condé, and then into those of Conti himself. Roquette's exaggerated show of devotion and his holier-than-thou remarks prompted Molière to write a play about people who shammed devotion for their own material gain: Le Tartuffe, subtitled "The Imposter," first performed in 1664. (By the early 1670s, Roquette, now a bishop, would find his way into MADEMOISELLE DE GUISE's little court, where he would be accused of being her "Tartuffe.")

Any role that the Prince of Conti may have played in obtaining a still more powerful protector for Molière's troop is not known. Shortly after the actor's return to Paris in that year, goes the tale, GASTON D'OR-LÉANS became the troop's "protector" and subsequently "presented Molière to the King [Louis XIV] and the Queen Mother," who granted him the honor of performing in the Louvre and, in 1660, at the Palais-Royal. Here again the tale is inaccurate. Gaston had protected the Illustrious Theater back in 1643; but in 1658 he was ill, disgraced, and exiled to Blois. Rather, it was PHILIPPE II D'ORLÉANS, Louis XIV's brother, who became such an enthusiastic supporter of Molière's endeavors that he lent his name to the troop, which became known as "Monsieur's Troop."

At this point, the present portrait of Molière puts this old tale behind it, in favor of facts related to the playwright's collaboration with Marc-Antoine Charpentier. The accuracy of the tale is not an issue here. What counts is the broad picture of frustrated talent that it paints, a picture that was based upon hard realities and that applied to many seventeenth-century artists. The youth chafes under the yoke his family is imposing upon him, discards that yoke, leaves home to test his mettle, increases his skills by practicing his art, and struggles to keep body and soul together until a powerful acquaintance offers him protection.

When details are changed here and there, the tale becomes a plausible account of Marc-Antoine Charpentier's first twenty-eight years. That is, Jean Pocquelin, the royal upholsterer, becomes LOUIS CHARPEN-TIER THE SCRIVENER; Grandfather Cressé and the schoolmaster are transformed into relatives and family friends such as Monsieur Dupin, the guardian of Marc-Antoine and ARMAND-JEAN CHARPENTIER; the protection of the Prince of Conti is turned into recommendations by ÉLISABETH-MARIE MALIER or MARIE TALON; and Gaston d'Orléans is replaced by his former sister-in-law, MADEMOISELLE DE GUISE, acting on behalf of Gaston's daughter, MADAME DE GUISE. To the extent that these parallels reflected similarities in education and careers, Molière may have empathized with Marc-Antoine Charpentier and found it especially satisfying to work with him.

Were it not for the ties of friendship and distant kinship that are known to have connected the Pocquelins and the Charpentiers, it would be more than imprudent to draw this type of parallel between the attitudes of the two families, and between Marc-Antoine Charpentier's and Jean-Baptiste Pocquelin's training, rebellion, tribulations, and eventual protection by great nobles. This parallel has its merits, however, because from the 1650s on, these two extremely creative individuals actually had a "friend" or relative in common. In January 1651, while Jean-Baptiste Pocquelin was wandering through southern France with his troop, Marc-Antoine's cousin, GILLES CHARPENTIER THE SECRETARY, the groom's "friend," signed the wedding contract of the playwright's sister, Marie-Madeleine Pocquelin, and André Boudet, the upholsterer grandson of two merchants from Meaux: Guillaume Boudet and SAMUEL CHARPENTIER THE WEAVER.

Gilles the Secretary's presence at the Pocquelin–Boudet wedding of 1651 is explained by old family ties at Meaux. These ties would soon stretch southwards, where Gilles' new actor "friend" was wandering from town to town. From Languedoc and the Prince of Conti, Molière and his troop moved westward, reaching Bordeaux by mid-August 1656. There they were warmly welcomed by the royal lieutenant for the province of Guyenne, the Marquis of Saint-Luc—who happened to be GILLES THE SECRETARY's employer. A few months later Saint-Luc recommended the troop to the city fathers of Agen: "A troop of actors who has spent some time in this city," he wrote in December 1656, "to the satisfaction of all who heard them declaim, is on the way to your city, and they asked me to recommend them to you during their stay [in Agen]." Saint-Luc ended his letter with a strong exhortation: "I beg you to treat them well, and to lend them your support in everything that depends upon the authority of your offices."[3]

A debt of gratitude on Molière's part toward the Charpentier clan as a whole could conceivably explain why the playwright gambled on Marc-Antoine Charpentier sixteen years later, asking him to write music for revivals of Le Mariage forcé and La Comtesse d'Escarbagnas. It may also help explain why Molière eventually snatched the commission for Le Malade imaginaire away from DASSOUCY and gave it to Charpentier. But such an explanation of how Charpentier and Molière came to collaborate in 1672 would be conjectural and an oversimplification.

Family ties and gratitude may well have made Molière more willing to look favorably on the Guises' composer; but a series of events beyond the playwright's control were reducing his options in 1672. In March, Lully had been granted a royal privilege giving him a monopoly over operas. Molière could read the handwriting on the wall. It mattered little that, since 1667, his troop had been honored with the title "The King's Troop," Lully was now the royal favorite, and he had cut his ties to the troop. Molière had to find another composer, and quickly. By early April, Charpentier had been given the nod. For him the timing was perfect: the Guise princesses were in mourning for the DOWAGER DUCHESS OF ORLÉANS, and he had time on his hands.

Judging from the content of the composer's two chronologically organized sets of notebooks, he had been writing exclusively devotional music with Latin texts ever since his return to France late in 1669. Why, then, did Molière turn to him for worldly songs in the vernacular? The obvious answer is that somewhere, somehow, Charpentier had proved his skills at setting French lyrics to music. For that to be the case, he either had to have acquired this experience before he left Paris for Rome circa 1666, or else he had to have written French vocal music while in Rome, perhaps for JACQUES II DALIBERT, Queen Christina of Sweden's impresario, but more likely for the DUKE OF CHAULNES.

Rehearsals for the revived plays began in late June 1672, and Charpentier went to Molière's country home several times to confer with the playwright. (Careful to keep his activities for the Guises separate from his outside ones, the composer did not ask GAIGNIÈRES, the Guises' equerry, to drive him to Auteuil. Instead, he billed the troop for the rental of a "coach."[4]) It was agreed that Charpentier would be paid 110 livres for his efforts, plus eleven livres for each performance—the latter being the amount per performance that dancer Pierre de Beauchamps had received for conducting the orchestra and supervising the dancers for *Psyché* in 1671, and that several hired singers received as wages for each show.[5] The double bill opened on July 9 and was played every other night until August 7.

The troop promptly got caught up in a verbal and harmonic joust with the Italian troop that performed on alternate days at the theater of the Palais-Royal. In a French-language play entitled *Le Collier de perles*, which opened on July 30 with music by Molière's colleague Beauchamps, the Italians poked fun at Molière's *Le Bourgeois gentilhomme*. Charpentier and Molière invented some new incidental music[A] in which *commedia*

[A] Cahier XV, H. 494 [9–11].

dell'arte characters mock Harlequin's braying and Beauchamps' harmony.[6] The musical jest lasted only a few days, because the run was cut short when Molière fell ill and the theater closed for a week. (In all of 1672, this was only time the playwright was sick enough to force a cancellation.)

At some point between August 7 and August 14, DASSOUCY went to visit the ailing Molière and came away with an invitation to compose the music for *Le Malade imaginaire*, the new "machine play," *pièce à machines*, scheduled to open in March 1673. "If you will deign to remember the promise you made when I went to see you during your most recent illness," Dassoucy would soon remark in an open letter to Molière.[7]

Not long afterward, Dassoucy learned that Molière had changed his mind and had invited Charpentier to compose for *Le Malade*. In a furious letter alluding to the playwright's illness, Dassoucy referred to "today," and to Molière's having "lost Monsieur de Lully." Contrary to what is sometimes asserted, Dassoucy was not writing this letter in March 1672, when Lully was awarded his monopoly and broke with Molière; nor was he referring to Charpentier's music for *Escarbagnas* and *Le Mariage forcé*, which had closed after the August 7 performance, when Molière fell ill. By "today" he was referring to the royal decree dated September 20, 1672, that granted Lully the publication rights for every one of the comedy-ballets for which he had composed music.[8] Although he had paid for Lully's work and would normally have been considered the owner, the music had been snatched away. Molière had indeed "lost Lully"—and everything associated with him. In other words, the playwright broke his agreement with Dassoucy in late September 1672, and the disputed commission involved the music for *Le Malade imaginaire*, which was in fact a *pièce à machines*, while *Escarbagnas and Le Mariage* were not.

Dassoucy describes the playwright's decision as just so much "incense for false divinities," so much "censing of heroines and goddesses," a response to "so many irritated virgins" who had to be "pacified."[9] Veiled though these allusions may be, in the parlance of the day they were far from ambiguous: they referred to women of high rank. For example, Mademoiselle de Guise was commonly called a "virgin," a "noble maid," a "heroine" born into a "heroic" family made up of "demigods." Their Royal Highnesses of the House of Orléans were likewise described as "great heroines," "goddesses," "divine" beings.[10] Dassoucy is therefore saying that some of the principal heroines and goddesses of the realm—a category that in 1672 included only a handful of women, among them MADEMOISELLE DE GUISE, MADAME DE GUISE, MADAME DE MONTMARTRE, and MADEMOISELLE DE MONTPENSIER—had pressured the playwright until he yielded. In view of the playwright's problems with Lully, yielding had its advantages: it could turn these powerful, determined women into potential allies. As Dassoucy himself admitted, he had no such heroines to call upon.

Dassoucy doubtlessly was unaware of a rather compelling reason why Molière might feel obliged to comply with the goddesses' demands. The House of Guise owed his maternal relatives a sizeable amount of money. Back in the mid-1650s the playwright's maternal uncle, Louis Cressé, merchant upholsterer of Paris, had submitted a bill for work done and materials supplied. It is not clear whether Cressé was ever paid, even in part. And now, in 1672, a certain Jean-Baptiste Cressé was awaiting payment of a bill for three thousand livres for fabric supplied decades earlier to Duke Henri de Guise by his father-in-law. Under the circumstances, it would have been most imprudent for Molière to anger Mademoiselle de Guise, whose benevolence offered the only assurance that the Cressés would finally be paid. The playwright therefore "censed the heroine"; and in May 1676, at a time when the princess was generally not paying old debts, she borrowed three thousand livres in order to settle the Cressé claim.[11]

Molière had convinced the King to prevent Lully from restricting incidental music to two songs and two instruments per show; but by August 1672, surely in response to Escarbagnas and Le Mariage forcé, the Florentine had managed to obtain an order limiting theatrical troops to a maximum of six vocalists and twelve instrumentalists. Perhaps the protection of the heroines and goddesses of the Houses of Orléans and Guise made Molière especially courageous. At any rate, for Le Malade imaginaire he and Charpentier ignored the decree. The payroll shows that twelve violins were joined by "three symphonists" and "seven male and female musicians." ("Musicians" was a term that denoted singers, as contrasted with instrumentalists.) In other words, the troop wittingly broke the law.[12] Charpentier received a "recompense" for his work, but the exact amount does not appear in the account books, nor does any daily wage. The show opened on February 10, 1673. During the fourth performance, February 17, Molière began hemorrhaging and died shortly after being carried off the stage.

The troop was determined to go on, despite the loss of its leader, and despite one thousand livres still owed for props for Le Malade. In a public show of support, PHILIPPE II D'ORLÉANS and his wife, "accompanied by their entourage," attended the performance on March 5. (Although the troop no longer bore his name, the prince was still protecting them.) Then, on April 30, a royal decree not only reduced the number of voices to two, it restricted instruments to six. The troop was also forbidden to hire any "outside" singers or use "any dancers."[13] To make matters worse, a month later they were expelled from the Palais-Royal to make room for Lully's *Cadmus*. They managed to find new quarters on the Left Bank, in the Hôtel de Guénégaud, on the rue Mazarine; but they could not come up with the necessary payment of fourteen thousand livres. On July 13, 1673, André Boudet, royal upholsterer (and "friend" of GILLES THE SECRETARY), rescued them by advancing the money for two years.[14]

During the four months separating March 5 and July 13, 1673, the troop had begun to lean toward the Duke of Orléans for protection. This probably was not obvious to the average spectator; but the people in the royal administration who made it their business to be informed could scarcely have been unaware that the actors were gravitating into the Orléans–Guise orbit and could be expected to test Lully's monopoly of stage music at every opportunity. The first sign of this had been PHILIPPE II D'ORLÉANS' show of support on March 5; next, André Boudet had loaned the actors money; and now, in lieu of a fixed stipend that often amounted to considerably more than an actor's percentage of ticket sales, Marc-Antoine Charpentier (a protégé of a Guise and an Orléans) was not only working for half an actor-member's share, and was planning to revise *Le Malade* so that the troop would appear to be striving to comply with the latest rulings.

The troop was fighting back. On January 7, 1674 (four months before a scheduled opening of the revised version of *Le Malade*), it "obtained a lettre de cachet from the royal administration, forbidding all actors but the King's Troop [that is, themselves] to perform *Le Malade imaginaire* until the play has been printed."[15] By October the actors had found two playwrights who were willing to join Charpentier in twitting Lully and testing his privilege. One was JEAN DONNEAU DE VISÉ, who had longstanding links to GASTON D'ORLÉANS; the other was THOMAS CORNEILLE, whose brother Pierre had lived at the Hôtel de Guise in the 1660s, as Duke Henri's protégé.

The actors' resistance did not blacken Molière's memory at court. Not only did the troop perform his plays there, but Louis XIV sometimes overlooked Lully's restrictions, lest they dim the luster of command performances. For example, if the engraving of the performance of *Le Malade imaginaire* in the gardens of Versailles on August 21, 1674, is only somewhat accurate, the orchestra that day was made up of several dozen instrumentalists—this despite the fact that, for the new run of the previous May, Charpentier had prepared a stripped-down version "with the restrictions," as contrasted with the original version of 1673 "in its splendor."[A]

Nor did Lully's monopoly totally dim the luster of the original during subsequent performances at court. For example, when the troop performed *Le Malade* at Versailles on January 11, 1686, there were sixteen actors, at least eight dancers, seven string players, and a harpsichordist.[16] That Marc-Antoine Charpentier copied these particular revisions[B] into an arabic-numbered notebook suggests that they were a gift of sorts from MADAME DE GUISE to her royal cousin, the King. Indeed, the troop's financial records do not give the impression that Charpentier was paid for these revisions for *Le Malade*.

[A] Cahier XVI, H. 495, etc. ("dans sa splendeur"), and H. 495a ("avec les défenses").
[B] Cahiers 44-45, H. 495b.

II

Monsieur Du Bois is so happy with the Music

DU BOIS THE CHAPEL MASTER

Philippe Goibaut, Sieur du Bois et de la Grugère,
known as "Monsieur Du Bois"

The biography of Philippe Goibaut du Bois written by one of his colleagues in the French Academy bears certain similarities to a contemporary biography of MOLIÈRE—and to that of DOCTOR VALLANT as well. Full of distortions and downright errors of fact and chronology, it draws a portrait that is a stereotype of the self-made man, seventeenth-century style. Du Bois is portrayed as a man of modest origins who made his way up the social ladder thanks to his charm and energy:

> Since he left no children whom the information being provided about his origins can harm or displease, and since moreover we must ... make those of us whose birth is obscure feel that it depends solely on them to raise themselves by means of letters, I will have no qualms about saying that Monsieur Du Bois, this author of so many serious works, began as a dancing master.

> He was engaged in that capacity for the household of the Duke [Louis-Joseph] of Guise, who as a child became so accustomed to seeing him and came to feel such friendship for him, that he wanted no one else as his governor. It is not a rare thing for men to have totally different talents, talents that are more essential than the ones their profession permits them to use. It did not take long for this to be noted in Monsieur Du Bois; and if, in his first métier he was skilled at forming his disciple to physical exercise, later events revealed that he was infinitely more skilled at giving him moral lessons, and inspiring in him a love of virtue.

> In order to be able to do his work well, he had the courage to learn the elements of Latin at the age of thirty. He applied himself to

150

PHILIPPE GOIBAULT
S.^r Du Bois, de l'Académie Fr.^{se}
Décédé le 1.er Juillet 1694. âgé de 75 ans.

Paris chez O. louvre rue d'Anjou la derniere P.Cochere a gauche entrant par la rue Dauphine . C.P.R.

Philippe Goibaut, sieur du Bois.
Known as "Monsieur Du Bois," he was selected to be governor to
Louis-Joseph de Lorraine, After the Duke's death, Goibaut served as
chapel master to the two Guise princesses. His translations from
the Latin won him election to the French Academy. He died at seventy-five
in his apartment at the Hôtel de Guise, July 1, 1694.

Latin under the guidance of Messieurs of Port-Royal, who not only had Mademoiselle de Guise under their thumb, but everyone who came near that virtuous princess. He chose these men as directors of his own conscience and his studies. Thanks to their discipline he became a model of the regular life [*vie réglée*]. He even adopted much of their way of writing: that grave, sustained, periodic style, but which is a bit slow and too uniform.

After he had wisely raised the Duke of Guise, he experienced the pain of seeing him die in the flower of his youth. From that time on, absolute master of his free time, he devoted himself entirely to translating the works he judged to be the most useful, either by Saint Augustine, or by Cicero. At the same time, in order to have someone with whom to share the tedium or the pain of his solitude, he decided to marry. He came from Poitiers, and chance having brought to Paris one of his old acquaintances, the widow of one of his old countrymen, he married her.[1]

This portrait of Monsieur Du Bois is a telling example of how the veil surrounding MADEMOISELLE DE GUISE's protégés prevented outsiders from fully understanding the hierarchy in the household, and the activities carried on by each individual. The academician based his biography upon snippets from a variety of sources, interpreted by people who were not part of the exclusive Guise circle. Although some of the statements in these opening paragraphs of the Du Bois biography are not totally false, they twist the facts and distort the sequence of events that brought him to the Hôtel de Guise. His contemporaries could not explain Goibaut's enthusiasm for music, so they imagined that he was a former dancing master who reverted to his art and, in the process, became the Guises' chapel master. (Note how the veil of silence still prevented people from speaking publicly about the GUISE MUSIC, five years after Mademoiselle de Guise's death.)

The biography is accurate in stating that Du Bois came from Poitiers. The son of a barrister, he was baptized there in March 1620. He eventually inherited the seigneury of Bois in Poitou, worth fifteen thousand livres, as well as other lands worth twenty-four thousand livres. That he received an education appropriate to his social status is demonstrated by the library of some two hundred volumes in Greek, Latin, and French that he had amassed while still living in the provinces. He also was something of a musician, for he owned a "bass viol with two bows," a "theorbo of Padua," and an "ebony guitar."[2] The small violin that was the dancing master's basic tool is conspicuously absent from this inventory of the possessions of the thirty-five-year-old country gentleman who was about to wed.

When he married in 1655—an event that took place in Poitiers, not in Paris, as his biographer asserted—Philippe Goibaut bore the titles "squire, lord of Bois La Grugère, and maître d'hôtel in ordinary to the king." His bride was Françoise Blacvod, the granddaughter of a Scottish physician named Adam Blackwood who had come to France with Mary Queen of Scots (the daughter of a Guise princess), and who had been rewarded with a position as councillor in the presidial of Poitiers.

The Blackwoods' link to the House of Guise had been strengthened during the early decades of the seventeenth century, when Adam Blackwood's son became Olivier d'Alesso's in-law. D'Alesso was not only the son of an ardent supporter of the Guises during the League, he was the first cousin of Marie Versoris-Verthamon, whose granddaughter by marriage, MARIE TALON, would sign ÉLISABETH CHARPENTIER's wedding contract in 1662. In other words, one of Madame Du Bois' relatives was protecting the family of LOUIS CHARPENTIER THE SCRIVENER a mere four years before Philippe Goibaut du Bois was engaged as "governor" or "preceptor" to LOUIS-JOSEPH DE LORRAINE, DUKE OF GUISE. the adolescent nephew and ward of MARIE DE GUISE THE REGENT.

"Belonging" to the House of Guise in this way explains why Françoise Blacvod's money-hungry heirs credited her with obtaining the couple's entry into the Guise household:

> [She] made Monsieur Du Bois come to Paris to make the most of the talents of his mind, which were languishing in the provinces, and to enable him to take advantage of the credit she had acquired with the House of Guise. It was she who obtained for him the honor of being the governor to the Duke of Guise, the last of that name, and who had him kept on by the late Mademoiselle de Guise, with the huge pensions that permitted him to increase his fortune, which amounted to more than one hundred thousand livres in property.[3]

Françoise Blacvod's role in Du Bois' nomination may be a fable; but assuming there is some truth in it, Her Highness clearly did not select Du Bois solely because he had married a woman of proven loyalty to the House of Guise. After all, Madame Goibaut's death in May 1676 did not result in her spouse's dismissal.

Du Bois was a man of charm, quick intelligence, and strong religious convictions—the latter strengthened by contact with Blaise Pascal, the Duke of Roannez, and the "*pascalins*" around Roannez during visits he had made to Paris in 1660–1661 and 1663–1664. (The term *pascalin* was coined to denote "the men of intellect who can be viewed as Pascal's disciples or who are at least struck by his example and take inspiration from his way of proceeding."[4]) In 1665, during the repression of Jansenism that was especially painful for the nuns at the ABBEY OF PORT-ROYAL, Du Bois used his pen to defend Pierre Nicole, a Jansenist; and in 1666 he was invited to work on the translations for the so-called "New Testament of Mons" being prepared by a group of Jansenists. It probably was the *pascalins* and their link to Port-Royal that prompted the Goibauts' move to Paris early in 1666.

Before the end of that year, Mademoiselle de Guise had singled out Du Bois, who was working on a treatise about how best to educate the Dauphin. The conditions surrounding his selection doubtlessly resembled those encountered by DOCTOR VALLANT a few years later. The Doctor was informed by a third party that Her Highness wanted him to refrain from "taking on other engagements," because she "wanted [him] to attach [him]self to her and to put [him] on her household list at the start of the new year."[5]

The exact date of the first encounter between Du Bois and Mademoiselle de Guise is not known. There is, however, evidence to suggest that the princess was in contact with him by early April 1666, when she proposed that an unnamed "male householder" who knew Italian might act as a middleman with the Medici staff in Florence, which had been instructed to purchase a harpsichord and a spinet for the Grand Duchess. In the end, the Florentines declined to work with this individual, who turned out to be unfamiliar with the Tuscan dialect and handwriting.[6]

Mademoiselle de Guise is said to have sought Louis XIV's approval before appointing Du Bois—later described as "the person whom [the King] had approved ... to govern a young prince whose blood, after having flowed in the veins of all the sovereigns of Europe, had gloriously been joined with his own, in the person of one of the most virtuous princesses on earth."[7] (The virtuous princess was Louis XIV's first cousin, ISABELLE D'ORLÉANS OF ALENÇON, the daughter of GASTON D'ORLÉANS.) The Goibauts promptly took up residence at the Volière, a riverside house in the Tuileries gardens, adjacent to the royal aviary, where Mademoiselle de Guise and the Duke were then residing.

It is difficult to deduce the exact nature of Du Bois' duties as the governor-preceptor to a sixteen-year-old prince who would soon marry. (The wedding was celebrated in May 1667). Judging from a long letter to the Duke, one of Du Bois' tasks was to shape the youth's conscience and make him think about what he read and heard, so that he would succeed at the important role for which his blood had destined him. (On this point the Academician's biography of Du Bois is accurate.) The letter —which merits quoting at length, because it is so revealing of Goibaut's thinking and way of expressing himself—was prompted by the prince's reading of Montaigne's *Essays* and his rather categorical assertion that

polite conversation was a good enough teacher, so a great noble did not
need to read books:

> Since Your Highness attacks me with my own words, I could also
> defend myself by his. He will recall that he wrote me yesterday that
> there was nothing more diversified than Montaigne's book. It is
> certain that there has never been a man less likely to be accused of
> being a man with a métier than he, and it would be difficult to guess
> it when reading his works. He criticizes all those who are ever so
> little involved in one, and he gives them no rest, not even those with
> the finest métier in the world, that is to say, those who command
> others. And he warns them a hundredfold not to think of creating
> kings without recalling that [kings] are men, and not to be afraid to
> lower themselves so they can live.
>
> In truth, he is right, Monseigneur; and when it pleases Your
> Highness to think about it, he will see that all our time is spent on
> physical exercise, ceremonies, business. One thinks of that alone and
> does not live at all. And that is what makes one a man with a
> métier. One's capital consists of things that should only be viewed as
> superficial ornaments that add some luster to life, but one neglects
> what makes it truly worthwhile. One wants to be a good hunter, a
> good dancer, a good equerry; and one doesn't worry about knowing
> how to make good judgments and to have upright, just, and honest
> sentiments about everything. ...
>
> I would agree with you, Monseigneur, if one could find
> conversations like the ones one might wish for; and it is certain that
> if that were the case, one would scarcely need books. But we know
> only too well that this is not the case; and one needs only see what
> people who do not read are like, who pass their life going from house
> to house and from *ruelle* to *ruelle*. There is no doubt that they can,
> at best, become as clever as the people with whom they associate; ...
> and that is why people who live in the world are all more or less the
> same: they all model themselves after one another, and thus they are
> limited to a certain level above which they are incapable of rising
> without some extraordinary help, which in most cases is the help of
> books.
>
> In truth, I see that there are some people who are born with such
> great mental advantages that they need no help to elevate
> themselves, and find in themselves sufficient force to get by without
> what they might get from reading; but that is so rare, that one must
> not take them as a model. These people have to spend their life
> meditating, and they must have a métier that permits them to
> devote themselves to it entirely; and this is not suitable for people of
> high rank, who do not have enough leisure and are obliged, early in

life, to acquire the things they need in order to play their role in the world. They should therefore know how to manage their time and collect, from their surroundings and from reading and conversation, and from their own reflection, a great fount of skill and knowledge, so that they can act with a just confidence that they will succeed.[8]

Mademoiselle de Guise is thought to have put Du Bois to work writing the memoirs about the late Duke Henri of Guise's expedition to Naples that appeared under the Duke's name in 1668. By the time the memoirs were published, Mademoiselle de Guise, her nephew, and their householders had left the Volière and had moved into the newly renovated Hôtel de Guise. The Goibauts lodged in the stable wing, in an apartment on which Mademoiselle de Guise had lavished special attention during the renovations of 1666-1668. The floor plan survives for the Du Bois' three-story, twelve-room apartment, which boasted the most modern amenities, including a *buffet*.[9]

Immediately adjacent to Du Bois' apartment—but occupying only the upper floor where light abounded—was a seven-room apartment sandwiched between the Goibauts' quarters and the six-room apartment of GAIGNIÈRES, the equerry-collector, situated above an indoor riding ring that eventually was turned into an orangery. During the summer of 1687—just when Marc-Antoine Charpentier became the official composer for one or another of the JESUIT HOUSES of Paris—this top-floor lodging would be vacated, and BISHOP ROQUETTE's nephew would move in. In short, this central apartment seems to be the one that Mademoiselle de Guise "gave" Marc-Antoine Charpentier circa 1670, and that he occupied throughout his service to the House of Guise. If that is the case, it was in these two adjacent apartments in the stable wing that music was composed, copied out into partbooks, and rehearsed far from Their Highnesses' apartments in the main building.

No sooner had Philippe Goibaut moved into his apartment than he became the Guises' de facto impresario and chapel master. By the fall of 1669—when young MADAME DE GUISE's brother-in-law, Cosimo III de' Medici, the future Grand Duke of Tuscany, was received at the Hôtel de Guise—Du Bois had acquired something of a reputation as a connoisseur of courtly song. After his return to Florence, Cosimo exchanged a few letters with Du Bois, but for some reason he hesitated to ask a favor of the Guise protégé. In November 1670 Cosimo therefore commanded the Medici agent in Paris to obtain "a few scores of the most merry *canzonettes* ... that are sung by ladies in their *domestiche conversazioni*," that is, during their household musical sessions. He wanted "not only the words, but also the music." The agent was authorized to get help from *Monsù Bué* (the Tuscans' preferred phonetic rendering of Du Bois' name), but only as a last resort. In the end, a lady with "very good taste in such matters and [who] knows the best musicians at court," came to the agent's rescue and was rewarded for her troubles with a diamond.[10]

For twenty years Du Bois (collaborating closely with Marc-Antoine Charpentier) adapted his musical activities to a model that had been observed at the House of Guise since the late sixteenth century, when a household composer dedicated two song books to the Duke and Duchess, in gratitude for their having "treated him so well." For his protectors' edification, the musician had selected texts by the best poets and set them to music. He had paid for the publication himself, in order "to show you in particular, and the public in general, the devoted affection I have shown and will always show to your House, which protects not only music and letters, but all the virtues." This same point of view shaped Goibaut's dedication to MADEMOISELLE DE GUISE of a translation of Saint Augustine in 1686. His point of departure was "a work of great value" that he was making available in French, in order to "give some public mark of my respect and my gratitude" to "this House that is so distinguished among the sovereign Houses of Europe." He was taking the opportunity to thank the princess publicly for having given him "the means to finish this work, through the sweetness of the repose that her kindness permits for all those who have the honor of belonging to her."

The sixteenth-century householder had informed his protectors that he had begun training a group of musicians to perform the pieces he had composed: "Seeing the pleasure that you and ... your wife take in music, and the affection you both show for it," he had taken it upon himself "to set up our little concert [of musicians] and train it to serve you." These compositions, and their performance, were intended to provide a "most agreeable recreation from the cares and troubles" that the Duke experienced while "seeing to [his] business." In 1680 the emerging GREAT GUISE MUSIC—organized and directed by Du Bois but trained by skilled musicians such as LOULIÉ and vocal coach Montailly—used song as a means to soothe their weary mistress after an exhausting day. "Monsieur Du Bois," she wrote, "got the notion of entertaining me, because I had a lot of business to conduct all day."[11]

The sources do not reveal whether Du Bois was enthusiastic about Italian music prior to 1666, or whether repeated encounters with Italian visitors to the Hôtel de Guise piqued his curiosity. (If he was in fact the "male householder" who, in April 1666, had claimed a competence in Italian that he did not actually possess, he clearly was fascinated with the culture of the Italian peninsula long before he met Mademoiselle de Guise.) The Chevalier de Méré, a *pascalin* who had known Du Bois since

1660 and who was known for his verbal jabs and hurtful witticisms, suggests that by the mid-1670s Goibaut had made a concerted effort to become informed about the Italian musical scene. "Monsieur Du Bois," he wrote, "is inventive. He learned music by himself from an Italian book, and he did not know much Italian." Méré also made a denigrating comment about Goibaut's musical skills that should probably be taken with several grains of salt: "Monsieur Du Bois reads music well: that is what he does best. He learned that from musical theory, just as Monsieur Guillemeau retained, from [his study of] medicine, the skill of making good soup."[12] In short, Du Bois appears to have been a good sight-reader; but if Méré is to be believed, he was not an especially insightful performer. Yet perform in public Goibaut clearly did, or Méré would have been unable to pass judgment on his musical skills, or lack of them.

The GUISE MUSIC clearly was Goibaut's project—to the point that he eventually would be described as the Guises' "chapel master." Still, when Charpentier first arrived at the Hôtel de Guise in early 1670, Goibaut does not appear to have had a very clear idea about the role the composer should play in the household. He set him to writing a variety of little devotional pieces—and, as Fate would decide, an entire corpus of funeral music, first for LOUIS-JOSEPH DE LORRAINE, DUKE OF GUISE (1671) and then for Madame de Guise's mother, the DOWAGER DUCHESS OF ORLÉANS (1672). Mademoiselle de Guise kept Du Bois on, once MADAME DE GUISE and her son moved to the Luxembourg Palace in 1673, and Du Bois put the composer to work on music for the nearby MERCY convent, in whose devotions Mademoiselle de Guise was becoming increasingly involved. As 1675 dawned, the mission of the Guise Music was, however, far from clear, although there is no evidence that the princess envisaged dismissing the half-dozen musicians then in her employ.

The little Duke of Alençon died in March 1675. Watching helplessly as the child lost consciousness, Goibaut and DOCTOR VALLANT consoled the grief-stricken Guise women as best they could. Then, six months after the child's burial, someone—it cannot be determined who—got the idea of expanding the princesses' devotions to include oratorios, plus works for a small group of musicians that could be used and reused during Marian devotions (especially for Our Lady of MERCY) and for the INFANT JESUS.

By 1676 the works that Marc-Antoine Charpentier was copying into his arabic-numbered notebooks had become a mirror of the Guise women's devotional preoccupations. Although it is impossible to say who decided that a piece of music should be written for a given devotional event, it presumably was Goibaut, rather than Charpentier or Mademoiselle de Guise, who made such decisions. It almost certainly was Du Bois who supplied texts to the composer, sometimes piecing together passages found in the Scriptures or in liturgy, and sometimes writing original devotional texts. (These texts doubtlessly were then approved either by Her Highness's almoner or, for the original texts, by BISHOP ROQUETTE.) Du Bois also presumably arranged for the venue and directed the performance. In addition, in consultation with the princesses he probably played a decisive role in selecting new members for the GUISE MUSIC.

In sum, although he did not do it single-handedly, Philippe Goibaut du Bois created a unique cultural entity, the GUISE MUSIC. During what would become a cultural moment—a discreetly veiled cultural moment, reserved for the elites of the realm—a Latinist, a composer, and a group of talented young people would collaborate to express the prayers and the preoccupations of two powerful women. This does not mean that the collaborators necessarily became friends. In fact, since the hierarchy within the household had to be respected, it is unlikely that Monsieur Charpentier presumed to speak familiarly with Monsieur Du Bois, his social superior, or that either Charpentier or Du Bois talked to the musicians as equals.

For just over a decade, 1675 to 1687, the Music would glorify the Virgin, the Holy Child, the Holy Sacrament, and Louis XIV the God-Given; it would speak out in favor of converting Protestants by reason rather than force; it would perform Italian music regularly; and it would thumb its nose at Jean-Baptiste Lully's monopoly over the operatic genre. If the householders did all this, it was because Mademoiselle de Guise had authorized Philippe Goibaut du Bois to send her composer and her musicians down this challenging path.

That, at any rate, is the picture suggested by the rather veiled remark of the colleague who welcomed Du Bois to the French Academy in 1693. He hinted that shortly after LOUIS-JOSEPH DE LORRAINE's death in 1671, Mademoiselle de Guise had begun entrusting Philippe Goibaut with the selection of talented but needy young men and women from good families, to serve in her household or in her Music, or to profit from her generosity by occupying one of the comfortable apartments in the stable wing of the Hôtel de Guise:

> The generous princess, his aunt, I mean Mademoiselle de Guise, whose name is too fine not to be uttered, asked you for advice. And what could a soul as great and as lofty as hers desire, if not the advice of a wise man? And what advice did you give her? The indigent nobility, lifted so often by her beneficence! Poor men of letters, her illustrious pensioners, you have felt the repercussions. I would call as witnesses the Manes of those who are no longer with

us, and the gratitude of those who are still alive, if I did not want to spare your modesty.[13]

Later, Du Bois acknowledged publicly his gratitude to Mademoiselle de Guise for making it possible for him and other protégés to carry on a variety of cultural activities:

> It is [Your Highness] who gave me the means to finish this work, through the sweetness of the repose that her kindness permits for all those who have the honor of belonging to her. ... For a long time I have longed for the opportunity to give her some public mark of my respect and my gratitude.[14]

Among the "means" she provided Du Bois throughout the 1670s and 1680s was a copyist-valet named Claude Neri.[15] And the "work she made it possible for him to finish"—and publish prior to her death—included four translations of Saint Augustine's works from Latin (1676, 1678, 1684, 1686); a plainsong setting of a Latin hymn (pre-1688); a translation of Thomas à Kempis' *De Imitatione Christi* (1687); and a discourse on converting Protestants by reason rather than by force (1685, reprinted in 1686). To this list should be added various unpublished works related to Blaise Pascal and Jansenism and, it would seem, the bulk of the devotional texts that were not borrowed from liturgy and that Marc-Antoine Charpentier set to music between 1670 and 1687 and preserved for posterity in his arabic-numbered notebooks. In addition, since it was customary for gentlemen in a princely court to write verse in the vernacular for their lord or lady, it cannot be ruled out that Du Bois wrote some, but certainly not all the libretti for Charpentier's pastorales and chamber operas.

The so-called "discourse" on converting Protestants (the actual title was "Conformity in the Conduct of the French Church") was written at ARCHBISHOP HARLAY's request late in 1685, shortly after the Revocation of the Edict of Nantes.[16] In it Du Bois expressed thoughts that for several years had been animating a whole faction of the Assembly of the Clergy that was opposed to forcing Catholicism upon the Huguenots of the realm. That Harlay turned to Du Bois is very revealing of the reputation that Mademoiselle de Guise's protégé had acquired. A readership had developed; and now those readers would weigh the merits of the discourse simply because Du Bois had written it. This commission made Goibaut the visible partner of an invisible Jean Racine, who in July 1685 had been asked to ghostwrite the speech that Archbishop Colbert of Rouen, the assembly spokesman, was scheduled to make before Louis XIV. Playwright and Royal Historiographer Racine talked of bringing "brothers" back into the fold, not by "iron and fire" but by the "gentleness and wisdom" with which the King governed.[17] (As early as 1682, these wayward "brothers" had been evoked in letters addressed to the Protestants by Archbishop Harlay and BISHOP ROQUETTE. "You are our brothers," the prelates had asserted.[18])

In November 1685, a copy of Goibaut's "discourse" about this peaceable approach was sent off to Florence, along with the libretto (and perhaps the score) of Charpentier's latest oratorio in honor of Saint Cecilia. "Attached are the discourse on Saint Augustine's two letters that Monsieur Du Bois, chapel master of Mademoiselle de Guise, translated by order of Monseigneur the Archbishop of Paris. I will send his libretto for our Italian musicians," scribbled the Tuscan agent in Paris.[19] This postscript is the proof that Du Bois wrote the libretti for Charpentier's oratorios honoring Saint Cecilia. It is therefore not surprising that these libretti emphasize the Saint's gentle conversion of her bridegroom, Valerianus, and the couple's subsequent conversion of Tiburtius—who was, of course, his *brother*.

Du Bois wrote the libretti for these oratorios, and Charpentier wrote the music; but words and music fused into a single voice, and that voice was not theirs, it was the voice of the two Guise women—especially MADAME DE GUISE. As early as 1676,[A] when her cousin the King asked her to persuade a Huguenot woman to convert, she had used this musical voice during a service at the Jesuit Noviciate, to state publicly her opposition to the use of force. In a succession of oratorios honoring Cecilia she maintained this position, until the Revocation of 1685.[B]

Without MADEMOISELLE DE GUISE's approval, Du Bois could scarcely have taken the public position he did in the discourse. One can therefore presume that she too favored this peaceful approach to the Huguenot problem. In other words, the last Guise was rejecting the violence that had characterized her ancestors during the Wars of Religion; and through her protégé's pen and eloquent style, she was making her position clear.

The introduction to the discourse on "conformity" is therefore extremely revealing about the thoughts of both Mademoiselle de Guise and Madame de Guise during the late 1670s and the 1680s—thoughts that spill over to the oratorios in honor of Saint Cecilia. "One will see," Goibaut wrote, "that Saint Augustine himself was of the opinion that one must use only the force of Truth to bring heretics back." In a passage that calls to mind Cecilia's proud martyrdom, Du Bois painted martyrdom in a way not unlike a Stoic precept: "It is not the *suffering* that

---

[A] Cahier 13, H. 394.
[B] Cahier 13, H. 394; cahiers 19–20, H. 397; cahier 42, H. 413; cahier 47, H. 415.

makes the martyr," he wrote, "but the *cause.* ... When one suffers for Truth, it is called Constancy." He concluded with a veritable prayer that should be seen as reflecting the two Guise women's own prayers: "May it please God's mercy to finish this great work [of conversion], and to bless intentions as pure as are those of the Church, in the desire it feels to bring back to Jesus Christ such a great number of souls, and to preserve them from death."[20] Du Bois could not have written this introduction without first conferring with theologians, principally ARCHBISHOP HARLAY and BISHOP ROQUETTE. In fact, it must not be forgotten that Harlay himself, who held a doctorate in theology from the Sorbonne, had asked Du Bois to write the discourse in the first place.

Once the expeditious conversion of the Protestants in the realm had become her royal cousin's official policy in 1685, MADAME DE GUISE ceased commissioning oratorios favoring persuasion rather than force. That said, in 1686 someone—it can only have been Goibaut himself— commissioned a new prologue[A] for the oratorio of 1685. With its allusion to a "rule of life," *regula vitæ,* the prologue echos words that Du Bois used that very year when dedicating to Mademoiselle de Guise a translation of Saint Augustine's letters, complete with an engraved portrait of the princess. She had long observed, he pointed out, "a rule of life that is always consistent and worthy of being proposed as an example for all persons of her rank."

That this prologue exists is precious evidence of Du Bois' position in the Guise household. It also reveals the strength of his convictions. That is to say, Madame de Guise clearly was unwilling to oppose her cousin's policy about Huguenots, hence her decision not to sponsor further oratorios about Saint Cecilia. Yet a full year after the Revocation, Monsieur Du Bois still hoped that reason would prevail. And he knew that Mademoiselle de Guise shared this hope. Madame de Guise having authorized him to reuse the oratorio for Saint Cecilia, Goibaut wrote a Latin text that used expressions similar to the ones he employed when dedicating Augustine to his protectress. He then commissioned music from Charpentier (and apparently remunerated him), and he probably conducted the Guise Music himself for this final performance of the oratorio—perhaps at festivities during which he presented Mademoiselle de Guise with a copy of the book.

For over fifteen years, one of Goibaut's greatest pleasures was supervising the GUISE MUSIC. Echoes of his exuberance have been preserved in correspondence sent back to DOCTOR VALLANT in Paris during

---

[A] Cahier XLIX, H. 415a.

Her Highness's (and her Music's) progress through Champagne in October 1680. From her estate of Marchais—with its nearby chapel of Notre-Dame de Liesse, situated northwest of Rheims, not far from the city of Laon— MADEMOISELLE DE GUISE noted, in her phonetic French:

> The Music is doing wonders, and Monsieur Du Bois is so happy with it, and is so busy, that he has not complained thus far of any inconvenience. I think he would not feel great ones, so happy is he with making them sing most of the time that we spend when we are not at Liesse.[21]

The endless music eventually drove her to distraction. Having crossed out several words, she confessed to Vallant:

> I can't refrain from telling you that the Music is distracting me in such a way that I don't know what I am writing. Monsieur Du Bois got the notion of entertaining me, because I had a lot of business to conduct all day. He is succeeding so well that I can almost think only of what I am hearing, and that causes me to make so many mistakes in my letter that I don't know if you can read it.[22]

Here is solid proof that it was not Marc-Antoine Charpentier who directed the Music, it was Du Bois. This, despite the fact that the composer seems to have made that journey and performed with the Guise Music. (At any rate, a high tenor, *haute-contre*, sang in a piece honoring the Virgin[A] almost certainly written for Liesse.)

It is likely that Du Bois was responsible for many of the devotional Latin texts that Charpentier was setting to music with increasing frequency after the mid-1670s. A certain number of works are, of course, based on texts from the Scriptures or from liturgy. And some of the texts set to music by Charpentier appear to have been written for specific events. More common, however, are what could be described as "patchwork" texts—that is, texts constructed of lines borrowed from one liturgical text or another and assembled into a whole. Gluing scriptural or liturgical texts together, and connecting them with a few words of one's own, was a familiar practice. Producing this sort of patchwork text was something to be proud of, not ashamed:

> The motet [in honor of Saint Louis] ... was made up of various passages from the Scriptures, applied to the life of the saintly King. Monsieur [François] Charpentier of the French Academy put them together to create this canticle. It requires a great deal of erudition and reading; and since nothing is more difficult than to create

---

[A] Cahiers 29–30, H. 400.

> something with continuity out of several separate pieces, one can
> pride oneself on having very fine judgment when one succeeds at
> this sort of writing.[23]

Relying on this approach to text-writing, Du Bois appears to have assembled the words for many, but not all of Charpentier's Latin oratorios. He surely did not do so unaided. BISHOP ROQUETTE, a doctor of theology, could advise him on questions of theology and orthodoxy. And Marc-Antoine Charpentier—who, although probably not a skilled Latinist, had a certain familiarity with the language and was a master at fitting its prosodic rhythms to music—presumably suggested slight modifications, the better to enhance the expressiveness of the whole. Du Bois' willingness to listen, or his irritation at such temerity, must remain a matter for conjecture.

The Chapel Master himself tried his hand at setting the texts of other Latinists to plainsong melodies and acquired a certain reputation in that field. In a volume of hymns with words by Jean Santeul, Du Bois was put on a par with the most illustrious chapel masters of the realm, among them Henri Du Mont, Jean Mignon, and Pierre Robert.[24] Goibaut's presence in the book may be partly explained by a long acquaintanceship, if not friendship with Jean Santeul, who was DOCTOR VALLANT's friend. Du Bois himself was an associate of Santeul's brother Claude, who was acting as consultant to the Latinists working on the translations of Saint Augustine being sponsored by the monks at Saint-Maur.[25] Strictly speaking, therefore, Marc-Antoine Charpentier was not the only Guise composer to set Latin texts to music during the 1670s and 1680s.

Although Du Bois worked continually with Charpentier for seventeen years, the older man clearly possessed the greater power in the household. In fact, for his own devotions or to please a friend, he may well have asked Charpentier to compose music—and to consider it part of his ordinary duties. For example, it most likely was Du Bois, rather than one of the princesses, who requested the corpus of works for Tenebrae[A] at the ABBAYE-AUX-BOIS, scheduled for performance in early 1680. Du Bois and DOCTOR VALLANT (for many years he had been the nuns' physician) were in close touch with two laywomen boarding at the abbey. One was the widowed daughter-in-law of Madame de Sablé, Vallant's former employer; the other was a certain Madame de Saint-Aubin. (It has not been determined whether she was the composer's cousin, Marthe Croyer, the widow of HAVÉ DE SAINT-AUBIN.)

[A] Cahiers 26–29.

The power relations between Du Bois and Charpentier can be deduced from the composer's arabic-numbered notebooks for 1677. From approximately March to June of that year, Du Bois was confined to his apartment: "Monsieur Du Bois has been shut up for forty days after a surgical operation that was performed on him, and I have been obliged to visit him almost twice a day," noted VALLANT.[26] During these Goibaut-less weeks, Charpentier may have replaced Du Bois as director of the daily performances of the Guise Music. He did more than that: he wrote pieces for himself.

That is to say, from January 1670 to March 1677 Charpentier wrote only three pieces for a male trio: *haute-contre* (high tenor), tenor, and bass. Two of these pieces, written for the the Virgin,[A] date from 1674 and were surely destined for the MERCY, the venue at which this *haute-contre*, who must be Charpentier, generally performed. The third work was a pastorale[B] performed for PHILIPPE II D'ORLÉANS in 1676, presumably by Charpentier and Guise musicians De Baussen and Beaupuis. But during Goibaut's illness, four compositions calling for an *haute-contre*, doubtlessly the composer himself,[C] crop up in the notebooks. After the last of them, a motet for Saint Louis—in all probability intended for performance at the MERCY around August 25—this voice disappears. With the exception of one *haute-contre* solo that beyond all doubt was written for the MERCY,[D] this high tenor does reappear in this series of notebooks until the early 1680s, when Charpentier began singing with the emerging GREAT GUISE MUSIC.[27] The reasons why Marc-Antoine Charpentier generally did not perform with the Guise Music are not known, but it cannot be ruled out that Du Bois preferred it that way.

Indeed, Charpentier did not reign supreme in the Guise chapel and chamber. Over the years, the Guise Music (the Core Trio and eventually the expanded Great Guise Music) performed works by a variety of composers, including at least one Italian. In 1686 Mademoiselle de Guise's repeated request for "all" the works of Giovanni Battista Mazzaferrata was finally heeded by the Grand Duke of Tuscany's agents, but only because Du Bois kept pestering them—ostensibly on Her Highness's behalf, although he was clearly very eager to get his hands on the books. The Guise singers promptly set about preparing some of the pieces, which Mademoiselle de Guise declared to be "very beautiful," *bellissime*.[28]

[A] Cahier 8, H. 159, H. 20.
[B] Cahier 13, H. 479.
[C] Cahier 16, H. 58 and H. 319, and cahier 17, H. 320 and H. 321.
[D] Cahier 22, H. 25.

By then Du Bois had accumulated quite a musical library. An inventory of his possessions made in 1694[29] mentions fifty-six volumes, but few of them are identified. The top book in one packet was a volume of Henri Du Mont's "motets"—perhaps his *Motets à deux voix avec la basse continue* of 1668, but more likely, considering the size of the Music after the early 1680s, his *Motets à deux, III et IV parties, pour voix et instruments, avec la basse continue*, published in 1681. At the top of another packet was a copy of Lully's "motets," doubtlessly his *Motets à deux chœurs pour la Chapelle du roi*, published in 1681. The third package is described as containing an astonishing number of religious works by Michel Lambert, "nineteen volumes of motets by Lambert." (Did this package contain one or two volumes of vocal music by Lambert—perhaps some motets in manuscript that were never published—and, lower in the pile, books containing the works of other composers?)

Faithful advisor and servant of Mademoiselle de Guise though he was, Philippe Goibaut was never entirely disinterested. A letter to the princess dated 1677 suggests a typical discourse between the princess and her protégé. Du Bois began by preparing her for the favor he was about to request:

> My condition, moreover, is such that there is nothing in the world that I would want to change. Your Highness leaves me nothing to wish for, and in that which she does me the honor of giving me, I find in abundance the wherewithal to supply all the conveniences I might need, and even that of a coach, which is the greatest and the most necessary of all.

Then he dropped the other shoe:

> But, I cannot have that convenience, Mademoiselle, if Your Highness does not deem it good that I keep my coach and my horses inside the Hôtel [de Guise]. That is the only favor I must ask of her, and if I dare take this liberty it is not in order to save the rent on a coach house and stables, nor to avoid having my coach and horses far from me. It is uniquely because one cannot cause a coachman to live an orderly life unless one has him right before one's eyes, and because those sorts of people, on the pretext of being with their horses, are continually outside, exposed to all sorts of disorders, which for me would be a greater worry than not having a coach.[30]

This bit of moralizing, worthy of Molière's *Le Tartuffe* (and not all that different from the discourse of Her Highness's "Tartuffe," BISHOP RO-QUETTE) was merely a preamble to Du Bois' crowning argument. This arrangement, he asserted, would surely prove felicitous for Mademoiselle de Guise, for her horses "will no longer be troubled by having to drive either me or Monsieur Vallant around." (VALLANT frequently spent the night at the Hôtel de Guise, lodging with Du Bois.) It is not clear whether the princess was convinced by his reasoning, for the loan of a coach house and horse stalls was not the sort of detail preserved in descriptions of the contents of the Hôtel de Guise nor in the inventory of Du Bois' personal possessions. Be that as it may, Du Bois lavished attention on his coach, which was renovated in 1680, down to its gilded nails. During Mademoiselle de Guise's tour of her lands in Champagne, he begged Doctor Vallant to relay his wishes to the coach-repairer:

> I beg you to tell Chevreux that he should take good care of
> everything old that he removes from my coach, and that he should
> make a list of all the iron that can be reused and the iron that must
> be remade. ... Please tell Chevreux that I want no more gilded nails
> on my coach than there originally were. ⸗

During Goibaut's early years in service to the Guises, Méré made some harsh statements about him, and about how cleverly he could plead his cause:

> Monsieur Du Bois is brazen; he is brazen to the point of cheekiness.
> ... He is very self-serving in his plots, but if it were to his interest to
> write against the [Jansenist] people at Port-Royal, he would write
> against them. He is methodical in paying court, he is brazen when
> he is with the uninformed. ... He is insinuating and gentle, but this
> gentleness appears to come from a delicacy of spirit; he appears to be
> astute.[31]

Here again it is difficult to determine how much of Méré's appraisal of Du Bois is witticism, and how much captures the man himself. Still, a Jansenist acquaintance, Antoine Singlin, made a similar judgement about Du Bois: he has "wit, and even piety," but "he would be very delighted if things work out to his advantage." Méré and Singlin turn out to have been perceptive indeed. As late as 1677, Du Bois named the Jansenist nuns of Port-Royal-des-Champs as his principal heirs; but after the Peace of the Church had been broken, this bequest was omitted from his will of 1680, and it did not reappear in his final testament. In fact, toward the end of his life Du Bois was accused of attempting to conceal his old associations with the Jansenists:

> Monsieur Du Bois, who was naturally timid as far as his person and
> his worldly interests were concerned, ... was so careful to watch out
> for himself concerning P[ort]-R[oyal] that he pretended to have had
> no tie to the people who were connected with it, and he concealed
> the tie he used to have.[32]

Despite the assertion by the Academician who wrote Goibaut's biography, no evidence has been uncovered to support the statement that "Messieurs of Port-Royal had Mademoiselle de Guise under their thumb." (The facts suggest the opposite, for her confessor, who died in June 1670, had been Father Annat, S.J., one of the Jansenists' bitterest enemies.) One of the first notebooks in the arab-numbered series into which Marc-Antoine Charpentier copied out his compositions for the Hôtel de Guise, does however contain a motet for the Feast of Saint Augustine[A] of August 1670, an especially holy day for committed Jansenists. Had Her Highness been won over to Jansenism in the space of those few months? That is implausible. Rather, this piece probably was written at Du Bois' request, for he still felt a strong pull toward Port-Royal. If he slowly turned his back on Jansenism and focused instead on the conversion of another type of "heretic," Huguenots, was it owing to the strong and very focused religious preoccupations of MADEMOISELLE DE GUISE and MADAME DE GUISE during the decade 1676–1686?

By the early 1680s, Philippe Goibaut was becoming as thick as thieves with Father François de la Chaise, one of the FOUR JESUITS in this portrait gallery. A decade earlier, Méré had alluded to a "plot" of Goibaut's, apparently a Jansenist one. The early months of 1688 would find Du Bois in another "plot,"[33] along with La Chaise and BISHOP ROQUETTE. Exerting what was viewed as undue influence upon a dying woman, the trio convinced MADEMOISELLE DE GUISE to add codicils to her will, giving each of them large legacies. "For the good and agreeable services he has rendered for twenty-two years," Du Bois, "who is near me," was willed a life pension of four thousand livres and a one-time payment of six thousand livres.

A few days later, GAIGNIÈRES expressed his dismay at the behavior of the clique around the dying princess:

> There is no way to keep from talking about all the statements that Monseigneur the Bishop of A[utun] and Messieurs Du Bois and La Chaise are making and are causing to be made by their friends and associates in the plot, concerning the donations in the will and codicils of the late Mademoiselle de Guise.

After MADEMOISELLE DE GUISE's death in March 1688, the GREAT GUISE MUSIC was disbanded. In the space of a few days or weeks, Du Bois suffered two painful losses: his protectress and his musicians. Mercifully, he was not evicted from his apartment, for Her Highness's will stipulated

[A] Cahier 2, H. 53.

that protégés and householders could remain in their lodgings. Despite his legacy, Du Bois was beside himself with grief. "Don't you find that he resembles Adam expelled from Paradise on earth?" someone quipped.[34]

Did he perhaps find consolation in several objects that recalled happier days? In addition to the portraits of Mademoiselle de Guise, MADAME DE MONTMARTRE, and Saint Charles Borromeo (the subject of one of Charpentier's oratorios) that hung near his writing table, he had in his possession a little silver "dial," *cadran*, that had belonged to LOUIS-JOSEPH DE LORRAINE and "that he made me wear," plus a "little silver book with a screw closing" that had belonged to Mademoiselle de Guise. Did the "Little Jesus in wax, in a box bearing five lines of verse,"[35] make Du Bois nostalgic about the heady days when the Guise women were creating two pedagogical institutes dedicated to the INFANT JESUS?

Du Bois was elected to the French Academy in November 1693, owing perhaps to the real or perceived merits of his publications, or perhaps to a protector such as Madame de Guise. He attended meetings regularly, amassing sixty silver tokens in less than eight months, one for each session attended. Now that Mademoiselle de Guise was gone, he turned for protection to MADAME DE GUISE, to whom he dedicated a translation of Saint Augustine's sermons in 1694. In his open letter to her, he alluded to "the protection and, if I dare say, the very special kindness with which Your Royal Highness has honored me for so many years."[36] This was Philippe Goibaut's last publication and his last quest for protection. He died in his apartment at the Hôtel de Guise on July 1, 1694, and was buried at the Church of Saint-Jean-en-Grève. He had not lived long enough to collect his legacy from Mademoiselle de Guise.

III

The play was so prodigiously successful

CORNEILLE THE YOUNGER

Thomas Corneille, playwright, librettist,
and co-editor of the *Mercure galant*

Thomas Corneille, the younger brother of famed playwright Pierre Corneille, had been writing for the theater since the 1640s. Following in his older brother's wake, Thomas left their native Rouen in 1662, to settle near him in Paris. The brothers were so close that to some extent Pierre's creative accomplishments shaped Thomas's career. In the foreground of this portrait of Thomas Corneille, a sketch of his brother is therefore propped on the worktable.

By 1648 Pierre Corneille had entered the protective orbit of Chancellor Pierre Séguier. There he became close to artist CHARLES LE BRUN, who had recently returned from Rome and was organizing the new Royal Academy of Painting. Two years later, Pierre Corneille asked DASSOUCY to write music for *Andromède*, and the pair remained in contact until at least 1653, when Dassoucy addressed a friendly poem to Pierre. By 1662 Corneille had gravitated into the Guise circle. In October of that year he was living with his wife and son at the Hôtel de Guise, where he was fed and lodged at Duke Henri's expense.[1] Thus Pierre Corneille, who had been traveling back and forth between Paris and Rouen for some thirty years, became a Parisian.

Since Thomas also moved to Paris in 1662, it cannot be ruled out that he too lodged at the Hôtel de Guise. After all, he had dedicated his *Timocrate* to Henri de Guise in 1656. Be that as it may, the Duke's death in June 1664 ended Pierre's protection by the HOUSE OF GUISE. Pierre had apparently hoped that MARIE DE GUISE THE REGENT would keep him on, for he sent a sonnet of condolence to the new Duke, fourteen-year-old LOUIS-JOSEPH DE LORRAINE, whom he described as a "young hero" in whom "so many heros live again."[2] (Here, as in DASSOUCY's open letter to MOLIÈRE, the heroic ideal was applied to a Guise.) The sonnet brought, perhaps, a reward; but it did not bring a commitment. Mademoiselle de Guise was about to embark on a total renovation of the Hôtel de Guise and could not lodge Corneille and his family in the Volière, the relatively small hôtel where she was living at the time.

Pierre Corneille found other lodgings, and until 1681 he and Thomas lived in the same house. By the early 1670s, Pierre was in his late sixties and in failing health. He stopped writing for the theater in about 1674, although his plays continued to be performed in Paris and at court.

Two years earlier, Thomas Corneille and JEAN DONNEAU DE VISÉ had begun a joint publishing venture, a monthly journal called the *Mercure galant*. The first issues appeared sporadically, but regular publication began in 1677. If Thomas strove to keep his activities as a journalist separate from his theatrical career, he was not entirely successful. Although he was more or less the silent partner in the *Mercure*, with Donneau the focus of public attention, allusions to the Corneilles and to their friends and collaborators routinely found their way into the journal. (Whether Charpentier became the journalists' actual friend or remained a professional associate cannot be determined. That said, this portrait gallery describes them as "friends.")

Meanwhile, after MOLIÈRE's death in 1673, the remnants of his troop had reached out to Thomas, whose tragedies had been performed in various Parisian theaters. Thomas Corneille began by writing several plays for the troop (now known as the "Guénégaud Troop") that did not call for music. Then, in October 1674, the actors voted in favor of a costly new venture on which Marc-Antoine Charpentier and Thomas Corneille (assisted by Donneau de Visé) would collaborate: *Circé*, a "machine play" that was neither an opera nor a tragedy, but a blend of both.[3]

Circé[A] opened on March 15, 1675. In one awesome entertainment, plants grew, mountains rose, statues moved and flew about, and gardens were transformed into rocks that crashed into a vast ocean. It was a resounding success. Donneau later recalled that

> the play was so prodigiously successful that it was performed without
> interruption from the beginning of Mardi Gras until the month of
> September. ... During the first six weeks the theater was full by
> noon, and since there were no more seats, people would pay half a
> gold *louis* just to get in; and they were happy when that same
> amount, which was the price of the best box seats, got them a seat in

[A] Cahiers XVIII–XIX, H. 496.

the third tier. ... Performances would have gone on longer if the interests of one individual [Lully] had not forced them to reduce the number of singers.[4]

The King remained aloof, but his brother, PHILIPPE II D'ORLÉANS, supported the troop by attending a performance: "Their Royal Highnesses were marvelously satisfied with this fine spectacle, whose decorations, flights, and machines are extraordinary," noted the *Mercure galant* in gratitude for this gesture of support by the godfather of Donneau's son —and, although they did not say it, in appreciation for his gift of three hundred livres to help the troop with its expenses.[5]

Lully protested about *Circé*, for the orchestra consisted of a dozen instruments and a harpsichord, and the names of seven singers were marked on Charpentier's score, three of them professionals who did not belong to the troop. In addition, ten "marchers" were paid to perform dance-like motions, twenty "fliers" soared about in the machines, and eight "jumpers" did acrobatics. Four days after the first performance a royal decree reminded the troop that, among other restrictions, the decree of April 1673 permitted only two singers, who must be full-time actors in the troop. *Circé* continued to be performed with a somewhat reduced crew; but even so, more musicians were participating than were permitted by the decree (seven singing actors, three professional singers, and ten "marchers"). This reduction of forces prompted the reflection that if the troop were permitted to use all the singers, dancers, and instruments they wanted, "*Circé* would clearly attain the level of all the operas performed up to now."[6]

Lully's persistence in enforcing his monopoly comes as no surprise, but Thomas Corneille's determination to test those restrictions leaves one perplexed. What were his motivations? Rancor against the Florentine? Complicity with some of Lully's rivals? Encouragement by the House of Orléans? Or by the House of Guise? For some inexplicable reason, this brother of a former Guise protégé had allied with Marc-Antoine Charpentier and JEAN DONNEAU DE VISÉ in what would prove a long but losing battle to preserve music and song in the spoken theater.

November 1675 brought *L'Inconnu*,[A] a comedy by Thomas Corneille with musical embellishments by Charpentier. Pressed for time, the playwright asked Donneau de Visé to be his silent collaborator in the venture. "There were reasons to perform this piece quickly," recalled Donneau. He did not elaborate on the reasons for the haste, but it probably had something to do with Lully, and with the troop's convic-

---

[A] Cahier XXIV, H. 499.

tion that they must not appear to be slackening in their fight against the monopoly. "To speed things up, I wrote the play in prose, and while I was writing the prose for the second act, [Corneille] was turning the first act into verse," Donneau continued. "And since prose is easier than poetry, I had time to write the poetry for the *divertissements*, especially the dialogue between Love and Friendship that did not displease the public."[7] In other words, although the play was published under Corneille's name, it was a joint venture based on a story Donneau had published in 1669.

Corneille's next play, which opened in August 1676, was another "machine play," *Le Triomphe des dames*, for which Charpentier composed the music, since lost. It was a calculated challenge to Lully's monopoly. The troop hired six string instruments and twenty-eight "marchers or assistants"; and they went out to the royal court several times to beg permission to engage two professional singers.[8] Their request was denied.

The story of Charpentier and Corneille's struggle against Lully's monopoly—a tale of gradual strangulation—has been told elsewhere.[9] Not only were the troop and its in-house artists being hampered, it must sometimes have seemed to the Corneille brothers that Pierre was paying the price for his brother's daring. In what may be nothing but a simple chronological coincidence, Pierre's pension went unpaid from 1674 (when preparations began for *Circé*) until shortly after the revival of Pierre's *Andromède*[A] in 1682, which for all intents and purposes marked the end of the troop's resistance to Lully. (Pierre Corneille's pension was not, of course, the only one being reduced or withdrawn during the 1670s, to pay for international wars.)

In the very midst of this resistance to Lully's monopoly, the Florentine invited Thomas Corneille to provide the libretto for *Bellérophon* in 1679. The collaboration did not go well. Lully humiliated Corneille by forcing him to rewrite endlessly.[10] Meanwhile, Thomas was preparing several tributes to his ailing brother. The first involved Pierre's *Polyeucte Martyr*, written back in 1640. It was performed at the College of Harcourt in 1680, with ballet music, *Le Combat de l'amour divin*, by Charpentier. (The composer reused music he had written for a very brief revival of Molière's *Le Dépit amoureux*[B] in 1679). It clearly was Thomas Corneille's project, rather than the Jesuits' or Charpentier's. (Contrary to what has been asserted, this college was not a JESUIT HOUSE, nor was it administered by the Jesuits. It was an independent school and remained so until the

---

[A] Cahier XXXIV, H. 504.
[B] Cahier XXIII, H. 498.

Revolution. In other words, it is highly unlikely that this student production was organized by Charpentier's JESUIT FRIENDS.)

Some months later, Charpentier's setting of Pierre Corneille's *Stances du Cid* appeared in three consecutive issues of the *Mercure galant*, January, February, and March 1681. Pierre was in such poor health at the time that his death appeared imminent.[11] In other words, this public tribute to an ailing Pierre Corneille was made possible by Thomas Corneille and JEAN DONNEAU DE VISÉ, and it probably was Thomas who suggested the project. Charpentier apparently wrote the pieces for himself, an *haute-contre*, a high tenor.

Pierre survived until October 1684. Despite advancing senility, he probably was aware that his *Andromède* was being revived in July 1682, with Charpentier's music replacing the late DASSOUCY's outdated compositions from the 1640s. The revival was an overt reply to Lully's *Persée*, based on the same tale, which had opened the previous April. Once again the actors were twitting the Florentine and his privilege. By now they were very familiar with the clauses of the royal decrees of April 1673 and March 1675, which restricted them to two singers who were regular actors in the troop, and prevented them from hiring outside singers or employing dancers. Yet Charpentier's score shows that six actors and actresses sang; and the subject-book mentions a hired professional singer. A week after the opening, the authorities presented the troop with yet another reminder that they were infringing on Lully's monopoly. *Andromède* continued to be performed sporadically until 1683.

Corneille and Donneau de Visé coauthored two more plays for the troop, one of them with music by Charpentier. Their *La Divineresse* of November 1679 was a great success, coinciding as it did with the POISON AFFAIR. Special effects abounded, but somewhat surprisingly there was no music. (Did Charpentier prefer to remain aloof from this work, in view of the poison investigations being conducted in the circles around the Guise princesses?) Their second play about magic, *La Pierre philosophale*,[A] with music by Charpentier, opened in 1681 but closed after only two performances. In May of that year, Charpentier accompanied the actors to Versailles for a command performance of *L'Inconnu*. Lully's monopoly was suspended for that performance: the troop was permitted to hire dancers and singers, and it was paid 332 livres by the royal administration to cover costs.[12]

A revival of the original version of Thomas Corneille's *Psyché* in the fall of 1684 constituted yet another overt challenge to Lully. First per-

---

[A] Cahiers XXIX–XXX, H. 501.

formed in 1671 as a "tragicomedy with ballet," with music by Lully, this verse play had been reworked in 1678 and turned into a libretto for Lully. Now Corneille and the troop were reviving the original play, with new music by Charpentier. The music has not survived, so it is impossible to deduce whether they limited their challenge to the similar subject matter, or whether the troop flouted the restrictions, as had been their wont since 1674. Be that as it may, Charpentier's music for a revival of Donneau de Visé's *Vénus et Adonis*[A] in September 1685 stayed within the imposed limits. The troop clearly had gotten the message. That project marked the end of Charpentier's association with the troop.

Between 1673 and 1685 Charpentier had, of course, worked with playwrights other than Corneille and Donneau. He collaborated with several different authors after August 1680, when a royal decree created the Comédie Française by merging the Guénégaud and the Bourgogne troops. For example, 1681 brought a revival of *Endimion*, with incidental music by Charpentier.[B] (Its full title was *Les Amours de Diane et d'Endimion*, the old play by Gabriel Gilbert that had been read aloud at the Hôtel de Guise in 1656 for Queen Christina of Sweden, in the presence of Mademoiselle Marie de Guise and Duke Henri. Why this play was revived shortly after Gilbert's death remains unexplained, as does any connection the revival may have had with the Guises, the Queen, or JACQUES II DALIBERT, her secretary.)

Most of Charpentier's music for the theater was copied into the arabic-numbered series of notebooks that contain his "extraordinary" production. That is to say, having copied his music for MOLIÈRE into this series,[C] and his compositions for Corneille and Donneau de Visé's *Circé*[D] into the same series, Charpentier continued that practice until *Vénus et Adonis*,[E] his final work for the Comédie Française.

There are two intriguing exceptions to this pattern. During the summer of 1685 he "adjusted for the third time" some music for *Le Malade imaginaire*,[F] and he also wrote a *Dialogue d'Angélique et de Médor*,[G] apparently for Dancourt's play by that name, which opened in August 1685. For some reason he copied these particular pieces into the arabic-numbered notebooks where he preserved his Guise commissions. An oversight? Or a Guise gift to the troop? Since the *Dialogue* satirized

[A] Cahier XLVIII, H. 507.
[B] Cahier XXXI, H. 502.
[C] Cahier XV, H. 494; cahier XVI, H. 495 and H. 495a; cahier XVII, H. 495.
[D] Cahiers XVIII–XIX, H. 496.
[E] Cahier XLVIII, H. 507.
[F] Cahier 44, H. 495b; cahier 45, H. 495b.
[G] Cahier 45, H. 506.

Lully's recent *Roland*, was this music inserted into *Angélique et Médor* as a tease, in the manner of his and MOLIÈRE's interaction with the Italian actors back in 1672? This conjecture is supported by the fact that, as an "unusual expense," the troop purchased the "opera *Roland*," so that they could use it as a point of departure for "the sort of parody" they were going to prepare.[13] (Was this parody written for the command performance before Louis XIV at Marly on August 7, 1685, when five coaches, five torchbearers, eighteen actors, and an extra horse bore the troop to court?[14]) That the *Dialogue* and the retouching of *Le Malade* were gifts to the troop seems borne out by the records of the Comédie Française, which do not mention payments to Charpentier that summer.

Charpentier collaborated one final time with Thomas Corneille; and in a sense Pierre Corneille contributed to the project too. In 1693, Thomas reworked his brother's *Médée* and turned it into a libretto for Charpentier, much as he had earlier reworked and condensed his own *Persée* for Lully. Owing to what was described as a "plot," *cabale*, the opera closed after less than a dozen performances.

From 1682 on, Thomas Corneille's attention was being increasingly diverted from the theater toward the *Mercure galant*. In January of that year he and DONNEAU DE VISÉ formalized their longtime collaboration on that publication. "Up until now," read the notarized act, "[Thomas Corneille] has worked conjointly with me, and has worked on composing and distributing the said *Mercure*."

Three years later, Corneille was unanimously elected to his late brother's armchair in the French Academy. He became increasingly preoccupied with the Academy's projects and the debates that animated its members. Poor sight forced him to give up the *Mercure galant* in about 1700, and the Academy in 1705. He retired to his family home in Normandy, where he died in 1709.

Having got the idea to create a monthly publication

DONNEAU DE VISÉ AND THE PRESS

Jean Donneau de Visé,
playwright and editor of the *Mercure galant*

This portrait of one of Marc-Antoine Charpentier's collaborators in the theater focuses less on the works that Jean Donneau de Visé created with the composer, than on the public image he slowly constructed of the man known as "Monsieur Charpentier."

That image was shaped by conventions that prevented a journalist from revealing links of patronage, authorship, and friendship, and that forced him to evoke interpersonal relations that could not be explicitly mentioned. For example, a great noble was occasionally willing to have his or her name linked publicly with that of a householder or a protégé. If not, the journalist generally named the noble and wove into the article a compliment about the "fine music" performed that day. On the other hand, if a journalist was determined to praise an artist, and if he could rest assured that the great noble was amenable, he would recount how much that artist's talents had been appreciated by an audience made up of "people of quality"—among whom, the informed public realized, was the artist's protector, who had agreed to remain anonymous.

From his birth, Jean Donneau de Visé "belonged" to the House of Orléans. He was the son of Antoine Donneau de Visé, marshal of lodgings to GASTON D'ORLÉANS. His link to the House of Orléans remained so strong that PHILIPPE II DUKE OF ORLÉANS stood as godfather for Jean Donneau's son in 1666. At the time Donneau was writing plays for MOLIÈRE's theater, which had not yet become the "King's Troop" but was known as "Monsieur's Troop," that is, the troop protected by Philippe II d'Orléans.

Like THOMAS CORNEILLE, his close collaborator, Donneau de Visé was an established playwright when he began writing for the troop that had

177

been created by Molière and that came to be known as the "Guénégaud Troop" after the playwright-actor's death in 1673. However, rather than write entire plays, Donneau tended to lend Corneille a hand. For example, in 1674 he provided the plot for Corneille's *L'Inconnu* by using, as a point of departure, one of the *Nouvelles galantes* he had published in 1669, and by turning the plot into a prose play that Corneille then transformed into verse. In the process, "since prose is easier than poetry," Donneau got so far ahead of his colleague that he "had the time to write the poetry for the *divertissements*."[1]

Thus it was that Donneau became one of Marc-Antoine Charpentier's colleagues during the fall of 1674. Over the next decade he continued to collaborate with the composer, often as Corneille's coauthor. For example, in 1676 the three men teamed up for *Le Triomphe des Dames*. Corneille and Donneau's *La Divineresse* of 1679, with its evocation of the POISON AFFAIR was a great success; but for some reason the authors either did not want music, or else Charpentier preferred to distance himself from so a touchy subject as the Poison Affair, whose tentacles had found their way to the Hôtel de Guise and the Luxembourg Palace. In 1681 the trio collaborated on *La Pierre philosophale*,[A] a play about magic and alchemy; but despite Charpentier's music and Donneau's special effects, it was hissed off the stage.

Donneau's principal preoccupation was a monthly journal called the *Mercure galant*, for which he had received a royal privilege in 1672. Publication remained sporadic until 1677. Donneau was known to the public as the creator and moving force behind the *Mercure*, but from the outset Thomas Corneille had been active in preparing each issue. In 1681, when the two men decided to become official partners in the venture, Donneau informed the notary who was drawing up the act that:

> I, Visé, having got the idea to create a monthly publication that contains all sorts of news, with the title *Mercure galant*, for which I obtained the privilege, I made a verbal agreement with [Corneille] who, as a result, has worked conjointly with me up until now, and has taken care of composing and distributing the said *Mercure*, which we have kept going and sustained against everyone who wanted to harm it, and we state that until the present we have equally shared all the rights and profits accruing from it.[2]

Regular publication of the *Mercure* had begun with the April 1677 issue, well into Donneau and Corneille's creative association with Charpentier.

[A] Cahiers XXIX-XXX, H. 501.

It was not long before the composer was mentioned in the periodical. The January 1678 issue included an air by Charpentier (*Quoy, rien ne vous peut arrester*), which "I"—that is, the spokesman that sometimes was Donneau, sometimes Corneille, and sometimes a blend of the two—introduced as follows:

> I think that you will give me a very big thank-you for this air, because it is by Monsieur Charpentier, famous for a thousand works that have charmed all of France, and among them the air for the Moors in *Le Malade imaginaire*, and all the airs in *Circé* and in *L'Inconnu*.

(As was their wont, Donneau and Corneille were tacitly praising themselves here, as well as Charpentier, for the latter two plays were their creations.) "He lived a long time in Italy," the article continued, "where he often saw Carissimi, who was the greatest music master that we have had for a long time."[3]

In other words, in this time when first names were generally not known outside the family, in order to introduce the "famous Monsieur Charpentier" to their readers, his collaborators first summarized the activities that set him apart from other individuals with that rather common surname. The article does not say it, but any reader familiar with Parisian theater knew that Charpentier had worked first with MOLIÈRE and then with the Guénégaud Troop, and that he had participated in the creation of two extravaganzas by Thomas Corneille: *Circé* and *L'Inconnu*. Fully informed readers perhaps realized that Donneau de Visé, the silent coauthor of *Circé*, was also being complimented.

To round out the picture, the journalists added a few details about the composer that their general readership might not know: Charpentier had lived in Italy, where he had frequently visited with CARISSIMI. If Corneille and Donneau were privy to these details and could state them so unequivocally, it was because they had been told this by the composer himself. (SÉBASTIEN DE BROSSARD, the close friend of ÉTIENNE LOULIÉ, a member of the GUISE MUSIC, was equally certain about Carissimi and Rome: "Monsieur Charpentier ... remained for several years in Rome, where he was the very assiduous disciple and supporter of the famous Carissimi."[4] The Parisian Jesuits who wrote the *Journal de Trévoux* concurred: "He was Carissimi's pupil."[5]) Corneille and Donneau were so sure of these facts that they repeated them again and again: "The music was charming. You know the Italians excel at that. Monsieur Charpentier, who lived in Rome for three years, learned a great deal from it. All his works offer the proof"; "Monsieur Charpentier, who learned music in Rome under Carissimi, deemed the best master in Italy, was employed to work on this fête" at the Royal Academy of Painting; "He studied music in Rome under Carissimi, who was the most esteemed music master of Italy"; "Monsieur Charpentier learned music in Italy, under Carissimi."[6]

Having thus outlined the composer's public image, his friends began refining and elaborating it. Without the praise that regularly appeared in the *Mercure*, would "Monsieur Charpentier" have become so interesting a public personage that Pierre Landry would want to fit an image of him into the Almanac he engraved for 1682?[7]

There was self-congratulation and flagrant promotion. However, there were things that could be said, and things that could not. For example, the journalists often had to proceed by dropping hints and by inserting clues that would permit informed readers to understand who the unnamed patron of an event might be, or conversely, who the unnamed composer might be. In the case of Marc-Antoine Charpentier and his protectors, if one or another Guise princess was mentioned, it would have been inappropriate to mention the composer. The journalists therefore tended to mention the patron, and it was up to the reader to deduce the composer's identity. Take, for example, the article about a *Te Deum* sung at the MERCY in August 1682: "Mademoiselle de Guise attended, with a large number of persons of the highest rank," they wrote.[8] Since the Guises never allowed their name to be linked to Charpentier's in the *Mercure*, it was impossible to mention the person who had written the *Te Deum*. Yet Charpentier's notebooks contain the remnants[A] of music for this event.[9] These conventions are not unlike the ones employed by the engravers who produced popular images: anyone who knew how to read the clues could identify the various ladies and gentlemen standing around the King or the Queen.

In subsequent issues of the *Mercure galant*, the "famous" composer was portrayed as working with the Guénégaud Troop, often for plays written by one or both of the journalists. In addition to the statement of January 1678 that dropped the titles of *Le Malade imaginaire*, *Circé*, and *L'Inconnu*, Charpentier was mentioned in an article about Donneau's *Les Amours de Vénus et d'Adonis*. The special effects—which originally had not been accompanied "either by dances or by voices"—were now benefitting from music by Charpentier,[B] "who for many years has been doing these sorts of things successfully. ... A lament[C] was added that charmed everyone who heard it and who were musical connoisseurs."[10]

[A] Cahier 36, H. 428, H 291.
[B] Cahier XLVIII, H. 507.
[C] Cahier XLVIII, H. 507 [14–16].

The December 1693 article about Thomas Corneille and Marc-Antoine Charpentier's *Médée* likewise evoked the "twenty years" and the "thousand places" where Charpentier's music had charmed theater-goers. Here too the journalists cite their own works and Molière's: *Le Mariage forcé*, *Le Malade imaginaire*, *Circé*, and *L'Inconnu*. Convention kept Corneille and Donneau from referring to themselves by name in this article, for the emphasis was on the composer. They settled for talking about Corneille obliquely: "One might say that the opera [that is, the libretto] of *Médée* and the one for *Bellérophon* by the same author, are as full of themes as any [spoken] play we possess."[11] Sometimes, however, the journalists remained silent about Charpentier's music, preferring to emphasize the quality of a play they themselves had written. This is the course they took in January 1681, in discussing *La Pierre philosophale*.

On nine separate occasions, starting in January 1678, the public was treated to engraved pieces by Charpentier. One of these published airs, *Ne frippez pas mon bavolet*, was added to the 1679 revival of Corneille and Donneau's *L'Inconnu*; another is a setting of Pierre Corneille's *Stances du Cid* that continued for three issues.

Some articles link Charpentier to individuals who belonged to the same protective network as he did. Two of these articles provide engraved music. The first piece is a rondeau setting of a poem by "Mademoiselle Castille," that is, twenty-four-year-old Marie-Henriette de Castille, the daughter of Henri de Castille of Villemareuil, the late intendant for GASTON D'ORLÉANS' household, who was a close relative of MADEMOISELLE DE GUISE's friend, Madame Nicolas Foucquet.[12]

The second air, *Brilliantes fleurs naissez*, features lyrics by Jean de La Fontaine, who had begun his career in Nicolas Foucquet's circle and then moved to the Luxembourg Palace, where he resided until the death of his protectress, the DOWAGER DUCHESS OF ORLÉANS, in 1672. In 1676 Charpentier had used this same air for the "little eclogue"[A] performed at the baptismal party of PHILIPPE III D'ORLÉANS, Duke of Chartres, in the presence of MADAME DE GUISE and MADAME DE TOSCANE. The *Mercure galant*'s decision to publish La Fontaine and Charpentier's old song was a subtle compliment to the Duke of Chartres. That is, when this air was finally published in October 1689, Charpentier and former Guise musician, ÉTIENNE LOULIÉ, were embarking on a very prestigious pedagogical project: Chartres' musical education.

In sum, at least two of the songs by Charpentier that appeared in the *Mercure galant* honored individuals whom the informed public knew were

---

[A] Cahier 13, H. 479.

linked to either MADEMOISELLE DE GUISE or MADAME DE GUISE, Charpentier's protectresses. (Some informed readers also realized that these two individuals had extremely close ties to the disgraced Nicolas Foucquet.)

Another article involves an individual who, like Donneau de Visé, had "belonged" to one of the Guise princesses before he was born: ARMAND-JEAN DE RIANTS, who hosted Charpentier's *Amours d'Acis et de Galatée* in 1678.[A] Corneille and Donneau not only dared to call the work an "opera," they also named guests who were closely linked to the House of Guise. In this way it was made clear to the informed public that this "opera," which was flouting Lully's monopoly, had been created for a Guise friend by a Guise protégé; and that the performances were being given for a cohort of other Guise friends. (In October 1679 the music was reused for a revival of Thomas Corneille's *L'Inconnu*.[13])

A year later came an article linking Charpentier to CHARLES LE BRUN, the son of a former Guise sculptor. For the Feast of Saint Louis, August 25, 1679, "Monsieur Le Brun, first painter to His Majesty, who every year celebrates [that feast day] with special zeal, had a mass sung on that day, in the parish of Saint-Hippolyte. The symphony was composed by Monsieur Charpentier."[14] Judging from the fact that the music was copied into an arabic-numbered notebook, the composer—with the approval of his protectresses—appears to have offered Le Brun, free of charge, a motet "in honor of Saint Louis," a motet "with a symphony."[B] This was the first of two projects involving Charpentier and Le Brun that are mentioned in the *Mercure galant*. It is not known how the composer and the painter first met, nor whether it was Charpentier, Mademoiselle de Guise, Madame de Guise, or Monsieur Du Bois who came up with the idea. The second collaboration with Le Brun came in February 1687, a mass organized by the Academy of Painting to celebrate Louis XIV's recovery from an anal fistula. (The *Gazette de France*, too, mentioned Charpentier in its description of that particular fête.[15])

Another article alluded to Charpentier's Tenebrae music[C] performed at the ABBAYE-AUX-BOIS during Holy Week of 1680. This corpus seems to have been a gift to the convent where VALLANT was physician, ÉTIENNE LOULIÉ's sister was a nun, and two of MONSIEUR DU BOIS' friends resided.

April 1681 marked the start of a series of articles linking Charpentier to the DAUPHIN. That month PHILIPPE II D'ORLÉANS invited the royal family and the court to a grand fête at his country estate, Saint-Cloud. No sooner had Louis XIV arrived at his brother's château than

[A] Cahier XXIV, H. 499.
[B] Cahier 22, H. 323.
[C] Cahiers 26–27, H. 96–110.

he furloughed all his own musicians; and until his return to Saint-Germain, he would listen only to Monseigneur the Dauphin's Music. Every day the music sung at the mass were motets by Monsieur Charpentier, and His Majesty would listen to no others, no matter what was proposed to him. These motets have been sung for the Dauphin for two years.[16]

In short, Corneille and Donneau knew for a fact that Marc-Antoine Charpentier had begun composing for the Dauphin during the first half of 1679. (This dating is corroborated by the presence of the names of the Pièche sisters[A] in both series of the composer's notebooks for 1679.)

In 1682, for the annual assembly of the Order of the Holy Spirit that was held each January 1, the *Mercure galant* recounted how the DAUPHIN took communion in the chapel at Saint-Germain-en-Laye. "His musicians were heard during the mass. The music was composed by Monsieur Charpentier, whom I have mentioned so often. Mesdemoiselles Pièche demonstrated their fine voices, as usual."[17] The following May, PHILIPPE II D'ORLÉANS again invited the court to Saint-Cloud, and this time the fête lasted the better part of a week. It rained almost continually! Once again Louis XIV furloughed his own musicians, and Charpentier's compositions, sung and played by the Dauphin's Music, were performed in the chapel, to which "all the lords and ladies, all dressed up, often came two or three hours before the scheduled mass."[18]

In 1683 the *Mercure galant* informed readers that Charpentier had fallen ill and had been forced to withdraw from the competition for two sub-masterships at the royal chapel: "Sieur Charpentier was very sick" when the time came for the fifteen candidates to be locked up in a room to compose their masterpiece: "He therefore could not participate in the contest."[19] Not long after that, the *Mercure* pointed out that the composer's services to the Dauphin had ended:

I want to inform you that the King ... gave Monsieur Charpentier a pension. You know he always composed the music that was sung at Monseigneur the Dauphin's mass, whenever that prince did not attend the King's mass. Since I have told you about him whenever his music caused a stir, I have nothing more to say.[20]

(It was Jean-Baptiste Colbert who determined which names that would appear on a royal pension list, just as it apparently was he who decided, early in 1679, that the DAUPHIN would be allowed to engage Charpentier as his composer and pay him from his *menus plaisirs*. In fact, two of the

---

[A] Cahier 22, H. 170 ("Demoiselles Pieches") and cahier XXV, H. 174 ("Piesches").

notebooks containing works for the Dauphin's Music[A] were made from paper with Colbert's coat of arms as a watermark.)

The seemingly routine, offhand statement about Charpentier's pension is generally quoted outside its broader context—a long discussion of the state of French opera in 1683 and the disadvantages of Lully's monopoly over the genre.[21] Coated with honey to make it somewhat more palatable, the article was a scathing and quite ironic attack against the Florentine. Its point of departure was a little "opera in the form of a concert, that [Academician Perrault] wrote to entertain his friends," with Claude Oudot supplying the music:

> Some people said that Monsieur Lully was to be pitied for having been left to compose every opera, for he had only asked the King for his privilege so that he could teach music to students, as the name 'Academy' suggests, every academy being created to receive the works of those who wish to become better at an art.

True, the journalists continued, operas by novices would doubtlessly lack Lully's consummate mastery, but

> a city like Paris, which appears to be a world in itself, would not be reduced to having only one opera a year, which bothers many music-lovers; because after having seen the same opera fifteen or sixteen times in the space of a month, they are deprived of this diversion for the rest of the year; and this lack of new operas often forces Monsieur Lully to have old ones performed that have been seen for five or six consecutive summers, ... which is not to France's honor.

Indeed, they continued, Paris should be like Venice, with a multitude of different operas each year. (The Mercure's mention of Venice suggests that Charpentier and his friends were corresponding with JACQUES II DALIBERT. Dalibert's proposals to create operas at Turin in 1678 were based upon his experiences in Venice, where he attended operas and talked with Venetian impresarios.[22])

This jab at Lully was followed by an exhortation to other composers to create their own operas, in order to lighten his burden:

> It only remains to exhort those who give such agreeable concerts to work on full operas, not only for their pleasure and for the glory of their country, but so that, by sparing Monsieur de Lully, we will be able to enjoy him longer. I must inform you that, before leaving [for the front] the King gave Monsieur Charpentier a pension ....

[A] Cahiers XXVI and XXVIII.

Following as it does this exhortation to create more operas, without a new paragraph to separate it from the broader argument, the allusion to Charpentier and his pension was to be read within the context of a thinly veiled challenge to Lully. Charpentier heeded his friends' exhortation, producing a number of works that he boldly called "operas." The first was *Actéon*, performed in the spring or summer of 1684 and revised for the fall hunting season. (Its title calls it a "pastorale in music," but it begins with an "overture to the opera *Actéon*"). Then came *Les Arts florissants, Opéra*, performed in the summer of 1685, probably for the Academy of the INFANT JESUS; *La Descente d'Orphée aux enfers*, doubtlessly performed at court in 1686,[23] because some members of the Dauphin's Music joined the GREAT GUISE MUSIC (the work is so clearly an opera that no such designation was required); and finally the "opera" *David et Jonathas*, performed a year after Lully's death.

Corneille and Donneau continued to mention their composer friend after he had ceased writing for the Dauphin. Charpentier's name appeared in a description of a memorial mass sung in December 1683 at the LITTLE CARMEL to honor the late QUEEN, who had frequently visited the convent with Madame de Guise:

> A great number of prelates and persons of quality formed the
> assembly, and the nuns of this convent omitted nothing in this
> ceremony, which was doubly sad for them, that could mark their
> pain and their just gratitude. The music, which was very touching,
> was composed by Monsieur Charpentier.[24]

(Since the Florentine agent's correspondence confirms that Madame de Guise was in Paris at the time, she almost certainly was one of the "persons of quality" attending the service. By refraining from naming her and other illustrious mourners, the journalists could name the composer.)

After a few years of silence about Charpentier, in March 1688 the *Mercure* praised the "opera" he had written for the College of Louis-le-Grand. The article summarized the public facet of the composer's career to date and almost gleefully categorized the work as an "opera":

> I want to tell you about three operas. One was performed for the
> Jesuits on February 28. ... In addition to the tragedy of Saul, which
> was recited in Latin verse, there was one with French poetry entitled
> *David et Jonathas*; and since this verse was put to music, this work
> was rightly called an opera. One cannot receive more applause than
> it did, both during rehearsals and during the performance. The
> music was by Monsieur Charpentier, whose works have always had
> very great success. The play *Circé*, and those of *Le Malade imaginaire*
> and *L'Inconnu*, for which he wrote the music, as well as several other

[plays], are the proof. One could say that if what he did in those works was approved by so many people, they would have been even more pleasing had they been performed by the finest voices and in greater number. For a long time he worked for the Dauphin, at the time when this prince had a daily private mass, his studies preventing him from attending the King's mass. The rewards that [Charpentier] received, mark their satisfaction with him. He lived for a long time at the Hôtel de Guise, and he did some things for Mademoiselle de Guise's Music that were very highly esteemed by the most able connoisseurs. He composes perfectly well in Italian, and the Italian songs in the plays I mentioned above prove it. Also, he learned music in Rome under Carissimi, who was the most esteemed music master of Italy, and under whom the late Lully[25] also studied this fine art. The poetry of this opera by Monsieur Charpentier was by Father Chamillard. ... One need only read the verse to know that this father is no less skilled in the delicacy of French poetry than he is in Latin verse.[26]

This article typifies the *Mercure*'s portrayal of Marc-Antoine Charpentier. It reflects primarily the "extraordinary" facets of his career that had been allowed to become public knowledge. It tells of his training in Rome and his work for the Dauphin. Now that Lully was dead, the journalists dared to employ the word "opera" and to allude to the restrictions that the Florentine had imposed for the troop's principal "machine plays," *Le Malade imaginaire*, *Circé*, and *L'Inconnu*.

The article adds something new, however—something the informed public knew but that the press could not mention until 1688. For the first and only time, the *Mercure galant* told of the composer's longtime protection by MADEMOISELLE DE GUISE. (It should be noted that his name never was associated publicly with MADAME DE GUISE's.) Between 1677 and 1688, whenever the journalists said that one or more of the members of the Houses of Guise or Orléans had attended an event involving "lovely music," they were careful not to name the composer. The above allusion to Mademoiselle de Guise appears in the same issue as her obituary; but even then a proper distance is maintained between the princess and the protégé. Her Highness's obituary, with its reference to her fine Music—and its silence about Marc-Antoine Charpentier—came first. A dozen pages later came the article about Charpentier and his opera, with its reference to the last Guise. If Corneille and Donneau mentioned her at last, it was because she was dead and the GREAT GUISE MUSIC was being disbanded.

Nor was Charpentier named in articles that praise musical events organized by a duke, a prelate, an abbess. For example, the *Feste de Ruel*,[A] which was summarized at length in the *Mercure*,[27] honored the DUKE OF RICHELIEU and the centenary of the birth of his illustrious granduncle, Cardinal Richelieu. Hence it would have been inappropriate to name the composer. The lengthy and very detailed article about the thanksgiving mass[B] celebrated at Montmartre for Louis XIV's recovery[28] honored Mademoiselle de Guise's "generosity." Thus the composer could not be named. The mass sung at Port-Royal[C] and praised in the *Mercure*,[29] honored ARCHBISHOP HARLAY and his sister, the ABBESS OF PORT-ROYAL. The composer was not named.

Similar conventions were observed once Charpentier had been named music master for one or another of the THREE JESUIT HOUSES. Articles about regularly scheduled services at Saint-Louis sometimes alluded to music but usually did not name the composer. If Charpentier's name was dropped, it tended to occur in an article about a special event —for example, the "opera" performed at the College in early 1688.

This focus on special commissions, and this silence about day-to-day obligations, characterizes the *Mercure galant*'s final articles about Charpentier. In April 1691 Corneille and Donneau told of Tenebrae services[D] at the College of Louis-le-Grand. Charpentier's music

> appeared admirable and continually increased the attendance at the
> church of the College of Louis-le-Grand, to hear the Tenebrae sung
> there on the three accustomed days. This music is all the more
> impressive because it expressed perfectly the content of the words
> being sung, and made their emotional force understandable.[30]

In 1692 came praise for his music for the Feast of Saint Louis[31] on August 25: "The music, which was by Monsieur Charpentier, charmed the entire assembly, particularly a motet[E] composed especially for this feast day. One cannot add anything to the reputation he acquires day after day."[32] Although copied into the series of "ordinary" compositions, the motet was so special a creation that the journalists could not refrain from praising their composer friend.

In April 1695, the *Mercure* described another special event, the funeral mass[F] for the Duke of Luxembourg at the Jesuit Church of Saint-

---

[A] Cahiers XLVII–XLVIII, H. 485, H. 440.
[B] Cahier LI, H. 196; and cahier 50, H. 431.
[C] Cahier LI, H. 5.
[D] Cahier LV, H. 120–122?
[E] Cahier 63, H. 418?
[F] Cahier LXVIII, H. 10, H. 269?

Louis.[33] The church "was all hung in black from the top of the capitals to the floor." All exterior light having been blocked out, "the church was lighted only by tapers and candles." The words of the officiating prelate were "answered by a great number of the best musicians of Paris. It was composed by Monsieur Charpentier." A related special commission had been mentioned a month earlier. The students of the Jesuit college of Rennes had performed a three-act play, the lost *L'Apothéose de Laodomas à la mémoire de M. le Maréchal Duc de Luxembourg*, "with incidental music appropriate to the subject, whose words were found very agreeable, as well as the music composed by Monsieur Charpentier."[34]

The editors of the *Mercure galant* continued to observe these conventions after the composer left the Jesuits for the SAINTE-CHAPELLE. Every November[35] they would inform their readers that Parlement had opened and that Charpentier had composed the music for the event—known as the "Red Mass" because the parlementaires wore their splendid red robes that day. This was an extracurricular duty for which the musicians and the master of the Sainte-Chapelle were remunerated by the judges and barristers. The composer could therefore be named.

Donneau de Visé had begun losing his sight in around 1700. By 1703 he referred to the eye problems that had been afflicting him for the past year. In November he apologized for the typographical errors that had found their way into the volume, owing to his proofreader's carelessness. The March 1706 issue brought bad news: he was now totally blind—like Thomas Corneille, who had lost his sight in 1704. Eye problems and the journalists' advancing age help explain why the *Mercure galant* failed to mention Charpentier's death in February 1704. Or were they too upset to write their old friend's obituary? In April they compensated for the lacuna by telling their readers about a mass composed and directed by "Monsieur Bernier, music master at the Sainte-Chapelle, in the place of the famous Monsieur Charpentier, who recently died."

As the capitalized names scattered throughout this portrait reveal, each article about Marc-Antoine Charpentier was replete with resonances for his contemporaries—and for his twenty-first-century admirers as well. It suffices to know how to read the little facts.

V

There is a concert almost every day

THE GUISE MUSIC

The Core Trio and the Great Guise Music

The press did not talk about the young musicians who performed at the Hôtel de Guise, at the Luxembourg Palace, in various Parisian churches and chapels, and at the court of Louis XIV. Not until March 1688—when the Guise Music was about to disband after MADEMOISELLE DE GUISE's death—were these skilled performers mentioned by Corneille and DONNEAU DE VISÉ, Marc-Antoine Charpentier's friends at the *Mercure galant*. Her Highness, they asserted, "even had her kept Music. This Music was so good that one can say that the ensembles of several great sovereigns do not come close to it." A month earlier, when the princess had become bedridden, they had broken the silence by referring to her Music: "This splendor-loving princess has a very good Music, and there is a concert at her residence almost every day."[1] Still, they had not dared to mention Charpentier.

Mademoiselle de Guise's testament and the papers of her estate confirm that the musicians mentioned in 1688 were the same individuals whom Charpentier named throughout his arabic-numbered notebooks, 1684–1687.[A] Their names also appear in some of the roman-numbered notebooks for those years, performing a few Latin motets and vernacular pastorales, most of the latter celebrating the birth of the INFANT JESUS.[B]

Archival documents provide some crucial information that Charpentier's manuscripts conceal: these musicians were very young. Many of the performers of 1688 had entered Mademoiselle de Guise's service in the early 1680s as adolescents.[2] This clear preference for youthful voices

---

[A] Cahiers 41–50.
[B] Cahiers XLII–XLIII, H. 412; cahier XLIV, H. 482; cahiers XLIV–XLVI, H. 483, H. 484; cahiers XLVIII–XLIX, H. 483b; cahiers XLIX–L, H. 483b, H. 195.

suggests that the Guise Music was shaped by the same esthetic as the King's Chapel:

> Everyone present ... said to themselves that they had never heard better singing. ... Mademoiselle de Lalande is only fifteen. One has never heard a bigger voice than hers. It has an unparalleled sweetness and is totally flexible. She has a lightness in her throat and a cleanness that it would be difficult to describe, with a marvelous rhythm, accompanied by an admirable pronunciation that comes from the fact that she knows several languages. And what is admirable, and is found in few people, is that one scarcely notices her open her mouth to sing, while most singers who sing things that demand a great deal of expression cannot give everything that is required without grimacing.[3]

Owing to the musicians' youth, song in the Guise chapels presumably was light, sweet, and agile. The singers' technique was faultless, because the princess had hired a highly reputed singing teacher named Montailly; and MONSIEUR DU BOIS was there to ensure that their Latin pronunciation would be impeccable.

These skilled young people of the 1680s were not the musicians who had worked with Charpentier and PHILIPPE GOIBAUT DU BOIS to develop the Guise Music during the mid- and late-1670s, and who in 1675 began performing the oratorios that Charpentier wrote for small ensembles.[A] Rather, the singers of the 1680s constitute a final flourish—what in this gallery is known as the "Great Guise Music." This expanded ensemble represents the culmination of an adventure that began with a small group of musically talented domestics that either already existed when Du Bois came to the Guise household in 1666, or was created shortly after his arrival. By 1688 the Guise Music rivaled or surpassed the ensembles kept by a grand duke of Tuscany, an abdicated queen of Sweden, a king of England, an elector of Bavaria.

When Charpentier came to the Hôtel de Guise late in 1669, he appears to have been confronted by a very small group of talented domestics with whom Du Bois had been working for two or three years. Thus he probably had little or no control over the combination of voices and instruments for which he was expected to compose. One factor did work in his favor: in view of MADAME DE GUISE's rank as a "granddaughter of France," the musician-chambermaids conformed to the ideal embodied in the maid of honor to the wife of her first cousin, PHILIPPE II D'ORLÉANS: "She is attractive, and she knows Italian, sings with ease,

---

[A] For example, cahier 12, H. 393, cahier 13, H. 394, cahier 14, H. 395.

dances becomingly, and loves instrumental music with a passion. She plays the harpsichord, theorbo, and guitar very well."[4]

Conforming to that ideal did not necessarily mean that these early performances were impeccable. In fact, the nascent Guise Music probably resembled that of another duchess, whose Music was composed of her almoner, her equerry (who had been a page in the King's Music), her valet, and two of her maids-in-waiting. At a mass attended by the Queen Mother, these householders performed pieces not unlike the ones Marc-Antoine Charpentier would compose for the Guises over the years: "This Music sang a very fine motet, a little *élévation* for the precious body of My God, and a *Domine salvum fac Regem*, all with very accurate and fine voices. The girls' [voices] trembled a bit, but it was not disagreeable."[5]

Nothing suggests that Marc-Antoine Charpentier had a say in selecting the new performers who entered Mademoiselle de Guise's service during the late 1670s and early 1680s. Rather, he worked with the raw materials given him. When writing for the householders of 1670—and for the succession of teenagers who gradually found their way into this group portrait of the Guise Music—the composer had to nourish their raw talents and treat them tactfully and gently, so that skills would blossom. He had to make the best of the vocal timbres and ranges of each singer, just as he had to take into account the instrumentalists' dexterity. Above all, he had to avoid vocal or instrumental lines that could not be performed to perfection, for the least error on a musician's part would be a public humiliation for the princesses.

The contours of this small group of amateur performers can be glimpsed in Charpentier's first arabic-numbered notebooks of 1670, which contain pieces for lay musicians.[A] That is to say, these compositions call for recorders, and there is no evidence that nuns played that instrument, even in the most lax of the female religious orders.

The performers of these first works almost certainly were three of MADEMOISELLE DE GUISE's or MADAME DE GUISE's chambermaids, joined by two recorder-playing valets and by MONSIEUR DU BOIS on the viol. Save for the wind instruments, the makeup of the ensemble was very much like the one for which Mademoiselle de Guise's sister, the ABBESS OF MONTMARTRE, prided herself. Still, they were clearly lay musicians, for along with a high soprano voice (*haut-dessus*) and a somewhat lower soprano (*dessus*), there were one or two recorders plus MONSIEUR DU BOIS

[A] Cahiers 1 and 2, H. 306 (for Saint Bernard of Clairvaux) and H. 307 (for Saint Augustine); cahier 1, H. 91–93 (Tenebrae).

Dame qui joüe de la Viole en chantant.

Elle sçait marier fort agréablement   Et peut auec cet art obliger un Amant
La beauté de sa voix, auec sa Viole ;   De se faire Écolier d'une si douce École,

A lady sings as she accompanies herself on the treble viol.
Some of Marc-Antoine Charpentier's pieces for the Guise Music mention
these "little viols." This lady is trying to charm a lover: *Elle sçait marier fort
agréablement la beauté de sa voix avec sa Viole; Et peut avec cet art obliger un Amant
De se faire Écolier d'une si douce École.*

playing his bass viol. Treble viols, presumably played by girls, sometimes were used instead of recorders.

By Lent of 1673, when the Music resumed singing after a year and a half of mourning for LOUIS-JOSEPH, DUKE OF GUISE and the DOWAGER DUCHESS OF ORLÉANS, the composition of the group changed.[A] During the hiatus, the woman with the very low voice had left the ensemble. She may have been Mademoiselle de Guise's chambermaid daughter, Marie Naudot, who began her noviciate at Montmartre in around 1673.[6] Or perhaps she was one of MADAME DE GUISE's chambermaids and followed her mistress to the Luxembourg Palace that spring. Her place was taken by a woman with the somewhat higher voice known as a *bas-dessus*, a mezzo-soprano.

One or perhaps two new sopranos had entered Mademoiselle de Guise's service and were preparing devotions for the Virgin,[B] and some Tenebrae music[C] for Holy Week 1673—almost certainly at MONTMARTRE, where the two Guise princesses were in retreat in order to prepare themselves spiritually for the mass that would mark the end of their mourning for Madame de Guise's mother. The wife of PHILIPPE II D'OR-LÉANS was borne in a litter to hear these Tenebrae on Wednesday, April 28.[7] Having written each part with the specific strengths and weaknesses of the singer in mind, Charpentier identified the girls: "Mademoiselle B" (*haut-dessus*) was to perform with "Mademoiselle T" (*dessus*) in the new *Ave regina cœlorum*; and "Mademoiselle Magdelon" (*haut-dessus*) and "Mademoiselle Margot" (*dessus*) were to sing a *Misererei* and a *Recordare* during Tenebrae.

It is difficult to say which of several possible Marguerites and Magdelaines were nicknamed "Margot" or "Madelon." There was Marguerite de Mornay, who in the spring of 1672 decided to leave Mademoiselle de Guise's service for convent life, but whose actual date of departure is not known.[8] There was also a chambermaid named Magdeleine Boisseau, who could conceivably be both "Magdelon" and "Mademoiselle B." And there was Marguerite-Agnès de la Bonnodière, who remained in Mademoiselle de Guise's service until 1688, at which time she was described as a "maid of honor." In short, the identity of some of these singers and instrumentalists will probably never be known.

One of the newcomers of 1673 is however identifiable. "Mademoiselle T" was Isabelle Thorin, a chambermaid in her late teens who performed until the dissolution of the Great Guise Music in 1688, when she was

---

[A] Cahier 5, H. 18.
[B] Cahier 5, H. 19.
[C] Cahier 6, H. 157, H. 95.

listed as the senior female musician. Isabelle almost always sang a *dessus* part.

Isabelle Thorin's arrival at the Hôtel de Guise was the first step toward a stellar ensemble. Then, in October 1673, nineteen-year-old ÉTIENNE LOULIÉ was "permitted" to leave the SAINTE-CHAPELLE, where he had been receiving a solid education in musical theory and musical practice. There is no evidence that he sang. Rather, he played recorder, viol, and keyboard. Loulié remained with the Guise Music until it disbanded in 1688, at which time he was the senior male musician. The arrival of this skilled instrumentalist coincides with the composition of four preludes for two treble instruments and continuo.[A]

Three more male musicians joined the Music in 1674: Pierre Beaupuis, a bass; Toussaint Colin, an instrumentalist; and Henri De Baussen, who usually sang tenor. All of them were Loulié's age, and all were awarded similar legacies for length of service in Her Highness's will of 1688. It would be surprising if one or another of these singers did not also play the recorder or the viol. Taking advantage of the variety provided by these newcomers, during the summer of 1674 Charpentier composed briefly for a male trio consisting of *haute-contre*, tenor (De Baussen), and bass (Beaupuis), sometimes accompanied by two treble instruments, perhaps recorders, perhaps small viols.[B] Since Charpentier sang the *haute-contre* part with the Great Guise Music during the early 1680s, the *haute-contre* of the 1670s was presumably the composer himself. His regular participation in the Music appears to have been considered inappropriate, or perhaps it displeased someone. At any rate, this *haute-contre* promptly disappeared from the notebooks and did not return until the early summer of 1677, when DU BOIS was ill for several months.[C]

The first half of 1676 brought what would become the signature vocal combination of the Guise Music—what this portrait gallery calls the "Core Trio": two sopranos (*haut-dessus* and *dessus*) performed with a bass, two treble instruments, and continuo.[D] This rather atypical combination of voices is probably explained as much by the personnel available in 1676 as by esthetic preferences. Still, the results clearly pleased both Her Highness and Du Bois, and for the next decade this "Core Trio" dominated the Guise Music. (For MADAME DU BOIS' funeral in May 1676,

---

[A] Cahier 7, H. 509–12.
[B] Cahier 8, H. 159, H. 20.
[C] Cahiers 16–17, H. 23 (with two other males), H. 319 (with a woman and a man), H. 320 and H. 321 (a pair of solos for *haute-contre* and two treble instruments, probably for the MERCY). For larger choral events *haute-contres* were, of course, used in the chorus, and they sometimes sang solo or in a trio.
[D] Cahier 12, H. 163.

Gentil-homme jouant de la violle.

Ce galant veut charmer auec son instrument   Mais quoy que dans ses airs eclate la tendresse
Les tourments que luy cause vne fiere maitresse   Elle n'egale pas ce que son cœur ressent.

Chez IBonnart vis auis les Mathurins au coq auec priuil'. 1689.

A gentleman playing the viol.
Both Philippe Goibaut du Bois, the Guises' chapel master, and Étienne Loulié,
a member of the Guise Music, played this instrument. The gallant young man
in this illustration strives to please his sweetheart: *Ce galant veut charmer
avec son instrument Les tourments que luy cause une fière maîtresse, Mais quoy
que dans ses airs éclate la tendresse, Elle n'égale pas ce que son cœur ressent.*

Charpentier wrote a *Pie Jesu*[A] for this combination of musicians.) Within the Guise Music, which by then had increased to a total of five singers, another permutation was however possible. For devotional events where female voices would have been inappropriate, the bass was joined by an *haute-contre* (Charpentier) and a tenor (De Baussen).

Irrespective of whether the Core Trio resulted from a conscious preference for this particular blend of vocal ranges, or whether Charpentier and Du Bois had to make do with what the princesses sent their way, the appearance of this group in the notebooks coincides with a changed focus for the devotions of the two Guise women. The spring of 1676 marked the end of mourning for MADAME DE GUISE's son. Having recently obtained chapels in the churches of the THEATINES and the MERCY, having lent their moral and even financial support to two educational ventures placed under the protection of the INFANT JESUS, and having prepared lodgings for themselves at MONTMARTRE, MADEMOISELLE DE GUISE and MADAME DE GUISE proceeded to worship to music in one or another of these venues.

It doubtlessly was to improve the quality of the Core Trio that young Geneviève De Brion, an extremely gifted *haut-dessus* born in 1665, came to the Hôtel de Guise as a chambermaid in the late 1670s, when she was just entering her teens. There she joined another adolescent newcomer, Anne Jacquet. Anne apparently played an instrument—doubtlessly the harpsichord, for she was the sister of Élisabeth Jacquet (the future "Jacquet de La Guerre"), who at the age of ten had astonished the royal court with her singing and keyboard improvisations.

In late 1675 one or both of the Guise princesses set Marc-Antoine Charpentier to composing rather elaborate devotional works. Quite a few of them were oratorios for ensembles so large[B] that they must have been composed of hired musicians. The scant available evidence suggests that these ambitious works were sponsored by MADAME DE GUISE, who is known to have called upon the King's Music at the time of her husband's and her mother's deaths, and who apparently began turning to this royal ensemble for some of her special musical devotions in 1675. There is no evidence that the Guise chambermaids and male musicians participated in these grand events. For them, Charpentier composed a whole corpus of pieces for the two sopranos and a bass that now typified music in the Guises' private chapels. Works for the Core Trio can to be found in

[A] Cahier 12, H. 427.
[B] This trend began in cahier 9 with *Judith sive Bethulia* (H. 391).

Fille de qualité joüant du Clavessin.

A young noblewoman playing the harpsichord.
Guise musicians Étienne Loulié and, in all probability, Anne Jacquet played
keyboard instruments. Madame de Guise played the harpsichord as a girl. Her
apartment at Alençon contained a harpsichord. Madame de Toscane was
a serious harpsichordist and played daily at Montmartre. Whether Mademoiselle
de Guise played the harpsichord in her music room has not been determined.

Charpentier's arabic-numbered notebooks from 1675 all the way to the mid-1680s.

During the early 1680s the Music grew again. This expansion appears related to MADEMOISELLE DE GUISE's loss of a lawsuit with MADEMOISELLE DE MONTPENSIER in early 1681, a humiliation that caused the last Guise to embark on a politics of grandeur. She and Madame de Guise seem to have had a tacit agreement about the musicians. They would be paid from Mademoiselle de Guise's revenues, and they would be remembered in her will. Yet the Music would be allowed to perform for Madame de Guise wherever and whenever Her Royal Highness wished, just as DOCTOR VALLANT and the Guise gardener served both households although they were paid by Mademoiselle de Guise's treasurer. Charpentier would be available for any task that Madame de Guise might give him, just as Vallant was.

The arrangement proved extremely convenient. MADAME DE GUISE was spending much of her time at court, where it would have been inappropriate to maintain her own musicians; and during her summers at Alençon she had no need for musicians more skilled than her own chambermaids, who presumably could sing and play the harpischord or viol. In October 1682 she offered the King the first of several musical entertainments. Charpentier, joined by a few of the Guise musicians, journeyed to Versailles to perform with the Dauphin's Music[9] during the festivities known as the "Fête of the Apartments."[A]

With the creation of this expanded group, whoever had been discouraging Marc-Antoine Charpentier from singing with the Music either relented or began to view the ensemble from a different perspective. Pieces for *haute-contre*, tenor, and bass reappeared in the composer's notebooks.[B] Then, in the summer of 1684, the Great Guise Music appeared in all its splendor—and the composer joined them.[C] From 1682 until Mademoiselle de Guise's death in March 1688, these young and the no-longer-quite-so-young domestics performed at various venues in Paris and at court.[D]

To form the Great Guise Music, Mademoiselle de Guise had hired two young chambermaids in 1681 or 1682: fifteen-year-old Antoinette Talon and sixteen-year-old Jeanne Guyot. She had also taken on, to be

---

[A] Cahier 37, H. 480.
[B] Cahier 33, H. 82 (Litanies of Virgin), late 1681; cahier 38, H. 331–32 (for the MERCY, Sept. 1683?) and H. 471 (*Orphée*).
[C] Cahier 41, H. 333. With H. 75, the next piece in that notebook, the musicians' names begin to appear.
[D] Cahier "II" (probably the missing cahier 48), H. 488 (with the Pièches); and perhaps cahiers 44–45, H. 486.

"near her," seventeen-year-old Marie Guillebault de Grandmaison, whose social rank was just a bit too lofty for her to be a chambermaid. Three men also joined the ensemble: "Joly," who left the household before the summer of 1685; seventeen-year-old Germain Carlier, a bass; and seventeen-year-old François Anthoine, an *haute-contre*. A singing teacher was also engaged: Nicolas Montailly, a pupil of the famed practitioner and teacher of the art of sung declamation, Bénigne de Bacilly. Charpentier began marking their names in his manuscripts, to avoid confusing one *haut-dessus* or one *dessus* with another. (Remember, each vocal and instrumental line presumably was written with the special talents or weaknesses of that particular performer in mind.)

It is not clear who chose these young people. Obviously, they all were unusually talented for their age. On the other hand, the reason why they were selected, in preference to other equally talented young Parisians, is rather clear. Most of these adolescents came from families with longstanding ties to the House of Guise or, somewhat less often, to the House of Orléans.

Isabelle Thorin's arrival at the Hôtel de Guise had coincided with MADAME DE GUISE's decision to move to the Luxembourg Palace. Since the family name Thorin is found in the duchy of Alençon,[10] she perhaps was chosen by Madame de Guise but stayed on at the Hôtel de Guise after Her Royal Highness's departure. Still, a Thorin was the spouse of one of Anne Jacquet's forebears in the 1580s, so a distant cousinship between the two Guise musicians cannot be ruled out. Anne Jacquet[11] herself boasted both Guise and Orléans ties. Her mother's first husband had been GASTON D'ORLÉANS' domestic, but one of her paternal relatives was painter Philippe de Champaigne, who descended from a Guise household officer during the League. In addition, it cannot be ruled out that Mademoiselle Jacquet was related to Guise musician Toussaint Colin, for the Jacquets had Colin cousins.

Antoinette Talon,[12] the daughter of a skilled woodworker, was raised in Madame de Guise's parish of Saint-Sulpice, where MARIE TALON's in-laws, the Voisins, were members of the charitable organization headed by Madame de Guise. No link between Antoinette and Marie Talon has, however, been found. Marie Guillebault, or "Guilbault," de Grandmaison had close relatives in Angers, on the Loire River.[13] She may have been related to Jean Guilbaud, a captain in Duke Henri of Guise's regiment in the late 1650s. Or was she related to ÉTIENNE LOULIÉ, the Guise musician, who had sword-polisher cousins named Guillebault?

Jeanne Guyot[14] was for all intents and purposes an orphan, for her father became a priest after her mother's death. Her mother was née Dupin, but it is not clear whether she was related to the guardian of

ARMAND-JEAN CHARPENTIER and his brother Marc-Antoine. (Were the Guyots old friends of the Charpentiers? The name is extremely common, but a Madame Guyot owed money to LOUIS CHARPENTIER THE SCRIVE-NER.[15]) Or was Jeanne Guyot related to one of the Guyots who were administering the barony of Ancerville for Mademoiselle de Guise? It is not clear whether Geneviève De Brion[16] had any affective links to either Mademoiselle de Guise or Madame de Guise. Was she distantly related to Marc-Antoine Charpentier? It cannot be ruled out, for Brion was the name of the tawer son-in-law of PASQUIER CHARPENTIER THE MEASURER.

The male musicians likewise appear to have been selected on the basis of family ties to the House of Guise or the House of Orléans. There is tantalizing evidence to suggest that ÉTIENNE LOULIÉ was a distant cousin of Marc-Antoine Charpentier's cousins, the CROYERS.[17] The grandfather of Pierre Beaupuis[18] came from a town only thirteen kilometers from Guise. Was Toussaint Colin[19] related to an official in the Guise barony of Ancerville? Or to Guise musician Anne Jacquet? Or was he related to the household officer who had supervised the pantry of the late Duke Henri and was still owed large amounts of money? With so common a family name, tracing potential links is almost impossible.

Germain Carlier's paternal grandfather[20] had lived in Ribemont, just seventeen kilometers from Guise, and his father had been closely linked to GASTON D'ORLÉANS in 1650. In the late 1670s Germain's brother become a religious at the MERCY, where not only the Guises but also the Bailleuls and Madame HAVÉ DE SAINT-AUBIN worshiped. François Anthoine[21] may be related to Jean Anthoine, a Parisian who was doing business with the Guise officers at Joinville in the mid-1660s. Any affective ties underlying Henri De Baussen's[22] selection have not been determined. Montailly[23] was a hired teacher, rather than a domestic.

In 1688 all these young people were named in Mademoiselle de Guise's will. By then Isabelle Thorin was a mature woman and was presumed to be too old to marry. Thus, as senior musician, she received both a cash legacy (5,000 livres) and a pension (300 livres). Jacquet and De Brion were willed 5,000 livres in cash each, and their juniors got 4,000 livres. The men were less amply rewarded. For fifteen years of service, Loulié, Beaupuis, Colin, and De Baussen were given 3,000 livres each. The more recent arrivals, Carlier and Anthoine, were awarded 2,000 livres. Montailly got a pension of 300 livres.

The musicians had to wait for a year for a partial payment of their legacies. When the money was paid, the young women used it for their dowries. Geneviève De Brion wed royal musician Pierre Pièche, a member of the DAUPHIN's Music during Charpentier's service to the prince. She soon was admitted to the King's Music. Anne Jacquet moved to her husband's home town of Joinville and gave birth to a son who grew up to be an organist. ÉTIENNE LOULIÉ first taught music to PHILIPPE III D'ORLÉANS, next conducted research on what would come to be the science of acoustics, then wrote several handbooks on musical theory, and ended his days supervising musical copyists and investigating "early" music. Henri De Baussen became a skilled music engraver, having doubtlessly acquired a facile musical hand while copying partbooks for the Guise Music. Pierre Beaupuis performed with the Opera and for the Jesuits during Charpentier's tenure there. He died old and penniless. Germain Carlier did not survive beyond the early 1690s. The other musicians either went on to live uneventful lives, or disappeared from view after their brief moment in the sun.

Panel 7

DISCREET COMMISSIONS
IN PRESTIGIOUS LOCALES

Their Devotion Shaped His Creativity
but He Was Rarely Mentioned

Six paintings hang in this panel. Each portrays one or another Parisian convent inhabited by clerics wearing the distinctive habits of their order. In the background of each picture looms one of the churches that stud Paris. To these edifices well-dressed worshipers hasten, as if anxious to find somewhere to sit.

Prosp. de l'Eglise des Religieux de la Mercy
Auprés l'Hostel de Guise

The Mercedarian Convent of Notre-Dame de la Mercy.
In the foreground is the medieval entry door of the Hôtel de Guise, shown as a ruin. The rue de Braque runs along the right side of the church. In the 1660s Nicolas de Bailleul and Elisabeth Grimaudet, friends of the Charpentier family, lived on the rue de Braque.

I

All she gave us was three hundred livres

THE MERCY:
OUR LADY OF MERCY AND RANSOM

The Mercedarian convent of Notre-Dame de la Mercy
et de la Rédemption des Captifs, on the rue du Chaume

After the little Duke of Alençon's death in 1675, each grieving
Guise princess turned to a monastic community that had been
protected by a woman with whom she had an affective bond. In
a sense, each princess was picking up and re-knotting a thread that had
loosened after the death of the convent's benefactress. MADEMOISELLE DE
GUISE chose a convent run by a Spanish order, the Mercedarians. The
convent of Our Lady of Mercy and of the Ransom of Captives, known
familiarly as "*La Mercy*," had been created in 1613 through the efforts of
her godmother, Queen Mother and Regent Marie de Médicis. It stood at
the corner of the rue du Chaume and the rue de Braque, just opposite
the medieval entrance door of the Hôtel de Guise.

Construction of the convent had dragged on for two decades, but the
church was finally dedicated in 1657. The masters and householders of
the Hôtel de Guise had offered decorative objects to embellish the new
church: a stained-glass window from Duke Henri, altar hangings from
different Guise princesses, and paintings and ornaments from Guise
officers. Other donors included President Nicolas de Bailleul who, prior
to his death in 1652, had offered a black chasuble bearing his arms; and
his son, Louis de Bailleul, who would give a processional banner in 1674.[1]
In 1664 Marc-Antoine Charpentier's own cousin, Madame HAVÉ DE
SAINT-AUBIN, founded a series of masses there; and in 1672 a somewhat
more distant CROYER cousin founded other masses.[2]

As its name suggests, devotions at Notre-Dame de la Mercy centered
upon the Virgin Mary, especially during the week in mid-August that

brought both the Feast of the Assumption (August 15) and the Feast of Our Lady of Mercy (celebrated on the Sunday closest to the Assumption).

The Mercy quickly gained a reputation for the fine and often innovative music performed there, under the sponsorship of private individuals. In 1658 a certain Monsieur Bernard, who would be one of the principal benefactors of the Mercy for the next decade, sponsored a "concert in music" to honor Louis XIV. The music, which was "sweet and beautiful," was performed by "Messieurs de La Barre and Bertaut" (Berthod was a soprano castrato), and by "several of the chanters of the said convent of the Mercy, too."[3] In other words, not only were some of the Mercy fathers skilled at plainsong, they sometimes joined lay singers for special events.

In 1659, motets by Henri Du Mont were performed in the splendid new church.[4] At around the same time,

> Monsieur X– went into debt to give vespers services to his mistresses. To do so, he used the rood screen of the fathers of the Mercy, opposite the Hôtel de Guise. Everyone ... talked about these vespers, because they used violins, which one was not accustomed to hear in churches at the time.[5]

In August 1660, Bernard sponsored a lavish service for the Feast of Saint Raymond Nonat, honoring simultaneously this Mercedarian saint and Louis XIV's wedding. The service included a *Te Deum* and "a partsong motet, admirably harmonic ... invented by Baptiste," that is, Jean-Baptiste Lully, and performed by "a great number of the most beautiful voices, along with the [King's] twenty-four violins and other instruments." In addition to Louis XIV's mother and bride, the guests included ISABELLE D'ORLÉANS OF ALENÇON and her sisters.[6] Four years later, for the same feast day, a *Te Deum* by an unnamed composer was begun in plainsong by the Mercedarians and finished in music.[7]

The Mercy exerted a pull on MADEMOISELLE MARIE DE GUISE that went beyond mere proximity to the Hôtel de Guise. Not only had she been born on the Feast of the Assumption, the most solemn day of the Mercy's liturgical year, but her godmother, Queen Marie de Médicis, had founded the convent. Still more compelling for a devotee of the Virgin was the fact that the Mercy was considered "the ornament" of Marian devotions in Paris[8]—far more so than the THREE JESUIT HOUSES with their confraternities of the Virgin, and far more than the Benedictines, the Cistercians, or even the Capuchins who had been brought to France by Mademoiselle de Guise's maternal grandfather, Ange de Joyeuse.

There is no evidence that the princess had forged a close personal or devotional bond with the convent prior to LOUIS-JOSEPH DE LORRAINE's death in August 1671. Such a bond cannot, of course, be ruled out. Indeed, she may well have joined the Confraternity of the Scapulary of Our Lady of Mercy[9] when she moved into the renovated Hôtel de Guise in 1667. If she did belong to this confraternity, her nephew apparently did not; for when the Mercedarians marched in the young Duke's funeral procession in 1671, it was "in gratitude for the favors received on several occasions" from the House of Guise,[10] rather than in sorrow for the loss of a specific member of their flock.

In August 1672 a devotional bond between the convent and the princess became official. A "lady" described as being a "person of quality" was instrumental in creating a Confraternity for the Dying Sick, *malades agonisants*, and in obtaining indulgences "at a privileged altar, in favor of the faithful dead."[11] (The term "person of quality" was used exclusively to denote noblemen and women, and the only true noblewoman mentioned in the Mercy's archives for the 1670s and 1680s is Mademoiselle de Guise.)

The rapidity with which Her Highness's bond to the Mercedarians developed can be deduced from Marc-Antoine Charpentier's arabic-numbered notebooks. In April 1674 he composed a mass for instruments "in the place of" an organ.[A] The story of the crisis that threatened the Mercy's beatification services for Saint Peter Pascual that spring has been told elsewhere.[12] Suffice it to say here that delivery of the church's new organ having been delayed, Charpentier composed a mass where instrumentalists imitated the different stops of the missing organ. MADE-MOISELLE DE GUISE contributed to this event personally by donating the candles and the altar hangings, and she and MADAME DE GUISE attended some if not all the services that week. For these festivities, or perhaps for another service at the Mercy, Marc-Antoine Charpentier composed a psalm and a *Sub tuum præsidium*[B] for high tenor (*haute-contre*), tenor, and bass—a trio that would perform at the Mercy for the next decade. (The vocalists almost certainly were Charpentier himself, singing with De Baussen, and Beaupuis, members of the GUISE MUSIC.)

A year later, only a few months after the death of little Alençon, the last male of the House of Guise, MADEMOISELLE DE GUISE informed the fathers that she "wished to have a chapel in their church," and that the chapel must have a door opening onto the street so that she "would not

---

[A] Cahiers 7–8, H. 513.
[B] Cahier 8, H. 159, H. 20.

have to be seen or pass through the church." The contrast could scarcely be more marked between her ideal chapel and the one that Madame de Guise was then having prepared in the looming transept of the unfinished Italianate church of the THEATINES, known for its lavish devotions sponsored by highborn princesses. Mademoiselle de Guise spent some three thousand livres to renovate her chapel at the Mercy, which—judging from the content of the pieces for small ensembles that Marc-Antoine Charpentier began copying out into his arabic-numbered notebooks—was dedicated either to the Virgin, the INFANT JESUS, or the Mother and the Child together. By mid-1676 the embellishments to the chapel were finished, and the princess's musical devotions began to be reflected in Charpentier's arab-numbered notebooks.

In an apparent response to this new chapel and the devotions conducted there, a cluster of works for two or three singers, sometimes accompanied by instruments, were copied into these Guise notebooks in 1676, 1677, and 1678. In the main, these compositions were appropriate for the vespers of the Virgin and for Her "Little Office" celebrated as matins–lauds[A] and vespers–complins[B] every Saturday at the Mercy.[13] Since two high voices—presumably women rather than choirboys—often sang with a bass, these pieces can scarcely have been written for monks. They were intended for the devotions of a private individual or a sodality.

In fact, many of the texts that Charpentier set to music reflect the lay person's view of the mass or other liturgical services. There is one or another of the familiar psalms commonly recited by worshipers or followed silently in the prayer book as the priest read aloud; there are antiphons and hymns, primarily for vespers; and there are the Litanies of the Virgin known as the Loreto Litanies.[C] There are also numerous *élévations* to be sung during the Elevation, when the host was being lifted, the one part of the mass that the layperson could see clearly and that therefore had special meaning[D]—especially because the *élévation* was a form of adoring prayer that both ISABELLE D'ORLÉANS and MADEMOISELLE DE GUISE are known to have practiced.

[A] Psalms: cahier 12, H. 163, and cahier 37, H. 187; plus cahier 50, H. 345, for the Great Guise Music.
[B] Antiphons and hymns: cahier 16, H. 22, H. 23; cahiers 18-19, H. 287; cahiers 20-21, H. 60; cahier 25, H. 26; cahier 26, H. 27; cahier 32, H. 63; cahiers 41, H. 75. *Domine salvum fac regem*: cahier 13, H. 286; cahier 40, H. 293, H. 294. Psalm: cahier 15, H. 165.
[C] Cahier 33, H. 82; cahiers 41-42, H. 83, for the Great Guise Music.
[D] Cahier 17, H. 239; cahier 21, H. 241; cahier 22, H. 242, H. 243; cahier 24, H. 244, H. 245, H. 246, H. 247; cahier 32, H. 250; cahiers 38-39, H. 252, H. 253; cahier 40, H. 254; cahier 41, H. 255; cahier 50, H. 258.

A smaller proportion of these works were for men: a trio, a duo, a solo voice.[A] These particular pieces presumably were destined for services at a male convent, rather than a female one; and they either were sung by the religious themselves or by members of the GUISE MUSIC, discreetly concealed in a chapel to give the impression that the fathers were singing. One of these works for men is Charpentier's setting, for two male voices (one of them an *haute-contre*, probably the composer himself), of a text approved in March 1679[14] for the Mercedarians' exclusive use. The text was to be chanted on the Feast of Our Lady of Mercy in mid-August.[B]

For the *haute-contre* of this male trio, Charpentier had already written a devotional diptych[C] for August 1677. One piece was a motet for August 10, the Feast of Saint Laurence, when the Mercedarians commemorated the founding of their order with a procession of thanksgiving. The other was a motet for the Feast of Saint Louis, August 25. For the full male trio, he wrote a similar diptych in August 1683: a lament for the late QUEEN MARIE-THÉRÈSE and a companion piece honoring Saint Louis and, through him, Louis XIV.[D] The two works in the latter diptych appear to have been performed at the "solemn mass" in the Queen's memory sung at the Mercy on an unspecified date in August, but probably around August 20, when MADAME DE GUISE came to Paris from Alençon for four days, to attend a service for the Queen.[15] (A few months later the funeral oration given for Marie-Thérèse at the LITTLE CARMEL would be based on a similar diptych: it "contrasted all the King's grand deeds with the pious deeds of the Queen."[16])

A second cluster of Marian compositions appears in Charpentier's arabic-numbered notebooks for 1680, when MADEMOISELLE DE GUISE was preparing to journey with her musicians to the Church of Notre-Dame de Liesse, adjacent to her chateau of Marchais, near Laon. Although these new works for a small ensemble almost certainly were intended to be inaugurated during this progress through her lands, they expanded an existing corpus of music for the Virgin that could be sung in a variety of different venues and be repeated year after year. Indeed, the excursion to Liesse offers proof that Her Highness did not limit her devotions to one venue, nor to a single, exclusive performance in a specific church. Finally, between 1684 and 1687, came a few pieces for the Great Guise Music that correspond to Mademoiselle de Guise's devotions at the Mercy.

[A] Cahier 16, H. 22, H. 23; cahier 26, H. 27; cahier 33, H. 82; cahiers 38–39, H. 252.
[B] Cahier 22, H. 25.
[C] Cahier 17, H. 320, H. 321.
[D] Cahier 38, H. 331, H. 332.

Several sodalities met at the Mercy, among them the Confraternity for the Dying mentioned above, of which the unnamed "lady of quality" was the driving force. The members of this confraternity were, of course, expected to remember the dead in their prayers; but the group's principal mission was to "do many pious and charitable good deeds," and to "pray for peace and concord among the Christian princes, for the extirpation of heresy, and for the exaltation of the Church."[17]

Most of the confraternity's devotions consisted of attending the matins and vespers of the Little Office of the Virgin, as well as the Feast of Our Lady of Mercy in mid-August. Actually, the services mentioned in the handbook for confraternity members overlap the services cited in the rituals and ceremonial books outlining the Mercy's own liturgy. For example, the confraternity handbook states that the group's principal holy day was the Feast of Our Lady of Mercy. In addition to the usual devotions conducted by the fathers, a solemn mass was said on that day at the privileged altar of the Dying; the Litanies of the Virgin[A] were "sung" (as they were at the vespers of the Little Office); the Holy Sacrament was exposed for the entire day, leading up to the Benediction of the Holy Sacrament, *salut*, that ended these festive devotions.

The "same lady" who had created the confraternity had provided for weekly masses for the dead, and for prayers for the dead on the principal Marian feast days. To receive additional benefits, members could attend the "high mass of the Virgin" sung every Saturday morning, as well as a weekly mass for the dead sung on Monday mornings. Members were also advised to "turn to" Saint Mary Magdalene,[B] "who strove to love more, who burned unceasingly in her heart until her last breath, so that we can learn that those who are dying can obtain perfect love" through repentance.[18]

From 1676 and on into 1687, Charpentier's arabic-numbered notebooks reflect the priorities of this confraternity. Of course, not every composition evoking international peace, charity, and the elimination of "heresy" (Protestantism) was written for performance at the Mercy, or exclusively for the Mercy. Many of these compositions were appropriate for other venues as well. And some of them (for example, the oratorio "for peace"[C] and its companion *élévation* of early 1676) required so many musicians that performance in so small a sanctuary as the Mercy would be less than ideal—although the magnificence derived by having the musicians occupy as much space as the elite worshipers might conceivably

---

[A] Cahier 33, H. 82; cahiers 41–42, H. 83.
[B] Cahier 49, H 343.
[C] Cahiers 11–12, H. 392, H. 237.

have outweighed practicality. Even so, these ambitious works almost certainly were commissioned by MADAME DE GUISE.

The program to eliminate "heresy" is reflected in Charpentier's numerous oratorios about Saint Cecilia,[A] the converter of heathens. In sermons given at the Mercy in the 1660s, Cecilia was portrayed as an "alliance" between purity and the temptations of the flesh, a "union" of female weakness and the strength of God's spirit. (In this respect Cecilia had much in common with Judith and Esther, the "strong women" about whom Charpentier would write other oratorios.) The Mercy practiced what it preached, for in May 1661 a Protestant girl converted to Catholicism there, in the presence of a "fine and grand company"—just as another Protestant woman would do in November 1676 at the Jesuit Noviciate, thanks to MADAME DE GUISE's urging; and as a Huguenot girl boarding at MONTMARTRE in the 1680s did at MADEMOISELLE DE GUISE's urging,[19] at an unspecified venue.

The charitable program being emphasized by the new confraternity was similar to that of the Confraternity of Saint Charles Borromeo[B], which had branches not only at Saint-Jacques-de-la-Boucherie but also at the Church of the THEATINES.[20] Members would go out and visit the poor and the sick, and contribute money for food and medications.

This is not to say that one or both Guise princesses, and their composer, contributed music to every devotional activity at the Mercy during these years. For example, Charpentier's arabic-numbered notebooks contain neither a *Te Deum* nor any other music corresponding to the redemption procession in which children dressed as angels led a group of ransomed galley slaves to the Luxembourg Palace in July 1681, where MADAME DE GUISE invited them in. Nor, at first glance, do his notebooks appear to contain music appropriate for the festivities that followed the birth of the Duke of Burgundy in August 1682:

> The fathers of the Mercy, near the Hôtel de Guise, distinguished themselves on Sunday, the thirteenth of this month, by three rounds of explosive charges and by especially inventive fireworks, but above all by a *Te Deum* that the King's Music sang in their church. Mademoiselle de Guise attended, along with a very large number of persons of the highest quality.[21]

That DONNEAU DE VISÉ, Charpentier's friend at the *Mercure galant*, alluded to MADEMOISELLE DE GUISE, suggests that the princess offered music for the event—surely a piece composed by her protégé, who had

---

[A] Cahier 13, H. 394; cahiers 19–20, H. 397; cahier 42, H. 413; cahier 47, H. 415.
[B] Cahier 24, H. 398.

become so illustrious that he was currently composing for the DAUPHIN, the newborn prince's father. A closer look at the arabic-numbered notebooks for that year, reveals that some pages are missing at the start of one notebook: after a fragment[22] comes a *Dominum salvum fac regem*[A] for a large ensemble that could well be the King's Music. Whether the lost pages contained a *Te Deum* must remain a conjecture.

One of Mademoiselle de Guise's final musical devotions at the Mercy took place in 1687, on Holy Saturday.[23] The invited guests were the "distinguished people of the neighborhood." But when the news got out that a "fine concert of voices and instruments" would accompany the service, the little church was besieged by music-lovers who stole the seats reserved for the convent's benefactors. Since it was a Saturday,[24] the liturgy was the Little Office of the Virgin, which, for lauds, included the Song of Zacharias.[B] In the composer's notebooks a setting of that text is followed by a very personal *élévation* that alludes to the Crucifixion.[C]

A year later, Mademoiselle de Guise was dead, the GREAT GUISE MUSIC had disbanded, and the fathers of the Mercy were expressing their disappointment at the legacy from their illustrious benefactress. They had "given" the chapel to her, noted one of the monks, "and all she gave us, when dying, was three hundred livres in annual rents on the Duchy of Guise." (The princess's nine bequests to religious communities ranged from fifty to one thousand livres, for an average of three hundred and fifty livres.[25]) Having gotten wind of the tens and even hundreds of thousands of livres she had willed as lump sums to several abbeys, in order to found seminaries or to help the poor, the Mercedarians felt rejected.

[A] Cahier 33, H. 180 (reused?); cahier 36, H. 291.
[B] Cahier 50, H. 345.
[C] Cahier 50, H. 258.

II

My ears were charmed and my heart was moved

THE THEATINES OF
SAINTE-ANNE-LA-ROYALE

The Theatine church of Sainte-Anne-la-Royale
on the quay near the rue des Saints-Pères

Shortly after her son's death in March 1675, MADAME DE GUISE
approached the Theatine fathers at the convent of Sainte-Anne-la-
Royale, situated on the Left Bank of the Seine, just opposite the
Louvre and the Tuileries. She was seeking a church that could become
the focal point for an unspecified "devotion" that she preferred to
conduct at a considerable distance from her private chapel in the
Luxembourg Palace and her private chapel in her parish church, Saint-
Sulpice. She was not seeking to buy or rent a chapel emblazoned with
her coat of arms. In this church famous for its musical "devotions,"
especially during the Christmas season, she wanted to embellish an
existing chapel, the chapel of the Order's founder, Saint Gaetano of
Thiene.[1]

The Theatine church had just the right devotional resonances for a
"granddaughter of France" whose dynastic links to the House of Guise
had recently been severed, who was intent on proclaiming her ties to the
royal family, and who was anticipating the imminent return to Paris of
her sister, the Grand Duchess of Tuscany, MADAME DE TOSCANE. "Saint
Anne the Royal," *Sainte-Anne-la-Royale*: by its very name the church
created a tie between Madame de Guise and her paternal aunt, Queen
Anne of Austria. In marked contrast to the little church of the MERCY,
where MADEMOISELLE DE GUISE was involved in negotiations for a chapel
where she could worship unobserved, the Theatine church offered
Madame de Guise the grandeur appropriate to her station. It also
provided a touch of Italy that could not fail to please, or at least impress

213

the Grand Duchess. The Italian colony in Paris worshiped there, lingering after services to talk about poetry, music, and things Italian.[2]

In 1644 a group of Theatine fathers had been brought from Italy by Cardinal Mazarin.[A] On July 16, 1648, the eve of the Feast of Saint Anne, Mazarin, Queen Mother Anne of Austria, and little Louis XIV had participated in the festivities that marked the founding of the convent and the installation of the Theatine fathers. The church was named for the Queen Mother.[3] Although Mazarin willed the convent three hundred thousand livres to help build a large Italianate church, the structure was still little more than a vast transept in the 1670s. This had not prevented the Theatines from sponsoring worship services that might more accurately be called devotional entertainments. Indeed, the high altar, with its niche for the Holy Sacrament, was an exercise in perspective, in the manner of a stage setting.

One of the principal devotional events at the church was the annual Advent novena. Each year a Neapolitan-style crêche like the one invented by the Order's founder, Gaetano of Thiene, was set up; and from December 16 until Christmas there was music daily—performed by the King's Music whenever (or because?) members of the royal family were present. For example, in 1660 the Queen and the ladies of the court attended the opening event of this "august devotion," where the Music of the King's Chapel sang; and when the same musicians performed on Christmas Eve, the women were joined by Louis XIV, preceded by one hundred Swiss guards beating their drums. In 1665 the Queen, PHILIPPE II D'ORLÉANS and his wife, and ISABELLE D'ORLÉANS OF ALENÇON lent their prestige to a "solemnity ... made still more famous by the King's Music." In 1666 Mademoiselle d'Alençon represented the Queen and was treated to "excellent music"; and in 1668 this Advent "devotion" was "more august than ever, owing to the ornaments with which the good fathers had embellished their church," to honor the royal family's visit.[4] The decor changed daily, with different tableaux from the Christmas Story being set up and paid for by high noblewomen.

As the 1670s approached, the novena continued to attract the elite of the capital to daily vespers, sermons, and Benedictions of the Holy Sacrament, *saluts*. In 1669 the worshipers included King Casimir of Poland and PHILIPPE II D'ORLÉANS and his wife, who remained for the Benediction "sung by excellent musicians." This annual "devotion" was described as "among the most solemn, owing to the large daily atten-

---

[A] Cahier 9, H. 315 (which may have been in the *gros cahier* in 1726).

dance by persons of the highest quality, and also the one with the most pomp, owing to the care the fathers took to decorate their new church."[5]

The convent's emphasis on the Nativity meshed perfectly with MADAME DE GUISE's principal preoccupation during the first half of 1675: the INFANT JESUS. Not only did the annual novena culminate in Christmas, it coincided with her birthday, December 26—just as the principal mid-August feast days at the MERCY coincided with MADEMOISELLE DE GUISE's birthday and name day, August 15.

There was, perhaps, another link to the Theatines that could bring solace to the two daughters of GASTON D'ORLÉANS. Every October 10 the fathers honored one of their sixteenth-century members, Blessed Andrea Avellino. Having suffered a fatal stroke while celebrating mass, Avellino became a protector from strokes and sudden death. The DOWAGER DUCHESS OF ORLÉANS had suffered a series of small strokes prior to being carried off by a massive one in the spring of 1672. It would have been in Madame de Guise's character to go Sainte-Anne-la-Royale and pray for her mother's recovery, as the latter's worsening health provoked sporadic aphasia and unconsciousness.

Another devotional activity may have attracted MADAME DE GUISE to Sainte-Anne-la-Royale: the charitable Confraternity of Saint Charles Borromeo.[6] She was one of the "princes and princesses, dukes and duchesses, presidents and presidents' wives, and other persons of all ranks" who belonged to this organization that assembled regularly in the different parishes of Paris. If Madame de Guise was not already the "superior" of the charitable association for the parish of Saint-Sulpice when she made her proposal to the Theatine fathers in 1675, within a matter of months she was given that responsibility.[7] Like the other charitable sodalities participating in this citywide movement—among them the recently founded Confraternity of the Dying at the MERCY—the Confraternity of Saint Charles had taken the INFANT JESUS and the Virgin as its protectors. Members met weekly; and after worshiping together they would go out to feed the poor, visit prisoners, and care for the sick. The Confraternity of Saint Charles also worked to convert "heretics" and to help new converts.

One of the most vital figures in this movement was Madame de Miramion, to whom MADAME DE GUISE was extremely close, having recently been swept up in this pious widow's charitable activities. Miramion's correspondence with her own spiritual advisor reveals the importance of Charles Borromeo within the devotional and charitable program she had created. She requested a special communion service and a Benediction the Holy Sacrament on his feast day, for herself and the sisters of charity she directed."[8]

Madame de Guise began chafing at the slowness with which the Theatines were complying with her wishes. On July 7, 1675, she made her dissatisfaction known to the Superior,[9] who promised that the paneled altarpiece proposed by stage-designer Vigarani would be completed by October 7 at the very latest. The altarpiece probably included a new or existing representation of Saint Gaetano, generally depicted carrying the INFANT JESUS.[10]

Marc-Antoine Charpentier's arabic-numbered notebooks suggest the reason for Her Royal Highness's impatience that July. Not only was MADAME DE TOSCANE scheduled to reach Paris in a matter of weeks, but an oratorio, *Judith sive Bethulia*,[A] was being prepared for performance by a large hired ensemble, and the performance was scheduled for late September—probably September 26, 27, or 28. (It was based on texts that were only recited when September had five Sundays, as was the case in 1675.)

Judith was the first of Marc-Antoine Charpentier's oratorios. Madame de Guise's "devotion" clearly involved music, for in the arabic-numbered series of notebooks this initial oratorio was followed by fifteen more, usually for large ensembles but sometimes for the Core Trio[B] of the GUISE MUSIC. (By contrast, no oratorio was copied into the roman-numbered notebooks until 1681.) The composer himself did not use the Italian term. Rather, he often called this sort of work a *canticum*, "song." That the texts of these oratorios are in Latin, rather than in the vernacular, shows unequivocally that these works were destined for the elite.

The earliest of these oratorios extol "strong women," *femmes fortes*, with whom Anne of Austria had been paralleled in 1661, that is, women who had agreed to be God's tools.[C] These presentations of strong women were followed by oratorios about incidents in the lives of Saint Cecilia and Saint Charles Borromeo, thereby paralleling MADAME DE GUISE's charitable and converting activities.[D] Three oratorios honor the Virgin[E] or tell of Christmas or Epiphany,[F] key feasts for the Confraternity of Saint Charles, and for devotees of the INFANT JESUS as well. One oratorio prays for peace among the nations of Europe,[G] a goal espoused by several

---

[A] Cahiers 9–11, H. 391.
[B] Cahier 12, H. 393; cahier 13, H. 394; cahier 14, H. 395.
[C] Cahiers 9–11, H. 391; cahiers 17–18, H. 396.
[D] Cahier 13, H. 394 (probably performed at Jesuit Noviciate); cahiers 19–20, H. 397; cahier 24, H. 398; cahier 42, H. 413; cahier 47, H. 415.
[E] Cahiers 29–30, H. 400.
[F] Cahier 12, H. 393; cahier 14, H. 395; cahiers 42–43, H. 414.
[G] Cahier 11, H. 392.

sodalities, among them the Confraternity of the Dying at the MERCY. Several oratorios evoke sin and punishment,[A] and two recount events in the lives of male figures from the Old Testament.[B] The latter stand out from the rest, for they were intended "for the Jesuits"[11]—that is, they apparently were performed in 1681 and 1682 at one of the THREE JESUIT HOUSES in Paris, just as the earliest oratorio honoring Saint Cecilia had been sung during a conversion at the Jesuit Noviciate in which MADAME DE GUISE had been instrumental.[12]

In addition to the oratorios, Charpentier's arabic-numbered note-books for 1676 and 1677 contain three psalms[C] for the Guise Core Trio that are part of the Office of Saint Charles Borromeo. (They were also recited on Saturdays during the Little Office of the Virgin.)

By their content, most of these oratorios and psalms reflect MADAME DE GUISE's devotional activities, but quite a few were equally appropriate for MADEMOISELLE DE GUISE's devotions and preoccupations. That is to say, both women were devoted to the Virgin and the Infant Jesus; both worked actively to convert heretics, as Saint Cecilia worked to convert her heathen husband and brother-in-law; and both were linked to churches that extolled Charles Borromeo as a model for Christian charity.

Although distressingly little information seems to have survived about services at the Theatines between 1675 and 1684, MADAME DE TOSCANE and one or more members of her entourage are known to have been in contact with the Theatines in May 1682, the very month when Father Alexis Du Buc was "preaching conversions" there every Sunday.[13] Nor is there any doubt that musical devotions were in fact taking place at Sainte-Anne-la-Royale during the late 1670s and early 1680s. A neighbor later recalled that, "When I was young, the sound of music told me that there was a ceremony at the Theatines. ... I went in, and my ears were charmed by the voices, and my heart was moved in the presence of these holy mysteries."[14]

The possibility of sponsoring musical performances in a prestigious setting had doubtlessly been one of MADAME DE GUISE's principal concerns when she approached the Theatines in 1675. If she singled out this church, it surely was because the fathers were enthusiastic supporters of elaborate musical services. Witness the week-long festivities prepared by Vigarani for the canonization of Saint Gaetano in August 1672. (For

---

[A] Cahier 29, H, 399; cahiers 30–31, H. 401; cahier 37, H. 407.
[B] Cahier 32, H. 403 (which ends with a text for the Saturday prior to the fifth Sunday after Pentecost); cahier 34, H. 404.
[C] Cahier 12, H. 163; cahiers 14–15, H. 164, H. 165.

one of the masses held that week, did Marc-Antoine Charpentier compose his mass for four choirs[A] inspired by what he had heard in Rome?) Costly tapestries covered every surface, the chapels were hung with gold-embroidered crimson satin, the altars were laden with silver and silver-gilt plates and vessels. A velvet- and brocade-draped architectural element had been constructed around the high altar, which stood on a high pedestal decked with silver vases full of flowers. Above the Holy Sacrament hung a gilded sunburst surmounted by an embroidered, crown-capped canopy. "Two choirs of musicians" occupied tapestry-covered stalls, performing a *Te Deum*[B] with an "excellent symphony." The same musicians performed at vespers; and then, to the sound of oboes and "other instruments," a tall lighted cross was set ablaze on the quay, and fireworks were set off above the Seine.[15]

Moved by the death of her close friend, QUEEN MARIE-THÉRÈSE, in August 1683, MADAME DE GUISE decided to "renounce the world and its pomp."[16] By early 1684 she was spending increasingly less time in Paris and would retreat to her duchy of Alençon for five or six months at a time, once her winter obligations at court had ended. Judging from the content of Marc-Antoine Charpentier's arabic-numbered notebooks, it was not long before she stopped sponsoring these devotions. His penultimate oratorio—for the Great Guise Music—was written for Christmas 1684; and the final one, in praise of Saint Cecilia, came a year later, in November 1685.[C]

The gradual cessation of oratorios in the series of notebooks that contains Marc-Antoine Charpentier's compositions for the Guises, may also be related to a rising star, an Italian composer named Paolo Lorenzani. By April 1683 the Florentine agents in Paris were reporting that Lorenzani was in contact with the Theatines.[17] Perhaps the fathers were simply responding to Madame de Guise's reticence about sponsoring musical devotions, now that she felt such distaste for "pomp." Then too, Charpentier was no longer the rising star: his service to the DAUPHIN had recently ended without his being named to a position at court; and illness had forced him to withdraw from the competition for a sub-mastership at the royal chapel.

Whatever the Theatines' motives, their negotiations with Lorenzani made them decide to "establish in our church a devotion for the dead in the manner of the oratorios of Rome, with music twice a week." On June 20, 1685, the arrangement became official,[18] and by October the new

---

[A] Cahiers XII–XIV, H. 4, H. 285.
[B] Cahiers X–XI, H. 145 and H. 162?
[C] Cahiers 42–43, H. 414 (Dec. 1684); cahier 47, H. 415 (Nov. 1685).

"devotion" was in full swing. The *Mercure galant* described one of these services: a *De Profundis*, a "sung psalm or motet," a brief sermon, another motet, and the Benediction of the Holy Sacrament.[19] Although this new devotion differed in detail from the "devotion" that Madame de Guise had been conducting at the church for almost a decade, her devotion at the Sainte-Anne had presumably consisted of music, a sermon, and either the Benediction of the Holy Sacrament or the Litanies of the Virgin.

The new devotion for the dead was not without its critics. In fact, the Archbishop of Paris was informed that

> the Theatines, under the pretext of a devotion for the Souls in Purgatory, are having a veritable opera sung in their church, where everyone goes to hear the music. The door is guarded by two Swiss guards, and chairs are rented for ten sous; and with every change [in program], ... posters are put up, as if it were a new play.

Both the Florentine resident and MADAME DE TOSCANE's Italian musician-chambermaid, Cintia Galoppini, promptly became enthusiastic participants in the new devotion, declaring that Lorenzani's motets were "the most beautiful that one could ever hear."[20]

That no such complaints about "veritable operas" were made about Madame de Guise's devotions at the Theatines, suggests that they were carried out with great discretion and at her own expense, with no admission fee. Indeed, if the Theatines were criticized in 1685, it was not so much because they had decided to sponsor this new "devotion," as because they were so patently eager to recoup the lump sum they paid Lorenzani each week—and perhaps have something left over for themselves as well.

III

People flocked to the abbey, the music was very moving

THE ABBAYE-AUX-BOIS
AND THE LITTLE CARMEL OF THE RUE DU "BOULOIR"

The Abbaye-aux-Bois of the Faubourg Saint-Germain;
and the Carmel royal de Sainte-Thérèse,
on the rue du Bouloi near the Louvre

In addition to the music he wrote for services at the ABBEY OF MONT-MARTRE and the ABBEY OF PORT-ROYAL, Marc-Antoine Charpentier composed for two other Parisian convents for women. For the convent known as the Abbaye-aux-Bois, he composed quite a few works for a trio of nuns. By contrast, the commission he received from one of the Carmelite convents was for a triumphalist service that included the always grand King's Music.

The Abbaye-aux-Bois

In the 1640s a group of nuns wearing a distinctive habit—a black veil, a white mantle, a red scapulary, and a gray robe with a rope belt—fled to Paris from the Cistercian abbey of Notre-Dame-aux-Bois, in the diocese of Noyon, to escape the conflicts along the northern frontier. They settled on the rue de Sèvres in buildings recently abandoned by another order. Although it no longer was in the woods, the abbey continued to be called the *Abbaye-aux-Bois*, the "Abbey in the Woods."

In the mid-1650s, Marie-Magdaleine d'Albert d'Ailly became coadjutrix there. Abbess de Lannoy was in poor health and gradually sank into senility, so for three decades the Coadjutrix was for all intents and purposes the Abbess. It is not clear whether the fact that she was the sister of the DUKE OF CHAULNES, French Ambassador to Rome in the late

1660s, has any bearing on Marc-Antoine Charpentier's apparent gifts of music to the abbey, including his music for Tenebrae[A] of 1680.

Two of the nuns at the abbey during the 1660s and early 1670s attract our attention. One was Élisabeth Desnots, a skilled singer whose voice was so low that she could sing parts normally destined for a high tenor, *haute-contre*. The other nun of interest was the sister of ÉTIENNE LOULIÉ, a member of the GUISE MUSIC. Nothing is known of the latter woman's musical talents—or her lack of such talents—although it is tempting to imagine that she was one of the two nuns who sang with Mother Desnots.[1]

By the autumn of 1677, Marc-Antoine Charpentier was writing for the abbey: two motets[B] for the trio of nuns of which Mother Desnots was a part. One of the compositions alludes to the nuns' little cabinet organ, which was approximately four feet high and three and one-half feet wide, with seven stops in the upper keyboard and five in the lower.

Then, as Lent of 1680 approached, the composer embarked on a more ambitious project, a corpus of lessons for Tenebrae services, plus responses for each day.[C] For at least one of these works a harpsichord was specified. Although a change in the breviary forced him to abandon the responses—"I didn't finish the others because of the change in the breviary"—he copied the incomplete corpus into the arabic-numbered notebooks that normally were reserved for Guise commissions, just as he had done with the motets written back in 1677.

It is not clear why he deemed the arabic-numbered series appropriate for these works, rather than the roman-numbered one where he generally put his outside commissions. Nor does the brief statement about these Tenebrae services published in the *Mercure galant* shed light on why he treated these pieces as somehow related to his room and board:

> We also had very lovely music in Paris on those days, and people flocked to the Sainte-Chapelle and the Abbaye-aux-Bois. The music at the Sainte-Chapelle was by Messieurs Chaperon, Delalande, and Lalouette; and at the Abbaye-aux-Bois by Charpentier.[2]

Two explanations for this apparent aberration can be proposed but not proved. Charpentier may have been making personal gifts to the convent where Loulié's sister was a nun. After all, the two men appear to have been distantly related through the CROYERS. (This explanation is considerably weakened by the fact that he copied personal gifts to

---

[A] Cahiers 26–29, H. 96–104, H. 106–119.
[B] Cahier 19, H. 288, H. 322.
[C] Cahiers 27–28, H. 96–110; cahiers 28–29, H. 111–19.

PORT-ROYAL into a separate unnumbered "fat notebook," *gros cahier.*) Or does the explanation lie in MONSIEUR DU BOIS', DOCTOR VALLANT's and MADAME DE GUISE's friendships with a certain Madame de Saint-Aubin, who had been living at the abbey since the mid-1660s?[3] (There is no evidence that she was the wife of HAVÉ DE SAINT-AUBIN, but there is no evidence to the contrary either.)

The Little Carmel

During these same years MADAME DE GUISE had become a frequent visitor to the so-called "Little Carmel," also known as the "Carmelites of the rue du Bouloi" (or "Bouloir"). The Little Carmel had been created in 1656 as a subdivision of the Carmel of the Annonciation, the "Great Carmel." In 1663 Louis XIV gave the Little Carmel an independent status. He named it the "Royal Carmel of Saint Theresa," *Carmel royal de Sainte-Thérèse,* and he proclaimed that the convent would henceforth be the spiritual retreat for his bride, QUEEN MARIE-THÉRÈSE. In this way, the Queen became the Little Carmel's official founder and protectress.

References to MADAME DE GUISE's visits to the Little Carmel crop up periodically in the pages of the *Gazette de France,* starting in the late 1660s. Readers would be informed that the Queen, accompanied by Madame de Guise, had visited the "Carmelites on the rue du Bouloir," sometimes eating a noon meal there before attending a service. The Queen tried to spend every October 15 at the Little Carmel, to celebrate the Feast of Saint Theresa of Avila,[A] her patron saint.

The Florentine agents' correspondence reveals that not only were these visits more frequent than the *Gazette* suggests, they also continued up until the Queen's death in 1683. As of 1676, MADAME DE TOSCANE would frequently be present as well. There was quite a bit of sociability at the Little Carmel; but while the Queen and the princesses were chatting, the nuns were busy spying on the Grand Duchess and reporting her every foible to the Florentines.[4]

By 1682 one of the Carmelites had begun pointing out that Madame de Toscane inexplicably "hated" them all. In a letter he sent off to Florence, Sainte-Mesme, her governor-guard, feigned ignorance about the cause of her annoyance: "We do not understand why Madame the Grand Duchess behaves as she does toward the Carmelites, whom she no longer wants to see, and where she does not even want us to set foot."[5]

The situation had worsened by November 1684. Madame de Guise too was angry with the nuns: "We are still in disgrace with [Madame de

---

[A] Rés. Vmc. ms. 27, H. 374 (a separate volume for the Dauphin's Music).

Toscane] and with Madame de Guise," commented one Carmelite. "But," she added, "Mademoiselle consoles us."[6] MADEMOISELLE DE MONTPENSIER had begun a power play and was making her half-sisters' visits to the Little Carmel as unpleasant as possible. To achieve her goal, Montpensier had abandoned the Grand Carmel, which she used to visit almost daily; and by May 1681 she was not only assiduously visiting the Little Carmel, she would gossip privately with the nuns about her stepsisters. The information she gave them was promptly passed on to Florence.[7] Hence Madame de Toscane's eventual refusal to visit the Carmel.

Music and pomp were not ruled out at either Carmel, despite the extremely austere rule the nuns themselves had embraced. A newsletter of the mid-1660s, written in doggerel verse, described an Assumption Day service at one of the Carmelite houses. Instrumentalists brought in for the occasion played a "symphony." Male singers performed music written especially for the service:

> At the pious Carmelites, ... they say that eight panegyrists from the pulpit, each in turn, by their flowery eloquence have been casting a bright light on the Assumption of Mary. Then they sang the Benediction of the Holy Sacrament, where harpsichord and lutes, violins and theorbos equaled celestial bodies. ... The famous La Grille [a male musician of the Royal Chamber], who sings as sweetly as a girl, made his lovely voice heard and charmed the greatest of kings.

Robert Cambert "directed the musicians, having composed the music for all these ravishing concerts."[8]

On December 20, 1683, music by Charpentier was performed at the Little Carmel, during a memorial service for QUEEN MARIE-THÉRÈSE. That the music was copied into a roman-numbered notebook suggests that it was commissioned and paid for by the Carmelites. This reading of the circumstantial evidence provided by Charpentier's notebooks is confirmed by the notice that DONNEAU DE VISÉ, the composer's friend, published in the *Mercure galant*:

> The Carmelites of the rue du Bouloir having had a solemn service said for this princess on the twentieth of the month, the pontifical mass was celebrated by the Bishop of Auxerre, and the funeral eulogy was given by Abbé des Alleurs, the Dauphine's almoner. He lived up to expectations, and he contrasted all the King's grand deeds with the pious deeds of the Queen. The assembly was composed of a great number of prelates and persons of quality, and the nuns of the convent neglected nothing in this ceremony, doubly sad for them, that could demonstrate their pain and their just gratitude. The music, which was very moving, was composed by

Monsieur Charpentier. Twenty-four paupers whom [the Queen] had clothed went to the oratory, each with a candle in hand. Immediately after the death of this great princess, [the nuns] had ordered the entire church draped in black mourning, with three velvet swathes bearing coats of arms that will remain there all year.[9]

The mourners "of quality" almost certainly included MADAME DE GUISE, who had returned to Paris from Alençon earlier that month. By avoiding mention of her name, the editors of the Mercure galant could praise their composer friend.

There are strong parallels between Charpentier's music and the memorial mass composed by Cambert two decades earlier. Charpentier's commission included a string overture or "symphony," an élévation and an oratorio for mixed female and male voices and instruments, plus a De Profundis.[A] One can conjecture that, as they did at actual funerals, the nuns, "wearing their mantles, and with their great veils lowered, and lighted candles in their hands ... went processionally in silence, with the cross, two candlesticks, the holy water, and the censer." After the nuns had formed two choirs, the priests would begin a chant, and the nuns would continue in plainsong as they moved about the choir.[10]

The service for the late Queen was commissioned shortly before Madame de Guise's break with the Little Carmel. In 1684 she and Madame de Toscane transferred their affections to the Great Carmel. There, in 1675, a childhood friend, Louise de la Vallière, had taken the veil in the presence of several tearful princesses, among them the Queen and Madame de Guise.[11] Sister Louise de la Miséricorde, as she was now known, spent the rest of her life repenting her liaison with Louis XIV. She continually compared herself to Mary Magdalene:

Above all, Lord, view me unceasingly as the Magdalene, and see to it that, like that penitent saint, I water Your feet with my tears, and that by trying to love You a great deal, I will try to erase the multitude of my crimes.[12]

One of her greatest solaces was kneeling before the altar of the Holy Sacrament, like the Magdalene at Christ's feet, "adoring her divine Spouse." She would rise at three in the morning and spend two hours there, praying and meditating.[13]

In 1686 and 1687 Marc-Antoine Charpentier composed two pieces for female voices that may well have been written for performance at the Grand Carmel, and that he copied out into the arabic-numbered

---

[A] Cahiers XXXVI–XXXIX, H. 524, H. 408, H. 409, H. 189.

notebooks containing primarily works for the Guises. Owing to the fact that these pieces come too late to have been gifts from Madame de Guise to the Queen, another recipient must be proposed: La Vallière. The first piece honors Saint Theresa of Avila, the founder of the Carmelites; the second is the love song that a "weeping" Mary Magdalene pours out to Jesus, her dear "heart."[A]

So close to the nuns at the Grand Carmel did MADAME DE GUISE become during the 1680s and early 1690s, that she entrusted them with her will. In it she asked to be buried in the convent cemetery, in the habit of a Carmelite. In 1696 her body was conveyed from Versailles to Paris, and the nuns gave it a "holy and modest" burial, their veils lowered in mourning.

[A] Cahier 49, H. 342, H. 343.

PORTAIL de l'EGLISE de la Maison Professe des R.P. Jésuites en la rue St. Antoine

The Church of Saint-Louis and, immediately to its left, the Jesuit profess house.
Fathers Verthamon, La Faluere, Voisin, and La Chaise resided at the profess house during the 1670s and 1680s. Marc-Antoine Charpentier was music master at Saint-Louis in the 1690s.

IV

Vespers sung by the Opera

THREE JESUIT HOUSES

The Church of Saint-Louis on the rue Saint-Antoine,
the Chapel of the Noviciate on the rue du Pot-de-Fer, and
the Chapel of the College of Louis-le-Grand on the rue Saint-Jacques

The reverend fathers of the Society of Jesus maintained three establishments in Paris. The first was the spacious and splendid Church of Saint-Louis, sometimes called "Saint-Louis of the Jesuits." The second was the Noviciate, situated on the Left Bank not far from the Luxembourg Palace. The third was the College of Louis the Great, *Louis-le-Grand*, located in the Latin Quarter.

The profess house at Saint-Louis
The Church of Saint-Louis rises high above the rue Saint-Antoine, not far from the Place Royale (today's Place des Vosges) and the surrounding noble residences of the *Marais*. From a side door of the church one could go directly to the Jesuit profess house, where the Provincial administered and oversaw all the schools, seminaries, and chapels that the Society had established in the "province," that is, in France and in the Spanish Netherlands. The activities of the profess house itself were overseen by the Superior, who was appointed for a three-year term.

The records sent off every three years to the General in Rome by the fathers in Paris reveal that several friends of the Charpentier family were in residence at Saint-Louis during the 1670s and most of the 1680s. Pierre de Verthamon—one of the FOUR JESUIT FATHERS who appear to have shaped Marc-Antoine Charpentier's career—was selected to be Superior of the profess house of Saint-Louis in 1678 and again in 1681. (Father Verthamon came from a family that had long been faithful to the Guises. He was the uncle of MARIE TALON, ÉLISABETH CHARPENTIER's friend.)

227

Verthamon resided at the profess house virtually full time from the late 1660s, when he returned from Rome, until his death in July 1686. His attention was, however, diverted to the Latin Quarter during his three years as Rector of the College of Louis-le-Grand, 1672–1675.

The same records show that another of the FOUR JESUITS portrayed in Panel 4, François de la Faluère—who, like Verthamon, had been secretary to the General in Rome during the 1660s—retired to the profess house in about 1675 and died there in November 1678. During the same two decades, a third Jesuit—Louis Voisin, MARIE TALON's brother-in-law—likewise lived at Saint-Louis.

Saint-Louis had its own music master, a layman who was paid for carrying out his weekly duties and who was permitted to keep the money he earned by giving music lessons or writing "extraordinary" music, that is, music for events that were not part of his official tasks. There was no Sunday mass at Saint-Louis. In its place, musical vespers were held on Sunday afternoons and on the major feast days of Jesus and the Virgin—plus Pentecost, All Saints' Day, and all the high holy days celebrated by Parisians. The few high masses celebrated at Saint-Louis were reserved for a dozen holidays (Palm Sunday, Pentecost, and so forth) and for special events such as canonizations or extraordinary pontifical masses. It is possible that the master's "ordinary" duties also included celebrations in honor of Saint Louis, after whom the church was named. His duties also included writing for a few matins services: matins on Christmas eve, matins for All Saints' Day, and the Holy Week matins known as Tenebrae.

Each year several special events were held at Saint-Louis that were not part of the music master's obligations. Just as the Superior could prevent the music master from working outside the profess house, so could he permit him to work for another Jesuit establishment—or forbid him to do so. He could also authorize outsiders to write music for special events at Saint-Louis or at one of the other two Jesuit houses.[1] Since the money for these events did not come from the Jesuits' annual budget, but from paid admissions and chair rental,[2] these lavish musical events were in every sense of the word "extraordinary." That is to say, they occupied a place outside the "ordinary" musical events for which the salaried music master was expected to provide music.

When an "extraordinary" event took place at Saint-Louis, it was in a sumptuously decorated edifice, the decorations augmented by flowers, candles, and representations of angels and various symbolic figures. The church would be lighted all the way to the top of the dome, and these grandiose services would sometimes be followed by great bonfires in front of the church.

During the mid-1660s, the singers who had been performing in Pierre Perrin and Robert Cambert's operas became regulars at Saint-Louis. In January 1672, shortly before Lully snatched the opera privilege from Perrin and Cambert, Cambert himself performed on the organ during a week of services celebrating the canonization of Saint Francis Borgia. His opera singers performed during some of these services: "All the musicians from the opera are creating a frenzy there." There was also a magnificent musical ensemble composed of the best voices from the King's Music and helped by the musicians of the church, who were "excellent."

The circumstances of Cambert's hiring provide a rare glimpse at the respect for precedence that the Jesuits were expected to observe when commissioning a piece of music from an outside composer. First of all, if Cambert was working for them in the first place, it was because the fathers had gone to see the Marquis de Sourdéac, the director of the opera, and had "begged" him to allow it. Sourdéac agreed to "order" Cambert to work for them, as long as he did not neglect his ordinary obligations. He likewise "ordered" the opera singers and instrumentalists to participate in the services, as long as there was no conflict with their duties at the opera. From start to finish, Cambert simply obeyed orders: "I did not fail to obey all the orders I was given, principally those of the Jesuits, as soon as they were given."[3]

In other words, the Jesuits first approached the employer. If the employer was willing to share the employee with these outsiders, he "ordered" the employee to do the task. At the same time he insisted that this outside commission not conflict with the employee's ordinary obligations. Now, Marc-Antoine Charpentier was already composing special works for the Jesuits when Cambert was ordered to work for the reverend fathers. Thus it is very certain that Mademoiselle de Guise had "ordered" him to do so, having first been approached by the Jesuits.

From roughly January 1670 to early 1675, Marc-Antoine Charpentier's roman-numbered notebooks contain quite a few works conceived for a large ensemble. These compositions can only have been commissioned for performance in one among a half-dozen large Parisian churches. Saint-Louis of the Jesuits immediately comes to mind, because these works call for a mixture of voices and instruments that closely resembles the ensemble for which Charpentier composed during the 1690s, while music master at Saint-Louis.[4]

Several of these works for large groups coincide chronologically with special events at Saint-Louis. Others pieces set texts written by a Jesuit father. For example, for the Feast of Saint Nicaise of Rouen,[A] December 14, 1671, Charpentier set a text by Father Commire, S.J.[5]; and in mid-1675 he would set to music this Jesuit's *Mementote peccatores*, since lost.[B] Being invited to collaborate with Commire was a testimony to the composer's prowess at setting Latin verse to music. He was considered a worthy partner for this poet, whose "writings had made him famous among the men of letters of his day. ... Perhaps since the century of Augustus, no one has better understood the genius of lyric poetry."[6]

It is therefore certain that Charpentier was working with the Jesuits as early as 1671. Only a few months later came a mass[C] and associated pieces that he copied into his roman-numbered notebooks for early 1672. In view of the proven link to Saint-Louis for 1671, it appears likely that these compositions were written for the festive week of January 17, 1672, with its organ-playing and music by Cambert, and its daily masses and vespers to mark Saint Frances Borgia's canonization. Within the broader framework of these festivities, it may be significant that BISHOP ROQUETTE gave a eulogy for the saint on January 20.

Other works of Charpentier's are more difficult to link to specific services, but they too are works for large ensembles and tend to be psalms—and a very special type of psalm at that. That is to say, these particular psalms were recited either during matins other than the matins routinely held at Saint-Louis, or else they were for weekday vespers,[D] as contrasted with the Sunday vespers that were the music master's "ordinary" responsibility. Sometimes a work clearly was for a special event: a *Te Deum*, an *Exaudiat*,[E] or a sung mass with its *Domine salvum fac Regem*[F] could scarcely be routine.

Mid-1675 brings a gap of three notebooks in the roman-numbered series. When that series resumes, Charpentier is composing for the DAUPHIN, and the Latin works for these large ensembles have disappeared —not to return until 1688 and notebook LVI, made of paper produced by a Jesuit mill and dating from the first year or two of the composer's tenure as music master for the Jesuits. In other words, for a period of only

---

[A] Cahier IX, H. 55-57.

[B] Cahier IX (on Jesuit paper: recopied?), H. 55-57; cahier XIX, H. 425a.

[C] Cahiers VI-VIII (on Jesuit paper: recopied?), H. 3, H. 236, H. 283, H. 514; and perhaps H. 73 (for vespers).

[D] Cahier VI (recopied on Jesuit paper), H. 158; cahier IX (recopied on Jesuit paper), H. 160, H. 161 (both show names of Beaupuis and Dun); cahier XIX, H. 167.

[E] Cahier X (on Jesuit paper: recopied?), H. 145; cahier XI, H. 162.

[F] Cahiers, XII-XIV, H. 4, H. 285 (assuming, that is, that these works were not written for the THEATINES).

three or four years during the early 1670s, the Guise composer appears to have been invited to compose "extraordinary" music for Saint-Louis.

These were, of course, the very months (early August 1671 to March 1673) when the House of Guise was in deep mourning for LOUIS-JOSEPH DE LORRAINE, DUKE OF GUISE and the DOWAGER DUCHESS OF ORLÉANS, thereby silencing the GUISE MUSIC and the Guise composer. This prolonged period of mourning was followed by MADAME DE GUISE's departure from the Hôtel de Guise in June 1673, and by a time of uncertainty about the future of the Music. Then, with MADAME DE TOSCANE's return to France during the summer of 1675, the princesses embarked on "devotions" that took the form of musical events at the MERCY and at the THEATINES—with the end result that Charpentier was no longer idle. In short, his Jesuit friends (along with MOLIÈRE and his successors) appear to have kept the Guise protégé occupied, and re-munerated, throughout the musical drought at the Hôtel de Guise, 1671–1675.

The Noviciate

The Jesuits maintained a second house, the Noviciate, situated not far from the Luxembourg Palace. There were no weekly worship services for the public in this splendid chapel. Rather, it was a venue for the devotions of one or another Jesuit-sponsored confraternity. And, as ÉTIENNETTE CHARPENTIER THE LINENER's testament reveals, young girls were given "instruction" there. Now and then a special extraordinary service for a Jesuit saint, or the consecration of a prelate, would be held at the Noviciate. Among these special events was the conversion of a Huguenot woman, in the presence of MADAME DE GUISE, on or around Saint Cecilia's Day,[A] November 1676.[7] In addition, a work in Charpentier's roman-numbered notebooks just possibly was written for a special service at the Noviciate for the Feast of Saint Francis Xavier, December 6, 1672.[B]

The College of Louis-le-Grand

The third Jesuit house in Paris was the College of Clermont, a secondary school for boys, *collège*, that after 1674 went by the name *Louis-le-Grand*, "Louis the Great." MOLIÈRE had studied there as an extern. The college chapel was rather small, so it is unlikely that the compositions for large ensembles that Marc-Antoine Charpentier copied into his notebooks between 1671 and 1674 were intended for perfor-mance there. (Given the Jesuits' fondness for music and splendor, the

---

[A] Cahier 13, H. 394.
[B] Cahiers XII–XIV, H. 4, H. 285.

possibility cannot, of course, be ruled out.) Nor did Father Verthamon's three years as rector at the College, 1672–1675, bring a cluster of less ambitious works that correspond to the little we know about devotions at the school.

In the mid-1680s the fathers at Louis-le-Grand approached Mademoiselle de Guise and requested permission to employ her composer. Every year during the Mardi Gras season, the pupils presented a tragedy in Latin. They marked the end of the school year in August with a similar Latin tragedy, plus a ballet. With the 1680s, music began being added to the spoken tragedy performed each winter. In 1683 the music was a "pastorale"; but from 1684 on, these compositions were described as "tragedies in music to serve as *intermèdes* to the Latin play." The expression *tragédie en musique* was, of course, synonymous with "opera." In other words, the Jesuits began sponsoring operas in February 1684. Did they not realize that they were challenging Lully's monopoly over the genre?

Did Lully view the "tragedy in music" of 1685—set to music by Claude Oudot—as a conscious test of his determination to defend his privilege against some priests and schoolboys? Was Oudot a *bête noire*? Back in 1683 his "opera in the form of a concert" had been praised in DONNEAU DE VISÉ's *Mercure galant*, in the context of an overt criticism of Lully's monopoly. The article—which had alluded to Marc-Antoine Charpentier, and to his compositions that had "caused such a stir"—had included an exhortation to "those who give such agreeable concerts" and who "wish to become better" at the art: they should "work on full operas."

That is exactly what the Jesuits began doing after the *Mercure*'s appeal of June 1683. They started commissioning operas. Early in 1684 the students performed their first "tragedy in music," by an unidentified composer; in 1685 Oudot himself wrote the opera (he would continue to work for the Jesuits, composing a *Te Deum* for them in 1687); and a "tragedy in music" by an unidentified composer was performed in 1686. Meanwhile, Charpentier's *Orphée* had been performed at court in early 1686, probably for the DAUPHIN; and entertainments by "composers other than Lully" were being given for Monseigneur that winter. In this context, Charpentier's two devotional operas for the College of Louis-le-Grand, performed for Mardi Gras of 1687 and 1688, take on a new meaning. They appear to be part of the challenge that frustrated composers had begun mounting against Lully back in 1683.

In 1686 the Jesuits appear to have made a more or less formal arrangement with Charpentier to compose for these school fêtes—

presumably going to the Hôtel de Guise and "begging" Mademoiselle de Guise to "order" him to work for them, as Sourdéac had ordered Cambert many years earlier. (Does a commitment to Jesuits explain why, in the spring of 1686, the composer stopped marking his name beside the *haute-contre* part in his compositions for the GREAT GUISE MUSIC?)

For the festivities of Mardi Gras 1687, the boys prepared a Latin play, *Celsus martyr*, by Father Pallu, S.J., which was paired with a sung tragedy "to serve as *intermèdes* to the Latin play." This lost devotional opera had French lyrics by Father Bretonneau, S.J., and music by Marc-Antoine Charpentier. Then, in February 1688, came Charpentier and Bretonneau's *David et Jonathas*, performed with *Saül*, a Latin play by Father Chamillart, S.J.

When *David et Jonathas* was performed, Lully had been dead for a year. Although the challenge proclaimed in the *Mercure galant* in 1683 had lost its immediacy, Charpentier's longtime friends at the *Mercure*, Corneille and DONNEAU DE VISÉ, praised "this work [that] was rightly called an opera." His contribution, they concluded, could scarcely have received more applause. These laudatory remarks about *David et Jonathas* were part of a long article describing the utility of student "operas":

> The College of Louis-le-Grand being full of boarders of the highest rank, who upon leaving take possession of the highest dignities in the State, the Church, the Sword, and the Robe [the judiciary], these youths must become accustomed to demonstrating the daring and refined air that is necessary when speaking in public. It is to this end that the Jesuits take the trouble to practice this [art of public speaking] by having them prepare two tragedies each year. ... In the past these tragedies were intermingled solely with dancing, because dance is very necessary to give grace and to make the body agile; but now that music reigns, it was deemed appropriate to incorporate music, in order to make this entertainment complete.

Charpentier's participation in these theatricals apparently ended late in 1689 or in 1690. That is, one of the fathers sent an autograph copy of the composer's *Salve Regina* to Quebec, with the notation: "Music master at our Parisian college, 1689."[8] Not long after, the composer moved to Saint-Louis—perhaps as a result of a compact between the dying Mademoiselle de Guise and Father La Chaise, one of the FOUR JESUITS who appear to have contributed to shaping Charpentier's career. Although Charpentier continued to work for the Jesuits for a decade, 1688 marked the end of his sacred tragedies for Louis-le-Grand. He had vacated his apartment at the Hôtel de Guise in 1687 and was probably already living across the Seine, on the rue Dauphine, where he resided in 1692, when he was listed as one of the principal composers of the capital.[9] (His apartment at the Hôtel de Guise was given to BISHOP ROQUETTE's nephew, Roquette d'Amades.)

Music Master at Saint-Louis

In 1689 Charpentier set to work creating a corpus of works from which he could pick and choose, as his ordinary obligations at Saint-Louis might require. These he copied into the series of notebooks with arabic numbers. In other words, he continued the classification practice he had observed throughout his service to the Guises, when he copied his "ordinary" works into arabic-numbered notebooks, and his "extraordinary" ones into the roman-numbered series. However, many of the works composed after 1689 can be used in so many different situations that it can be difficult to discern clearly just what his ordinary duties were. For example, an arabic-numbered notebook contains a piece "for the Virgin" with a text about "boys whom the Lord has entrusted to me"[A]—*cum pueris quos dedit mihi dominus, Audite filii*. The work seemingly was written for an event involving the pupils at Louis-le-Grand, the most studious of whom are known to have been honored by induction into a Marian sodality.

The general nature of much of this corpus makes it difficult to discern whether there was indeed a strict separation between ordinary and extraordinary. For example, why are some pieces for the Virgin found in roman-numbered notebooks while the one about boys is in an arabic-numbered one? What for us is a mystery, or a contradiction, may not be a mystery or a contradiction at all.

An explanation must lie in the fact that once Charpentier had entered the service of the Jesuits, his work was governed by the rather special slice of liturgical time observed at Saint-Louis—a liturgical time in which Sunday morning masses played no part. Into his arabic-numbered notebooks he now copied out works for Sunday vespers, texts appropriate for the vespers or Little Office of the Virgin, music for martyrs and for Jesuit saints, and so forth.[10]

By contrast, doubtlessly obeying very unambiguous rules set down by the reverend fathers, into the roman-numbered notebooks he copied special commissions, just as he had done during his years at the Hôtel de Guise. Except that now most of these "extraordinary" works were for the Jesuits, rather than for the theater or for one or another of the convents of the capital. These roman-numbered notebooks contain Litanies of the Virgin, settings of texts for weekday vespers, *élévations*, settings of texts

---

[A] Cahier 66, H. 371.

suitable for the Benediction of the Holy Sacrament, music for Corpus Christi processions, celebrations of saints other than martyrs, and music for catechisms.[11]

It is noteworthy that neither series contains a succession of oratorios similar to the series that Charpentier wrote during his years at the Hôtel de Guise. In fact, in the notebooks filled between approximately late 1688 and May 1698 there are only three works that musicologists would categorize as "dramatic motets," or "sacred stories," that is, oratorios. Two of them are for Christmas.[A]

While these devotional works that Marc-Antoine Charpentier wrote for the Church of Saint-Louis were being performed, worshipers trained their eyes on the resplendent high altar,

> which, to tell the truth, is a bit too low, which makes it sad and gloomy. However, on feast days, when it is brightly lighted, the defect is less noticeable. The tabernacle, which is uncovered on those days, is made of silver with leaves and ornaments of silver gilt, whose workmanship surpasses the cost of the materials. In no church in Paris can one see more reliquaries, silver vases, candlesticks, chandeliers, perfumers, and other such things, and all these things are of silver or silver gilt. There are even a few made of gold.[12]

Charpentier's music added luster to this splendid setting. The principal weekly service was Sunday vespers. An allusion to one such service, dated September 1689, early in the composer's tenure, tells of "a troop of musicians [singers] dressed up almost like actors."[13]

Although seventeenth-century descriptions of devotions at Saint-Louis are not plentiful, an account of the service marking the end of the annual Advent catechism has survived. (The Lenten catechisms doubt-lessly were similar.[B])

> I must share with you the fine things we saw and heard at Saint-Louis yesterday. ... We arrived just as the catechism was about to begin. There were a very great number of people, yet we got rather good seats. The bad thing is that it cost each of us a sou for a chair. Considerable preparations had been made: Jesus in the manger, the Angels, the Shepherds, and the Innocents. And it was very clear to us that this catechism was one of their most solemn ones. ... Once the Father had entered, he demanded full attention from his listeners, giving them to understand that everything he was about to say was not only for children but for adults, even the most aged and

---

[A] Cahier 58, H. 416; cahier 63, H. 418; cahier LX, H. 417. (Cahier 74, H. 421, dates from the years at the SAINTE-CHAPELLE.)

[B] Cahier LVII, H. 69, H. 352, H.70; cahier LXVI, H. 370.

learned among them. First he summoned the Angels, who
announced that the Savior of mankind had been born. After that,
the Shepherds stated their homage.[14]

One costumed character after another, chosen from among the best
catechumens—"three boys and two girls"—recited a little speech and was
awarded a prize for his or her good work. In short, for the less privileged
children who could not attend the College of Louis-le-Grand, the fathers
wrote little devotional plays to be acted out by catechumens. Not only
boys, but also girls like ÉTIENNETTE CHARPENTIER THE LINENER, learned to
declaim brief texts, acquiring a certain degree of self-mastery that would
serve them in their trade when they grew up.

Descriptions have also survived for a few of the other special services
that the Jesuits organized.[15] Although generally written by critics of the
Society of Jesus, when taken with the appropriate pinches of salt these
descriptions suggest the type of service for which some of Marc-Antoine
Charpentier's music of the 1690s was destined. Among these events were
Benedictions of the Holy Sacrament, saluts, where children once again
participated: "The good fathers promised their friends the most charming
serenades by the best symphonies, and a group of little costumed
schoolboys who will present a totally comical review."[16] There were the
annual Corpus Christi processions,[A] where the flowers at the temporary
altar, reposoir, added a spiritual perfume to the event, "a procession so
devout and luminous, and so full of perfumes and orange blossoms
strewn on the ground, that everyone was charmed."[17]

The Jesuits also organized spiritual "exercises" or "meditations" where
music played an important role. According to one of the Society's critics,
a little book of "spiritual exercises" was published in 1688 for use by a
confraternity of the Virgin[18] that met privately every week for an hour
and a half, "to a concert of voices and instruments." "Would you ever
have believed that the spiritual exercises that are so prized among the
Jesuits would be transformed into operas, and the meditations into
music?" The critic then summarized these musical devotions:

> When five o'clock has sounded, for the first quarter-hour the
> instruments play, and a devout motet is sung, after which everyone
> kneels and the priest says the prayer Mentes, etc. After that he also
> recites the points to be observed when examining one's conscience.
> The audience follows him, and when they reach the second point, a
> Veni Creator[B] is sung. After that, everyone thinks privately about

---

[A] Cahier 70, H. 372; cahier LIV, H. 348; cahier LVIII, H. 358 (flowers).
[B] Cahier LV, H. 66; cahier XVII, H. 69; cahier LXI, H. 362.

what he may have done that day or that week, and then the priest recites the act of contrition, after which comes a *Miserere*.[A] The second quarter-hour is taken up by the exhortation, and the priest explains two points in it upon which to meditate.[B] ... The third quarter-hour is far more remarkable: one meditates while the instruments alone are playing. ... During the fourth quarter-hour the Litanies of Our Lady[C] [of Loreto] are sung in music, which is followed by a motet. During the fifth quarter-hour the rosary of the Good Death is recited, and that of Our Lady of Bonsecours, and everyone says *Sub tuum*,[D] etc., except that the musicians sing *Sancta Maria*, etc., three times. ... During the sixth quarter-hour the musicians sing the *Exaudiat*,[E] and they finish with a *De Profundis*[F] for the dead.

Interestingly enough, two of the texts sung during the devotions of this real (or purported?) confraternity for the Virgin were set to music by Marc-Antoine Charpentier for catechisms.[G]

Now that he was immersed in liturgical time and was no longer writing for the theater or composing for the DAUPHIN, Marc-Antoine Charpentier's name rarely appeared in the *Mercure galant*. When DONNEAU DE VISÉ and Corneille mentioned him, it often involved a special event rather than a day-to-day obligation. For example, he was praised for the expressiveness of the Tenebrae service sung at the College in April 1691, clearly an extraordinary event for which he received extra compensation.[H] He was lauded for his motet for the Feast of Saint Louis,[I] celebrated at the Church of Saint-Louis on August 25, 1692. (Judging from the fact that he copied this motet into an arabic-numbered notebook, music for this saint's day was part of his ordinary obligations.) The *Mercure galant* also told how he had written music for the Duke of Luxembourg's funeral[J] at Saint-Louis in April 1695, a special commission that was given to him for reasons that elude the historian but that surely are more significant than the simple fact that he was the music master there. In addition, the *Mercure* informed its readers that a tragedy by

---

[A] Cahier 43b, H. 193 ("of the Jesuits," but originally for the GUISE MUSIC); cahier LVIII, H. 193a; cahier LXV, H. 219.
[B] BN, Vm¹ 1175 bis, H. 380-89 (BROSSARD's copy).
[C] Cahier LIV, H. 84; cahier LVIII, H. 85; cahier LXI, H. 86; cahier LXII, H. 87, H. 88; cahier LXV, H. 89; cahier 66, H. 90.
[D] Cahier LVII, H. 352; cahier LVIII, H. 527.
[E] Cahier 63, H. 180a, H. 180b (reuse of cahier 33, H. 180).
[F] Cahier 57, H. 205; cahier 66, H. 222.
[G] Cahier LVII, H. 69 (*Veni Creator*), H. 352 (*Sub tuum*), H. 70 (*Veni Creator*).
[H] Cahier LVII, H. 123-25.
[I] Cahier 63, H. 418.
[J] Cahier LXVIII, H. 10, H. 269.

Charpentier, the lost *Apothéose de Laodomas*, had been performed at the Jesuit college of Rennes in May 1695, to honor Luxembourg. (It is impossible to say whether ÉTIENNETTE CHARPENTIER's friend and protectress, FRANÇOISE FERRAND and her husband, the First President of the Parlement of Brittany at Rennes, had anything to do with commissioning this allegorical work; or whether the invitation was extended by the DUKE OF CHAULNES, the former ambassador to Rome who was now royal governor for Brittany.)

On the other hand, the *Mercure* did not inform their readers that Charpentier wrote music for one or another of the prelates who were consecrated in the different Jesuit establishments during the 1690s. The silence is understandable. Here, as with the Guises, the glory went to the new prelate. The composer could not be named. Nor did Charpentier have some sort of monopoly over consecrations at Saint-Louis or the Noviciate. For the years 1694–1696 alone, *Gallia Christiana* shows at least two consecrations at Saint-Louis and four at the Noviciate; yet in his decade with the Jesuits the composer received only three[A] such commissions. In theory this task was not part of the music master's ordinary duties. A prelate presumably selected his own composer. That said, it is interesting to note that two of Charpentier's three[19] compositions for consecrations were copied into arabic-numbered notebooks, as if the bishop were a Jesuit or had been offered the music as a gift from the reverend fathers.)

Marc-Antoine Charpentier was not the only composer working for Saint-Louis during the 1690s. In 1694 the Jesuits paid Paolo Lorenzani 106 livres, 9 sous, surely to remunerate him for contributing to an extraordinary event.[20] The fact that this commission was extended to the Italian during Charpentier's mastership adds compelling evidence in favor of the conjecture that he had received several such extraordinary commissions back in the early 1670s.

Working for the Jesuits gave Charpentier sufficient time to teach privately,[21] compose an entire opera, *Médée*, and participate in the education of PHILIPPE III D'ORLÉANS, DUKE OF CHARTRES. He turned the drudge-work over to copyists: "You must also copy it into all the part-books, after the pauses of the *Benedictus*," or, "Be careful to use the bass clef."[B] Some of these copyists—perhaps with the Music Master's permission, but perhaps behind his back—made copies of some of his works and passed them on to SÉBASTIEN DE BROSSARD.[22] (It is not known whether

---

[A] Cahier XLVI, H. 537 (Dec. 1695 or early 1696); cahier 66, H. 536 (fall 1694), H. 432 (fall 1696).

[B] Cahier VI, H. 3, fol. 32v; cahier 43b, H. 193, fol. 13.

Brossard wanted the works from "curiosity," that is, for his burgeoning collection of musical manuscripts and treatises, or whether he intended to perform them.)

As the Roman Jesuits' protection of the exclusivity of CARISSIMI's music demonstrates, appropriating someone else's property was undesirable behavior. And making one's own work available to someone who had not commissioned it was tantamount to theft and could lead to dismissal, disgrace, and a blighted career. When reusing or revising older works, Marc-Antoine Charpentier was therefore very careful not to revive, for the Jesuits, compositions that had not belonged to them in the first place.

For example, during the 1690s he recopied[23] onto Jesuit paper, and perhaps reworked some older compositions, particularly those in notebooks VI through XI. (He put these new copies back in their original chronological slot, the early 1670s.) In reviving these pieces he almost certainly was not infringing upon the rights of the original patron, because some, if not all the works in these six recopied notebooks appear to have been Jesuit commissions[A] in the first place. Reusing old Guise compositions constituted no risk, of course, for upon Mademoiselle de Guise's death in March 1688 they had become his property, and he could with impunity adapt for the Jesuits a whole corpus of works about the Holy Sacrament and the Virgin.[B] Hence the revival and revisions of some of these pieces during the 1690s. As for the compositions for PORT-ROYAL[C] that he reworked, they almost certainly were his own personal gifts to the abbey, copied into his unnumbered "fat notebook," *gros cahier.* Thus he was free to adapt some of these works for male voices and to add instrumental preludes.[24]

On the whole, Charpentier seems to have disposed of considerably more free time while working for the Jesuits than for the Guises. During his eighteen years with the Guises, he filled just over one hundred notebooks, most of them made of seven or eight large folded pieces of paper, for an average of five or six notebooks a year. The loss of quite a few notebooks from the mid-1690s on, makes it difficult to calculate his output during the decade with the Jesuits. Even so, his official obligations filled at most two notebooks a year, and his work for special events was scarcely more copious. In sum, although the job was scarcely a sinecure, he was less rushed than he had been throughout the 1670s and 1680s. He

---

[A] Cahier VI, H. 54; cahier IX, H. 160, H. 162.
[B] Cahier 5, H. 18; cahier 16, H. 21, H. 23; cahier 24, H. 244, H. 247; cahier 26, H. 27; cahier 33, H. 180; cahier 39, H. 190, H. 253; cahier 41, H 333; cahier 43b, H. 193; cahier 50, H. 258.
[C] For example, cahier "d," H. 81, H. 226.

had, however, traded the wishes and devotional priorities of one master, MONSIEUR DU BOIS, the Guise chapel master, for the liturgical demands and traditions of another master, the Society of Jesus.

That is not to say that he was obliged to work solely for the Jesuits. Indeed, he was allowed to accept an occasional non-Jesuit commission. In 1693 he wrote a funeral mass that may well have been commissioned by MADAME DE GUISE for MADEMOISELLE DE MONTPENSIER's funeral at Saint-Denis[A]; and in 1693 the KING (or perhaps the DAUPHIN) commissioned music for a ceremony of the new Military Order of Saint Louis.[B]

During his tenure as chapel master, Charpentier called upon Pierre Beaupuis, the bass of the now disbanded GUISE MUSIC, who had moved on to the Royal Opera. He also engaged a half-dozen other opera singers, plus a few members of the King's Music. Musical performances at Saint-Louis during Marc-Antoine Charpentier's tenure became the principal target of Lecerf de la Viéville's critique of music at that church in general:

> I must say something about one of the houses of Paris that is
> inhabited by the wisest of men, men with the most irreproachable
> morals, as even their enemies, whom they do not lack, will agree:
> one never hears vespers without part of them being sung by the
> Opera. The loft is garnished by opera singers in street clothes, who
> execute and theatrically declaim one or two psalms, as if testing
> themselves out, in order to be in the mood for the roles these
> gentlemen will be playing an hour later. And this church is to such a
> degree the Church of the Opera, that a person who does not go to
> the one can be consoled by going to vespers at the other, where it
> will be cheaper; and to a new opera singer it would even seem that
> as yet he has only half the rank, and half the job, until he has been
> installed [in the choir loft] and has been made to sing.[25]

On May 20, 1698, the music master of the SAINTE-CHAPELLE died. Within a month, Marc-Antoine Charpentier had replaced him. There is no evidence that he ever again composed for the Society of Jesus.

[A] Cahier LXIII, H. 7, H. 263, H. 213.
[B] Cahier LXIII, H. 365.

V

Prepare a motet and some other prayers

THE SAINTE-CHAPELLE OF THE PALACE OF JUSTICE

The Chapter of the Sainte-Chapelle du Palais
on the Île de la Cité

At the opposite end of the island from the Cathedral of Notre-Dame, stands the "Palace," *Palais,* a medieval fortress that was the principal seat of the royal law courts. In the large central courtyard of this massive castle, a chapel lifts its spire to the heavens: the *Sainte-Chapelle,* the Holy Chapel constructed by Saint Louis. This was one of several royal chapels in the Paris basin. The Sainte-Chapelle has two levels. In a lower chapel the inhabitants of the "Palace courtyard" worshiped. The upper church, which was reserved for the king and his officers and guests, was effectively a large reliquary with glorious stained-glass windows. The chapel was administered by the Treasurer (the superior) and the Chapter (composed of some two dozen clerics). A music master, a grammar master, an organist-treasurer, and some eight choir boys contributed to the beauty of the services sung there.[1]

On May 20, 1698, François Chaperon, music master since 1679, died after an illness of some three weeks—just enough time for news of a possible vacancy to spread, and just enough time for candidates to begin casting around for protectors who would speak on their behalf to the chapel's Treasurer, who had the final say in naming a master because he "represents the king". Owing to alleged pressure from PHILIPPE III D'ORLÉANS, Duke of Chartres, Marc-Antoine Charpentier was selected in June, rather than SÉBASTIEN DE BROSSARD.

Brossard later asserted that Treasurer Fleuriau had asked "one of his relatives in Strasbourg" to tell Brossard to come quickly; but by the time Brossard reached the capital a week later, "Sieur Charpentier had so effectively pressed the Duke of Chartres, his disciple, that Abbé Fleuriau was obliged to give him the position."[2] The chapter records make no

Palais.

The Sainte-Chapelle in the Palace of Justice.
The choir school occupied a lower floor of the turreted building at the rear of the courtyard and to the left of the chapel. It was reached from a landing on the arcaded stairway that led to the Chamber of Accounts, *Chambre des Comptes.* The cemetery that encircled the apse of the chapel is concealed by a ring of shops.

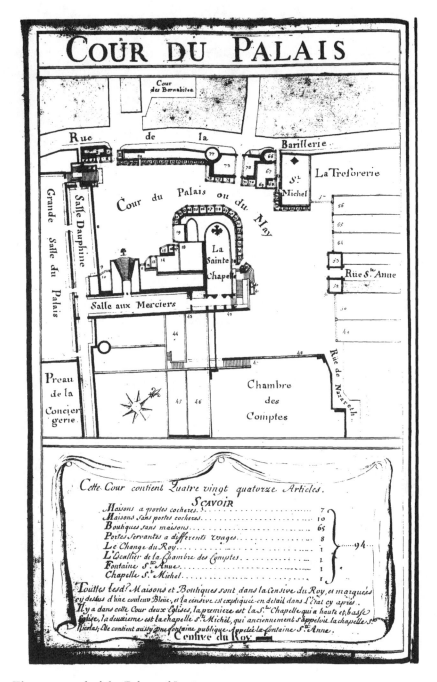

The courtyard of the Palace of Justice.

The "Red Mass" of the Parlement was sung in the Great Hall, *Grande Salle*. The chapel choristers also contributed to the devotions of the sodality that met in the Chapel of Saint Michael, top right. Marc-Antoine Charpentier was buried in the shop-encircled cemetery just behind the apse of the Sainte-Chapelle. Élisabeth Jacquet de La Guerre lived in a house near the rue Sainte-Anne, right.

mention of outside pressure or politicking. Rather, they state that on June 18, a full month after Chaperon's death, Fleuriau informed the chapter that,

> having been informed about the good life-style, manners, and capabilities of Master Marc-Antoine Charpentier, native of the diocese of Paris, he had chosen him and named him to replace the music master of the choirboys, vacant owing to François Chaperon's death; that it being the turn of Abbé [Le Cirier] de Neuchelles to present an ordinary cleric to serve in the church under his prebend, he had presented the said Charpentier to him. Although he was very convinced that [Charpentier] composes and knows music to perfection, in conformity with the foundations and customs of the Sainte-Chapelle he had nonetheless asked the Chanter to examine him; who having found him capable, [the Treasurer] decided to receive [Charpentier] as a cleric [clerc] prior to the high mass. That he will have him take the usual oath in the sacristy, in the presence of the said Abbé de Neuchelles and others who may be present. And finally, that he will assign him the place in the choir that was occupied by the said deceased, which is the last one in the upper stalls, on the right side. Which was done and carried out, as is stated above.[3]

Having been tonsured[4] on June 18, 1698, as a sign of dedication, submission, and admission, Marc-Antoine Charpentier moved into the choir-school apartment, situated within the forbidding walls of the Palace of Justice.

A few months later, Marin de La Guerre replaced his father in the combined post of revenue collector and organist. Henceforth Marc-Antoine Charpentier would collaborate closely with La Guerre, who happened to be the brother-in-law of Anne Jacquet, a former member of the GUISE MUSIC. La Guerre's wife was Anne's younger sister, Élisabeth Jacquet de La Guerre. For the next six years Charpentier lived just across the great courtyard from this respected and creative female composer and her organist spouse. Any Italianisms in Jacquet de La Guerre's compositions should therefore come as no surprise.

Succeeding François Chaperon meant reimbursing his heirs, just as Chaperon had reimbursed the estate of his predecessor, René Ouvrard, for "an advance on the reimbursements paid every three months for the food for the choirboys, the music master and the grammar master, and their domestics." To pay this obligation, Chaperon had "borrowed three thousand livres," which he "gave to Sieur Ouvrard" with the intention that this "advance, paid by me when I became master, should be returned to my heirs after my death by the Chambre des Comptes," that is, the

Royal Chamber of Accounts that administered the chapel.[5] Reimburse-ment by the Chamber was the sort of wishful thinking that comforted many a seventeenth-century creditor, but each successive master clearly was obliged to pay some three thousand livres for what amounted to the purchase of his office. This doubtlessly is why, on January 12, 1699, ÉTIENNETTE CHARPENTIER THE LINENER loaned her brother 2,700 livres, and exactly one year later, January 12, 1700, loaned him another 122 livres, which were followed on April 24 by an additional 70 livres—for a grand total of 2,892 livres.[6] The sum borrowed and never repaid was 108 livres short of the amount due the Chaperon heirs. In other words, Étiennette purchased her brother's mastership for him.

Having assumed his new responsibilities on July 1, 1698, Charpentier now worked full time for the Crown, as personified by Louis XIV. For the rest of his life he would be one of many bees who buzzed about their appointed tasks in that hive known as the Sainte-Chapelle, all of them working together to ensure that the Virgin, Christ, and all the saints in Heaven would look favorably upon the king and the Monarchy. With no distinctive ritual of its own, the chapel adhered to the Roman breviary, moving through the liturgical day, the liturgical week, the liturgical year. This routine was occasionally broken by a visit from the king, a member of the royal family, or a prestigious guest such as a foreign sovereign. The music master would be notified to "prepare a motet and some other prayers, along with the *Domine salvum fac Regem* in music."[7] The chapel would be decked out with carpets; the royal prayer stool would be draped with crimson velvet; and crimson-velvet armchairs would be brought out, as would stools and cushions for the ladies of the royal entourage. As the royal coach entered the courtyard, the members of the Sainte-Chapelle would assemble by rank to conduct their illustrious guests into the chapel.[8] For his artistic and pedagogical efforts, Charpentier was paid "wages," *gages*. These wages—combined with the "gratifications" received for any special services ordered by the Chapter—totaled between three and four thousand livres a year.[9]

Charpentier, the grammar master, the housekeeper, and eight choirboys were housed in an eleven-room apartment just across the courtyard from the Sainte-Chapelle. As was customary, on his first day of residence the composer went through each room of the apartment with a representative of the Chamber of Accounts, acknowledging that the lodging contained the items belonging to the king that had been present when his predecessor began his tenure. The furnishings provided by the Crown were shabby and minimal. The apartment was a rabbit-warren of large and small rooms. There was a kitchen with a large table, benches, and eight porringers for the children; a classroom with two tables, two benches, two chests, and a wardrobe containing the boys' linens; and a vestibule hung with shabby cloth from Bergamo and furnished with an old square table with a holey table-cover. The music master's bedroom contained a curtained bed, several chairs, and a table. In an adjacent small room or *cabinet*, music books and papers were stored. The grammar master occupied a similarly equipped bedroom and *cabinet*. The boys' room contained eight beds. The servant's room, with its cot, had shabby wall-hangings, and five old chairs. If the music master wanted comfort and elegance, it was up to him to furnish and decorate his rooms, as Chaperon had done[10] with great panache and in the taste of a would-be learned celibate.

Music Master Charpentier henceforth wore the "cassock and long mantle" that set him and the grammar master apart from the rest of the clerics.[11] If he dressed like his predecessor, this meant a black wool mantle, a cassock of black crepe or black poplin, a square bonnet of black wool, a black serge cope, a black woolen camail with a purple plush lining, and a linen amice.[12] He and the grammar master were expected to be attentive to the "exact pronunciation of every word" of the Latin texts sung or recited during services; and it was their duty to "imbue [the choir boys] with Christian precepts," make sure that the children behaved modestly and piously in the church,[13] and escort them to the chapel and back to their residence on the other side of the courtyard. With the housekeeper's help, the two men were expected to ensure the cleanliness of the boys and their clothing, and to eat with them every day. Before the start of the fall season, they would take the children out into the country for a short vacation.

In short, Marc-Antoine Charpentier was now a pedagogue as well as an artist who worked with sound. None of these constraints or obligations could have come as a surprise, for ÉTIENNE LOULIÉ, a member of the GUISE MUSIC, doubtlessly had shared with him his experiences as a choir boy at the Sainte-Chapelle.

When Charpentier posed his candidacy, he surely was forewarned that the personnel at the chapel was given to backbiting and to squabbling over precedent. A lengthy battle was still being fought over the use of a reading stand, *lutrin*, and its position in the choir. Nor was it a secret that Music Master Chaperon had been rebuffed by his colleagues a decade earlier, for failing to share with them the proceeds from a special service in the Palace of Justice in which the clerics had participated. During the dispute, Chaperon's colleagues had denigrated the role music played in religious services. Music, they had argued, "is not the essence of the church service, it only adds decorum and solemnity." True, Chaperon bore the title "*master* of music," but he was little more than a "mercenary of the Evangel." Along with the "wages" paid from the royal coffers, the Chapter had given him mastery over the choir boys and over any outside musicians he might hire; but his mastery did not extend to them, the chaplains and the clerics whose income came from "livings," *bénéfices*, created by Saint Louis. Nor, they asserted, was the music master in any way the peer of his clerical colleagues. It was therefore appropriate that the Chapter share in the proceeds from any musical event in which they participated, for in such instances the master had no authority over them. Viewed in the context of the attack upon Chaperon's "mastery" over musical devotions at the chapel, the Tenebrae sung there in 1680 take on a new meaning. Chaperon did not work on them alone. He either hired Delalande and Lalouette to assist him, or else these composers were forced upon him.[14]

Such problems and potential snubs aside, moving to this new post permitted Charpentier to fall back upon a whole corpus of existing music composed by his predecessors. That is to say, everything written for masses at the Sainte-Chapelle, or commissioned by the Chapter for special events, was promptly confiscated upon the death of each successive music master, on the grounds that the compositions were royal property and must remain in situ.

The choirboys had to pass an audition: "Today the company, having heard several children whom the Music Master brought to the meeting, to choose the best voice," one of them would be "named to fill the empty place as choirboy."[15] Master Charpentier proved to be far from enthusiastic about two boys who had been admitted shortly before his predecessor's death. Two months sufficed to convince him that the latest comer was hopeless. Although no choirboy had been dismissed for having a tin ear throughout the 1670s, 1680s, and 1690s, this particular child was "sent away, given that he has neither a voice nor a good ear," and a replacement was found. Eight months later, Charpentier managed to have another boy dismissed: although the child had been at the chapel almost a full year, "he learns nothing."[16] The lad was promptly replaced.

For the adult singers, the Chapter had its own standards. When Music Master Chaperon proposed Éloi Antheaume as a cleric in October 1694, offering "to him music to perfection," the Chapter had replied that although the candidate "has a very fine sound to his voice, it is not usual to accept a cleric who does not know much music." They decided to engage Antheaume as a paid singer until he learned partsong. Four months later, having "greatly perfected his music," Antheaume was received as a cleric.[17] Satisfied or not, Charpentier could not insist that a cleric with marginal skills be dismissed. Rather, as he had at the Hôtel de Guise, he had to work around the strengths and weaknesses of each singer. And he must never disregard the petty jealousies that could poison the atmosphere in this hermetically sealed environment. There was one consolation: for truly special, "extraordinary" events, he could hire outside musicians.

On the other hand, one problem had no remedy. The acoustics created by the medieval builders were inimical to partsong:

> The nave is not suitable for partsong [*musique*], because it is too open and fitted with stained glass that shatters the different voices. Still, one sometimes hears music there that is rather pleasant to the ear; but when that has happened, it means that the Master was very able. Knowing how to accommodate his composition and his parts [*voix*] to the inconvenient nave, he could thereby demonstrate his merit. But one so rarely finds good voices and a good composer there, because there are no livings available for the singers, and the Chapter is not as mindful about it as the Chapter of Notre-Dame.[18]

One of the great "extraordinary" events prepared each year by the music master of the Sainte-Chapelle was the Mass of the Holy Spirit[19] for the opening of the Parlement, sung every November 12 in the Great Hall, *Grande Salle*, of the Palace of Justice. On that day the red-robed judges of the different chambers of the Parlement, joined by the barristers and the procurators, assembled for what was popularly called the "Red Mass." Jesters had christened it the "Bowing Mass," or the "Crayfish Ballet,"[20] for during the very lengthy Offertory[A] the First President of the Parlement would bow repeatedly to the altar, then bow to each of the judges in turn, according to seniority. To avoid turning his back to the altar, he continually scuttled backwards, like a crustacean. For the Red Mass of 1702 Charpentier composed an oratorio about Solomon the Judge.[B] That the procurators of the Parlement commissioned such an Italianate work should not be taken as evidence that the Chapter of the Sainte-Chapelle approved of that particular art form.

After Charpentier's death the Chapter would conclude that some, if not all the music he had written for the Parlement was sufficiently "extraordinary" to make confiscation inappropriate. That is to say, neither his vocal interlude for the "long Offertory" nor the oratorio about Solomon were part of the mass itself. The former was performed during the Crayfish Ballet, and the latter was based on a text that did not appear in the breviary for mid-November. By contrast, the Chapter apparently confiscated any motets the Music Master may have prepared

[A] Cahier 74, H. 434.
[B] Cahier LXXV, H. 422.

for the mass itself, doubtlessly arguing that "this extraordinary ceremony is carried out by the entire corps of the Sainte-Chapelle, where the ordinary chaplains, the clerics, the master of the choirboys, and generally all the musicians are in attendance."[21]

Compositions have survived for several other devotions at which the choristers sang, even though the service was not commissioned by the Chapter of the Sainte-Chapelle. That some of these works were copied into arabic-numbered notebooks, and others into roman-numbered ones, suggests just how difficult it must have been for Master Charpentier to deduce which was which. Indeed, how did one go about deciding which works were not only "extraordinary" but so extraordinary that the Chapter could not claim a share of the proceeds. In addition to the motet for the "long Offertory," the works that Charpentier thought to be "ordinary"[A] include an *élévation* for an unnamed *haute-contre*,[B] high tenor; a Christmas oratorio for three high voices, perhaps choirboys[C]; and a *Te Deum*[D] where none of the singers are identified. Shortly after that, he set three psalms[E] as motets for Holy Week, to be performed by the chapel choristers. He copied these pieces into an arabic-numbered notebook, apparently believing that the service was part of his ordinary duties. In every instance, the Chapter and the Chamber of Accounts disagreed. On the other hand, they concurred that—like the oratorio for the Parlement —the mass for the Feast of the Assumption,[F] August 15, 1702, and the *Domine salvum fac regem* that concluded it, were extraordinary, despite the fact that singers from the Sainte-Chapelle had taken part.

That the music for the Assumption mass was not confiscated in 1704 suggests that the event was sponsored by an outside group that met or worked in the Palace and worshiped in the Chapel of Saint Michael.[22] Revisions of the mass to accommodate changes in the chapel personnel demonstrate unequivocally that this mass was an annual event, sponsored by one of a handful of organizations entitled to call upon the musicians of the Sainte-Chapelle.

On February 24, 1704, at the end of vespers, Treasurer Fleuriau summoned the Chapter to his lodgings, to discuss Marc-Antoine Charpentier's death at seven that morning. It was decided that he would be buried the following day after vespers, and that vespers for the dead

[A] Cahier 74, H. 273, H. 421, H. 148.
[B] Cahier 74, H. 273.
[C] Cahier 74, H. 421.
[D] Cahier 74, H. 148.
[E] Cahier 75, H. 228–30.
[F] Cahier LXXIV, H. 11, H. 303.

would be sung around his body. The service was held in the lower
chapel, because funeral services were not permitted in the upper one.
Later, the nine lessons of matins would be sung; on the following day
lauds for the dead would be sung; and before the daily mass, there would
be a "high mass for the dead," at which the Chanter would officiate.[23]

On the afternoon of February 25, Marc-Antoine Charpentier's body
was carried across the great courtyard and "through a little door between
the shops at the bottom of the ... stairway to the Sainte-Chapelle." This
door, and the cemetery to which it led, was "wide enough for two men
to pass through, shoulder to shoulder." The corridor-like cemetery
encircled the apse of the church, "separating the chapel, for its whole
length, from the shops that open onto the courtyard of the Palace."[24]

Two weeks later, the Treasurer again convoked the Chapter. The
bills for Charpentier's funeral were coming in, and they were "excessive."
Each cleric who had attended the vigils of the nine lessons and the
funeral mass was expecting to be paid for his participation. To this must
be added the payments to the beadle, the embroiderer, the gravedigger,
the candle-seller, the cross-bearer, the bell-ringer, and the Augustinians
who had carried the body. A price list was established to serve as a model
for future obsequies of chaplains, clerics, and other officers.[25]

When Master Chaperon died in May 1698, his heirs had wanted to
have seals placed on the doors of the apartment, a notary's first step in
inventorying someone's possessions. To ensure that the "boxes of
handwritten music that were there" would not be placed under seal,
Treasurer Fleuriau "had them brought to his quarters so that they could
be inventoried and entrusted to the person whom he shall deem an
appropriate successor as music master." When the inventory was taken
a week later, the notary nonetheless gave the impression that the
manuscripts were in their normal place: "Concerning the books and
music papers that are in the aforesaid cabinet, no inventory nor
evaluation was made," because "the things there appertain to the music
school of the Sainte-Chapelle and belong to the king."[26]

The Chapter records suggest that the Treasurer did not need to go
to such lengths in February 1704. That is, there was no allusion to a
temporary removal of all manuscript music. Marc-Antoine Charpentier's
personal property was not inventoried. Instead, ÉTIENNETTE CHARPENTIER
THE LINENER handled the estate[27] as she apparently had for her sister and
younger brother. She turned over to the Chamber of Accounts and to
the Chapter of the Sainte-Chapelle everything that was deemed to be
royal property, and she took home the boxes and bundles of autograph
manuscripts that would come to be known as the *Mélanges*.

Panel 8

ELITE PATRONS

Some of the Princesses' Friends
Allowed His Name to be Linked to Theirs

The five portraits in this panel depict individuals from the elite levels of society. Some of them wear court dress, others are garbed in the more modest garments appropriate for barristers or royal officials. A few are ecclesiastics. In each painting, the sitter is surrounded by the attributes of his rank or profession.

In the first portrait a man in elegant dark clothes stands in a schoolroom and gestures through the open door to a chapel where a manger scene has been set up. From the shadows a Minim father looks on approvingly.

In the second portrait the subject has draped his black robe over an armchair. He turns toward a luxuriously furnished room where a well-dressed audience watches an opera being performed on a makeshift stage.

The attributes in the third portrait are brushes, paint pots, canvasses, and sketches strewn over a table.

In the fourth, an archbishop with his crosier smiles at a crosier-bearing nun, who points through an open door to the church at the Abbey of Port-Royal of Paris.

The final portrait depicts a man in costly court dress who gestures toward his garden. A marble bust of Cardinal Richelieu peeks from the foliage. In the background an equestrian statue of Louis XIV can be discerned.

I

In adoration before the cradle

DOMESTICS OF THE INFANT JESUS

Nicolas Le Jeune de Franqueville,
founder of the Academy of the Infant Jesus;
and Father Nicolas Barré, Minim,
founder of the Daughters of the Infant Jesus

During the months that followed the death of the last male of the House of Guise in March 1675, two educational institutions were created in Paris. Both were placed under the protection of the Infant Jesus. One of these ventures was supervised by the Seminary of Saint-Sulpice and had Madame de Guise as its patroness. The other, situated in the Guise parish of Saint-Jean-en-Grève, was Mademoiselle de Guise's project.

The Academy of the Infant Jesus

In September 1675, just six months after the death of MADAME DE GUISE's only son, the Duke of Alençon, a young barrister named Nicolas Le Jeune de Franqueville purchased a house on the periphery of the parish of Saint-Sulpice, not far from the convent of Notre-Dame de Liesse. The purchase price of thirteen thousand livres was ostensibly provided by several individuals who signed the document[1] but who appear to have been strawmen.

In reality, the project was the creation of Alexandre Le Ragois de Bretonvilliers, curate of Saint-Sulpice. Bretonvilliers was the nephew of Séraphim Le Ragois, a longtime servant of both the House of Orléans and the House of Guise. Alexandre was the brother of Madame Louis de Bailleul, a family "friend" of Jean Édouard, the dancing master who had wed ÉLISABETH CHARPENTIER a decade earlier.[2]

Said to be the wealthiest ecclesiastic in France (his annuities provided some forty thousand livres a year for charitable ventures), Bretonvilliers

253

had been put in charge of the Seminary of Saint-Sulpice in 1652, when poor health forced Jean Olier to pass his responsibilities to a younger and more vigorous man. Like Olier, Bretonvilliers was especially devoted to the Virgin. His motto—and that of the Seminary—was "Jesus living in Mary."[3]

At first glance the purchase of this house has nothing to do with either Bretonvilliers or Saint-Sulpice. Appearances are deceiving, however, because the people from whom Le Jeune de Franqueville had borrowed the purchase price were two first cousins, Cornille François and Pierre Neret. They happened to be the nephews of Curate Olier of Saint-Sulpice, the man who had left such a profound mark upon the spirituality and the charitable activities of Curate Le Ragois de Bretonvilliers. That François and Neret were also cousins by marriage of JACQUES II DALIBERT suggests that, like the Le Ragois–Bailleul family, the pair had strong affective ties to the household of Madame de Guise's late parents, GASTON D'ORLÉANS and the DOWAGER DUCHESS OF ORLÉANS.[4]

In reality, the house was being acquired at Bretonvillers' instigation, although the transaction was conducted in such a way that the notaries would be unable to identify the true purchaser. A reliable source asserts that it was Bretonvilliers who created the "Academy of the Infant Jesus, under the direction of Monsieur Le Jeune de Franqueville"; and that it was he who, with his own money, "had a magnificent house built, and acquired a very large enclosed plot of land."[5] (Although the building and grounds were usually called the *Hôtel de l'Enfant Jésus*, the school was known as the "Academy of the Infant Jesus," *Académie de l'Enfant Jésus*.)

In the parish of Saint-Sulpice there were already several academies where boys of high social rank could learn to dance, ride, and wield a sword. These establishments emphasized preparation for the courtly and military life. By contrast, the founders of the Academy of the Infant Jesus sought to keep their pupils in the "innocence of their baptism," and to "preserve them from the corruption of the century by raising them in a noble way that was worthy of their birth."[6] (The "innocence of their baptism" and the "corruption of the century": these expressions come as an echo of MADEMOISELLE DE GUISE, who in 1671 expressed her determination to protect MADAME DE GUISE's infant son from the "world.")

The Academy opened its doors to "the finest youth of the kingdom"—some eighty children in all—who were "the sons of dukes and peers, provincial governors, and presidents" in the Parlement. The boys studied "the humanities, rhetoric, philosophy, writing, dancing, and all the other exercises suitable for persons of their rank and age."[7] The directors of the school had a very precise mission. They were preparing France's future: "This academy is a sort of seminary to create good

Christians in all the three Estates," that is, the clergy, the nobility, and the Third Estate (commoners). These future servants of the Crown studied German and Latin, the two diplomatic languages of the day, because they were being prepared "to succeed their fathers in their property and their offices."[8] It is evident that the founder did not think that the Jesuit *collèges* should be the only serious educational alternative for elite sons.

The boys who boarded at the school were automatically enrolled in a confraternity devoted to the Infant Jesus that met regularly in the school chapel:

> Every Sunday they sang the Office of the Infant Jesus together, and
> a priest from Saint-Sulpice would go conduct their catechism. On
> the twenty-fifth of each month, two of them would take turns all
> night in adoration before the image of the Infant God, in whose
> confraternity they were all enrolled and where each had a task.[9]

The children were raised "in such a great devotion for the Infant Jesus" that they commemorated His birth on the twenty-fifth of every month: "They are in adoration before the cradle of the Infant God, two by two, from midnight until dawn, confessing and taking communion and singing the Office of the Infant Jesus."[10] This office for the "domestics of Jesus the Holy Child," devised by the Carmelites of Beaune, in Burgundy, used a fifteen-bead rosary.[11] It was a royal devotion: royal in that it drew a parallel between the Infant Jesus and Louis XIV, the God-Given Child King; and royal in that the entire royal family and aristocracy made a public show of this veneration—for example, during the annual Advent novena at the THEATINES.[12]

All "domestics" of the Christ Child were expected to create a devotional space consecrated to Him, a "special place in their houses, in the form of a chapel where He is portrayed as an infant."[13] This "special place" often took the form of a manger scene, sometimes set up in a wardrobe cabinet, sometimes in a chapel. The chapel at the Academy of the Infant Jesus was fitted with these essential devotional objects. The eyewitness description of the services conducted in the school chapel, quoted above, refers not only an "image of the Infant God" but to a "cradle," a *crèche*, a manger scene. Two notarial documents provide further details about the "large chapel with stone paving" and an "Italian-style ceiling." There was a "large painting depicting the Infant Jesus."[14] Since it is not described as a *Nativity*, the painting presumably portrayed the swaddled Child surrounded by cherubim and clouds.

The decoration of the school chapel fits into a larger framework, the "devotion" to the Infant Jesus. In the Carmelite church at Beaune, the faithful could come at any time of year and seek inspiration as they contemplated a Neapolitan-style manger scene, with life-sized statues. Like the boys at Franqueville's academy, the nuns of Beaune belonged to a sodality and recited the Litany of the Infant Jesus daily. Once a month they would go in procession to the "hermitage of the Infant Jesus," wearing their mantles and bearing candles.[15] In Paris, at Christmas time the faithful could admire a similar manger scene at the Hospital of the Pitié. After Twelfth Night the tableau became a "naive representation of the house of the Holy Virgin, consisting of wax figures that represent Saint Joseph, the Virgin, and Little Jesus at work."[16]

Evidence is scanty about MADAME DE GUISE's devotion to the Infant Jesus, but she is known to have belonged to the Confraternity of the Holy Infant Jesus and the Slavery to the Very Holy Virgin, created at her parish church of Saint-Sulpice in 1663.[17] Her private chapel in that church was decorated with a painting of the Nativity by Charles de la Fosse.[18] Her membership in this confraternity, combined with the recent loss of her son and her charitable activities in the parish, suggest that Curate Bretonvilliers consulted Madame de Guise before creating the new academy, and that the institution was a memorial to the dead prince.

Although no evidence has been found about MADEMOISELLE DE GUISE's membership in a confraternity of the Infant Jesus, the objects in her private apartment at the Hôtel de Guise reveal an especially strong devotion for the Christ Child. She owned a model of the Santa Casa of Loreto, made of exotic woods and trimmed with gold and jewels. Contemplating this devotional dollhouse, she could watch the Virgin making soup in a "cauldron of enameled gold" or spinning with her "wheel and distaff ... decorated with enameled gold and little diamonds and rubies." She could meditate as she contemplated a "Saint Joseph who is working ... before his carpenter's table ... with his tools, trimmed with gold and little diamonds and rubies," and an "Infant Jesus holding a broom."[19]

The Daughters of the Infant Jesus

While Le Jeune de Franqueville was creating the school in the parish of Saint-Sulpice, MADEMOISELLE DE GUISE embarked on a pedagogical venture of her own. The aims of her school differed markedly from those of the academy for young nobles. Focusing on the poverty and humiliation that the Child had accepted when He became man—and seeing the Infant Jesus in all the poor and deprived children of the realm who, despite their wretched outward appearance, were a "hiding place for God"—she created an institute that would prepare schoolmasters and schoolmistresses to work in the poorest urban neighborhoods, and in the rural areas where most children received no education at all, not even their catechism. The idea for the project may well have come from BISHOP ROQUETTE OF AUTUN.

Impressed by the work being done in Rouen by Nicolas Barré, a Minim father who was training girls from respectable bourgeois families to be schoolmistresses, she attempted to lure him to Paris. It was no easy task, but in the fall of 1675 Barré finally capitulated, in part because his superior had ordered him to do so, and in part because he could not refuse a command audience with a "princess of royal blood." In other words, MADAME DE GUISE had come to Mademoiselle de Guise's rescue. Barré went to the "palace"of the "Royal Highness" who had summoned him; he talked first with the princess and the gentlemen around her, and then with a group of clergymen. From start to finish, the scenario smacks of a pre-arranged testing of Father Barré:

> One of the princesses of royal blood had him come [to Paris] in order to test his doctrine and to tempt him by proposing several difficulties in the spiritual and mystic life. ... No sooner had he entered the palace than he was shown into the presence of the noble princess, who ... confided to him everything that her heart wanted to clarify. Father Barré answered all her questions fully, nothing escaped his insights or remained unanswered. ... Several monks and ecclesiastics who were around the princess, having seen how much she honored this monk and how much she enjoyed consulting him on theological subjects, asked to see him, to attend these conversations, and with the princess's permission to ask questions. ... The august princess, having acceded to their wishes, admitted them to these conversations.[20]

It soon became evident to Barré that although he had been interviewed by Her Royal Highness Madame de Guise, he had in effect agreed to work with Mademoiselle de Guise.

Only a few weeks later, in October 1675, Barré's institute opened its doors in Mademoiselle de Guise's parish of Saint-Jean-en-Grève and began training both male and female teachers. "We sent two [daughters] to the parish of Saint-Jean, where they were protected by the Curate and by Her Highness Mademoiselle de Guise," recalled one of the participants.[21] The princess soon sent teachers to her lands in northeastern France. The teachers trained by this institute came to be known sometimes as the "Daughters of the Infant Jesus," *Filles de l'Enfant Jésus*, and sometimes as "Father Barré's Girls," *Filles du Père Barré*.

In setting up this institute, Her Highness received guidance from an experienced group of educators. Some years earlier, with the cooperation of the Seminary of Saint-Nicolas-du-Chardonnet, Madame de Miramion had created a similar institute, the Daughters of Saint Genevieve. She and Mademoiselle de Guise are alleged to have vowed to merge their efforts, should one of the institutes encounter financial or administrative problems. The accuracy of this tale is confirmed by three documents that Mademoiselle de Guise signed in December 1676. Loans to and by the Seminary of Saint-Nicolas, and repayments and transfers of existing loans, conceal an exchange of funds in favor of each woman's teaching establishment,[22] in a way that was typical of the Barré organization and that calls to mind the strawmen who only a year earlier had purchased the house for Le Jeune de Franqueville. Miramion would soon work closely with MADAME DE GUISE in bettering the lot of the Parisian poor.

Domestics of the Infant Jesus

The tragedy that plunged the Hôtel de Guise and the Luxembourg Palace into mourning in March 1675 brought an abrupt about-face in the princesses' preoccupations. To find meaning in life, they turned to the Child and His Mother. Transforming her own domestics—the members of the GUISE MUSIC—into "domestics" of the Virgin and the Child, MADEMOISELLE DE GUISE hung on the walls of her music room two paintings of the Virgin, a depiction of the Infant Jesus, and a Descent from the Cross.[23] The music performed in that room would henceforth be so many prayers ascending to Heaven.

Until December 1676, neither series of Marc-Antoine Charpentier's notebooks contained music that specifically honored the Infant Jesus' high feasts: December 25, Christmas; January 1, Circumcision; January 6, Epiphany; and February 2, Purification. Advent 1676 brought a marked change in the content of the arabic-numbered series. In rapid succession came five motets or Latin oratorios for the Core Trio of the Guise Music. Three of these works celebrated the Infant Jesus through the feasts of the Circumcision, Epiphany, and the Purification; and in what surely is a bouquet to Madame de Miramion and her institute, the fourth honored Saint Genevieve.[A]

It is likely that these pieces were performed annually for the next eight years. The different motets for the Christ Child conceivably were sung over and over in one or more of the Guise chapels—that is to say, the chapels of the Hôtel de Guise and the Luxembourg Palace, the Church of the MERCY, the THEATINE Church of Sainte-Anne-la-Royale, the Abbey Church of MONTMARTRE, and the chapel at the Academy of

---

[A] Cahier 13, H. 316; cahiers 13–14, H. 317, H. 395, H. 318.

the Infant Jesus—plus, in all probability, the Guise chapel at Saint-Jean-en-Grève and MADAME DE GUISE's chapel at Saint-Sulpice.

For the better part of a decade the Guise Core Trio was there to perform these pieces; and then, in 1684, newcomers swelled the ranks of the GUISE MUSIC, transforming it into the Great Guise Music. At that point, Charpentier wrote a new piece for Christmas[A] and copied it into an arabic-numbered notebook. Concurrently with this work, he set two French-language Christmas pastorales to music,[B] also for the Great Guise Music. For Christmas 1685, he expanded one of the pastorales by adding a "second part"[C]; and for Christmas 1686 he wrote yet another "second part."[D] Strangely enough, he copied all these pastorales into the roman-numbered notebooks that contain outside commissions. In other words, a friend or friends of one or both Guise princesses commissioned the Christmas pastorales in 1684, and then requested two successive additions to one of them.[E] That Mademoiselle de Guise's musical chambermaids were allowed to perform is firm evidence that Her Highness approved of the patron and the venue. Who might this patron or these patrons have been? And why the shift from Latin to the vernacular?

This spate of vernacular Christmas music coincides with several important new responsibilities being entrusted to Father Barré's teachers. As the movement to convert Protestants gained momentum prior to the Revocation of the Edict of Nantes of 1685, the royal administration asked Barré to supply teachers for the new converts in the South. In 1684, in 1685, and on into the summer of 1686, teachers were sent to the provinces as fast as they could be trained.[24] Then, in the fall of 1686, a dozen of Barré's teachers began instructing the girls at Saint-Cyr, the prestigious new school for nobly-born girls founded by Madame de Maintenon; and several of Barré's male teachers accompanied missionaries overseas to teach native populations.[25] This chronology, and this blossoming of Mademoiselle de Guise's training program, suggests why these French-language pastorales were commissioned. They appear to have been written for festivities at the Institute of the Infant Jesus, where the teachers being trained knew little or no Latin. Another coincidence in dates reinforces this conjecture. Austere Father Barré died in 1683, and by 1684 the Institute was being administered by Ennemond Servien de

---

[A] Cahiers 42–43[a], H. 414.
[B] Cahiers XLIV–XLV, H. 482, H. 483.
[C] Cahier XLVIII–XLIX, H. 483a.
[D] Cahier XLIX, H. 483b.
[E] Cahiers XLVIII–XLIX, H. 483a, and cahiers XLIX–L, H. 483b.

Montigny, a highly entrepreneurial figure with considerable private wealth. (Servien was a member of the well-known ministerial family by that name.)

From the late 1670s on, compositions that correspond to events at Le Jeune de Franqueville's academy crop up in the arabic-numbered note-books that generally contain works for the Guise princesses. Among these pieces are prayers for the royal family[A] written for the Jubilee of March 1677, when the Archbishop ordered that prayers for LOUIS XIV be said in every church in Paris. Between March 3 and March 25, the QUEEN and the DAUPHIN visited each church. No evidence has been found of a visit to the school chapel, which was not technically a church; but on March 10 Father Tronson of Saint-Sulpice went to the Academy "to say mass and give the little gentlemen a brief exhortation about the Jubilee."[26] Another devotional work conceivably performed at the Academy was a Latin oratorio[B] for the Great Guise Music that recounted the Christmas Story. Composed for Christmas 1684, it was copied into an arabic-numbered notebook.

In 1685 a contract to renovate the school buildings was signed, a new edition of Franqueville's Latin method was in press,[27] and ÉTIENNE LOULIÉ, a member of the GUISE MUSIC, was devising handbooks on how to teach young boys viol and recorder. In other words, the arts were literally flourishing at the Infant Jesus that summer, when Charpentier wrote Les Arts florissants for the Great Guise Music.

The librettist for this "opera" was clearly aware that a Ballet des Arts was being prepared for the summer fête at the College of Louis-le-Grand. Yet the final result had nothing in common with the subject-book distributed to spectators at the Jesuit-sponsored entertainment.[28] Nor is it likely that the Great Guise Music ever performed at Louis-le-Grand. Emphasizing Peace as it does, the libretto evokes Lully and Racine's Idylle sur la Paix, which was performed for the Colberts at Sceaux in mid-July. In fact, for the partbooks Charpentier made this parallel explicit and called the work an "idyl." Since Madame de Guise was at Alençon all summer, it is highly unlikely that Les Arts florissants was written for performance at court, in the context of yet another twitting of Lully's privilege.

What, therefore, is one to make of this unusually didactic entertain-ment? It praises Louis XIV far more than usual, yet it does not suggest that he was witnessing the performance. It weaves the theme for Sceaux

[A] Cahiers 14–15, H. 164, H. 165.
[B] Cahiers 42–43[a], H. 414.

and the theme for Louis-le-Grand into an edifying whole. Was it performed at the Academy of the Infant Jesus during the festivities that marked the end of the school year?

This conjecture is strengthened by the juxtaposition, on the same stave, of the final measures of the opera and the opening measures of a work about boys. It is as if the two compositions were very closely linked in the composer's mind—for the same venue, but not necessarily for the same event. The motet about boys clearly was intended for youths and their teachers or spiritual advisors. That is to say, it evokes boys' induction into a confraternity of "servants" or "domestics" of the Virgin[A]: *Hodie Maria virgo suscepit nos omnes in servos suos*, "Today Mary the Virgin receives all of us as Her domestics." The text likewise alludes to teachers—or perhaps to ecclesiastics from Saint-Sulpice—and to the boys who have been entrusted to them: "Here we are, and the boys whom the Lord has given us," *Ecce nos et pueri quos dedit nobis Dominus, serva eos in nomine tuo, serva eos Maria in nomine tuo*. Who could these "domestics" be, if not the pupils and teachers at the Academy of the Infant Jesus? In other words, at Franqueville's academy—as at Louis-le-Grand, where outstanding students were honored by induction into a Marian sodality —select pupils apparently were given the special privilege of being domestics not only of the Child but of His Mother as well.

Marc-Antoine Charpentier moved out of the Hôtel de Guise in mid-1687, and the Great Guise Music disbanded shortly after MADEMOISELLE DE GUISE's death in March 1688. In her will, Mademoiselle de Guise remembered the institute she had founded with a annual payment of six hundred livres. Madame de Guise's will of 1695 made no mention of Franqueville's academy.

[A] Cahiers 46–47, H. 487, H. 340 (and H. 548?).

An opera was given at his hôtel with the usual splendor

RIANTS THE PROCURATOR

Armand-Jean de Riants,
procureur royal at the Châtelet of Paris

Armand-Jean de Riants was born into a parlementary family in
1623. He began his career as a royal page, became a councillor
in the Parlement of Paris in 1654, and in 1657 acquired the office
of royal procurator at the CHÂTELET, a position he occupied until 1684.

As a mature man, Riants preferred to conceal christening names that,
for his contemporaries, proclaimed an affective link to the Richelieu
family. He therefore would invert his baptismal names: "Jean-Armand."
Acts drawn up by several different notaries nonetheless show unequivocally that he was "Armand-Jean de Riants."[1] In short, Riants was
probably the godson of Cardinal RICHELIEU, who died in 1642. (Marc-
Antoine Charpentier's brother, ARMAND-JEAN THE ENGINEER, showed a
similar reticence about this distinctive combination of christening names.
He generally went by the name "Jean.")

Was Armand-Jean de Riants the godfather of LOUIS CHARPENTIER THE
SCRIVENER's second son, born in 1645? The possibility cannot be ruled
out, in view of family ties that linked the Riants family to the husband
of MARIE TALON, ÉLISABETH CHARPENTIER's friend. Riants' age was right,
for he was in his early twenties when the Charpentiers' younger son was
christened. Still, owing to the gap in our knowledge about Riants'
activities during the mid-1640s, neither Armand-Jean can be linked to
the other, nor to another Armand-Jean in the Richelieus' circle. It is,
however, certain that Riants was acquainted with several officials at the
CHÂTELET who were either friends or relations of the Charpentiers. For
example, throughout the 1660s he co-signed document after document
with Civil Lieutenant FERRAND, a friend and protector of ÉTIENNETTE
CHARPENTIER THE LINENER.

Riants married Anne Marceau, the daughter of a judge-provost at Troyes, and the couple set up housekeeping on the rue des Lions in the parish of Saint-Paul, on the outskirts of the *Marais*. Debts began to pile up. For example, in November 1657 Riants and his brother borrowed 15,800 livres. This loan, which was not repaid until 1670, is probably related to Armand-Jean's acquisition of his office at the Châtelet in September of that year.

In 1678 Royal Procurator Riants and his wife celebrated Mardi Gras by hosting an "opera"[A] by Marc-Antoine Charpentier, that other Armand-Jean's brother. What made Riants decide to participate in what amounted to a challenge to Lully's monopoly over the opera as a musical genre? And what made Riants think that MADEMOISELLE DE GUISE and MADAME DE GUISE would permit him to be linked in the press to their composer? The answer to the latter question appears to be that the Riants family had "belonged" to the House of Guise since the late sixteenth century.

In 1575, President Denis Riants' widow[2] signed André d'Alesso's wedding contract, declaring that she was the groom's maternal aunt. This tidbit of information seems irrelevant at first, for although Denis Riants was Armand-Jean de Riants' great-grandfather, the wedding predates Charpentier's opera by a century. The tidbit becomes somewhat less irrelevant when one learns that the groom's brother, François d'Alesso, was an ardent supporter of the League, and that their uncle had been Prior at the Guise pilgrimage church at Liesse.

The apparently tenuous thread that stretches from the Guises of the 1570s to the Guises of the 1670s was quite tangible in Armand-Jean de Riants' day, for in 1671 François d'Alesso's great-grandson, Jean d'Alesso, was in the immediate entourage of LOUIS-JOSEPH DE LORRAINE, DUKE OF GUISE.[3] In fact, Alesso was one of the intimates who traveled to England with the Duke that year.

This is not the only strand linking the Alesso–Riants family to the Hôtel de Guise over the decades and the generations. Early in the seventeenth century an Alesso granddaughter, Catherine Chaillou, married Frédéric Versoris. Frédéric was the son of Pierre Versoris, one of the Guises' principal advisers during the League. (MARIE TALON's husband was Pierre's great-grandson.) The Alessos were also related to the Blacvods,[4] and therefore to Madame GOIBAUT DU BOIS of the Hôtel de Guise. In short, Armand-Jean de Riants was part of a complex family tree

---

[A] Cahier XXIV, H. 499.

that had sprung from a group of fervent League supporters: the Riants, Alesso, Versoris, and Blacvod families.

It is in this context that the opera performed in 1678 at Armand-Jean de Riants' hôtel—he now resided on the rue Saint-Antoine in the *Marais*—takes on meaning. If the opera is significant to an understanding of Marc-Antoine Charpentier's creativity, rather than a simple entertainment commissioned or hosted by an ambitious man, it is owing to interpersonal contacts in the 1660s. During those very years, (a full three generations after the pro-Guise Riants–Versoris–Alesso–Blacvod family tree began to take shape) an Alesso and a Blacvod were residing at the Hôtel de Guise; Mademoiselle de Guise stood as godmother for old Pierre Versoris' great-grandson; and old Versoris' great-granddaughter-in-law, MARIE TALON, signed ÉLISABETH CHARPENTIER's wedding contract as a "friend" of the bride. In this context, it is not all that surprising that Mademoiselle de Guise would look favorably upon Armand-Jean de Riants' request that Marc-Antoine Charpentier be allowed to write an opera and have it performed at his home.

In their *Mercure galant*, the composer's friends and colleagues, Corneille and DONNEAU DE VISÉ, described the fête at which a "little opera" about Acis and Galatea was performed:

> During Mardi Gras several types of entertainments were given here, but one of the greatest we witnessed was a little opera entitled *Les Amours d'Acis et de Galatée*, several performances of which were given at his hôtel, with the usual splendor, by Monsieur de Riants, royal procurator at the Old Châtelet,. Each time more than four hundred listeners assembled. Among them several persons of the highest quality sometimes had difficulty finding a seat. All those who sang or played instruments were enthusiastically applauded. The music was composed by Monsieur Charpentier, two of whose airs I have already published here. Thus you are already familiar with his felicitous talent. Madame de Beauvais, Madame de Boucherat, Messieurs the Marquesses of Sablé and of Biran, Monsieur Deniel, Monsieur de Sainte-Colombe, so famous on the viol, and a quantity of others who understand to perfection all the fine points of song, were among the persons admiring this opera.[5]

Perhaps the most noteworthy thing about this article is the fact that the word "opera" is used twice. In other words, the editors of the *Mercure galant*—surely in complicity with Marc-Antoine Charpentier—were stating publicly that the Royal Procurator had dared infringe upon Jean-Baptiste Lully's monopoly over that musical genre, by allowing an "opera" to be performed in his stately home on "several" occasions. In this little rebellion, the composer and the host were joined by several individuals who likewise allowed their names to be mentioned in the press.

To the well-informed it would be evident that the people singled out were linked to either the Guises or the Orléans. There was the wife of Louis de Beauvais, a rich financier who had loaned money to Mademoiselle de Guise but had not yet been repaid[6]; and there was the wife of Louis Boucherat, the future chancellor of France who, calling himself a family friend, had signed the wedding contract of JACQUES II DALIBERT's sister in 1647.[7] (By 1679 Dalibert, that former householder of GASTON D'ORLÉANS, had acquired quite a reputation as an operatic impresario.) There was Riants' brother-in-law, the Marquis de Sablé, whose grandfather, Urbain de Laval, had been a Guise supporter during the League. But even closer to home, the Sablés—among them the famous Marquise who had long been DOCTOR VALLANT's patient—were Riants' in-laws. That is to say, Armand-Jean's late sister had married Madame de Sablé's son. (When the opera was being performed, Sablé's second wife and widow, Madame de Bois-Dauphin, lived at the ABBAYE-AUX-BOIS for which Marc-Antoine Charpentier had recently been composing.[B]) And there was the famous Monsieur de Sainte-Colombe, the protégé of MADEMOISELLE DE GUISE's late brother, Duke Henri. As for Marc-Antoine Charpentier, his position as the Guises' resident composer was scarcely a secret. In short, informed readers were to understand that the opera was a Guise- and Orléans-centered challenge to Lully's monopoly.

The *Mercure galant* did not mention the librettist, a longtime Orléans protégé. From 1664 to 1672 Jean de La Fontaine had been a gentleman in ordinary to the DOWAGER DUCHESS OF ORLÉANS. The lyrics of this "opera" begin with an air entitled *Brillantes fleurs naissez*. Written in 1661 while La Fontaine was Nicolas Foucquet's protégé, this poem had been part of *Le Songe de Vaux* and the sumptuous fête that led to Foucquet's arrest and disgrace. For Charpentier's opera the opening line was modified, the "fountains" of Vaux being replaced by "brilliant flowers." The composer had set this updated version of the poem to music prior to the fall of 1676, when he wove it into a pastorale-opera[C] performed at Saint-Cloud, PHILIPPE II D'ORLÉANS' country estate. Now, two years later, La Fontaine used these updated words for the opening air of his *Galatée*. In other words, there had been a give and take between the poet and the composer during the years preceding Riants' fête, and this interaction probably began at the Luxembourg Palace between 1670 and 1672.

[B] Cahier 19, H. 288, H. 322 (fall 1677).
[C] Cahier 13, H. 479.

When La Fontaine published the first two acts of his incomplete *Galatée* in 1682, he prefaced the work with a telling statement:

> I did not begin this work with the intention of turning it into an opera with the usual accompaniments, that is, visual effects and other divertissements. My only aim was to practice writing this sort of comedy or tragedy mixed with songs, which at the time amused me. ... The changeableness and anxiety that are so natural to me prevented me from completing the three acts into which I wanted to condense this subject.[8]

Hence the ironic adjective, "little," used by the editors of the *Mercure*.

In other words, La Fontaine had made the first two acts of *Galatée* available to Charpentier, who began "turning it into an opera"; but when the potential consequences of this challenge to Lully's monopoly began to dawn on the poet, his "natural anxiety" may well have caused him to "change" his mind and abandon the project. Tainted by his services to Foucquet during the 1650s, La Fontaine had been trying to rehabilitate himself in the King's eyes. His reasons for backing out of the project, or at least for keeping his name out of the *Mercure galant*, are therefore not difficult to deduce. Having expressed his irritation with Lully a few years earlier in three satyrical poems that could conceivably have been circulated in manuscript by anyone eager to bring about his disgrace, La Fontaine decided to dissociate himself from an "opera" that could dash his hopes for election to the French Academy.[9]

It is not clear from the *Mercure galant* whether Riants simply made his residence available, or whether he actually commissioned the opera and was therefore expected to remunerate Charpentier—and pay the requisite fine should Lully decide to cause trouble. That the composer copied the music into a roman-numbered notebook suggests that he expected to be remunerated by someone, just as the fact that he reused the music for a revival of *L'Inconnu* in October 1679 suggests that Riants did not give him the customary "gratification."

By 1680 Riants was in fact deeply in debt. This did not stop him from organizing events that would attract the King's attention, a tested but not always successful way to solicit royal largesse. In 1683 alone, he sponsored two religious services. One was held at his parish church, Saint-Germain-l'Auxerrois, in thanksgiving that Louis XIV had not been seriously injured in a fall. The other took place at the Châtelet, in memory of the late Queen. Immediately after her death, noted the *Mercure galant*, Riants "ordered services held at the Great and Small Châtelet for the repose of this princess's soul. He ransomed several prisoners and offered meals and money to those who were willing to receive it." So deeply was Riants in debt by November 1684 that his wife obtained a legal separation of their property. His furniture eventually had to be sold to pay his debts.[10]

A few months earlier, in August 1684, Riants had resigned his office in the Châtelet. His retirement, combined with his bankruptcy, attracted the attention of Louis XIV, who granted him a pension of six thousand livres in gratitude for three decades of service.[11] (A year earlier, Marc-Antoine Charpentier too had been rewarded with a pension upon termination of his services to the DAUPHIN, but the amount is not known.)

Riants' wife died in February 1686 and was buried in the church of the Cordeliers. By 1693, he had withdrawn to the Abbey of Saint-Victor, where he lived in one room. If he remained in touch with Marc-Antoine Charpentier, he did not remember him in his will.

III

Do me the favor of sending me some money

LE BRUN THE PAINTER

Charles Le Brun, First Painter to the King
and Chancellor of the Academy of Painting for life

Born in 1619, Charles Le Brun was the son of Nicolas Le Brun, a sculptor who had come to Paris from the Picard village of Crouy-en-Thelle. Not quite two modern kilometers from that village was a hamlet called Bellé, where a certain Jean Broquoys owned a house and fuller's mill. Jean had a daughter named Anne, born like Nicolas Le Brun in about 1580. When Anne grew up, she married a young man from Meaux, LOUIS CHARPENTIER THE BAILIFF. In short, Marc-Antoine Charpentier's paternal grandmother was both the neighbor and the contemporary of Charles Le Brun's paternal grandfather. This may be a coincidence of little or no consequence in the interpersonal and inter-professional links between the First Painter and the Guise composer. On the other hand, it may shed light on why Charles Le Brun is present in this gallery.[1]

At the time of Charles' birth, his sculptor father lived in Paris, on the rue Saint-Martin in the parish of Saint-Nicolas-des-Champs. That very year, 1619, Nicolas Le Brun was hired by the Duke and Duchess of Guise (MADEMOISELLE MARIE DE GUISE's parents) to make a stone fountain for the Hôtel de Guise.[2]

The pencil and the brush attracted young Charles Le Brun far more than the chisel and the hammer. By the time he was twelve, he is said to have drawn so well that Pierre Séguier offered the boy his protection and gave him quarters in his hôtel. That may be a legend, but there is not the shadow of a doubt that Charles had become Séguier's protégé by 1634. (In other words, LOUIS CHARPENTIER THE SCRIVENER's cousin, CHARLES SEVIN—an aide to Séguier and his daughter—presumably was acquainted with Charles Le Brun.) Extending his protection to other members of the family, as a conscientious patron was expected to do, Séguier made a point of hiring Nicolas Le Brun to carve ornaments for his garden.

By 1638 Charles Le Brun had become a "painter to His Majesty," although not until 1642 did he complete the formalities that gave him a mastership in the Painters' and Sculptors' Corporation. He then set off with painter Nicolas Poussin, who was on his way back to Rome. Séguier had promised Charles an annual pension and had given him letters of recommendation to two extremely powerful people, the Pope, and the Pope's nephew, Antonio Barberini. Thanks to these letters, Le Brun was given access to the Vatican and the Farnese Palace, where he was permitted to copy artworks for Séguier. Meanwhile, Poussin was teaching the young man some of his painting techniques.

But the Pope died and the nephew was exiled. Le Brun wrote Séguier, hinting that he would prefer to return to Paris. The Chancellor ordered him to remain in Rome. That required more money than Le Brun had in his purse, so in December 1644 he politely poured out his woes to Séguier, in a "very humble request" that calls to mind Marc-Antoine Charpentier's financial troubles in Rome and his rescue by DASSOUCY:

> After having been here some time without money, ... I went into
> debt; so that having paid my debts with part of the money it pleased
> Your Grandeur to send me, and having had some winter clothes
> made, very little of the aforesaid money is left. ... [Thus] I am so
> brazen as to importune Your Grandeur by very humbly begging him
> to not abandon me in my need, and to do me the favor of sending
> me some money.[3]

Without Barbarini protection, the young painter now found the doors closed when he went to copy paintings and frescoes for Séguier. Yet the Chancellor did not send him money to pay the bribes that would open those doors. After consulting with Poussin, Le Brun started out for Lyons. Only then did he inform Séguier that he was on his way back to France:

> Not having the money to [make the trip], I was forced to borrow
> from my friends, ... in order to clothe myself and make the aforesaid
> journey, which now obliges me to beg Your Grandeur to help me by
> the accustomed liberalities, so that I will have the means to pay for
> the expenditures I have made during my trip, and those I will have
> to make before I reach Paris.[4]

Back in Paris, Le Brun embarked on what would be a brilliant career. He was put in charge of organizing the Royal Academy of Painting. Prestigious commission followed prestigious commission; but none of the milestones in his career, nor the identity of his different patrons, sheds light on why Charles Le Brun allowed his name to be linked publicly with Marc-Antoine Charpentier's in 1679 and again in 1687.

Séguier's high royal office, and his protection of the French Academy, gave him virtual control over royal patronage of arts and letters. Did Pierre Séguier play a role in young Marc-Antoine Charpentier's musical apprenticeship in Rome?[5] The possibility certainly cannot be excluded, because the Chancellor was acquainted with at least two members of the Charpentier family, CHARLES SEVIN and GILLES CHARPENTIER THE SECRETARY. In fact, only a year before Marc-Antoine set out for Italy, Séguier had intervened to save the latter from prosecution.

On the Feast of Saint Louis, August 25, 1679, Le Brun sponsored a sung mass at the parish church for the royal Gobelins tapestry works where he resided:

> Monsieur Le Brun, First Painter of His Majesty, who every year celebrates [the Feast of Saint Louis] with special zeal, had a musical mass sung that day, in the parish of Saint-Hippolyte. The symphony was composed by Monsieur Charpentier. The church was hung with the richest tapestries made at the Gobelins. They represented the history of the King and were admired, as was the music, by all those who assembled in that place. ... Trumpets and oboes participated in the festivities and made it known afar what was happening at the Gobelins.[6]

For 1679 no music in honor of Saint Louis is to be found in Charpentier's roman-numbered notebooks, where he generally saved his non-Guise commissions. The other series of notebooks contains a motet for that saint, a motet "with a symphony"[A] that corresponds to the above description. The work was written for the two women's voices and the bass voice that had been typifying the Core Trio of the GUISE MUSIC since mid-1675, and that now was also characterizing the DAUPHIN's little ensemble, created only a few months earlier.[7] If this work by Charpentier was in fact sung at Saint-Hippolyte that day, was it performed by the Guise Music? Or by the Dauphin's Music?

This is one of a handful of works that, on the surface, appear to have found their way into the "wrong" series of notebooks during a moment of carelessness. This very small category of apparently misplaced works includes Charpentier's music for the nuns at the ABBAYE-AUX-BOIS—where, it turns out, friends of MONSIEUR DU BOIS, DOCTOR VALLANT, and MADAME DE GUISE were living. A similar explanation doubtlessly exists for

---

[A] Cahier 22, H. 323.

why Marc-Antoine Charpentier copied the music for the Feast of Saint Louis into the arabic-numbered notebooks.

In view of Le Brun's family ties to the very stones of the Hôtel de Guise, it is tempting to imagine MADEMOISELLE DE GUISE displaying her generosity toward Louis XIV in this way, and her special gratitude to the DAUPHIN for having asked her protégé to work for him. After all, the Feast of Saint Louis was the Dauphin's name day too.

Although most readers of the *Mercure galant* would not realize that Her Highness had loaned her composer to Le Brun for his mass at Saint-Hippolyte (and was perhaps lending him her household musicians as well), informed readers would have realized that the House of Guise was behind this event where the son of a former Guise sculptor was linked publicly with Monsieur Charpentier of the Hôtel de Guise. Indeed, it is very tempting to imagine that it was Nicolas Le Brun's servant–master ties to the House of Guise, rather than Charpentier's ties to the vicinity of Crouy-en-Thelle, or the men's common links to Chancellor Pierre Séguier, that brought the Guise composer into collaboration with the First Painter. Should that be the case, Le Brun may well have engaged the Dauphin's Music to perform that day, thereby honoring not only King Louis XIV but Louis the Dauphin as well.

The second musical event linking Charles Le Brun to Marc-Antoine Charpentier took place on February 8, 1687, when the Royal Academy of Painting—of which Le Brun was chancellor for life—organized a pontifical *Te Deum* mass at the Church of the Oratory, in thanksgiving for Louis XIV's recovery from life-threatening surgery. "The church was hung with rich tapestries, with nine huge paintings and twenty-four bas-reliefs, and vast illuminations." The press recounted how Le Brun had "himself worked on a painting" that represented one of the "principal actions" of the reign. A manuscript newsletter had been whetting appetites by promising that "the decorations will be magnificent, and the music will be the best of all the music yet heard" during this plethora of thanksgiving services.[8] Charpentier was mentioned, but not lauded, by both the *Gazette de France* and the *Mercure galant*: "Choirs of music sang the *Te Deum* and the *Exaudiat* composed by Sieur Charpentier"; "Monsieur Charpentier, who learned music in Rome under Carissimi, ... was employed to work on the music for this festivity."[9] No *Te Deum* and no *Exaudiat* are to be found in either series of the composer's notebooks for late 1686 and early 1687.

In the greater scheme of things at the Academy of Painting, Charpentier was far from the major artistic figure contributing to the beauty of this mass. The allusion to him in the *Gazette de France* totaled seventeen words, just thirteen percent of the total word-count of the article; and the *Mercure galant* devoted twenty-six words to him, a mere six percent of the total word-count in an article that discussed the paintings at some length.

The expenses incurred by the Academy suggest that, for the academicians as for the press, the music was but a small element in a splendid whole. In fact, Charpentier's stipend represented approximately fourteen percent of the total expenditures for such items as ushers, tickets, chairs, paintings of the King's "principal actions," and other decorations. To be precise, Charpentier was paid a lump sum of 350 livres, from which he was expected to pay the performers.[10] This represented fourteen percent of the total expenditure of 2,378 livres—virtually the same percentage of the total word count that the *Gazette* had allocated to Charpentier in its article about the mass.

No explanation has been found for why Charpentier received the commission, nor about any role that Charles Le Brun may have played in his selection.

IV

She is to her sex what her brother is to his

HARLAY THE ARCHBISHOP AND
MADAME HARLAY OF PORT-ROYAL

François II de Harlay de Champvallon, Archbishop of Paris;
and Marguerite de Harlay, Abbess of Port-Royal, his sister

In January 1671 Louis XIV nominated François II de Harlay de Champvallon, archbishop of Rouen, to be the new archbishop of Paris. On February 14, at the Convent of the Visitation, he received his pallium from MADEMOISELLE DE GUISE's confident, BISHOP ROQUETTE OF AUTUN. That Harlay chose Roquette comes as no surprise, for the Archbishop prided himself on his ties to the House of Guise.

Harlay's uncle, François I de Harlay de Champvallon, had, to use an seveteenth-century expression, been "raised" by Cardinal Joyeuse, Mademoiselle de Guise's maternal granduncle. "Before dying, the Cardinal begged the King to give him, as a successor, Monsieur de Harlay-Champvallon; he had been brought up at his side." In fact, the maternal side of Mademoiselle de Guise's family "thought of him as a relative."[1] Thus François I de Harlay became Joyeuse's coadjutor at Rouen in 1613 and succeeded him in 1615. In 1651, François I resigned in favor of his nephew, François II.

Not only was François II, the new Archbishop of Paris, "related" to MADEMOISELLE DE GUISE through her mother, he also boasted about a distant cousinship to MADAME DE GUISE. Back in the late fifteenth century a certain Jean Luillier de Manicamp had fathered two children. The daughter had married a Harlay, and her bloodline led directly to the Archbishop. From Luillier's son came a line of direct descent that produced the bride of François de Lorraine de Vaudemont, a member of the ducal family of Lorraine. One of the children born to Vaudemont was Madame de Guise's own mother, Marguerite de Lorraine, DOWAGER DUCHESS OF ORLÉANS.[2]

273

Although Harlay knew BISHOP ROQUETTE well by the time he was translated to Paris, and although the two prelates would continue to work closely during successive assemblies of the clergy, there is no firm evidence that Harlay commissioned any of the religious works in Marc-Antoine Charpentier's roman-numbered notebooks. One tantalizing work does, however, correspond to an event in the life of the new Archbishop of Paris. On the Feast of the Purification, February 7, 1671, the Confraternity of Our Lady at the Church of Sainte-Magdelaine held a pontifical mass to induct Harlay into their midst. The following day all the members assembled for a "Mass of the Holy Spirit," that is, a mass at which *Veni creator Spiritus* was chanted or recited to solicit divine inspiration. An "excellent music" was heard during the service, which included a *Te Deum*.[3] Charpentier's roman-numbered notebooks for 1671[4] contain a setting of this invocation of the Holy Spirit.[A]

The conjecture that Harlay perhaps commissioned a work from Charpentier as early as 1671 is somewhat strengthened by the fact that ROGER DE GAIGNIÈRES, Mademoiselle de Guise's equerry, was sufficiently familiar with Harlay by 1677 to write him some prodding albeit polite letters about a possible abbey for Bussy Rabutin's son. Gaignières even went to see the Archbishop. Although Harlay gave Gaignières "caresses and compliments," he dragged his heels and did not produce the requested letter to Father La Chaise, one of the FOUR JESUITS depicted in this gallery. The reason for Harlay's hesitation can be deduced. Within the so-called "council of conscience," *conseil de conscience*, where the two prelates had been advising the King about the distribution if livings to the French clergy, La Chaise was just then wresting power from Harlay. Nine months passed before Harlay finally "recalled, while talking to [Gaignières], that a month earlier he had promised Madame de Guise that he would give an answer."[5] In short, in addition to knowing BISHOP ROQUETTE, Harlay was in contact with both MADAME DE GUISE and Gaignières by mid-1677 at the latest—and doubtlessly with Mademoiselle de Guise as well.

In addition, during the different assemblies of the clergy of France held during the 1670s and 1680s, Harlay worked closely with BISHOP ROQUETTE. And we know with certainty that Harlay was in contact with the Hôtel de Guise during the mid-1680s, for in 1685 he asked PHILIPPE GOIBAUT DU BOIS to write a discourse on converting Protestants by gentle persuasion rather than force.

[A] Cahier VI, H. 54.

During the 1680s, Harlay would play a crucial role at the Abbey of Port-Royal, over which he had jurisdiction. A masterful politician, he managed to subdue Jansenism slowly, without raising too many hackles:

> He was not even hated by the most fervent Jansenists: he knew how to pad adroitly the blow being aimed at them. His friendly and engaging manners were like a magic charm that calmed or suspended the fury of the opposing parties, and no man ever knew better how to make himself everything for everybody, in order to win all of them over. It would have been fortunate if he had wanted to attach people to religion rather than to his person.[6]

Madame de Longueville's death in April 1679 ended the decade of calm known as the "Peace of the Church." Just one month later, Harlay went out to Port-Royal-des-Champs, the house "in the fields," and informed the nuns that all postulants and boarders must be sent away, and that no novices could be admitted for the foreseeable future. The death knell began tolling for the Jansenist house of the abbey. The Archbishop's pronouncements did not, however, affect the Parisian house, which had become a separate establishment in 1668 under Abbess Dorothée Perdreau. It was in this convent on the rue Saint-Jacques that MARIE CHARPENTIER THE CONVERSE, the composer's sister, was a nun.

Abbess Perdreau's death in 1685 gave Archbishop Harlay the opportunity to place his own sister, Marguerite de Harlay, on the abbess's throne at Port-Royal, to do his bidding. Marguerite initially protested that "her age, which was over sixty, and her poor health, would not permit her to follow the strict observance established at Port-Royal." A month later she capitulated, the King having ordered her to Paris.[7] She was consecrated on March 21, 1685.

In Charpentier's roman-numbered notebooks—immediately after a piece for the *Rendez-vous des Tuileries*, which opened on March 3, 1685—there is a Latin "dialog" about the four seasons of the year,[A] for two high treble voices (*haut-dessus*) and continuo. The texts draw upon the Song of Songs. In breviaries the liturgical year is, of course, divided into four "parts," each generally published as a separate tome: Spring, Summer, Fall, Winter. There are also four liturgical colors: white, red, green, purple (plus black for the dead, which has no specific "season"). It is therefore possible, even probable, that these dialogs were commissioned by the Archbishop for his sister's benediction. If not by Harlay himself, then this work was commissioned by the unidentified benefactor of the

---

[A] Cahier XLVI, H. 335–38.

abbey at whose behest Marc-Antoine Charpentier had written several works for Port-Royal a few years previously.

That is to say, back in 1681 he had composed a *Pange lingua* for the nuns of Port-Royal—specifically, for nuns with high treble voices, *haut-dessus*.[A] Then, in the fall of 1684, he composed an *élévation* [B] for a trio of these high voices consisting of two nuns, plus a boarder named Mademoiselle Du Fresnoy. That a boarder was present to perform with the nuns proves that Charpentier's pieces "*pour le P.R.*" could not have been written for the Jansenist house "in the fields," from which all boarders had been expelled several years earlier. The patron who commissioned the *Pange lingua* and the *élévation* has not been identified, but it was someone in the Guises' good graces. That is to say, this patron dared to beg Mademoiselle de Guise for permission to approach her householder, and he or she managed to obtain the princess's approval—an honor she did not always bestow, as DOCTOR VALLANT could attest from personal experience. In short, since Marc-Antoine Charpentier was composing for the nuns of Port-Royal as early as 1681, any commissions he received from Abbess Harlay represent the continuation, not the creation of a link between the abbey and the Hôtel de Guise.

(On the other hand, it is extremely unlikely that two pieces[C] that Charpentier had composed back in the summer of 1670—one for Saint Augustine, so revered by the Jansenists, and the other for Saint Bernard, the founder of the Cistercians—were written for the nuns at either house of the abbey. In both works, two women are accompanied by recorders, an instrument apparently not played by nuns. That the composer copied these works into his arabic-numbered notebooks suggests that they were intended for someone in the Guise circle, probably MONSIEUR DU BOIS, who had not yet broken his ties to the Jansenists at Port-Royal-des-Champs. Performance by the nascent Guise Music at the Parisian convent is plausible, if not documented.)

Into one of his roman-numbered notebooks Charpentier copied out a mass "for Port-Royal," for the two nuns and the boarder who had performed the *élévation* back in 1684. Since the introits, graduals, and communions in this mass honor both Saint Francis and Saint Marguerite (albeit separately), and since the notebook dates from the summer of 1687, the mass in question must be the one discussed in DONNEAU DE VISÉ's *Mercure galant*. The service was held on July 20, to rejoice over

[A] Cahier XXXI, H. 62.
[B] Cahier XLII, H. 256.
[C] Cahier 1, H. 306; cahier 2, H. 307.

François Harlay de Champvallon's recovery from an illness that "had been of great concern to the people in his diocese."

The mass was celebrated in the "rather bizarre, but very gallant and comfortable" church designed by Lepautre. Above the high altar hung Philippe de Champaigne's *Last Supper*. The Holy Sacrament was suspended from a gilded bronze crook, causing it to hover above the altar, "as it did in the Early Church. ... It is so artful that not only does the Holy Chalice seem suspended in the air, it also descends noiselessly and without a squeak."[8]

That day several devotions to music were held in this chapel, with its awesome and mystifying altar. A "sung" mass, complete with several motets, was the high point of the day. The mass was sandwiched in between the offices of terce and sext, and nones and vespers, chanted by the Franciscan monks (Cordeliers) of the Great Convent. After refreshments came the Benediction of the Holy Sacrament, *salut*, chanted by the monks but embellished with partsong:

> The Archbishop of Paris is presently in perfect health. The Cordelier fathers of the Great Convent, who during his illness had offered daily public prayers in their church to ask God for his recovery, ... wanted to give a special thanksgiving; and to make the solemnity more striking, the Abbess of Port-Royal, worthy sister of this illustrious prelate, agreed to allow it to take place in her church on the twentieth of last month, the Feast of Saint Margaret, whose name she bears. The Guardian Father [of the Cordeliers] and his officers, accompanied by about thirty monks, went to the church of Port-Royal on the morning of this feast. They began by singing terce, and then the high mass was sung with all the ceremonies of the Great Convent, and several motets in music for the Holy Sacrament, Saint Margaret, and the King, after which sext was sung. After the service, they were served a magnificent repast, along with the directors and the almoners. Nones and vespers were sung at the usual hour, in plainsong and in faux-bourdon; and after that, Father Le Blanc, vicar of the Great Convent, gave the panegyric in honor of Saint Margaret with great success. He said of the Abbess of Port-Royal, that she knew how to lead without commanding, that she governed without reigning, and that she was to her sex what Monsieur de Paris [Archbishop Harlay] is to his. A Benediction of the Holy Sacrament to music ended the festivities. It was chanted by the same fathers, who had recited all the offices that day in a manner that demonstrated their zeal for the Archbishop and for the Abbess of Port-Royal.[9]

Although only Saint Margaret was honored that day—which was as it should be, since it was her feast—Charpentier provided for a potential reuse of this mass on the Feast of Saint-Francis in mid-September. That his friends at the *Mercure galant* did not name the composer of the "motets in music" comes as no surprise. The festivities honored the Harlays and praised the Cordeliers, so it would have been inappropriate to mention Marc-Antoine Charpentier. Even so, readers who knew about the composer's family tie to Port-Royal would have little trouble deducing who had written the motets. It is noteworthy that Charpentier's music for the mass was not performed by the usual three *haut-dessus*, but by three slightly lower voices, *dessus*. Does this mean that the music for this mass was performed by laywomen positioned in the church proper, rather than by the two nuns and their boarding student, singing from behind the curtained grill of the nuns' choir, as was their wont? Judging from the *Mercure galant*, it was the Cordeliers, not the Harlays, who remunerated Charpentier.

Charpentier wrote several other works specifically labeled "for Port-Royal"—apparently between August and December 1687, that is, just after he had left the Hôtel de Guise and had begun composing for the Jesuits. He used paper the Jesuits were providing; but instead of making these pages a part of one or the other of his numbered series of notebooks, he put them into an unnumbered notebook or bundle, just after his "Epitaph." (The bundle would later be called the "fat notebook," *gros cahier.*[10]) In other words, the works in this notebook or bundle were not related to his work for the Jesuits. Nor were they paid commissions. Rather, he gave the pieces to the abbey as a personal gift. Destined for the usual trio of high voices, these compositions—two psalms and a *Magnificat*[A]—were appropriate for vespers and/or the Saturday service known as the Little Office of the Virgin. (One of the psalms was subsequently modified for male voices, presumably for performance at the Church of Saint-Louis, one of the THREE JESUIT HOUSES of Paris.)

In this context, the subject of another piece that he copied onto Jesuit paper and appears to have stored away in the same "fat notebook" assumes significance. This work, which calls for two high sopranos rather than three, seems to have been written for the Feast of Saint Augustine,[B] August 28, 1687.[11] In honoring this saint whom the Jansenists held in great veneration, the composer had come full circle. In 1670, at the start of the Peace of the Church, he had copied a motet for Augustine into one of his earliest Guise notebooks. Now, in the waning months of 1687—with the Peace broken, Jansenism repressed, and the former

---

[A] Cahier "d," H. 226 (Sunday vespers), H. 227 (Monday vespers), H. 81 (all vespers).
[B] Cahier "d," H. 419.

Jansenist stronghold of Port-Royal of Paris under the control of the Harlays, who had vowed to extirpate this heresy—Marc-Antoine Charpentier set a text about the "death" of this "good servant who has fought to defend the faith." This composition may well have been intended as a gift to the Parisian house of Port-Royal, where Jansenism, was subsiding. Ironically, by the time performance rolled around, Marc-Antoine Charpentier had been appointed music master to the Jesuits, those fervent opponents of Jansenism.

Marguerite de Harlay was given to arranging splendid services at Port-Royal, where expense was not a concern. Once the separation of the two houses had become official in 1669, the abbey could count on an annual income of ten thousand livres, in addition to the high rents they collected on a cluster of large buildings just outside the abbey walls. In addition, the Paris house had received all the silver in the sacristy and two-thirds of the furniture. (The far more populated house at Port-Royal-des-Champs had to get by on just under twenty thousand livres.) During Madame Harlay's tenure as abbess, the "income presumably increased considerably, because they were still free to receive boarders[A] and novices"—the former paying room and board, the latter contributing pensions.[12] Abbess Harlay's propensity for allowing expenditures to exceed income brought the abbey to the brink of insolvency. "Ruined by the mad expenditures of their abbess," in 1696 the nuns would try, but in vain, to regain control over some of the property that was held by Port-Royal-des-Champs.[13]

With the final months of 1687, Port-Royal disappeared from the composer's notebooks, despite the fact that his sister Marie lived on at the abbey into the eighteenth century, and despite the fact that the Archbishop and his sister went about their administrative and devotional tasks for eight more years. Marguerite de Harlay turned the indebted abbey over to a Benedictine nun from Alençon in April 1694 and died the following year. Having lost the power he had long wielded over the clergy of France, François was carried off by apoplexy on August 6, 1695, at his country house. He was remembered for

> his profound knowledge, the eloquence and ease of his sermons, the excellent choice of subjects, and the able conduct of his diocese, as well as his administrative abilities and the authority he had acquired over the clergy—all of which stood in marked contrast to his private behavior, his gallantry, and his manners worthy of a great courtier.[14]

[A] Cahier XLII, H. 256; cahier "d", H. 226, H. 227, H. 81 (Mlle. du Fresnoy, a boarder, sings with nuns).

V

The King's departure upset the Duke's plans

RICHELIEU OF RUEIL

Armand-Jean du Plessis de Richelieu,
Duke of Richelieu and peer of the realm

In 1631 Armand-Jean du Plessis, Cardinal Richelieu, gave his two Christian names to his two-year-old grandnephew. The Cardinal's will named this godson as the prelate's "universal heir," on condition that he adopt the name and the arms of the Du Plessis family. Thus Armand-Jean de Vignerot de Pont-Courlay came to be called Armand-Jean de Vignerot du Plessis de Richelieu. And thus, at the age of thirteen, he became Duke of Richelieu.

Like his illustrious granduncle, who had given his name to a host of little Armand-Jeans (ARMAND-JEAN DE RIANTS appears to have been one of these godsons), the Duke of Richelieu honored an additional host of little Armand-Jeans by agreeing to be their godfather. These two successive generations of Richelieu godsons created a pyramid effect. The first generation of godsons, born prior to 1642, and the second one, born during the 1640s, eventually passed their distinctive christening name to their own godsons. Thus it is impossible to say whether Marc-Antoine Charpentier's brother, ARMAND-JEAN THE ENGINEER, baptized in 1645, was the godchild of the Duke or the godchild of one of the Cardinal's godsons. Be that as it may, it is virtually certain that LOUIS CHARPENTIER THE SCRIVENER was in contact with the Richelieus or with someone who "belonged" to them.

The Duke of Richelieu's wedding to a widow in 1649 shocked the family and the royal court, as did his insistence upon controlling his estates himself, although he was still a minor. Having no head for such matters, Richelieu promptly went deeply into debt.[1] Had his mother not conveniently died in 1674, and his aunt, Madame Combalet, Duchess of Aiguillon, in 1675, the Duke would have lost control of much of his property. Their deaths temporarily staved off his creditors, and they increased Richelieu's holdings by giving him title to the Cardinal's beloved estate of Rueil. By the time he inherited Rueil, the Duke was in his early fifties. And he was childless. It was little consolation that he was appointed "honorary knight" to the Dauphine in 1680, and that the Duchess became one of her "honorary ladies."

In May 1684, the Duchess died. By July 30 the Duke had remarried. The bride brought a dowry of four hundred thousand livres, including one hundred thousand livres in cash. Rueil was promptly refurbished, and in late August the newlyweds held a special fête for PHILIPPE II D'ORLÉANS, his wife, and their entourage.[2] To fill his rapidly emptying purse, Richelieu sold his office in the Dauphine's household in February 1685, for three hundred thousand livres.

Although his first child, born in June 1685, was a girl, the Duke was in such a festive mood that he got caught up in an unofficial competition where cities vied with cities and nobles with nobles, to see who could offer Louis XIV the most splendid statue. Richelieu commissioned a representation of the King on horseback.

He began planning the fête during which the model of this equestrian statue would be unveiled. The event would commemorate the centenary of the birth of the "Great Armand," September 5, 1585. In this way the Duke could not only draw a parallel between himself and his granduncle, he could also parallel the statue that would be unveiled on a September day in 1685, and with the bronze equestrian statue of Louis XIII that the Cardinal had erected in the Place Royale (today's Place des Vosges) on a September day back in 1639. The festivities came to be called the *Feste de Ruel*, the "Fête of Rueil."[3]

The Duke approached Marc-Antoine Charpentier, who began preparing a pastorale to be performed in the gardens, and an air for the King to be sung at the unveiling.[A] Richelieu's reasons for selecting the Guise composer are not clear. Although the first names of Marc-Antoine's brother suggest a long-standing link with the Richelieu circle, and although some of the composer's SEVIN cousins were administering the Duke's finances in 1685, the commission may simply be explained by the fact that the Duke's late wife had been one of the ladies of honor at MADAME DE TOSCANE's little court at MONTMARTRE.[4] In other words, the Richelieus had not only had an opportunity to hear Charpentier's music, they also had been seeing MADAME DE GUISE and MADEMOISELLE DE GUISE

[A] Cahiers XLVII–XLVIII, H. 485, and the partbooks, H. 485a.

at Montmartre—and at any court functions the Grand Duchess of Tuscany was permitted to attend.

For the Fête, Richelieu commissioned a second "opera," this one from SÉBASTIEN DE BROSSARD, the friend of Guise musician ÉTIENNE LOULIÉ. Brossard had recently been in contact with the Duke's householders, the SEVINS,[5] and he appears to have been keeping informed about, if not actually participating in Madame de Richelieu's salon.[6]

By late August a model of the statue was attracting visitors to Rueil. One of them commented upon the precarious state of the Duke's finances:

> We went to lunch at Rueil, where the Duke of Richelieu showed us the model of an equestrian statue of the King that he plans to have cast in bronze. Gobert made it and is gambling on the event; he is advancing the money and is sure he will succeed.[7]

The sculptor was indeed taking both a financial and an artistic risk. Not only was he working without an advance to cover his expenses, he was more or less guaranteeing that the statue would move at the slightest touch:

> The King is mounted on a horse, which according to the most savant connoisseurs surpasses that of the Pont-Neuf [bridge in Paris], in all its proportions and its pose. There is something noteworthy in this equestrian figure, which is excessively heavy: all the weight of the horse rests on its hind feet, and the front feet are in the air, and the sculptor balanced it so perfectly that it can be set in motion with one finger.[8]

As September 1685 approached, the Duke of Richelieu was anxiously awaiting confirmation of the anticipated royal visit. So were his domestics, his sculptor, his composers, and the musicians they were rehearsing. Silence. Then disaster! On September 3 Louis XIV and his court set out for Chambord, not to return until mid-November.

The article by Corneille and DONNEAU DE VISÉ, Marc-Antoine Charpentier's friends at the *Mercure galant*, downplays the Duke's disappointment. Rather than blame the King, the article told a white lie, implying that it was Richelieu's slowness in having the statue moved and painted that had led to the cancellation of the Fête:

> The Duke of Richelieu ... was expecting to be honored by receiving the King at Rueil; but since the most agreeable entertainment of this fête was supposed to be the image of this great prince, and since it required time to transport the most extraordinary figure ever made, the King's departure for Chambord upset all the Duke's plans.

(Actually, the statue had been in place at Rueil since August 28, when Dangeau went out to inspect it.) "And so," the *Mercure* continued, "the Duke of Richelieu having invited several persons of quality to Rueil for a noon repast," the guests found a series of madrigals posted around the statue. One of the posters bore the words to Charpentier's air for the King. However, because the Duke was being praised, neither Marc-Antoine Charpentier nor Sébastien de Brossard could be mentioned.

There is no reason to think that Charpentier's pastorale was ever performed. Indeed, he kept the partbooks that he generally turned over to his different patrons, who in this way could be sure that the commission would remain exclusive and not find its way into the public domain. Nor did Brossard get to conduct his little opera: "There was supposed to be a performance of my opera *Pyrame et Thisbé*, which I wrote expressly for [the Fête]; but the King's departure for Chambord upset all [the Duke's] plans."[9]

Without the anticipated gratification from Louis XIV, Richelieu was ruined. His only alternative was to withdraw from court, in order to reduce his expenditures—which he did shortly after the failed Fête. The statue was never completed, although the painted plaster version remained in the garden. Later that year, a visitor to Rueil noted that

> to the right, as one looks at the garden, above the grotto there is a bronzed plaster model of an equestrian statue of the King, who seems to be galloping. There is a pond surrounded by numerous fountains and waterfalls, which are decaying, however. The great cascade at the end of the alley creates a fine effect, although it is no longer so radiant. ... Otherwise there is nothing noteworthy, beyond a triumphal arch in trompe-l'œil, which looks very realistic. There is also a dragon that revolves and wets everyone who comes up to see it. ... The château is old and not very imposing.[10]

The Great Armand's ne'er-do-well heir and godson died at eighty-six, having finally produced a son in March 1696.

Panel 9

THE ROYAL HOUSES
OF BOURBON AND ORLÉANS

Madame de Guise's Cousins,
Madame de Guise's House

Each individual or group portrayed in this panel is depicted in an ornate, gilded room with frescoed ceilings. Gilded lilies of France decorate almost every object.

The first painting shows a couple accompanied by three young princesses. Through a window a domed entryway can be seen, and through another window, a vast garden. In the background a young woman is striding out of the picture. Busts of Kings Henri IV and Louis XIII stare out from the background shadows (*pace* Largillière!).

The same busts peer out from the shadows in the second painting, which likewise is a group portrait. The subjects are King Louis XIV, the Queen, and their son the Dauphin.

The third painting is a double portrait. A father and his son stand proudly in a sumptuous room where a makeshift stage has been set up. The adolescent prince holds some music paper.

The fourth and fifth paintings form a pair. The royal princesses portrayed here are recognizably sisters. One is strikingly beautiful, yet she stands disconsolately in a vast Italian palace. The other, who has assumed a posture she hopes will conceal her crooked spine, holds the portrait of a beautiful young man. She has removed a jeweled fleur-de-lis from her court gown and is pinning a double-beamed cross of Lorraine in its place.

I

But all that glory had passed

MONSIEUR AND MADAME D'ORLÉANS

Gaston de France, Duke of Orléans, known as "Monsieur,"
and Marguerite de Lorraine, his wife, known as "Madame,"
who became the Dowager Duchess of Orléans,
the parents of Madame de Guise

Gaston of France was the younger of the two surviving legitimate sons of King Henri IV and Queen Marie de Médicis. Born in 1608, the prince, known as "Monsieur," was witty and lively. He was the antithesis of his morose older brother Louis, who succeeded his assassinated father in 1610. Resentful about what he saw as repeated rebuffs by his brother, now Louis XIII, Gaston became continually caught up in court intrigues and conspiratorial plots.[1] Time and again his supporters were punished in his stead; and now and then the prince would seek refuge abroad, in the Spanish Netherlands or the Duchy of Lorraine.

Among Gaston's most loyal supporters was Claude de Bourdeille, Count of Montrésor, who entered Monsieur's entourage in around 1630 as Master of the Royal Hunt. (Montrésor eventually became MADEMOI-SELLE MARIE DE GUISE THE REGENT's morganatic husband.) Over the years, Montrésor's role was to help stir up the malcontents at court and push them to commit violent acts. At the crucial moment, he would disappear into the wings, escaping the punishments meted out to the conspirators.[2]

By his wedding in 1626 to wealthy Marie de Bourbon-Montpensier, Gaston became Mademoiselle de Guise's brother-in-law. His bride died less than a year later, giving birth to MADEMOISELLE DE MONTPENSIER, also known as the "Grande Mademoiselle." (This strong-willed and outspoken princess has stalked out of this family portrait and has gone to lord it over her inferiors in Panel 11.)

While exiled in 1631 for plotting, Gaston eloped with Marguerite de Lorraine, the Duke of Lorraine's adolescent sister. This second marriage strengthened Monsieur's ties to the Guises, for Marguerite's sister had married Louis, bastard of Guise, Mademoiselle de Guise's second cousin. In other words, although the ducal and the Guise branches of the House of Lorraine had gone their separate ways in the early sixteenth century, MADEMOISELLE DE GUISE and Madame d'Orléans were close cousins by marriage and would remain strong allies over the years, whenever a dynastic issue arose involving the House of Lorraine.

In October 1634 Gaston was permitted to return to France. There, abetted by Montrésor, he resumed his political activity—or rather, his political plotting. His wife had remained in Brussels, because Louis XIII and Cardinal Richelieu refused to recognize the marriage. Marguerite de Lorraine did not see her husband again until 1643, shortly after Louis XIII's death. Complying with the dying monarch's wishes, the couple went through a second nuptial mass, Madame sobbing all the while "because she believed she had been living in mortal sin until then."[3] This decade of rejection, combined with the possibility that she might be an adulteress, left psychological scars that deepened with the years.

In 1645 the couple produced a daughter, Marguerite-Louise d'Orléans, known in her youth as "Mademoiselle d'Orléans." (Because she later married Cosimo III de' Medicis, son of the Grand Duke of Tuscany, she is known as "MADAME DE TOSCANE" in this portrait gallery.) A year later, the Duchess of Orléans announced that she was again pregnant. The baby was born on December 26, 1646. It was another girl. Gaston could not hide his disappointment, for should young Louis XIV and his brother die, the Crown would pass to a male of the House of Orléans. This new daughter was therefore a "sorrowful subject for the Duke of Orléans. He passionately desired a son."[4]

The arrival of Mademoiselle d'Alençon was extremely distasteful to MADEMOISELLE DE MONTPENSIER, who admitted that, when she received the news, "I was even more pained than at [the birth] of the first one." She did manage to express compassion for her disappointed father: "I felt regret, because I know [this birth] ran counter to His Royal Highness's hopes, and that it was not to the advantage of his House."[5] Named *Élisabeth* by her godfather and first-cousin, PHILIPPE II D'ORLÉANS, the princess would prefer a variant of that name: *Isabelle*, ISABELLE D'ORLÉANS OF ALENÇON.

Detesting her half-sisters even more than she detested her stepmother (Madame d'Orléans) and her aunt (Mademoiselle Marie de Guise), Montpensier made life difficult for them all. Her bitterness toward the young princesses became legendary, especially the scorn she showed Mademoiselle d'Alençon:

> [Isabelle] was badly treated by Mademoiselle, her only sister from her father's first marriage, who was powerfully rich and who had never been able to digest the fact that Monsieur, her father, had remarried, nor tolerate his second wife or her daughters.[6]

The death of Gaston's only son in 1652, at two, followed by the demise of another daughter in 1656, saddened Monsieur and Madame; but Montpensier shed no tears over the departure of a baby sister she viewed as superfluous: "Since I had never seen her, my affliction was middling; the affliction of Their Royal Highnesses was great, for they love their children very much."[7]

The so-called "Fronde of Monsieur," a rebellion of the early 1650s, having failed, Gaston d'Orléans withdrew to his châteaux (principally Blois), and to Orléans, the capital city of the Duchy of Orléans, which he had received as an apanage in the 1620s and could transmit to a son but not to a daughter. (After Gaston's death, Orléans was given to Louis XIV's brother, Philippe II de France who, as head of the House of Orléans, is depicted in this portrait gallery as PHILIPPE II D'ORLÉANS.) Some of Gaston's domestics were left behind in Paris to tend to his business in the capital; others were permitted to retain their titles in his household, although they no longer carried out the usual duties; and a small group followed him to Blois.

Despite the Duke's disgrace, these faithful householders were retained. Indeed, whenever death caused one Orléans household to be dissolved, many servants were passed on to another member of the House of Orléans. In addition, these domestics often wangled positions for their friends and relations. This was the case in 1660, when some of Gaston's servants were gathered in by his wife; in 1672, when MADAME DE GUISE incorporated some of her late mother's domestics into her own household; and in 1702, when GILLES CHARPENTIER THE SECRETARY's children moved from the household of the late PHILIPPE II D'ORLÉANS to that of his son, PHILIPPE III, once Duke of Chartres and now Duke of Orléans.

The papers of Gaston's estate reveal that during the 1640s and 1650s, the following people whose names recur in this portrait gallery "belonged" to Monsieur in one way or another: JACQUES HAVÉ DE SAINT-AUBIN, his gentleman in ordinary, who was LOUIS CHARPENTIER THE SCRIVENER's close cousin; Claude and Marc Malier, Madame's first almoners, the brother and the nephew of ÉLISABETH-MARIE MALIER, a friend of ÉLISABETH CHARPENTIER's husband; René Grimaudet, Gaston's lieutenant general at Blois, the brother of ÉLISABETH GRIMAUDET, another

friend of ÉLISABETH CHARPENTIER's husband; Nicolas Guichard, valet to
Gaston, whose son Henry would be integrated into the household of the
next Duke of Orléans, PHILIPPE II D'ORLÉANS; Nicolas Pinette de Charmoy,
intendant of Gaston's household and financial guardian of the princesses,
who moved to Madame d'Orléans' household and whose son, Jacques,
became MADAME DE GUISE's private secretary; Denis Doujat, Gaston's
advocate general, who happened to be the maternal grandfather of MARIE
TALON, ÉLISABETH CHARPENTIER's friend; Pierre Perrin, Gaston's introducer of ambassadors and one of the creators of French opera, whose
debts would be paid by MADAME DE GUISE in 1672[8]; Anne-Alexandre de
l'Hospital de Sainte-Mesme, Gaston's first equerry, who was taken into
Madame d'Orléans' household in 1660 and was appointed MADAME DE
TOSCANE's "honorary knight" in 1675; Jacques I Dalibert, superintendent
of Gaston's finances, and his son and assistant, JACQUES II DALIBERT;
Macé Bertrand de La Bazinière, Gaston's councillor and financier, who
was the second husband of MARIE TALON's mother-in-law.[9] Thus, when
Marc-Antoine Charpentier left for Rome in about 1666, and when he
returned to Paris at some point in 1669, at least four proven "friends" of
the Charpentier family were in a position to recommend the young
composer to Gaston's daughter, ISABELLE OF ALENÇON, who wed LOUIS-
JOSEPH, DUKE OF GUISE, in 1667.

While the remnants of Gaston's Parisian household were casting
about for other masters, his entourage at Blois was cut off from the King's
court and from the fashionable life of the capital. Gaston's court was
passé, it was growing old with its master:

> His court had formerly been filled with several high nobles of the
> realm, all of whom wanted the honor of belonging to him, ... but all
> that glory had passed. ... Nothing remained for him but the bitter
> memory of the vanity of his thoughts and the uselessness of his
> actions. After the failure of his unfortunate undertakings, he had
> remained in a certain state of disgrace that causes men to be classed
> among the dead before they actually are.[10]

When Monsieur and Madame received Louis XIV at Blois in 1659,
neither the dance performed by the little princesses in his honor, nor the
magnificent buffet that Gaston had readied, could conceal the fact that
the King's uncle was living like a provincial noble, and that his daughters
were deficient in the social skills valued by the royal court. MADEMOISELLE
DE MONTPENSIER, who was feeling especially lofty because she was traveling with the royal party, was the first to criticize her sisters—and her
father:

We wanted to make [the little princesses] dance, ... for people
thought highly of my sister [the graceful Mademoiselle d'Orléans];
she danced very badly. The youngest [the talkative Mademoiselle de
Valois...] would not say a word. Since my father's household officers
were no longer in style, no matter how magnificent the meal, it was
not considered good, and Their Majesties ate very little. All the
ladies of the court of Blois, who were very numerous, were dressed
up like the dishes in the banquet, out-of-date. The Queen [Mother]
was in such a great hurry to leave, and the King too, that I never
saw anything like it. That didn't seem very gracious, but I think my
father felt the same way, and that he was very pleased to be rid of
us.[11]

Struggling with real or imagined ill health, and given to indolence,
Madame d'Orléans slowly sank into inertia mingled with intense piety:

For important events she had proved her mental acuity, but usually
she showed none at all. Full of reason and good judgment, she
surrounded herself with foolish and ridiculous people, and she
yielded to their puerile caprices. Courageous, resolute, and active in
important events, she ordinarily was indolent and indecisive. She
almost never left her residence, and she feared the least agitation. ...
She was scrupulously devout.[12]

... so devout that she had herself painted holding a book opened to the
Litanies of Loreto.[13]

She rejected the company of the wives of the city fathers of Blois,
whose conversation did not measure up to that of the Lorraine-born
householders who had followed her into exile. Even so, the Duchess of
Orléans presumably was acquainted with the wife of René Grimaudet de
la Croiserie, one of Gaston's councillors and his lieutenant general in the
baillage and gouvernment of Blois. René's sister, ÉLISABETH GRIMAUDET,
went to ÉLISABETH CHARPENTIER's house in 1662 and signed her wedding
contract as a friend of the groom. If the Charpentiers were not already
in the Orléans' orbit when the marriage was being negotiated, they
entered it on Élisabeth's wedding day. And so, as of August 1662, if not
before, the family of LOUIS CHARPENTIER THE SCRIVENER "belonged," albeit
somewhat tangentially, to the House of Orléans.

Left to their own devices, the little princesses played by the hour with
their young attendants, among them Louise de la Vallière,[14] Louis XIV's
future mistress. Louise moved to Paris with Madame and her daughters
in the early 1660s; and decades later, as a Carmelite nun at the Great
Carmel, she would pray with the other nuns while MADAME DE GUISE was
interred in the convent cemetery.

Although there was a troop of actors in Blois, neither Monsieur nor Madame attended the theater. Whenever Montpensier paid a brief visit, she therefore made a point of watching plays with her half-sisters, "who were awed, having no entertainments."[15] By the end of the 1650s, "Mesdemoiselles d'Orléans, d'Alençon and de Valois ... were so weary of being at Blois, and their youth made them desire a trip to Paris so passionately, that they undoubtedly were easily consoled to see their exile ending" upon their father's death in 1660.[16]

The princesses had received an education appropriate for their rank in society, for their parents hoped to arrange advantageous marriages for them. Another option was, of course, the Church, for which ISABELLE D'ALENÇON had been destined since she was a toddler. An opportunity to establish another daughter in the Church arose in 1653, when Monsieur and Madame were offered a prestigious royal abbey, Fontevrault. Montpensier informed her father of the offer, and Gaston replied:

> Talk to Madame about it. As for my daughter of Orléans, you can well imagine that we won't put her there. [As for] my daughter of Valois, she entertains me, and that is why I refused to send her to you. ... That leaves only my daughter of Alençon. Madame, who placed her at Charonne with Mother Madeleine, will never agree to having her removed. Do what you can to win her over, but I personally would be very pleased.[17]

Isabelle might be expendable for Gaston; but Madame was determined to see her on the abbess's throne at Remiremont, for which she herself had once been destined, not at Fontevrault. As the Duke had suspected, Madame did not mention Isabelle; and as he had predicted, she proposed her third daughter, Mademoiselle de Valois, knowing full well that Monsieur would never part with her. Owing to Madame's stubbornness, Fontevrault slipped from their grasp, and they were left with four daughters on their hands. The oldest, MADEMOISELLE DE MONTPENSIER, was extremely rich but no longer young; and the remaining three, although young, were, to use Montpensier's expression, "beggars."

Toward the end of his life, Gaston attempted to return to Louis XIV's good graces, but it was not to be. During one of his rare visits to court, the King and the Queen Mother greeted him cooly, then ignored him.[18] He died at Blois in January 1660. Marguerite de Lorraine was at his bedside, surrounded by his most faithful servants, including JACQUES II DALIBERT and his father. Acting in Madame's name, and fiercely refusing to part with any object that might be included in the estate, her chambermaids refused to surrender a sheet for the Duke's shroud. Despite her tears, Marguerite de Lorraine had sufficient presence of mind to order her domestics to lock up the silver.

The household was disbanded on the day of Gaston's death. Shocked by the abruptness of their dismissal, the dead man's officers refused to stand guard beside his body, as was customary: "As a result, while Monsieur's body was at Blois, in the evening they closed the door and the priests went away, although it is customary to pray to God continually for people of that rank; but there was neither light nor firewood, so it was very cold." The corpse was carried to the royal necropolis at Saint-Denis, "with a few guards, a few almoners, and a few other household officers. This was done without pomp and without expense," just as the prince had wished.[19]

Marguerite de Lorraine, now Dowager Duchess of Orléans, immediately dispatched a messenger to the King to request his protection for herself and her children. She was responding to a clause in Monsieur's will that begged Louis XIV to continue the yearly pensions of one hundred thousand livres that each daughter had hitherto received, "in order to see to their needs until all three of them are married, ... and to marry them according to the dignity of their birth and the honor they have to belong to him, [and] to give them suitable dowries."[20]

Instead of remaining at Blois and retreating for forty days to the customary darkened room draped in black, Madame set off for Paris, incognito and masked. Accompanied by their childhood friend, Louise de la Vallière, the three princesses followed her, "with dignity," in a second coach. If Montpensier is to be believed, the widow immediately confiscated her stepdaughter's apartment in the Luxembourg Palace and "planted herself there"; and her three daughters moved into Madame's old apartment, showing "no civility" toward their half-sister.[21] Montpensier made it clear that she would consider herself the owner of the palace until Madame paid the 1,200,000 livres owed her by Gaston's estate.[22] She promptly chased her sisters from the apartment their mother had expropriated for them. When Montpensier finally received the money in 1665, the palace was officially divided in two: the half to the left of the entry portico would be hers, and right half, plus the duchy of Alençon, went to Madame.[23]

At any rate, that is how Mademoiselle de Montpensier tells the story. The Dowager's letter to Cardinal Mazarin paints a slightly different picture. "I do not claim to make any arrangement with Mademoiselle," she wrote. Then, having proposed separate apartments so that she and her daughters could keep their distance from her, she added: "A few days ago she wrote me a letter that makes me think she does not believe that I intend to live on good terms with her. I am sending you the original."[24]

Montpensier further showed her scorn by ordering the construction of a wall through the palace garden, so that she would not encounter or have to cast her eyes on Madame and her brood when they strolled on their half of the terrace.

Casting off her inertia, Madame did battle with anyone who threatened her or her daughters. Doing her utmost to call attention to the girls, she pushed ahead marriage negotiations with the Houses of Savoy and Tuscany. Judging her to be a "woman who would spoil everything she got involved in," Cardinal Mazarin decided to give Madame "only what she needed to live according to her rank, considering that she had the honor of being Monsieur's wife."[25] But he did agree to arrange suitable marriages for the three princesses. Madame must have feared just that sort of lukewarm response to the optimistic yet pleading letters she had been sending the Cardinal since Gaston's death: "I confess," she wrote Mazarin on one occasion, after alluding to her late husband, "that it is impossible to bring up this unfortunate event without redoubling my regrets." She continued:

> But since I have daughters for whom I will always have maternal feelings, and since I must cherish them even more because they are all that remains to me of Monsieur, in some way I feel relieved to see that you are promising them another father who can do more for them than the father they have lost. I know that we need your favorable mediation if we are to hope for [the King's] favor. I am fortified by the many expressions of good will that you have given me in such a difficult situation[26]

The young princesses were promptly swept up into the festivities accompanying Louis XIV's marriage to Marie-Thérèse of Spain in 1660. By order of the King, and at his expense, ISABELLE D'ALENÇON and Mademoiselle de Valois headed south to attend the wedding and carry the bride's train beside Mademoiselle de Montpensier.

Once back in Paris, the girls resumed their mourning, which continued until Gaston's End of the Year Service in March 1661. This ceremony doubtlessly served as a model for the Dowager of Orléans' End of the Year Service in 1673, and also for the annual memorial services that ISABELLE D'ALENÇON organized at Charonne each March and April on the anniversaries of her parents' deaths. In March 1661 "three thousand ears" listened to music written and conducted by Gaston's household composer, Étienne Moulinié, and "sung by a great number of excellent musicians." That day, "in addition to a perfect theorbo player and excellent harpsichordists, and in addition to the marvelous Hotman" playing the viol, Mesdemoiselles Moulinié and Tournier "charmed by their divine voices."[27]

Casting off their mourning, the princesses turned to their half-sister for amusement, as they had at Blois: "Since my sisters were young," Montpensier recalled, "and since they loved to skip about and dance, on evenings when there was neither a ballet nor a play at the Louvre, they would dance. I had violinists, so the ball was quickly arranged in a room far from Madame's chamber."[28] The princesses were given seats of honor at court festivities: in the fall of 1660 they watched Cavalli's *Xerse* at the Louvre, and for Mardi Gras of 1662 ISABELLE D'ALENÇON and Mademoiselle de Valois danced in Cavalli's *Ercole amante*.

Rumors of impending marriages had been circulating since early 1660. Hoping to spoil her sisters' chances of wedding one or another of the eligible European sovereigns, MADEMOISELLE DE MONTPENSIER spread lies about them, describing them as humpbacked, ugly, pitted by small-pox.[29] Skirting disgrace on several occasions, JACQUES II DALIBERT managed to convince negotiators that Montpensier was prevaricating. Thanks in large part to Dalibert, Mademoiselle d'Orléans married Cosimo III de' Medici in 1661, thereby earning the name by which she is known in this gallery: "MADAME DE TOSCANE." Louis XIV gave her a dowry of 900,000 livres, in return for a renunciation of her rights to Monsieur's estate. Two years later, Mademoiselle de Valois married the Duke of Savoy, and she too was dowered with 900,000 livres. Not until 1667 did ISABELLE D'ALENCON find a husband. Louis XIV agreed to Madame's proposition that Isabelle wed LOUIS-JOSEPH DE LORRAINE, DUKE OF GUISE, so that one daughter would be near her in her old age. The King dowered Isabelle with a mere 300,000 livres. If widowed, she would be allowed to choose a château.[30] (She would opt for Alençon, and for her mother's half of the Luxembourg).

With all her daughters married, the Dowager of Orléans once again had time to think of her soul. She moved closer spiritually to the Franciscan fathers, and to the "Clarices," that is, the Franciscan nuns of Saint Claire, especially those of the convent of the Ave Maria at Alençon. Although her health did not permit her to travel to Alençon, Marc-Antoine Charpentier's roman-numbered notebooks suggest that the Dowager commissioned music for the week-long services held at Alençon in December 1670 to celebrate the canonization of Saint Peter of Alcantara. At any rate, quite a few pieces in those early notebooks were written for a choir with *dessus* but no *haut-dessus*—that is, it had sopranos but no trebles. This choir appears nowhere else in Charpentier's notebooks. The very fact that the event was mentioned in the *Gazette de France*[31] suggests that the Dowager contributed to the festivities, commissioning music for the pontifical mass[A] of Saturday, December 27, which opened the festivities, and music for the daily vespers services.[B] All the liturgical texts used in this little group of compositions were recited at vespers during the week that separates Christmas from the New Year.[32] The festive week ended on January 3, 1671, with a Benediction of the Holy Sacrament, *salut*, "sung by excellent musicians."

Meanwhile, the Dowager's spiritual attachment to the Franciscans was deepening. On Sunday, June 14, 1671, during a mass in the chapel of the Luxembourg Palace, she took the vows of the Third Order of Penitence[C] in the presence of the General of the Franciscans. With several ladies from her entourage, she donned the Franciscan habit.[33] The Feast of the Impression of the Stigmata,[D] September 17, was now one of Madame's principal devotional days.

Lethargic though she was by nature, and more concerned about her soul than about things of the world, Madame acted decisively when her son-in-law, LOUIS-JOSEPH, DUKE OF GUISE, succumbed to smallpox in the summer of 1671. She promptly "prepared a superb apartment in her palace" for her grandson, the infant Duke of Alençon—the King having "taken upon himself the care of the child."[34] Meanwhile MADAME DE GUISE and MADEMOISELLE DE GUISE were fighting bitterly over the child's guardianship. Mademoiselle de Guise appealed to the Dowager, arguing that the child must not be turned over to the worldly people at court who were certain to influence a young widow. To get her way, she threatened to reveal the existence of her children by Montrésor, thereby throwing the estate into chaos. The appeal, or the threat, or both, promptly won Mademoiselle the Guise the right to supervise the child's education.[35]

MADAME DE GUISE was a frequent visitor to her mother's court at the Luxembourg and made a point of being there every week when the Tuscan agent brought the latest news from Florence. Among the Dowager's householders was poet Jean de La Fontaine, to whom Madame of Orléans had given a lodging within the palace. In an overt bid for a transfer of protection—from the ailing Dowager to her son-in-law, LOUIS-JOSEPH DUKE OF GUISE, via her "heiress," Madame de Guise—the poet dedicated his *Fables nouvelles* to the Duke in 1671, shortly before the prince's death: "You are the master of my leisure and of every moment of my life, since they belong to the august and wise princess [the

---

[A] Cahiers VI–VIII, H. 1, H. 236, H. 283.
[B] Cahiers I–V, H. 149, H. 150, H. 72, H. 152.
[C] Cahier 2, H. 17, H. 282.
[D] Cahier 2, H. 310.

Dowager] who deemed you worthy of possessing the heiress [Madame de Guise] of her virtues."[36]

After several small strokes, the Dowager died during the night of April 3, 1672, while Madame de Guise struggled to don a dressing gown. The two Guise princesses immediately withdrew to the Abbey of Montmartre. Dressed in the habit of the Third Order of Saint Francis, the body was carried in great pomp to the royal necropolis at Saint-Denis to await burial. The procession continued on to MONTMARTRE, where Bishop Marc Malier presented Madame's heart to the Abbess and her nuns, "enclosed in a silver heart, on a black velvet cushion, on which was a silver-gilt crown covered by black crepe."[37] "Surrounded by some 150 torches of white wax carried by mounted pages and a great number of footmen," Malier stopped before the entrance to the abbey:

> [The Bishop] was received at the door to the cloister by all the nuns, carrying candles and led by the Abbess. After a brief speech [by the Bishop], to which she replied, he accompanied this cushion inside the nuns' choir, where the accustomed prayers and censing were done.[38]

No musical service took place that day, for the "ceremony was postponed until May 11, when the big service would take place."[39] No service was said at Saint-Denis either, although Madame de Guise had asked Bishop Malier of Tarbes to officiate a few days later at a "solemn service," after which the body would be placed in a chapel to await burial in May.

On Wednesday, April 13, the day of the first Tenebrae service of Holy Week, the King was announced at Montmartre, to express his condolences:

> [Louis XIV was] received at the door of the convent by the Abbess and by Mademoiselle de Guise, who led him to the nuns' choir, where they had prepared a prayer stool for him; and His Majesty, having heard the mass, went to visit Madame de Guise, who was in her bed [where condolences were customarily received], and expressed to her the sorrow he felt at Madame's loss. ... Then His Majesty passed though Mademoiselle de Guise's chamber, and on through that of the Abbess, who took him back to the place where they had received him.[40]

Had Louis XIV delayed his visit by one day, he could have heard a Jerusalem[A] that replaced the one Charpentier had composed in 1670.[B]

[A] Cahier 2, H. 94.
[B] Cahier 1, H. 93.

Was the King treated that day to a repeat performance of the piece the Guise composer had written for Holy Wednesday[A] of 1671?

For a month Madame's coffin lay in state beneath a canopy of black velvet in the black-draped Saint-Denis, surrounded by an "infinity of silver candlesticks" and covered by a "pall belonging to the Crown on which sat a silver-gilt crown and a ducal mantle of blue satin with three rows of golden fleurs-de-lis, bordered in white ermine with black tails." On the afternoon of May 10, "vespers and the vigils of the dead"[B] were said.

The next day, May 11, at eight in the morning, the solemn funeral mass was celebrated. Wearing his pontifical vestments, Bishop Malier officiated. Madame de Guise, who "led" the mourners because she was the dead woman's daughter, was accompanied by her half-sister, Mademoiselle de Montpensier, and by the daughter of Philippe II d'Orléans, head of the House of Orléans. The three princesses participated in the Offertory, their long trains carried by royal heralds and by gentlemen from their households. At the Elevation, six monks from the abbey appeared, bearing torches. After intercessory prayers for the deceased, the four officiating prelates wafted incense over the coffin and "the [Royal] Music began the De Profundis." The sound of their voices wafted down from the rood-screen. Standing at the foot of the coffin, Malier sprinkled it with holy water, then signaled that it was time to carry it to the burial vault. Louis XIV paid all the funeral expenses, "contrary to custom, it being the heirs' duty to pay."[41] In other words, money was not an issue during this sumptuous funeral, nor was the availability of skilled musicians and their remuneration, for the King had loaned his musicians to Madame de Guise.

The sources do not identify the person who composed the "mass sung in music by the Royal Chapel, which had been placed in the loft."[42] That no royal composer was mentioned suggests that this individual belonged either to the Lorraines or to the Orléans—as had Moulinié, when he composed the music for Gaston's End of the Year Service, and as did Bishop Malier, the officiant in May 1672. Charpentier's notebooks reveal that, around mid-April 1672, he wrote a De profundis and a Requiem æternam[C] to round out the funeral mass he had composed for LOUIS-JOSEPH DE LORRAINE in 1671. In other words, something compelled the composer to transform the mass for the Duke of Guise into a complete funeral mass. That is to say, these two particular texts were reserved for

---

[A] Cahier 1, H. 92.
[B] Cahier 4, H. 311.
[C] Cahier 3, H. 2 and H. 234, reused; cahier 4, H. 156.

actual burials, and the service in honor of the late Duke of Guise had been a memorial mass, not a real funeral.[43]

Although her role in planning the funeral service at Saint-Denis cannot be documented, MADAME DE GUISE personally arranged other services for her late mother. Her household records show that she "supplied the money for the burial [and] funeral services" that, with the doctor bills, totaled just over nineteen thousand livres.[44] One of these services was a "solemn service in the Abbey of Montmartre, where Madame's heart is," held on May 14 and paid for by Madame de Guise.[45] Charpentier's *Plainte*, which is addressed to the "friends" of a mourner, was perfectly suited for vigils commemorating the loss of a mother. Was his *Messe des trépassez* or his *Plainte*,[A] or both, performed at Montmartre on Saturday, May 14, 1672? And again on May 21, when the nuns at Charonne showed their gratitude toward their founder, Marguerite de Lorraine, by holding "in their church a service with a handsome mausoleum, and all the pomp due the memory of so great a princess"?

This mass of May 21—which was "sung by the Music" (that is, the royal musicians) and presumably was preceded by the vigils usually sung on the eve of a burial—involved a burial of sorts: the interment of Madame's entrails. Once again Bishop Malier officiated, in the presence of MADAME DE GUISE and a "great number of princesses," plus the Medici agent for Paris.[46] That the royal musicians participated in this mass supports the conjecture that Charpentier's mass for the dead, and perhaps the *Plainte*, were reused at Charonne. In other words, the musicians who had performed at Saint-Denis on May 10 and May 11 probably went out to Charonne on May 21 (and had perhaps gone to Montmartre on May 14). That none of these sources mentions a court composer such as Lully, strengthens the likelihood that the music at these services was written by Marc-Antoine Charpentier, the household composer to the Dowager's grieving daughter.

Marguerite de Lorraine and Gaston d'Orléans lived on in Madame de Guise's memory. Each year, on the anniversaries of their deaths, memorial masses were sung in their honor at Charonne.[47]

[A] Cahier 3, H. 2; cahier 4, H. 311.

II

With the accustomed brilliance and pomp

THE KING, THE QUEEN, AND THE DAUPHIN

Louis XIV, King of France;
Marie-Thérèse of Austria, Queen of France;
and Louis de Bourbon, Dauphin of France, known as "Monseigneur"

During the 1640s several children were born into the senior branch of the House of Bourbon, all of them grandchildren of King Henri IV and Queen Marie de Médicis. Two of these "grandchildren of France" were the sons of King Louis XIII and his wife, Anne of Austria. While still a child, the older boy ascended to the throne as Louis XIV. The younger son, Philippe, became PHILIPPE II D'ORLÉANS upon the death of his uncle Gaston in 1660 and received the Duchy of Orléans as an appanage for himself and his male heirs.

The remaining grandchildren of France were the offspring of Louis XIII's brother, GASTON DE FRANCE, DUKE OF ORLÉANS. Among them were three princesses whose portraits appear in this gallery. The eldest was MADEMOISELLE DE MONTPENSIER, the child of Gaston's brief union with MADEMOISELLE MARIE DE GUISE's half-sister. Montpensier was almost two decades older than her first cousins and her half-sisters. The latter —two of whom appear in this portrait gallery—were born to Gaston's second wife. One was Marguerite-Louise d'Orléans, depicted as a mature woman in the portrait of "MADAME DE TOSCANE"; the other was ISABELLE D'ORLÉANS OF ALENÇON, later known as "MADAME DE GUISE." (A portrait of a third sister, "Mademoiselle de Valois," has been omitted from this gallery, because she died as a young bride in distant Savoy.) Since Princess Isabelle would be one of Marc-Antoine Charpentier's protectresses, this portrait of the royal family is seen through her eyes, and primarily through her contacts with them.

These first cousins did not always get along well, but they tried. And when the interests and prestige of the House of Bourbon or the House of Orléans were an issue, they watched out for one another. As cousins do, they stood as godmother and godfather for nieces, nephews, and close cousins. However, godparents tended to be chosen from within one's House. For example, Philippe II d'Orléans was Isabelle d'Orléans' godfather; and Isabelle d'Orléans and Marguerite-Louise d'Orléans later stood as godparents for two of Philippe's children, among them PHILIPPE III D'ORLÉANS, DUKE OF CHARTRES.

It is in this context of family ties that Louis XIV's invitation to his exiled and rather provincial first cousins of the House of Orléans, to participate in his marriage festivities on the Spanish frontier in June 1660, takes on a special meaning. Louis and his minister, Mazarin, were committed to finding prestigious husbands for these daughters of GASTON D'ORLÉANS, and the princesses' presence at the wedding would be the first step toward bringing them before European eyes. For the same reason, during the months that followed the girls were among the young women embellishing the stage in the Italian operas given at court, and dancing in the ballets of French-style entertainments. In February 1662 ISABELLE D'ALENÇON and her sisters danced in *Ercole amante*; in January 1665 Isabelle sat with the royal family at the Twelfth Night banquet; and a month later she was one of the "belles" riding one of Vigarani's "machines" during a ballet-mascarade.

The King kept his promise to find suitable husbands for his cousins and to dower them as befit their rank as grandchildren of France. His late uncle's householder, JACQUES II DALIBERT, played a pivotal role in marriage negotiations with Turin and Florence. By 1663 two of Gaston's four daughters were married, one to the Duke of Savoy and the other to the heir apparent to the Grand Duchy of Tuscany. Finding husbands for the remaining two was proving difficult. MADEMOISELLE DE MONTPENSIER later would claim that she had doomed herself to spinsterhood by being too selective. By contrast, humpbacked ISABELLE OF ALENÇON was eager to marry, but she had been passed over by both Savoy and Tuscany. Thus Louis XIV was visibly relieved when her mother came to him in 1667 and said she would accept LOUIS-JOSEPH, DUKE OF GUISE, as a son-in-law. He was still more relieved when MARIE DE GUISE THE REGENT did not insist upon a large dowry.

During the 1660s Isabelle d'Alençon, convent-raised and apparently doomed to spinsterhood (she would soon be twenty), had become close to Louis XIV's Spanish wife. The princess and the extremely devout Queen took to visiting the LITTLE CARMEL on the rue du Bouloi, of which Marie-Thérèse had been declared the "founder" shortly after her arrival in France. Some of these visits were brief, but the Queen would occasionally have a "succulent, opulent" meal prepared for the nuns, and would dine with them.[1] These devout highnesses sometimes stayed on for a religious service, for example a taking of the veil.[2]

Drawing an implicit parallel between their new "founder," Queen Marie-Thérèse, and her mother-in-law, Queen Mother Anne of Austria, the nuns held a memorial service for Anne in 1666, with a eulogy by BISHOP ROQUETTE.[3] (A similar service, with music by Marc-Antoine Charpentier, would be held at the LITTLE CARMEL in December 1683, this time for Marie-Thérèse herself.) From the early 1660s until her death in 1683, the Queen's friendship with Isabelle d'Alençon strengthened; and neither Isabelle's marriage nor her responsibilities at the Hôtel de Guise kept her from joining her friend at the Carmel. Marie-Thérèse made a special point of being there every October 16, for the Feast of Saint Theresa.[A]

By March 1669, as part of a thinly-veiled power play, Princess Isabelle (now MADAME DE GUISE) began ingratiating herself with the Queen: "Madame Colbert currently controls the Queen, although all the princesses of the House of Lorraine are assiduously paying court to her, and Madame de Guise is the leader." The Queen was not taken in by all this attention: "She complained a lot about the princesses of the House of Lorraine, especially Madame de Guise, and she said that [Madame de Guise] bored her so much that she could not tolerate her any longer."[4]

To some extent, Madame de Guise's politics succeeded. The King made sure that she and her husband were part of the royal party at court events, both worldly and devotional. For example, on January 1, 1669, the Feast of the Circumcision, Madame de Guise was at the King's side during the annual vespers sung at the Jesuit Church of Saint-Louis, and a few months later during Tenebrae services at the Church of the Feuillants.[5] In February 1671 the royal couple were the guests of honor at festivities organized by MADEMOISELLE DE GUISE for the wedding of a princess of the House of Lorraine.

During the three periods of mourning that darkened MADAME DE GUISE's life between 1671 and 1675, Louis XIV always went to visit her at MONTMARTRE, to express his condolences in person. And he repeatedly paid the funeral costs. Once mourning had ended, Madame de Guise would be mentioned in the *Gazette de France* as attending a public event with the royal party. Thus she christened a bell with the King and Queen

---

[A] Cahier 49, H. 342; and H. 374, in a notebook containing music for the DAUPHIN's Music, copied onto paper with a crown in the watermark.

in April 1673; and in August 1674 she was at their side during a *Te Deum* sung at Notre-Dame for the Feast of Saint Louis.

She reciprocated by discreetly honoring her royal cousin with musical gifts. For example, in June 1672 Marc-Antoine Charpentier composed an instrumental overture[A] for a Corpus Christi procession at Versailles in which Madame de Guise marched:

> The procession was held here, with the accustomed brilliance and pomp, the places where it passed being decorated with the richest tapestries belonging to the Crown; and Monseigneur the Dauphin ... attended with a very exemplary devotion, as did Madame [the wife of Philippe II d'Orléans] and Madame de Guise, with a great number of ladies.[6]

This was the first of a succession of compositions by Charpentier for the portable altar, *reposoir*, set up at court each year for the two Corpus Christi processions.

In July 1673, during citywide celebrations for the capitulation of Maastricht, MADAME DE GUISE organized a public rejoicing at her new residence, the Luxembourg Palace. There were "fireworks, which were accompanied by the distribution of wine to all passers-by, so that the joy was more evident there than anywhere else in the city." (If Charpentier composed for this event, he did not copy the pieces into his notebooks for that year.)

The death of MADAME DE GUISE's young son in March 1675, and the return to France a few months later of her sister, MADAME DE TOSCANE, ushered in a new relationship with her cousin's court. Louis XIV went to great lengths to show sympathy in her time of desolation. From the northern frontier he replied to a congratulatory letter she had sent him:

> There is no need to tell you that your compliments about the capture of Lunbourg [Limbourg] pleased me greatly. You will be able to judge, if you reflect upon the pleasure I receive from everything that comes from persons for whom I feel great friendship. Keep me always in your friendship, and believe that your friendship could never be more true or more tender than the friendship I feel for you. *Louis*[7]

Avoiding when possible the Luxembourg Palace where her child had died, Madame de Guise mingled winters at court, summers at Alençon, charitable activities in Paris, and visits to her sister at MONTMARTRE.

[A] Cahier 7, H. 508.

After a few years this pattern changed, and the Dauphin appears to have been one of the reasons.

As the 1670s progressed, the Dauphin began to be mentioned in the *Gazette de France*, often in the company of his parents and Madame de Guise. He turned sixteen in 1677 and was reaching the end of a long educational program that had begun in the mid-1660s, when pedagogues such as GOIBAUT DU BOIS were writing treatises on how to educate a prince. The Dauphin's governor, the Duke of Montausier, browbeat the boy until assertiveness was replaced by blandness, timidity, fatalism.

His preceptor, Bishop Jacques-Bénigne Bossuet, was no less authoritarian in overseeing the youth's education. The best pedagogues in the kingdom were appointed to teach him Latin, physics, astronomy, mechanics, hydraulics, mathematics, and fortifications. A whole series of classical editions would be published "for the use of the Dauphin," *ad usum delphini*. But Monseigneur cared little for study. He preferred hunting; and when he could not hunt, he did not conceal his boredom. He did, however, enjoy music. At six, he had insisted that musicians sing during a mass recited in his sickroom, and he continued to ask for music whenever he was ill. In like manner he demanded music at his daily mass[8] while he was studying—for he spent most of the day shut up in his private apartment, leaving it only for mass and for a noon meal with his father.

In March 1677 the adolescent Dauphin played a central role in a devotional event that involved most of the churches in Paris. Archbishop Harlay had ordered public prayers for Louis XIV "in all the churches of this city and diocese, ... for the safety of the King's person, and for the prosperity of his arms." In conjunction with these prayers, in the space of three weeks Monseigneur and his mother visited each church on foot, as part of a "jubilee" being celebrated "for the Holy Year and for the royal family."[9] Marc-Antoine Charpentier's arabic-numbered notebooks contain several works[A] for this jubilee, doubtlessly for performance at one or more of the Guise princesses' preferred venues: the MERCY, the THEATINES, and perhaps their own parish churches, Saint-Jean-en-Grève and Saint-Sulpice, as well. In fact, repeated performances in several venues are likely. For example, on March 9 the Queen did a "station" at the LITTLE CARMEL, but the source does not name the ladies who accompanied her that day. On March 10 she went on foot with MADEMOISELLE DE MONTPENSIER from the Luxembourg to Notre-Dame Cathedral; on March 12 she went to the Hôtel de Guise and apparently walked with MADEMOI-

---

[A] Cahiers 14–15, H. 164; cahiers 15–16, H. 165, H. 166.

SELLE DE GUISE to one or more unspecified churches; and on March 13 she lunched at the Luxembourg and did several stations with MADAME DE GUISE. The jubilee was quite a social event. Upon entering a church, the women would chat with friends, then sit quietly before proceeding to the next church.[10]

In 1678 MADAME DE GUISE, MADAME DE TOSCANE, and MADEMOISELLE DE MONTPENSIER began paying court to Monseigneur. In February, and again in March, the three sisters went to court to "see" the Dauphin and "be happy" with him around the dinner table.[11] Madame de Toscane must have told him about her musical entertainments, for a few months later Monseigneur attended a ball at the residence of Toscane's friend, Bishop Furstemberg of Strasbourg.[12]

These meals with the Dauphin took place shortly before his first solo audience with foreign dignitaries.[13] During the weeks that followed, the prince began lunching with his father almost daily. For a time, the enthusiasm that was gripping him carried over to his studies.[14] Then, in December 1678, he mustered up enough courage to propose a successor for Guillaume Estival, a singer in the royal chapel who had just died. As it turned out, the prince had more or less promised to obtain this position for an unspecified individual, and had mobilized his mother and Madame de RICHELIEU to talk to the King about it. Louis XIV vetoed the idea, adding that the youth had no business getting involved in such things.[15]

This frustrated and naive attempt to have someone appointed to the royal chapel coincided chronologically[16] with the first composition on which Marc-Antoine Charpentier marked the names of the Pièche sisters,[A] members of the new little ensemble that would come to be known as "the Dauphin's Music." Had the three princesses been pressuring the Dauphin on Charpentier's behalf—not for the chapel post, but for the position as Monseigneur's composer? To whet the prince's appetite, did Madame de Guise offer him a piece by Charpentier? Is that why the composer copied this first work for the Dauphin's Music into an arabic-numbered notebook, rather than a roman-numbered one?

Soon after this apparent gift, Charpentier marked the Pièche girls' names on another psalm[B]; but this time he copied the piece into a roman-numbered notebook. During the months that followed, he copied out a whole series of pieces for the Dauphin's Music, occasionally using paper with Jean-Baptiste Colbert's crest as a watermark. This suggests that the

---

[A] Cahier 22, H. 170: "The *Superflumina* for the Demoiselles Pieches."
[B] Cahier XXV, H. 174: "Piesches."

royal minister had played an important role in the decision to allow
Charpentier to compose for the Dauphin.[17] Indeed, at some point in
1679[18] Colbert had apparently approved remunerating Charpentier from
the funds of the Dauphin's *menus plaisirs*. That is, at any rate, the picture
painted by a contemporary treatise on royal ceremonial:

> There never was any music at the mass of the children of France,
> not even for the dauphins before they married. It is true that
> Monseigneur the Grand Dauphin, son of Louis XIV, had a small
> Music of two or three voices, that is, a *basse-taille*, two *haut-dessus*
> sung by *demoiselles*, and two *basses de violons*. This Music sang at all
> the low masses that he came to hear in the chapel. But since this
> prince also liked music, he wanted to pay for it himself from his
> *menus plaisirs*, and this little musical group was in no way dependent
> upon the King's Music. [...] When the Dauphin married, he
> disbanded this little Music and gave the musicians who had been a
> part of it the same positions for life.[19]

In other words, the Dauphin's Music was a more or less ad hoc entity
that depended largely upon the prince; and it was relatively short-lived,
for it was disbanded soon after the Dauphin's marriage in early 1680.
Monseigneur had been given a household of his own a few months prior
to the wedding,[20] but for several years he would refuse to give up
Charpentier, to whom he remained tenaciously loyal. Equally unwilling
to see his Music disbanded, he made sure that the musicians would
remain close at hand, in the King's Music, always ready to perform for
him. In fact, Charpentier would write for them throughout the 1680s,
primarily for Corpus Christi; and for this work he probably was paid, as
before, from Monseigneur's *menus plaisirs*.

Articles by Corneille and DONNEAU DE VISÉ, the composer's friends
at the *Mercure galant*, confirm the statements made in the treatise on
ceremony just quoted. These journalists do not suggest that Charpentier
occupied a post in the Dauphin's household. Rather, they portray him
as writing primarily music for one very specific event: the Dauphin's daily
worship. "For a long time [Charpentier] worked for the Dauphin, at the
time when this prince had a daily private mass, his studies preventing
him from attending the King's mass."[21] In other words, as he had when
just a child, Monseigneur was insisting that music accompany a mass
—this despite the fact that he technically was not entitled to worship to
music until he was a married man.

From late 1679 until mid-1683 Charpentier wrote piece after piece for the Dauphin's Music,[A] which consisted of three vocalists: Magdaleine Pièche, a high soprano, *haut-dessus*, whose part was written with a treble clef; Marguerite Pièche, a soprano, *dessus*; and Antoine Frizon, a bass. They were accompanied by two treble instruments (flutes played by Antoine and Pierre Pièche), and continuo. In other words, the treatise on ceremony is slightly inaccurate: Frizon was not a *basse-taille*, that is, a baritone; Marguerite Pièche was not an *haut-dessus*; and the preferred instruments appear to have been flutes rather than violins.

It almost certainly was the composer, not Monseigneur, who chose the musicians. Charpentier knew these individuals from his collaboration with MOLIÈRE in the early 1670s, when the little Pièche sisters, ages seven and nine, had charmed audiences with their dancing, and Frizon had sung in *Le Malade imaginaire*. In proposing this rather atypical trio to the Dauphin, he was duplicating the Core Trio of the GUISE MUSIC. In fact, he was replicating the Guise singers' youthful voices, for the Pièche sisters were then sixteen and eighteen, the same age as Mademoiselle De Brion of the Guise Music. With his protectresses' permission, he could reuse, for Monseigneur, any or all of the devotional pieces he had written for the Core Trio since 1676.

The chapel where the Dauphin's Music performed at Versailles was not the one we know. The earliest works for the Music were sung in a chapel built in 1672. The musicians were positioned in a tribune above the altar, directly opposite the tribune occupied by the royal family. From the tribune a door opened directly to the Dauphin's apartment. In 1679 a large organ was installed. Then, in April 1682, a new chapel with tribunes for the musicians and an organ (perhaps a cabinet organ) was inaugurated. It was in this more spacious setting that Marc-Antoine Charpentier's later works for the Dauphin's Music were performed.[22]

So caught up was Monseigneur in his Music, and so eager was he to please his bride, that he began taking singing lessons:

> This young prince, who continually demonstrates his gallantry
> toward the Dauphine, is studying everything that is to her taste, in
> order to make his taste conform to hers; and on his own he decided
> to learn how to sing, for he noticed that it pleased her when
> someone loves singing, this princess having both a fine voice and
> extensive training. He had no sooner come up with the idea than he
> carried it out; and although it will seem incredible, he came to such
> a clear understanding of the difference between the pitch of one note

[A] Cahiers XXV, XXVI, XXVI, XXVIII, *passim*; cahiers XXX–XXXI, H. 178, H. 61, H. 179; cahier XXXII, H. 327, H. 328; cahier XXXIII, H. 405, H. 181; cahier XXXV, H. 429, H. 184, H. 329; BN, Rés. Vmc Ms. 27 ("Pieche").

compared to another, that by his second lesson he was able to sight read a rather difficult air.[23]

As if basking in the glory accruing to her from Charpentier's new position, in early 1680 MADAME DE GUISE began to play a more active role at court. In February she journeyed with it to Châlons, to greet the Dauphine and be present when she wed the Dauphin. Throughout that spring the *Gazette de France* mentioned Madame de Guise as part of the newlyweds' entourage. She therefore presumably was included in the fête that PHILIPPE II D'ORLÉANS organized in May 1680, to welcome the Dauphine. This was the first of three late-spring receptions held for Monseigneur and his wife at the Duke's country estate of Saint-Cloud.

Madame de Guise delayed her departure for Alençon that year, in order to march in the Corpus Christi procession on June 27, 1680, beside the King, the Queen, the Dauphin, and the Dauphine.[24] That she was singled out by the *Gazette* suggests that Charpentier had composed something for this event.[A]

In late September 1680, as the POISON INVESTIGATORS were hard at work, the Dauphin came down with a tenacious fever and dysentery. Relapse followed relapse, and rumors of poison began to circulate. A quinine-based remedy concocted by an Englishman named Talbot finally restored his health. Madame de Guise remained at Alençon until mid-November that year, then she hastened to court. For the Dauphin's Music Marc-Antoine Charpentier had written a celebratory piece about this recovery,[B] and he copied it into an arabic-numbered notebook. This suggests that Madame de Guise had commissioned the work, and it of course explains why Her Royal Highness returned to court so hastily.

During the winter season 1680–1681, Madame de Guise was something of a fixture at court, where attention focused increasingly upon the Dauphin, the Dauphine, and the entertainments prepared for them. The Dauphin, "in his extreme youth, where the generosity and the kindness of his heart were continually appearing, thought only of his pleasures and left the cares of the Crown to the King his father." By contrast, the Dauphine was proving to be "a princess with a great deal of wit, but she did not permit its breadth to be seen in all sorts of situations. She kept her eyes on the King, wanting to let his wishes entirely rule hers, and to do nothing that would appear disagreeable to him."[25]

In mid-May of 1681 came PHILIPPE II D'ORLÉANS' second fête at Saint-

---

[A] Cahier XXVI, H. 175? (a psalm for Corpus Christi); H. 248?; or perhaps H. 275, in BN, Rés. Vmc Ms. 27?
[B] Cahier 31, H. 326.

Cloud for the Dauphin and the Dauphine. The King, the Queen, and all the court attended the event, which lasted several days. Among the guest artists was Charpentier, whom the two Guise women were graciously sharing with the Dauphin. Louis XIV honored his son by furloughing his own musicians and "listening only to the musicians of Monseigneur the Dauphin." In so doing, he honored his son's composer (and through the composer, the Guises): "Each day the music sung at the mass consisted of motets by Monsieur Charpentier, and His Majesty would listen to no others, no matter what was proposed to him."[26]

MADAME DE GUISE was at court that May, so she almost certainly attended this fête. That year too she delayed her departure for Alençon until after the two Corpus Christi processions. In the *Mercure galant* Corneille and DONNEAU DE VISÉ described the procession at length, but they mentioned neither the Dauphin, nor Madame de Guise, nor Charpentier. The central figure was the King, who stood bareheaded for three hours in the hot sun, "without even using a parasol." Their description merits a closer look, for the details it contains shows the sort of setting in which Marc-Antoine Charpentier's music for the royal court was performed.

The procession first moved through the two courtyards of the chateau of Versailles, "hung with the finest tapestries belonging to the Crown. All the balconies and windows, up to the roof of the château, were decorated with Persian rugs with gold and silver backgrounds." It then advanced to the "altar that had been placed at the bottom of the great and magnificent Stairway" of the Ambassadors, where masses of flowering plants were tucked into silver urns that had been inserted into the ornate bronze railings or that stood on the marble pedestals of the stairway. The altar cloth was made of "cloth of gold of surprising beauty," and the tabernacle was decorated with rubies, emeralds, and diamonds. "A crown three feet in diameter made a dome over it. The crown was covered with gems and emitted such a dazzling fire that its brilliance could scarcely be endured." The tabernacle had been positioned in such a way that the "cascades" of a nearby fountain could be seen through it,

> and nothing was more agreeable than the sight of this water and the
> gems, which the lights caused to glimmer. ... The Music of the
> King's Chapel had been placed at the top of the stairwell. It would
> be very difficult to find a more advantageous place for harmony. So
> the instruments and the voices were heard with great pleasure.[27]

Within this resonant setting, the Dauphin's Music (now part of the "Music of the King's Chapel") caused the harmonies of Charpentier's

Pange lingua[A] to float down to the Monarch and his son, like angelic song.

In late September 1681 the court set off for Strasbourg to accept its "submission." They did not return until November. By then MADAME DE GUISE had returned from her summer at Alençon and had settled in for a winter divided between Versailles and Saint-Germain-en-Laye. (She did, however, go to Paris for a few days around Christmas.) One can therefore surmise that, in late November or early December, Charpentier's *Exaudiat*[B] was performed at Versailles[28] as Madame de Guise's gift to her royal cousin; and around that time the *Menuet de Strasbourg* was performed at a court ball and was preserved—along with a portrait of "Monsieur Charpentier"—in Landry's Almanac for 1682.[29]

The final days of 1681 were exhilarating for the Dauphin and hectic for his composer. On December 29 a Parisian performance of *L'Inconnu* called Charpentier away from Saint-Germain-en-Laye,[30] where he was rehearsing music for January 1, 1682, when the Dauphin would be inducted into the Order of the Holy Spirit. (The music has either been lost or it was so multipurpose that it cannot be identified.) Corneille and DONNEAU DE VISÉ linked the composer's name to Monseigneur's in the *Mercure galant*, but they did not present Charpentier as one of the Dauphin's householders. It clearly was the King who had commissioned the music for this event arranged to honor his son. The Dauphin,

> having entered the chapel of the Chateau of Saint-Germain, took communion ... . His Music was heard during the mass. The music was by Monsieur Charpentier. ... Mesdemoiselles Pièche demonstrated their fine voices, as usual. Monseigneur the Dauphin's devotions having been completed, he returned to his apartment and donned the uniform of a novice.[31]

Wearing the doublet and hose created by King Henri III, his black feathered cap "studded with all the gems of the Crown, save a diamond known as the *grand Sancy*," Monseigneur was made a knight of the Order of Saint Michael. He then donned the heavy cape of the Order of the Holy Spirit, with its embroidered flames—its weight proved almost too much for him—and marched to the royal chapel for a Mass of the Holy Spirit, with its *Veni creator Spritus*. The day ended with musical vespers in the royal chapel.

A few weeks later, on Easter Day,[C] and still at Saint-Germain-en-

---

[A] Cahiers XXX–XXXI, H. 61.
[B] Cahier 33, H. 180 ("for Versailles").
[C] Cahier XXXIII, H. 405.

Laye, the entire royal family attended high mass in the chapel of the chateau, "sung by the Music." The *haut-dessus*, *dessus*, and bass voices suggest that the performers for this Easter music were the Pièches and Frizon, who at Monseigneur's insistence had been incorporated into the King's Music. For as we have seen, "when the Dauphin married, he disbanded this little Music and gave the musicians who had been a part of it the same positions for life," in the King's Music. Later that day, vespers were sung.[32]

In the spring of 1682 DONNEAU DE VISÉ once again linked Charpentier to the Dauphin in the *Mercure galant*. Owing to repairs at the chateau of Saint-Germain, the entire royal family moved to Saint-Cloud for two weeks, along with the usual swarm of courtiers. To entertain them, PHILIPPE II D'ORLÉANS organized several days of festivities. It rained continually, and the principal amusement consisted of listening to music—church music:

> The King having furloughed all his musicians, the Dauphin's Music alone performed during the mass, where Monsieur Frizon sang daily. This music was accompanied by Sieurs Converset and Martinot, and Sieur Garnier was organist. The group is said to consist of the Pièche family, because five members of that family belong to the ensemble, that is, two girls and three boys. Throughout Their Majesties' sojourn at Saint-Cloud, nothing except music composed by Monsieur Charpentier was sung in the chapel.[33]

Although the Dauphin's Music was the only ensemble to sing during mass, other musicians performed during those two weeks. Nicolas Le Bègue, one of the four royal organists, played a "Symphony Mass" on the organ, with Philippe d'Orléans' violinists as echos. Balls and French and Italian plays also kept the courtiers diverted.

When the Dauphin's first son was born in August 1682, MADAME DE GUISE prepared public rejoicings for her cousins' good fortune, this time in Paris, at the Luxembourg Palace:

> Madame the Duchess of Guise had very fine fireworks set up on the terrace and on the dome. They consisted of rockets, fire-pots, and fireworks, grenades, and sparklers, all combined into one grand blaze. At the same time, lanterns were lighted on all sides, in the windows of the palace: so that it seemed to be burning well into the night. At ten o'clock the fireworks were lighted, and they lasted for almost an hour, and after this public entertainment, Madame de Guise gave a magnificent supper for several ladies. Meanwhile, she had bread and wine distributed to the many people who had assembled in the square; and so that nothing would be lacking in these public and private expressions of her joy, she entertained

everyone with a fine instrumental concert that lasted until after midnight.[34]

That same day, across of the Seine, the fathers of the MERCY "distinguished themselves by shooting off three canisters and by very unique fireworks, but above all by a *Te Deum* that the King's Music sang in their church. Mademoiselle de Guise was present, along with a great number of persons of the highest rank." Having almost certainly sponsored the *Te Deum*, MADEMOISELLE DE GUISE blended a lay celebration with the devotional one at the Mercy. That is, she illuminated the facade of the Hôtel de Guise, just across the street from the convent door.[35] The outer pages of the arabic-numbered notebook that Charpentier made and used that summer have been lost, but it may well have begun with a *Te Deum*, followed immediately by a work that ends with the words ... *et invocate sanctum nomen ejus*, and finally by a complete *Domine salvum fac Regem*[A] for a large ensemble that may well have been the King's Music.

The Dauphin's education was all but over by the final months of 1682, and his Bavarian bride was becoming quite outspoken about her musical and theatrical tastes. Mirroring this change in focus, MADAME DE GUISE ordered some entertainments for the coming winter season, when she would be in residence at Versailles. One of these court events was the "Fête of the Apartments,"[B] an innovation by Louis XIV himself that began in November of that year and continued well into January. Three times a week, from six until ten in the evening, a variety of entertainments were held in the principal rooms of the Great Apartment: billiards, cards and games of chance, refreshments (including fruits, sorbets, wine and liqueurs, and hot coffee and chocolate), plus "symphonies" and "dancing." Throughout the fête, only a few guards were present, and

> the King, the Queen, and all the royal family stepped down from their grandeur, to gamble with some of those present, who have never before been so honored. ... [The King] goes to one game or another. He allows no one to rise or stop the game when he approaches.[36]

During this fête, an "opera" was performed every Saturday.[37] Charpentier's little opera-like entertainment about the "pleasures of Versailles," which alludes to all these entertainments, almost certainly was written for the Dauphin's Music—joined by a high tenor, *haute-contre*, surely the composer himself, in the role of "Gaming," *Jeu*. The two Pièche

[A] Cahiers 36–37, H. 428, H. 291.
[B] Cahier 37, H. 480.

brothers accompanied them on flutes. Charpentier and the Music ended their entertainment by speaking directly to the King: "Great King, all covered with laurels, if our flutes and our voices prove incapable of relaxing you after your martial tasks. ... Take our wishes as deeds, and may your flourishing weapons achieve your aims."

Perhaps intentionally, perhaps accidentally, this little chamber opera amounted to a farewell gift to the Dauphin. Early in the spring of 1683 a royal order to reward Charpentier with a "pension," that is, an annual payment, began making its way through the administration. The pension became official shortly before the publication of the June issue of the *Mercure galant*. Being an official pensioner of the King did not, of course, preclude future work for the Crown; and Charpentier did in fact receive several commissions from the King or his son.

In fact, in early 1683 Charpentier clearly was still composing for the Crown, if not specifically for the Dauphin. His "dialog" for three male voices was written for Circumcision Day,[A] January 1, when the entire royal family attended the annual mass of the Order of the Holy Spirit, celebrated in the royal chapel of Versailles and "sung by the Royal Music." Later that day they attended vespers, "also sung by the Music."[38] That same spring he composed some instrumental music and a motet for the Dauphin's Music, for performance during the annual Corpus Christi procession,[B] June 17. That Charpentier mentioned an organ should not come as a surprise, nor be considered a slip of the pen. That year the *reposoir* was erected inside the new royal chapel—hence the organ. By the time the procession took place, Charpentier had become so ill that he had to withdraw from the competition for a sub-mastership in the royal chapel. As it turned out, he would not compose anything for over four months.[39]

While recuperating that summer and early fall, he was asked by the nuns of the LITTLE CARMEL to write music to honor their founder, Queen Marie-Thérèse, who had died on July 30, 1683. Charpentier was the logical choice, owing to his ties to MADAME DE GUISE and his recent service to the Dauphin, who as a child used to visit the convent with his mother on Saint Theresa's Day. On December 20, 1683, his compositions were performed at the Little Carmel, during the pontifical mass[C] in the Queen's memory.

After the Queen's demise, Madame de Guise began turning her back on the world. She spent increasingly less time at court. This does not

---

[A] Cahier XXXV, H. 406.
[B] Cahier XXXV–XXXVI, H. 523, H. 329.
[C] Cahiers XXXVI–XXXIX, H. 188, H. 524, H. 408, H. 409, H. 189 (and H. 251?).

mean, however, that she stopped asking Charpentier to compose for her cousins. For example, his arabic-numbered notebooks contain one piece that is clearly her gift to the Dauphine—or rather, to the Dauphine's brother, Maximilian Emmanuel of Bavaria, who had recently wed. The text was an *epithalamio* in Italian,[A] the language of culture that the Dauphine and her brother valued so highly. (Maximilian's Music consisted primarily of Italians, among them several castrati.)[40] Composed during the summer of 1685, this piece coincides chronologically with the Dauphine's dispatching of a French courtier, the Marquis of Bellfonds, to Munich, to congratulate the newly-weds.[41]

In 1686 Charpentier received another court commission, perhaps at the Dauphin's behest, perhaps at the King's. For one of the two Corpus Christi processions held at Versailles—the "big" procession that fell on June 13 that year, and the "little" one held a week later—he wrote a "grand motet[B] for the *reposoir* of Versailles in the presence of the ... King."[42] On June 13, 1686,

> the King, accompanied by Monseigneur the Dauphin, Monsieur, and Madame [of Orléans], participated in the procession that went from the parish church to the inner courtyards of the château. His Majesty attended high mass in the same church. In the afternoon he attended music in the chapel of the château, for vespers sung by the Music; and in the evening there was the Benediction of the Holy Sacrament.

A week later, "the King was again on foot in the procession, despite the excessive heat."[43]

That same year, Marc-Antoine Charpentier's opera, *La Descente d'Orphée*,[C] was performed by the combined GUISE MUSIC and Dauphin's Music. The opera appears to have been part of a not-too-subtle attack upon Lully's privilege, encouraged by the fact that the King had decided against subsidizing the Florentine's annual opera. Charpentier himself sang the title role, in this his last appearance with the Great Guise Music. Where and when was the opera performed? Certainly at court, and almost certainly during the first half of 1686. A probable date is early February, and the likely venue was the Dauphin's apartment: "Monseigneur gave a supper for the King, for the Dauphine, and for some ladies. There were only twenty at table. Afterwards there were very agreeable *divertissements*."[44] Or perhaps *Orphée* was performed at Fontainebleau in

---

[A] Cahiers 45–46, H. 473.
[B] Cahier XLIX, H. 344.
[C] Cahier "II," H. 488 (judging from its paper, this is the lost cahier 48).

October, when "little operas were sung before the King that were composed by other royal music masters than Baptiste."[45] After all, Marc-Antoine Charpentier was one of those "royal music masters." For that is the title attributed to him in the privilege that PHILIPPE III D'ORLÉANS, the composer's former pupil, granted to JACQUES ÉDOUARD in 1716: "the late Sieur Charpentier, one of the music masters to the late King."

One year later, in June 1687, in what was becoming a tradition, Charpentier wrote two pieces for the temporary altar,[A] reposoir, being set up for the annual Corpus Christi procession. The ensemble performing one of these works included the Pièche sisters and Frizon, along with several unidentified singers. In short, the compositions were written for a performance at court by the King's Music. This suggests that the pieces were commissioned by Louis XIV, who allowed his son's protégés to be given prime roles. Of the two Corpus Christi Day celebrations, June 5 and June 12, the former is the more likely performance date. The King and Monseigneur had been at the northern frontier since early May; but something compelled the Dauphin to gallop back to Versailles, ahead of his father. He arrived on the evening of June 4, just in time for the procession the following day.[46] An explanation for his mad dash is that he knew that Charpentier, the Pièches, and Frizon were contributing to the event, and he did not want to disappoint them.

After a gap of several years came another commission for the Pièches.[B] Composed during Charpentier's tenure as music master at the JESUIT HOUSE of Saint-Louis, this psalm, which uses a text recited during Monday matins, cannot be dated with precision. Nor has the specific religious service been identified. It is, however, likely that Charpentier invited the Pièches to sing at a special service to which the Dauphin had been invited.

Finally, in 1693 came a commission for a motet in honor of Saint Louis,[C] composed for the new Military Order of Saint Louis, which held its first induction service on May 10, 1693, in tandem with a mass for the Order of the Holy Spirit.[47] This appears to have been Charpentier's last explicit commission from either the King or the Dauphin.

That is not to say that Marc-Antoine Charpentier never again wrote for Louis XIV. In December 1693 his Médée was performed at the Royal Opera, and the composer dedicated the published score to the King—a gesture that customarily required royal approval. This "epistle" to the King is a congeries of commonplace phrases and images. During the

---

[A] Cahier LI, H. 346, H. 196.
[B] Cahier 55, H. 201.
[C] Cahier LXIII, H. 364, H. 264, H. 365.

1680s these commonplaces had been woven into the lyrics of some of Charpentier's artistic creations: the "arts" patronized by Louis XIV had been praised in *Les Arts florissants*; the "vigils," that is, the midnight oil burned by the faithful servant, Cardinal Richelieu, had been evoked in the *Feste de Ruel*; the King's "pleasures" at the musical art, and the "relaxation" it gave him, had been evoked in *Les Plaisirs de Versailles*.

In 1688, the Lully family had woven these same courtly literary commonplaces into their dedication to Louis XIV of *Thésée*. That does not mean that Charpentier's "epistle" is pro forma and routine. His manner of assembling these commonplaces provides insights into the man himself, and how he viewed more than a decade of service to Crown. "Sire," he began,

> the special protection that Your Majesty has always given the fine arts obliges all those who practice them to consecrate to you the fruit of their vigils. And since music has often been one of your pleasures, it would scarcely merit this protection if, when it provides a spectacle for your subjects, it did not appear in public under Your Majesty's glorious auspices. You know, Sire, better than anyone in your kingdom, everything that [music] possesses that is moving and delicate; and if *Médée*, which I dare to present to you, has the good fortune to please you in some of its parts, I will have nothing more to desire in the goal I set for myself. Accept, Sire, this feeble mark of my zeal; and allow me, in offering you this work, to let everyone know that my sole ambition is to be able to contribute something to the relaxation that is so necessary to Your Majesty, during the painful and continual burdens he bears for the glory of the State and the advantage of his people. I am, with the most profound respect, Your Majesty's very humble, very obedient, and very faithful servant and subject, *Charpentier*

First of all, by alluding to "vigils," Charpentier informed the public that the work he had done for the King and the Dauphin had required him to burn the midnight oil. In other words, he had conscientiously spent his daytime hours tending to the ordinary obligations he owed his full-time employers, first the Guises and now to the Jesuits. As a result, only the evenings were available for writing music that might honor the King. Second, despite the troubles that Lully's monopoly had caused him over the years, he was suggesting that the "spectacles" to which he had contributed in the past—his theatrical music for MOLIÈRE, CORNEILLE, and DONNEAU DE VISÉ, and the little operas performed at court during the 1680s—had been authorized by the King and had been performed under his "glorious auspices." (Was he not stretching this point a bit? For example, it is unlikely that Louis XIV authorized or sponsored the little "opera" performed at RIANTS' residence, a venture that flouted Lully's monopoly. Still, since neither this "opera" nor the subsequent ones, until *Médée*, were published, we lack the "epistles" that might have provided more information about these commissions.) Third, if Charpentier had burned so much midnight oil during the 1680s, it was in order to "move" the King with his music (which had been primarily devotional) and to "contribute to his relaxation," as he had done during the secular entertainments written for the King and his court.

The Dauphin demonstrated his loyalty to his former composer by attending the opera "twice"; but a "cabal" sounded the death knell for *Médée* after only "eight or nine" performances.[48]

To his last day, Marc-Antoine Charpentier continued to be Louis XIV's "faithful servant." That is, from May 1698, when he became music master at the SAINTE-CHAPELLE, until his death in 1704, he wrote exclusively for the King, as embodied in his Parlement and in his Sainte-Chapelle. In fact, everything that Marc-Antoine Charpentier composed for the chapel was not only written for the King, it belonged to the King.

III

He knows the ornaments of artfulness

TWO PHILIPPES OF THE HOUSE OF ORLÉANS

Philippe II de France, Duke of Orléans, the brother of Louis XIV;
and Philippe III, Duke of Chartres, his son

A second son, Philippe de France,[1] was born to King Louis XIII and Anne of Austria in September 1640. While still a child, Philippe stood as godfather for his first cousin, ISABELLE D'ALENÇON, the daughter of GASTON D'ORLÉANS by his marriage to Marguerite de Lorraine. For the next half century, Philippe would be supportive toward this godchild and first cousin. In fact, during the 1670s and early 1680s, the protégés of these two Orléans cousins would constitute a creative circle that proudly stood apart from the artists around Philippe's older brother, KING LOUIS XIV.[2] True, in the eighteenth century Saint-Simon would assert that Isabelle was "considered as nothing" by Philippe d'Orléans (and by Louis XIV himself); but the facts contradict the memoir-writing Duke. The cousins probably were not emotionally close, but Monsieur was Isabelle's loyal supporter.

In view of this special relationship between the two cousins, this joint portrait of Philippe the father and Philippe the son focuses on the father's generosity toward Marc-Antoine Charpentier, and on the son's gratitude for having had the opportunity to learn some compositional secrets.

Philippe II d'Orléans

In 1661, Philippe married his English first cousin, Henrietta Stuart. Almost simultaneously with his marriage, he was granted the Duchy of Orléans, vacant owing to the recent death of his uncle Gaston, as an appanage that could be passed on to a son. The newly-weds, known as "Monsieur" and "Madame," created a court at their residence, the Palais-Royal, and held sumptuous fêtes for the "well-dressed youth" belonging to the principal noble families of the realm.[3] (Madame died in 1670 and Philippe took a second wife in 1671, the exuberant "Palatine.")

When ISABELLE D'ALENÇON wed LOUIS-JOSEPH DE LORRAINE, DUKE OF GUISE, in May 1667—thereby becoming "MADAME DE GUISE"—the couple became a fixture at the Orléans' court:

> The fête was very lovely. The Palais-Royal was beautifully furnished and lighted. There was a play and then a ball; and after people had danced for some time, some of the ladies went off to sup at two tables, at one of which Madame presided, ... and at the other, Madame de Guise. The others danced during the meal; and when it was finished, the first came back to dance, and the others went to eat at two other tables, at one of which Monsieur presided, and at another, Mademoiselle de Montpensier. Each table had fifteen place settings, magnificently served.[4]

A word-portrait of Monsieur published that very year presented him as

> not having that majesty equal to his brother's, nor that deep, generous goodness that appears in our Monarch. He does not have that lofty seriousness nor that natural pride. He is sweet, agreeable, cajoling by nature, civil and obliging, courteous toward women, always gay and active, curious about beautiful and rare things, and this carries over to his choice of clothes, furnishings, cabinets; and he knows perfectly well the ornaments that artfulness causes to appear in architecture, painting, music, perspective, and agriculture.[5]

He does not, the portrait concluded, have much training in the military art, although "he has sometimes worked at riding, but less assiduously than the King." (That would not prevent Philippe from fighting bravely in war.)

Philippe does not appear to have been especially devout, yet as early as 1665 he began organizing a rather distinctive type of fête at his country estate, Saint-Cloud. For several days, banquets and theatrical performances would be intermixed with religious services.[6] He continued to host this type of event until at least the early 1680s.

Connoisseur that he was of the "ornaments" that could be artfully incorporated into a building, Monsieur wove a somewhat hedonistic iconographic program into the facade of his château at Saint-Cloud, where extensive renovations took place during the late 1670s. On one façade Time lifted a cloth from an hourglass, accompanied by four cupids symbolizing the four parts of a day. The right wing of the structure bore niches with the figures of Eloquence, Music, Fine Food, and Youth; the left wing showed Force, Spring, Politics, and Abundance—plus Momus, who stood for Comedy, and a bacchante, who represented Dance. The iconographic program continued inside the château, which was resplendent with colored marble columns, painted ceilings, bas-reliefs, and symbolic statuary.[7] Within this elegant setting, Philippe (with the help of Impresario Henri Guichard[8] and Composer Jean Granouillet de Sablières) prepared several fêtes each year. At some of them, Monsieur's own Music[9] performed; at others, guest composers or musicians were invited to participate.

From late 1669, when the Guises extended their protection to Marc-Antoine Charpentier, and on into the mid-1680s, Philippe II d'Orléans encouraged MADAME DE GUISE's artistic and devotional undertakings. On several occasions he or his wife put in an appearance at a church where, judging from pieces copied into Charpentier's arabic-numbered notebooks, music by the Guise protégé was being performed. For example, the first Madame went to the ABBEY OF MONTMARTRE for Tenebrae[A] on April 2, 1670.[10] And although Charpentier's notebooks for 1676, 1677, and 1678 contain no new works for Holy Week, Tenebrae[B] again attracted one or both of the Orléans to the abbey on April 3, 1676, April 10, 1677, and April 8, 1678. (April 3, 1676, was the fourth anniversary of the death of Madame de Guise's mother, the DOWAGER DUCHESS OF ORLÉANS.) The Duke and Duchess of Orléans—and Madame de Guise— were among the dignitaries present at MADEMOISELLE DE GUISE's magnificent Te Deum, sung in MONTMARTRE's new church in January 1687 to rejoice over Louis XIV's recovery. In addition, once Madame de Guise had embarked on some "devotions" at the THEATINE church in the fall of 1675, Monsieur and Madame attended Christmas services there: December 24, 1675, December 24, 1676,[C] and again on either December 24 or 25, 1682.[11] These documented presences were doubtlessly complemented by others not mentioned in the press or diplomatic correspondence.

Although attendance at these services can be taken as a gesture of support for his cousin rather than for the composer, on at least one occasion Philippe II d'Orléans and his circle rallied around Marc-Antoine Charpentier himself. On March 5, 1673, when MOLIÈRE's troop resumed performances of Le Malade imaginaire only a few days after the playwright's collapse and death, "Monsieur and Madame came, with their entire entourage."[12]

Monsieur does not appear to have commissioned a single composition from Charpentier. To do so would scarcely have been appropriate.

[A] Cahier 1, H. 91–93.
[B] Probable reuse of cahier 1, H. 91–92, and cahier 2, H. 94 (first sung during mourning at Montmartre for the DOWAGER, April 14, 1672).
[C] Cahier 12, H. 393, H. 238, H. 286.

It would have been an insult to his own household composer, Sablières, and to the members of his Music.[13] Nor was music by Charpentier inevitably performed every time MADAME DE GUISE visited Saint-Cloud. On one occasion Philippe II d'Orléans did, however, invite his cousin-goddaughter to provide music by her composer (and the performers as well), for festivities he was planning.

The event in question was the party that followed the baptisms of his children, Philippe III d'Orléans, Duke of Chartres, and his infant sister, Mademoiselle de Chartres, on October 5, 1676. MADAME DE GUISE and MADAME DE TOSCANE stood as godparents that day, and the entire royal family, plus their cousins, the Bourbon-Condés, were present:

> Monsieur the Duke of Chartres and Mademoiselle de Chartres were baptized at Saint-Cloud in the chapel of the château, in the presence of Their Majesties, the Dauphin, and Monsieur and Madame, accompanied by all the court. The Duke of Chartres was held over the font by the Prince of Condé and the Grand Duchess of Tuscany, who named him *Philippe*, which is Monsieur's name. Mademoiselle de Chartres was held by the Duke of Enghien [Condé's son] and Madame de Guise, who named her *Élisabeth-Charlotte*, which is Madame's name. ...Their Majesties, with Monseigneur the Dauphin, having then gone up to the salon, they found a splendid repast. ... Their Majesties then were entertained with an opera in the same salon, which had been prepared with all possible magnificence.[14]

Marc-Antoine Charpentier's arabic-numbered notebook for that fall contains a pastorale[A] that "sings of the virtues of the most powerful of kings, a victorious King." This was an allusion to the campaign of the previous spring, when Philippe II d'Orléans had attacked a fortress on the northern frontier. (His royal brother subsequently heeded his generals and changed the attack into a siege that continued well into the summer, when the city surrendered at last.) In short, although the lyrics ostensibly praise Louis XIV, they discreetly commend his courageous brother who had been kind enough to fit Charpentier's pastorale into the party. Charpentier himself probably sang the *haute-contre* (high tenor) role of Lysandre, along with De Baussen and Beaupuis of the GUISE MUSIC.

This pastorale reused songs from *Le Malade imaginaire*, plus an air entitled *Brilliantes fleurs naissez*,[B] with lyrics by Jean de La Fontaine. In this way the pastorale tossed a bouquet to Philippe II d'Orléans, who had protected MOLIÈRE, and a nosegay to Madame de Guise's late mother, the

---

[A] Cahier 13, H. 479.
[B] *Mercure*, October 1689, pp, 297–98, H. 449.

DOWAGER DUCHESS OF ORLÉANS, who had taken La Fontaine into her household after the Foucquet Affair.

In October 1678, fraternal rivalry prompted Philippe to organize a five-day fête whose principal aim was to show off his new gallery. (Louis XIV's galleries at Versailles were still incomplete.) Having worked at deciphering the iconography in the reception rooms, the guests soon turned their attention to the meals, the ball, the rides and strolls through the new Le Nôtre gardens, and the games of chance that had been prepared for them. Violent rainstorms brought the fête to an early end.[15]

The Dauphin's marriage in the spring of 1680 prompted a similar fête, again at Saint-Cloud. In fact, every spring, for the next three years,[16] Monsieur offered several days of entertainments to the Dauphin and the Dauphine, with the King and Queen and the rest of the court as guests. The first such fête began on May 10, 1680.[17] It was modeled on the festivities of October 1678: a ball in the new Mignard gallery, elegant refreshments in the salon, a visit to the gardens, and two plays by the Bourgogne Troop. (There is no evidence that any of Marc-Antoine Charpentier's music was played at this event, although the possibility cannot be ruled out.)

The second fête[18] took place in April 1681 and lasted a full week. The weather was splendid. Six-year-old Philippe III, Duke of Chartres, was permitted to leave Paris, where he was studying, to revel in the festivities. The members of the royal family arrived to the sound of trumpets and drums, were greeted by their hosts on the grand staircase where the Duke's violinists and oboists were playing, and then processed through the splendid apartments to a room glistening with silver furniture and gold embroidery. There Nicolas Lebègue, "His Majesty's famous organist, played a most ingenious cabinet organ, and the pleasure of hearing him made the courtiers linger there for some time." (Spring was not the quarter during which Lebègue served the King, so he participated in the fête as guest artist engaged and remunerated by the Duke of Orléans.) The guests eventually moved on to the Mignard gallery, at the end of which Monsieur's "symphonists in ordinary" were playing: Sieur Baltasard, harpsichordist; Sieur Garnier, *dessus de viole*; and Sieur Jaquesson, lute. After a ride through the gardens, the guests watched three plays. On subsequent days there were banquets enlivened by "concerts" of oboes and violins; there were balls; and there were plays—among them MOLIÈRE's *La Comtesse d'Escarbagnas*, for which Charpentier had written incidental music[A] a decade earlier, and THOMAS CORNEILLE's *Dom Bertrand de Sigaral.*

Respecting the administrative separation between the King's Music and the Dauphin's Music (an ensemble that Monseigneur himself had created and was remunerating from his *menus plaisirs*), and apparently eager to honor his son and daughter-in-law, who were the guests of honor,

> upon arriving at Saint-Cloud [Louis XIV] furloughed his musicians and would only listen to the Dauphin's Music. ... Every day during mass these musicians sang motets by Monsieur Charpentier, and His Majesty refused to hear any others, although some were proposed to him. For two years [Charpentier's motets] have been sung before the Dauphin.

This is the first of two documented furloughing of the King's Music, in favor of the Dauphin's.

It is noteworthy that the Duke of Orléans' Music also performed throughout the week-long festivities and that the musicians were named in the *Mercure galant*, just as Charpentier was. In other words, Philippe II had agreed to put Charpentier on a par, publicly, with his own householders. Other entertainers were singled out by the *Mercure*, among them Lebègue. Although not specifically named, it was the Guénégaud Troop that performed Molière's and Corneille's plays—with *Escarbagnas* perhaps ornamented with Charpentier's music from 1672. All in all, Charpentier's contribution to the fête of 1681 was considerably less dominant than one is generally led to believe, when the sentence containing his name is cited out of context.

In May 1682, while the pregnant Dauphine was resting at Saint-Cloud, Monsieur prepared yet another fête.[19] Once again, Louis XIV furloughed the Royal Music, so that attention would focus on his son's musicians and on the pieces Marc-Antoine Charpentier had written for them. This time the weather was so bad that all outside activities had to be canceled, and the chief diversion turned out to be the daily mass, which was accompanied by music:

> All the lords and ladies were present, often all dressed up two or three hours before the mass. There were several gaming tables in the Gallery. ... In a way, the wretched weather even seemed to contribute to the pleasure. ... Throughout the day His Royal Highness's servants were in the salon, to offer drinks and refreshments to those who needed them. ... The King having

---

[A] Cahier XV, H. 494.

> furloughed all the members of his Music, the Dauphin's Music alone
> performed at mass, where Sieur Frizon sang every day. ... Nothing
> was sung in the chapel, during Their Majesties' stay at Saint-Cloud,
> that was not composed by Monsieur Charpentier.

As he had in April 1681, Lebègue performed, but this time it was during
one or more of the religious services, where he played a "symphonic
mass" on the organ, with Monsieur's violinists as echo. The Duke's
violinists also performed during meals, as they had a year earlier. Other
entertainments included balls, nine French plays, and a comedy by the
Italian Troop. In May 1686 the Dauphin was again received at Saint-
Cloud, but by then Marc-Antoine Charpentier had left his service.

Without Philippe II d'Orléans' explicit approval, Corneille and DON-
NEAU DE VISÉ could scarcely have called attention to Charpentier in their
Mercure galant for two consecutive years. Should this publicity of the
early 1680s, combined with Monsieur's support of MOLIÈRE's devastated
troop in March 1673, be taken as evidence that the Duke was a supporter
of the Guise composer? Not only is it possible, but it seems likely. First
of all, in the early 1690s Monsieur engaged Marc-Antoine Charpentier
to teach composition to his son, the Duke of Chartres. Second—as we
shall see later in this portrait—around that time two of the composer's
close cousins found their way into Philippe II's household. And finally,
in December 1693 Philippe II himself made a point of attending "four" of
the "eight or nine" performances of Charpentier's *Médée*, perhaps in an
attempt to quash the "plot" being mounted against the opera.[20] That the
Duke was favorably disposed to the composer can scarcely be doubted,
but the extent of that commitment remains a conjecture.

Philippe III d'Orléans

By the time *Médée* was performed, Philippe III d'Orléans, Duke of
Chartres, was reaching the end of an avant-garde experiment in how best
to educate a prince:

> Since care was taken, early on, to put people near him who could
> shape his morals and his mind, instruct him in all the knowledge
> worthy of the application of a prince of this high birth, and to whom
> he would be likely to become personally fond, they have been
> fortunate to see that the fine and fortunate genius of their pupil has
> reached that high level, and even surpassed their expectations and
> those of the public. So that this young prince is justly the delight of
> Monsieur and Madame, and he is already attracting special respect
> from the entire court.[21]

On June 2, 1686, the Feast of Pentecost, the twelve-year-old prince
had been admitted to the Order of the Holy Spirit during a service in the

royal chapel of Versailles.[22] (Charpentier does not appear to have composed for it.) By 1688, when Chartres was fourteen, his intelligence and his talents were becoming legendary:

> Monsieur the Duke of Chartres, who usually resides in Paris in order not to be distracted from his studies by the thousand potentially distracting things at court, where he only goes from time to time to see the King and attend fêtes and splendid ceremonies, gave several balls last month [during Mardi Gras], with a magnificence worthy of his rank. An infinite number of persons of the highest rank were present each time at the Palais-Royal; but nothing was as brilliant in these sumptuous fêtes as the mind and the good grace of this young prince. ... Few people of his age have said more things worthy of notice.[23]

By the time he was fifteen, Philippe III had been taught the "principles," the "elements," of mathematics and history, as well as the foreign languages essential for a prince of his rank.[24] Next he studied the arts of fortification and mechanics, under the tutelage of the respected mathematician Joseph Sauveur; and before the end of that year he was studying music, with special attention to the mathematical aspects of that art. The teacher was ÉTIENNE LOULIÉ, a former member of the Guise Music. By early 1691 Chartres had learned the "elements" of musical notation and probably was proficient on the recorder and viol as well.

At that point, attention turned to his military training, and Philippe III went off to war. For several years he divided his time between the northern frontier and the royal court. He was an extremely bright young man, with a real talent and love for music. Eager to learn the art of composition, between November 1692 and May 1693—roughly when work was beginning on *Médée*—Chartres studied with Charpentier, using as a textbook a little manuscript treatise drawn up by the composr himself. The result of these studies was *Philomèle*, a lost opera performed three times at the Palais-Royal in 1694. Wishing to keep this collaborative effort exclusive, Chartres would not allow the opera to be published.

In May 1698 Chartres showed his gratitude by pressuring the Treasurer of the SAINTE-CHAPELLE to have his former teacher appointed as music master: "Sieur Charpentier so effectively pressed the Duke of Chartres, his disciple, that Abbé Fleuriau was obliged to give him the position," recalled Loulié's close friend, BROSSARD, who had been eyeing the post for himself.

Chartres never lost his love for music. He continued his benevolence toward Charpentier by watching out for the composer's close relatives. For example, he incorporated at least one Charpentier cousin into his personal household. This gesture should not surprise us, for princes and princesses of the House of Orléans frequently engaged the close relative of someone who "belonged" to them or to another member of their House. In this way, the children, or nephews, or second cousins of some of GASTON D'ORLÉANS' householders turned up in Philippe II d'Orléans' household a generation later. For example, Nicolas Guichard had been Gaston's chamber valet, and now his son, Henri Guichard, was Philippe II's master of revels. Jacques I and JACQUES II DALIBERT had handled Gaston's finances and had loaned him huge sums of money, and before 1678 Jacques II's brother, Claude Dalibert, had been named Philippe II's almoner.[25]

Over the years, Marc-Antoine Charpentier's relatives found their way into Philippe II's household in a similar way. As early as 1669, the Duke's household list included Claude Sevin, gentleman in ordinary, a cousin of CHARLES SEVIN; and at some point prior to 1696, GILLES CHARPENTIER THE SECRETARY's two sons were placed on Philippe II's household roster. To be specific, René Charpentier was Philippe II's almoner, and Jean-Baptiste, his brother, was an "officer" in the Duke's household.[26]

Although the presence of two of the composer's cousins in the Duke of Orléans' household can be seen as, and probably was, an expression of gratitude for the lessons that Marc-Antoine Charpentier had given to Chartres, Monsieur was continuing a protection that spanned several decades, moving from JACQUES HAVÉ DE SAINT-AUBIN (who had been in Gaston's household during the 1650s), to Claude Sevin (in Philippe II's service from the late 1660s to the early 1680s), and now to the composer's cousins in the 1690s.

Philippe III d'Orléans of Chartres carried this protection a generation farther. He obtained the mastership of the SAINTE-CHAPELLE for Marc-Antoine Charpentier in 1698, and in 1734 one of his almoners was Jean-Baptiste-Thomas Charpentier, the son of Jean-Baptiste Charpentier and the grandson of GILLES CHARPENTIER THE SECRETARY.[27]

Upon his father's death in 1702, Chartres became Duke of Orléans. (After Louis XIV's death, he would serve as Regent to young Louis XV.) In 1709 Marc-Antoine Charpentier's nephews, JACQUES ÉDOUARD and Jacques-François Mathas, dedicated a little volume of the composer's motets to Philippe III d'Orléans. In other words, the Duke had agreed to allow the book to be dedicated to him; and by permitting this dedication, he ensured that Édouard and Mathas would be granted the requisite privilege to print and distribute the book.[28] In this dedication the pair expressed their hope that—in view of the "special protection" he had shown their late uncle—His Royal Highness would "not refuse to accept and protect" Charpentier's compositions, in memory of "a man who, during his life, received so many good things from you," a man who "had the honor of developing [in you] the principles of musical composition."[29]

If Édouard and Mathas had hoped that Philippe III d'Orléans would subsidize other volumes, their hopes were dashed. In 1716 JACQUES ÉDOUARD, acting alone, tried another tack. Having petitioned the Duke, he was granted a special privilege to create a theater that would perform works "in the Italian taste," but in the French language. Nothing came of the project. Aside from the presence of a Charpentier in Philippe III's household, 1716 apparently marked the end of His Royal Highness's contacts with Marc-Antoine Charpentier's immediate family.

IV

I accept this arrangement with joy

MADAME DE TOSCANE

Marguerite-Louise d'Orléans, Grand Duchess of Tuscany,
Madame de Guise's sister

Born on July 28, 1645, and known in her youth as "Mademoiselle d'Orléans," Marguerite-Louise d'Orléans[1] grew up at Blois under the tutelage of her temporarily exiled parents, GASTON D'ORLÉANS and Marguerite de Lorraine. MADAME D'ORLÉANS paid little attention to her children: "Madame only saw her daughters for a quarter hour in the evening and a quarter hour in the morning, and she never said anything to them but 'Stand up straight,' 'Hold your head up.' This is the only instruction she gave them," recalled their half-sister, MADEMOISELLE DE MONTPENSIER, who profoundly disliked and resented her stepmother, Madame d'Orléans. It was at Blois that young Marguerite became close to Louise de la Vallière, her principal playmate.

Just seven when her father left Paris in disgrace after the Fronde, Mademoiselle d'Orléans did not experience life at the royal court until 1660, when her widowed mother—now the DOWAGER DUCHESS OF ORLÉANS—was permitted to bring her daughters to Paris. Moving into the Luxembourg Palace, the Dowager began casting about for suitable marriages. Shortly before his death, GASTON D'ORLÉANS had made a final but failed attempt to arrange a betrothal between Marguerite-Louise and her first cousin, LOUIS XIV.[2] Mademoiselle d'Orléans was so hurt about being rejected that her mother refused to let her attend the King's wedding: she "did not want to make [her daughter] feel bad by attending his marriage to someone else, after having been so hopeful that she would wed the King."[3]

Of the three young Orléans sisters, beautiful and talented Marguerite-Louise was early singled out by the Medicis of Florence, and JACQUES II DALIBERT began negotiating her wedding with Cosimo III de' Medici.

328

A description that claimed to be "sincere" did not mention her reputation for being headstrong and quite spoiled:

> The Princess has excellent qualities of both mind and heart. She possesses the gentlest and most upright heart that one might wish; she is accommodating in the extreme, very witty without forgetting the rank that her birth merits; she speaks very well, she has an agreeable tone of voice, she sings very agreeably, she plays the spinet very well, she dances to ultimate perfection, she has a lovely body, ... her bosom is very beautiful and full. She has white skin and vermilion cheeks, lively eyes, brown hair in great abundance, ... she is rather gay but never out of control, very pious and very regular in her devotions, ... she possesses the gift of winning the hearts of those whom she receives.[4]

The recollections of one of the Dowager's householders reveal that Mademoiselle d'Orléans was adamantly opposed to the Medici proposal. "The Princess was as beautiful as an angel, and she did not want to go so far away. And so she had difficulty consenting to this marriage. She had thought she could wed Prince Charles of Lorraine, who had been courting her all winter."[5]

But consent she must, so Marguerite wed Cosimo III de' Medici in 1661. She never adjusted to life in Florence—where, with a retinue of forty-four retainers,

> she arrived with the intention of enraging her husband and her mother-in-law [Vittoria delle Rovere], at which, one might say, she succeeded admirably. I remember that she began by keeping the signet she had used before her marriage, not wanting, she would say, to mingle the fleur-de-lis with those little Florentine circles. It was a great beginning.[6]

With each of her pregnancies, she insisted that one of her mother's ladies-in-waiting make the trip to Florence, to be present at the birth. Nor was the emotional void filled by the operas performed each year at the Tuscan court,[7] including several dedicated to her: Jacopo Melani's *Ercole in Tebe* (1661), performed in Florence during her wedding festivities; Domenico Anglesi's *Il Mondo festeggiante* (1661), also performed for her wedding; Ziani's *Le Fortune di Rodope e di Damira* (1662); a revival of Antonio Cesti's *La Dori ovvero La Schiava Fedele* (1670). Always perverse, young "Madame de Toscane" tried to win the Florentines over to French music and dance.

As the years passed, her behavior became increasingly erratic. She would sneak off for tête-à-têtes with her French male servants; she would insist that she was fatally ill and must return to France; she corresponded secretly with the object of her obsessive affections, Prince Charles of Lorraine; and she eventually withdrew to one of the Medicis' country villas and refused to see anyone but a handful of servants.

At times Cosimo would try to appease her. It doubtlessly was to please his pregnant wife that he requested some French song books in November 1670[8]; that he went to great lengths to obtain a description of the banquet that MADEMOISELLE DE GUISE prepared for the Harcourt wedding a few months later; and that he had a French cookbook sent to him.[9] At other times he would threaten his wife or refuse to pay her allowance. By 1673, the Grand Duchess was declaring that rather than continue her life with Cosimo, she would live in a French convent and surrender all her rights over her children.[10] Not even the most persuasive envoys sent by Louis XIV could make her change her mind.

The King finally agreed to let this first cousin return to France, or rather, to the Royal Abbey of MONTMARTRE, which was of "a rank superior to others." Above all, the Abbess (who was MADEMOISELLE DE GUISE's sister and alter ego) had the requisite strength of character. It would be made to appear that Madame de Toscane was residing there of her own volition; but in reality she would be more or less a prisoner, under royal surveillance and only leaving the convent when the King summoned her.

In March 1675 the *Gazette d'Amsterdam* broke the news; and although some of the details in the article differ from the actual conditions laid down by Cosimo and Louis XIV, the announcement paints a reasonably accurate picture:

> They say that Madame the Princess of Tuscany is coming to travel about France, with the avowal and full consent of His Most Serene Highness the Grand Duke of Florence, who will give her eighty thousand crowns a year for her upkeep, for as long as she wishes to stay there. A superb apartment is being prepared for her at Montmartre, near the abbey, and the King has appointed the Countess of Sainte-Mesme and the Count her husband, who was first equerry of the late Madame [the Dowager of Orléans], to go fetch her. This princess will bring with her only two *demoiselles*, a page, a cook, and two bailiffs.[11]

Because the Abbess, MADAME DE MONTMARTRE, had initially been very dubious, Madame de Toscane accepted in writing the conditions imposed by her husband and her royal cousin:

> The Grand Duke, wishing me to live a very withdrawn life, and desiring that I go to Montmartre, I accept this arrangement with joy, having no stronger wish than to spend my life near Madame de

Montmartre; and I promise that I will only leave upon the King's orders; and I surrender my power to allow people to enter there, understanding that without that, there would be no cloture [for the nuns]; and as for the people I will take into my service, I will always defer to Madame de Montmartre.[12]

The Grand Duchess did not keep these commitments. Her conduct often brought chaos to the abbey. She had no intention of burying herself in a convent for the rest of her life, as her childhood friend, Louise de la Vallière, had recently done at the Great Carmel. She therefore continually attempted to stretch the limits her husband had imposed upon her, exclaiming, "I don't give a tinker's darn about him! I'll not keep a single one of the promises I made him."[13]

In July 1675 Madame de Toscane again set foot on French soil. The narrative of her return, published in the *Mercure Hollandois*, suggested that Louis XIV would find it difficult to exclude his beautiful cousin from his court:

They judged ... her beauty to have increased extremely in Italy, and that it was, however, a shame for such a beautiful princess to be shut up in a cloister for the rest of her life. The King also went to see her at Montmartre, and he said that he had the greatest trouble in the world refraining from seeing this princess whom, contrary to his feelings, he had permitted to live in a cloister for the rest of her days, and that he felt no greater joy than in seeing her at court, so that she could participate in the pleasures enjoyed there. He then praised her for her beauty.[14]

Madame de Sévigné and her circle were quite pessimistic about Madame de Toscane's fate: "They are preparing a prison at Montmartre for her, which would terrify her if she didn't have hopes of having it changed. She will be caught in her own trap. In Tuscany they are overjoyed to be rid of her." She seemed "very changed," "tedium seems written and engraved on her face." It was predicted that "she will be blotted out by Madame de Guise," that she would be "swallowed up by her Montmartre and by her Guise women."[15] Montpensier's impression upon seeing her half-sister again was similar: "I found her very much changed, something old, strained." In addition, she "talks a great deal and recounts all manner of things." It seems, she concluded, "that is the style in Italy."[16]

By returning to France, the Grand Duchess prompted a revolution in the music that Marc-Antoine Charpentier had been composing for the two Guise highnesses. To please—or perhaps to impress—her musician sister, in the spring of 1675 MADAME DE GUISE obtained a chapel at the

Church of Sainte-Anne-la-Royale, which belonged to an Italian order, the THEATINES. Using biblical texts scheduled to be recited on September 26, 27, or 28 of that year, MONSIEUR DU BOIS pieced together a Latin account of Judith's heroism. Charpentier turned this text into an oratorio—the first of a succession. MADEMOISELLE DE GUISE and MADAME DE GUISE (and to some extent Madame de Toscane) could now proclaim their devotional preoccupations to the select group of worshipers permitted to attend these events.

This first oratorio, performed by a large ensemble, appears to have triggered in the Grand Duchess a frenetic enthusiasm for music of all sorts, but preferably courtly music. She promptly began organizing musical entertainments. A scant month after her arrival, the Florentine agent found MADEMOISELLE DE GUISE's "people" and the Grand Duchess's "people" "conversing" and "passing their time at the [parlor] grill in musical concerts."[17] By February 1676 her guests were being treated to musical performances. For example, PHILIPPE II D'ORLÉANS and his wife were surprised with a "musical entertainment" that the Grand Duchess had secretly arranged.[18]

The identity of the performers in these musical events can be deduced. Madame de Toscane herself surely performed, for she was an accomplished musician and would often withdraw to a little room near the convent parlor and practice the harpsichord.[19] She also played the lute, the guitar, and the viol. Another performer was Cintia Galoppini, one of the two *demoiselles* who had come to France with her and who was described as an excellent musician.[20] There were Mademoiselle de Guise's "people" as well—that is, the members of the GUISE MUSIC. And there were, of course, the two or three Benedictine nuns at MONTMARTRE who "knew music marvelously well" and performed during devotions in the abbey church.

Laymen and laywomen were soon entering and leaving the Grand Duchess's new house that sat astride the abbey walls. The structure was walled-in on one side, to give the impression that she was confined to the monastery; yet friends could enter via a salon accessible from outside the walls. Now and then Madame de Toscane would escape her prison through this door, to the exasperation of the Abbess and the Count of Sainte-Mesme, technically her "honorary knight" but in reality more or less her jailor.

MADEMOISELLE DE GUISE and MADAME DE GUISE likewise had private apartments in the abbey, so the three women saw one another frequently. The two sisters—Madame de Guise and Madame de Toscane—took special pleasure in offending one another. This attitude spread to their servants and each would take her mistress's side. Exasperated by the princesses' disputes, Sainte-Mesme commented to his Tuscan contact: "I assure you, Monsieur, that our little courts are thorny; and minds that are on bad terms mingle there, and create obstacles that one has a great deal of trouble fending off."[21]

It took only five months for Madame de Toscane to win the right to dine outside the abbey, and she soon was spending at least one day a week in Paris. Often she would have a noon meal with MADEMOISELLE DE GUISE or MADAME DE GUISE, sometimes at the Hôtel de Guise and sometimes at the Luxembourg Palace. Various members of the House of Lorraine—primarily Mesdames d'Elbeuf, de Lillebonne, and d'Armagnac—would attend these social events, which were quite courtly and included dancing and musical *divertissements*.[22]

Men were sometimes present at these parties as well, among them Franz Egon von Furstemberg, Bishop of Strasbourg, and Abbé d'Harcourt, yet another Lorraine. After the meal and the entertainments, the guests sometimes would set off for MONTMARTRE, where they would spend the rest of the day listening to music or playing games.[23] One Sunday, Jean-Baptiste Colbert's brother-in-law, Charron de Ménars, conducted part-singing for the little girls who boarded at the abbey. The music went on for several hours, in the Abbess's presence.[24] On another occasion, a little opera by a German in the service of the Bishop of Strasbourg—the Florentines called him the "Baron di Ronsuer"—was performed in the Grand Duchess's lodging.[25] (She was seeing too much of the Bishop, and it was unhealthy, concluded an exasperated MADAME DE MONTMARTRE.[26]) Some of these courtly entertainments almost certainly included Italian music, for now that the Grand Duchess was back in France, she was boasting about the superiority of Italian music over French music. (If Marc-Antoine Charpentier's two lost operas in Italian[27] were not written in Rome, but in Paris, were they composed with Madame de Toscane in mind? Or at least revived for her?)

During some of her visits to Paris, the Grand Duchess would spend the afternoon at the Great Carmel, visiting Louise de la Vallière. The pair would weep together over their fates. Madame de Toscane also frequently accompanied Madame de Guise to the LITTLE CARMEL on the rue du Bouloi. The QUEEN was often there too, for this was her preferred retreat. One day Madame de Longueville appeared and, knowing how much Madame de Toscane loved music, asked rather pointedly whether Cosimo liked music as much as she did. The Grand Duchess replied rather sadly that he was a morose man who detested concerts and was only happy when he was alone.[28]

By the fall of 1676 Madame de Toscane had stretched her bonds still further and was being permitted to attend court functions. The first of these sorties was for the baptisms at Saint-Cloud of PHILIPPE III D'ORLÉANS, DUKE OF CHARTRES, and his sister, in October 1676. The description of the event in the *Gazette de France* focused on the members of the royal family who attended the fête, and only mentioning in passing the "opera" performed that day.[29] Madame de Toscane had a wonderful time. Not only had the baptisms been followed by games and an opera, there had been dancing too. To prepare for future balls, she promptly hired Monsieur Des Airs, the Dauphin's dancing master, to come to the abbey. After her dancing lesson, she would play the lute, the guitar, and the viol with him.[30] The Tuscan resident protested, but MADAME DE MONTMARTRE stood up for her. After all, the boarding girls were taught by laymen within the abbey walls, and they even took riding lessons there.

The Grand Duchess's hopes of being accepted at court—indeed, of being granted an apartment there—remained stillborn, however:

> The King did not value her very much. They found her boring, talking a great deal and not very agreeably, continually talking about her domestic affairs, the horses she was buying, where they came from; in short, details worthy of a horse-dealer or a country girl who goes to the fair with her husband; and she dressed just about that way.[31]

As if to compensate for this disappointment, Madame de Toscane got caught up in her sister's charitable activities. Eager to spend more time outside the abbey walls, she began going on "retreat" with MADAME DE GUISE.[32] These pious activities alternated with worldly ones. For example, on Tuesday she might lunch and gamble with Madame de Guise and the Bishop of Strasbourg; and the next day, after a noon meal at the Hôtel de Guise, she would go out and distribute food to the poor.

One of the Carmelite nuns who spied on the Grand Duchess for the Florentines, summed up these two contradictory facets of conduct. In the process, the nun made some pointed remarks that angered Madame de Guise and Madame de Toscane:

> It is true that I said that Madame de Guise was never supposed to arrange for public dancing and entertainments for the wife of a sovereign who has separated from her husband, and that this is shameful, for sovereigns can only appear in public with all the dignity of their rank. I mentioned only the balls to Madame the Grand Duchess. ... As for ridicule, I confess that I did say that it was difficult to conceive of Madame de Guise being able to leave the Gray Sisters [of Charity], and then take her sister to gamble and dance, and that it would be better to let her get a bit bored [and]

seek diversion in the little things one can innocently do in a convent.[33]

Sainte-Mesme did everything he could to keep Madame de Toscane entertained, so that she would not be tempted do something inappropriate. As the winter of 1677–1678 drew to a close, he rejoiced that:

Madame the Grand Duchess has been rather calm all winter long. She has had almost no visitors, and that forced us to be very assiduous about keeping her busy and entertaining her with all sorts of things, in order to prevent the effects of the chagrin that solitude might cause her.[34]

Madame de Toscane's hey-day at the Abbey of Montmartre ended with MADAME DE MONTMARTRE's death in 1682. MADEMOISELLE DE GUISE assumed the responsibility of supervising her conduct, but the Grand Duchess's behavior was increasingly unpredictable, and Mademoiselle de Guise's health was failing. By the mid-1680s, the Grand Duchess's musical "conversations" either stopped, or else the Tuscan agent ceased alluding to them. Her husband was sending her less and less money, and by the summer of 1689 she had to sell a pearl necklace.

Having inherited her share of MADAME DE GUISE's estate in 1696, Madame de Toscane at last was financially independent from Grand Duke Cosimo III. Outliving MADAME DE GUISE and MADEMOISELLE DE MONTPENSIER by almost three decades, Marguerite-Louise d'Orléans eventually moved to a convent at Saint-Mandé.

V

She embraced a holy rule of life

ISABELLE D'ORLÉANS OF ALENÇON

Élisabeth ("Isabelle") d'Orléans,
known in her youth as "Mademoiselle d'Alençon,"
and after 1667 as "Madame de Guise"

Princess Isabelle was the second of GASTON D'ORLÉANS' three daughters by his second wife, Marguerite de Lorraine. Born on December 26, 1646, Isabelle was separated from her family when she was just two.[1] In January 1649, during the rebellion known as the Fronde, her mother, and her half-sister, MADEMOISELLE DE MONTPENSIER, fled Paris with the King and his court, but little Isabelle and her baby brother were sent to the Dominican nuns of Poissy. (She would return to Poissy from time to time, usually to honor the convent by her presence at a high religious holiday.) For his role in the Fronde, Gaston and his family were exiled to Blois and to his duchy, Orléans.

Isabelle remained in Paris—not at court but at the convent of Notre-Dame de la Paix, which her mother had founded just outside the city, at Charonne. Isabelle had her own household there, and she received instruction in the arts and letters similar to the education her sisters were being given in Blois. She studied Italian with Lorenzo Ferreti, a Roman who dedicated his Italian-French dictionary to her and a younger sister in 1663, and she became proficient enough to write to her father in that language. Thus, in the late 1650s, she notified her father's secretary that "I honored myself by writing Monsieur in Italian, so that I am doing everything to please him."[2] She studied music, dancing, harpsichord, and guitar. She also took singing lessons from Sieur Gourlin, a high tenor, *haute-contre*, who belonged to her father's Music (which was directed by Étienne Moulinié). Gourlin visited Charonne regularly to instruct the princess.[3] By the time Isabelle was thirteen, she had also acquired "some principles" of Latin.[4]

Latin? Yes, for Isabelle had been given to the Church when she was not yet two. Louis XIV and Gaston d'Orléans had agreed that Madame could write the nuns at the Abbey of Remiremont (where she had been raised and had been coadjutrix) to inform them that, having learned of the death of her aunt the Abbess, "I have the desire to see my daughter of Alençon one day occupy the same place among you." The nuns voted in favor of naming Mademoiselle d'Alençon, the late Abbess's grandniece, as her successor. The Pope issued an age dispensation, and little Isabelle, still a toddler, became Abbess in 1648.[5]

The extremely devout Mademoiselle de Saujon, whose only thought was to leave the court and become a Carmelite, was put in charge of the girl's religious education. Curate Olier of Saint-Sulpice supervised Isabelle's training from a distance and offered advice about her spiritual development. "I pray you," he wrote Saujon, "to train your young princess little by little to lift her heart to God. Give her a few written-out *élévations* for morning and evening, and before she begins an activity."[6] In other words, the little princess's devotions were shaped by an approach to prayer known as the *élévation*,

> a sort of prayer ... that is done by means of admiration, adoration, reverence, a humble look, homage, and honor, and other similar practices, which purely and simply tend to honor and glorify God, without thinking about ourselves, without desiring or asking anything [for ourselves].[7]

(Echoes of this lyrical adoration can be discerned in quite a few of the Latin texts that Marc-Antoine Charpentier set to music between 1670 and 1687.)

If Isabelle d'Orléans was destined for the cloister, it was in large part because she had a crooked back. The sources are unanimous: she was "misshapen," she had a "spoiled torso." As a Florentine marriage negotiator observed, she did not, in truth, have a very "free" body, but with a stiff bodice fabricated by a clever tailor, it should "be possible to repair what is lacking."[8]

Although she had left the cloister by 1657 and was soon accepted at the court of her first cousin, LOUIS XIV, Isabelle's religious training marked her for life. It "filled her with the maxims of Jesus Christ." By the time she was thirteen, it was possible to predict that "she will have a sort of piety that is perfectly adjusted to the rules of Christianity, which ... insists upon occupying the center of the heart and refuses to be received only on the tip of the tongue, and in those actions that have no aim other than men's eyes." The author of one of the eulogies given after her death in 1696 summarized Princess Isabelle's education, and the repercussions this training had upon her personality:

> God ... caused her to enter one of those [religious] houses where
> Heaven spreads forth its most saintly and most favorable influences.
> It was there, among the faithful spouses of Jesus Christ, that
> Élisabeth learned, from her childhood, to know Him and adore
> Him. It was there that she lived happily, protected from the
> contagious air of the grand world and from the dangers to which the
> children of princes are exposed, even in their own homes, by seeing
> those very worldly people who have the honor of approaching them
> and who, under the pretext of serving them, often do them
> irreparable harm by making them know and love evil. ... She
> embraced a holy rule of life; she subjected herself to pious practices,
> and she always observed them inviolably.[9]

Interpreting her early widowhood as a sign from God, Isabelle d'Orléans would spend a quarter century at court, where she would indeed eschew the "contagious air of the grand world," and "embrace a holy rule." The years gradually transformed her into a nun at heart, who was not permitted to cast off the courtier's gown in favor of the Carmelite's habit. When only in her teens, she modestly told someone who alluded to the possibility of a lofty marriage: "My happiness is serving God. I come from a very Christian House. It is upon my religion that my glory depends."[10]

For reasons that are not clear, by the late 1650s her parents had second thoughts about giving Isabelle d'Alençon to the Church. They began casting about for a potential bridegroom. Gaston's death in 1660 speeded up the search, but making a match for Isabelle meant finding a bridegroom who was willing to overlook her physical appearance and focus instead on her spiritual strengths. The Medicis and the House of Savoy were proving increasingly wary, for MADEMOISELLE DE MONTPENSIER was telling them that one or more of her half-sisters was a humpback. They also asked for reassurances that Mademoiselle d'Alençon—who at the time was living at the convent of Charonne—did not feel a strong religious vocation. The reply was emphatic: "No, the Princess has no interest in and no taste for the life of a nun."[11]

At thirteen, Isabelle was one of the most educated and pious princesses in the realm. Despite the hyperbole woven into a word-portrait that was dispatched to Florence, it is clear that she wrote well and painted skillfully; that she spoke her native tongue correctly and knew Italian and some Latin. She liked history, had acquired a solid knowledge of geography, and was well acquainted with philosophy, especially "the part that is concerned with regulating morals."

Still, the most artful tailor could not conceal the crooked back that caused her to be un-regally short. Her blue eyes, her high forehead, her rosy cheeks, her long oval face, her average-length nose that was "a bit round at the extremity," and her curly chestnut brown hair could not disguise fact that her height "is yet, in her case, merely a hope of being tall." Nor could her "gait, as lofty as it can be," her "voice, a bit strong ... with a sound entirely suitable for uttering commands," and her "assurance, [which] is that of a princess," compensate for the twisted spine that would keep her from developing into a physically imposing woman.

Another word-portrait of Isabelle, painted considerably later, reveals that as the twig had been bent, so the tree had grown. Her character changed little over the decades. The tribulations of the 1670s did not alter her regal manner, any more than they could possibly change her "humpbacked and excessively misshapen" body. To the end of her life, the author of this portrait noted, she was "a very pious princess who was totally occupied with prayer and doing good deeds."

That did not mean that this granddaughter of France was too devout to exert her prerogatives. When residing in her Duchy of Alençon,

> she lorded it over the royal intendant, as if he were a little
> journeyman; and she treated the Bishop of Sées, her diocesan, the
> same way, making him stand for hours on end as she sat in her
> armchair, never letting him sit, not even behind her back and in a
> corner. She was very stubborn about her rank, but at the same time
> she knew [the respect] she owed others, she paid it, and she was
> extremely kind.[12]

When Isabelle abandoned convent life after her father's death in 1660, she immediately plunged into the festivities surrounding LOUIS XIV's wedding. Joining the royal family's southward progress, she rode in a coach with two of her sisters, among them MADEMOISELLE DE MONTPENSIER, whose description of the wedding festivities provides clues about thirteen-year-old Isabelle's first experiences at court. "Decorated with pearls," she was present at the ball that Louis XIV offered his entourage on the eve of his wedding—an event that Queen Mother Anne of Austria had "ordered" the princesses to attend, despite their mourning.

A problem arose the following morning, however, and made palpable the scorn that so many courtiers felt for Gaston's daughters. No one had been designated to carry their trains, and a call for volunteers brought no results. Montpensier eventually found a duke willing to be her train-bearer, but her sisters were less fortunate: "They looked for some dukes to bear my sisters' [trains]; no one was willing to do it." Without trainbearers, protocol prevented the girls from participating. In the end,

Isabelle d'Alençon's train was carried by a mere count (the late Gaston's equerry, Anne-Alexandre de l'Hôpital de Sainte-Mesme, who had just been incorporated into the household of DOWAGER DUCHESS OF ORLÉANS), while a simple marquis bore Mademoiselle de Valois' train.[13] During the festivities that followed, a friendship developed between Isabelle d'Alençon and QUEEN MARIE-THÉRÈSE, six years her elder. They would remain close until the Queen's death in 1683.

By the fall of 1663 two of Isabelle's sisters had married, one to the Duke of Savoy, the other to a Medici of Florence. In the youthful court of Louis XIV, Isabelle was the remaining marriageable granddaughter of France. (Her half-sister, MADEMOISELLE DE MONTPENSIER, was now in her mid-thirties). Isabelle was at the King's side throughout Les Plaisirs de l'Île enchanté; she gambled at court functions and often lost. On one occasion, her indiscrete remarks about the Queen infuriated the King. "Crestfallen, ashamed," she begged his pardon. Her punishment involved being sent to bed whenever the Queen went for a stroll after supper. This sort of conduct made the courtiers exclaim: "What! Someone who is good for nothing has only enough wit to plague people."[14]

By the mid-1660s, when she was in her late teens, Isabelle had formed affective and devotional ties to several Parisian religious houses. These ties strengthened during the years when Marc-Antoine Charpentier was living at the Hôtel de Guise. She of course continued her visits to Charonne, where she had been raised, but by 1665 she belonged to the small group of highborn ladies who several times a month would accompany the QUEEN to the LITTLE CARMEL on the rue du Bouloi.[15] In 1664 she thanked the nuns of the other Parisian Carmelite house—the Great Carmel, where she would be buried in a nun's habit in 1696—for having said a novena for her when she fell ill with smallpox.[16] She was also a devotee of Saint Francis: on October 4, 1664, she went to the Irish Recollets to hear a sermon and a Benediction of the Holy Sacrament in honor of that saint.[17] In this she appears to have been inspired by her mother, the DOWAGER OF ORLÉANS, who would take the vows of the Third Order of Saint Francis in the early 1670s.

Isabelle's chances of making a prestigious marriage were ebbing rapidly; and when her twentieth birthday had passed, people began to assume that she would remain a "Mademoiselle," like her half-sister, Montpensier. She was becoming an ornamental pillar at her mother's court, adding luster but always in the background. Finally, "preferring to marry the last Duke of Guise rather than not marry at all,"[18] she gleefully accepted the arrangement worked out by MARIE DE GUISE, THE REGENT, and the DOWAGER DUCHESS OF ORLÉANS. So enthusiastic was Mademoiselle de Guise about this chance to unite the House of Guise to the Royal

House of Bourbon, that she was willing to forgo the large dowries that Isabelle's two sisters had received from the King.

It was agreed that, after her marriage to LOUIS-JOSEPH DE LORRAINE, DUKE OF GUISE, who was more than three years her junior, Isabelle would assume the title "Duchess of Guise." However, any children born of the union would not bear one or another of the titles associated with the House of Guise; instead, they would take the name of a royal land, for example, the Duchy of Alençon.[19] Accepting to be a Guise did not mean that Isabelle would surrender the prerogatives and the pre-eminences due a granddaughter of France. She would be entitled to sit in an armchair; and in public she would have precedence over all princesses who were her inferiors by birth—a category that included the groom's aunt and guardian, MARIE DE GUISE THE REGENT, a mere "foreign princess natural-ized in France."

The nuptial mass was celebrated on Sunday, May 15, 1667, in the chapel of the Old Château at Saint-Germain-en-Laye. Mademoiselle de Guise's new protégé, ROQUETTE, BISHOP OF AUTUN, officiated. "The entire court, gay and natty," attended this rather impromptu event. (Neither the Dowager of Orléans nor Mademoiselle de Guise had dared delay, lest Louis XIV change his mind.) Up in the tribune, Madame de Montespan, the royal mistress, chuckled when she saw her dogs' pillows being used as improvised kneeling cushions for the bride and groom. During the repast that followed, attended by the King and the Queen, the groom offered his bride "a pair of earrings, rich, of course, and marvelously beautiful." The newlyweds then set off for the Luxembourg Palace, where PHILIPPE II D'ORLÉANS handed his goddaughter the traditional night-gown.[20]

The battle over precedence that marked court life was fought each day at the Hôtel de Guise. There, Isabelle, now known as "MADAME DE GUISE," would order her husband about from the armchair that marked her rank, as contrasted with the folding stool to which the Duke was entitled as a mere prince of the House of Lorraine. Every formality was "observed with the same exactitude, and it began anew each day, without the wife's rank lowering one tiny bit, and without Monsieur de Guise's increasing whatsoever, despite this grand marriage."[21] Insistent though she was about prerogatives and ceremony, Her Royal Highness the Duchess of Guise cast aside the coat of arms of the House of Orléans, with its fleurs-de-lis, in favor of the crest of the Guises, emblazoned with the double-beamed cross of Lorraine.[22]

In a sense, the young Duchess was transformed into a split personal-ity when she married. The half of her that was a granddaughter of France caused her to be haughty toward her husband and to show inordinate concern for the honors due her. Yet when confronted by MADEMOISELLE DE GUISE's iron will, she became compliant and humble, a behavior learned during scoldings by her mother and brow-beatings by her half-sister, MADEMOISELLE DE MONTPENSIER. The interpersonal relationships between the three women became legendary:

> [Isabelle was] very badly treated by Mademoiselle [de Montpensier], her sister, the only child of her father's first marriage, powerfully rich and never able to stomach the second marriage of Monsieur her father, nor tolerate his second wife or his daughters. Abandoned like this, considered nothing by the King and by [Philippe II d'Orléans], her only paternal relatives, ... she came under the thumb of Mademoiselle de Guise, who by her property and her rank occupied a high position in the world, and who had subjugated the entire House of Lorraine. [Mademoiselle de Guise] was, in addition, a very thoughtful person with a lot of plans that were worthy of the Guises, her forebears.[23]

The young Duchess had little influence at the Hôtel de Guise:

> Three or four months after she was married, they dismissed a chambermaid she loved very much and to whom she become accustomed, having had her since she came into the world. They also dismissed her equerry, and her secretary, who was the brother of this female domestic. I think it was done for grandeur, because [when French princesses marry] in foreign countries, French domestics are usually sent away.[24]

Isabelle not only lost her trusted domestics, strangers were imposed upon her as well. For example, she had to tolerate a certain Monsieur Alzeau and pay his wages and living expenses from her treasury. Not until mid-1675 did she summon the courage to defy Mademoiselle de Guise and dismiss him.[25]

Given these circumstances, it almost certainly was MARIE DE GUISE THE REGENT who selected Marc-Antoine Charpentier to be the household composer. Still, the choice was calculated to please Isabelle d'Orléans—or at least not humiliate her publicly. That is to say, selecting the talented relative of HAVÉ DE SAINT-AUBIN, gentleman in ordinary to Isabelle's late father, would have positive resonances among the high aristocracy, which tended to select householders from among families that already "belonged" to their House.

The young Duchess of Guise went to the Luxembourg Palace frequently to see her mother, the DOWAGER OF ORLÉANS. She would time her visits to coincide with the Tuscan agent's delivery of the latest news from Florence. Had she forgotten her Italian? Or was it from consideration for her mother that Isabelle insisted that the agent provide French translations of the latest cultural news from Florence? Of the items delivered during these weekly visits, her favorites were sweetmeats, medicines, and a host of surprises sent by MADAME DE TOSCANE and her husband, the Grand Duke, with whom Isabelle and the Dowager had become acquainted during Cosimo's visit to Paris in 1669.

If Isabelle got on so well with her mother, it was because they had many traits in common and had been raised in similar ways. They were extremely pious, and each was an expert at putting her foot in her mouth. Isabelle tended to act without thinking; and when criticized she would fabricate excuses or proclaim her innocence. "I've known her for a long time," her half-sister later remarked, "she is her mother's daughter."[26]

At the different entertainments held at the splendidly renovated Hôtel de Guise, the young Duchess was nominally the hostess; but the real hostess was MARIE DE GUISE THE REGENT, who generally put DUKE LOUIS-JOSEPH DE LORRAINE in the position of figurehead. It was he who received foreign visitors, it was he who stood beside the King at military reviews. Upon him all his aunt's hopes depended: he must sire a son to perpetuate the House of Guise.

Madame de Guise produced that son in August 1670. In accordance with her marriage contract, little François-Joseph de Lorraine bore the title "Duke of Alençon." The House of Guise now had an heir. Six months later the Duchess miscarried—of a second son, it was asserted—and almost died. Four months later, her husband, LOUIS-JOSEPH DE LORRAINE, DUKE OF GUISE, succumbed to smallpox.

The young widow was universally commended for her devotion during the Duke's dreadful illness and death. The Florentine agent told of "her constancy and her love for her beloved consort," and he alluded to the amazement people had felt upon seeing her "leave her palace with only two women, totally incognito, without footmen, going through the muddy streets without concern for herself, visiting churches to ask Divine Goodness to save him."[27] Her prayers were in vain.

Continued in Panel 10: MADAME DE GUISE

Panel 10

THE HOUSE OF GUISE

Their Composer was the Reflection of Their Glory
and the Audible Voice of Their Prayers

The illustrious persons portrayed in this panel are sumptuously dressed, but they wear black as a sign of their seemingly endless mourning.

The first painting, a group portrait, depicts a family reunion in a vast Italian palace. The mother and her lovely daughter are surrounded by handsome and virile young men. In the second portrait the daughter, now a mature woman, holds a beautiful boy by the hand.

The third painting depicts a Benedictine nun who holds the jeweled crosier of an abbess. She stands before a splendid entry gate surmounted by the arms of the House of Guise.

The beautiful boy, now a young man, is the subject of the fourth portrait. He stands before the fireplace of his reception hall, making a welcoming gesture to visitors. His costly court clothes are studded with small double-beamed crosses of Lorraine.

The fifth painting depicts a woman whose face is so deeply marked by sorrow that, were it not for her crooked back, she would not be recognized as the hopeful young princess of Panel 9.

The final portrait shows the beautiful princess of the first two paintings, but now she is elderly. She holds an engraving depicting a single tree standing in a decimated forest. Its motto reads: "The survivor bears witness to the fallen."

Madamoiſelle Marie de Lorraine et de Guyſe.

B. Moncornet excudit cum Privilegio Regis

Mademoiselle Marie de Lorraine of Guise.
This popular depiction of the princess was made in the early 1640s,
shortly after she and her family returned from Florence. Although no
longer young, she was one of the prime matrimonial candidates of the time.

I

As the twig is bent so grows the tree

MADEMOISELLE MARIE DE GUISE AND HER FAMILY

Marie-Louise de Lorraine, known as "Mademoiselle de Guise";
and her parents, Charles de Lorraine, Duke of Guise,
and Henriette-Catherine de Joyeuse

On the day after the Feast of Saint Cecilia, in the year of Grace 1617, the curate of Saint-Jean-en-Grève recorded the baptism of two-year-old Marie-Louise de Lorraine:

Born [on August 15, 1615], the oldest daughter of most illustrious Prince Charles de Lorraine, Duke of Guise, and Catherine de Joyeuse, baptized privately the same day in the low chamber of their hôtel; baptized on November 23, 1617, and named *Marie* by Queen Marie de Médicis, represented by Mademoiselle de Montpensier [the child's half-sister], the godfather [was] the Duke of Joyeuse, her paternal uncle.[1]

Marie: an appropriate name for a daughter born on the Feast of the Assumption of the Blessed Virgin Mary. *Louise*: a name that would resonate in the princess's musical devotions for August 25, the Feast of Saint Louis, King of France. The Feast of Saint Cecilia: an augur of sorts for a princess who would spend her final decade surrounded by singers and instrumentalists who honored in song this patroness of musicians, while transforming her into the patron saint of conversions to Catholicism.

For the Guise couple, the birth of a daughter on August 15 was a sign from God. The infant's paternal grandfather, the scar-faced Duke of the Religious Wars, was known to "have been very devoted to the service of the Holy Virgin, Mother of God, continually wearing his rosary and reciting it with care." He hung this rosary about his neck, like a piece of jewelry, "finding it glorious to wear in public the livery of his dear Mistress."

347

Scarface's son, Charles de Lorraine, Duke of Guise, continued this devotion to the Virgin. Imprisoned after his father's assassination in 1588, he escaped on August 15, 1591, having "chosen the day of the Assumption of our Lady, ... pointing out that the late Duke, his father, had always found it advantageous to commit his deeds to this Mother of Mercy."[2] Charles made his way to Paris, where he received a hero's welcome. The Jesuits promptly attributed his miraculous escape to the prayers being recited at Our Lady of Loreto by the Italian members of the Society. The Virgin, they asserted, had been "lifted to Heaven" on August 15; and now, on August 15, 1591, she had "lifted" Charles de Lorraine from prison.[3] Convinced of the efficacy of these prayers, the leaders of the League commissioned a miniature ship bearing the arms of the city of Paris and sent it off to Loreto, where it joined the costly votive objects displayed at the *Santa Casa*.[4]

As Henri IV gained power to sustain his throne, Duke Charles made peace with his sovereign. Members of the House of Guise began to appear at court functions as part of the King's entourage. Charles was soon named grand master of France, admiral of the seas of the Levant, and governor of Champagne and Provence. After Henri IV's assassination, Guise gravitated to the circle of Regent Marie de Médicis.

In 1611 Charles married a young widow, Henriette-Catherine de Joyeuse, the only child of Father Ange (Henri) de Joyeuse, a duke turned Capuchin who had acquired considerable renown as a general. This marriage had great political significance, for it united two families that had been active in the League and that exemplified the Counter Reform in France. The union was also calculated to strengthen the ties between the Lorraines of Guise and the royal family, for Marie de Bourbon-Montpensier, Henriette-Catherine de Joyeuse's daughter by her first marriage to the Duke of Montpensier, had been promised to Henri IV's younger son, GASTON D'ORLÉANS.

Henriette-Catherine had been raised in a very pious family. Her father had wanted to become a Franciscan but was compelled to wed for dynastic reasons. The Joyeuse marriage proved to be a love match. Although "this holy couple of lovers" outwardly lived in the "world," they had a special devotion for the Virgin and would go out incognito to feed the Parisian poor. After his wife's death, Ange de Joyeuse took the vows to which he had so long aspired. In September 1587 he became a Franciscan monk, a Capuchin; but, for most of the next twelve years, he found himself wielding the sword—for the League, for the Pope, for the Monarchy.[5]

Henriette-Catherine was a toddler when her father became a monk, an adolescent during his years as a military figure. When she wed the

Duke of Guise two decades later, she took her parents as a model. Emulating her mother, she worked at her husband's finances, for the turmoil of the League years had wreaked havoc with the Guise fortune. Turning next to the well-being of the householders who had served the family throughout these years, she again emulated her parents, who had always made sure that the "pensions of their gentlemen" and the "wages of their valets" were paid. Thus the 1640s found her struggling to repay the descendants of Claude de Champaigne, who had "managed the property of the Duke of Guise and given an accounting in November 1586."[6]

The spiritual needs of the household were another major concern for the Duchess of Guise, as they had been for her parents, who

> to their householders forbade lies, drunkenness, debauchery, immodesty, blasphemy, and generally every vice, under penalty of being sent away without hope of return. They gave each of them time to serve God and to carry out their duty toward their master, according to the work each did. The equerries were ordered to answer for the pages and the lackeys, the maîtres d'hôtel for the officers who were subordinate to them. The almoners were ordered to say mass every day, the domestics to attend and to confess and take communion each month. The Count's authority permitted him to establish these saintly rules for his household; but in getting them to be followed, his example was more powerful than his authority. ... The order observed in the Countess's entourage was no less exact for her women servants, ... and it was not without reason that their saintly behavior was admired throughout France. ... It is difficult ... to adjust humility to the pomp of one's trappings, one's palace, one's furniture. Frugality amidst abundance in all things, sobriety in the presence of fine food, courtesy in the presence of favor, moderation in the presence of passions and desires, and justice in the presence of power.[7]

The Duke and Duchess of Guise produced seven children who survived the childhood illnesses that so often were fatal: François, prince of Joinville, born in 1612; Henri, who would become an archbishop and eventually Duke of Guise, in 1614; Mademoiselle Marie de Guise, in 1615; Charles-Louis, Duke of Joyeuse, in 1618; Françoise-Renée, the future Abbess of MONTMARTRE, in 1621; Louis, also Duke of Joyeuse, in 1622; and Roger, Chevalier of Guise, in 1624.

Devoted as two generations of Guises and Joyeuses had been to the Virgin, Marie's birth on the feast of the Assumption must have been viewed as a favorable omen—for the child and for the House of Guise. She partook of the miraculous: the rosary worn by the scar-faced Duke and his prayers to the Virgin; the image of Our Lady before which Ange de Joyeuse would pray throughout the night; Charles de Lorraine's escape on the Feast of the Assumption. Her birth embodied a family devotional tradition: links to the Society of Jesus, that is, the Jesuits, recently reestablished in France[8]; to the Capuchins; to the Virgin and her feast days, especially August 15; to the *Santa Casa* of Loreto and to "the French Loreto," that is, the chapel of Notre-Dame de Liesse[9] adjacent to the Guise château of Marchais; and to the rosaries and litanies recited during Marian devotions.

Little is known about Marie de Lorraine's youth. Perhaps she was sent to one of the convents directed by her close relatives—for example, Saint-Pierre of Rheims, where her aunt was abbess until 1626 and where her sister Françoise-Renée was being raised; or Jouarre, over which another aunt-abbess presided until 1638. Or was she brought up by her mother, admired for being a "very honest and very devout woman"?[10] The Duchess of Guise is known to have played an active, almost meddling role in raising her son Henri.[11]

Mademoiselle Marie's spelling remained phonetic, but she wrote clearly and expressed herself elegantly. In all things she took as a model her mother, for whom she felt great respect and profound friendship. Her niece, MADEMOISELLE DE MONTPENSIER, is one of the few sources that accuses Mademoiselle de Guise of possessing a sharp tongue. Indeed, Marie de Lorraine was generally described as gracious and kind—traits corroborated by the cordiality and unpretentiousness of her letters. She appears to have avoided one of her father's less praiseworthy traits. Although charming and generous, Charles de Lorraine had a reputation for being something of a prevaricator: "He was a great dreamer and a great liar. He lied, and often, by repeating it enough, he ended up believing what he said."[12]

As a mature woman, Marie de Lorraine would emulate the "generosity" and magnanimity that her ancestors and relatives had shown toward the king, toward their own protégés and householders, and toward the poor. ("Generosity" did not simply mean giving generous gifts to the needy, it meant spending huge sums to entertain a guest or to honor a member of the royal family.) Duke Charles lived by the maxim, "The people of our House never repent over having spent money liberally."[13] The Duchess likewise demonstrated "liberality," but it took the form of amply rewarding her most faithful householders. In her will she remembered "many a church, many a hospital, and many a convent, servant, lady-follower, and gentleman-follower."[14]

From her ancestors, Mademoiselle Marie inherited the intelligence, the physical beauty, and the charm for which the Guises were famous.

"Good, handsome, well-built, and well-mannered," her father was known for "his valor and his goodness, for he was a benefactor." (He was, on the other hand, accused of having "a rather slow wit," because he was not good at epigrams.) Charles de Lorraine's good deeds "made him loved by everyone."[15] Henri, his older son, possessed many of these traits. He was "well-built, obliging, gentle, civil, agreeable"; he "speaks well, writes poetry, and understands fine things."[16]

Marie de Lorraine strove to fit into a similar Guise mold—a female one patterned after her aunt, Madame de Conti, who had embodied the traits to which Guise women aspired. Madame de Conti was respected for her intellectual gifts and her personal merits: "She was humane and charitable; she helped men of letters and was of service to whomever she could serve."[17] Emulating this model, Mademoiselle Marie grew up to be a person who was so "loveable ... that one cannot help honoring and respecting her entire life, once one has had the honor of seeing her even once." Those who met her were "charmed" by her "upright conduct that, although natural to her illustrious House, nonetheless set her apart in the extreme and increased the respect that is due her."[18] Some of this respect was hers by birth, but she had earned much of it by her conduct; for, in all things, she "honored her birth by the nobility of her manners."[19]

Imitating the best qualities of her family and avoiding the worst ones, Marie was steeped in the pride of being a Guise. Like her aunt, Madame de Conti—who "toward the end of her life became unbearable about the grandeur of her House"[20]—on her deathbed Marie would be thinking about the past glory of the House of Guise. Above all, she tended to see everything through the eyes of a Lorraine, that is, from the perspective of a "foreign" and "sovereign" princess whose family had been "naturalized in France." Her niece, MADEMOISELLE DE MONTPENSIER, repeatedly asserted that Mademoiselle de Guise considered the Duke of Lorraine to be her "sovereign," and that whenever the House of Lorraine assembled en masse to "combat" anyone who dared oppose their family politics, Mademoiselle de Guise was sure to be present.

Marie early learned how to behave toward her social inferiors—not only her householders but also the high royal officials who professed to be ready to "receive her commands" at any time.[21] Knowing how to give orders graciously but firmly was essential for a princess who would one day supervise a huge household. Marie was taught these skills, for she was being prepared for a prestigious marriage that would enhance the glory and fortune of the House of Guise, just as her sister, Françoise-Renée, was being prepared to reign over a prestigious abbey.

In August 1626 Marie de Lorraine's half-sister, Marie de Bourbon-Montpensier, wed GASTON D'ORLÉANS. But Guise hopes for increased intimacy with the royal family were dashed when the young Duchess of Orléans died in 1627, after giving birth to MADEMOISELLE DE MONTPEN-SIER. The Guises' attention now turned to adolescent Marie, who began to appear at court functions and for whom a grand marriage was expected. She made quite an impression and was judged "estimable in everything, and of great and absolutely perfect beauty."[22]

However, belonging to the House of Lorraine meant being suspect. As a late seventeenth-century biographical sketch of Charles de Lorraine pointed out,

> a very sad experience of the great power of the name *Guise* took place, even after the League was no more. This House was, in a way, a state within a state, and it was to be feared that the people's stupidity and false zeal would turn it into an idol, every time a religious war broke out.[23]

For this very reason the marriage negotiations of Marie de Bourbon-Montpensier and Gaston d'Orléans had encountered a serious snag: the future bride was the Duke of Guise's stepdaughter, and Cardinal Riche-lieu's advisors had doubts about Guise's fidelity:

> If Monsieur [Gaston] weds Mademoiselle de Montpensier, it will be very difficult to prevent the powerful House of Lorraine from gaining control over him, because there are so many lords and ladies in this House, who will swell Monsieur's household by being assiduous toward him and ... by using different artifices. ... In addition, this alliance involves a foreign House that has always been harmful and suspect to France, and that has even resisted the authority of our kings, having as its only goal getting ahead of the Bourbons day by day. ... The members of this family ... are more than capable of attempting anything, ... are only too disposed to support [plots], thanks to old intelligence networks they have inside and outside the realm.[24]

If Marie de Bourbon-Montpensier was temporarily held hostage to her stepfather's reputation, Marie de Guise was a hostage to her paternal blood line. She descended from a line of plotters against the state. The only suitor acceptable to the Monarchy would be a man lacking in courage, in charisma, in power. (Similar considerations would prompt Louis XIV to approve the marriage of his first cousin, ISABELLE D'ORLÉANS OF ALENÇON, to LOUIS-JOSEPH DE LORRAINE, DUKE OF GUISE, a youth who was perceived as lacking the strength of character typical to his ancestors. It was thought that the groom would not develop into a "very able man, and that one does not dare, as a good Frenchman, to wish that he were as honest a man as his fathers—so odious is the memory of them to all good Frenchmen!"[25])

In February 1631 the search for a potential husband for sixteen-year-old Marie was halted. Having been identified as a conspirator against Richelieu, Duke Charles of Guise realized that his disgrace was a matter of time. Preferring to leave the realm before a royal order forced him to do so, he went into exile. Or rather, he announced that he wanted to make a pilgrimage to Loreto and to Rome. Accompanied by his householders and by some eighty soldiers wearing the green livery of the House of Guise, the Admiral of the Levant boarded his fine galley and sailed east from Marseilles. "We now see the Duke of Guise outside France, and unable to give any other reason except that he is penitent about the ambitiousness of his forebears."[26] His pilgrimage completed, Charles headed for Florence, where he was received by the Medicis and sheltered according to his rank. Displaying portraits of his comely offspring, Guise prepared his hosts for the arrival of the rest of the family.

Not until March 1634 did Louis XIII inform the Duchess of Guise, her youngest sons, and Mademoiselle Marie that they had three days to pack up their belongings and withdraw to Rheims, where Françoise-Renée was a nun, there to await further orders. In August, the King made his wishes explicit in a letter to the Duchess:

> My Cousin: Diverse reasons cause me to inform you, by this letter, that I desire you to leave during the month of September, to go join your husband. Since I have no doubt that this is the place you most wish to be, it is the place where you can be most comfortably; for there, no one can, with your complicity, do any dealings that are prejudicial to my service. I pray you therefore to leave without fail during the said month of September, with your entire family, to make this voyage. *Louis*[27]

The King eventually granted the Duchess's request that Françoise-Renée be allowed to remain in her convent. By November the Guises had reached Marseilles, where two royal galleys waited to carry them to Livorno:

> The Duchess of Guise arrived in [Genoa] contrary to her intentions, the storm having forced her to turn around and go back more than twenty miles. She, the Prince of Joinville, the Duke of Joyeuse, the two little knights of Malta, and Mademoiselle de Guise, with their householders, are on two galleys from Florence, paid for by the officers of the Grand Duke, who came to meet them at Cannes, and who did not want to leave their galleys, no matter how bad the weather was.[28]

They took with them "the best and the most precious furnishings" of the family.[29]

Marie was not yet twenty when she set foot on Italian soil. Once they had reached Florence, the Guises and their entourage—"fifty-six mouths" in all—settled first in the Settimana Palace near the Pitti, and then in the Palazzo Vecchio.[30] Tallemant des Réaux encountered Marie there in 1638. "One day, on the *Corso*," he recalled, "the Dowager Grand Duchess and Mademoiselle de Guise passed by, and they were splitting their sides with laughter" at the sight of the outrageous garb of one of the gentlemen to the future Cardinal de Retz.[31] Long after her return to France, Marie continued to correspond with Grand Duchess Vittoria della Rovere, sending and receiving package after package, letter after letter.[32]

Two Florentine sources[33] from the 1630s and 1640s make it possible to sketch Mademoiselle Marie's activities in Florence. Having boarded the Medici galleys at Livorno, the Duchess, Marie, and the two youngest princes reached Porto Venere in mid-February 1635. Riding in three coaches sent by the Grand Duke, they made a triumphal entry into Pisa and were shown the principal churches. Since it was the Mardi Gras season, they remained there for several days, attended a play in the local dialect, then watched the *pallio* in front of the ducal palace. By late February they had joined Duke Charles and his older sons in Florence.

The Medicis took the entire family under its wing. The Guises were present at most of the receptions honoring illustrious visitors to the Medici court: cardinals, ambassadors, princes, and the French envoy who brought news of the birth of the future Louis XIV. One of these visitors, Claude Malier du Houssay, ambassador to Venice, sought out the Guises at the Palazzo Vecchio in December 1637. (Twenty-five years later his daughter, ÉLISABETH-MARIE MALIER, would sign ÉLISABETH CHARPENTIER's wedding contract.) The Guises were also included in Medici family outings, such as the trip to Prato to venerate the Virgin's holy belt and enjoy the hospitality of the "principal ladies of the region," who had prepared a buffet of jams and candied fruits decorated with lovely silk flowers.

As the goddaughter of a Medici, young and attractive Mademoiselle de Guise was given special treatment. She would sit at the Grand Duke's side to watch the Saint John's Day parade in the square before the Palazzo Vecchio. With the ducal family she and her mother attended polychoral masses at San Lorenzo or at the Cathedral, during Holy Week, on Easter Sunday, or at Pentecost. Moving through the private gallery that connected the Palazzo Vecchio to the Palazzo Pitti, Marie and her family could attend services in the ducal chapel, where the Medici musicians often performed.

Although Girolamo Frescobaldi left the court six months before Mademoiselle de Guise's arrival in Florence, other fine musicians in ordinary performed there between 1635 and 1643. One was Dominico Sarti, a soprano castrato who sang in oratorios and performed at the Church of SS. Annunziata on November 10, 1635. Giovanni Battista Gagliano, the Medici chapel master, wrote the music for a religious play, the *Martirio di S. Agata*, performed during Mardi Gras of 1641. In short, unless Marie excused herself that day, she knew full well what an "*oratorio*" was; and her familiarity with that devotional genre doubtlessly helps explain why Marc-Antoine Charpentier wrote his first oratorio, *Judith sive Bethulia*, in 1675. During her stay in Florence another Medici musician, a theorbo player named Angolo di Silvestro Conti, composed music for oratorios performed for the Compagnia dell'archangelo Raffaelo, a lay confraternity: *Il martiro di S. Bonifatio*, with words by Aglae, in May 1639, and *Il martiro de' Santi Giustina e Ciprino*, to a text by Carlini, in February 1640.[34]

The Guises are also mentioned as being among the nobles who assembled in the Cathedral to witness Grand Duchess Vittoria's coronation. Marie presumably had also attended the festivities after Vittoria's wedding to Grand Duke Ferdinand II de' Medicis, which included *Le Nozze degli dei*, a "fable" by Coppola set to music by five of the best composers of the city. It was performed in the courtyard of the Pitti Palace, with one of the Medici princes playing a leading role. The famous woman singer, Settimia de Giulio Caccini, had come to Florence to perform in this *favola*. Nor is it likely that Marie missed *Armida e l'Amor Pudico*, a *festa a cavallo* with floats and other "machines" held in the Boboli gardens as part of these wedding festivities. On the other hand, it has not been determined whether she attended the *tragicommedie* or *favole pastorale* performed between 1638 and 1641 at non-Medici events such as Antonio Salviati's marriage, or performances organized by the Accademia degli Ardenti il Rinovato. She and her mother were in mourning for Duke Charles in 1642, so they may have missed the Mardi Gras performance of *Li Buffoni*, a *comedia ridicola* written by a Roman woman, Margherita Costa.[35]

Eight years in Florence brought considerable sorrow. March 1637 saw the death of nineteen-year-old Joyeuse, whose body was carried to the Church of San Lorenzo by the nobles of the Medici court and interred in the ducal chapel. The sad procession was repeated in November 1639, when another son, handsome and witty Joinville, died of fever at twenty-seven. He was considered by many to be "the most accomplished prince of his day," a "prince offering great hope."[36] Then, in September 1640,

Duke Charles died near Siena, on the way to the spa of Radicofani: "While taking the said waters a fever came upon him and carried him off so promptly that the Duchess of Guise, his wife, arrived a mere four hours before his death."[37] His body was placed in a lead casket and carried back to Florence by monks. There, in a torch-lit procession, it passed through the crowd-lined streets leading to San Lorenzo, and the Medici chapel where his two dead sons awaited him. Thus ended the life of a man who had

> suffered for nine years a great deal of torment and persecution from ill fortune: exiled from France, having lost his government, his property ruined, [and himself devoured] by the loss of his two children ... and by the bad conduct of the third [Henri], who did not live according to the vows he had professed.[38]

Henri de Lorraine, the couple's second son, had become Archbishop of Rheims at an early age. "Pushed into the Church in his youth, at six or seven years of age, in order to help pay for the expenditures [of the House of Guise], he was neither suited to it nor called by God."[39] The handsome young Archbishop had several notorious liaisons, among them his clandestine marriage in June 1636 to Anne de Gonzague, who loudly proclaimed that she was "the wife of Monsieur de Guise." He not only neglected to inform his exiled parents of the wedding, he kept his sovereign in the dark, in order to safeguard his ecclesiastical benefices until one of his brothers could replace him, and until his parents could give him "some of the property of the House, in proportion to what he would need in order to maintain himself with all the dignity of a married prince."[40] When Richelieu forced Henri to give up his ecclesiastical income, the prince made his way to the Spanish Netherlands and began plotting against the Cardinal, and against France. There he became enamored of Countess de Bossut, a beautiful widow whom he promptly "married"—for the prince "made love as they do in novels."[41] "He squandered fifty thousand crowns during his exile [in the Low Lands], and then he wearied of her."[42]

On September 6, 1641, Henri, now Duke of Guise, was declared guilty of lese majesty and sentenced to decapitation in effigy. All his possessions were confiscated, and Louis XIII issued an order to "erase the coat of arms of the said Duke of Guise everywhere on the château [of Guise], churches, and elsewhere where they are to be found."[43] It also appears that the Crown ordered the façade of the Hôtel de Guise in Paris daubed with the humiliating yellow paint that signified treason. Henriette-Catherine de Joyeuse begged Louis XIII for permission to return to France, to save her remaining children's inheritances from certain disaster.[44] Taking pity, he gave her the property that belonged to her profligate son; but Duke Henri was permitted to keep the Hôtel de Guise, with all the courtyards, buildings, and gardens.[45] Louis XIII made this generous gesture in view of the "very moving loss" the Duchess had just experienced in the death of her husband, and in view of her distress over the potential "total ruin of her House," at a time when she had "two other sons ... whom she is raising to be our affectionate servants."[46]

During their exile, the Guises had borrowed money with the help of a small group of Parisians who had long been faithful to the House of Guise. At one point they borrowed from Chancellor Pierre Séguier's mother, and at another from Séraphim Le Ragois, the Duchess's intendant.[47] (During these same years, Marc-Antoine Charpentier's cousin, CHARLES SEVIN, was benefitting from Pierre Séguier's protection; and a generation later, Marc-Antoine's brother-in-law would be protected by ÉLISABETH-MARIE MALIER, whose son had married Le Ragois' niece.)

Charles de Lorraine's body was returned to France in July 1641, his widow having implored Cardinal Richelieu to allow the "bodies of the persons I have loved the most to be brought to France," and having begged him to protect her and her surviving children.[48]

As they awaited permission to return to France, neither their mounting debts nor their mourning prevented the Guises from making the obligatory pilgrimage to Rome and Loreto. On May 4, 1642, "the Duchess of Guise and two of her children left for Rome and the *Santa Casa* of Loreto, for devotional reasons" and did not return until June 10. The visit to Loreto left an indelible mark on Mademoiselle de Guise. It probably was after her return to France that she commissioned a miniature house modeled on the *Santa Casa* and peopled it with figures representing Jesus, Mary, Joseph and the Holy Spirit. The structure was made of exotic woods, precious metals, and gemstones. From the two Litanies of Loreto"[A] that Charpentier set to music for the Guise Music during the 1680s, it is evident that the princess was active in a confraternity of the Glorious Virgin Mary.

Mademoiselle de Guise's memories of her pilgrimage to Loreto must have resembled those of other seventeenth-century travelers. Having spied the dome from afar, the pilgrim made his way into a town that proved to be nothing but "a little place where there are scarcely more than two main streets where one sees nothing but shops selling only rosaries and medals."[49] After purchasing a few of these souvenirs, the typical pilgrim headed for the holy place:

[A] Cahier 33, H. 82; cahiers 41–42, H. 83.

I felt a singular pleasure at seeing an infinite number of pilgrims arrive. ... They are to be seen marching like squadrons, singing God's praises. No sooner do they arrive at the door of the church than they drag themselves on their knees to the *Santa Casa* and go all the way around it, uttering great sighs. I saw some who were singing the Litanies of the Virgin aloud. ... I was in the great nave [of the church] where the first vespers of the Feast [of the Birth of the Virgin, September 7] were being said. I saw the Bishop officiate with all the canons and the Jesuits. There were four choirs of music, and at the end of vespers they sang the Litanies of the Holy Virgin, which takes place every Saturday.[50]

The Duchess of Guise and her children had to bide their time for a year, while royal ministers tried to convince Louis XIII and Richelieu that these particular Guises posed no threat to the Monarchy and that, to the contrary, these fine young people would surely serve the Crown. Each tiny step forward in the negotiations tended to be countered by a misdeed by Duke Henri. For example, in April 1641 the King informed the Duchess that "I was upset that the conduct of your oldest son prevented me from showing you the marks of my good will. ... [His conduct] continues to be so bad that I cannot, and ought not, change my feelings in order to do what you desire." In their accompanying notes, the royal ministers told her that it was the "disorder into which the Archbishop of Rheims has thrown himself," it was the "bad conduct of your son," it was the "trouble in which Monsieur your son is involved" that were paralyzing their efforts and would continue to do so until "a felicitous wave of that tempest casts up Monsieur your son in a safe haven, as all your servants desire."[51] Everything seemed lost: "Monsieur de Guise's bad conduct has, in a single moment, ruined the fruit of more than a day's carefulness. I now have to begin all over again," her contact lamented.

Louis XIII finally relented, and in April 1643 two galleys loaned by the Grand Duke of Tuscany brought the Guises and their householders to Cannes.[52] Their arrival in Paris coincided with a declaration of amnesty for Duke Henri. Moving into the Hôtel de Guise with his mother and sister, the Duke ordered the family's magnificent furnishings removed from the storerooms where they had been gathering dust for almost fifteen years.

The Duchess began searching for a potential marriage partner for Mademoiselle Marie, who had just celebrated her thirtieth birthday.

Continued in this panel: MADEMOISELLE MARIE THE REGENT

II

She will be the sole executrix

MADEMOISELLE MARIE THE REGENT

Marie de Lorraine of Guise,
guardian of Louis-Joseph de Lorraine, Duke of Guise

Marie de Lorraine of Guise, thirty-two, appeared in all her glory at the festivities that Mazarin offered the court in 1647, the pièce de résistance of which was Luigi Rossi and Francesco Buti's *Orfeo*. "[She] was no longer young, ... her beauty, her fine looks, and her modesty, with pearls and black, caused her to be admired by everyone who saw her."[1] The granddaughter of the scar-faced Duke of the late sixteenth century attracted attention that day by dressing in black and white, as her grandparents had. The pearls were her mother's famous ones, treasured since her youth and worth more than thirty-five thousand livres.[2]

Mademoiselle Marie's oldest brother was also attracting attention during the late 1640s, but for quite different reasons. From his earliest years, Henri had demonstrated a disturbing trait. The handsome, swashbuckling prince could not say *no* to pleasure, could not tolerate a disciplined way of life. From the mid-1640s until his death in 1665, he spent huge sums not only on entertainments but also on preparations for two unsuccessful attempts to conquer the Kingdom of Naples, in the hope of one day wearing a crown.[3]

This ill-conceived venture threatened the future of the entire House of Guise, which was on the verge of bankruptcy. His mother tried to make him understand the crisis at home:

> I assure you that it is very difficult to find money here, and I had to pawn all my possessions and yours, and borrow money from private individuals, and pawn gems, in order to find the money I am sending you. ... I only regret that I cannot do more.[4]

The situation was perhaps worse than she imagined, for the Duke was covertly selling the treasures of the Hôtel de Guise bit by bit, in part to finance his expedition, in part to furnish a house for his latest amourette, Suzanne de Pons, and in part to pay the legal costs of having his marriage to Madame de Bossut annulled.

Upon learning that his mother and sister had prepared an apartment for Bossut at the Hôtel de Guise, the Duke turned violent. Furious at his mother's refusal to turn control of the family's fortune over to him,[5] he repeatedly expelled her and his sister, who would run crying to GASTON D'ORLÉANS and MADAME D'ORLÉANS. On one occasion the Duchess's quick thinking kept Henri from snatching away the pearls that had become Mademoiselle de Guise's signature.

Between 1643 and 1653, rumors circulated about possible marriages for Mademoiselle Marie de Guise, one of the wealthiest and most prestigious catches in the realm. For example, in 1645, she was proposed as a wife for the King of Poland. Negotiations broke down, however, partly because the Monarchy was dubious about the power that would accrue to the suspect House of Guise, and partly because the princess showed no enthusiasm for the match.[6] The reason for her coolness could scarcely be made public: she had given her heart to Claude de Bourdeille, Count of Montrésor.[7]

One of GASTON D'ORLÉANS' most devoted householders, Montrésor had "followed this great prince in all the fluctuations of his rather agitated fortune,"[8] and had been privy to all of Gaston's plots.[9] In March 1646 Montrésor was arrested for having once again participated in "intrigues." In his memoirs he evoked his fourteen months in the royal fortress of Vincennes, during which the Guises negotiated on his behalf; and he thanked Mademoiselle de Guise, in an open letter so personal that he dared not use her name:

> I know how much you tried to soften [my misfortunes] by the
> attentions that a true and sincere affection can produce. ... If I had
> been more fortunate, I would have been of service to you, instead of
> causing you pain. ... Whatever might happen as time goes by, I am
> sure that you will always have the same feelings of friendship for me,
> and that the exquisite probity that marks all your actions will not be
> altered by the false maxims of a corrupted century that, to its shame,
> prefers self-interest to honor. ... You have all the necessary qualities
> for being judged worthy of all the advantages a person of your birth
> can legitimately acquire. Take advantage of them, I beg you. You
> can do so by taking the same paths you have been following, since
> that depends absolutely on you. And believe that, by observing that
> generous perseverance that conforms to your natural inclinations,

you can be firmly assured that you have, in me, until the last
moment of my life, the most faithful and the most passionate servant
that you could chose, to honor your good graces.[10]

This disguised love letter suggests the depth of the couple's affection. In
veiled terms, Montrésor was thanking her for her "friendship," a term
that designated what today is frequently called "love"; for not breaking
off their affair; and for "persevering" along a path that only her honor
and virtue could make acceptable to the "world," that is, to the great
nobles of the royal court.

Although Montrésor came from a very old and respected noble
family and was the Duchess of Guise's cousin, he was Mademoiselle de
Guise's social inferior. However, by means of a so-called "marriage of
conscience," a morganatic marriage, persons of unequal social rank could
have their union blessed, while pretending to be platonic friends. This
was the only option available to a princess of Marie de Guise's rank, for
a public marriage meant renouncing her title and prerogatives as a
foreign princess, and becoming a mere French countess. Louis XIV and
Madame de Maintenon would opt for a morganatic marriage in the
1680s, and earlier in the century Princess Marie's paternal aunt had made
a similar choice, discreetly concealing her union with Bassompierre.

Three letters in Marie's hand, addressed to Montrésor and clearly
written during a forced separation, suggest that they were seeking royal
approval for just such a marriage in 1651. (She kept these letters all her
life, and GAIGNIÈRES thought them significant enough to preserve them
along with other Guise papers he spirited away at the time of her death
and added to his collection.) In the first letter she evoked her "solitude,"
but she clearly was not alone. Rather, she was surrounded by domestics
or religious who were preventing her from seeing Montrésor. The second
letter, which appears to date from December 1651, contains what can be
read as an allusion to GASTON D'ORLÉANS' unauthorized marriage to
Marguerite de Lorraine. Here Mademoiselle de Guise's principal concern
was to have a document approved by the royal council and sealed by the
chancellery. In the third, very emotional letter, which she signed "your
most desolate one," she expressed her fears that Montrésor would forget
her. When she wrote this letter, she had been a virtual prisoner for over
a year. She clearly was not in Paris, for she attributed her health
problems to the change of air.[11]

This lengthy separation probably was necessitated by a pregnancy,
for extremely reliable sources refer to several children born to the couple.
There was a son who was raised in Holland or possibly in the Spanish
Netherlands where, perhaps coincidentally, Montrésor had spent a good

part of 1644 and early 1645. Two daughters were also mentioned. One of them, Marie Naudot (or Nodot), "Sister of the Holy Martyrs," was a nun at the Abbey of MONTMARTRE.[12]

In the early 1650s, when Marie de Guise was in her late thirties, newsletters and correspondence virtually ceased referring to her. It was at this time that she purchased the feudal site of Montrésor from her secret husband, thanks to a cash "gift" from her mother.[13] The sale technically deprived Montrésor of his estates and his title; but it permitted Mademoiselle de Guise to use the title "Countess of Montrésor" legally, and to pass that title to one of their children should the day ever come when they could be publicly recognized. She only employed this title for notarial acts involving the property. Publicly she was known first as "Dame of Marchais and Liesse," then as "Princess of Joinville," and finally, after 1675, as "Duchess of Guise and Joyeuse, and Princess of Joinville."

Montrésor likewise withdrew from court. After 1653 he "lived in retirement and no longer got mixed up in any affairs."[14] The former plotter was described as having "chosen another sort of profession, having received benefices in the Church [the abbey of Lannoy] from the royal court, which deemed him, as it still does, a person of rare merit."[15]

Duke Henri refused to be polite to Montrésor. On one occasion he said he would shave his sister's head if she continued to see him, thereby threatening her with the humiliation meted out to prostitutes.[16] In 1656 yet another fuss broke out between the Duchess and her son, over Montrésor:

> One evening [the Duke] was in Madame de Guise's chamber and
> begged her to refuse to allow the Count of Montrésor to enter her
> lodging; and that if he set foot there, he would have him thrown out
> the window; that he could no longer tolerate all the tales being told
> about him and Mademoiselle de Guise; and on that subject he said
> some very unpleasant things to Madame and Mademoiselle de
> Guise, which forced them to leave the Hôtel de Guise.[17]

Mother and daughter found a new lodging that they called the "Hôtel de Joyeuse." It was located a few houses from the rear gate of the Hôtel de Guise. Montrésor lived only a short distance away.[18]

The hangings of the Duchess's room proclaimed to all visitors that she mourned for her husband and sons. Her bed was hung with black velvet curtains trimmed with violet-colored fringe. Her favorite painting of the Virgin was protected by a curtain of red, black and gold taffeta, and the window curtains and a screen were of red serge. In the antechamber where she received her guests, chairs and benches covered in black leather surrounded a canopy of black velvet trimmed with purple fringe beneath which she sat enthroned when she officially received visitors such as ambassadors. Marie de Guise's apartment adjoined her mother's. Like the Duchess, this sovereign princess sat under a black and violet canopy to receive guests. The somber colors of this ceremonial object contrasted with the eighteen stools upholstered in red velvet and trimmed with gold fringe that lined the walls of the room.

The mother's and the daughter's piety can be judged from the devotional objects that surrounded them. In an alcove hung with satin from Burgos they could meditate before three paintings: a "Virgin holding the Infant Jesus, with Saint Jean," a portrait of Saint Philip Neri, and the depiction of a "nun holding a cross." These paintings provide important evidence about Marie de Lorraine of Guise's private worship prior to 1670. First of all, she was already more than routinely devoted to the Virgin and the INFANT JESUS.

Second, although one can only conjecture that the nun was a Capucine, it is likely. The Duchess almost certainly belonged to the Congregation of the Third Order of Saint Francis, "composed of one hundred and twenty ladies of mark." It met at the Capucine convent, under the direction of the Capuchin monks of the nearby Franciscan convent that her father, Ange de Joyeuse, had founded.[19] Women who had taken the vows of the Third Order were permitted to be buried in the habit of a Capucine nun—as the Duchess would in fact be buried in 1656, and as her daughter would request to be interred.

Third, both women had been attracted to Phillip Neri's oratory movement, presumably during their stay in Florence. This means that they gathered regularly in their "oratory" with a small group of friends, to carry out "spiritual exercises" such as singing lauds or reciting litanies. In Italy the word *oratorio* was inseparable from Neri and his Oratory. Indeed, both words were derived from the same Latin word for *prayer*.

> Having the most able master compose music for recitatives and dialogues on the principal subjects of the Holy Scriptures, [Neri] had the finest voices of Rome sing these recitatives in his church. ... This pious exercise still goes on [in 1681], and the same thing is done in the congregations [confraternities] where the nobility assembles, and on certain feast days in diverse churches.[20]

Thus the Guise women's portrait of Neri can be seen as the harbinger of the oratorios that Marc-Antoine Charpentier would begin composing two decades later.

From this alcove—where they could reflect upon the content of the "little devotional books" that made up the bulk of their library, or could finger one of their costly rosaries—the two women could move to their private chapel hung in red. Kneeling on one of the black velvet cushions, they could contemplate, above the "table serving as an altar," a large painting of the Virgin, Joseph, and "Saint John the Baptist with a lamb, at the feet of Little Jesus."[21]

Their contemporaries talk about the two Guise women as if they were a single entity. For example, MADEMOISELLE DE MONTPENSIER's anecdotes about her aunt and her grandmother portray Marie de Guise as continually at her mother's side, serving as her spokeswoman. There was a reason for their complicity: the daughter was being trained to be the Regent for the House of Guise. The Duchess was in her seventies, and the great House was threatened not only with bankruptcy but with extinction. The death in 1653 of her youngest and most gifted son, the Chevalier of Guise, was especially painful for the Duchess; and then, in 1654, another son, the Duke of Joyeuse, had died at her home from septicemia provoked by a war wound. Of the five Guise sons, only spendthrift Duke Henri remained, and he was childless. There was, however, one grandchild, Joyeuse's beautiful four-year-old son, LOUIS-JOSEPH DE LORRAINE, the last hope of the House of Guise. The child's mother was insane, so the Duchess took him into her house and managed to get herself appointed guardian, with Séraphim Le Ragois supervising the financial aspects of the guardianship. (Le Ragois was the uncle of Madame Louis de Bailleul, whose mother-in-law and daughter would sign ÉLISABETH CHARPENTIER's wedding contract in 1660.)

As early as the mid-1640s, the Duchess had begun taking steps to protect her other children from Duke Henri. For example, she convinced Henri to relinquish the principality of Joinville in return for the more than 2,500,000 livres she had loaned him and that he had not repaid; and she had retained the right to transfer this property to another one of her children.[22] By another group of notarial acts she ceded to Mademoiselle de Guise "half the domains of Caen, Bayeux, and Falaise in Normandy." (Some of the income from these domains was being claimed by "Sieur Louis Cressé, merchant upholsterer of Paris," MOLIÈRE's maternal uncle, in payment of Duke Henri's outstanding debts.)[23] Above all, over the years the Duchess had put her trust in Montrésor, her cousin and secret son-in-law.

In February 1656 the Duchess of Guise died. Her funeral would be an example for Mademoiselle de Guise, who wanted it repeated at her own burial:

> Henriette-Catherine de Joyeuse, Duchess of Guise, aged seventy, died here in her residence from a chest infection, after having

received all the sacraments with unusual piety and perfect resignation. Her body was dressed in the habit of a Capucine nun, and in this state it was exposed the next day, on a bier, [and the following day] was borne on a hearse covered with a pall of black velvet, and several torches carried by her domestics, to the Church of the Capucines on the rue Saint-Honoré, where a service was held the next day, ... after which eight Capuchin monks carried her body to the crypt, where she was buried without pomp or ceremony, which she had specifically forbidden.[24]

A somewhat more irreverent eulogy told how "Madame de Guise, the good woman, ... died here ... overwhelmed with troubles, illness, and age. To her son, the Duke of Guise, she left everything she had been unable to take from him, and to Mademoiselle de Guise, her daughter, she left everything she could give her."[25] MADEMOISELLE DE MONTPENSIER wrote a lively description of the reading of her grandmother's testament, which named Marie de Lorraine of Guise as one of the three executors:

> The morning after Madame de Guise's death, Mademoiselle [Marie], her daughter, summoned all the relatives she had in Paris, to be present at the opening of the will and to select a guardian for little Joyeuse. ... A Capuchin father brought [the will], on behalf of the Mother Superior of the Capucines, to whom [the late Duchess] had given it. The will was read. ... It was in her hand, and at the end [there was] an evaluation of her property, to demonstrate the justice and equity with which she had distributed it to her children.[26]

The deceased had made many pious bequests, some 90,900 livres in all; but "none of her noble lineage was given an advantageous share." To protect the property owned by the House of Guise from Henri, she willed this black sheep an income worth some 60,000 livres and begged him to be content with this sum, for she had paid his debts in excess of 3,000,000 livres. To little LOUIS-JOSEPH DE LORRAINE, Duke of Joyeuse, she gave the lands of Ancerville and Éclaron, plus the charge of grand chamberlain that had belonged to his father.[27] To MADEMOISELLE DE MONTPENSIER, her granddaughter, she willed only the amount due her by law, that is, an annual income of 20,000 livres a year, plus the diamond worth 200,000 livres that had been given to Marie de Bourbon-Montpensier when she wed GASTON D'ORLÉANS—"for which she begs her to be content." Mademoiselle de Guise received the rest:

> And of all the other great riches she could call her own, both in furniture and in inheritances, her daughter, the very wise princess, ... whom she loved so tenderly for the virtues she possesses, is without difficulty the universal heir.[28]

Without difficulty? Scarcely. This testament would cause Mademoiselle Marie enormous problems, for MONTPENSIER contested it and would drag her aunt through the courts for the next twenty-five years.

Having prepared Marie for this role during the decade when they were more or less inseparable, the Duchess used her testament to make her daughter the virtual Regent for the House of Guise. The mother trusted that the daughter would fight valiantly and unremittingly to obtain even the smallest financial or political advantage for the family's sole hope, LOUIS-JOSEPH DE LORRAINE. The Duchess did not, of course, use the word *régente*: instead, she named Marie as her universal heir and legatee, "entrusted with carrying out her testament."[29] Mademoiselle de Guise, who had celebrated her fortieth birthday only six months earlier, shouldered a heavy burden. She would supervise her family's vast possessions and protect them, nay, increase them whenever possible, so that Louis-Joseph could one day rise above the other great nobles of the realm. She would spend many hours consulting her advisors on financial matters. But her focus would be the child who would one day reign at the Hôtel de Guise, as his ancestors had before him. She made sure that she would not have to face these challenges alone, for a week later Montrésor was appointed to be the little boy's financial guardian.[30]

Meanwhile, the Parlement was working out a stratagem by which Marie the Regent could carry out her responsibilities unimpeded by the obstacles being created by Duke Henri, which promised to be even more difficult to overcome than those being raised by MONTPENSIER. That is to say, the two men who had been named in the late Duchess's testament, to be co-executors with Mademoiselle de Guise, were preparing a coup that would give her sole control over the family finances. (One of them, let us recall, was Séraphim Le Ragois, whose close relative would sign ÉLISABETH CHARPENTIER's wedding contract only six years later.) In collusion with Guise friends in the Parlement, the duo now asked to be relieved of their obligations. Waiting until Duke Henri was distracted by more pressing matters, the Parlement issued a decree that was extremely favorable to Marie de Guise:

> While Monsieur de Guise was totally involved with the Queen [Christina] of Sweden [who was on her way to Paris], the Great Chamber of this parlement rendered a rather important decree against him. ... In the will of his mother, Madame de Guise, he had opposed the conditions in favor of Mademoiselle de Guise, his sister, whom [the deceased] had advantaged to his detriment, owing either to special affection or to hidden resentment over the scorn and bad treatment she had received from her son. It was declared (given the fact that Messieurs Poucet, master of requests, and Le Ragois, the

former intendant of the said lady's household, have renounced their nomination as executors of her last wishes, along with the said *demoiselle*, her daughter) that [Mademoiselle de Guise] will be the sole executrix, and as such will be given possession of all the property of the said estate, for a year and a day.[31]

Neither her mourning nor her responsibilities as executrix prevented Mademoiselle de Guise from assuming the social obligations expected of a princess regent. Scarcely five months after her mother's death, she briefly set aside her mourning to greet Queen Christina of Sweden. Narratives of the receptions honoring the Sacred Royal Majesty do not mention Marie de Lorraine of Guise; but this silence does not prove that she preferred mourning to satisfying her curiosity, and to speaking face to face with the extraordinary personage about whom court and capital were talking. As royal chamberlain, Duke Henri had left Paris in July 1656 to meet the Queen at Lyons. Among the events was a fête held at Essonnes.[32] Was Mademoiselle de Guise among the "numerous ladies who went to see the Queen"? One generally very reliable source places her there.[33]

A few days later, Christina made her solemn entry into Paris, accompanied by the Duke of Guise:

[Duke Henri's] wit and courage, along with so many other brilliant qualities, had made him worthy of this honor. ... He thus attracted attention, a bit behind the Princess [Christina], ... [being] dressed and mounted on that occasion with the splendor that is usual in all his showy actions and that, in addition to his personal equipment, was also to be noted in his stable composed of sixty costly rust-colored horses, marvelously well decked-out and harnessed, along with all his household officers.[34]

Although Mademoiselle de Guise did not ride in the coach that bore Christina into Paris, she probably was among the noblewomen who awaited the Queen at her lodgings. At any rate, "princesses" are mentioned, and after the royal family and the Condés, Marie de Guise was the leading princess in the realm:

The princesses, duchesses, and other ladies there were so advantageously dressed that they seemed to be so many divinities who had descended into such a lovely place. ... They formed a charming circle in the courtyard, beside the door.[35]

During her brief stay in Paris, Christina "went to see all the fine houses," one of the finest being the Hôtel de Guise, where Duke Henri received her. During this visit, a comedy by poet Gabriel Gilbert—whom Christina had recently appointed, or soon would appoint to be her resident in

France—was "read at the home of the Duke of Guise, in the presence of the Queen, ... who enjoyed it a great deal."[36] (The play almost certainly was Les Amours de Diane et d'Endimion,[37] for which Marc-Antoine Charpentier would write incidental music[A] in 1681.) Since it is difficult to imagine the Guises not feigning unity before Christina, Marie de Guise presumably was present at this reading.

Then again, she may have made a point of being conspicuously absent, the better to demonstrate her low opinion of Christina. The Queen's hunger for honors and praise repelled Mademoiselle Marie, who was singled out as a ringleader of an anti-Christina claque:

> Neither Madame de Chevreuse, nor Mademoiselle de Guise, nor any of the other princesses who were in this city wanted to see her, and they accused her of being too impolite, for a queen who had only a title but no court and no money, and who, under the pretext of a vain and useless knowledge of languages and letters, treated everyone with disdain and scorn."[38]

Whatever her personal feelings about Christina, prior to and during Marc-Antoine Charpentier's stay in Rome a decade later, Mademoiselle de Guise was in a position to correspond with the Queen, via Gilbert in Paris and Christina's secretary in Rome, JACQUES II DALIBERT.

In January 1657, shortly after Christina's visit to the French court, Abbé Buti and Jean-Baptiste Lully's Amor malato bcame the center of courtly attention. With French musicians and poets being shoved into the background by these Italians, Duke Henri of Guise—always ready to take a position diametrically opposed to that of the court—made a gesture in support of French culture.[39] He offered the court a sumptuous French-style ballet entitled Les Plaisirs troublés, performed in the Louvre on February 11, 1657, and rumored to have cost forty thousand livres.[40] On successive days Guise's ballet was presented at three venues: Chancellor Pierre Séguier's residence, the home of the First President of the Parlement, and finally the Hôtel de Guise. The music for this "rather dazzling ballet, ... of exquisite invention and danced by Monsieur de Guise," had been composed by Louis de Mollier, and the choreography was by Pierre de Beauchamps. The Duke made sure that every detail of the staging would awe the audience: "Most of the clothes were ... embroidered with diamonds and sequins, even the shoulder-knots."[41] The Grand Duke of Tuscany's agent, who attended the performance, was considerably less enthusiastic:

[A] Cahier XXXI, H. 502.

In one respect it is more costly and beautiful than the King's [ballet], but in many other ways it is inferior to it. The Duke was pushed by certain envious people who cannot bear having the King use Italians to direct his ballet, and who hope that if the King sees a ballet done by them, he will call upon their talents. But the Duke's financial officers do not want to give him the money he needs to run his household, ever since the huge expenditures for the ballet, where sums destined for more necessary things were employed, which is a subject of gossip and laughter at court.[42]

If Duke Henri's household managers were so daring as to grab his purse strings, it was because their master "was spending more than ten thousand crowns, although his finances are not so good that he can make useless outlays."[43]

Les Plaisirs troublés was Henri's last ballet. He had to be content with his functions as grand chamberlain, which involved organizing young Louis XIV's carousels. These responsibilities suited Guise perfectly, for "even when having fun, he resembled the knights errant. He loved tournaments and combats at the barrier, as we see them depicted in *Amadis* and in *The Wars of Grenada*."[44] Henri adored horses. The stables of the Hôtel de Guise sheltered thirty-nine splendid ones. When his contemporaries thought of the Duke of Guise, what inevitably came to mind were his twelve Moors, his fine horses, his consummate horseman-ship, and his luxurious lifestyle.[45]

The Duke was usually in residence at the Hôtel de Guise, surrounded by his sixty-two domestic servants.[46] Among the protégés benefitting from lodgings were Tristan L'Hermite, Philippe Quinault, and Pierre Corneille (and perhaps Pierre's brother, THOMAS CORNEILLE, as well). Henri's patronage of the arts was not restricted to things literary and musical. He commissioned artworks, including a window for the Church of the MERCY[47]; and it was he who paid the costs of his younger sister's lavish benediction service as ABBESS OF MONTMARTRE in 1657, during which the Royal Music performed motets composed by Jean Veillot, the music master for the abbey.

Although sisters and brother made public shows of fraternal love, Marie kept her distance from Henri, who could not, or would not refrain from making insulting remarks about Montrésor. Three months after their mother's death, Guise made a point of "going to see his sister every evening"; and he was consternated to encounter Montrésor each time. One evening, he became enraged at finding her "supping privately with Monsieur de Montrésor." As if that were not bad enough, Montrésor had the audacity to behave as if he were the head of the household and show the Duke to his coach! Addressing Montrésor as his "cousin"—which

Bourdeille indeed was—Guise stated that although nothing prevented Montrésor from paying other visitors this honor, "as for me, no one has the right to do me the honors in my sister's lodgings."[48] With her brother "so extremely unleashed against Monsieur de Montrésor," Mademoiselle de Guise decided to move as far as she could from the Hôtel de Guise.

In May 1657 she bought the position of captain of the "Volière," the royal aviary in the Tuileries, and began to renovate the captain's official residence. When she and little Joyeuse moved into the hôtel in December 1658, Montrésor came with them.[49] Using their joint guardianship of LOUIS-JOSEPH DE LORRAINE as camouflage, they were at last living as husband and wife. For five years, the couple must at times have imagined they were supervising their own son's education. Mademoiselle de Guise smothered her nephew with frustrated maternal love. Keeping close watch over his upbringing, she became obsessed about protecting him from the craving for worldly glory that had corrupted Duke Henri. At the same time she would do almost anything to further Joyeuse's advancement at court; and by her own example she was determined to teach him that the head of the House of Guise could live in both splendor and piety.

Furthering her nephew's advancement appears to have meant opening his horizons toward Italy—thereby consciously diverging from the culture of young Louis XIV's court, which was turning its back upon the Italian art forms promoted by Cardinal Mazarin and was instead creating a distinctive French style for all the different arts. This preoccupation with Italy may explain why Marie de Guise's correspondence with the Medicis in Florence intensified after her mother's death. Bundles of French clothes were sent off to Florence, and bundles of Italian fabrics were delivered to the Volière, thanks to the solicitude of the Tuscan agents in Paris. These exchanges also included plants and bulbs, portraits, jewelry—and a multitude of boxes and chests whose contents remain a mystery because the packages arrived safely at their destination and did not prompt the frantic epistolary exchange that followed the loss, delay, or damage of a shipment.

The Florentine archives contain abundant allusions to letters to be transmitted to Grand Duchess Vittoria or to Mademoiselle de Guise; but these letters apparently were destroyed, along with the rest of the women's intimate correspondence. Fragments survive, but they reveal little about Marie de Lorraine's musical taste. One can only surmise that Her Highness's request for Italian music in the mid-1680s was not an innovation, but the last of a long series of such requests. The surviving page of a letter she dispatched to Vittoria reveals the affective strings the

French princess could pull in order to obtain the commodities she was coveting:

> I have so much confidence in Your Highness's friendship, and she gives me such great liberty, that I dare to ask her for some fans, the Queen having indicated that she would like some; and as for me, I ask Your Highness for some of the fine perfumes that are made for her, with a little bottle of a certain essence that Count Rabat [a Tuscan agent] used to give to his lady friends. I also very humbly beg Your Highness for a little pot of that good orange blossom pomade. Monsieur the Count Rabat gave some. It is yellow, and with orange flowers. I do not know, Madame, what Your Highness will say about my daring, but she sees the liberty that confidence gives.[50]

The rest of the letter is missing, which suggests that Vittoria passed this particular page to her secretary, rather than copy out the details of her friend's request, and that she kept for herself the more personal pages at the end of the letter.

In the spring of 1663, it was the Grand Duchess's turn to ask a favor: Would Mademoiselle de Guise receive a young chambermaid and see that the girl learned to dress hair and sew the latest French fashions? A bargain was struck. "Caterinangiola" would come to Paris, and Vittoria would host a French girl and place her in a convent school in the environs of Florence.

Caterinangiola promptly became homesick, despite "the undescribable courtesy and caresses shown by Mademoiselle de Guise's entire court."[51] It did not help that she knew no French, that "none of [Mademoiselle de Guises's] servants are skilled in the Tuscan language, and that [Her Highness] herself needs help reading our handwriting."[52] In short, Marie de Guise could communicate orally in Italian, but she found it difficult to decipher the courtly rhetoric and the Florentine script employed by the Medici secretaries. (If the Florentine agents made a point of speaking to her in French during official audiences, it was in order to call her *Altesse* and thereby avoid the Italian cognate *Altezza*, which designated someone more prestigious than a French "highness.")

Louis-Joseph de Lorraine and "all the *demoiselles* of the Princess" did what they could to amuse the newcomer, doubtlessly acquiring some rudiments of Italian as the young Florentine progressed in French. Caterinangiola quickly won Mademoiselle de Guise's heart, and she must have brought cheer to her new mistress, who was mourning Montrésor's death. Her Highness eventually informed the Florentines that she wanted the girl to be her personal chambermaid and hairdresser for three months. After two years of being spoiled by the entire household,

Catarinagiola said farewell in May 1665 and set off for home with a piece of the princess's jewelry as a keepsake.

By her own example, the Regent of the House of Guise was teaching her nephew that a sovereign prince must never yield the precedence due him. To BISHOP ROQUETTE she sent an eloquent letter "concerning duchesses who claim precedence over unmarried princesses." This matter, she asserted, concerns "my person and our House." The issue was especially touchy because, although she had been married, she had been obliged to pretend that she was a maiden princess. Nonetheless, since all Guises received the honors due the House of Lorraine, and since they were of a higher rank than French dukes and peers (whose children did not inherit the honors given to their fathers), she insisted upon exerting her superiority over French duchesses. The duchesses' claims were, she asserted, of recent date. Thus she was sure that Louis XIV "would not want to allow an innovation of this consequence, to the detriment of persons who breathe solely to serve him and to please him in small things as in great ones."[53] For this reason she asked Roquette to speak to the King, "or to notify me if you cannot, so that I can go and do it myself."

This protest about precedence fits into a broader framework, for the different branches of the House of Lorraine were perpetually worrying about their rights and their prerogatives, compared to the other great nobles of the realm. Notorious as the Lorraines were for assuming "titles that were not their due," no one dared "touch the House of Lorraine ... or expose themselves to the cries of Mademoiselle de Guise, so lofty and so notable."[54]

It was, therefore, as a maiden princess of the House of Lorraine that forty-five-year-old Mademoiselle de Guise honored the Abbey of Jouarre, near Meaux, with her presence in May 1660. Surrounded by a variety of Lorraine relatives, Abbess Henriette de Lorraine greeted the Duke of Lorraine.[55] It was, by contrast, as Regent for the House of Guise that Marie of Guise accompanied thirteen-year-old LOUIS-JOSEPH DE LORRAINE to Éclaron and Joinville in October 1663, and went with the court to Fontainebleau in the summer of 1664.

Within a year, Louis-Joseph became Duke of Guise, for his uncle died at fifty in June 1664. "This prince died intestate. The King is buying his stable, on which [the Duke's] creditors have had seals placed. They will sell his silver plate and other furniture to pay his debts."[56]

The customary ceremonial for the lying-in-state of a great noble was observed. After the requisite hours spent praying around the body in the chapel of the Hôtel de Guise, a solemn procession took the corpse to the Church of Saint-Jean-en-Grève:

In the evening he was borne to his parish church of Saint-Jean, in a mourning coach followed by a great number of other coaches in which rode the princes of his House and his household officers, preceded by a quantity of torches of white wax carried by his domestics; and he will remain there in safe custody until he can be taken to Joinville, where his ancestors are buried. He was accompanied by 120 Capuchins, some of whom had attended him in his last illness, these good fathers having done this pious duty to demonstrate their gratitude toward the House of Guise, benefactor of their Order, ... and also for the dear memory they preserve of Father Ange de Joyeuse, the deceased's grandfather, who died in their Order, having worn the habit for twenty-five years. The fine qualities that made [the Duke of Guise] notable have made his loss a public misfortune, and the court and the people showed their great grief to an equal degree.[57]

Mademoiselle de Guise almost certainly helped plan these ceremonies:

The 21st of this month, a very solemn service was held in the Church of Saint-Jean for the Duke of Guise, which the Prince of Joinville [Louis-Joseph de Lorraine], his nephew, attended along with the princes of his House. ... The church was hung in black, with two drapes of velvet garnished with coats of arms; and the body was exposed in the choir on a bier elevated by two steps, beneath a canopy, also made of velvet and garnished with similar crests, the whole lighted by an infinite number of lights. Towards evening, he was taken from this church, to be conducted to Joinville, on a hearse pulled by two horses draped in black velvet, and with the pall, whose corners were carried by gentlemen of his household, mounted on horseback. He was preceded by thirty lesser officers, also mounted, then by one hundred Capuchins and a similar number of footmen, each carrying a white torch. Next marched ten pages, led by their equerry, also on horseback. The First Equerry, bearing the deadman's sword, covered by crepe, marched in front of the hearse, surrounded by several Capuchins and footmen, who also carried torches. The First Gentleman and the Maître d'Hôtel came next, with several other mounted household officers: and twenty mourning coaches filled with the princes of the deadman's House, and a few of his officers, ended the procession, which moved along the rue Saint-Antoine to the Faubourg Saint-Antoine, where the Capuchins left the convoy.[58]

As Fate would have it, the splendor of the requiem mass celebrated for Henri at Saint-Jean-en-Grève on June 21, and the pomp of the procession to Joinville that followed, prefigured the magnificence of LOUIS-JOSEPH DE LORRAINE's own requiem mass, held in the same church in 1671.

Mademoiselle de Guise the Regent rapidly and efficiently set about overseeing the financial decisions regarding her brother's estate, despite his failure to draw up a will, despite the clamors of his creditors, and despite the seemingly endless lawsuit with MADEMOISELLE DE MONTPENSIER that complicated every financial decision.

Henri's "widow," Madame de Bossut, promptly claimed her share of the estate. When her brother had been attempting to marry Mademoiselle de Pons, Marie de Lorraine and her mother had always insisted that Bossut was his legal wife. But now, with Bossut clamoring for money, Mademoiselle de Guise began arguing that the marriage was invalid. The issue of the validity of the union having been taken up by the Roman Rota, Bossut—who made a point of calling herself "Madame de Guise" —set off for Rome in 1665 to present her case. Mademoiselle de Guise remained in Paris, in obedience to the royal decree forbidding her "to appear before the Rota or before any judges outside the realm."[59] In March 1666 the Rota decided in Bossut's favor, and she was received by the Pope and "treated as a duchess."

Giving up any thoughts she may have had about journeying to Rome, Marie the Regent followed the affair closely, and Foreign Minister Lionne kept her informed of the latest news from Rome.[60] In other words, during part of Marc-Antoine Charpentier's stay in Rome, his future protectress consulted with Lionne or his representatives at least once a week. Through them, she learned what was going on in Rome, and especially at the Farnese Palace, seat of the French Embassy, where a young Frenchman named "Carpentier" would soon be doing odd jobs for Ambassador CHAULNES.

Having been assured by the King that the Rota's decision did not apply in France (thereby quashing Bossut's claims to her share of the Guise fortune), and having redeemed some of the property sold by her brother (she could not regain possession of a few especially precious items that had been incorporated into the royal collections), Mademoiselle Marie the Regent could now concentrate on "establishing" her nephew. Her first concern was to improve the setting in which LOUIS-JOSEPH DE LORRAINE, DUKE OF GUISE, would hold court. The Hôtel de Guise must be renovated and embellished.[61] Work began during the summer of 1666 and was completed the following year.

She also set about creating a household for the Duke. Instead of incorporating her late brother's household into her nephew's, she sought new staff, new household officers, new protégés. One of the first items on her list was the appointment of a governor or preceptor[62]—not a schoolteacher, but someone who could take the place of the youth's dead father and insane mother, and guide him on a straight moral path until he was twenty-five, the age of complete legal majority. In the fall of 1666, a provincial gentleman named PHILIPPE GOIBAUT DU BOIS moved into the Volière, having been recommended by Madame de Sablé.[63] It was BISHOP GABRIEL DE ROQUETTE who convinced the Regent to name his protégé and one-time valet, Jean-François Le Brun, to be the young Duke's treasurer[64]; and the Bishop's presence in Mademoiselle de Guise's circle probably explains how his brother, CHRISTOPHLE DE ROQUETTE, came to be selected as intendant for the household. It is not clear who recommended ROGER DE GAIGNIÈRES as the Duke's equerry.

The household was still being assembled in May 1667 when LOUIS-JOSEPH DE LORRAINE married ISABELLE D'ORLÉANS OF ALENÇON, the King's first cousin. There had been no time to prepare the usual festivities, so the guests celebrated afterwards in the QUEEN's apartment. There an incident occurred that reveals just how adamant about precedence and protocol Mademoiselle de Guise and the entire House of Lorraine could be. Proud that a prince of their House had made so prestigious a match, the Lorraines gloried in the bride's right to lord it over them. But then the Princess of Mecklenberg entered the room, called attention to herself by making witty remarks, and sat in a position that was superior to the one being occupied by Mademoiselle de Guise. Mecklenberg was fully aware that Mademoiselle de Guise was, by birth, a "foreign princess naturalized in France," while she was merely a princess by marriage. (Born a Luxembourg, she was the daughter of a French duke and peer.) The princes and princesses of the House of Lorraine immediately set about righting this breech of etiquette. Marie de Guise first attracted attention by rising and feigning a conversation with a Lorraine male relative, who deftly slid her chair to a more eminent place than the one occupied by Mecklenberg. Mademoiselle de Guise then sat down quickly. Realizing she had been tricked, Mecklenberg took out a handkerchief and began amusing the Dauphin. Handkerchief in one hand and heir to the throne in the other, she rose and chose a seat that was far more prestigious than the one being occupied by Mademoiselle Marie. "Her adroitness was observed by the entire court, and some were pleased and others displeased; but no one caused a fuss, because they were in such gallant company, and because it was such a festive day."[65]

The *Gazette de France* was soon mentioning the newlyweds among the guests at court fêtes. The Duke stood at the King's side during a military parade. And the House of Guise began giving parties in the splendid new gardens of the refurbished Hôtel de Guise. That did not mean that Marie the Regent had surrendered her power to this couple of legal minors. Like a puppeteer, she stood in the background and manipulated the appropriate strings.

For example, she promptly took charge of MADAME DE GUISE's household, dismissing Her Royal Highness's favorite chambermaid and her secretary, and imposing some of her own protégés upon the young woman. For her lady of honor, the bride initially was given a woman who "was not of the stuff required for her to enter the Queen's carriage and to eat with her; but she was just what Mademoiselle de Guise wanted, pliable. Thus [Mademoiselle de Guise] was more concerned about her own domesticity than about my sister's grandeur," recalled Montpensier.[66] As a result, the new Duchess of Guise did not dare go to court until her mother, the DOWAGER OF ORLÉANS, came to the rescue and chose a more suitable person. Mademoiselle de Guise also imposed Jean-François de Voisins d'Alzeau on Madame de Guise, as her "knight of honor"; and she saw to it that Her Royal Highness would be the one to pay his stipend, his food, and his firewood.[67]

Thus it surely was Mademoiselle de Guise who decided that the Duke and his bride would offer their protection to Marc-Antoine Charpentier. Belonging as he did to a family with links to both the House of Orléans and the House of Guise, Charpentier was an ideal candidate. That is to say, clients of the House of Orléans would see him as having been Madame de Guise's candidate, so the young woman would appear to be in control. Yet friends of the House of Guise would see the appointment as a gesture in favor of one of their friends. At any rate, that is the picture that emerges from Montpensier's description of how Marie de Lorraine had earlier helped the DOWAGER OF ORLÉANS select a governess for her daughters. Mademoiselle de Guise's first concern had been to find someone who "belonged" to the House of Orléans. After that, she investigated whether the candidate happened to be the friend of someone she personally knew and respected. If the candidate passed these first two tests, Her Highness weighed the usefulness of that particular individual's talents to the household in general, and to herself in particular:

> Madame [the Dowager of Orléans] hardly knew [the potential governess]; her husband had belonged to my father [Gaston d'Orléans]. He had been his page. He was an upright man; but that was not why Madame took her, but because [he] was Montrésor's friend, and because his wife was very good at arranging the paintings and precious objects in Mademoiselle de Guise's *cabinet*, for my aunt loves that.[68]

If Mademoiselle de Guise used similar criteria and a similar procedure to select Marc-Antoine Charpentier, one can surmise that she first checked with her friend, the DOWAGER OF ORLÉANS, to make sure that the young composer's cousin, HAVÉ DE SAINT-AUBIN, had served GASTON

D'ORLÉANS faithfully. The next step would have involved consulting with friends of her own House who knew the candidate, to make sure that young Charpentier was "upright." (The most likely references would have been members of the TALON–VOISIN–VERTHAMON clan, who had belonged to the House of Guise for a century.) The reply being favorable, she then probably discussed the matter with MONSIEUR DU BOIS, who would be working closely with the newcomer. If he approved, Her Highness would ask a third party to extend her invitation to the composer.

There is reliable evidence that the Princess made it a practice to select her householders well in advance. For example, when she appointed DOCTOR VALLANT as her physician in the early 1670s, she asked a third party to speak to him and request that he not accept any other offer until the new year, when she could put his name on her household roster. (Although the exact date of Charpentier's invitation cannot be determined, the content of the composer's earliest arabic-numbered notebooks leaves no doubt that he began working for the Guises at the start of a new year, specifically during the first weeks of 1670.)

Just when and how the Guises first became aware of Marc-Antoine Charpentier's talents remains a matter for conjecture. No evidence has been found to indicate whether Mademoiselle de Guise was instrumental in helping him make the trip to Rome, or whether she learned about him from the DUKE OF CHAULNES and his circle at the Farnese. Indeed, it is impossible to say whether, prior to his return to Paris, probably during the fall of 1669, she even knew that he existed.

The fall of 1669: the timing was felicitous, because only a few months earlier the Guises had hosted Cosimo III de' Medicis; and now, as the year ebbed, Madame de Guise announced that she was pregnant. A composer—and an Italian-trained composer at that—was just what the glory of the House of Guise required.

Having extended her protection to Marc-Antoine Charpentier, Marie de Lorraine would henceforth watch out for his well-being, as she did for all current and past householders. For example, upon learning that an injured householder had died, she commented, "I cannot lose anyone who has served me without bewailing them."[69]

Judging from the pieces in Charpentier's first two arabic-numbered notebooks—the series of notebooks that clearly contain his compositions for the House of Guise—the Guises had no clear idea of the role a composer might play in their household. In fact, it cannot be ruled out that the idea of hiring a composer came from MONSIEUR DU BOIS. One thing was clear from the outset: Monsieur Charpentier was not going to be a worldly composer. At any rate, he does not appear to have composed secular music for the Harcourt-Cadaval wedding, ballet, and ball held at the Hôtel de Guise in February 1671. Instead, from early 1670 on, the composer copied devotional work after devotional work into these arabic-numbered notebooks.

His first three pieces surely were written for Tenebrae[A] services at MONTMARTRE, where Mademoiselle de Guise's sister was abbess. (That recorders are specified for one of the pieces suggests that two laymen participated in these services, just as the King's Music had performed there some years earlier.) Two pieces[B] composed the following summer (one of them likewise called for recorders) correspond to the devotional practices of GOIBAUT DU BOIS, who at the time was still a fervent Jansenist. That is to say, the first piece was for August 20, the Feast of Saint Bernard of Clairvaux, patron saint of the Cistercian nuns of PORT-ROYAL; and the second was for August 28, the Feast of Saint Augustine, of whom the Jansenists were proud to be the "disciples." These same notebooks contain a composition that may have been a surprise for Mademoiselle de Guise,[C] because the text is appropriate for the Feast of the Assumption (August 15, her birthday and name day) and also for the octave of the Nativity of the Virgin, in early September.

In short, during his first year at the Hôtel de Guise, Marc-Antoine Charpentier was not ordered to write a corpus of works for a specific devotion or a specific liturgy. Rather, he composed something for the Abbess, something for the Chapel Master, and something for Mademoiselle de Guise herself.

The summer of 1670 brought great rejoicing, for a son was born to the ducal couple. God was looking favorably upon Marie the Regent's stratagems for elevating the House of Guise. Not only was the Duke gaining favor with Louis XIV, he now had an heir. The joy would prove short-lived, for in the summer of 1671 Louis-Joseph de Lorraine made a trip that would cost him his life.

Continued in this panel: MARIE DE LORRAINE, THE LAST GUISE

[A] Cahier 1, H. 91, H. 92, H. 93.
[B] Cahiers 1–2, H. 306; cahier 2, H. 307.
[C] Cahier 2, H. 426.

III

The renewal of the ancient piety of this illustrious house

THE ABBESS OF MONTMARTRE

Françoise-Renée de Lorraine,
Abbess of the Royal Benedictine Abbey of Montmartre,
known as "Madame de Montmartre"

The Duke and Duchess of Guise's youngest child, Françoise-Renée de Lorraine, born on January 10, 1621, was dedicated to the Church at an early age. She was educated at the Abbey of Saint-Pierre in Rheims under Abbess Renée de Lorraine, her paternal aunt. Then, in 1644, while still in her early twenties, Françoise-Renée became coadjutrix to Marie de Beauvilliers, Abbess of Montmartre. This was a prodigious honor for the House of Guise, because Montmartre was "one of the most powerful and richest abbeys in the realm."[1] On the day of Françoise-Renée's reception the family was present, to the nuns' joy, "seeing in this princess the renewal of the ancient piety of this illustrious house."[2]

During the first decades of the century, Abbess Beauvilliers had made many reforms.[3] The nuns abandoned their impractical white habit in favor of a black one. Visitors were edified by the absence of "the least remarks that revealed a worldly turn of mind, no novels, and nothing that could dissipate the internal reflection they esteemed so much." The furnishings in the romanesque Church of Saint-Pierre, on Montmartre Butte, were stripped of their ornamentation, and the abbess's throne was moved to the lowest possible position. "All these vain ornaments were removed." The Holy Sacrament henceforth was displayed on the high altar, in a splendid, gem-studded, golden sunburst—the only visual pomp permitted in the church.

Madame Beauvilliers instituted quite a few devotional practices that would be continued by her successor. Choosing the Virgin as protectress of the house, she made Marian devotions a pivotal part of worship. A

379

bas-relief of Mary, dressed as a Benedictine abbess, now decorated the center of the choir, because the Virgin was "seen as the Sovereign of all the nuns."

In thanksgiving for Mary's protection during the civil uprisings of the late 1640s, another statue of Her was placed in a side chapel where, "every Saturday the nuns sing a *salut*," a Benediction of the Holy Sacrament.[A] Madame Beauvilliers and her nuns also observed a "special devotion for the poverty of the INFANT JESUS, lodged in a stable and lying on the hay in the manger."

Other high feast days were celebrated with great pomp. Before the splendid gold reliquary of Saint Benedict, founder of the Order, an annual "mass in music" was sung "with special solemnity" for the Feast of his Illation on December 4, for the Feast of his Translation on July 11, and for his birthday on March 21. In addition, every seventh year, on May 1, the procession of Saint Denis was held, and the reliquary containing the saint's head would be carried in solemn procession from the Abbey of Saint-Denis to the Church of the Holy Martyrs, situated lower on the butte than the abbey proper. In this church decorated with "ornaments and magnificent tapestries," the religious who had marched to the abbey would chant the antiphon for that feast as they placed the reliquary on a special stand. Then "the aforesaid Abbess and nuns sang, in music, the response *Pretiosus*." A high mass followed, after which the procession made its way back to Saint-Denis.

Abbess Beauvillers abandoned the breviary of Fontevrault, where so much was "contrary to the Roman rite," and the abbey began to publish its own liturgies and ceremonials.[4] She had the good fortune to admit a novice who not only "sang like an angel" but taught the other nuns how to sing. This young nun "worked out the notation of the books used in the nuns' choir, and elevated their song to the perfection where it now is"[5]—now being 1667, when Françoise-Renée de Lorraine had already succeeded Abbess Beauvillers.

It is not clear whether this perfected "song," *chant*, of the nuns was plainsong or partsong, but during Abbess Beauvilliers' tenure, magnificent musical events were held, and the nuns themselves sometimes participated. For example, in 1625 "a mass in music was sung in honor of our great saint [Benedict], which was very edifying for the Queen and the princesses" who attended the service. On that day "the abbey was hung with tapestries from the entrance gate to the church. The entire cloister

---

[A] Cahier 2, H. 17; cahier 17, H. 239; cahier 22, H. 242, H. 243 (both were for *salut*, according to the liturgies for Montmartre); cahier 40, H. 254; cahier 41, H. 75 (for the GUISE MUSIC).

was decorated in the same way and was lighted by an infinite number of lights." A description of another service, held in the late 1640s or early 1650s, has survived:

> In the church choir there is a grill where the nuns sing and play
> music with the organ that one of them plays, and it is done with
> such excellence that the King's Music is not more accurate and
> measured than theirs. I have seen them sing at the open grill,
> [illegible] a dozen, their faces uncovered, all of them standing, except
> the one who was playing the wind instrument [an organ? rather than
> a recorder?], who was seated. One of the standing nuns beat time.[6]

The nuns were trained by Antoine Boesset. "The genius of sweet music, and so esteemed by Louis XIII," this composer died in 1643, "to the great regret of the nuns, to whom he had taught singing."[7] He was buried at Montmartre.

By the end of Beauvilliers' tenure, the abbey was famed for its discipline, its nobility, and its music: "They sent [the Coadjutrix of Charenton] to the Abbey of Montmartre, where she is boarding while she learns how to govern nuns. ... The [one hundred and fifty women there] are almost all of high rank, and some were born princesses. They sing music there very melodiously, with voices and instruments."[8]

While coadjutrix, Françoise-Renée gradually took over most of the administrative tasks of this prosperous house, whose excellent noviciate was attracting so many young women. After Abbess Beauvilliers' death in 1657, Françoise-Renée—called "Madame de Montmartre" in this portrait gallery—remained faithful to her predecessor's vision and proved to be a "humble and excellent abbess." Owing to her administrative skills and her family's wealth and influence, the abbey experienced unknown material prosperity.

The decor and the music at Françoise-Renée's benediction as abbess in May 1657[9] were splendid. The raw materials for the decorations almost certainly came from the storerooms of the Hôtel de Guise:

> The entire church, the cloisters and the passageways, [even] the
> choir of the church, were hung with the finest tapestries in Paris.
> The high altar had been decorated with such industry, such
> richness, and such magnificence that nothing could improve it. ...
> The number of persons of quality was so great, and the afflux of
> common people so extraordinary, that the officials and guards had a
> great deal of trouble maintaining the requisite order.

The service began with a *Veni Creator Spiritus* (a text used for benedictions and inductions) "sung by a nun accompanied by a viol that was played to perfection." After that the nuns intoned the Introit "with a melody that one would have thought belonged to angels wearing nuns' veils and habits." Next, the "King's Music," directed by Jean Veillot, composer and sub-master of the royal chapel, sang the *Kyrie* and "the rest of the mass." Later in the service "the nun who had begun with the *Veni Creator Spiritus* sang a motet in honor of the Very Holy Sacrament, which she did so artfully and so accurately that the entire company was awed." The service concluded with a *Te Deum* sung by the royal musicians.

The religious service was followed by lavish refreshments presided over by the Abbess, Mademoiselle de Guise, and Duke Henri. The day ended with vespers, also "sung as music." Another source provides details about the music performed that day:

> Several psalms, motets, *cantiques*, were sung by musicians who charmed by their sweetness. ... In addition to lutes and viols, among the forty who sang were Berthod [a French-born castrato who sang in the royal chapel] and Le Gros [a male vocalist of the royal chamber], whose voices are worth an empire.

The feast alone, it was said, cost forty thousand francs.[10]

Three years later, "music" composed by Veillot was performed by the nuns for the Feast of Saint Denis. (Veillot's repeated participation in services at Montmartre suggests that this "renowned singer" had replaced the late Boesset.) That day the Queen listened to "the harmonious voices of the devout nuns who, it is said, have a fine talent for excellent singing. Their music was lovely and good."[11]

These snippets of information make it possible to deduce what music was like at the Abbey of Montmartre when Marc-Antoine Charpentier entered the service of the House of Guise. The nuns not only excelled at plainsong, they also performed harmonic partsong (*musique*), accompanied by an organ, viols, and perhaps a lute. Two or three of the nuns were accomplished soloists, and another ten were skilled enough to sing as a chorus. To ensure a performance of the highest quality, the women were taught by a respected music master. For special celebrations, the King would send his Music to perform, and the music master of the abbey would compose a mass or several motets for these visiting musicians. Some of these services to music were carefully planned to coordinate with the royal calendar. For example, on one occasion Madame de Montmartre informed Louis XIV that she wanted him to come to her church during Holy Week, to hear the nuns' music. If a visit was possible, she would like him to choose the day.[12]

The House of Guise made many costly gifts to the abbey: a long covered walkway connecting the main convent at the top of the butte to the distant priory and Church of the Martyrs; the repair and embellishment of the existing buildings; silver lamps and other costly ornaments; and dowries for several novices. Almost eighty thousand livres in all.[13] In return for this generosity, just short of a year after Duke Henri's death, Mademoiselle de Guise, the Abbess, and the grateful nuns agreed not only to continue the "solemn office of the dead that they customarily say and celebrate" each September 30, in memory of Mademoiselle de Guise's parents and brothers, but also to "say and celebrate" a similar mass each June 2, for Henri. Until the time when Mademoiselle de Guise herself should die, they would in addition "say and celebrate on her behalf a solemn mass of Our Lady"[A] every August 23, the octave of the Assumption. After her death, this service for the Virgin would be replaced by an annual mass on the anniversary of her demise; and an annual "solemn service of the dead" would be said for the late Abbess on the anniversary of her death.

In other words, after 1673 the annual "celebrations" at Montmartre —some or all of them involving music—included two solemn masses for the dead and a mass for the Virgin every August 23. (To these would be added, in 1683, a "service" for the late Abbess each December 4; and, in 1689, a "solemn service" every March 3 in Mademoiselle de Guise's memory.) So many masses for the dead! It is not surprising that, by the late 1680s or early 1690s, Charpentier recopied, and perhaps even reworked, the funeral music[B] he had written in 1671 and 1672, first for LOUIS-JOSEPH DE LORRAINE and then for Madame de Guise's mother, the DOWAGER DUCHESS OF ORLÉANS. Although no record of a similar agreement between the nuns and MADAME DE GUISE has been found, it is likely that Isabelle d'Orléans remembered her husband and mother in a similar way every July 30 and April 3. After all, their hearts were kept at the abbey, and she is known to have sponsored annual masses for her late parents at another convent.[14]

During the years that immediately followed the deaths of LOUIS-JOSEPH DE LORRAINE, DUKE OF GUISE and the DOWAGER OF ORLÉANS, the two grieving princesses would withdraw to the convent for weeks at a time, especially during Holy Week.[C] They soon had personal lodgings constructed within or adjacent to the existing buildings of the abbey. There they could receive friends, as MADAME DE GUISE did on April 23, 1673, when she entertained her cousin the King.[15]

[A] Octave of the Assumption: cahier 2, H. 426.

[B] Cahier 3, H. 2, H. 234; cahier 4, H. 311, H. 156; cahier 5, H. 12.

[C] Cahier 1, H. 91–93; cahier 6, H. 95, H. 157.

Both highnesses increasingly gave themselves over to what were described as "devotions"; and judging from Charpentier's arabic-numbered notebooks, these devotions often involved music. Just as the princesses' social and devotional life centered increasingly upon the Abbey of Montmartre, so their composer presumably devoted considerable time to composing motets for the nuns—becoming in the process the de facto composer and music master there. (The task of training the nuns was probably turned over to ÉTIENNE LOULIÉ, a member of the Guise Music.)

Most abbeys had highborn "benefactresses" who enjoyed special privileges and for whom the convent often became an extension of their own household. These wealthy laywomen would send their musicians to perform for high holy days. If they had given money in return for a private chapel, they were considered "founders" and were generally granted unrestricted admission to the convent. For example, they could sleep there with one or two domestics, and they could sit in the choir with the nuns and sing.[16] Thus it was with Queen Marie-Thérèse at the LITTLE CARMEL; thus it was with MADAME DE GUISE at the Clarice convent in Alençon; and thus it surely was at Montmartre, where the invasion by benevolent laywomen was at times overwhelming. In fact, yet another lodging for a highborn princess was built along the edge of the abbey enclosure in 1675.

Madame de Guise's sister, MADAME DE TOSCANE, became a permanent resident at the abbey that year. Her presence, combined with visits from the two Guise women and their entourages, upset the daily routine, especially because persons of their elevated rank could bring with them any number of laymen or laywomen. The results appalled the clergy who supervised these abbeys:

> No house is so reformed that all the ladies of the court are refused permission to enter. Not to have this privilege is a sign that one has little authority. ... Now, not only do they enter [convents] but they remain there for a week or two, eat there and sleep there and bring with them five or six young women. Each nun adopts one of them: 'She is my cousin, my confident, my devout one.' Imagine everything that goes on during that time, what silence, what retreat, what attention to the rules, and what mortification there is in the house: they laugh, they express their feelings to their friend, they whisper about those who don't suit their humor, and so forth.[17]

This was the state of affairs at Montmartre during the 1670s and early 1680s. Madame de Toscane, Madame de Guise, Mademoiselle de Guise —and, when it pleased her, MADEMOISELLE DE MONTPENSIER—had free access to the abbey. And they trailed domestics and friends in their wake.

The Florentine who was arranging Toscane's return to France was astonished to find "many women and men together" in Madame de Guise's apartment. "Their manner of living is not as strict as it is in Italy," he concluded.[18] But with the Grand Duchess's arrival, the situation worsened. The sisters snapped at each another continually, causing the Abbess to be almost glad that they did not get along; because if they ever allied, they would "cause trouble, rather than repose."[19]

Still more perturbing for the Abbess was the fact that MADAME DE TOSCANE insisted upon dancing, singing, and performing secular music within the convent proper. This insistence on music became so contagious that the Abbess herself could occasionally be found "in an upper parlor, listening to music."[20] If Madame de Montmartre rejoiced about anything involving the Grand Duchess, it was that she had brought with her an Italian musician-chambermaid, Cintia Galoppini. By entertaining her mistress, Cintia freed the "two or three nuns who know music marvelously well" from having to neglect their duties in order to play and sing with Toscane.[21]

During the 1670s Mademoiselle de Guise became especially fond of several nuns. As early as 1672, when she created those annual masses for the dead, she referred to the "good affection" the nuns felt for her, and she promised to "continue her help and protection in their monastery's affairs, and in their needs." With these "needs" in mind, she created life pensions for several women—one of them her own daughter, Marie Naudot, or Nodot, now "Sister of the Holy Martyrs." Mademoiselle Naudot, who had taken her final vows in about 1672 or 1673,[A] "was formerly in her service" as a chambermaid, perhaps a singing one. Among the young women at Montmartre to whom Mademoiselle de Guise also paid special attention was a Protestant who had converted to Catholicism.[22] The girl eventually fled the abbey and rejoined her family, which had sought refuge in Holland.

Abbess Françoise-Renée de Lorraine was by no means a prisoner in her abbey. She could, and did, spend time in Paris on abbey business, lodging in the Hermits' Apartment on the mezzanine floor of the Hôtel de Guise.[23] Then, in the fall of 1680 she and her sister—accompanied by several ladies, MONSIEUR DU BOIS, and the GUISE MUSIC—set off in several coaches on a progress toward Guise and Rheims, visiting churches and abbeys along the way. The Music doubtlessly sang all the while, as the musicians of a great noble were expected to do during expeditions: "The coach in which the Music was riding, was between four others, [and] they

<hr>

[A] Or perhaps in 1671?: cahier 2, H. 17.

sang and played."[24] To Chapel Master Du Bois' great joy, the musicians performed marvelously. (The participation of a high tenor, *haute-contre*, in a piece[A] almost certainly written for this trip suggests that Charpentier went along.) Letters sent back to DOCTOR VALLANT[25] during those three weeks convey the Abbess's charm and wit. Her health improved as the distance increased between her and her doctor (and his purges); and although she inquired about ailing nuns, she was overjoyed at the prospect of seeing her old friends in Rheims.

The improvement in Madame de Montmartre's health proved temporary. Her planned successor was Marie-Anne de Lorraine of Harcourt, who had been raised at the abbey since the age of four, in preparation for the day when she would sit on the abbatial throne.[26] (She was the sister of the Harcourt girl whose wedding at the Hôtel de Guise in February 1671 had been the talk of the town.) Marie-Anne was too young to be enthroned, so Madame de Montmartre kept her worsening health a secret, to prevent rivals from snatching the abbey from the House of Lorraine. She claimed that rheumatism was keeping her in bed, but by late November 1682 news leaked out that she was near death. Mademoiselle de Guise dispatched a person of trust to Versailles, to plead Marie-Anne's cause.

Françoise-Renée de Lorraine died on December 4, 1682. Despite her grief, Mademoiselle de Guise, seconded by Madame de Guise and several princesses of the House of Lorraine, sent a volley of letters to the King and his ministers. She finally won the day by proposing that the pension of ten thousand livres that she had created for the late Abbess be transferred to Marie-Anne. She did not let the new Abbess forget her generosity: "She immediately resumed her visits [to Montmartre], in the same manner as she had during her sister's lifetime, and she even spent several days in retreat there during this Holy Week [of 1683]."[27] During the period of transition, Mademoiselle de Guise was for all intents and purposes abbess, advising and guiding Marie-Anne until she was old enough to assume her duties legally.[28]

That Mademoiselle de Guise grieved deeply for her sister is apparent in her reply to a letter of condolence sent by Carlo Gondi, the Grand Duke's former agent in Paris:

> You can, Monsieur, judge better than anyone else the state in which the loss of my poor sister has left me, for it was the only consolation in my life, and you knew the tenderness and friendship in which we lived together. God alone can give me the strength to endure such a

---

[A] Cahiers 29–30, H. 400.

separation, and the pain it causes me. I am, Monsieur, very obliged
to you for wishing me comfort, and you could not possibly have
those feelings for anyone who esteems you more than I do. *Guise*[29]

Mademoiselle de Guise's links to Montmartre remained strong until
the final months of her life. For the Feast of Saint Genevieve, January 3,
1685, Charpentier set a text from the liturgy of Montmartre.[A] A few
months later, Her Highness gave the abbey a "large relic of the True
Cross in a crystal reliquary trimmed in gold, to honor the Passion." In
addition to two new daily masses in honor of the Passion, and in memory
of all the dead members of her family, she made it official that the
Saturday mass for the Virgin[B] would "continue" to be sung, and not
revert to being simply recited.

Then, in January 1687, Mademoiselle de Guise selected the new
Church of the Martyrs abbey church, situated partway down the butte,
as a venue for a splendid service of rejoicing over Louis XIV's recovery
from surgery. The *Gazette de France* evoked the lights, the tapestries, the
gems, and the silver vases that decorated the church that day. Without
naming the composer, it added, as a near aside, that "the *Te Deum* was
sung by an excellent Music."

The description of the event published by Corneille and DONNEAU DE
VISÉ, Marc-Antoine Charpentier's friends at the *Mercure galant*,[30]
provides details about what clearly was a continuity in the organization
of high feasts at the Abbey of Montmartre, from the 1640s to the late
1680s. The text is especially precious because Bérain's decorations, and
the silver objects and fake gems he provided, probably were a more
elaborate version of the ornaments displayed year after year during
solemn services at the abbey, but not described in the press because no
member of the royal family happened to be attending. For these high
holy days there would be tapestries, probably loaned by Mademoiselle de
Guise; the altar and its steps would be decorated with "crystals" and
"gems," many of them loaned by Her Highness, who was famous for her
collection of "crystals"; there would be light-refracting silver vessels and
platters, surely loaned by Mademoiselle de Guise, whose collection
rivaled the King's[31]; and there would be a great number of costly candles,
paid for by the princess:

> The high altar ... was so brilliant that the eye could scarcely bear the
> sparkle. The tabernacle, six to seven feet high, was totally covered
> with gems. All the architectural elements [of the altar] were outlined

---

[A] Cahier 45, H. 29.
[B] Cahier 2, H. 309; cahier 5, H. 18, H. 19; cahier 16, H. 21, H. 59; cahier 32, H. 63.

in gems, as was the rest of the altar, where lively colors represented other architectural elements on transparent places that an infinite number of lights caused to glisten and that united agreeably with the tabernacle. All the steps to the altar were not only decorated with a large number of candlesticks, they were also loaded down with rich items and crystals lighted from every direction, and together with fake and real gems, they formed the brilliant mass I have just described for you. Above the architecture of the altar was a crown with fleurs-de-lis made of lights and gems. The statues of the saints that are in niches on each side of the altar were ornamented with gems on every portion of their clothing that could hold them, so that the altar, its sides, and its top all the way to the vault formed a façade of gems on which the eye could not linger. What was surprising was that all the elements that produced this great blaze of light were perfectly distinguishable, and nothing was blurred together. ...

[In] the nuns' choir ... on each side there were three rows of tapestries, one along the nuns' chairs, another stretching up to a gallery that forms balconies, and the third all the way to the vault. There were also three levels of lights, all around the choir. The entire molding around the nuns' chairs was edged with silver plaques, and between each pair of round plaques there was a place in the shape of a cross of Lorraine. Above could be seen pyramids, arches, and various other figures formed by lights. ... Three rows of lamps also ornamented this choir, that is, one row of crystal lamps on each side, and a row of silver lamps in the middle that was higher than the other two, so that the ensemble formed a sort of great arched vault of lights.

As the guests left the church they were greeted by the sort of light display that usually accompanied such services: "All the walls, all the windows, and all the surroundings of this convent were lighted by an infinite number of lights as big as torches."

One can only conjecture that it was Marc-Antoine Charpentier who wrote the *Te Deum*, because no such work is to be found in his notebooks for 1687. His arabic-numbered notebooks do, however, contain music celebrating the King's recovery. One work was a chamber opera for the Guise Music[A] almost certainly commissioned by MADAME DE GUISE for a fête at the Luxembourg Palace scheduled to take place a week later. That did not, of course, rule out a preview at Montmartre or at the Hôtel de Guise. There was a *Gratitudinis* for the Pièche sisters of the DAUPHIN's

[A] Cahiers 49–50, H. 489.

Music.[A] A psalm of thanksgiving for the Great Guise Music, sans Charpentier, was copied into a roman-numbered notebook, as if it were an "extraordinary" commission from the young Abbess.[B]

The composer's roman-numbered notebooks reveal that Abbess Harcourt commissioned another work shortly after the festivities of January 20, 1687: a setting of a text found in the various *Propres* published for Montmartre and recited on December 4, during the second vespers of the Feast of the Illation[C] of Saint Benedict. Six months later, MADEMOISELLE DE GUISE died, and the composer's link to the Royal Abbey of Montmartre was definitively severed.

[A] Cahier 50, H. 431.
[B] Cahier L, H. 195.
[C] Cahier LI , H. 347 (1687).

Louis-Joseph de Lorraine in 1659.

When this portrait was made, the nine-year-old Duke of Joyeuse
was being raised by his aunt and guardian, Mademoiselle de Guise.

IV

A worthy heir to the merit and service of his ancestors

LOUIS-JOSEPH, THE LAST DUKE OF GUISE

Louis-Joseph de Lorraine, Duke of Guise, Joyeuse, and Angoulême,
Prince of Joinville, and Count of Eu and Ponthieu,
the last Duke of Guise

Louis-Joseph (or, sometimes, Joseph-Louis) de Lorraine, born on August 7, 1650, was the only son of Louis de Lorraine, Duke of Joyeuse, grand chamberlain of France, and Françoise-Marie de Valois, the daughter of the Duke of Angoulême. By the time of his wedding, twenty-seven-year-old Joyeuse had proved himself on the battlefield; and now the granddaughter of one of King Charles IX's bastard sons was bringing him a dowry of five hundred thousand livres and the prestige of her bar sinister.

Ten months later Louis-Joseph was born. He had a younger sister, Henriette, who was baptized with him at Saint-Jean-en-Grève in September 1651, but who was "raised incognito under the name 'Mademoiselle d'Essey' so that her brother would be an only son." The girl appears to have been brought up near her mother, whose mental incapacities were so great that she was soon relegated to a convent: "She was shut up in the Abbey of Essey for feeblemindedness."[1]

In July 1654 the Duke of Joyeuse, a colonel in a light cavalry unit of the royal army, set off for the northern frontier with his horse guards and his "most handsome equipment." On August 22 he was wounded in a skirmish near Arras. Infection set in, and he died at his mother's residence in Paris a month later.[2] Joyeuse's premature death threatened to deprive his four-year-old son of some of his father's lands and offices. The child's guardians would have to fight and scheme if they hoped to save his property from the clutches of Joyeuse's older brother, Duke Henri of Guise. Joyeuse's coffin was carried in solemn pomp to Joinville where, after sung vigils for the dead, he was buried near his father and brothers in the Church of Saint-Laurent, in the presence of the local clergy and the officers of his mother's household.

Thus it was that little Louis-Joseph de Lorraine succeeded his father as Duke of Joyeuse. His paternal grandmother, Henriette-Catherine de Joyeuse, Duchess of Guise, was appointed to be his guardian, and Seraphim Le Ragois (the paternal uncle of Madame Louis de Bailleul, whose mother-in-law and daughter would sign ÉLISABETH CHARPENTIER's wedding contract eight years later) served as his other guardian, overseeing the boy's finances.[3] Upon the Duchess of Guise's death in March 1656, Marie de Lorraine (portrayed in this gallery, for this period of her life, as "MADEMOISELLE MARIE DE GUISE THE REGENT") was named guardian in her place, and Claude de Bourdeille, Count of Montrésor (who had secretly married Mademoiselle de Guise) became the boy's financial guardian.[4] A year later the Princess purchased the house in the Tuileries gardens known as the Volière, refurbished it entirely (at the cost of some ninety thousand livres), and moved in, bringing her nephew with her.

Upon Montrésor's death in 1663, the issue of the child's guardianship was again raised. A council composed of the highest nobles in the realm, who "had assembled as friends of the young Duke of Joyeuse," unanimously selected as financial guardian MADEMOISELLE MARIE THE REGENT:

> [Her] prudence and virtue [...] make her, more than any mortal, capable of this guardianship. In short, all Paris wishes that this prince, her dear nephew, will make admirable progress under the charming tutelage of this lovable and wise aunt, who takes his interests to heart.[5]

The decision made by these illustrious "friends" of the House of Guise was aimed at keeping Duke Henri away from the youth's inheritance. When Henri's died a year later, fourteen-year-old Louis-Joseph de Lorraine became Duke of Guise. His aunt Marie continued to supervise his education and his property, lavishing on him all the affection she could not give her own children by Montrésor.

It was as Regent of the House of Guise that Mademoiselle de Guise had journeyed to Joinville with her nephew a year earlier, in October 1663, just three months after Montrésor's death.[6] The estate managers had met them at his land of Éclaron and escorted them to Joinville, with stops along the way to meet the inhabitants. At the city gate of Joinville they were treated to a harangue by the Dean of the chapter of Saint-Laurent, attended a church service, and were conducted to the castle—whose entry door was decorated with a representation of Phaeton being led out of the darkness by Dawn. At Phaeton's feet was a girl who offered the city to the prince and who carried the motto: *Post tenebras spero lucem*, "After the dark I hope for light," an unambiguous statement of the hope that better times would return to the principality of Joinville. Louis-Joseph and his aunt remained there for two months. (Less than a decade later, Louis-Joseph de Lorraine would return to Joinville in a coffin, to be buried near his father.)

Louis-Joseph became Mademoiselle de Guise's reason for living. To capture his beauty for posterity, she dreamed of commissioning a bust of him from Bernini In fact, she took her nephew to the Italian's lodgings on September 28, 1665. "The Cavaliere studied his face closely and praised its features, which greatly pleased his aunt. He told her how, in painting, the material helps the artist, but that it hindered him in sculpture."[7]

To prepare a dwelling for the Duke that would be commensurate with his rank, Marie the Regent undertook massive renovations of the rather dilapidated Hotel de Guise in the winter of 1665 and the spring of 1666. (She had sought Bernini's advice, perhaps with the hope of enticing him into drawing up plans; but the artist only had time to make a few general suggestions before returning to Rome.) The building was gutted, and every modern convenience was incorporated into the renovated apartments. The archaic mullioned windows and renaissance dormers were replaced by French windows and classical dormers like those in Louis XIV's latest building projects. New tile floors were laid in the public spaces, with glazed Guise-green tiles forming a pattern with terra-cotta ones. Parquet floors made the private spaces more comfortable. The magnificent parade apartment on the noble floor was totally reworked. Coved plaster ceilings painted with emblematic pictures now concealed the old-fashioned beams. Beneath these reception rooms an elegant ground-floor apartment was created for Mademoiselle de Guise; and on the noble floor, in the very center of the garden façade, an apartment for the Duke. The gardens were entirely redone by André Le Nôtre.

In February 1667, shortly after Mademoiselle de Guise chose PHILIPPE GOIBAUT DU BOIS to be the Duke's "governor," she gave orders to have the stable wing transformed into a row of modern apartments. The largest one was for Du Bois and his wife. An apartment near the stables was prepared for the equerry and would soon be occupied by ROGER DE GAIGNIÈRES.

In May 1666, while work was proceeding apace on this veritable palace, Mademoiselle de Guise—once again acting as Regent for the House of Guise—organized a grand fête at her residence in the Tuileries gardens, to honor the King of England and PHILIPPE II D'ORLÉANS and his wife:

> Nothing can be seen that is more gallant, more superb, and more
> opulent, be it the food, which was almost limitless and certainly very
> edible, or the organization, or the buffet; and the scene where all
> this was done was her handsome palace in the Tuileries, which are
> now in flower, a palace that one would truly take to be an
> enchanted palace; so that [...] this wise Guise Highness knows, as we
> can see, how best to entertain the children of the gods.[8]

That same month, "with great sumptuousness" she entertained the
Queen, who was "accompanied by Mademoiselle d'Alençon."[9]

Rumors were circulating that the Duke of Guise would soon wed Her
Royal Highness ISABELLE D'ORLÉANS OF ALENÇON. Thus Princess Isabelle's
presence at this party fed the gossip mill. Six months later, in mid-May
1667, Louis XIV unexpectedly agreed to the union, making much of the
fact that it was not his idea. The DOWAGER DUCHESS OF ORLÉANS, he
asserted, had come to discuss with him a suitable match for her daughter.
After he had refused her first candidate (his identity was kept confidential), she said: "I want to see my daughter married before I die. If Your
Majesty is willing to let her wed Monsieur de Guise, I very much wish it."
The preamble of the wedding contract corroborates this assertion:

> His Majesty wishing to give Madame the Duchess of Orléans, his
> aunt, the consolation of seeing [Mademoiselle d'Alençon] established
> in France, cast his eyes on High and Powerful Prince Joseph-Louis de
> Lorraine, Duke of Guise, whose great qualities, joined to the
> advantage of an excellent education, give His Majesty every reason
> to hope that he will worthily sustain the glory of a House as
> illustrious as the one into which he was born, which has married
> into the greatest houses of Europe; and that he will be a worthy heir
> of the merit and service of his ancestors, as well as of the zeal and
> attachment that his father, the Duke of Joyeuse, always showed for
> His Majesty, having died in his service.[10]

The King laid down certain conditions. The bride would not bring
her husband a vast fortune: "Since the Duke of Guise possesses great
property, they assert that he should be content with the honor of making
this marriage, without claiming any property." Princess Isabelle would
assume the title "Duchess of Guise," but any children born of the union
would not be considered princes of the House of Guise. In assuming her
new title, the bride would lose none of her prerogatives nor the preemi-
nence due a "granddaughter of France." She therefore would have
precedence over all other princesses who were her inferiors by birth—a
category that included MARIE DE GUISE THE REGENT.[11] Indeed, although
she gave up the fleurs-de-lis of France and adopted the coat of arms of the

House of Guise and the Guises' green livery,[12] young MADAME DE GUISE's propensity for demonstrating her superior rank became legendary:

> Every bit of respect due a granddaughter of France was preserved: Monsieur de Guise could only sit on a folding stool in the presence of Madame his wife; every day at dinner he gave her napkin to her, and once she had been seated in her armchair and had unfolded her napkin, with Monsieur de Guise standing, she would order his place-setting brought to him, which was always ready on the buffet, and it would be put at the end of the table; then she would tell Monsieur de Guise to sit there, and he would sit. Every other formality was observed with the same exactitude, and this started anew every day, without the wife's rank lowering in any way, and without Monsieur de Guise's having increased even a tiny bit, despite this prestigious marriage.[13]

The fiancée had given "hoots of joy" when informed of the engagement. The next day, the sixteen-year-old Duke had paid her a formal visit at the Luxembourg Palace, "with demonstrations of affection and tenderness," calling her his "wife." The wedding was celebrated at Versailles a few days later. "There was no other ceremony," recalled the King. "So little had been thought out in advance that they had no cushions [to kneel on]. They went to look for some and found only those of Madame de Montespan's dogs." Montespan gave a similar account of the event: "I was on the balcony, when they rose at the Evangel, and when I saw my dogs' cushions honored in that way, and being put to use in such a wedding, it made me laugh."[14]

By late 1667 the renovations of the Hôtel de Guise had been completed and the newlyweds—and the aunt—moved into their splendid new apartments. Although he was now a married man, Louis-Joseph de Lorraine could not break free of his aunt's domination:

> Monsieur de Guise was not yet seventeen when he married; he was handsome and well-proportioned, but he had a rather insipid and delicate air about him. They had great difficulty raising him, and since Mademoiselle de Guise loved him dearly, they kept him that way: he did not go out in the evening dew; he never ate anywhere but at home, because he was fed whatever Mademoiselle de Guise ordered. He did nothing without her permission. ... Husband and wife did not dare talk to one another without her permission. He did not go to Saint-Germain without Mademoiselle de Guise; she slept in a little *cabinet* just off their room.[15]

Legal minor that he was, the Duke had little choice but accept the "governors," "directors," and household officers selected by his aunt. No list of Louis-Joseph's household has been found, but judging from the roll of pensioners and domestics remunerated by Duke Henri in 1660 (approximately sixty-two individuals), by Mademoiselle de Guise in 1688 (some seventy people), and by Madame de Guise in 1672 (forty-five domestics, in addition to those of her late husband), one can presume that Louis-Joseph de Lorraine's household consisted of fifteen principal officers such as secretary, treasurer, equerry, and chaplains; six gentlemen in ordinary who received pensions; five councillors; and some forty servants who cared for the living quarters, kitchens, stables, and the Duke's person.[16] To these sixty-odd domestics must be added the householders of Mademoiselle de Guise and Madame de Guise, for a grand total of well over one hundred twenty-five householders.

In February 1668 Louis-Joseph de Lorraine got his first taste of battle. He was a part of the small force that helped the Prince of Condé take the Franche-Comté in a lightning attack that was over in less than a month. "The Duke of Guise not having yet appeared in the army, he was given as director the Count of Sainte-Mesme, who was a very prudent person and very experienced in the art of war."[17] (Long a faithful householder of GASTON D'ORLÉANS, Sainte-Mesme had been willing to carry ISABELLE OF ALENÇON's train when no one else would. In 1675 he would be given the challenging task of supervising MADAME DE TOSCANE.)

Upon her nephew's return to Paris, MARIE DE GUISE THE REGENT began arranging for the supplies he would need for the summer's military campaign. On his behalf she signed numerous contracts with suppliers.[18] A meat-roaster agreed to supply meats (all sorts of poultry and wild fowl, including turtle doves, pheasants, skylarks, quail, suckling pigs, young wild boars, and rabbits, but no salt pork, beef, or veal) for "this year's entire campaign," wherever the Duke might be fighting. A baker signed a similar agreement: he would "supply and deliver to His Highness's kitchen and lodgings, during his march with the royal army and during the sieges that might take place before fortified cities, castles, and fortresses, all the necessary bread [...] for My Lord, his retinue, his household, and his followers." The contracts generally provided for a "boy" who would accompany the Duke to war and do the work.

In the end, these arrangements proved unnecessary, because a truce, followed by the Peace of Aix-la-Chapelle, ended Louis XIV's military ventures for that year. The bread contract was canceled on June 5, 1668. Autumn brought contracts involving the upkeep of the coaches, the harnesses, and the horses that he, his wife, and his aunt might use to go to court—or "to the army," should war break out again. A few months later, in October, Louis-Joseph went to inspect his duchy of Guise. While there, he received a query from Le Tellier, the royal minister in charge of the army, proposing that the area be disarmed. Guise's reply was something of a put-down: it would be wise to consult Louis XIV first, he observed.[19]

The Duke appeared at various military events, including a review of the royal troops in July 1669. That day "the Duke of Guise stayed very close to the King's person," in the "second place" of honor, just at Louis XIV's left.[20] (The position at the King's right was reserved for his brother, PHILIPPE II D'ORLÉANS.)

Louis-Joseph de Lorraine and his bride became part of "the very dressed-up young people" who participated in fêtes arranged by Madame de Guise's first cousins, Louis XIV and PHILIPPE II D'ORLÉANS. The King honored Guise by granting him the right to sit on a square cushion. "I am not surprised that they gave Monsieur de Guise a cushion," observed a wit. "His new alliance with the royal family is the cause for his being treated with correctness."[21] Cushion or not, the Duke and the Duchess remained under Mademoiselle de Guise's thumb:

> He never did anything without her permission, so that [Madame de Guise] was more submissive to Mademoiselle de Guise than she was to her mother [the Dowager of Orléans]. Husband and wife did not dare talk to one another without her permission. ... He had only recently stopped calling Mademoiselle de Guise "My Dear Aunt" in public.[22]

In the name of her nephew and his bride, Mademoiselle de Guise went to considerable lengths to display the magnificence of the House of Guise during the elegant and costly entertainments she sponsored. When a child was born to Louis XIV in August 1668, the three Guises

> prepared a very special rejoicing, having held a magnificent reception in their hôtel—which was lighted by an infinite number of lights—for forty of the principal ladies of the court; having made fountains of wine available all day long to passers-by, with violins and trumpets; and having provided very beautiful fireworks as entertainment, which was followed by a most agreeable ball.[23]

Another spectacular fête was the marriage at the Hôtel de Guise of Cadaval, a Portuguese nobleman, and Mademoiselle d'Harcourt, a Lorraine cousin who was escorted that day by the young Duke and Duchess of Guise. The event was especially festive because it coincided with Mardi Gras. The King, the Queen, and "all the high nobles of the court" attended the banquet and ball. A description of the fête reveals the extent to which Mademoiselle de Guise dominated her nephew's court. The banquet was held in her elegant ground-floor apartment, where she, not the Duchess, was the principal hostess. On the other hand, the young couple apparently presided over the ball, which took place on the noble floor:

> All the courtyards of the Hôtel de Guise were lighted with two thousand lanterns. The Queen first entered Mademoiselle de Guise's apartment, which was brightly lighted and very decorated. All the well-dressed ladies knelt around her, without worrying about who was entitled to a cushion. They supped in that apartment. There were forty ladies at table: the food was magnificent. The King came, and he very gravely looked at everything without sitting down at the table. They went upstairs [to the parade apartment], where everything had been prepared for the ball. The King danced with the Queen, and honored the assembly with three or four courantes, and then he went off to sup at the Louvre.[24]

The festivities also included a "ballet."[25] Allusions to the twenty-four-foot-long table so intrigued the Medicis in Florence that, behind his sister-in-law's back, Cosimo set about obtaining a description of the "most ingenious" decor and the sumptuous menu.

The Guises also hosted numerous foreigners, for Marie of Guise's high rank, combined with her years in Florence, had made her a fixture in the Italian network in Paris. For example, in 1664, when Cardinal Chigi arrived in the capital to present the Pope's formal apology for the Corsican Affair, he first paid his respects to the DOWAGER OF ORLÉANS, whose daughter had recently wed in Tuscany, and then he went to visit Mademoiselle de Guise.

Now that the Duke had wed, these formal greetings took on new importance.[26] One of the first envoys from the Italian peninsula to pay compliments to the Duke and his bride was Andrea Minerbetti, who journeyed to Paris during the summer of 1667 to present the Medicis' official congratulations on the marriage. Other envoys followed, whenever official statements of rejoicing or condolence were à propos.

A typical visit can be reconstructed from the envoys' official reports. Having been greeted by the "gentlemen of the household," the guest would mount the splendid new stairway to the parade apartment on the noble floor, between two rows of footmen and pages. There he would greet the Duke, who was usually standing. He would ask his guest to be seated while reading aloud the letters from Florence. Guise would reply to these missives "with eloquence" and with a "courteousness" that showed "great esteem" for the master and mistress back in Tuscany. On at least one occasion, Louis-Joseph de Lorraine expressed his "hope to one day be able to go to Italy." Sometimes he would escort his guest to the antechamber, where "all his court" would conduct the visitor down the great staircase to MADEMOISELLE DE GUISE's ground-floor apartment.

The guest would then be escorted to his coach by "all her people." During the envoy's stay in Paris, the Duke and his gentlemen would take the visitor around the city, and sometimes to court. Before leaving, the envoy would return to the Hôtel de Guise to take his leave.

In August 1669 Madame de Guise's brother-in-law, Cosimo III de' Medici, arrived in Paris, where he was received several times by the Guises,. He was driven to Saint-Germain-en-Laye in Louis-Joseph de Lorraine's coach pulled by "eight beautiful white horses," was entertained by a parade of the royal cavalry, and a few days later was treated to a nocturnal fête at Versailles, with music, flowing fountains, a ball, and refreshments.

Later that year, during this moment of magnificence, optimism, and blossoming at the royal court, Marc-Antoine Charpentier was invited to move into an apartment in the refurbished Hôtel de Guise. It is quite unlikely that the invitation came from the Duke or the Duchess. Rather, it would have been MADEMOISELLE MARIE THE REGENT who took the initiative, overjoyed at finding a composer who was familiar with the Italian style and had the requisite ties of loyalty to both the House of Guise and the House of Orléans. It is noteworthy that she did not set Charpentier to work composing secular music—for the sumptuous fête prompted by the Harcourt wedding of early 1671, for example. Rather, the new protégé's principal task was writing for the ducal chapel. That said, it cannot be ruled out that, had Louis-Joseph de Lorraine lived long enough to break free from his aunt's domination, Charpentier would have begun to compose for the Duke's revels.

On the Feast of Saint Augustine, August 28, 1670, a son was born to the Duke and Duchess of Guise. Christened François-Joseph de Lorraine, the infant was immediately given the title of "Duke of Alençon." So high was the Guise star rising that Jean de La Fontaine dedicated his *Fables* to Louis-Joseph de Lorraine early in 1671, pointing out that "you received my first paying of respects in such an obliging manner, that all on my own I gave myself to you, before even dedicating these works to you."[27] La Fontaine clearly was hoping to win the Guises' protection, for the health of the DOWAGER DUCHESS OF ORLÉANS, his protectress, was declining rapidly. His hopes were far from unreasonable, for this was just the sort of transfer from one branch of the House to another that had been going on for decades. Having had been one of the Dowager's gentlemen since 1664, and having written poems about young Isabelle d'Orléans and one of her *demoiselles*,[28] a bid to move to the Guise circle had every chance of being viewed favorably.

It was not to be. In May 1671 Louis-Joseph de Lorraine set off for Flanders with the King and the court. (MADAME DE GUISE remained behind, to recuperate after a miscarriage a few months earlier.) At Chantilly they were received by the Prince of Condé, who had prepared for his guests the magnificent fête during which Vatel, his maître d'hôtel, committed suicide.

At Dunkirk Guise was singled out by the French ambassador to London, Charles Colbert, or perhaps by the Duke of Monmouth himself. He and the "principal members of his household" were invited to visit Charles II and his queen.[29] The invitation should not surprise, for Charles was Madame de Guise's first cousin; but according to Mademoiselle de Montpensier, the principal reason for Louis-Joseph's visit to London was "to do like everyone else: for every young man went there."[30]

The Duke and his gentlemen—among them GAIGNIÈRES and Jean d'Alesso, a member of the TALON–Versoris–Alesso clan—lodged with the Ambassador. Charles II saw to Guise's every need personally, sending him a coach and six footmen, inviting him to dinner or to the theater, and taking him to Hampton Court on a barge that, in Guise's honor, had been furnished with "the finest furnishings belonging to the Crown. ... He was similarly entertained by the highest-ranking nobles, with all the imaginable magnificence." Charles II convinced Guise to delay his return to France for three days, "in order to entertain him with a play mingled with music and ballet, which he had prepared for him. He watched the performance from the royal box, and from Their Majesties' own bench." Louis-Joseph de Lorraine embarked for France on June 18, "marvelously satisfied with this court," and he rejoined Louis XIV and his court. Having received word of the illness and death of Louis's young son, everyone hastened back to Paris, stopping at Compiègne on July 9. Guise lodged there in a house infected with smallpox.

The Duke was back in Paris by mid-July, and by July 24 he was very ill with smallpox. He died on the morning of July 30. Gossip circulated about whether the death could have been avoided. A newsletter dispatched to Florence asserted that "most people think that the prince died because he was bled too much." Guy Patin, a physician, claimed that the Duke was not bled at all, but died as a result of some "medicines in the form of cordials and powdered pearls" given him by "a great charlatan of an apothecary," and that he had been sent to the other world by a "so-called physician who had been the chamber valet of the late Dowager of Guise," Mademoiselle de Guise's mother. Madame de Sévigné echoed Patin: Her Highness "was never willing to let him be bled. Excessive blood caused a paroxysm in the brain."[31]

Louis XIV was reported to have been deeply saddened by the loss: "The King, who was very fond of him, is extremely afflicted." He declared that mourning for Louis-Joseph de Lorraine would merge with that for his own son, and he expressed his "wish" that "the body of the Duke of Guise lie in state for forty days in his parish church, Saint-Jean-en-Grève, before being borne to his lands at Joinville in Champagne."[32]

But first, the body lay in state at the Hôtel de Guise on July 31, where it was "exposed beneath a pall garnished with embroidered crests bearing the deceased's coat of arms." The entrance courtyard of the hôtel, the vestibule just across the courtyard, and the great entry door were likewise draped in black. As night fell, the body was taken through the crowded streets to Saint-Jean-en-Grève, the parish church, "by the light of a great number of torches of white wax carried by the livery, all dressed in mourning and marching at the head of the convoy." To show their gratitude to the House of Guise for past favors, monks from the Capuchin monastery founded by the dead man's maternal great-grandfather, and monks from the MERCY marched with other clergy. Then came the body, accompanied by Equerry GAIGNIÈRES, the gentleman of the chamber, and two almoners, "in a coach of mourning pulled by six horses draped in black, surrounded by the dead prince's pages, each with a torch," and followed by coaches bearing the princesses and princes of the House of Lorraine and other great nobles. (The Duke's wife and aunt were members of the House of Lorraine; but they did not take part in the procession, for they had withdrawn to MONTMARTRE, to which the dead prince's heart was carried for burial.[33]) The deceased's gentlemen and officers brought up the rear. The body was placed in the choir of the church, under a black pall bearing his coat of arms. After the "vigils of the dead" had been said, the body was moved to the Guise chapel at Saint-Jean, until it could be taken in pomp to Joinville.

On August 22—considerably short of the forty days ordered by Louis XIV—a pontifical mass[A] was conducted at Saint-Jean-en-Grève. Bishop Malier of Tarbes officiated. (He was ÉLISABETH-MARIE MALIER's nephew, and the DOWAGER DUCHESS OF ORLÉANS' principal almoner.) At seven in the evening the coffin was placed on a hearse pulled by eight horses "draped in black, studded with crosses of Lorraine made of silver brocade," and the slow and mournful procession set off for Joinville. "The convoy marched with a silence that made this spectacle even more lugubrious."[34]

In a sense, the late Duke was present at the Hôtel de Guise throughout the year of mourning that followed. Not until the End of the Year Service, bout de l'an, did a dead person cease hovering over the family and the household, not only as a memory but as a devotional force.

[A] Cahier 3, H 2.

Homme en grand deüil.

Ce jeune-homme habillé de deüil,   *Son Épouse n'est pas si tost dans le Cercüeil,*
Brûle d'vne nouvelle flame :   *Qu'il cherche ailleurs vne autre feme.*

A man in deep mourning.

The entire household, from the grieving family down to its pages and scullions,
would wear mourning robes supplied by the master or mistress. The higher the mourner's
rank, the longer the train. A princess of Madame de Guise's rank would wear a robe with
a ten-foot train, carried by a page or a gentleman. During mourning the gentlemen and
principal officers in a great household would drag one- or two-foot trains behind them.
The mourner in this print is already thinking of a new wife:
Ce jeune-homme habillé de deuil, Brûle d'une nouvelle flame: Son Épouse
n'est pas si tost dans le Cercueil, Qu'il cherche ailleurs une autre femme.

During that year of mourning the Duke's widow and his aunt would create devotions in his memory. One of them was at the MERCY chapel just across the street from the entry door of the Hôtel de Guise. Then, as the first anniversary of the Duke's death approached, the two princesses once again withdrew to MONTMARTRE, where on July 29, 1672, MADAME DE GUISE was "present for her funereal duties," the service known as the "vigils of the dead."[A] The following day

> they celebrated the End of the Year of the Duke of Guise in the abbey church of Montmartre, with all possible pomp, the Bishop of Autun [Gabriel de Roquette] having officiated pontifically, in the presence of the princes and princesses of the House, several bishops, and other persons of the highest rank.[35]

This "pomp" presumably included music by Marc-Antoine Charpentier—almost certainly his setting of the "prose for the dead,"[B] an integral part of the requiem mass, and perhaps a repeat of the funeral mass[C] he had composed in 1671 for the service at Saint-Jean-en-Grève.

A hint of what this End of the Year Service might have been like has been preserved. To mark the end of the year of mourning for his brother, Étienne Moulinié, household composer to GASTON D'ORLÉANS, prepared "a beautiful musical service" in which, "several famous voices" were heard. "In this great musical concert more than twenty excellent singers put their talents to use, along with four female voices that were deemed almost divine."[36] The service in question doubtlessly was a simplified version of the End of the Year that Moulinié composed and directed for Gaston in 1662. Any service organized by MADAME DE GUISE presumably resembled the one that Moulinié had prepared for his brother, but on a far grander scale.

Isabelle d'Orléans, Duchess of Guise.
"Second daughter of the late Gaston-Jean-Baptiste of France, Duke of Orléans,
and Marguerite de Lorraine, sister of Charles, Duke of Lorraine.
Born December 6 [sic], 1646, on May 15, 1667, she married Louis-Joseph
de Lorraine, Duke of Guise, Joyeuse, and Angoulême, who died on July 30, 1671.
By him she had a son, born on August 28, 1670, named François-Joseph
de Lorraine, Duke of Alençon, Guise, Joyeuse, and Angoulême, peer of France,
Prince of Joinville, Count of Alais and Ponthieu, who died on March 16, 1675."

V

The King is the master of everything that lies within my control

MADAME DE GUISE

Isabelle d'Orléans, wife and widow of the last Duke of Guise,
earlier known as "Mademoiselle d'Alençon"

On the morning of July 30, 1671, "with extreme regrets and lamenting by his consort and his aunt," LOUIS-JOSEPH DE LORRAINE, DUKE OF GUISE, succumbed to smallpox amid the splendor of the refurbished Hôtel de Guise. Isabelle d'Orléans, his widow, and MADEMOISELLE DE GUISE, his aunt, immediately withdrew to the ABBEY OF MONTMARTRE for the customary forty days, leaving the Duke's year-old son and heir, the Duke of Alençon, shut up in his quarters while the residence was purified by smoke. Consequently, neither woman would be present on August 22 for the pontifical mass for the dead[A] that preceded the body's removal to the Guise necropolis at Joinville. Devoured with resentment at the Guises' alleged opposition to her marriage to Lauzun, MADEMOISELLE DE MONTPENSIER sent condolences but refused to come and sprinkle the Duke's body with holy water.[1]

MADEMOISELLE DE GUISE and Isabelle were present when the Duke's heart was brought to Montmartre, a ceremony that presumably coincided with the transfer of his body from Hôtel de Guise to the Church of Saint-Jean-en-Grève, where it would lie in state for several weeks in anticipation of the requiem mass at Saint-Jean and the departure of the funeral convoy for Joinville. It almost certainly was Mademoiselle de Guise who wanted his heart at Montmartre, as a way of keeping a part of her nephew near her, rather than in far-off Joinville. During the summer of 1671 Madame de Guise was therefore in the process of creating a closer tie to the abbey than she might otherwise have envisaged.

[A] Cahier 3, H. 2, H. 234.

Mourning for Madame de Guise and her household of forty-five domestics cost thirty thousand livres.[2]

The two princesses were "touched to such a degree that one cannot console them, their loss bringing tears to everyone's eyes"; yet they spent those weeks at Montmartre fighting over little Alençon's guardianship. At twenty-four years and eight months, Isabelle d'Orléans was a few months short of legal majority. The child's guardianship had to be given to someone else. When MADEMOISELLE DE GUISE claimed that right, the widow pulled rank. She argued that Mademoiselle de Guise was behaving as if she were the equal of a granddaughter of France, but that it was impossible to weigh a person of Madame de Guise's blood against someone of Mademoiselle de Guise's rank. Had she, Isabelle, not honored the House of Guise by agreeing to wed the late Duke, her social inferior?[3]

Madame de Guise attempted to talk with Jean-Baptiste Colbert face to face, but either he was not available or she dared not see him for fear of breaking down:

> I beg you, Monsieur, to look over the attached memorandum and support my reasoning before the King. I got myself all ready to go to your home to tell you [my reasons], but I couldn't see you. Your affectionate Friend, *Isabelle d'Orléans*[4]

In mid-September, she had a long talk with Louis XIV and told him that as long as she had a separate apartment, she believed she would be able to tolerate living at the Hôtel de Guise. But Mademoiselle de Guise must not be allowed to foment intrigues about little Alençon, and she must give an accounting of the huge debts she claimed to have incurred while acting as the late Duke's guardian.[5]

Suddenly, the tone of the women's correspondence with Colbert changed—and for a reason the princesses apparently did not share with the Minister but which he could probably guess. If any formal demand for a financial accounting was made, or if she was "molested" in any way, Mademoiselle de Guise threatened to "make public her secret marriage contracted with the late Montrésor, by whom she had children nursed and raised in Holland." Were she to recognize these children, Alençon and his mother would be deprived of the one hundred twenty thousand livres produced annually by her estates. Thus it was promptly decided that Mademoiselle de Guise "should be given a say in the child's guardianship," and that the widow would receive a financially "decorous treatment," in return for her compliance.[6]

To this end, Isabelle d'Orléans surrendered all the property she had owned jointly with her late husband, and she signed a written statement that she would be satisfied simply to take back her dowry and surrender rights granted her by her wedding contract (a dower of forty thousand livres per year, the right to reside in one of the Guise châteaux, and similar arrangements). She retained the right to have the duchy of Guise transmitted to her son.[7] Conveniently, this surrender of her rights to Guise property would be signed shortly after her own mother's death. This renouncement therefore was mitigated by the fact that, in the interim, she had reached the age of majority and had inherited half the Luxembourg Palace, which liberated her from MADEMOISELLE DE GUISE's domination.

Although still in mourning, Isabelle d'Orléans became the subject of rumors. Would she wed her recently widowed first cousin, PHILIPPE II D'ORLÉANS? When Philippe invited her to festivities honoring their English cousin, the Duke of York, gossip sprung up about a match between Isabelle and the exiled heir to the English throne.[8]

If match-making was in fact going on, it ended abruptly in early April 1672, when the DOWAGER DUCHESS OF ORLÉANS succumbed to a stroke. Both Guise princesses once again withdrew to MONTMARTRE for the customary forty days of mourning. They were at the abbey for Tenebrae services, for which Charpentier composed a *Jerusalem*.[A]

Several services for the dead were held for the Dowager that month, for her heart was taken to Montmartre, her entrails to the convent of Charonne, and her body to the royal necropolis at Saint-Denis. Still more majestic services were held in mid-May, including her actual burial at Saint-Denis. For some of these events, music composed for the late Duke probably was reused; but that spring saw Charpentier writing additional funeral music—music that would be suitable for the Duke's approaching End of the Year Service as well as for services being planned for the Dowager.[B] This corpus of music to commemorate the dead would constitute the raw materials for the annual memorial services that were "sung" at Charonne every March and April for Madame de Guise's late parents, the DOWAGER DUCHESS OF ORLÉANS and GASTON D'ORLÉANS.

Mourning, punctuated by disputes over who would raise the last male of the House of Guise, had kept the two princesses from thinking about any music but funeral music. It being a great noble's duty to keep domestics and protégés active, lest they be tempted by pleasures of the flesh, the distraught women either pressured MOLIÈRE to engage Charpentier for revivals of *La Comtesse d'Escarbagnas* and *Le Mariage forcé*, scheduled for July 1672, or else they replied in the affirmative when

---

[A] Cahier 2, H. 94 (and probable reuse of cahier 1, H. 91–92).
[B] Cahier 3, H. 2, H. 234; cahier 4, H. 311, H. 156; cahier 5, H. 12.

François-Joseph de Lorraine, Duke of Alençon, in 1674.
This portrait was "offered" to the four-year-old prince and
his mother by Ranagny, "a faithful domestic."

Molière begged their permission to let the composer try his hand at theatrical music. That fall—for reasons that remain mysterious in two such unworldly women—the princesses descended upon the playwright like so many irritated "virgins," "heroines," and "goddesses," pressuring him to snatch from DASSOUCY the commission for *Le Malade imaginaire*, and give it to Charpentier. Were they motivated in part by annoyance with Lully, that former Guise–Orléans protégé who had had the temerity to snatch the opera privilege from Pierre Perrin, GASTON D'ORLÉANS' former householder? It surely cannot be ruled out, for Madame de Guise was protecting Perrin and had paid his debts only a few months earlier.

While still in mourning for her husband and her mother, Isabelle d'Orléans set about creating a place for herself at court, acting as the de facto Regent for her son, the better to ensure that his interests would be protected. She marched in the Corpus Christi procession at Versailles on June 16, 1672,[9] and she appears to have wheedled from the King a commission for Charpentier to compose some instrumental music[A] for the temporary altar, *reposoir*, to which the procession wended its way that day. In short, the advantages of a shared protection of Monsieur Charpentier were becoming evident to her. The composer would stay on at the Hôtel de Guise, but she could request music for herself or her friends, to be performed at venues of her choice. MADEMOISELLE DE GUISE apparently was perfectly content to share the composer in this way; and as the GUISE MUSIC gradually developed, she shared the musicians too.

In September 1672, just two months after her husband's End of the Year Service at MONTMARTRE, which marked the end of mourning, Isabelle d'Orléans engaged architect Jacques Gabriel to design and build an elegant pavilion and chapel on a piece of land the King had given her near the château of Versailles. It would cost forty-three thousand livres, and it must be ready for occupancy within two months. That same fall, work was also being done on a private apartment for her at MONT-MARTRE, where she could retreat each year on the anniversaries of her husband's and mother's deaths.

Towing little Alençon's nanny goat behind in its special cart, mother and son began going back and forth between the new house at Versailles and the Luxembourg Palace, into which she and her householders had moved in April 1673.[10] Saint-Sulpice being the parish church for the Luxembourg, it is likely that Madame de Guise had something to do with the privileged altar for the dead created there by a papal bull dated March 7, 1673, and located in the chapel of the Virgin.[11]

[A] Cahier XI, H. 515.

Although Isabelle d'Orléans was reaching a modus vivendi with MADEMOISELLE DE GUISE, all was not roses. For example, in May 1673 the young widow came up with a project that could not fail to wound. She began talking about selling part of the Hôtel de Guise and building several small houses in part of the new Le Nôtre gardens. Worse, she went so far as to commission plans that would have destroyed many of Mademoiselle de Guise's innovations and decorations.[12] The project was never carried out, perhaps because it coincided with Isabelle d'Orléans' move to the Luxembourg, where—for the "little" Corpus Christi procession[A] of June 8, 1673—she proclaimed her presence by preparing a temporary altar, *reposoir*, beneath the domed entryway:

> Madame de Guise ... received the procession of Saint-Sulpice
> beneath the dome of her palace, where she had ordered a
> magnificent altar prepared, with an excellent instrumental concert,
> and voices, after which this princess accompanied the procession to
> the parish church, where she attended the entire service.[13]

This *reposoir* was not an innovation. Rather, she was continuing one of the practices of her late mother, at whose side Princess Isabelle used to greet the procession.

Splendid though her apartment at the Luxembourg was, it came with a built-in problem: MADEMOISELLE DE MONTPENSIER, her half-sister, occupied the other half. The feuding sisters eventually found a way to avoid seeing one another. They had a wall built through the middle of the palace gardens.[14]

Although she now lived on the other side of the city and was often at court, Isabelle d'Orléans did not turn her back upon the Church of the MERCY, which had already been something of an extension of the Hôtel de Guise when she married the Duke. In April 1674 she was at MADEMOISELLE DE GUISE's side during a service there, basking in the cleverness of Charpentier's instrumental mass[B] that imitated the organ whose delivery had been delayed. In fact, Madame de Guise remained in Paris longer than usual that spring, to enjoy the pageantry of the week-long canonization festivities organized by the Mercedarian fathers.

On the other hand, there is no evidence that Isabelle d'Orléans publicly lent her prestige to Charpentier and the Guénégaud Troop—for example, by attending the revival of *Le Malade imaginaire* on May 4, 1674, which featured the stripped-down musical interludes imposed by Lully. Nor, during Charpentier's lengthy collaboration with THOMAS

[A] Cahier 7, H. 508 (and perhaps cahier 5, H. 235, reused).
[B] Cahiers 7–8, H. 513.

CORNEILLE and JEAN DONNEAU DE VISÉ, does she appear to have made even one special trip to Paris to see the plays for which Charpentier was composing instrumental music. Rather, it was her cousin, PHILIPPE II D'ORLÉANS, who made an occasional public gesture of solidarity.

March 16, 1675, brought tragedy. The four-year-old Duke of Alençon was dropped by his nursemaid, hit his head, and soon became feverish. "He was a very unhealthy child, who could not stand at six [sic] years. They were often worried about his health."[15] Having weighed with DOCTOR VALLANT the merits of bleeding and purging, the two princesses told the physician that he "should do what [he] deemed appropriate, and that they were turning the child over to him." Throughout the night the women hovered in the background, and Vallant would go off into a corner to discuss the case with the two men on whom Mademoiselle de Guise was leaning in this time of trouble: GOIBAUT DU BOIS and BISHOP ROQUETTE OF AUTUN.

The child died at dawn, in his little canopy bed with white curtains. Three days later his body was taken by night to Montmartre and, if his funeral resembled that of other princes of his day, was buried the next day in a white-draped church.[16] Circé had just opened, but Charpentier managed to write a Languentibus in purgatorio for three voices.[17]

MADEMOISELLE DE GUISE was accused of having spent part of the stay at Montmartre weeping, and part of it plotting and urging Isabelle d'Orléans to "give up a lot of things she was supposed to receive from her son's estate, in return for very little money."[18] It is not clear from the surviving sources whether she did in fact take advantage of Madame de Guise; but the estate was settled with an astonishing rapidity. Once again, Mademoiselle de Guise had threatened to recognize her children by Montrésor.

As her intestate son's sole heir, Isabelle d'Orléans was in a position to lay claim to Guise property; but she and her advisers were primarily worried about Mademoiselle de Guise's children. Madame de Guise therefore agreed to cede to Mademoiselle de Guise all her rights to the succession—a decision that met with "the great satisfaction of Mademoiselle de Guise and MADAME DE MONTMARTRE." Three weeks after the child's funeral, while the two women were still in retreat at the abbey, MADEMOISELLE MARIE, THE LAST GUISE, paid Isabelle d'Orléans sixty-six thousand livres, in return for which Her Royal Highness surrendered her rights to the property that Alençon had inherited from his father. (The cost of Mademoiselle de Guise's silence amounted to only sixty-five percent of the 102,207 livres that Her Highness had paid to renovate the Hôtel de Guise a decade earlier.) Madame de Guise would never lack money, for Louis XIV had granted her the revenues from some of the non-Guise properties that had been held by her husband and son.[19]

From spite, or from joy over her independence, Madame de Guise promptly began to dismiss some of the protégés who had been imposed upon her at the time of her marriage.[20] That Charpentier remained at the Hôtel de Guise while working part time for Isabelle d'Orléans over the next decade, suggests that it was MARIE THE REGENT who had selected him in the first place, and that it was primarily she who felt responsible for him. Even so, now that she was distancing herself from the Hôtel de Guise and its occupants, Her Royal Highness felt a certain responsibility for his well-being. She had been watching out for her late father's domestics[21]; and the composer's cousin, HAVÉ DE SAINT-AUBIN, had, after all, been one of GASTON D'ORLÉANS' householders.

Like Mademoiselle de Guise across the Seine, Isabelle d'Orléans therefore cast about for musical projects that would keep the composer busy and at the same time demonstrate her commitment to him. She began with music for her devotions[A]; and she got PHILIPPE II D'ORLÉANS to agree to let Charpentier contribute to a baptismal fête at Saint-Cloud.[B] As the decade ended, she convinced the King to allow this protégé to compose something for the Dauphin[C]; and finally, in the 1680s she finagled the court performance of some of Charpentier's little "operas."[D]

This, at any rate, is the tableau that emerges from Charpentier's autograph manuscripts, and from events in Her Royal Highness's life. The tableau starts in the first half of 1675, when the two Guise princesses were mourning and sparring. During those months, Marc-Antoine Charpentier added nothing to his arabic-numbered notebooks, save for the lost piece about Purgatory written for the Duke of Alençon's funeral. The absence of music does not mean that the princesses were idle. They were deeply involved in creating two educational institutions that were memorials to little Alençon. Both establishments were dedicated to the INFANT JESUS.

Extending the protective role of the Christ Child still further, Isabelle d'Orléans approached the THEATINE fathers of Sainte-Anne-la-Royale, who agreed that she could embellish a chapel, with the understanding that it would be connected to a special "devotion" of hers. There was a sense of urgency about the arrangements, not only owing to the imminent return to France of her sister, MADAME DE TOSCANE, but be-

---

[A] Starting with cahiers 9–11, H. 391.
[B] Cahier 13, H. 479.
[C] Cahier 22, H. 170.
[D] Cahier 37, H. 480.

cause the unspecified "devotion" clearly involved Italianate oratorios,[A] and the first one was scheduled for the final week of September 1675.

Although the themes of some of these "sacred stories" are so general as to make them appropriate for all manner of religious services (the Virgin talks with men, or Christ talks with sinners), the texts of most of them not only mirror Madame de Guise's devotions, they change as her focus changed. "Strong women" such as Judith and Esther give way to Charles Borromeo the charitable. Honored year after year are the Infant Jesus and Saint Cecilia the converter. That the texts of these oratorios were in Latin, rather than in the vernacular, indicates that the works were intended for the elite. In fact, the choice of this language points to Isabelle d'Orléans, who had studied Latin as a girl. The first of these oratorios, *Judith sive Bethulia*, dates from late September 1675. After 1680 this genre became infrequent in Charpentier's arabic-numbered notebooks; and between 1684 and late 1687 he copied no oratorios at all into the notebooks of this series that contains his music for the two Guise princesses.

Our modern perspective tempts us to question whether a princess of Madame de Guise's rank and religious education would really turn to saints and seek guidance from parallels with Biblical figures. There is considerable evidence that this particular royal princess did indeed think this way. For example, shortly before her son's death, or perhaps shortly after it, she commissioned two nearly life-size paintings that drew an explicit parallel between religious imagery and the roles being played by people dear to her. One represented a "Saint Michael that is the portrait of the King with a dragon under his feet," the dragon of Heresy. The other painting depicted "the Guardian Angel who leads a child by the hand, which are the portraits of Monsieur de Guise and Monsieur d'Alençon."[22] She also relied on relics and the intervention of saints. While in labor, she wore a relic of Saint Marguerite, the patron saint of pregnant women.[23] And when she was ill during the summer of 1677 with the chills and fevers of malaria, she prayed to Saint Genevieve, who had miraculously cured people who were burning and shivering from rye ergotism. Although no allusion to a bout of fever during the summer of 1676 has been found, Isabelle d'Orléans had apparently begged the saint's intervention that summer, and Charpentier was ordered to set a text

---

[A] Categorized as "*histoires sacrées*" by Hitchcock: *1675*: cahiers 9–11, H. 391; *1676*: cahier 11, H. 392; cahier 12, H. 393; cahier 13, H. 394; *1677*: cahier 14, H. 395; cahiers 17–18, H. 396; cahiers 19–20, H. 397; *1680*: cahiers 23–24, H. 398; cahier 29, H. 399; cahiers 29–30, H. 400; cahiers 30–31, H. 401; *1683*: cahier 37, H. 407; *1684*: cahiers 42–43, H. 413, H. 414. *1685*: cahier 47, H. 415.

honoring Saint Genevieve.[A] The text—which uses the first person, as grandchildren of France tended to do when addressing a saint—begs her to protect "me" from "future infirmity," and alludes to a "flaming" and "ardent" love for Jesus. This suggests that the piece was written for November 26, the Feast of Saint Genevieve of the Ardent.

Devotions were a major element in the Guise women's almost frenetic activity during 1675; but founding educational institutions and obtaining and decorating chapels served another purpose. It provided an excuse for staying away from the Luxembourg—and the bedroom where little Alençon had died. When Isabelle d'Orléans left the seclusion of Montmartre late in the summer of 1675, "there were tears upon returning to the Luxembourg." Mademoiselle de Guise also stayed away: "She came only once that year [1675], when [Madame de Guise] was ill."[24] Memories of the little boy's final hours were so painful that Isabelle d'Orléans contemplated selling her half of the palace. She never implemented the plan, for Louis XIV opposed the sale and asserted that he wished to remain "master" of the Luxembourg. At the news, she exclaimed, "What! Force me to live against my will in the house where my son died!" In October she capitulated and informed Louis XIV that "the King is master not only of the house, but of everything that lies within my control."[25] This renunciation of her own wishes in favor of the wishes of the God-Given, her cousin, coincides with the first of Charpentier's oratorios about "strong women"[B] who make themselves the instruments of divine will.

Being God's instrument did not mean that Madame de Guise was always able to hold her tongue. During her visits to MONTMARTRE, she could not refrain from backbiting. The Abbess would scold her about her behavior toward MADAME DE TOSCANE, and about the way she encouraged her sister to overstep the limits that had been set by the King. The sisters frequently exchanged "pungent words"; and matters were even worse when MADEMOISELLE DE MONTPENSIER put in an appearance. "They are happier to say goodbye than to say hello. ... We know from experience that they are incapable of remaining on good terms for very long, and it is no small thing that each of them tries to keep up appearances, without asking for more." Isabelle d'Orléans did try to be amiable, and she visited her isolated sister more often than she really wanted to: "Madame de Guise could not keep from showing the vexation and

---

[A] Cahier 13, H. 317.
[B] Cahiers 9–11, H. 391, late September 1675 (when Mme. de Guise was in Paris).

boredom she feels at having to go and stay at Montmartre, out of compassion for her sister."[26]

Nor did being God's instrument exempt even the most pious granddaughter of France from attending to her worldly obligations and insisting upon the respect due a person of her rank. For example, although it was her intention to spend most of her time at Alençon, doing good deeds or carrying out devotional activities, Isabelle d'Orléans made the requisite triumphal entry into the city in September 1676. The Duchess was greeted with bells, artillery, and a *Te Deum*.[27] Like QUEEN MARIE-THÉRÈSE, she prayed for hours on end in her private apartment. Her piety did not go unnoticed: "Madame de Guise continues in her great devotion. She loses no chance to do good, and she takes pleasure in being agreeable, and in seeing to her household affairs."[28]

Her devotions finished, like her friend the Queen she played the public role expected of a princess of the blood: she visited convents, especially the LITTLE CARMEL, where she and the Queen often dined and prayed together; she stood at the Monarch's side at numerous state events; and she offered secular musical gifts to the King and his court[A] —and, on at least one occasion, to PHILIPPE II D'ORLÉANS[B] and his court. During the late 1670s and early 1680s she planned courtly entertainments in Paris for MADAME DE TOSCANE. There would be music, and the ladies would gamble, their losses going to charity.[29] Some of these entertainments doubtlessly were repeated at MONTMARTRE, where the Grand Duchess had a little court all her own, and at the Hôtel de Guise as well.

By late 1675 Madame de Guise had established the devotional program she would follow for two decades—a program that for the next ten years would form a conspicuous vein in Marc-Antoine Charpentier's arabic-numbered notebooks. The first devotion was to the INFANT JESUS, a devotion she shared with MADEMOISELLE DE GUISE. In the composer's arabic-numbered notebooks, the year 1676 marks the creation of a small corpus of works for the principal holy days of the Christ Child: Christmas, Circumcision, and Epiphany[C]—plus some Litanies of Loreto[D] and diverse works for the feasts of the Virgin.

Closely linked to this devotion for the Infant Jesus was the one that honored Louis XIV the God-Given, whose divinity had been prefigured

---

[A] Cahier 37, H. 480, October or November 1682, for the "Fête of the Apartments"; cahier 44, H. 486, circa April 13, 1685, when the "apartments" ended for the year and Mme. de Guise left for Alençon.
[B] Cahier 13, H. 479, October 5, 1676, for the Duke of Chartres' baptism.
[C] Cahier 12, H 393; cahier 13, H. 316; cahier 14, H. 395, H. 318.
[D] Cahier 33, H. 82; cahiers 41–42, H. 83 (for the Great Guise Music).

by the Infant Jesus. Her cousin's well-being was a central point of Isa-belle's devotions. Although the venues for Marc-Antoine Charpentier's music have not always been identified—they probably were multiple, a given work being performed for both Mademoiselle de Guise and Madame de Guise—his arabic-numbered notebooks contain several musical prayers for the King and the royal family. In addition to a few *Domine salvum fac regem*'s whose use was too general to be discriminative, there is a "song for peace" and its *élévation*,[A] written at the start of peace negotiations with Holland in early 1676; prayers for the KING and the DAUPHIN[B] during the universal prayers and Jubilee of March 1677; pieces that coincide with negotiations and signatures of peace treaties, specifi-cally a work for the Treaty of Nimwegen, May to September 1678 (reused[30] late in 1678 or early in 1679 for the treaty with Spain); an *Exaudiat*[C] written "for Versailles"[31] in the fall of 1681; pieces for the Feast of Saint Louis,[D] August 25; and works that celebrate the recoveries of the DAUPHIN and of the KING[E] or that lament the QUEEN's death.[F] There is also an oratorio in honor of Saint Michael the crusher of Heresy[G] that Charpentier copied into a roman-numbered notebook in 1683. It is not clear who commissioned this "extraordinary" oratorio, but there is pre-sumably a relationship between it and the painting of Louis XIV as Saint Michael that Madame de Guise had commissioned a few years earlier.

A third element in Isabelle d'Orléans' devotional program involved the conversion of Protestants. Over the years, Charpentier composed a number of works for the Feast of Saint Cecilia,[H] November 22. Celebrat-ing this saint's feast day to music was scarcely an innovation for this granddaughter of France. In fact, Isabelle d'Orléans may have been present on November 22, 1663, when her new friend, Queen Marie-Thérèse, and her entourage attended vespers "sung by four choirs of the finest voices from the King's Music, with four [choirs] of instruments, among them the twenty-four violins [of the King], composed in its entirety by the music master of the Queen Mother, who was very satisfied with it, as was the whole company."[32]

[A] Cahiers 11-12, H. 392, H. 237.
[B] Cahiers 14-15, H. 164, H. 165, H. 166; cahier 20, H. 168; cahier 33, H. 180.
[C] Cahier 33, H. 180.
[D] Cahier 17, H. 320; cahier 22, H. 323 (for CHARLES LE BRUN, 1679); cahier 37, H. 332 (part of a diptych with a lament for the Queen, August 1683).
[E] Cahiers 31-32, H. 26 (for Dauphin's Music); cahiers 49-50, H. 489; cahier 50, H. 431 (for the Dauphin's Music).
[F] Cahier 38, H. 331 (and H. 332, for Saint Louis).
[G] Cahier XXXIX, H. 360.
[H] Cahier 13, H. 394; cahiers 19-20, H. 397; cahier 42, H. 413; cahier 47, H. 415; cahier XLIX, H. 415a (prologue: commissioned by M. DU BOIS?).

Rather, it is the Saint Cecilia portrayed in Charpentier's oratorios who is innovative, compared to her image in surviving seventeenth-century French musical works, paintings, and devotional poems. In each of Charpentier's oratorios the text depicts Cecilia as converting, by gentle reasoning, first her pagan husband and then her brother-in-law. This was the position being argued by ARCHIBISHOP HARLAY, BISHOP ROQUETTE, and MONSIEUR DU BOIS; and this is the position that Isabelle d'Orléans took in November 1676 at the JESUIT NOVICIATE, when a Huguenot woman abjured Protestantism "between the hands of Father de La Barre, in the presence of Madame de Guise, who by the King's orders had given her shelter in her palace, ... where she received instruction for several days." Note the emphasis on the "King's orders." Isabelle was her cousin's instrument; and, as she had so recently declared, Louis XIV was the "master" of everything she did. There was an additional reason to celebrate that November day. That same week, Madame de Guise and some ladies at Alençon had received authorization to open a house for women converts.[33] Charpentier's subsequent oratorios for Saint Cecilia—written in 1677 (when Madame de Guise's house for new converts was blessed by the Bishop of Sées[34]), 1684, and 1685 (the Revocation of the Edict of Nantes)—reflect Isabelle d'Orléans' fervent converting, especially at Alençon. By December 1685 it was possible to assert that "all Alençon is now Catholic."[35] The latter statement was, however, made in a context of forceful conversions that ran counter to the position that both Guises had espoused until then.

The fourth element in her devotional program began to emerge in 1676, when Isabelle d'Alençon embarked on a whirl of charitable activities involving both Paris and Alençon, where she had founded a house for the Daughters of Charity. Profoundly committed to addressing the problem of poverty in Paris, by 1678 she had been made the "Superior" for the charitable activities in her parish of Saint-Sulpice. There she worked closely with MARIE TALON's brother.[36] All across Paris, devout women and men were joining sodalities whose mission was to feed the poor and tend the sick and the prisoners. Two of the most active of these new organizations were the Confraternity for the Dying (created at the MERCY in 1673, thanks to MADEMOISELLE DE GUISE's efforts) and the Confraternity of Saint Charles Borromeo,[A] which had a sodality at the THEATINES, where Madame de Guise had been given a chapel in 1675. Each Wednesday—often after a noontime meal and musical entertainment at the Hôtel de Guise—Isabelle d'Orléans would set off for the

[A] Cahiers 23–24, H. 398.

"assembly for the poor," to which she contributed food and medicines. Sometimes she and MADAME DE TOSCANE would go out beyond the Saint-Martin Gate, to a "retreat" run by the Daughters of Charity directed by Madame de Miramion. There, in a large house that resembled a convent, many women resided, feeding and nursing the poor. Madame de Guise was deeply involved in the administration this house, and here too she worked closely with an old Charpentier friend, MARIE TALON.[37] She carried on similar activities at Alençon.[38]

In March 1678 her enthusiasm for these charitable activities prompted her to ask her Tuscan brother-in-law, Grand Duke Cosimo III, to "contribute" to her projects to help the sick. Convinced of his eagerness to help the poor of Paris, she requested a shipment of Italian medicines for stomach problems, feverish colic, and nerves—and also some theriaca, an antidote for poisons. When she received no answer, she wrote him personally. A few weeks later she asked whether she might have some gloves and some Florentine silk, in addition to the medications. (She loved to be surprised by "presents," often requested in this way rather than coming as surprise gifts. When informed that a shipment had arrived, she would react "with great gusto and with unconcealed happiness.") The case of medicines finally arrived in July.[39]

It was not mysticism that prompted Isabelle d'Orléans to embark on these four devotional programs. Rather, she had pondered these matters carefully and had sought guidance from books and from her spiritual advisors. As MONSIEUR DU BOIS put it, she had "long been nourished in the sacred truths of religion and was accustomed to dip these truths from their sources."[40] Some of these "sources" can be identified. At the time of her death, her chapel at the Luxembourg Palace contained one hundred forty-six devotional books, including several missals and De Sacy's translation of the Bible (Although her ownership of this great Port-Royal translation does not prove that she actually read it, it suggests an interest in sustaining faith by history.) In addition to several translations by Du Bois himself, she owned the sermons of Saint Gregory the Great, Saint John Chrysostom, and Saint Bernard; the lives of Saint Eudes, Saint Francis Borgia, Saint Louis, Saint Basil, Saint Gregory of Naziane, and Saint Philip Neri; the letters of Saint Jerome, Saint Bernard, and Le Maistre de Sacy. Neri's presence in this library reveals that, like MADEMOISELLE MAIRE DE GUISE, Isabelle d'Orléans was acquainted with the oratory movement, and consequently with the oratorios that were a part of Neri's devotions. It is, however, impossible to say whether this interest predated 1675 and Charpentier's first oratorio.

Her preoccupation with the monastic life is suggested by the presence of Saint Bernard's "duties of the monastic life" and Mabillon's treatise on "monastic studies." Through her copy of the "lives of the saints of Port-Royal," and her "fourteen volumes containing diverse treatises against the Jesuits," she kept informed about the Jansenist–Jesuit conflict. Especially revealing is the title of one manuscript volume: "Saintly and Christian prayers drawn from the Scripture and the Church Fathers, to ask God for the grace to faithfully accomplish all the duties of Christianity."[41] Although described as "prayers," the title of this volume suggests that it contained the sort of Oratorian–Sulpician *élévations* that had been part of her religious education as a child.

These devotions had to be conducted concurrently with her social responsibilities at court, where she had embarked on what appears to have been a conscious program to promote Marc-Antoine Charpentier. Each year during his approximately four years of service to the DAUPHIN, Madame de Guise would neglect Paris from early November to early May, and spend the time at her cousin's court. She was there in the spring of 1679, when Charpentier wrote his first piece for the Dauphin's Music.[A] She was there in the fall of 1679, when the POISON INVESTIGATORS were scrutinizing people in high positions. In February and March of 1680, she was part of the delegation that went to fetch the Dauphine at Châlons and witnessed her wedding to the Dauphin. She returned from Alençon in November 1680, just in time to rejoice over the Dauphin's recovery[B] from malaria. She was likewise at court during the final weeks of 1681, when Landry's Almanac depicted "Monsieur Charpentier" offering her his *Menuet de Strasbourg*[42]; and she also was there for New Year's Day 1682, when the Dauphin was admitted to the Order of the Holy Spirit. She remained at court that year in order to be present for the birth of the Dauphin's son in August, and then she hastened to Paris to celebrate the event at the Luxembourg with fireworks, wine, and music.[43] And she was at court in October of that year, when Louis XIV invented the "Fête of the Apartments."[C]

This pattern changed rather abruptly in the spring of 1683, just as Charpentier ceased composing for the DAUPHIN and was rewarded with the pension that became official in June. Having supported the composer morally by being present when his works were performed, it is as if Isabelle d'Orléans concluded that it was time for him to leave the nest. As a sign of their willingness to see their protégé take flight after some thirteen years in their service, she and Mademoiselle de Guise had authorized him to participate in a competition for a sub-mastership in the

---

[A] Cahier 22, H. 170 (which slightly antedates cahier XXV, H. 174).
[B] Cahier 31, H. 326 (for the Dauphin's Music).
[C] Cahier 37, H. 480.

royal chapel. (He would scarcely have dared take such a step without their permission.) In late May 1683, Madame de Guise set off for Alençon —just when Charpentier fell ill and withdrew from the competition.

Judging from the composer's arabic-numbered notebooks, he wrote little for Madame de Guise after that, although she seems to have lent moral support to some opera-like entertainments that Charpentier wrote for court performances[A] by the Great Guise Music in 1685 and 1686. That is to say, it is not clear how much of a role Isabelle d'Orléans played in twitting Lully's privilege, and how much was the DAUPHIN's idea.

On the other hand, it almost certainly was the princess who ordered Charpentier to set to music Madame Deshoulières' "Idyl on the Return of the King's Health"[44] for a fête[B] she was planning at the Luxembourg for January 30, 1687, to celebrate Louis XIV's recovery from surgery. The poem, which had been published in the *Mercure galant* the previous September, had apparently been written in early 1686, when the King was feigning recovery from the anal fistula that would eventually put him under the surgeon's knife. "The verse ... is not new," the editors had confessed. "It was written for the King's recovery after the disease of which His Majesty was healed, prior to the fever he experienced." (Louis' malarial fever began in early August 1686 and was cured by a dose of quinine around August 15.) In short, the text predates Charpentier's "Idyl" by approximately a year.

The poem—with its allusions to the gilded wainscoting, the fountains of wine, the fireworks, and the illuminations of the palace exterior— evoked just the sort of public display the two Guise women were wont to organize for celebrations honoring the royal family. It is highly unlikely that the poem was appropriated without the poetess's permission. Rather, as courtly etiquette obliged, Madame de Guise presumably had someone inform Madame Deshoulières of her "desire," her "pleasure," to have Monsieur Charpentier put these words to music; and the poetess in turn would have thanked Her Royal Highness for the great honor being paid her. It is highly unlikely that Marc-Antoine Charpentier would have presumed to approach Deshoulières with such a request on his own authority, even though he and the poetess had a friend in common, THOMAS CORNEILLE. He could, of course, have been delegated to be the princess's spokesman.

Isabelle d'Orléans' prestige, and her longstanding link to the Carmelite house known as the LITTLE CARMEL presumably were a factor

---

[A] Cahiers 44-45, H. 486; cahier "II," H. 488.
[B] Cahiers 49-50, H. 489.

in the nuns' decision to ask Charpentier to compose for a memorial service for the QUEEN.[A] (He presumably sought Mademoiselle de Guise's permission before accepting the commission.) Madame de Guise left Alençon briefly in mid-August,[45] returning to Paris for a service in the Queen's memory.[B] Since Isabelle d'Orléans had been absent all summer, that particular service almost certainly was organized by MADEMOISELLE DE GUISE. Returning to Alençon for another month, Madame de Guise was back at court the following October, just when the Marquis of Bellefonds set off for Munich to congratulate the Dauphine's brother on his marriage.[46] (The envoy's baggage presumably included a gift from Her Royal Highness to the Elector: an *epithalamio*[C] by Charpentier.)

The Queen's death in 1683 provided Madame de Guise with an opportunity for which she had long been awaiting. She had only remained "in the world" because Marie-Thérèse had begged her to keep her company in the difficult task of blending devotion and courtly duties. She was now free to live like a nun and, if the King approved, to take the habit of a religious. The King did not approve. By 1684 she had broken with the LITTLE CARMEL, owing in part to a power play by MADEMOISELLE DE MONTPENSIER, who was ingratiating herself with the nuns. This, combined with the fact that some of the Carmelites were relaying MADAME DE TOSCANE's conversations to the Florentines, prompted Isabelle d'Orléans and her sister to shift their allegiance to the Great Carmel, where Louise de la Vallière was a nun.

At about the same date, Isabelle d'Orléans appears to have given up her "devotions" at the THEATINE church. At any rate, this is the most plausible explanation for why oratorios more or less disappear from Charpentier's arabic-numbered notebooks at the end of 1685. This may also help explain why the Theatine fathers hired Paolo Lorenzani as their music master in June 1685. They were filling a void. By contrast, Madame de Guise continued to visit the ABBEY OF MONTMARTRE. For example, she spent Christmas eve and Christmas day there in 1684, doubtlessly to hear a composition that Charpentier had written for the GREAT GUISE MUSIC.[D]

Although she humbled herself by caring for the poor and praying for hours with the nuns of several convents, she maintained her noble demeanor and pomp, to the point of having one of the "little Turks" who followed great ladies and carried their trains. Her correspondence is characterized by a somewhat haughty tone, born of the imperiousness

---

[A] Cahiers XXXVI–XXXIX, H. 188, H. 524, H. 408, H. 409, H. 189.
[B] Cahier 38, H. 331.
[C] Cahier 45, H. 473.
[D] Cahiers 42–43a, H. 414.

Femme de Qualité allant a l'Eglise;

A noblewoman going to church.
She is accompanied by her *demoiselles*, her almoner (whose position in her
household is made clear by the purse hanging at his waist), and her little Turk.
In her will Madame de Guise bequeathed one thousand écus to Achmet, "my little Turk,
... so that he will have money to live and be raised as a good Christian."

inculcated into royal princesses. Sometimes this imperiousness was born of a fear of being slighted. Personal warmth had no place in the note she addressed to Gondi, the former Tuscan agent in Paris whom she knew quite well:

> I do not dare, Monsieur the Abbé, to write the Grand Duke [Cosimo], for I get no answers from him. I pray you to inform him that if I do not write, it is because I believe that he does not take pleasure in my letters, since he does not reply; but that this does not prevent me from loving him and esteeming him infinitely, and that I remain totally his, and ready to demonstrate it when the occasion arises. My manna [a medicine] has almost run out. I pray you to send me some as soon as possible, and to rest assured that one cannot esteem you more than I do. *Isabelle d'Orleans*[47]

The defensive and humiliated tone of this otherwise impersonal letter stands in marked contrast to the cordiality in MADEMOISELLE DE GUISE's letters to the same individual.

Madame de Guise could be curt, even wounding—perhaps from timidity rather than arrogance. For example, it may have been to hide her tears that, shortly after her husband's death, she "suddenly dismissed" the Florentine agent, saying that she "must dash off to see her son." This type of abrupt response to foreigners or strangers was repeated over the years. Having come face to face with MADAME DE TOSCANE after a separation of almost fifteen years, she abruptly ordered the coach taking them to Paris to halt, and she left her astonished sister alone for two hours while she prayed in a little church. She fled in a similar manner, in order to avoid having to meet the Prince of Orange —and was rebuked for it by Louis XIV. When the Florentine Pietro Guerrini came to Paris in the fall of 1684 he immediately went to the Luxembourg to "bow before Madame de Guise." Declining to receive him, she sent one of her domestics to tell him that if he wanted to see her palace in a better state than it was now, she would inform him of the day when he could visit, "to sense (she said) that it has no peer." Guerrini therefore headed for the Hôtel de Guise, where MADEMOISELLE DE GUISE received him warmly—as she had received the Florentine from whom Madame de Guise had fled back in 1671.[48]

A contemporary word-portrait of Isabelle d'Orléans captures the different facets of her public image in about 1690. Having first remarked that her torso is "less attractive and easy" than that of MADAME DE TOSCANE, and that her face is "neither beautiful nor ugly," the description moves on to her activities:

> Her humor is very charitable, and since her widowhood her mind is totally preoccupied by excessive devotion, which she has demonstrated, among other things, by the supposed conversions of the Protestants she knew about and who happened to live in her domain or patrimony, such as Alençon and elsewhere. I won't mention the zeal and the charity that cause her to visit hospitals regularly, where she tends the sick, feeds them, buries the dead, and carries on other similar functions.[49]

Like MADEMOISELLE DE GUISE, Isabelle d'Orléans had her spiritual advisors, among them Rancé, Abbot of La Trappe, who wrote his "Christian Instructions" and "Christian Conduct" for her. In her chapel at the Luxembourg were copies of Rancé's rules for the Abbey of the Trappe, and his treatise on "holiness" and the "duties of monastic life."[50]

Isabelle d'Orléans' apartment in the Luxembourg Palace suggested these preoccupations. Adjacent to a somewhat oriental room furnished with a "sofa" and with stools covered in "Turkish needlepoint," was a portrait gallery peopled by all the Bourbons back to Henri IV, by the Medicis, and by members of the House of Orléans and the House of Lorraine. Her son's room was kept more or less as it had been in 1675, as a sort of shrine.[51] The main-floor rooms of her residence at Alençon were equally elegant: rich furniture and a billiard table for her guests. Her private apartment contrasted markedly with these public rooms. The furnishings were modest, even convent-like. True, her antechamber housed a harpsichord and a chess set, but devotional mottos decorated the walls here and in the other rooms. Her bedroom was a veritable nun's cell: a single bed, simple iron firedogs, two desks, and writing equipment. A silver-gilt pounce-box was the only touch of luxury in these Spartan quarters. The chapel was equally sparse: a painting of the Virgin, wooden candlesticks, a dried bouquet, simple linen altar cloths, and a wooden prayer stool. A cedar-wood cabinet held her library: two hundred and fifty volumes, principally poetry and history.[52]

In 1693 Madame de Guise perhaps commissioned one final work from Marc-Antoine Charpentier: funeral music[A] for MADEMOISELLE DE MONTPENSIER. Despite their estrangement and their mutual detestation, *noblesse* literally obliged Isabelle d'Orléans to call upon the composer who had written music for the funerals of LOUIS-JOSEPH DE LORRAINE, the DOWAGER DUCHESS OF ORLÉANS, and the Duke of Alençon—and probably for MADEMOISELLE DE GUISE as well.

[A] Cahier LXIII, H. 7, H. 263, H. 213.

By contrast, it is not at all clear that Charpentier's music accompanied her to her last rest. In her testament dated March 1695, she wrote:

> I beg the King to approve of my being buried among the Carmelites
> of the Great Carmel, with no ceremonies, as if I were a Carmelite;
> and I forbid having my body opened, for that is useful to no one.
> But I beg them not to bury me until twenty-four hours have passed,
> and that I not be placed in my bier until the soles of my feet have
> been given two razor slashes. And without keeping my body any
> longer than that, I want it to be placed at the Carmelites. Since I
> want no other ceremonies, I ask this of the King, for it would be
> useless to keep me longer without all that pomp.[53]

(Her Royal Highness was haunted by the prospect of being buried alive: she had made the same request in an earlier will, dated 1684.)

A year later, almost to the day, March 17, 1696, Isabelle d'Orléans died from a respiratory infection. Her last wishes were respected:

> She received the sacraments and died as piously as she had lived.
> The King loved her and went to see her twice, the last time on the
> morning of the day she died; and that evening he went to Marly so
> that the ceremonies could take place. But she had forbidden them all
> and did not want to be buried at Saint-Denis, as someone of her
> birth should be, but at the Carmelites of the Faubourg Saint-
> Jacques, and as a simple nun. She was obeyed. They did not know
> until her death that she had long had a cancer, which seemed ready
> to break open. God spared her the pain. She observed every Lent
> and fasted, and her entire life was equally penitent.[54]

Despite her instructions to the contrary, Isabelle d'Orléans was embalmed. Her burial involved the modicum of ceremony without which no granddaughter of France could be laid to rest: a torchlight procession from Versailles to Paris, mourning clothes for her entire household, and a modest amount of funeral pomp (and perhaps music?) for which the Carmelites requested a reimbursement of 3,594 livres. They were given an additional 150 livres for "a marble tomb to put in our cloister at the place where the body of Her Late Royal Highness reposes."[55] Madame de Guise, the would-be nun, had remembered Carmelite sisters in her will: "I give the Carmelites of the Great Convent one thousand écus for an annual service [conducted] in their manner, and as they would for a sister."[56]

VI

The survivor bears witness to the fallen

MARIE DE LORRAINE
THE LAST GUISE

High and Powerful Princess Mademoiselle Marie de Lorraine,
Duchess of Guise and Joyeuse, Princess of Joinville,
Hereditary Seneschal of Champagne

The death of LOUIS-JOSEPH DE LORRAINE, Duke of Guise, on July 30, 1671, was a horrible blow to Marie de Lorraine's hopes and plans. "Mademoiselle de Guise has not yet stopped weeping," the Florentine agent noted in late September 1671:

> And in truth her House merits extreme compassion, because everyone knows that the care and the application she gave to saving her nephew are worthy of her birth, and she lost him in his finest age, with the danger of seeing her illustrious and glorious branch of the family become extinct.[1]

After Louis-Joseph's death, she and MADAME DE GUISE immediately withdrew to the Abbey of MONTMARTRE. Thus it was not they, but their householders, who organized the Duke's lying-in-state; and it surely was their almoners and chaplains, aided by MONSIEUR DU BOIS and Marc-Antoine Charpentier, who spent three feverish weeks preparing the pontifical requiem mass[A] to be celebrated on August 22 at the Guise parish church, Saint-Jean-en-Grève. The women apparently did not attend it or witness the departure of the Duke's body for Joinville; but they almost certainly were present when his heart was received at Montmartre.

In their darkened quarters at the abbey, the grieving women spent much of August and a good part of September fighting over the

[A] Cahier 3, H. 2, H. 234.

426

guardianship of the little Duke of Alençon, dispatching messages to the Luxembourg Palace and to the royal administration. Although she was still underage, MADAME DE GUISE was doing everything possible to gain legal control over her child. So was Marie de Lorraine. Alluding to their "friendship," she begged the DOWAGER DUCHESS OF ORLÉANS to side with her, so that the child would not be influenced by the "world," that is, by the threat to morals posed by life at the royal court:

> I beg you very humbly, Madame, not to side with those who seek this post. I expect this from the honor of your friendship for me and the friendship you want to have for my grandnephew. ... For insurmountable reasons I can never agree that this post be given ... to a person of the world. I will assume the function, as I did with success and approval as guardian for his father.[2]

She was pressuring Jean-Baptiste Colbert as well, pointing out that since "no one else was acquainted" with the financial situation of the House of Guise, she and her treasurer, Jean-François Le Brun, should be the principal guardians.

To this proposal Madame de Guise retorted that although Marie de Lorraine was not her social equal, "she wants to attribute to herself a total equality that does not exist." Meanwhile, Mademoiselle de Guise's opponents were telling Colbert that she had absconded with part of the Guise wealth by mingling accounts and refusing to present a written accounting of the late Duke's finances. Two million livres hung in the balance, they asserted.[3] This obfuscation and refusal to submit financial records calls to mind her mother's handling of MADEMOISELLE DE MONT-PENSIER's inheritance back in the early 1650s.

In mid-September an exasperated Marie de Lorraine pulled out her trump card. If an accounting was demanded of her, or if she was "molested" in any way, she would make public the existence of her children by Montrésor. The dispute was rapidly resolved. On October 7, 1671, by royal letters-patent, Marie de Lorraine was entrusted with the "education" of the Duke of Alençon. She and Colbert would direct the child's finances, with the help of an independent barrister of their choosing.[4]

Thus Marie de Lorraine became Regent for the year-old child who was now head of the House of Guise. So determined was she to play a decisive role in the child's development, that she was prepared to follow him and his mother to England, should Madame de Guise marry the Duke of York, which seemed a distinct possibility in early 1672.[5] For this tiny child there was no reason to create a splendid court, complete with music, as she, MARIE THE REGENT, had done in the late 1660s. Rather, she saw to it that Marc-Antoine Charpentier was kept busy, remaining in her service and honing his skills until they should be needed by the House of Guise.

Shortly before Christmas 1671—certainly with Her Highness's approval—an unidentified patron began commissioning church music[A] from the composer. The patron seems to have been one of the THREE JESUIT HOUSES of the capital,[6] where MARIE TALON's uncle, Father Verthamon (one of the FOUR JESUITS portrayed in Panel 4), held a position of power. Some of these pieces—plainsong settings of texts by Father Commire, S.J., in honor of Saint Nicaise, a founding archbishop of Rouen—can only have been destined for the Jesuit seminary at Rouen founded by Mademoiselle de Guise's granduncle, the Cardinal de Joyeuse.[7] These commissions,[B] apparently all for the same patron, continued throughout the initial months of this period of mourning; but after Easter 1672, and the death of the DOWAGER OF ORLÉANS, they stopped abruptly.

So deep was the women's mourning, and so total their withdrawal from society, that not until mid-November 1671 could they bear to listen to the Grand Duke of Tuscany's official condolences, conveyed by Carlo Gondi, the new Medici agent. Mademoiselle de Guise did, however, speak to Gondi briefly, asking him to tell the Medicis that it was impossible "to exaggerate the obligations of her entire House" for their generosity "during the time she was in Florence." Gondi made a point of speaking to her in French, calling her *Votre Altesse*, "Your Highness," in order to avoid *Altezza*, a more elevated title in Florence than in France.[8] This initial visit, imposed and shaped by protocol, was followed by less formal ones; and long after Gondi left Paris, Mademoiselle de Guise would continue to correspond with him.

It did not take long for Marie de Lorraine to make several important changes in her lifestyle. One of her first steps was to settle a law suit, thereby making the County of Montrésor hers.[9] Next, she sold the house and garden at Saint-Germain-en-Laye known as the "Hôtel de Guise," and she sold the "Hôtel de Guise" at Versailles as well.[10] These sales constituted what amounted to a rupture with the "world," that is, with the royal court. The Hôtel de Guise would henceforth be the center of her courtly activities and her devotions.

Yet she never broke her ties with the Capucine convent where her mother was buried, nor with her parish church, Saint-Jean-en-Grève, situated just behind the Hôtel de Ville. In fact, as a memorial to her late

---

[A] Cahier IX, H. 160, H. 161, for a large ensemble; and H. 313, H. 314, for a smaller group.
[B] Cahiers VI–VIII, H. 3, H. 236, H. 283, H. 514 (an elaborate mass); cahier VIII, H. 73 (*Magnificat*); and cahier VIII, H. 13, H. 312, H. 284 (for an Easter event).

nephew, she set about having a confraternity created at Saint-Jean, for the purpose of helping members win the "grace of a good death." Devoted to the "perpetual adoration of Jesus Christ in the Very Holy Eucharist," the Association for the Perpetual Adoration of the Very Holy Sacrament of the Altar became official on December 18, 1672.

Although the House of Guise was not mentioned in the confraternity bylaws,[11] Archbishop HARLAY (who in March 1670 had been granted the right to create one such sodality in Paris) almost certainly selected Saint-Jean-en-Grève with Mademoiselle de Guise in mind. That is to say, he declared that one of the principal feast days would be "Expiation Day at the said church," an annual event held in early September.[12] Founded by Marie de Lorraine's mother to expiate a sacrilege to the host, these devotions consisted of a procession around the church, solemn vespers followed by a Benediction of the Holy Sacrament, and prayers for the king and for the House of Guise.[13] Superimposed as it was upon an existing Guise-created and Guise-sponsored devotion, the new confraternity was less an innovation than an amplification of an existing event, the better to express Marie de Lorraine's priorities. As it turned out, the priorities of this new sodality would set the tone for Mademoiselle de Guise's devotions for the next fifteen years. In addition to doing "some pious and charitable works every day," members were expected to attend various services at Saint-Jean-en-Grève—among them the annual Reparation procession, the Corpus Christi procession, Epiphany, and the Feast of Saint Michael, destroyer of Heresy.

Members were expected to devote themselves to several types of prayers: prayers for the dying, agonisants; prayers for "heretics" (that is, Protestants), "schismatics" (Jansenists), and "infidels" (Muslims and Amerindians); prayers for the "extirpation of heresy" and for "peace in the realm"; and prayers "for the prosperity of the King, the Queen, the Royal House, and the State." These prayers took the form of élévations, a type of prayer promoted by the Oratorians and Sulpicians. It consisted of "admiring, adoring, revering, [and] paying homage," in order to honor and glorify God without "desiring or asking for anything."[14] The devotions of young ISABELLE D'ORLÉANS OF ALENÇON had been based upon just this sort of prayer. Thus, after 1672, the two Guise women shared a manner of praying that would give rise to the many élévations that Charpentier set to music.

Between 1672 and 1687, into his arabic-numbered notebooks Marc-Antoine Charpentier would copy works for several musicians that mirrored the devotional program of the new confraternity. There were pieces related to the Adoration of the Holy Sacrament or to Corpus

Christi[A]; works specifically labeled "*élévation*"[B]; oratorios focusing on Saint Cecilia as a converter of heathens[C]; prayers for the royal family and for peace in the realm[D]; and an oratorio honoring the charitable acts of Saint Charles Borromeo.[E] In addition, it cannot be ruled out that an oratorio for Saint Michael,[F] copied into a roman-numbered notebook in 1683, was commissioned by a member of the confraternity, for performance on the Archangel's feast day, September 29.

It almost certainly was to works in this devotional corpus that JEAN DONNEAU DE VISÉ and Thomas Corneille were referring when, in 1688, they broke their silence and informed readers that Marc-Antoine Charpentier had composed for the late Marie de Lorraine: "He wrote some things for Mademoiselle de Guise that were very highly esteemed by the most able connoisseurs."[15] "Some things." In other words, only *some* of the music in the arabic-numbered notebooks was for the last Guise. The rest was for MADAME DE GUISE. Many of the pieces were, of course, written with both women in mind, for Madame de Guise's devotions during those fifteen years were strikingly similar to Marie de Lorraine's.

In addition, it is possible, indeed quite probable, that many of the compositions appropriate for the Confraternity of the Holy Sacrament were performed not only at Saint-Jean-en-Grève, but at other venues as well. That is to say, almost concurrently with the creation of that sodality, Mademoiselle de Guise began making overtures to a convent just across the street from the Hôtel de Guise.

Casting about for a church to which she could be carried in her sedan chair, with its red-and-gold brocade interior and white brocade curtains that could be pulled to conceal the occupant's identity, she settled on the Mercedarian Fathers of the convent of Notre-Dame de la MERCY. Involving herself devotionally with this convent was scarcely an innovative step. For over two decades the fathers had counted the Guises among their benefactors, and Marie de Lorraine doubtlessly wanted to continue this generosity. But now the convent appealed for several reasons. Its proximity to the Hôtel de Guise made it easy for her to

---

[A] Cahier 5, H. 235; cahier 16, H. 58; cahier 22, H. 242, H. 243; cahier 24, H. 245, H. 246, H. 247; cahier 32, H. 250; cahier 40, H. 254; cahier 41, H. 255.
[B] Cahiers 11–12, H. 237; cahiers 12–13, H. 238; cahier 21, H. 241; cahier 22, H. 242, H. 243; cahier 24, H. 244, H. 245, H. 246; cahier 32, H. 250; cahiers 38–39, H. 252, H. 253 (?); cahier 50, H. 258.
[C] Cahier 13, H. 394; cahiers 19–20, H. 397; cahier 42, H. 413; cahier 47, H. 415.
[D] Cahier 11, H. 393 (for a large ensemble), H. 237; cahiers 14–16, H. 164, H. 165, H. 166; cahier 17, H. 320 (Saint Louis); cahier 20, H. 168 (for a large ensemble); cahier 22, H. 323 (Saint Louis); cahier 33, H. 180 (for a large ensemble); cahier 38, H. 331, H. 332 (Saint Louis); cahier 40, H. 293, H. 294; cahiers 49–50, H. 489, H. 431.
[E] Cahiers 23–24, H. 398.
[F] Cahier XXXIX, H. 410.

worship there discreetly; its principal devotion was to the Virgin, her patroness; and the little church had a reputation as a venue for musical devotions. In addition, the Mercy needed her: death had taken Monsieur Bernard, a "co-founder" who had sponsored musical events during the 1650s and 1660s.

Not long after the death of LOUIS-JOSEPH, DUKE OF GUISE, an anonymous woman described as a "lady," *dame*, and a "person of quality"—that is, a high noblewoman—received papal approval to create at the Mercy a branch of the Confraternity for the Dying Sick, the *agonisants*. The unnamed woman can only have been Marie de Lorraine, for no other noblewoman was mentioned in the convent's archives. The confraternity became official in August 1672, a few months prior to the official recognition of the new sodality at Saint-Jean. The goals of these two organizations overlapped in many ways. What differed was the focus: at Saint-Jean, via *élévations*, Mademoiselle de Guise could adore the Holy Sacrament; and at the Mercy, she could venerate the Virgin, whose namesake she was.

Neither sodality had yet been recognized by the archidiocese when Marie de Lorraine was forced to put on hold any plans she may have had to set Marc-Antoine Charpentier to writing for devotions at either Saint-Jean-en-Grève or the Mercy. The DOWAGER DUCHESS OF ORLÉANS died in early April 1672, and the Guise women once again withdrew to MONTMARTRE.

Charpentier therefore began rounding out a little corpus of compositions for the dead.[A] To be specific, the first weeks of April probably saw the revival and rehearsal of some of the funeral music he had written in 1671, for the reception of Madame's heart at Montmartre and her entrails at Charonne. Concurrently with that, he was writing new music for the End of the Year Service of LOUIS-JOSEPH, DUKE OF GUISE, scheduled for July 1672. In addition, he hastily composed a piece for the Tenebrae[B] of Maundy Thursday, April 14, 1672—almost certainly performed at MONTMARTRE for the princesses.

Five weeks of retreat at the abbey ended on May 14, with the splendid funeral services that MADAME DE GUISE had organized for the DOWAGER OF ORLÉANS at Charonne, Montmartre, and Saint-Denis. At the latter church a reprise of the Louis-Joseph de Lorraine's requiem mass appears to have been performed, completed by a newly composed *De Profundis*[C] that was de rigueur for an actual burial.

[A] Cahier 4, H. 311 (which may date from Aug. 1671 rather than 1672); cahier 5, H. 12.
[B] Cahier 2, H. 94.
[C] Cahier 4, H. 156.

The two Guise princesses had to reorganize their lives yet again, for in April 1673 MADAME DE GUISE moved into her late mother's half of the Luxembourg Palace. During this period of transition and mourning, Charpentier copied into his arabic-numbered notebooks little but funeral music and some pieces for Holy Week,[A] when the princesses were at MONTMARTRE preparing themselves spiritually to commemorate the anniversary of the DOWAGER OF ORLÉANS' death.

He was not inactive, however. During the months when the Guise women were thinking of other things, Charpentier was chosen by MOLIÈRE to replace Lully's music for two plays[B] scheduled to be revived in July 1672. For reasons unknown and somewhat mystifying, Mademoiselle de Guise permitted him to work with the excommunicated actors of Molière's troop. Having apparently assumed that the collaboration would continue, Her Highness was not pleased to learn that the playwright had asked DASSOUCY to collaborate on his next production.

At any rate, that is the picture painted by Dassoucy, who recounted how some irritated noblewomen more or less forced Molière to dismiss him and engage Charpentier for Le Malade imaginaire. Described as "virgins," "heroines," "divinities," "goddesses"—terms generally reserved for princesses of the House of Orléans and the House of Lorraine—these irritated women can be identified with reasonable certainty: Mademoiselle de Guise, Madame de Guise, and perhaps MADEMOISELLE DE MONTPENSIER who, although generally feuding with Mademoiselle de Guise, took so much pleasure in twisting people's thumbs that her participation cannot be ruled out, especially in view of her old mistress–servant link to Lully.

The women's intervention is eloquent evidence of just how responsible they felt toward the young man to whom the House of Orléans and the House of Guise had offered protection during the early years of a brilliant matrimonial union that had proved disappointingly brief. Uncertain about the future, they were opening doors for Charpentier, placing him in an artistic milieu where his talents would permit him to rival Lully—the Florentine whom Mademoiselle de Guise's late brother, the Chevalier of Guise, had brought to Paris to teach Italian to Montpensier, and who had been impertinent enough to beg his leave when she was relegated to her country house after the Fronde.

MOLIÈRE's death a few months later spoiled Marie de Lorraine's plan, if it indeed existed. Although Charpentier continued composing for the playwright's successors (principally THOMAS CORNEILLE), it became clear that the House of Guise would have to continue protecting him. He

---

[A] Cahier 6, H. 157, H. 95 (Friday, Mar. 31, 1673).
[B] Cahier XV, H. 494.

could not possibly make a career in the theater or the opera, for Lully was determined to quash all rivals. On the other hand, Charpentier was in a position to annoy the Florentine by challenging his monopoly. Mademoiselle de Guise clearly enjoyed the prospect. If she had not, she would scarcely have permitted him to collaborate with Corneille and the actors for over a decade.

Thus Charpentier stayed on at the Hôtel de Guise after MADAME DE GUISE moved out in the spring of 1673. Judging from the composer's arabic-numbered notebooks, neither MONSIEUR DU BOIS nor Marie de Lorraine quite knew what to do with him in 1673 and 1674. MADAME DE GUISE, on the other hand, got the idea of having him help her celebrate her move to the Luxembourg Palace. She ordered her householders to create a temporary altar, *reposoir*,[A] under the grandiose entryway to the palace, where she greeted the Corpus Christi procession organized by her parish church, Saint-Sulpice.

It probably was for Marie de Lorraine that Charpentier wrote a few preludes and several pieces for the Virgin[B] in 1673. In this climate of uncertainty about what to do with him, a crisis at the MERCY convent in April 1674 may have been a turning point for Mademoiselle de Guise. She rescued the reverend fathers when an organ could not be delivered owing to litigation over the donor's estate. To ensure the success of the week-long canonization festivities at their church, she ordered Monsieur Charpentier into the breach. Someone—it is not clear who—came up with the idea of creating an instrumental mass that would simulate the organ.[C]

In this way Her Highness discovered the pleasures to be derived from sharing her composer, and eventually her musicians, with a select public drawn from among the elites of the capital. In fact, she soon offered the Mercy two vocal pieces for a male trio, performed that summer or fall in honor of the Virgin.[D] The performers probably were members of the GUISE MUSIC, rather than Mercedarian fathers or musicians hired by the convent.

Since no trace of a high tenor, *haute-contre*, other than Charpentier has been identified at the Hôtel de Guise prior to 1686, the composer apparently joined newly arrived De Baussen and Beaupuis for these pieces. Until the emergence of the GREAT GUISE MUSIC in the 1680s, he

[A] Cahier 7, H. 508.
[B] Cahier 5, H. 18, H. 19, H. 235; cahier 7, H. 509, H. 510, H. 511, H. 512.
[C] Cahiers 7–8, H. 513.
[D] Cahier 8, H. 159, H. 20.

would restrict his public participation with the Music to singing at the Mercy[A] (usually with De Baussen and Beaupuis) or before the King.[B]

In March 1675 death once again crushed Marie de Lorraine's hopes and silenced the GUISE MUSIC. Four-year-old François-Joseph de Lorraine, Duke of Alençon, the last male of the House of Guise, died while she, MADAME DE GUISE, MONSIEUR DU BOIS, BISHOP ROQUETTE, and DOCTOR VALLANT tiptoed in and out and hovered around his little white bed. The body was carried to MONTMARTRE for burial, and there the princesses spent several weeks grieving.

The estate was quickly settled, for once again Mademoiselle de Guise threatened to recognize her children. Within a month, MADAME DE GUISE accepted a financial settlement and renounced her rights to Guise lands and titles. Marie de Lorraine was now Duchess of Guise. Her heirs were named in the agreement: the Gonzagas of Nevers (among them the Prince of Condé's wife) would receive a sizeable share of Guise possessions, and MADEMOISELLE DE MONTPENSIER would inherit the Joyeuse property.

By late May 1675, Mademoiselle de Guise was back at the Hôtel de Guise and sufficiently mistress of her emotions to go through the painful ceremony of listening to a Florentine envoy express the condolences of the House of Medici. With great politeness she received their spokesman, surrounded by "all the people of her House, and she was in bed, in conformity with the style observed here when receiving this sort of compliment. She had summoned to her bedchamber a great number of ladies, to attend this function." Marie de Lorraine listened intently. Then, bursting into tears, she once again expressed her affection for the Medicis and thanked them for their compassion over "such a bitter accident, the most devastating blow that had struck her House."[16]

Marie de Lorraine can only have felt relief at not having to make good on her threat to recognize her children. The Florentine agent realized just how momentous her decision had been:

> Everyone is wondering what Mademoiselle de Guise will do about the children she says she had by Montrésor, her husband 'by conscience,' who live in Flanders. She can only act during her lifetime, by means of a declaration; but that would mean that she would promptly lose her rank of princess.[17]

While the two Guise women were in retreat at MONTMARTRE that spring, news arrived that MADAME DE TOSCANE, Madame de Guise's older

---

[A] Cahier 8, H. 159 (Little Office of Virgin), H. 20 (Virgin); cahier 16, H. 23 (Virgin), H. 319 (Trinity); cahier 17, H. 320 (Saint Louis), H. 321 (Saint Laurence, their foundation day); cahier 22, H. 25 (antiphon for the Mercy); cahier 33, H. 82 (Litany of Loreto); cahier 34 (use not clear).
[B] Cahier 13, H. 479 (pastorale performed for the King).

sister, would be returning to France in midsummer and would be more or less imprisoned at the abbey. A conversation between the two princesses can be imagined: Madame de Guise expresses a desire to show her musician sister that the French can do as well as the Italians whom she has been praising in her letters. But since the Grand Duchess will only be permitted to attend devotional events, what sort of things might Monsieur Charpentier write that will amaze and impress her? Marie de Lorraine reflects for a moment—and proposes an *oratorio* like the ones she heard so long ago in Florence.

Perhaps no such conversation took place. Madame de Guise had, of course, graced the stage in a few Italian operas back in the early 1660s, and her late father's household composer, Moulinié, had demonstrated some interest in Italian music. Even so, there is no evidence to suggest that she knew much about Italian musical genres prior to 1675. Be that as it may, MADAME DE GUISE promptly arranged to have a chapel given her at the Church of Sainte-Anne-la-Royale, in the convent of Italian fathers known as the THEATINES. Only a few months later Marc-Antoine Charpentier wrote the first[A] of a succession of oratorios.

In September 1675, when that first Italianate oratorio was performed, Marie de Lorraine did not yet have a chapel where musical devotions calling for such a large ensemble could be performed before an elite public. In fact, not until July of that year had she approached the MERCY and requested a chapel, which was still being renovated in April 1676. In other words, although the idea that Marc-Antoine Charpentier should write some oratorios may well have been triggered by Marie de Lorraine's reminiscences, it seems to have been Madame de Guise who moved from reminiscence to fact. Nor is it likely that Mademoiselle de Guise hired the large ensembles required for some of these oratorios and for the other rather grandiose works that Charpentier copied into the arabic-numbered notebooks from late 1675 until the early 1680s—when the emergence of the GREAT GUISE MUSIC finally made this sort of performance feasible for Marie de Lorraine. In sum, these ambitious works probably were written for Madame de Guise, the "granddaughter of France" who had access to the King's Music.

Besides, Marie de Lorraine was preoccupied by other things during the six months that followed little Alençon's death. She was caught up in a flurry of activities as she concentrated upon what was known as the "regulated" life,[18] the life of the devout woman. She ordered the construction at MONTMARTRE of a new entrance gate with lodgings and parlors where lay persons could assemble and converse with the nuns, plus an

[A] Cahiers 9–11, H. 391.

entire pavilion adjacent to it, presumably for herself.[19] Then, during the summer of 1676,[20] once work had been completed on her chapel at the MERCY, she began to worship there—to music. At that point, works honoring the Virgin, generally for two or three singers plus instruments, began to appear in Charpentier's arabic-numbered notebooks. (In the mid-1670s, the GUISE MUSIC was still a relatively small group.)

Marie de Lorraine also embarked on a program of helping the less fortunate. The principal project was the creation of a teachers' training school dedicated to the INFANT JESUS. For, like MADAME DE GUISE, she was now focusing her devotions on the Holy Child. This devotion to the Child—which is reflected in Charpentier's arabic-numbered notebooks for the next decade—was, in a sense, superimposed upon the devotions for the Virgin and for the Holy Sacrament that had made their appearance in that series of notebooks in 1672 and 1673.

The first teachers began their training late in 1675, and a school for boys and girls opened soon afterward in Mademoiselle de Guise's parish, Saint-Jean-en-Grève. Over the next decade, the twenty-two teachers she was instrumental in training, and whose costs she subsidized, would work not only in her parish but also in the poorer neighborhoods of Paris and in the principal towns of her lands.[21]

Although each princess chose her venue for private worship and public musical worship, Mademoiselle de Guise and MADAME DE GUISE had a similar conception of the "regulated" life and the "devotions" it entailed. As a result, a great number of the works that Marc-Antoine Charpentier wrote between 1676 and 1686 were suitable for the devotions of both princesses. From the outset, many of these works were almost certainly conceived for several performances within a matter of days, one for Marie de Lorraine and one for Madame de Guise—and perhaps another for MADAME DE MONTMARTRE and her nuns, and another for the teachers and students of one or both of the schools dedicated to the INFANT JESUS. To these venues should be added Saint-Jean-en-Grève and its annual expiatory procession. In short, after the summer of 1676, venues and devotional events were not lacking, and they doubtlessly were exploited to the maximum.

As a pious woman living the regulated life, Marie de Lorraine was concerned for the poor and the sick. Charity was one of the principal obligations imposed upon members of the two new confraternities. It is not clear, however, that she joined MADAME DE GUISE and MADAME DE TOSCANE each week as they went about their charitable activities, which were perhaps deemed too rigorous for a noblewoman well into her sixties. It is likely that Mademoiselle de Guise had to be content with contributing money to one or another of the existing charitable confraternities in Paris, and with founding hospitals in her lands, to be run by the same

Daughters of Charity with whom Madame de Guise had contracted in 1676 for Alençon.[22] Charpentier's oratorio about the charitable work done by Saint Charles Borromeo[A] therefore expressed Marie de Lorraine's devotional preoccupations, just as it did those of MADAME DE GUISE. Here, as in some of the other works for a large ensemble, the costs of one or more performances of the oratorio conceivably could have been shared by the two princesses. And since these works were almost certainly performed for a small assembly of elite worshipers, it added to the magnificence of the event when the musicians took up half the Mercy chapel or half the lower gallery of the Hôtel de Guise.

In addition to sharing these charitable aims, the two sodalities that met in the vicinity of the Hôtel de Guise, one at Saint-Jean-en-Grève and the other at the Mercy, had another common mission: to extirpate heresy. Charpentier's successive oratorios in honor of Saint Cecilia[B] extol this converting activity, although in Cecilia's case it was heathens, not heretics, who were converted.

Like Madame de Guise, Marie de Lorraine fulfilled the social obligations expected of a woman of her rank and age. Although she rarely visited the royal court now—her advancing age making it difficult to stand for hours in the presence of the royal family— she went with MADAME DE MONTMARTRE to Fontainebleau during the summer of 1675, to fetch MADAME DE TOSCANE; and in 1682 she made the trip to court to thank Louis XIV for his support in obtaining papal approval for Mademoiselle d'Harcourt's nomination as Abbess of Montmartre, despite her youth. In addition, she occasionally went to court because Madame de Toscane had begged her to. That is, the Grand Duchess had come to realize that her conversations in the Queen's apartment were being reported to the King and to the Florentines. The best way to avoid being spied upon was to have at her side Marie de Lorraine, whose rank did not permit her to enter Marie-Thérèse's *cabinet*. Toscane could therefore politely decline the honor, saying that she could not possibly abandon the last Guise.[23]

Little is known about life at Mademoiselle de Guise's court between 1676 and 1687, but fragmentary evidence makes it possible to imagine the rooms where she spent the final decade of her life. Having ceded her elegant ground-floor apartment to her women servants and her "music girls," she now occupied the apartment on the noble floor that she had prepared for her nephew and his bride in 1667. This gave her an unobstructed view onto the gardens that Le Nôtre had created for her. A billard table occupied its predictable place in the large antechamber at

---

[A] Cahiers 23–24, H. 398.
[B] Cahier 13, H. 394; cahiers 19–20, H. 397; cahier 42, H. 413; cahier 47, H. 415.

the top of the stairs by which her guests entered the apartment. From the walls of that room, framed portraits of MADAME DE MONTMARTRE and the last four dukes of Guise scrutinized the billiard players. Her bedroom was quite small, as was the little "chapel" adjacent to it, which contained two small lecterns (one of them a writing stand), a prayer stool, some reliquaries, and an altar over which a silver and gold Holy Spirit was suspended.[24]

Dressed primarily in black that could be livened by white-and-blue-striped underskirts, she served a noontime repast to MADAME DE TOSCANE and MADAME DE GUISE each Wednesday.[25] Musical entertainments—variously described as "the divertissement of music," and as "dancing"—were an integral part of these events. As she aged, and as she turned her back on the court, her social circle shrank. Most of the guests came from one or another branch of the House of Lorraine: Madame de Toscane, Madame de Guise, the Lorraines of Armagnac, the Lorraines of Elbeuf, the Lorraines of Lillebonne, and the Lorraines of Harcourt. That Marie de Lorraine clung to these relatives appears to be explained less by the pleasure of their company than by her preoccupation with passing the name *Guise* to a male from one of these branches.

It is painful to imagine the conversations at these lunches. Talk was carefully constructed to be polite and witty, but it was also extremely cautious, lest a witty retort be directed at oneself. When the squabbling sisters were present, verbal exchanges had to be cold and pro forma, the better to avoid an incident. From time to time, a few non-relatives brought variety to these weekly events: PHILIPPE II D'ORLÉANS and his wife and daughter, BISHOP ROQUETTE OF AUTUN, or Bishop Furstemberg of Strasbourg. Some of Charpentier's chamber operas[A] may have been performed at these gatherings, as well as at the Luxembourg Palace or at court. Saint-Mesme described one of these events:

Mademoiselle de Guise offered a repast on Shrove Tuesday to Mademoiselle [de Montpensier], Madame the Grand Duchess, and Madame de Guise. Mademoiselle [de Montpensier] had not been invited, but knowing that her sisters were coming, she wanted to be part of the group, where Mesdames d'Elbeuf and de Lillebonne [two Lorraine princesses] and their daughters were present. It was a very grand repast, not so much in quantity as in presentation. Two hours after the meal, Mademoiselle [de Montpensier] left, and all the others went to Montmartre to spend the rest of the day.[26]

[A] Cahier 38, H. 471; cahiers 44–45, H. 486; cahiers 49–50, H. 489; and also cahiers 46–47, H. 487 (probably written for the INFANT JESUS)—and perhaps even cahier 37, H. 480, since Mme. d'Armagnac was in disgrace and could not go to court.

The venue for these entertainments was a large salon known as the "music room," situated just beyond her bedroom. This salon opened onto the dining room and the gallery. After an elegant meal, her guests could withdraw to the salon, with its white damask hangings and gold fringe, or to the gallery, according to the nature of the musical entertainment. In addition to a harpsichord, the music room contained "an oak bench and six lecterns on their stands, of the same wood," plus curio cabinets filled with her famed collection of precious objects. The decorations on the walls suggested Her Highness's devotions: a Virgin, a Descent from the Cross, the Mystic Marriage of Saint Catherine, the Death of the Virgin, the Infant Jesus by Nocret, and a crucifix.

As they moved about her apartment, her guests could admire the princess's collection:

> Mademoiselle de Guise ... has one of the most curious collections [cabinet] in Paris, where there are several pieces in filigree decorated with gems, and very fine miniatures. One can also see a very large number of pieces made from Saint-Lucie wood [a wild plum from the Mediterranean], which represent diverse devotional subjects, very delicately carved, to say nothing of a few other similar curiosities.[27]

Like all of Marie de Lorraine's outings, the excursions that followed many of the Wednesday entertainments were managed by GAIGNIÈRES, her equerry, to whom she wrote from Montmartre in May 1679:

> Choose two [sedan-chair] bearers, who will set off tomorrow from this abbey as far as Montmartre Gate, where my bearers will take the chair. I will return at six o'clock, and you will please wait for me with my girls in my large two-horse coach. I will go to the residence of Madame d'Armagnac [a Lorraine princess]. The six-horse coach with doors must come between four and five. Monsieur Vallant will bring it, and he will follow me all the way to Montmartre Gate.[28]

The "girls" in question were her chambermaids, among whom were several "music girls." In other words, it seems that Mademoiselle de Guise took members of the GUISE MUSIC with her when she called upon friends.

Sometimes everyone would go for a ride in the Vincennes Woods, stopping perhaps for refreshments at her little country retreat known as the "Ménagerie," near Bercy. The tiny house, decorated entirely in red leather and red-checked fabric, had been turned into a gallery with portraits and precious objects. In the garden, large satin umbrellas protected visitors as they talked and contemplated the oleanders and jasmines in wooden boxes.[29] The Ménagerie clearly was a picnic spot, for it had only a small kitchen and a cot for a domestic in the stairway to the attic. There is no evidence that the house was intended specifically as a musical venue, although the possibility that some of Charpentier's pastorales were performed in this pseudo-rustic setting certainly cannot be ruled out.[A]

The Wednesday lunches were distinct from the "conversational" entertainments at the Hôtel de Guise in which the GUISE MUSIC participated several times a week—"almost daily," asserts one source.[30] The little that we know about these concerts comes from Pietro Guerrini, a Florentine who visited the Hôtel de Guise regularly during his nine-month stay in Paris, 1684–1685. Rebuffed by MADAME DE GUISE and feeling quite homesick, he sought comfort at the Hôtel de Guise, going "several times a week to spend an hour or two at Mademoiselle de Guise's, where there is singing and instrumental music, and conversations that are gallant and studious; and the aforesaid Highness is very satisfied to find me there."[31] It is not clear what he meant by *conversazione*, "conversations."[32] Since he did not include the term "*in musica*"— which would show quite clearly that he was talking about the operas, cantatas, and serenades that Italians grouped under the general category *conversazione in musica*—it is not clear whether these "conversations" were the sort of discussions of poetry and morals that had become fashionable through translations of Castiligione's *Courtier*; or whether Guerrini was alluding to a musical genre consisting of dialogues set to music, for example cantatas, serenades, and chamber operas.[33] At least one of Charpentier's settings of Italian words, a *serenata*,[B] was written while the Florentine was visiting the Hôtel de Guise. This suggests that the "conversations" were done to music or interspersed with music. Indeed, during these same years Her Highness is known to have commanded the Florentines to provide her with "all" the Latin and Italian vocal works of Giovanni Battista Mazzaferrata, a composer from Ferrera.[34]

During her final decade, Marie de Lorraine made a point of demonstrating her loyalty to the Monarchy, as if she were determined to expunge the taint of treason that still hovered over the House of Guise, as it had when the doors were painted yellow after the disgrace of her brother, Duke Henri. The earliest of these events in honor of the royal family probably took place at the MERCY in March 1677, during the Jubilee conducted by the QUEEN and the DAUPHIN, and during the public prayers for LOUIS XIV[C] that coincided with it. If so, the event was not singled out in the press.

By contrast, Mademoiselle de Guise received both direct and indirect credit for celebrating the birth of the Dauphin's son in 1682. As at the Luxembourg, where MADAME DE GUISE sponsored fireworks, music,

---

[A] Cahiers 44–45, H. 486, for example?
[B] Cahier 43b–44, H. 472 (in Italian, early 1685, when Guerrini was in Paris).
[C] Cahiers 14–16, H. 164, H. 165, H. 166.

flowing wine, and a lighted facade, "the same things were done with great brilliance at the Hôtel de Guise." Meanwhile,

> the fathers of the Mercy, near the Hôtel de Guise, distinguished themselves on Sunday [August] 13 by discharging three rockets, and by very unusual fireworks, but above all by the *Te Deum* that the King's Music sang in their church. Mademoiselle de Guise attended, with a very large number of persons of the highest rank.[35]

Since Marie de Lorraine was mentioned, convention obliged the editors to refrain from naming the composer of the *Te Deum*.[A]

The Queen's death in August 1683 was commemorated by a "solemn mass" at the MERCY that MADAME DE GUISE came all the way from Alençon to attend. Falling in mid-August as it did, this service included two companion pieces for the male trio—probably Charpentier, De Baussen, and Beaupuis—that performed from time to time at the Mercy. One work was a lament for the late Queen, with a Latin text by Pierre Portes.[36] The other honored Saint Louis,[B] and through him Louis the God-Given, whose saint's day was August 25.[37] Mademoiselle de Guise's final event celebrating the Monarchy was the splendid *Te Deum* sung at MONTMARTRE in January 1687, to rejoice in Louis XIV's recovery from an anal fistula. Private festivities held that day may have included a performance of Charpentier's "Idyl" for the Great Guise Music, an entertainment that MADAME DE GUISE used for her own fête ten days later.

Demonstrating her loyalty to the royal family did not mean that the last Guise refrained from protesting when the Monarchy threatened her sovereignty. For example, she became enraged at the royal intendant for Guise who, she was convinced, was usurping her rights. In the fall of 1680 she and MADAME DE MONTMARTRE therefore set off on a progress to Guise lands in northeastern France. Marie de Lorraine hoped bring about, at Guise, a public humiliation of Royal Intendant Lafitte.

Lafitte had been grabbing power from the Governor of Guise (who was proving so faithful to the princess that Laffite described him as "a phantom obliged to mimic her movements and implement her plans") and from the town fathers as well (owing their appointment to her, they faithfully carried out her wishes). Among Laffite's transgressions was moving the market and requiring local notables to obtain his express permission if they wished to hunt. He also accused Her Highness of cutting timber without royal authorization. An exasperated Mademoi-

---

[A] Cahier 36, H. 291 (which may have been preceded by a *Te Deum*, for some pages were lost at the start of the notebook).
[B] Cahier 38, H. 331, H. 332.

selle de Guise protested that, in 1677, "he began [his tenure] by acting as if he were the lord of Guise, as if he owned it; and he usurped the lord's most enviable and delicate rights."

Lafitte traveled to Paris to confer with her—and proceeded to paint her as a "tyrant." She interrupted him several times, at which point BISHOP ROQUETTE OF AUTUN entered, joined the conversation, and dared to offer Lafitte advice: "You have to reach an accommodation with Mademoiselle de Guise, it will be to your advantage." The Intendant retorted that he "was not accustomed to receiving anything from anyone but [the King]." Things went from bad to worse, with Lafitte alluding to the need for strong royal authority in a city that had long been governed by the treacherous Guises. On that bitter note, he returned to Guise, and the princess methodically prepared his humiliation. She ordered a pair of splendid new benches for the mayor and the *bailli*, each ornamented with the arms of the House of Guise; and at some point in 1680, she commanded that the old "governor's bench" should be moved to the back of the church, so that the new benches could be placed symmetrically in the choir.

Late in September of 1680, Marie de Lorraine, MONSIEUR DU BOIS, MADAME DE MONTMARTRE, the Abbess of Jouarre (a Lorraine who had spent August in Paris to see to her abbey's business), and the GUISE MUSIC set off in at several coaches, on a progress through Champagne. The musicians performed almost constantly all along the route— especially at the Abbey of Jouarre, and at the Marian Church of Notre-Dame de Liesse. Judging from a piece for the Virgin[A] that Marc-Antoine Charpentier copied into his notebook for that summer, the composer made the trip, along with two women, two men, and a continuo player—perhaps Du Bois himself.

As so many pilgrims to this Marian site had done before them, princess and householders presumably carried out a predictable ritual:

> Upon arriving at Notre-Dame de Liesse, as soon as the pilgrim spies its Holy Chapel, he should be filled with interior joy. Then falling to his knees and humiliating his heart and his thoughts, he should show the respect he bears for it and the feelings he has upon seeing it. And he should also salute the Holy Virgin whom everyone comes from all corners to honor, by reciting or singing a *Salve Regine* or some other hymn, *cantique*, or prayer in Her honor. ... He must demonstrate the affection he bears Her by some offering for the upkeep and decoration of Her church, as his means permit. ... The pilgrim who, under these conditions, throws himself at the feet of the Holy Virgin, represented by Her celestial Image [that is, the

---

[A] Cahiers 29–30, H. 400.

miraculous statue of Our Lady of Liesse], and who addresses his
prayers to Her with all possible devotion, will not leave without
being forgiven and consoled.[38]

This ritual completed, they could admire the interior of this little French
Loreto, with its high altar that "glitters all over with white and black
marble, as does the rood screen in this sacred manor," and its "very rich
sunburst" that sheltered the Host. The Guise Music presumably sang
Charpentier's compositions from the loft atop the marble rood screen.

Circa October 9 they reached Guise, where the new benches were
inaugurated, doubtlessly to music by Charpentier. Protesting that he was
acting in the King's name, Intendant Lafitte insisted on sitting on the
castoff bench near the back door. Throughout the recriminations that
followed, Marie de Lorraine feigned naive innocence about her alleged
insult, asserting blandly that "she had never had any thought beyond the
decent appearance of the church."[39]

Marie de Lorraine was confronted by another crisis a few months
later, but this time it was she who was humiliated. In January 1681
MADEMOISELLE DE MONTPENSIER was declared the victor in litigation over
the late Duchess of Guise's will that had dragged on for more than two
decades. To the 500,000 livres that Mademoiselle de Guise had been
sentenced to pay her niece back in 1658, she now had to add an
additional 440,000 livres! Pay she must and pay she did; but she was
determined to disinherit her overbearing and greedy niece by spending
everything she could, and by writing a will so clever that nothing would
be left for Montpensier—who had been declared one of the heirs to the
Guise estate by the settlement with MADAME DE GUISE back in 1675.

To simplify to the maximum the execution of her testament, Her
Highness followed CHRISTOPHLE DE ROQUETTE's advice. She covertly began
paying the debts she had inherited from her parents and her profligate
brother, as well as the ones she had incurred for her late nephew. She
gave money to found masses and devotions at MONTMARTRE, and she
presented the abbey with several precious objects. She added paintings
to the gallery adjacent to the music room and dining room, asking help
from Gondi, the former Florentine agent with whom she had had so
many pleasant conversations during his mission in Paris. He should, she
ordered, look for "two paintings by ancient masters that are agreeable to
look at and that have, if possible, devotional subjects or at least very
modest ones. I want them to be able to be held in esteem by everyone
and to be incontestably original." The only other consideration was their
size, which was not to exceed the dimensions she was providing. There
was no hurry, she added, apologizing for the "liberties" she was taking in
asking him to help her. The letter ended with expressions of friendship

that reveal much about the personality of the last Guise: her "pleasures" were commands, stated with cordiality:

> Being so useless to you, I truly am ashamed to ask you for a pleasure that will cause you so much trouble; but you wanted me to do so with confidence, ... so be persuaded that I will have a true joy to serve you, if you would do me the kindness of saying how I can be useful in some way that you think suitable.

In the end, Mademoiselle de Guise found two paintings on her own. She sent Gondi a cordial letter to inform him of her success and to evoke old times:

> It has been so long, Monsieur, since I had news from you, that I cannot help asking for news of you and your court, to which I am still just as attached. The newsletters sometimes tell us things; but one is not content, for they are so general. I cannot tell you more news about me other than, by the grace of God, my health is the same, with no added indispositions. I also think I must tell you that last summer I was fortunate to find two paintings that fit the two places in my gallery, ... so I am no longer searching for that size, and I send you a thousand thanks for the trouble you took to find some for me, and I pay you another thousand excuses for the frustration it gave you. All that remains is to ask you to continue your friendship always, and to assure you that no one can wish it more than I do, nor value it more. I want to show it to you by some service, if you think I can do one, ... you will do me great pleasure in employing me. Guise [40]

Her Highness can literally be heard speaking in these letters, for she commented, "You see, Monsieur, that I write to you just as I spoke to you while you were here. I am sure you will not be displeased, since this confidentiality is based on my esteem for you"—indeed, "my affection." This letter that overflows with "confidentiality" was written late in 1686, as Marie de Lorraine's health declined and her world kept shrinking. This confidentiality was the pseudo-confidentiality that characterized pseudo-personal statements uttered in elegant salons or expressed in courtly letters.

That Mademoiselle de Guise could not go beyond these courtly expressions of friendship made still more painful the death of her principal confidant, her sister, MADAME DE MONTMARTRE, four years earlier. As she had told Gondi at that time, "My poor sister ... was the only consolation in my life, and you knew the tenderness and friendship in which we lived together."[41] She could not count on receiving that sort of "tenderness" and "friendship" from her niece, MADEMOISELLE DE MONTPENSIER, nor from her nephew's widow, MADAME DE GUISE. Nor—with the exception, perhaps, of a few chambermaids and her two maids of honor—was a truly affectionate relationship possible with her paid householders. Discipline within the household depended on everyone's strict observance of the master–servant relationship upon which the domestic hierarchy was predicated. Her very businesslike letter to an anguished GAIGNIÈRES in May 1679 demonstrates her determination to observe these conventions.

She could scarcely unburden herself to her Lorraine cousins, who were eagerly awaiting the day when they would profit from her death. It is therefore understandable that, after MADAME DE MONTMARTRE's death, Marie de Lorraine turned increasingly to MONSIEUR DU BOIS and BISHOP ROQUETTE, and finally to Father La Chaise, one of the FOUR JESUITS portrayed in this gallery. And that she turned ever more to music, another form of consolation.

The creation of the Great Guise Music coincides chronologically with the loss of the lawsuit with MADEMOISELLE DE MONTPENSIER in January 1681 and the ABBESS OF MONTMARTRE's death in December 1682—events that prompted Marie de Lorraine to live the rest of her life in maximum splendor, and to find, in music, the affection and the spiritual nourishment that her dear sister had once provided. Having her Music and her composer, paying their wages and their upkeep, and sponsoring concerts in prestigious venues, became her way of asserting to all the nobles of the court and to Louis XIV himself, that she was able to do prestigious and splendid things, despite her age and her increasing infirmity, and despite the impending end of the House of Guise. By the summer of 1684 a half-dozen young people had been added to the GUISE MUSIC and had begun performing[A] with their elders. Marie de Lorraine even engaged a singing teacher for them. The Great Guise Music was born.

Around that time she had a list of her domestics drawn up, with a legacy or a pension for each, according to the length of service. To exasperate MADEMOISELLE DE MONTPENSIER, and to make it difficult for her heirs to sell the Hôtel de Guise, she eventually decreed that any householder residing there at the time of her death could not be expelled, for she was making them a "gift" of their lodgings. In addition, she tried several strategies, none of them successful, to ensure that the name *Guise* would not die and would be passed on to a male of the House of Lorraine.[42]

Survivor that she was, Marie de Lorraine lived magnificently in her splendid residence, surrounded by some seventy householders. She eagerly awaited the delivery of jasmine plants, and bulbs, and music books from Florence; she sent one of her maids to the lodging of the

[A] Cahier 41, H. 333.

Marie de Lorraine, Duchess of Guise and Princess of Joinville.
This portrait by Mignard predates the engraving, perhaps by as much as a decade.
In 1684 Philippe Goibaut du Bois chose to reproduce this portrait in his edition
of Saint Augustine's *Lettres*, dedicated to Mademoiselle de Guise and published
in 1686. The emblematic last tree is accompanied by a motto:
Succisas dat conjectare superstes, "The survivor bears witness to the fallen"

Grand Duke's agent to request jasmine-scented chocolate; and she demonstrated her gratitude to the Medicis and their officers by sending them French-style clothes, ribbons, and coifs. Although she must have known that she was fatally ill, she ordered the replacement of the worn-out green woolen surface of the billiard table in her antechamber. She settled a lawsuit with the late Duke Henri's second "wife," Mademoiselle de Pons.[43] She dispatched CHRISTOPHLE DE ROQUETTE to inspect her lands. With the financial aspects of her estate in mind, she settled debt upon debt, so that when she died only a hundred-odd long-term debts remained unpaid.[44]

Marie de Lorraine had become a legendary figure for the court and for the elite society of her day. The world came to her, to consult her on political and courtly matters. In a letter sent back to Florence, she and Renaudot, editor of the *Gazette de France*, were cited as expert sources about the politics of a marriage being negotiated between a French noble family and the ruling house of Portugal.[45] At Louis XIV's request, she helped keep MADAME DE TOSCANE under control after MADAME DE MONT-MARTRE's death.[46] Remaining open to the world outside the high walls of the Hôtel de Guise that protected her from prying eyes, she sought information from her visitors. Apparently worried about the safety of the son who had been raised in the Low Countries, she asked the Tuscan agent whether he had heard that a fortuneteller was predicting war in Flanders. The very thought made her grow pale. Whispering "Jesus," she made the sign of the cross.[47]

Marie de Lorraine's health was failing. She concealed a cancer, permitting those close to her to talk merely of the "little bit of gangrene" on her arm that was scraped off from time to time. Eager to show his gratitude, but surely motivated by gossip about how generous her bequests were likely to be, PHILIPPE GOIBAUT DU BOIS dedicated one of his translations of Saint Augustine to her in 1686, complete with a splendid engraved portrait. Du Bois elected to reproduce Mignard's portrait of her, as if he preferred to preserve for posterity the Marie de Lorraine of the early 1670s. Together, the portrait and the dedicatory letter depict the patron–protégé relation, and the silence that surrounded it.

Succisas dat conjectare superstes, "The survivor bears witness to the fallen," reads the motto under the portrait, a motto doubtlessly invented by Du Bois himself. Although Marie de Lorraine—the survivor, the last tree in the great forest that had been the House of Guise—had avoided public praise for decades, Du Bois broke the taboo. He wrote a word-portrait of Marie de Lorraine to complement the engraved one:

> This House [of Lorraine] that is so distinguished among the
> Sovereign Houses of Europe, and whose dignity Your Highness
> sustains so well, might have supplied me with enough subjects that

would even be related to religion. ... The great princes from whom Your Highness descends were the principal supports of religion in this kingdom. ... But I know, Mademoiselle, that what can be of greater utility for the Church is always what is most in Your Highness's heart; and my knowledge of [that heart] does not permit me to doubt that she will, without comparison, be more touched by the gift I am offering her than by something that concerned only the glory of her name and of her House. It is the effect of that foundation of religion and faith that everyone reveres in Your Highness and of which she shows such noteworthy marks: a rule of life that is always consistent and worthy of being proposed as an example for all persons of her rank; the spirit of justice and equity she demonstrates in the conduct of her affairs; the limitless charity that is extended to all the needy about whom she learns; the care she has taken to do good and to maintain it in her lands by founding hospitals, sending missionaries, and paying for charitable schools; but especially that constancy and that resignation that is so Christian and so exemplary, which it has pleased God to test so harshly, and whose value is heightened by Your Highness's natural sensitivity, beyond anything words can express. I sense the pain I am causing her, and I dare go no further; but I could not contain myself entirely, nor resist the pleasure of making everyone understand that what is owed to virtue derives far more from [my] profound respect than from attachment and gratitude.[48]

This dedication contains a personal testimony to the patronage dispensed by Marie de Lorraine. If this book exists, Du Bois continued, the public "owes it to Your Highness, for it is she who gave me the means to finish my work, by the sweetness of the repose that her kindnesses permit all those who have the honor of belonging to her to enjoy." In the place of Philippe Goibaut du Bois, it could be Marc-Antoine Charpentier speaking here; or ÉTIENNE LOULIÉ , the senior member of the GUISE MUSIC; or the respected collector, ROGER DE GAIGNIÈRES, her equerry; or DOCTOR NOËL VALLANT, her physician.

Although Her Highness ordered the notary to draw up pensions for several householders who had demonstrated loyalty to the House of Guise over the years, Marc-Antoine Charpentier does not appear to have been among them. This suggests that he was not the sort of former domestic servant who expected a pension, and that he had received the customary "gratification" that a protector gave to a protégé living "near" him. The amount perhaps was less than the composer would have liked, for Marie de Lorraine was said to be somewhat niggardly toward her householders. (At any rate, Charpentier had to borrow from his sister a decade later, to purchase his position at the SAINTE-CHAPELLE. But perhaps he simply did not know how to manage the money he earned?)

One of the last extant pieces Charpentier composed for Marie de Lorraine appears to have been an extremely intimate *élévation*[A] for Holy Week 1687, almost certainly performed at the MERCY. In it, "I," sung by a woman, cries out to "Thee": "My most clement Savior, my most powerful Creator, who was crucified for me. Behold, I am thine, and I always will be."

By mid-1687 it had become clear that cancer would soon defeat the combative princess. Rumors began circulating:

> Mademoiselle de Guise is very dangerously ill from an inflammation that has degenerated into a tumor on her arm accompanied by a fever, and they even say she has cancer. On this occasion there is a great stir among the principal members of the House of Lorraine, and among a few others who will inherit part of her vast wealth. They say she has been informed that the King expects that, in disposing of her property, she will not make any bequest in favor of individuals who might be suspect to him.[49]

She was especially devious about concealing her illness from MADEMOI-SELLE DE MONTPENSIER:

> She hid her illness so well that no one knew she had a cancer. ... It was not talked about [at] the Hôtel de Guise, for whenever Mademoiselle [de Montpensier] came to see her, she would say she simply had rheumatism in her arm, and she would sit up on a little bed. In sum, she did not want to think about death, nor to have anyone think it was near.[50]

That particular observer was mistaken: Marie de Lorraine had been contemplating her death and planning her estate for several years. As she lay propped up on her daybed, pretending that all was well, she perused financial records old and new. She drew up a list of the family portraits in her possession. She consulted genealogical treatises and charters involving the House of Guise.[51]

There was a great deal of stir and a lot of plotting going on during the final months of 1687. Several issues were at stake. Some of the plotting was being done by Marie de Lorraine herself, in order to disinherit MADEMOISELLE DE MONTPENSIER. This involved calculating her total worth in real and personal property. Once this figure had been reached, a revised list of current domestics was drawn up, with either a cash legacy or a pension, according to the length of service. She made a considerable number of large pious bequests and foundations, most of them involving lands in Lorraine or religious establishments traditionally in the gift of the House of Lorraine. For a time she balanced between

[A] Cahier 48, H. 258.

having her personal property sold at auction and giving it to the King. In the end she opted for the auction. She granted MADAME DE GUISE lifetime rights to Marchais, the Guise château adjacent to Notre-Dame de Liesse; and MADEMOISELLE DE MONTPENSIER was willed her collection of crystal and agate vessels set in gold and encrusted with jewels and enamels, some of which survive in the collections of the Louvre.

In 1686, in the preamble to her autograph will, Mademoiselle de Guise set the stage for the battle over her estate. In the name of all the dead trees in the Guise forest, she was heeding God's will as she set about distributing her vast property:

Jesus † Maria

> In the name of the Father, the Son, and the Holy Spirit, I, Marie de Lorraine, Duchess of Guise, being by the grace of God healthy in body and mind, and desiring to employ what life remains to me to prepare for death, and considering that disposing of the property of my House, all of which is today in my hands, is one of the principal things for which I will have to render an accounting to God, I have resolved to write my will; and to that end having withdrawn into my *cabinet*, and having asked God for the light needed for this final act of my life, as I should have done for all the others, that is, according to His orders and with the sole goal of pleasing Him, and also to satisfy the obligations of my conscience and the consciences of all those from whom God permitted me to inherit, I have written my will as follows ....

During her final days, several important modifications were made to the testament. Some changes simply reflect the fact that her advisors had underestimated her total worth. That is to say, unless certain legacies were increased, Montpensier would not get the slap in the face she deserved. The amounts willed the domestics were therefore increased,[52] and two Lorraine women were willed a huge "gift" in cash, to be paid after all the other legacies. Only then would Montpensier and the other legal heirs receive their share of whatever remained. The existence of this surplus may have encouraged MONSIEUR DU BOIS, BISHOP ROQUETTE and Father La Chaise, one of the FOUR JESUITS portrayed in this gallery, to exert pressure on the dying woman, perhaps consciously and maliciously, perhaps unwittingly. Whatever their motives, their perceived "plot" resulted in codicils by which each man was granted a large cash payment in addition to previous bequests. (GAIGNIÈRES made sure that a record was kept of these goings-on, and he eventually dashed to Versailles to inform the King about the shocking new clauses.)

In addition to expressing her fondness for the three purported plotters to whom she had turned for affection and consolation, in each codicil she reiterated her wish that Marie Naudot, Sister of the Martyrs, the nun at MONTMARTRE who was generally believed to be her daughter, be assured of a pension. In the midst of a host of Lorraine-centered legacies—and in addition to the large legacy to the Jesuits—the dying princess remembered three institutions to which she had been intimately linked. The convent of Notre-Dame de la MERCY would receive three hundred livres a year, an income that the reverend fathers would consider a humiliating pittance. The Institute of the INFANT JESUS would receive six hundred livres, a sum that amounted to a full subsidy of three woman teachers each year. In addition to the pension that she had promised Louis XIV would be created for her cousin the Abbess, MONTMARTRE was willed four hundred livres a year for a daily mass in the memory the princess, her sister, her ancestors, her brothers, and her "dear nephew," Louis-Joseph de Lorraine.

The final codicil contained a shocking legacy, a veritable slap in the King's face. Drawing a not-too-subtle but tacit parallel between the tapestries known as "Emperor Maximilian's Hunt" that the Crown had refused to let her redeem after Duke Henri's death (they are now in the Louvre), and the "Tapestries of the Ages" based on cartoons by Giulio Romano, which had decorated the bedchamber of Louis-Joseph's father in 1654, she willed the Romano hangings to Louis XIV. And in another thinly disguised parallel between the Guise "Marriage Bed" with its coats of arms and dynastic implications, which she had been unable to wrench away from the King back in the 1660s, she willed Louis XIV an almost-complete set of embroidered red bed hangings, enhanced with pearls, upon which she had been working for eighteen years.

The will was viewed, and condemned, as a gesture worthy of the granddaughter of the scar-faced Duke who, for his pride and ambition, had been "executed" at Blois in 1588. Exactly one hundred years later, Marie de Lorraine was putting the House of Lorraine above the interests of the French royal family. The marginalia in one printed copy of her testament reveals that a century had not sufficed to modify the image of the Guises as traitors. Her donation to the poor in the duchies of Lorraine and Bar earned the rejoinder: "Why to the poor of Lorraine, since the property is in France and was acquired at the expense of so many poor people who still live here?" Her founding of a seminary in Lorraine or Bar: "In 1589 we cruelly felt the peril that kings can encounter, if there are monks who are devoted to people who are, by heredity, opposed to all the princes of the Royal House." Her creation of scholarships for girls from Lorraine and Bar, to be educated at Montmartre: "Good! As long as the duchies of Lorraine and Bar remain royal property, but if not, it is a hereditary plan of this House to help people from Lorraine at France's expense." A mass to be said at Saint-Mihel in honor of the Lorraines: "She would be willing to have all of France taken

Haute et Puissante Princesse Mademoiselle Marie de Lorraine
Duchesse de Guise et de Joyeuse, Princesse de Joinville. Restée seule
de la branche de Guise, héritiere de toutes les vertus et de tous les biens des princes ses ancêtres. Née à Paris le 15 d'aoust 1615 de Charles de Lorraine Duc de
Guise, et de Henriette Catherine seule heritiere de la maison de Joyeuse : qui
auoit epouse en premieres noces Henri de Bourbon Duc de Montpensier.

Picart Rom.ⁿ ad viu del 1680.

Mademoiselle de Guise in 1686.
"High and powerful princess Mademoiselle Marie de Lorraine, Duchess of Guise
and Joyeuse, Princess of Joinville. She alone remained of the House of Guise.
She inherited all the virtues and all the possessions of the princes her ancestors.
She was born in Paris on August 15, 1615, to Charles of Lorraine, Duke of Guise,
and Henriette-Catherine de Joyeuse, the sole heir of the House of Joyeuse,
whose first husband was Henri de Bourbon, Duke of Montpensier."

to Lorraine, and one can judge what this House would be capable of doing, ... if they were allowed to elevate themselves and assume the rank they had a century ago. ... [The mass is] a good safety measure for preserving the memory of the League and warding off the outlawing of their House in 1588." Her wish to have the Guise name live on: "[It] has always served the French royal standard by assembling rebels, just as the tail of Mohammed's horse brought the Infidels together." And finally, her bequest of family portraits to the Lorraine male who would assume the name *Guise*: "Very few would remain if she had excluded the individuals who were proscribed and rebels against our kings, their masters and benefactors."[53]

Marie de Lorraine died on Ash Wednesday, March 3, 1688. People held their breath as they waited for her will to be made public. Would she would finally acknowledge the existence of her children by Montrésor? She did not mention them, "neither in her will nor in any more covert way."[54]

Within a half hour, MADEMOISELLE DE MONTPENSIER and the Condés sent a notary to place seals on the doors of the Hôtel de Guise. The overzealous notary sealed the doors to Mademoiselle de Guise's apartment, leaving her body to lie unattended, on the deathbed, for four full days. When doctors were finally admitted, they managed to remove her heart so that it could be carried to Montmartre for burial, but her body was so decomposed that it could not be dressed in the habit of a Capucine, as she had wished. "Although she had made legacies of many millions of livres, and although she was surrounded by a huge court, ... no one thought of embalming her"; and while her funeral was being planned, "they put her in a cellar without candles and without priests."[55]

"With great pomp" the funeral was held at the Capucine convent on March 13. Furious about the will, Montpensier and Condé refused to come and sprinkle the coffin with the traditional holy water; nor did they and their householders go into mourning. The procession from the Hôtel de Guise to the Capucines is known to have consisted of several six-horse coaches bearing princes and princesses of the House of Lorraine, fifteen deaf mutes, and six "ordinary" coaches devoid of mourning drapery, in which rode a few of Condé's and Montpensier's householders.[56] The ten-day interval between Mademoiselle de Guise's death and burial left adequate time to prepare a revival of some of the music that Marc-Antoine Charpentier had written for LOUIS-JOSEPH DUKE OF GUISE in 1671 and 1672, but the scanty descriptions of the event make no mention of music.

MADEMOISELLE DE MONTPENSIER had indeed been disinherited, although the Parlement nullified some of the clauses in the will. She did not live long enough to see the end of the legal formalities, for she died in 1693. The legacies were paid out in dribbles for more than three decades, and no one received the full amount due him, for all the heirs had been forced to pay the legal expenses.

March 2, 1688

Panel 11

They Too Bear Witness

They Preserved Evidence, They Influenced

F ive paintings fill this final panel. All the subjects are shown writing, sorting papers, or peering intently into an adjacent room. Unlike the individuals portrayed in the other panels, the people depicted here did not directly affect Marc-Antoine Charpentier's creativity. Rather, they served as record-keepers. Sometimes they were catalysts, causing modifications in his career or shaping his intellect.

The court gown worn by the woman in the first painting reveals that she is a highborn princess. She holds a thick manuscript entitled *Memoirs*. She does not seem to mind being segregated from the other high nobles in Panel 9 and Panel 10—all of whom she detests.

The second painting is a group portrait. A scrivener takes notes during an interrogation being conducted by several dignified men. All have paused and are staring through the open door at a terrified wretch who fights the stake to which he is tied, as the executioner lights the pyre at his feet.

In the third painting a gentleman is sorting documents and drawings. He has stopped working on the collection before him and gazes through the window at the garden façade of the Hôtel de Guise.

The next painting is another group portrait. A prelate talks with a man who is poring over account books. In the background stand two young men, one a layman, the other a cleric.

A black-garbed physician is depicted in the fifth portrait. He is sitting in his *cabinet*. Stacks of thick Latin tomes lie flat on the shelves that line the walls. The doctor has been sorting his papers and has paused to read a letter.

The final painting shows two young men, one dressed in gray and red, the other in a cassock. They are sitting at a table strewn with books and papers. Some of the papers are musical scores, others are scholarly treatises. In the shadows a variety of musical instruments can be discerned.

I

The misfortunes of my House

MADEMOISELLE DE MONTPENSIER

Anne-Marie-Louise d'Orléans, Duchess of Montpensier,
known as "Mademoiselle," or the "Grand Mademoiselle,"
Mademoiselle de Guise's niece and Madame de Guise's half-sister

Anne-Marie-Louise d'Orléans[1] began her *Memoirs* with a lament: "The beginning of the misfortunes of my House occurred shortly after my birth, since it was followed by my mother's death: which greatly diminished the good fortune that my rank should have led me to expect."[2] Her tormented personality caused Mademoiselle to blame many of these misfortunes on relatives in whose veins flowed the blood of the House of Lorraine.

So strong was Mademoiselle de Montpensier's dislike for her aunt, MADEMOISELLE DE GUISE, her cousin LOUIS-JOSEPH DE LORRAINE, DUKE OF GUISE, and her half-sisters, MADAME DE GUISE and MADAME DE TOSCANE, that she has refused to allow her picture to hang beside theirs in Panel 9 and Panel 10 of this gallery, where members of the Houses of Bourbon, Orléans, and Guise can be contemplated. The princess reasoned as follows: while alive, she avoided seeing or speaking to these individuals, often because they had failed to take the initiative and visit her first, in hopes of mending a bridge or smoothing over a perceived slight.[3] So why should she, a ghost, confront them now, in this imagined portrait gallery?

Montpensier's derogatory words about her relatives have been woven into their portraits. The evidence she preserved about Marc-Antoine Charpentier's protectresses is not, of course, always derogatory. But when it is, her negative remarks usually overlie statements of fact, like a bitter, poisonous frosting. The accuracy of many of Montpensier's assertions is confirmed by other reliable evidence. Still, she omitted from her memoirs some very important incidents involving her sisters or her aunt. By their absence, these omissions are important. The bitterness, the search for dominance, and the unconcealed animosity that the Grande Mademoiselle showed toward one relative or another, appears to have prompted those individuals to modify the path they had been following through life.

Anne-Marie-Louise d'Orléans was proud to say that no Lorraine blood—at least no recent Lorraine blood—flowed in her veins. This granddaughter of a Bourbon, a Medici, a Bourbon-Montpensier, and a Joyeuse was born on May 27, 1627, to GASTON D'ORLÉANS and his first wife, Marie de Montpensier, the half-sister of MADEMOISELLE MARIE DE GUISE. Her mother died only a few days after giving birth, and neither of the little princess's grandmothers was around to fill the affective void in her life. Her paternal grandmother, Queen Marie de Médicis, was disgraced in 1630 and withdrew to the Low Countries; and four years later, her maternal grandmother, the Duchess of Guise, was exiled to Florence. Although both grandmothers were absent, it was rank, rather than the distance between Florence and Paris, that caused the little princess to think of the Duchess of Guise as somehow inferior. Her Guise grandmother was "my far-away grammy. She is not a queen."[4]

Mademoiselle did not see her father much either: he was sometimes in disgrace for his plots, sometimes in favor, and sometimes in exile —where he eloped with beautiful Marguerite de Lorraine. In 1643 this second marriage was finally recognized, and sixteen-year-old Mademoiselle came face to face with the new DUCHESS OF ORLÉANS. A terrible disdain for her stepmother soon held Anne-Marie-Louise in its talons, eventually turning into open animosity. Her scorn for this particular Lorraine was transferred to her maternal relatives, the Lorraines of Guise, perhaps because Marguerite de Lorraine's sister had married MADEMOISELLE MARIE DE GUISE's bastard cousin. Whatever the reasons for Mademoiselle's animosity, by the mid-1640s, she was viewing the Lorraines in general with a jaundiced eye; and when she began her memoirs in 1659, she dipped her pen in poison.

When the Lorraines of Guise had returned from exile in 1643, Mademoiselle was initially ecstatic about having a grandmother and an aunt nearby: "I went to visit her at the Hôtel de Guise, which she said made her very happy. ... The next day Madame de Guise came to dine with me, and after that, for a long time I visited her almost every day." Montpensier was especially happy to find that Marie de Guise agreed with her on certain issues. "I had such a strong friendship for Madame and Mademoiselle de Guise that I could not keep from seeing them every day."

The young princess's enthusiasm soon soured, as so many things did in her life. Having been punished by her governess for attempting an evening visit to the Hôtel de Guise, "I imagined that this could not have happened without Madame de Guise's involvement. So I no longer was so eager to see her, and after that I felt a certain coolness toward her."[5] The coolness turned to animosity, and by 1644 Mademoiselle was suspicious about everything involving her stepmother, her grandmother, and her aunt, Mademoiselle Marie de Guise, who was some ten years her senior. She accused her aunt of "behaving badly," being "angry," and "whispering" things to the Duchess of Guise, in order to put people who disagreed with them in a bad light, or to "ruin plans" that Mademoiselle herself favored.[6] Montpensier's animosity increased over the years, and it seems to have given her great satisfaction.

Whether she was born that way, or whether this attitude was fed by backbiting at court, Mademoiselle early proved to be headstrong, cantankerous, vindictive. "Granddaughter of France" that she was, she saw great nobles, grands, as essentially different from ordinary mortals. Her conduct was therefore to be revered, and never questioned: "The intentions of the great nobles must be like the mysteries of the Faith," she observed. "One must revere [these mysteries] and believe that they always are for the good and safety of the country."[7] Her interventions at the Bastille and at Orléans during the rebellion known as the Fronde partook of these mysteries, about which she had considerable time to meditate while exiled to her country house at Saint-Fargeau during the early 1650s. (Eager to leave that remote place, a young householder named Lully asked permission to leave her service. He soon found his way into Louis XIV's good graces.)

Her father and stepmother were exiled too, at Blois, where they were surrounded by their young children. Montpensier not only deplored the arrival of each successive child born to the DUKE AND DUCHESS OF ORLÉANS, she found it difficult to say anything favorable about her half-sisters.

Relegated to Saint-Fargeau by royal order, Montpensier could not keep abreast of what GASTON D'ORLÉANS was doing. Her appeals for records of his stewardship of her property went unanswered, and the reason soon became clear. Consciously confusing thine and mine, Gaston had absconded with some of her revenues in order to accumulate money for dowries that would permit her half-sisters to make prestigious marriages. The father soon sued the daughter, and the daughter sued the father. At the mere mention of Montpensier's name, Gaston would shout: "She does not like her sisters, she said they were 'beggars,' and that after my death she would watch them beg for alms and not give them any." He would also bring up Mademoiselle's cutting remarks about her stepmother: "My mother was of the House of Bourbon, and she brought four hundred thousand livres a year to the House [of Orléans]; and my stepmother is a Lorraine, and she got nothing" as a dowry—or, to be exact, nothing but a few pikes and muskets to arm one of Gaston's rebel regiments.[8]

A settlement between father and daughter clearly had to be worked out. The litigants turned to the Duchess of Guise, who agreed to act as arbiter. Montpensier was dubious, convinced as she was that "my grandmother has never liked me."[9] After months of seemingly doing nothing, the Duchess summoned Gaston and Mademoiselle for an urgent reconciliation ceremony and insisted that both parties sign an agreement without reading it first. The next day Montpensier realized she had been duped. Gaston ended up owing her nothing, while she was liable for "her" share of his debts.[10] The arbiters accused the Duchess of Guise of altering their findings. After a terrible spat with her grandmother and her aunt, Mademoiselle attributed their deceit to the fact that they were pro-Lorraine, even though the Duchess's first husband had been a Bourbon-Montpensier:

> I told [my grandmother] that it seemed that she preferred the House of Lorraine to the House of Bourbon; that she was right to try to give property to my sisters; that they would get little from Madame [d'Orléans], and that this demonstrated to me that I was a great lady who had enough to get by on her own, and that the fortune of my family was going to be built on what could be grabbed away from me; but that I was superior enough to them for them to accept my kindnesses; and so it was better to let them count on my generosity than to trick me out of it; that this was the better way, according to God and to men.[11]

This rejoinder to her grandmother became the central theme of her relations with MADEMOISELLE DE GUISE for the next three decades. Her hatred for the House of Lorraine would also contaminate Montpensier's relations with her half-sisters.

This animosity toward Mademoiselle de Guise is exemplified in, and was in large part caused by a financial dispute that ended in a lengthy lawsuit, souring their relations for the next thirty years. The Duchess of Guise died in 1656, while Montpensier was at Saint-Fargeau: "Mademoiselle de Guise apologized for not having informed me of her illness, but she had been too upset." Montpensier preferred her own interpretation of this silence:

> But I think that the real reason was that she was afraid that ... [my grandmother] might repent about what she had done to drive a

wedge between me and [my father], and about the dispositions of her will, which were not fair.[12]

Mademoiselle had been willed 20,000 livres a year, which represented the income on an investment of 300,000 livres. She also was willed a diamond worth 200,000 livres that had "come to me from Mademoiselle de Guise, who had given it to my mother when she married, and this diamond had been given to my grandfather, the Duke of Joyeuse, by King Henri III, one of whose favorites he was."[13] In her will, her grandmother requested that Montpensier be content with this legacy. Initially, she accepted the conditions of the will. Thus Mademoiselle de Guise began borrowing money in December 1657—511,500 livres in all, a total just slightly in excess of the 500,000 livres she had agreed to pay her niece. (Montpensier had agreed to return the diamond, for its cash equivalent.) The money came from twenty-six individuals, virtually all of whom "belonged" to the Guises.[14] Some descended from householders at the time of the League. Another group (they loaned a total of 233,500 livres) were the in-laws, the cousins, and the husband of MARIE TALON, who only five years later would sign ÉLISABETH CHARPENTIER's wedding contract.

Once she had thought it over, Mademoiselle de Montpensier decided that she was not "content" with her legacy after all. Although she accepted the 500,000 livres her aunt had borrowed, she claimed an equal share of the estate. Year after year lawyers for both sides conferred, but nothing was decided.[15] Decree followed decree: 1662, 1663, 1665, 1670, 1679, and finally 1680, when the Parlement ordered Mademoiselle de Guise to pay her niece an additional 440,000 livres.[16] Mademoiselle de Guise appealed, but the appeal was rejected in January 1681. Rejected because Montpensier, by her own admission, had used a verbal thumbscrew on her cousin the King:

> Mademoiselle de Guise, who does not give up easily, defended herself again. ... Her influence over the First President, and over others, is such that I encountered a thousand problems in the Great Chamber [of the Parlement]. ... This wretched affair forced me to talk to the King in private twenty times, almost an hour each time, and several other times that were much too long for my taste, because I was afraid of boring him. ... I won, my victory is total: the battlefield is mine; I get the booty. If I had wanted only the honor, Mademoiselle de Guise would have been very pleased; but it is just that I should profit from her wealth and not leave it to her to dispose of.[17]

Having become the official owner of the rough diamond willed her by her grandmother, Montpensier began thinking aloud about having it cut—which would make it of "inestimable value"—and inserted into a clasp with all her other fine diamonds.[18] The threat was calculated to hurt Mademoiselle de Guise, just as a resentful MADAME DE GUISE's plans to tear down parts of the Hôtel de Guise in 1673 had been aimed at wounding and humiliating her.

MADEMOISELLE DE GUISE was not simply wounded, she was furious. She set about spending her money, living splendidly in her magnificent hotel, with seventy-odd householders tending to her needs. One of the aspects of this politics of grandeur was the expansion of the GUISE MUSIC. A bevy of new musicians began to be hired during the months that followed her defeat in the Parlement. Her Highness began preparing a testament that would disinherit her niece and give most of her wealth to the House of Lorraine and to charitable foundations. After her death in 1688, one of the attorneys administering her estate offered a tongue-in-cheek justification of the last Guise's will—which he knew full well had been crafted to disinherit her detested and detestable niece:

> Mademoiselle de Guise loved her name [Lorraine]; that is a
> praiseworthy passion for great nobles. ... Her wealth was incapable of
> making a granddaughter of France [Montpensier] and princes of the
> blood [the Condés] more illustrious. She used her wealth for pious
> legacies, for alms, for rewards to her domestics, for gifts to the
> princes and princesses of her blood and her name. Are not these
> sentiments natural enough, without imputing them to hatred for the
> heir?[19]

To complicate matters for her so-called "natural" heirs, Mademoiselle de Guise stated her wishes in such a way that they were to be paid last: "And so, no matter how one goes about it, it will take sixty years to get to the end" of the settlement of the estate.[20] In other words, it was clear from the outset that Mademoiselle de Montpensier could not possibly live long enough to receive any of her aunt's fortune. To assert their claim to the estate, Montpensier and Condé had a notary waiting near the Hôtel de Guise, where the last Guise lay dying. Within a half hour of her death, the notary placed seals on the doors—imprisoning Mademoiselle de Guise's body in her bedchamber for several days. To demonstrate their resentment, the heirs not only refused to come and sprinkle the body with holy water, they denigrated the dead woman by refusing to participate in her funeral procession. In fact, instead of sending their most showy coaches, each heir dispatched "three ordinary coaches with no drapery," bearing a few of their gentlemen and domestics.[21]

Mademoiselle's relations with her stepmother and her half-sisters were as full of animosity as her relations with her aunt; but in many ways the situation was worse, because after GASTON D'ORLÉANS' death in 1660 these antagonistic women lived under a single roof, the Luxembourg Palace. Some of her antagonism toward her half-sisters probably stemmed from frustrated marriage plans:

> In her youth the Grande Mademoiselle had thought she would marry the Emperor, the King of England, the Duke of Savoy. Her imperious humor caused her to break all these marriage plans. Finally, in 1660, she wanted to marry Prince Charles of Lorraine. Every evening she would invite him to supper with violins; there would be dancing half the night. But, unfortunately for her, Mademoiselle d'Orléans, her sister, was present at all these parties, beautiful as the day, at sixteen. Mademoiselle appeared to be her grandmother. Prince Charles fell in love with [Mademoiselle d'Orléans]. The old princess soon realized it and canceled all her parties. Mademoiselle d'Orléans wed the Grand Duke [of Tuscany], and Prince Charles left France. Mademoiselle then contemplated marrying Monsieur [Philippe II d'Orléans], who received the proposition with such scorn that, enraged at all princes, she got the idea of making the fortune of a French nobleman [Lauzun] who was her good servant, and who went along with whatever she wished.[22]

Montpensier appears to have seen ISABELLE D'ALENÇON's union with LOUIS-JOSEPH DE LORRAINE in 1667 as strengthening the entire House of Lorraine, whom she blamed for every unfortunate event in her life—especially for having convinced Louis XIV at the last minute to forbid her marriage to Lauzun in December 1670. Shortly before the King made his position known, she had returned home to see "the whole House of Lorraine assembled, for they now marched only as a corps, to fight me." Madame de Guise and Mademoiselle de Guise were, she was convinced, the ringleaders of this plot against her[23]—which probably explains why she refused to attend the Harcourt–Cadaval wedding at the Hôtel de Guise in February 1671. It was a Lorraine marriage, hosted by Lorraines. This doubtlessly also explains why she refused to talk to the Duke of Guise a few months later. And it definitely explains why she did not send a personal letter of condolence to the Dowager of Orléans, Madame de Guise, and Mademoiselle de Guise after the Duke's death: "They had behaved so badly toward [Lauzun] and toward me, that I did not feel obliged to observe the proprieties with them."[24]

On one occasion Mademoiselle almost felt tenderness toward a Lorraine. In the winter of 1672, as death hovered over her stepmother, the DOWAGER DUCHESS OF ORLÉANS, Montpensier saw the Dowager being carried out into the garden of the Luxembourg to catch a bit of sun:

> I watched her through the window. If she had asked me, I would
> have gone to see her; but since I did not have anything for which to
> beg her forgiveness [as was customary when someone was dying],
> and since it was I who had been mistreated by her, I was afraid that
> if I went, she would think it was in order to rejoice at seeing her in
> that condition—which I never would have done, being a Christian
> and not liking to see death, because I am so afraid of it, and
> therefore would never wish it on anyone.[25]

Anne-Marie-Louise d'Orléans left Paris without saying a last farewell to her stepmother.

The negative side of Mademoiselle's personality had by then become legendary:

> This princess ... is proud, go-getting, free-speaking, and cannot
> tolerate anything that runs counter to her way of thinking. She is
> the richest unmarried woman in Europe. ... She is handsomely tall, a
> bit masculine, and elevated by a gait that is free and bold. She has a
> majestic carriage and is rather easy to approach. Her humor is
> impatient, her mind active, and her heart ardent in everything she
> undertakes. ... She does not know what dissimulation is, and she
> expresses her feelings without taking anything else into
> consideration.[26]

The return to France of her half-sister, MADAME DE TOSCANE, in 1675 modified the dynamics between the sisters to some extent. Montpensier usually avoided going to see MADAME DE TOSCANE at MONTMARTRE, for she knew the visit would probably end in a quarrel; yet on at least one occasion she appeared uninvited at one of the weekly entertainments at the Hôtel de Guise that her sisters attended.[27]

By 1680 all three sisters were devoting themselves to charitable and devotional activities. Although, Mademoiselle de Montpensier does not appear to have accompanied her sisters each week to Madame de Miramion's charitable establishment run by the Sisters of Charity, she began putting in an appearance at the LITTLE CARMEL. In fact, perhaps through insensitivity, but perhaps through malice, she abandoned the Great Carmel to which she had been faithful for years, and she concentrated on the Little Carmel, where a power vacuum had been created by the QUEEN's death in 1683. MADAME DE TOSCANE and MADAME DE GUISE soon abandoned the Little Carmel and began visiting the great one, where their friend, Louise de la Vallière was a nun. "We are still in disgrace with Madame de Guise," wrote one of the nuns of the Little Carmel, "but Mademoiselle consoles us." Mademoiselle was not only their consolation, she was their entertainment. She told them about gifts she was planning to give Lauzun, she made them privy to a large donation she was preparing to give one of Louis XIV's bastard sons; and she promised to show the nuns the huge diamond that was hers at last. Soon Anne-Marie-Louise d'Orléans was spending the night at the Little Carmel.[28]

Her search for a meaning in life was sincere, although her way of going about it was perhaps less than considerate. After her definitive break with Lauzun in 1685, Mademoiselle began writing devotional books. Shortly before her death she came full circle, and in her comments on the *Imitation of Jesus* she returned to the theme of "misfortune" with which she had begun her *Memoirs*:

> Greatness of birth and the advantages bestowed by wealth and by nature should provide all the elements of a happy life. But experience should have taught us that there are many people who have all these things and are not happy; that there are moments when one believes oneself happy, but it does not last. ... The events of my own past would give me enough proof of this. ... But alas! Since the veil has fallen from my eyes, I have known that all the grandeur, all the vanity, and all the pomps and pleasures of the world have been illusions, and that however much effort we make to possess and enjoy them, they are destroyed in a moment. And I have certainly seen that we are only actors who play a role in the theater, and that the persons portrayed are not our true selves.[29]

Anne-Marie-Louise d'Orléans died on April 5, 1693. After the customary prayers in the Luxembourg Palace, her body was taken to the royal necropolis of Saint-Denis to await burial. There, on May 7, the King's Music performed during a requiem mass sung in her honor. Marc-Antoine Charpentier's notebooks appear to contain that music,[A] presumably commissioned by MADAME DE GUISE.

By an irony of Fate, the so-called "Guise portrait gallery" in the Château of Eu, which Mademoiselle bought from Mademoiselle de Guise in 1660, has survived, almost intact. As in our imaginary portrait gallery, there is a notable gap. The portrait of Marie de Lorraine of Guise is missing!

[A] Cahier "b," H. 7, recopied into cahier LXIII.

II

A veritable river that carries everything with it

THE POISON INVESTIGATORS

The anonymous scriveners who recorded facts
about "La Charpentier," Belot, and some people with familiar names
who were investigated during the Poison Affair

During the late 1670s and early 1680s, the so-called "Poison Affair" spread terror in the capital and at court. This group portrait depicts the anonymous scriveners who recorded the interrogations, and the wretches they questioned. As in any witch hunt, some of the things to which the suspects confessed were imagined. Still, the threat was real—for the suspect and for his friends and associates. Anyone linked by surname, address, or profession was suspect in his turn and could find himself tied to a stake in the Place de la Grève, trembling as the executioner lighted the pyre.

Although the Poison Affair did not surface until 1676, it took shape in the late 1660s, when the Marquise of Brinvilliers began using slow poison to eliminate her father, her two brothers, and her husband. The deaths would perhaps never have attracted attention had her lover not died, leaving a little chest with a label stating that it should be turned over to Brinvilliers, and that an attached pacquet should be given to a financier named Reich de Pennautier.

Suspicions were raised when the Marquise attempted to gain access to the chest, which had been placed under notarial seals along with the rest of the dead man's possessions. When the police officials from the Châtelet opened the chest, they found more than papers: they discovered concoctions made with arsenic. The long illnesses and painful deaths of Madame de Brinvilliers' relatives at last made sense. Brinvilliers fled the country but was captured and brought back to Paris for interrogation. Prior to her execution in mid-July 1676, she tried to implicate Pennautier, who was briefly detained but released.

The police continued their investigations. Only a few days after Brinvilliers' execution, the police questioned a certain Alexandre Belleguise, who had been the cashier of Pennautier's late colleague, Pierre Dalibert, receiver for the clergy. The fact that Dalibert—who after a brief illness in July 1671 had succumbed to what appeared to be apoplexy—was Jacques I Dalibert's nephew and JACQUES II DALIBERT's first cousin[1] does not appear to have been a consideration in the investigation.

Still, owing to the recent investigations of the Fouquet Affair, the authorities were well aware that Jacques I Dalibert had used the name *Belleguise* for some of his financial speculations.[2] They also knew that Jacques II was in living in Rome, in Queen Christina's household, for the Queen had sent him to Paris in the mid-1660s to represent her interests to the royal administration. And everyone knew that Christina was fascinated with alchemy. Suspicion that travelers to and from Italy might be involved in a poison plot was heightened when the police learned that Brinvilliers' lover had shared a lodging with an Italian who had been in Christina's service. This Italian was a very shady individual reputed for his skill with poisons.[3]

Italy in general—and Rome in particular—was synonymous with poison for the typical Frenchman, elite or popular. In fact, around the time of Pierre Dalibert's death, a poet captured this public image by linking Paris, Rome, and poisons:

> I cannot, without horror and without pain, see the great waves of
> the Tiber mingle with the Seine and drag to Paris its brats, its jokers,
> its language, its poisons, its crimes, and its morals, and [see] everyone
> joyously, in this time so full of vice, make their malice even richer by
> the crimes of Italy.[4]

When Brinvilliers was arrested in April 1676, Marc-Antoine Charpentier was just embarking on a series of oratorios[A] for MADAME DE GUISE's "devotions." Although these works were Italianate in style, it is unlikely that this preoccupation with Italian music, prompted by MADAME DE TOSCANE's return to France, rendered either the composer or the princesses suspect to the police. Still, it would not be surprising if Charpentier's name found its way to the police office around that time, for he not only had lived in Rome, he had links to JACQUES II DALIBERT (either through both families' service to the House of Orléans during the 1660s, or through encounters at the Farnese when the DUKE OF CHAULNES was ambassador to Rome, or both).

[A] Cahiers 9–11, H. 391, H. 392; cahier 12, H. 393.

When questioned, Belleguise replied that he had been employed by Pierre Dalibert for some twenty years and had stayed on to work for Pennautier. During his interrogation Belleguise insisted that Pennautier "had no better friend than Dalibert, and that he had never poisoned him, nor thought about it." Questioned in July 1677, Pennautier protested his innocence: despite rumors that Dalibert had been poisoned, he had kept Belleguise in his employ, because he did not want to part with a good accountant.[5]

The tentacles of the investigation were not, however, reaching toward the Hôtel de Guise and the Luxembourg Palace. Indeed, it is unlikely that MADEMOISELLE DE GUISE and MADAME DE GUISE were trying to allay suspicions about their loyalty, and the loyalty of their composer, when they sent up musical prayers for the KING and honored the Jubilee being carried out by the QUEEN and the DAUPHIN.[A] These musical tributes presumably were sincere and offered with no ulterior motive.

In September 1677 the Poison Affair took an ominous turn. An anonymous message left in a confessional warned of a plot to kill Louis XIV and the Dauphin. Scouring Paris for potential plotters, the police arrested a certain Louis Vanens in December. Two years earlier, Vanens had participated in what may have been a successful plot to poison the Duke of Savoy, the late brother-in-law of MADAME DE GUISE and MADAME DE TOSCANE. Vanens' arrest revealed the existence of a Parisian network of alchemists, counterfeiters, and magicians. These shady individuals proved to have been, at one time or another, in the pay of respectable financiers, clergy, and royal officeholders—all of them eager to have black masses said, and love potions and poisons concocted.

Two of Vanens' colleagues, Monsieur and Madame La Miré de Bachimont, were promptly arrested at Lyons and imprisoned. In their lodging the police found alembics, ovens, and all manner of deadly substances. Madame de Bachimont was doubly suspect owing to her family ties: she was a cousin of the disgraced and imprisoned royal minister, Nicolas Foucquet. The Bachimont interrogation began in May 1678. In June the couple's domestic servant was brought in for questioning. Her name was Marie-Anne Gaignières, and she was the widow of a Lorraine-born soldier who had served in the regiment of one of the males of the Harcourt branch of the House of Lorraine. Described as "poor" and an object of the Bachimonts' charity, "La Gaignières" had apparently been won over to the plot by Vanens' promises of wealth. Vanens was not only busy concocting poisons, he also kept trying to turn base metals

---

[A] Cahiers 14–15, H. 164; cahiers 15–16, H. 165, H. 166.

into gold and had behaved "so opulently and so generously that he even attracted La Gaignières to his side, in the hope that he would enrich them all."[6] When a search of Marie-Anne Gaignières' quarters turned up some chemistry books, she was imprisoned in the fortress of Vincennes, where she remained for four years.[7]

Simultaneously with their investigation of the Vanens–Bachimont group, the royal investigators focused on three other individuals, two of whom they arrested. The third suspect was a woman of wealth and prestige, Madame Louis de Bailleul, née Le Ragois de Bretonvilliers, whose mother-in-law, ÉLISABETH-MARIE MALIER, had signed ÉLISABETH CHARPENTIER's wedding contract in 1662. The investigators may have been following a perceived link to Foucquet and his circle, for Madame de Bailleul's father had been one of the financiers fined for peculation by the royal investigators.[8] Madame de Bailleul avoided arrest: "Rather than be brought in for questioning, Madame de Bailleul was to be given a personal summons."[9] Any role she may have played in the poison scandals soon was moot, for she died on January 31, 1678.

Through the investigators' interest in Madame de Bailleul, the Poison Affair touched the Charpentier family directly. It was bad enough for this family friend to have come under suspicion; but it was scarcely a secret that, during Foucquet's heyday, her husband, Louis de Bailleul, had used an individual named Jacques Charpentier as a strawman for his investments. (Jacques Charpentier had earlier been interrogated by the panel investigating Foucquet, and the records of the interrogation have survived to this day in Jean-Baptiste Colbert's papers.) Once the Foucquet Affair had calmed down, Bailleul had continued to deal with Jacques Charpentier and was still signing contracts with him in 1676.[10] Under the circumstances, bearing the surname *Charpentier* was scarcely reassuring. (The situation in which Marc-Antoine Charpentier and his siblings found themselves late in 1677 is analogous to the one that ROGER DE GAIGNIÈRES would experience in May 1678, when news of the imprisonment of Marie-Anne Gaignières risked becoming public knowledge. It is not clear whether Roger was related to the suspect, but the shared surname brought the risk of humiliation and—more ominous —the possibility that he himself might come under suspicion owing to some perceived or imagined association.)

Alchemist Vanens had been in contact with another shady character, a fortune-teller known familiarly as "La Voisin," who had been teaching men and women of good society the charms of poison as a way of getting rid of an unwanted spouse. La Voisin's arrest in March 1679 revealed the extent to which a fascination with poisons and alchemy had spread into the higher levels of society. Eager to keep the details from the public, the royal administration created a special board of inquiry known as an "Ardent Chamber," which would conduct its investigations in great secrecy and whose decisions could not be appealed.

Only days after the creation of this Ardent Chamber, and shortly before its first meeting on April 10, 1679, Louis XIV agreed to have one of the Queen's householders arrested. A postscript was added to the order: "As for Blot, His Majesty judged it appropriate to wait a few more days before sending someone to talk to Madame de Guise about it, to see if he might not fall into the hands of [the police], thanks to the expedients taken to that end."[11] The person being sought was Belot, a bodyguard who was said to have been making poison from toads.[12] MADAME DE GUISE clearly knew him very well, but it is not clear how or why. In fact, was Madame de Guise herself suspected of importing poisons from Italy in those packages of medications and aromatic concoctions that she was continually receiving from Florence?[13]

Executions had become commonplace in May, June, and July 1679, when Belot was being sought out and questioned. It was an anxious time: "Everyone is frightened. Thank God that I have never bought any makeup or had my fortune told!" exclaimed Madame de Scudéry.[14]

La Voisin had begun to talk, especially about a mysterious woman who went by the nickname "Catho" and who was the wife of a glove-maker on the Pont-Neuf. Catho's dubious activities reached deep into the royal household, and to the royal mistress, Montespan. When Belot was interrogated on June 8, 1679, he was asked if he knew Catho. He replied that "he had heard of her, and saw her only with La Charpentier, with whom Catho had gone to Rome. La Charpentier has since died."[15] (The woman who bore the surname *Charpentier*, perhaps by birth, perhaps by marriage, was Catho's aunt.) As a result of his fascination with poisoned cups and toad venom, Belot was promptly executed.[16]

Thus, during the summer of 1679 the investigators not only possessed irrefutable evidence that poisoners had infiltrated the royal household, they had also learned that one suspect was closely linked to Madame de Guise. In addition, through Catho and her aunt, La Charpentier, they · were keeping close watch on persons linked to Rome—as Marc-Antoine Charpentier was. From the old records of the Foucquet Affair, the investigators of course knew that Jacques I Dalibert's wife was née Étiennette Charpentier, and that Pierre Dalibert had lived on the same street as La Charpentier, the rue des Vieux-Augustins.[17] None of these potentially suspicious links were, however, noted in the summaries of the interrogations.

By a quirk of Fate, almost simultaneously with Belot's arrest and execution, Marc-Antoine Charpentier was singled out to compose for the

DAUPHIN.[A] This link between Madame de Guise and a poisoner could scarcely have come at a worse time for the composer's career. Does that explain why music for the Feast of Saint Louis, 1679, is to be found in one of the composer's arabic-numbered notebooks[B]—which contain almost exclusively works for one or another of the Guise princesses? To demonstrate her loyalty to the Monarchy did Madame de Guise arrange to have this music woven into the festivities that CHARLES LE BRUN was planning for Louis XIV's feast day? Was it to proclaim the composer's devotion to the royal family that Corneille and DONNEAU DE VISÉ, Charpentier's collaborators in the theater, mentioned the event in the *Mercure galant* and named their composer colleague?

A few months later, in October and November 1679, the investigation focused on yet another Charpentier: Marguerite Charpentier, the widow of Jean de Refuge, who had been the secretary of Le Ragois de Bretonvillers, master of requests in the Parlement. In short, although Madame de Bailleul was dead, suspicion still hovered over the Le Ragois and Bailleul families—and by extension, over the Charpentiers who worked for or with them.

Marguerite Charpentier was taken to Vincennes and interrogated. Seals were placed on the doors of her lodging, and all the "waters, powders, and drugs" in her quarters were described and examined by experts. Reports were also drawn up about her visits to apothecaries. The investigation of her suspicious activities was still going on in August 1681, but her ultimate fate is not recorded.[18] (Another Marguerite Charpentier was imprisoned in Vincennes and investigated in November 1679, but she does not appear to have had ties to anyone in Marc-Antoine Charpentier's immediate circle.[19])

Marguerite Charpentier was linked to Marc-Antoine Charpentier by circumstantial evidence. Although these two people probably did not know one another and do not appear to have been related in any way, they shared a suspect surname, *Charpentier*, and both had been protected by the Le Ragois–Bailleul family. Until it could be proved otherwise, the investigators may well have speculated that Marc-Antoine Charpentier was somehow linked to their prisoner, Marguerite Charpentier.

Unaware, perhaps, that Marguerite Charpentier existed, the Guise composer continued to produce works for the DAUPHIN. He did not, however, collaborate with CORNEILLE and Donneau de Visé on *La Divineresse* ("The Fortuneteller"), which opened in November 1679 and

---

[A] Cahier 22, H. 170 ("Demoiselles Pieches," early 1679); cahier XXV, H. 174 ("Piesches": for June 1, 1679?).
[B] Cahier 22, H. 323.

was a resounding success. Was it deemed prudent for him to keep a low profile during these months when several Charpentiers were being interrogated about their possible links to the fortuneteller named La Voisin? These were awful weeks, as people were arrested and interrogated by the investigators. The Poison Affair had become "a veritable river that carries everything with it."[20]

In a letter to the police chief dated February 1680, Louis XIV alluded to "the person who knows how to use poison and whom you believe is dangerous to be left at court."[21] In other words, the plot against the royal family mentioned in the anonymous note two years earlier was now a confirmed threat. People connected to the poisoners had gained access to the royal court and were posing a great danger to the royal family and the royal ministers. Whenever someone near the royal family felt ill, there was now a panic, for "such things are of dangerous consequences in the royal household." In fact, "everything a bit unusual is thought to be poison."[22] Several duchesses were questioned about reported links to La Voisin. Among them was Madame d'Armagnac, who had been exerting her influence to get one of the poisoners' friends appointed as physician or surgeon to the DAUPHIN.[23] In other words, one of MADEMOI-SELLE DE GUISE's close relatives in the House of Lorraine, a woman she was continually visiting and inviting to the Hôtel de Guise, was suspected of trying to obtain access to the Dauphin for a potential poisoner.

Marc-Antoine Charpentier had, of course, been granted just this sort of access to the DAUPHIN's own person. To argue otherwise is to presume that he simply shipped his compositions off to the Pièches and let someone else direct the music according to their reading of the page, rather than his own. Then, in September 1680, the Dauphin fell ill with a tenacious fever that continued into December, when it was cured by the quinine-based remedy prepared by an English physician named Talbot. In view of the anxieties about the safety of the royal family, it is understandable that "the King had [Talbot] mix his remedy in his presence and entrusted Monseigneur's health to him."[24]

In this context, when Madame de Guise had Charpentier write a piece celebrating the Dauphin's recovery[A] late in 1680, it may have been her way of further disassociating herself from Belot and from Madame d'Armagnac, and of dissipating a perceived link between Marc-Antoine Charpentier and Marguerite Charpentier (who remained a prime suspect until at least 1681). In like manner, the composer's collaboration with CORNEILLE and Donneau de Visé on La Pierre philosophale, which opened

---

[A] Cahier 31, H. 326 (for the Dauphin's Music).

in February 1682, can be seen as a public demonstration of Charpentier's disdain for the black arts: the piece is a spoof on the Rosecrucians and the "secret science."

The Dauphin remained in good health, but fears did not dissipate, even after La Voisin's execution in February 1681. By December of that year the investigators were reviewing the Marquise of Brinvilliers' old testimonies and were becoming increasingly worried about plots to kill Louis XIV—plots analogous to the one in which the late Jacques Pinon du Martroy, yet another Foucquet relative, appeared to have been implicated. Not only was Pinon alleged to have made a pact with the Devil, he was said to have had a henchman in the royal kitchen, ready to poison the King, whom Pinon blamed for confiscating his property during the Foucquet Affair. Pinon was executed, but in effigy, for he had been dead of natural causes for some time.

Pinon himself presented no obvious link to the residents of the Hôtel de Guise or the Luxembourg Palace. But then, in February 1682, the investigators learned that the deadman's sister might have been his accomplice. She bore that suspicious surname, *Charpentier*.[25] This time the name was especially suspicious, for the Charpentiers from whom she descended were linked to the House of Guise. That is to say, Pinon's sister Jeanne had wed Louis Charpentier, master of accounts; and Louis' aunt, Catherine Charpentier, had married Pierre Mérault, the brother of the treasurer of MADEMOISELLE MARIE DE GUISE's mother.[26] Although there apparently was no blood link between Catherine Charpentier's brother Louis, and LOUIS CHARPENTIER THE SCRIVENER, the royal administration could scarcely have been unaware of the Charpentier-Pinon link to the House of Guise. The shared christening name, *Louis*, had every reason to make them still more suspicious.

Despite rumors that might have been circulating about possible Guise involvement in the Poison Affair, Marc-Antoine Charpentier continued to compose for the DAUPHIN. Indeed, unless Landry's Almanac for 1682 is based on pure fantasy, "Monsieur Charpentier" was present at a court ball late in 1681. He is in fact known to have been at court on December 29, 1681, rehearsing music for the mass during which the Dauphin would be admitted to the Order of the Holy Spirit. It is likely that he was also allowed to approach Monseigneur on Easter Sunday 1682, as well as during the festivities that PHILIPPE II D'ORLÉANS prepared for the Dauphin the following May.

Now that La Voisin was dead, attention turned to her daughter, who had been privy to many of her secrets. The details that she provided led to still more interrogations—and to an accusation directed at yet another Charpentier. Just before her execution in January 1682, a woman named

Desloges stated that her lover, Nicolas Charpentier, surely was a "sorcerer." An architect and bourgeois of Paris, he had bragged about causing Mazarin's death back in 1661.[27] This particular Charpentier does not appear to have had any links to either of the Guise highnesses, nor to their composer.

The Ardent Chamber was dissolved on July 21, 1682, and the records kept by the anonymous scriveners were sealed and kept secret until they were burned 1709.[28] Just as Mademoiselle de Guise had promised ROGER DE GAIGNIÈRES, the names of the prisoners—who, let us recall, included Marie-Anne Gaignières—were kept confidential to the end. During the three years of its existence, the Chamber had given rise to a veritable reign of terror, investigating 442 individuals and arresting 367 of them. Of these detainees, 218 had been jailed and 36 executed.

In August 1682 Louis XIV decided the fate of all these prisoners. Some of them knew so much that they could not be released. Among them was "La Gaignière, who is a woman who knows a great deal of secrets, she was the confidante and correspondent of Bachimont, Vanens, ... and several others. She could be placed in the General Hospital." Thus, on October 21, having "long been a prisoner in Vincennes," she was taken to Lyons to be confined to the General Hospital.[29]

The final months of 1682 not only brought the Poison Affair to an end, they ended the DAUPHIN's formal education as well. Henceforth Monseigneur would attend mass with his father. A personal composer was no longer necessary. Marc-Antoine Charpentier nonetheless wrote for the Corpus Christi procession of June 17, 1683, a piece composed just prior to falling ill. One can only conjecture whether this four-month illness was provoked by worries that the Ardent Chamber might summon him, some desperate wretch having mentioned his name under torture.

Marc-Antoine Charpentier continued to compose sporadically for the DAUPHIN, but 1683 apparently brought an abrupt end to any personal relationship that might have developed between the composer and the prince.

III

That pretty apartment one cannot see without being envious

GAIGNIÈRES THE "CURIEUX"

François-Roger de Gaignières, equerry to the Guises
and governor of Joinville

Grandson of a merchant from Lyons, and son of a secretary to a nobleman, Roger de Gaignières[1] "belonged" to the Lorraines from his youth—to the Harcourt branch, not the Guise one. Raised by his father in the Harcourts' grand Parisian residence, he developed into a young man of taste and wit, filled with curiosity about the history of the great noble families of France.

In the late 1660s, when Gaignières was in his mid-twenties, MARIE DE GUISE THE REGENT chose him as equerry to her nephew, LOUIS-JOSEPH DE LORRAINE, DUKE OF GUISE. Gaignières moved into the renovated stable wing of the hôtel, where an apartment had been created for the person who would hold this post. It was situated in the center of the long stable wing, just over the indoor riding ring and adjacent to the stables and coach house. (The ring eventually was transformed into an orangery.) One of his neighbors was Latinist PHILIPPE GOIBAUT DU BOIS, the adolescent Duke's new governor-preceptor. Another neighbor—who came to the Hôtel de Guise at just about the time that Gaignières moved into his lodgings—was composer Marc-Antoine Charpentier, who settled into his top-floor apartment that adjoined Gaignières' on one side and Du Bois' on the other.

A handbook written by the equerry of another powerful duke sheds light on the master–servant relationship that shaped Gaignières' every action:

> He must observe continual care about his everyday behavior, even
> his clothes, which are related to his master's humor. For if he always
> tries to be gallantly dressed while serving a lord who is accustomed
> to dress modestly, the magnificent equerry with his glitter and

475

feathers will often be taken for his lord. ... And although this can happen once or twice, as a joke, if it continues, it will irritate the master. ... So, I think one should always try to model oneself upon and dress according to the inclination and taste of the person one serves. ...

Above all, one must not play the clown nor joke with the lord, for that sort of intimacy customarily gives rise to a scorn that sooner or later falls upon the person who stupidly allows himself to do this. And if, by chance, the equerry has a humorous word to say to his lord, I advise him not to say it while serving him. And if his master should encourage him or even force him to act too intimately with him, in words or in deeds, if [the servant] is wise, by his modesty he will show his honest fear at consenting too freely to this dangerous familiarity that, with time, can easily be transformed into hatred.[2]

If the equerry felt he should correct his master's riding technique, he was to do it with great discretion. And in his master's presence he was expected to be well-dressed and booted, "to show his gratitude for the honor he is receiving by having his master present." Throughout the Hôtel de Guise similar considerations governed householders' conduct toward their superiors—that is, a musician's demeanor toward Monsieur Du Bois, or Du Bois' demeanor toward the princesses. The watchword was modesty, reticence, elegance, respectfulness.

Roger de Gaignières accompanied his young master on a trip to England during the summer of 1671. The twenty-one-year-old Duke caught smallpox and died shortly after returning to Paris. (As if preserving a bit of his late master, Gaignières kept a letter that Du Bois had dispatched to him from Paris, early in the voyage.[3]) It was Gaignières who, with two almoners and the late Duke's principal gentleman, rode in a black-draped coach as his master's body was borne from the Hôtel de Guise to the Church of Saint-Jean-en-Grève. It was he who conducted the coffin to Joinville, stopping along the way at each town and village for a memorial service.

MADEMOISELLE DE GUISE kept Gaignières on after the Duke's death, and the Equerry's principal duties appear to have been reduced to delivering messages for her, driving her about the city, and dispatching a sedan chair or a coach to fetch her at MONTMARTRE or take her to visit one of the Lorraine cousins whose residences studded Paris. He also appears to have served as her master of ceremonies.

At some point in the 1670s—almost certainly after the Duke's death —Roger de Gaignières began to metamorphose into what was known as a *curieux*, a "curious person," that is, a collector. Was this curiosity fed by Mademoiselle de Guise? Fascinated by the history of the House of

Lorraine, she can be imagined saying to him: "Monsieur de Gaignières, you will give me great pleasure if you can find the first name and coat of arms for my cousin, that Lorraine of Vaudemont who married a Bourbon-Montpensier back in the sixteenth century. I also desire to know where he and his wife were buried, and what the tomb looks like. And will you please determine how he is related to my cousin the Dowager of Orléans, who is a Vaudemont?" Her wish being his command, Gaignières promptly hies himself off to the Royal Library, to consult the histories by Duchesne or the new genealogy of the royal family by Father Anselme. With each question from Her Highness and each visit to the library, the Equerry's curiosity is piqued until he begins asking friends to send him drawings of tombs and coats of arms.

Gaignières' relatively light duties gave him abundant time to compile what would become a famous collection: drawings of coats of arms, genealogies of the principal families of the realm, illustrations of their tombs, epitaphs, portraits of the great nobles, and fashions over the centuries—plus any artistic treasures, such as "Julie's Garland," that he managed to get his hands on. He would trade one item for another. Concerning one of his prize volumes, Gaignières commented: "I got it from ... Mademoiselle de Guise's maître d'hôtel. I gave him a big wardrobe cabinet in which I used to put my books."[4]

Some of Gaignières' correspondence has survived. It provides precious insights into what it was like to be one of Mademoiselle de Guise's householders. Thanks to these bits of information, one can imagine what the lives of MONSIEUR DU BOIS, Monsieur Charpentier, and DOCTOR VALLANT were like at the Hôtel de Guise. One of Gaignières' friends depicts him as grieving for his master, Louis-Joseph de Lorraine:

> I assure you that I was very strongly moved, for love of you, by the
> death of Monsieur de Guise, and that I viewed you as an
> unfortunate man to whom things happen that appear impossible,
> and that surprise in a strange way. If your friends' sharing this grief
> and pain could diminish yours ...."[5]

By 1675, Gaignières had turned his apartment above the orangery into a special world full of beautiful things. Intrigued by descriptions of the apartment—"My wife said so many nice things about your lodging, its convenience, and your magnificent furniture"—a friend promised to come to the Hôtel de Guise himself, "and to stroll about with you in all its different apartments." In other words, in addition to visiting Gaignières, the friend was hoping to tour at least the parade apartment of the Hôtel de Guise. Another friend alluded to "that pretty apartment one cannot see without being envious." Many of these visits appear to have included an audience with MADEMOISELLE DE GUISE, about whom one friend wrote in 1679:

> [You are] near such a loveable princess as Mademoiselle de Guise, whom one cannot keep from honoring and respecting all one's life, when one has had the honor of seeing her once. I left charmed by her politeness, which, although natural to her illustrious House, nonetheless sets her totally apart and increases all the respect that is due her.[6]

Gaignières' friends and correspondents, from mid-1670s on, included César-Philippe, Count of Chastellux; Abbé Verthamon (surely a relative of MARIE TALON, although he has not been located on the Verthamon–Voisin–Versoris family tree); Louis Courcillon, known as the Abbé Dangeau (the younger brother of the memoir-writing Marquis); and Madame de Sévigné's relative, Coulanges. Dangeau would lunch with Gaignières at the Hôtel de Guise, and the two would write to Carlo Gondi, the former Florentine agent who was now secretary to the Grand Duke of Tuscany.

These messages to Gondi are expressed with a cordiality that suggests frequent conversations during the Florentine's years in Paris. For example, on one occasion, Dangeau asked Grand Duke Cosimo III de' Medici and his agents to send him "everything you have in your country that will help me acquire an exact and 'curious' knowledge of Tuscany, for geography, topography, and government, as well as for political and natural history, and everything that can be related to it."[7] Gaignières' requests, which Gondi was expected to transmit to the Grand Duke, were equally all-inclusive. He wanted drawings of:

> fêtes, magnificences, special maps, mausoleums, portraits, and other things illustrating his country. I am sure that when [the Grand Duke] learns of this, he will not be displeased, being given to collecting to such a degree as he appeared to be when I had the honor of seeing him here [during Cosimo's visit in 1669]. [8]

Thus was Roger de Gaignières transformed into a living reference book that Mademoiselle de Guise could consult at her convenience.

Did he also become a model that other Guise householders were being encouraged to emulate? Or was his curiosity simply a personal response to the intellectual and creative activities of his neighbors and associates at the Hôtel de Guise? It is not at all clear. The Equerry nonetheless occupied a central position in research-institute-before-the-letter that was the Hôtel de Guise from 1675 to 1687. During that decade, PHILIPPE GOIBAUT DU BOIS produced translation after translation; ÉTIENNE LOULIÉ began deepening his knowledge of musical theory and dipped into

the history of music; and Marc-Antoine Charpentier honed his understanding of the art of composition, copying out and commenting upon
Francesco Beretta's polychoral mass, and decanting his compositional
insights into a little treatise that eventually would be used to teach
PHILIPPE III D'ORLÉANS.

During the 1670s Gaignières was also corresponding with Roger de
Bussy Rabutin, exiled to his estate in the eastern province of Burgundy.
Although Bussy saw BISHOP GABRIEL DE ROQUETTE quite frequently
whenever the prelate was in residence in his diocese, when it came to
requesting an abbey for his son, Bussy preferred to have Gaignières act
as his go-between with ARCHBISHOP HARLAY. Harlay replied that he
would have to transmit the request to Father La Chaise (who appears in
this gallery in the portrait of FOUR JESUIT FATHERS). La Chaise was in the
process of wresting from the Archbishop the "control sheet" for distributing livings to French clerics.[9] Gaignières wrote Harlay note after
note. Finally, after almost a year of his polite nagging, the Archbishop
and La Chaise either paid attention, or Bussy gave up. At any rate, Bussy
ceased corresponding with Gaignières about the abbey. (That Gaignières
did not offer to speak personally with La Chaise suggests that the Jesuit
was not yet the familiar at the Hôtel de Guise that he would be from the
early 1680s on.)

There was great interaction and emulation among these men, and
they in turn influenced MADEMOISELLE DE GUISE. For example, in the mid-
1670s Her Highness set about embellishing her gallery. Gaignières
therefore took her to Coulanges' residence, to see his gallery. Coulanges
was absent, but they inspected it anyway. When he learned of the visit,
Coulanges chided his friend:

> You have taken Mademoiselle de Guise to my cabinet when my
> cabinet is so out shape that it cannot live up to its reputation. But I
> fully understand your plan: you wanted to make yours look better,
> make your paintings shine, and you easily succeeded; but you will at
> least have to admit that your triumph was not difficult, and that you
> got it cheaply. Still, I am extremely annoyed at the news, for my
> cabinet was neither clean nor polished, no little portraits around the
> door, no little mirrors, ... no portraits over the fireplace, an infinity
> of others missing in the lower rows, no porcelains anywhere, and not
> even me to praise my merchandise and compensate for their least
> little flaws by means of a story or an eloquent remark. On the other
> hand, this *me* would have been very ashamed to appear before a
> great princess, after having been so remiss in paying her my respects
> and my submissions ....[10]

Late in 1679, Mademoiselle de Guise rewarded Roger de Gaignières by making him governor of Joinville, an appointment that one friend described as a "present."[11] Only a few months earlier, she had given him a still more crucial gift. Into a routine and quite impersonal business note, she wove the promise that the name of a woman known as "La Gaignières," arrested by the POISON INVESTIGATORS, would be kept confidential:

> You have given me great pleasure by telling me what you know about those wretched criminals; and the list of those who are accused will not appear. I promise you. ... If you have learned something special today, you will give me great pleasure to inform me tomorrow morning, so Madame [de Guise] can be informed.[12]

After several years as a prisoner in the royal fortress of Vincennes, Marie-Anne Gaignières—who came from the region around Lyons, as the Equerry did—avoided execution. She was not freed, however: in the fall of 1682 she was taken to Lyons and locked up in the General Hospital. Of all the notes that Mademoiselle de Guise presumably wrote him over the years, this is the only one that survived. (Were the others discarded by the royal librarians when they sorted the Equerry's papers? Or was this really the only note that he saved, apparently because these few confidential sentences, tacked on to impersonal instructions about sending a coach, had a special meaning for him?)

During the final days of February 1688, as MADEMOISELLE DE GUISE lay dying, Gaignières witnessed the development of a "plot" by which MONSIEUR DU BOIS, BISHOP ROQUETTE OF AUTUN, and Father La Chaise, the JESUIT, were wheedling as much money from Her Highness as they possibly could. That, at least, is how Gaignières interpreted their secretive behavior. Day after day he and one of his assistants watched and jotted down what they saw, in an almost illegible scribble.

Bishop Roquette had come to Paris from his diocese and was shuttling back and forth between the Hôtel de Guise and Versailles, where he would confer with the King and transmit messages to ailing Mademoiselle de Guise. Father La Chaise was also paying court very assiduously to the sick woman, whom he would visit for five or ten minutes at a time. Having gotten wind of the content of some of the last-minute codicils, Gaignières dashed to Versailles on Saturday, to prepare Louis XIV for the impending crisis. A few hours later, Roquette appeared at the Hôtel de Guise and hastened to Mademoiselle de Guise's room, where two new codicils were signed.

On that Saturday, MADAME DE GUISE came to the Hôtel de Guise and was informed that the dying princess would be given the last sacraments at dawn. "They were very careful to hide it from Mademoiselle [de Mont-pensier], who learned it at Versailles." (MONTPENSIER had made it very clear to Roquette that she did not trust him.) Gaignières' memorandum for Monday, March 1, noted that "papers were burned, at the request of La Chaise and Du Bois," and that Mademoiselle de Guise was given extreme unction—"as a precaution," asserted Du Bois. Still another codicil was drawn up, and the dying princess signed it with a trembling hand. Later that evening, Gaignières conferred with her treasurer, Jean-François Le Brun, who decided to inform the heirs in person that the Guise officers were willing to accept the King's decision to allow the will to be executed. At the Luxembourg Palace, Madame de Guise informed him that Bishop Roquette had gone back to Versailles. There, Louis XIV—who was aware of the machinations in which the Bishop was enmeshed—had said with a certain irony: "Monsieur d'Autun, it is not our doing that Mademoiselle de Guise did not make other types of bequests." By then everyone suspected that many clauses in the testament would be nullified by the Parlement.

As Mademoiselle de Guise sank into unconsciousness, Gaignières noted that:

> There is no way of preventing people from talking, especially about the things that the Bishop of Autun and Messieurs Du Bois and La Chaise are saying, and are causing to be said by their friends and all those associated with the plot, on the subject of the donations in the will and the codicils.

The three plotters were not simply talking, they were acting. "Father La Chaise came and ... Monsieur d'Autun showed him a paper. I entered and begged him to tell Mademoiselle de Guise that I asked her forgiveness"—a customary ceremony between a servant and his dying master or mistress. In other words, they were preventing Gaignières from approaching Her High-ness. Shortly after that, Du Bois and one of the executors named in the will "burned more papers and received money on Monday and Tuesday."

The following day, Ash Wednesday, "she spoke twice at five in the morning," lost consciousness a half hour later, and "died at ten o'clock precisely." Within minutes seals were placed on the doors, at MADEMOISELLE DE MONTPENSIER's request. MADEMOISELLE DE GUISE's body was therefore imprisoned in her apartment for four days.[13]

The Equerry clearly had been serving as Mademoiselle de Guise's master of ceremonies over the years. He consulted the royal master of ceremonies about whether the mourning draperies should be black, for a married woman, as Madame de Guise proposed, or white, for a virgin. They eventually decided upon white, thereby maintaining the public fiction that

Marie de Lorraine had never wed. As equerry, Gaignières rode in the principal mourning coach when her body was taken to the Church of the Capucines on March 13, 1688.

The correspondence that Roger de Gaignières saved, especially the letters of condolence addressed to him in 1688, further deepens our understanding of the mistress–servant relationship within which not only Gaignières but Du Bois and Charpentier lived for roughly two decades. A few months before Mademoiselle de Guise's death, Gaignières wrote:

> She is not a princess around whom one can do disfavors to anyone.
> We are blessed that she is not like most great nobles, she is not
> prejudiced and would not condemn someone without hearing him
> out, nor condemn one side without having heard the other. So do
> not worry about her, since one would never get in her good graces
> by talking to someone's detriment.[14]

His correspondents generally concurred with this characterization of Mademoiselle de Guise: "She was a great princess who honored her birth by the nobility of her manners." His friends nonetheless felt that Gaignières had been badly treated in her will: "I see that you are now delivered from a servitude to which your honor alone has long kept you committed," wrote one. "But since you did not belong to her for personal advantage," you should not think of the money you received, but of your grief, commented another. A third friend referred to Gaignières' "disgrace,"and to the "injustice that has been done to you, ... the harsh blow you received"[15] by being willed nothing more than the customary horses and a modest annual pension of twelve hundred livres. Another friend, who thought that Her Highness had been niggardly, commented:

> I do not know whether Mademoiselle de Guise, at her death,
> demonstrated more liberality than she did during her lifetime. She
> had all the leisure, during her illness, to think about what she had to
> do for, and about, the persons who rendered her as many services as
> you did.[16]

Madame de Sévigné too sent him a letter of condolence:

> I tried several times, Monsieur, to gain admission to the Hôtel de
> Guise to express to you my sincere compliments, and to tell you of
> the pain I myself feel at the irreparable loss we have suffered; but you
> know, Monsieur, that the doors are closed. I sent one of my lackeys,
> who found no one in your lodging; so in the end I am reduced to
> telling you, by this note, that no one can be more sensitive than I to
> everything that touches you.[17]

A former householder to another prince painted a still more profound picture of the master–servant relationship:

> No one knows better than I, by my all too mournful and unfortunate experience, what it is to lose the persons to whom one is attached, more by a strong and praiseworthy inclination to serve them than in view of recompense. ... I have never been able to forget the late Monsieur de Nemours, my dear Master, and for me he is always as present as while he was alive; and if I can say that I never received any possessions, beyond the honor that he paid of loving me, his death afflicted me to a point that for a long time I did not think I would ever be consoled.[18]

Now that he was free from his "servitude," Gaignières was offered a "pretty apartment" in the Farnese Palace by the French ambassador to Rome. Having admitted that the apartment he was proposing was "less well-furnished and decorated than yours at the Hôtel de Guise," the Ambassador added with some irony: "But you would be three hundred leagues away from Monsieur Du Bois, and that pleasure is something to think about."[19] The implication is that the Equerry and the Impresario did not always get along—a reading that is supported by a remark made by Madame de Sévigné only a few months later: "Monsieur Du Bois is charmed over your greetings; but Monsieur de Gaignières' horses are making noises under his head: it is killing him."[20]

During the debacle that followed Mademoiselle de Guise's death, Gaignières served as middleman for potential purchasers of her furniture. He did his best to find jobs for her domestics. Thus, in April 1688, the coadjutor to the archbishop of Rouen wrote him, inquiring about "furniture." Then, in reply to a proposal that the Equerry had made in an earlier letter, he commented: "I was very happy to learn what you told me about Beaupuis. I am certain that I will be happy with him in the future."[21] In the end, Beaupuis, a member of the GUISE MUSIC, stayed on in Paris, where he sang for the Jesuits and for the Opera. On the other hand, François Anthoine, another member of the Music, soon turned up in Rouen.

As the last Guise's possessions were being readied for auction, Gaignières ferreted out documents that her heirs were likely to throw away or burn. For example, it surely was in March 1688 that he added the following items to his collection, many of them quoted in one or another of the portraits that hang in this imaginary gallery. There were papers about Duke Henri's Neapolitan adventures; letters from the Dowager Duchess of Guise to Henri informing him that she had pawned her valuables to help him; Montrésor's correspondence during the late 1640s and on into the late 1650s; Mademoiselle de Guise's emotional letters to Montrésor; the correspondence about the guardianship of the Duke of Alençon; and papers concerning Mademoiselle de Guise's dispute with Intendant Lafitte. Without Gaignières, all this information would have been lost.

For almost a decade Gaignières exerted the right granted him by Mademoiselle de Guise's will, to stay on at the Hôtel de Guise. In the early 1690s he was made "Instructor to the Children of France,"[22] having participated in the education of several royal princes, just as Charpentier and LOULIÉ, the former Guise musician, had done for PHILIPPE III D'ORLÉANS. Gaignières eventually built a house for himself and his now quite huge collection.

After several projects aimed at preserving the collection had aborted, he sold everything to the King in 1710, to ensure that his treasures would not be dispersed. Although the collection remained in Paris, it was split up after Gaignières' death in 1715, with his manuscripts going to the Royal Library, his portraits and engravings to the Louvre, and his printed books and pamphlets to the archives and library of the Foreign Ministry. In addition, all manner of papers were appropriated by Clairambault, whose collection is cited in so many footnotes in this book. Clairambault's papers eventually made their way to the Royal Library.

Gabriel de Dauhun (signature)

h. Em. de Roquette d'amades. R. (signature)

IV

The conduct of this prelate has been a continual enigma

THE FOUR ROQUETTES

Gabriel de Roquette, Bishop of Autun;
Christophle de Roquette d'Amades, his brother,
Mademoiselle de Guise's intendant;
and Christophle's sons, Henri-Auguste-Louis de Roquette, Abbot of Gildas,
and Henri-Emmanuel de Roquette d'Amades

Gabriel de Roquette was born in Toulouse in 1624, to a city councilman and barrister before the Parlement of Languedoc. His maternal and paternal ancestors had served in the judicial and financial administrations of the city and the province. Living in Toulouse and participating in the municipal government as the Roquettes did, they could scarcely have failed to work closely with the maternal relatives of Jacques I and JACQUES II DALIBERT.[1]

Gabriel de Roquette had been destined for the Church, while his brother Christophle was being taught the skills that would permit him to earn a living within the royal financial administration or in the service of a great noble. No sooner had Gabriel finished his studies in Toulouse than he moved to Paris, where his maternal aunt, Marguerite de Senaux, Superior of the Dominican convent known as *Les Filles de la Croix,* "the Daughters of the Cross," was in Queen Mother Anne of Austria's good graces. With his aunt's help, Gabriel had found his way into the circle around the Prince of Conti and, perhaps more important, around the prince's mother, the Dowager Duchess of Condé. Gabriel was described as "having a sweet and devout little mien." He was profoundly ambitious.[2]

It is not clear how Gabriel de Roquette extended his field of influence from the Hôtel de Condé to the Hôtel de Guise, but as early as 1646 the beginning of a link can be discerned between the attractive young priest from Toulouse and the women of the House of Guise. When Roquette's sister took the veil in 1646, in addition to the Queen Mother and Madame de Condé the witnesses included the Duchess of Guise, her daughter MADEMOISELLE MARIE DE GUISE, and her granddaughter MADE-MOISELLE DE MONTPENSIER. Also present was the Countess of Brienne, a benefactress of the convent. Her husband was, or soon would be Christophle de Roquette's employer.[3]

In 1646 the ingratiating young abbé had not yet trained his ambitious eyes on the Guise women who had so recently returned from exile in Italy. He was busy making himself indispensable to the elderly Dowager of Condé, who rewarded him generously; and after her death in 1650 he gravitated to her son, Conti. Roquette may well have played a role in the prince's conversion in 1657. It was around Conti—probably at the time of this conversion—that Roquette became acquainted with another of the prince's protégés, the actor-playwright known as MOLIÈRE, from whom the now-pious prince withdrew his patronage, rather than promote so sinful a thing as theater-going. Roquette remained close to Conti until the prince's death in 1668.

By the early 1650s Gabriel de Roquette had brought his brother Christophle into his network of powerful and rich people. Having purchased an office as royal councillor, Christophle found a lodging in the parish of Saint-Sulpice and became the principal financial clerk of Henri-Auguste de Loménie de Brienne, secretary of state for foreign affairs.[4]

Christophle's wedding contract of 1654 suggests the protective web within which he and his brother were circulating. In addition to several of Roquette's Parisian cousins who had purchased prestigious offices in the Parlement, the guests included the entire Loménie family, the Bishop of Montauban, and the Bishop of Tours, first almoner to GASTON D'OR-LÉANS.[5] The couple's continuing protection by the Loménies can be seen in the christening names of one of their sons: Henri-Auguste-Louis. The Secretary of State almost certainly was his godfather.

It was not too long before Christophle de Roquette obtained an entrée to the Bourbon-Condé household, probably owing to his brother's favor with Conti. (One source asserts that Christophle was Conti's household intendant.[6]) Next, the Roquette brothers worked their way into the circle around another ministerial family, the Le Telliers.[7] By 1666 Abbé Roquette was described as "governing the entire Le Tellier household." He remained close to them until at least 1674.[8]

Then, shortly before Conti's death in 1668, Christophle de Roquette's name cropped up in the Guise circle, where he soon was appointed the household intendant to the adolescent Duke of Guise.

(Christophle had more or less lost his protector when Loménie de Brienne was disgraced in 1663.) The Roquette family's increasing influence at the Hôtel de Guise can be discerned in notarial documents drawn up for Mademoiselle de Guise. By March 1667, Christophle was in her pay and was working at paying off the debts of the princess's late father. In 1668 Her Highness appointed Jean de Roquette, a relative, to conduct her business in Languedoc. By April 1669 Christophle was fully ensconced, signing a wedding contract alongside the Guises and their principal householders, among them MONSIEUR DU BOIS.[9]

Since Gabriel's name does not appear in these notarial documents, one can only conjecture whether it was he who introduced Christophle to MADEMOISELLE DE GUISE, or whether the brothers entered her circle more or less together, in 1666 or 1667. That was just the time when Gabriel de Roquette—who had attracted much attention by his brilliant funeral oration for Anne of Austria—was basking in his recent nomination as Bishop of Autun. If Gabriel did not yet "belong" to Mademoiselle de Guise by 1667, he was close to it, for it was he who officiated at the marriage of ISABELLE D'ORLÉANS OF ALENÇON and LOUIS-JOSEPH DE LORRAINE, DUKE OF GUISE in May of that year. (A month earlier the Duke of Guise had been among the illustrious guests at Roquette's consecration.[10])

The nomination to the bishopric of Autun, which came in May 1666, represented the summit of a pyramid up which Gabriel had been slowly climbing since the late 1640s. He had been vicar general for Conti when the prince was Abbot of Cluny; he had been granted several priories; the King had given him an abbey near Toulouse; he had been ordained a priest and earned a doctorate in theology; and now he was a prelate. He nonetheless aspired to climb even higher, to obtain an archbishopric or a cardinal's hat.

But in the interim, he had to win papal agreement for his nomination, and at the time the Pope was more or less pretending that the candidates proposed by Louis XIV did not exist. In August 1666 Gabriel de Roquette got in touch with the DUKE OF CHAULNES, the French ambassador in Rome. The Ambassador wrote Condé about him, promising "that I will ... do everything I can for Abbé de Roquette's business"; and he informed the prince that Christophle de Roquette was doing everything he could to help. (Christophle knew Condé well enough to write him in January 1670, at which time he described his brother, the Bishop of Autun, as Condé's "friend."[11]

The Bishop was consecrated at the Cathedral of Notre-Dame in April 1667, and by the end of the summer he was in his diocese, conducting his first visitation. It soon became apparent that village priests were inadequately trained and ignorant of the rudiments of theology, and that

Euesque

L'esprit le bon air le merite,
Qui l'ont conduit a l'Euesché

Pouront peut estre dans la suite
Le conduire a l'Archeueche. 1686.

A bishop.
"His wit, his fine air, his merit, Which led him to the bishop's palace,
Will perhaps, one day, Conduct him to the archbishop's palace."
L'esprit, le bon air, le mérite, Qui l'ont conduit à l'Évesché,
Pouront peut estre dans la suite, Le conduire à l'Archévesché.

the schools they ran were disastrous. Heeding Louis XIV's recent order that all bishops create seminaries in their dioceses, in October 1667 Roquette urged the faithful to come together and join with him in this worthy project. As this zealous reforming bishop traveled through his diocese, he showed dismay at the scarcity of male and female teachers who possessed impeccable morality and were at the same time versed in the rudiments of spelling and arithmetic.[12] By 1669 the Bishop had expanded his reforms to include the creation of "charitable" schools, that is, separate schools for boys and girls that were paid for by the townspeople.

By the early 1670s, Gabriel de Roquette was one of MADEMOISELLE DE GUISE's confidants. He is not mentioned as participating in the requiem mass celebrated for LOUIS-JOSEPH DE LORRAINE, DUKE OF GUISE on August 22, 1671, at which Bishop Marc Malier officiated; but on May 14, 1672, Roquette was among the prelates joining Malier for the funeral service for the DOWAGER DUCHESS OF ORLÉANS at the Royal Abbey of Saint-Denis.[13] In July 1672 it was Roquette who officiated at MONTMARTRE[14] during the End of the Year Service for the Duke of Guise. In sum, when Roquette is mentioned as playing an important role in a religious service, there is a strong possibility that Marc-Antoine Charpentier composed music for the event. That is not to suggest that the Bishop commissioned music for these events. Rather, the music was requested by the Guises; and the presence of Bishop Roquette, like the sound of the music, was a ornament that permitted Their Highnesses to put their personal stamp upon the event.

It is nonetheless tempting to propose that Roquette commissioned a mass[A] from Charpentier for January 20, 1672, when he had the honor of giving a eulogy during the week-long canonization service at the Jesuit Church of Saint-Louis.[15] That would explain why Charpentier copied the mass into a roman-numbered notebook. Yielding to this temptation would probably be unwise, however, for Roquette was still alive in the 1690s when the composer recopied the mass onto Jesuit paper, presumably for reuse by the reverend fathers at one or another of the THREE JESUIT HOUSES in Paris. (The composer avoided modifying and reusing, for a third party, anything he had written for a patron who was still alive.) In short, if Charpentier's mass was for the event at Saint-Louis, it probably was commissioned by the Jesuits themselves, in hopes of ingratiating themselves with Mademoiselle de Guise.

[A] Cahiers VI-VIII, H. 3, H. 236, H. 283.

In March 1675, Gabriel de Roquette was a bystander when MADAME DE GUISE's son died. Although the Bishop apparently stayed away from Alençon's bedside, he shared confidential information about the little prince with DU BOIS: "Monsieur Du Bois having arrived, I told him that things were going very badly," noted DOCTOR VALLANT, somewhat disgruntled about the Bishop's loose tongue:

> He replied that the previous evening Monsieur d'Autun had told
> him that I was not optimistic about this illness. It is true that on
> Friday evening I had told Monsieur d'Autun that I was very worried
> about this illness, but that I did not dare reveal it to Their
> Highnesses, for fear of overwhelming them.

MADEMOISELLE DE MONTPENSIER was not duped by Autun's unctuous concern: "My sister [Madame de Guise] cried, and Mademoiselle de Guise was very afflicted," she noted, "but she did not become disconcerted. The Bishop of Autun was there."[16]

As the two princesses tried to decide the course to follow now that the last male of the House of Guise was dead, Roquette of Autun hovered in the wings. Realizing how painful MADAME DE GUISE found the apartment where her son had died, he enmeshed his longtime protectors, the Condés, in an ingenious scheme that created quite a stir. Madame de Guise would sell her half of the Luxembourg Palace to the Condés, thereby putting them in a stronger position to acquire the entire palace upon Mademoiselle de Montpensier's death; Mademoiselle de Guise would sell the Hôtel de Guise; and she and Madame de Guise would move into the vacated Hôtel de Condé. Louis XIV quashed the project, claiming the Luxembourg for the Crown. Montpensier blamed Roquette, describing him as "a busybody, a man of bad faith, on good terms with everyone, and who has Mademoiselle de Guise under his thumb."[17]

The royal veto did not decrease Roquette's stature in MADEMOISELLE DE GUISE's eyes. Gabriel de Roquette had earlier served as her ambassador to Louis XIV, having been asked to "speak to the King" on behalf of her claim to precedence over duchesses. And now, in 1675, although he was not named, he and Bishop Malier of Tarbes presumably were among the anonymous "ecclesiastics" who interviewed Father Barré when two educational institutions devoted to the INFANT JESUS were being created under the protection of MADEMOISELLE DE GUISE and MADAME DE GUISE. In fact, in many ways the schools set up by Mademoiselle de Guise and Barré resembled the charitable schools that Roquette had been creating in his diocese. Since the slightest tinge of Jansenism risked killing the project,[18] the presence of a well-connected theologian such as Roquette was essential to any investigation into the orthodoxy of the Minim's religious beliefs. (An investigation was advisable, for the notoriously Jansenist curate of Saint-Merry was named Barré; and at the time MONSIEUR DU BOIS was a close friend of the Jansenists at Port-Royal-des-Champs.)

By the late 1670s, Bishop Roquette felt so sure of himself that he could go wherever he pleased in the Hôtel de Guise, and state his opinion freely. Or perhaps his eruption into MADEMOISELLE DE GUISE's interview with Royal Intendant Lafitte was staged in advance? Lafitte had just called Her Highness a "tyrant," when Roquette appeared and threatened him, saying that it would be to Lafitte's advantage to reach an accommodation with the princess.[19] In the public's mind, Roquette's name became associated not only with the use of this sort of innuendo, but with concealment, secrecy. For example, marginalia in one of the position papers printed by lawyers after Her Highness's death suggests that Autun played a role in concealing the existence of Mademoiselle de Guise's son.[20]

In view of Gabriel de Roquette's closeness to MADEMOISELLE DE GUISE and to GOIBAUT DU BOIS by the mid-1670s, it is likely that he was consulted in 1676 about the orthodoxy of presenting Saint Cecilia primarily as a sweet and gentle converter, and only secondarily as the patron saint of musicians. Then, at the Assembly of the Clergy in 1682, Roquette and ARCHBISHOP HARLAY signed an open letter to their Calvinist "brothers," asking them to return to the Catholic Church so that force could be avoided. Next, in 1685, Harlay asked DU BOIS to write a discourse about the merits of conversion by reason rather than force. In short, the positions taken by Bishop Roquette and Archbishop Harlay during the 1680s—and probably earlier—served as underpinnings for the texts of Marc-Antoine Charpentier's different oratorios honoring Saint Cecilia.

Gabriel de Roquette had been careful to keep a certain distance from the Hôtel de Guise. For example, when Church affairs brought him to Paris, he did not lodge with his brother at the Hôtel de Guise, nor in one of the apartments in the stable wing. Instead he rented rooms. In the 1670s he lived on the rue d'Orléans, which ran at right angles to the Hôtel de Guise; but in about 1680 he moved farther afield, lodging near the Church of Saint-Merry, in the residence of Everhard Jabach, the famous collector.[21]

All the while, Christophle de Roquette was administering MADEMOI- · SELLE DE GUISE's large household and trying to pay the debts incurred by several successive dukes. In September 1679 Her Highness gave him full power to go to her lands in northeastern France "to examine the conduct of the officials, to give an accounting of their administration, ... to collect what they owe," and to arrange for the cutting of wood, and so forth. Christophle's records of this inspection tour have survived. They reveal a man as sincere as his brother appears to have been self-interested and ambitious.[22] For example, having inspected the schools she had created at Joinville, he sent unpleasant news: "I have not yet said anything to Your Highness about the men and women teachers, which is one of the subjects you wanted to be enlightened about by the Truth." The women were doing very well, but the conduct of the men was a "scandal," he reported. "The vicar does not hold out much hope. [He] finds poor Father Barré to be a good chap, but easy to deceive. In a word, [the men are] not working out as the women are, and I don't know whether it would be appropriate to remove them." Mademoiselle de Guise replied: "If the schoolmasters are not useful, they must be dismissed."

Intendant Roquette wove personal advice into this correspondence with the princess. Indeed, over the years a certain confidentiality had developed between mistress and servant. For example, he proposed that she pay off all Guise creditors. She could then, "by a will written in her own hand, dispose of all the property that remains. To do it more calmly and advantageously for [your] interests, it is necessary that I explain two things to Your Highness that are infinitely necessary," he continued. The principal concern was secrecy, "for if things got abroad," her creditors would swoop down and prevent the sale of any property.

When news of MADAME DE MONTMARTRE's failing health reached him in December 1682, the Intendant wrote Mademoiselle de Guise. His words go to the heart of the master–servant relationship within which he had been working for over fifteen years:

> On such a desolate occasion I cannot get over being struck with fear about [Madame de Montmartre's] health, and about Your Highness's death. All my trust is in the grace that I hope God will show to a House where He is so well served, and to such a great number of householders, most of whom would be inconsolable if Your Highness fell ill.

Madame de Montmartre died the day after this paragraph was written.

Christophle de Roquette died in 1685, leaving two sons. One of them, Henri-Auguste-Louis, was being groomed to be his uncle Gabriel's coadjutor:

> Abbé Roquette is well-built, he sings and paints very methodically, has a very quick wit, and has demonstrated it, having studied with the Jesuits with unusual success. Few cassock-wearers are his equal; he currently is preparing his *licence*. He speaks with ease in public, and whether he is defending himself or attacking, the advantage is

always on his side. So many fine qualities are not surprising. One cannot be the nephew of the Bishop of Autun and lack wit.[23]

"Eager to support his intentions, ... and convinced ... that he is capable of rendering service," in 1684 Mademoiselle de Guise gave the young cleric a life pension of five hundred livres a year.[24]

Christophle's other son, Henri-Emmanuel de Roquette d'Amades, stayed on at the Hôtel de Guise after his father's death. Perhaps he had been assisting his father and simply stepped into his empty shoes. On the other hand, since no household position follows his name in the papers of the Guise succession, he may simply have been "near" Her Highness, as MONSIEUR DU BOIS was. Be that as it may, Mademoiselle de Guise was fond enough of Henri-Emmanuel to will him a life pension of twelve hundred livres per year. In addition, at some point in 1687 she permitted him to leave the "room and cabinet off the grand staircase, with a view onto the garden," situated in the hôtel proper, where almost all her household officers lodged, and to move into an empty apartment in the stable wing, located just between DU BOIS' and GAIGNIÈRES' lodgings.[25] In other words, Roquette d'Amades now occupied Marc-Antoine Charpentier's recently vacated apartment.

Throughout his ascension in the Church, Gabriel de Roquette had demonstrated an amazing single-mindedness, cloaked in civility and flattery. Early on he realized that he could advance his career by ingratiating himself with the wealthy and the devout, and by taking advantage of their generosity and gullibility. He was said to have been the principal model for the hypocrite "Tartuffe," in MOLIÈRE's controversial play of 1664. At any rate, people were soon identifying Tartuffe as Gabriel de Roquette: "They say that Molière wrote Le Tartuffe ou l'Hypocrite to criticize this Abbé [Roquette], as a result of the feelings against him that he is said to have contracted in the past, at the residence of the Prince of Conti, where both of them lived."[26]

In Molière's play, a shabbily dressed and shoeless Tartuffe, who has come to Paris from a provincial city, has attracted the attention of a rich bourgeois by sitting near him in the parish church and praying with great gesticulations, sighs, and demonstrations of piety. The bourgeois takes "the poor man," le pauvre homme, into his household, where Tartuffe proceeds to turn the bourgeois and his mother into excessively devout prudes. In addition, he wheedles a large financial donation from his benefactor and, by a subterfuge, gains ownership of the man's house. As a last straw, he attempts to seduce his host's wife. Tartuffe is, of course, a hypocrite and a sham who is not devout at all. For contemporaries it was easy to draw the intended parallel between the Dowager Duchess of

Condé, the conversion of the Prince of Conti, and the gifts the two of them showered on the pious young abbé from the provinces whom they had taken into their households.

The parallel between Tartuffe and Gabriel de Roquette remained in the public's thoughts. One of the DOWAGER OF ORLÉANS' householders noted that Roquette "had all the characteristics that the author of *Le Tartuffe* showed as the model of a fraud," and he asserted that the Bishop was not above mounting a "plot" against anyone who crossed him. In fact, this source asserted, Roquette was so hypocritical and obsequious that he once pretended not to recognize humpbacked Conti at a mascarade ball, and acted as if a handsome and well-formed man were the misshapen prince, his protector.[27] If another tale of Roquette's hypocrisy is true, it strips the man bare. A visitor having admired a handsome buffet in Roquette's lodging, the Bishop replied: "What you see there belongs to the poor." That is, he had paid for it with money put in the poor box. The visitor's reply was witty and biting, but Roquette was unperturbed: "He pocketed this sort of slap in an engaging way, he did not frown, he simply became more obsequious toward the person who had given him the verbal slap."[28]

Madame de Sévigné was particularly fond of drawing a parallel between Tartuffe and Roquette: "The Bishop of Autun having given the panegyric for M*** at the Jesuits, who had hired all the musicians of the Opera, they are saying in Paris that the Jesuits gave two plays in one day: the Opera and *Le Tartuffe*." She nonetheless admired the oratorical skills and tact that he had mustered for the funeral oration of Condé and Conti's late sister, Madame de Longueville. He did it "with all the capacity, all the grace, and all the skill of which a man is capable. This was no *Tartuffe*, ... this was a prelate of consequence, preaching with dignity, saying or not saying everything that must be said or hushed up" about the dead woman's checkered career and lovers.[29]

Two of these allusions to Tartuffe involved parallels between Mademoiselle de Guise and the devout woman whom the hypocrite had duped in the play. Roquette, asserts one of these texts, was the "leader of those falsely devout people who go by the name of 'Tartuffes.' [He] was promoted by the Prince of Conti and later became attached to Mademoiselle de Guise, whose entire household was under his domination." The second allusion consisted of scabrous doggerel lyrics, wondering whether Mademoiselle de Guise's virginity had resisted not only Montrésor but her "Tartuffe" as well.[30]

These parallels between Roquette and Tartuffe predate the fall of 1687, when MADEMOISELLE DE GUISE fell ill and the Bishop looked out for his own interests. He set about worming his way into the ailing princess's testament. To manage this, he teamed up with MONSIEUR DU BOIS and Father La Chaise, one of the FOUR JESUITS of Panel 4. As GAIGNIÈRES watched helplessly, the three men isolated Her Highness physically and psychologically, with the end result that three dictated codicils were added to the autograph testament she had drawn up a few years earlier on Christophle de Roquette's advice. She signed each codicil with an increasingly trembly hand; and with each codicil the trio received a larger legacy than in the preceding one.

In the first codicil Roquette d'Amades was given a pension of 1,200 livres, and the Bishop's seminary at Autun was willed 25,000 livres toward its completion. It was also in this codicil that Mademoiselle de Guise stated a most ingenious bequest that would allow Roquette d'Amades and Monsieur Du Bois to remain in their apartments at the Hôtel de Guise: "she wishes that all of her householders who lodge in her hôtel shall keep their lodging for the rest of their lives, as a legacy and gift." In the second codicil Roquette d'Amades' pension was increased to 2,200 livres. In addition, the dying princess suddenly and quite miraculously remembered a request made years earlier by the late Christophle de Roquette: Would she pay his debts of 22,000 livres, which had been co-signed by his brother, the Bishop? Mademoiselle de Guise stated that she wished to do just that.

Her bequests to Gabriel de Roquette—in the form of the money for his seminary and the reimbursement of those co-signed debts—came to the astonishing total of 47,000 livres. The Roquettes apparently were content. At any rate, they received nothing additional in the third and final codicil, signed on the eve of her death.

Judging from the records of the Comédie Française, during the final month of Mademoiselle de Guise's life ÉTIENNETTE CHARPENTIER and ÉLISABETH CHARPENTIER were having such fun with the gossip circulating about the Roquettes, that they attended a performance of Le Tartuffe.[31] The legacies to Roquette of Autun and his relatives were indeed feeding the gossip mills. Even more, marginalia in the papers of the Guise estate repeatedly blamed the Bishop for Mademoiselle de Guise's most aberrant legacies:

> The people who had Mademoiselle de Guise under their thumb
> suggested extraordinary arrangements to her, for their own
> individual interest; and seeing that she was dying, they used
> constraint, seduction, and fraud in order to share among themselves
> all the property of her estate.

The jurist who made this observation blamed the notaries who had permitted the fraud to take place. They were, he asserted, guilty of going along with:

> everything that the people with whom Mademoiselle de Guise was obsessed wanted them to do. ... The Bishop of Autun participated in these codicils ... and [the plotters] embroiled ... all Mademoiselle de Guise's domestics, in order, on the one hand, to win protection for these notarial acts, and on the other to involve all Mademoiselle de Guise's householders in the secret.[32]

This is an allusion to the last-minute increase in the legacies given to her householders, and to the clause permitting them to stay on indefinitely at the Hôtel de Guise.

During the spring of 1688, that is, during the months while Mademoiselle de Guise's estate was being debated in the courts and outraged comments were on many lips, Gabriel de Roquette was conspicuously absent from Paris. Friends wondered if it was owing to the contestation over the Guise will; but others attributed it to the fact that "the King does not like it very much when bishops are away from their dioceses." Whatever the Bishop's reasons for staying in Autun, scales were falling from the eyes of his associates, who now alluded to "his usual flummery," "those manners" of his that are "so stiff":

> The truth must be said: Monsieur d'Autun has been very good at shaping his fortune, and his fortune has been very good at shaping him too. He had won the friendship and trust of many illustrious people; he has the honor of having reformed his diocese; he narrates things agreeably, he dines well, but he is not natural, almost everything about him is false. He has nothing interesting to say, no relaxed air when dealing with others; he constrains others because he himself is constrained.[33]

Echos of Roquette's participation in the Guise plot, and the parallel between him and Tartuffe, surfaced a few years later in a comment about his participation in the Assembly of the Clergy of 1690, where he was the eldest of the eleven prelates attending. Roquette was now:

> an old man of seventy-three, who nonetheless preached at the opening of the assembly. Perhaps he would have done better to abstain than to demonstrate, on this occasion, his worn-out imagination and his voice that was only half audible, sad remnants of a talent that, thirty years before, had caused a stir in worldly circles. ... Throughout his life the conduct of this prelate has been a continual enigma: one could never guess whether there was any

truth in what he was saying. ... 'The poor man,' [*le pauvre homme*, the famous phrase from Molière's *Le Tartuffe*], how zealous he is![34]

La Bruyère, who knew Roquette from the Condé circle, painted a similar but far more devastating portrait of the Bishop, under the nickname *Theophile*, God-loving:

> What is *Theophile*'s incurable illness? He has had it for thirty years, he doesn't get well: he wanted to, he wants, and he shall want to govern high nobles. Death alone will take from him, along with his life, his thirst for empire and for ascendency over minds. Is this his zeal for his neighbors? Is it a habit? Is it an excessively high opinion of himself? There is no palace into which he does not insinuate himself; he does not stop in the middle of a room, he goes to the window niche or a small private room; people wait for him to speak, at length and actively, before having an audience with him, in order to be seen. He knows family secrets; he is involved in everything sad or advantageous that happens to them; he warns, he offers himself, he participates in the festivities, he has to be admitted. To fill his time or his ambition, it is not enough to have the care of ten thousand souls [in his diocese] for which he is answerable to God, as he is for his own soul: there are higher-level souls, souls of greater distinction, for which he need not account and with which he voluntarily burdens himself. He listens, he watches over everything that can serve as pasturage for his mind, with its intrigue, mediation, and manipulation.[35]

Into a portrait of *Onuphre*, a Tartuffe-like sham, La Bruyère wove some observations that almost certainly were inspired by Bishop Roquette's mannerisms and conduct:

> He would pass for what he is, a hypocrite, and he wants to pass for what he is not, a devout man. ... *Onuphre* is not devout, but he wants people to believe he is, and by a perfect, albeit false imitation of piety, he quietly sees to his own interests. ... He takes it upon himself to be the legitimate heir of any old person who dies rich and childless. ... There are people who, according to him, must in good conscience be disparaged, and these people are the ones who do not like him, the people he wants to harm, and whose estate he covets. He obtains his goals without even having to open his mouth: ... he smiles or he sighs; people ask questions or press him, he does not answer, and his is right: he has said enough.[36]

The Bishop lived on until 1707; but to the disappointment of his nephew, Abbé Henri-August-Louis de Roquette, he ceded his responsibilities to a different nephew, a Senaux:

An old bishop died who, his whole life long, had done everything to make his fortune and be a personage: it was Roquette, a man of very little means, who had caught hold of the bishopric of Autun and who, at the end, could do nothing better than govern the Estates of Burgundy by his suppleness and his manipulations around Monsieur the Prince [of Condé]. He had adopted all the different colors [of household liveries]: Madame de Longueville, Monsieur the Prince of Conti her brother, Cardinal Mazarin, and he was especially given over to the Jesuits. All sugar and all honey, linked to important women of that time, and involved in every intrigue; sometimes very sanctimonious. It is from him that Molière got his Tartuffe, and no one was deceived. .... Despite all his efforts, he remained at Autun and was unable to make a greater fortune. ... The good opinion of him that remained, and his manipulations, disappointed Abbé Roquette, his nephew, who had found his way into high society, who preached, and who had spent his life with [his uncle]. He obtained the coadjutorship for another nephew, and Abbé Roquette, with his sermons, his intrigues, his white hair, and so many hopes, could not become a bishop. He ended up in the household of Madame de Conti, the daughter of Monsieur the Prince of Condé, becoming her almoner, and his brother was her equerry.[37]

The Abbé died in 1725, having spent the final two decades of his life in circumstances that recall the careers of GILLES CHARPENTIER THE SECRE-TARY's two sons in the household of PHILIPPE II D'ORLÉANS.

V

Mademoiselle de Guise wants to attach me to her person

VALLANT THE PHYSICIAN

Noël Vallant, physician to the Guises,
the Abbey of Montmartre, and the Abbaye-aux-Bois

Noël Vallant, one biography asserts, was born in Lyons[1] in about 1630, to a silk-cloth merchant of the city. This eulogistic and perhaps apocryphal biographical sketch of Noël's early years recounts how his family was planning to have him carry on his father's trade. Fascinated by literature and the sciences, the youth insisted that he wanted to be a physician—a profession that required a considerable financial investment but that could guarantee neither wealth nor renown. As in the stereotypical biography of MOLIÈRE, the boy turned to outsiders, in this case his teachers, in order to win over his father. The father capitulated.

Noël earned a master of arts diploma at Lyons and in 1653 went off to study at the renowned Faculty of Medicine of Montpellier. After completing his studies in 1655,[2] he set off for Paris, literally to seek his fortune. Success in the medical profession came within his grasp in 1659, when he entered the service of Madame de Sablé, née Magdaleine de Souvré de Courtenvaux.[3]

This protectress was the widow of Philippe-Emmanuel de Laval, Lord of Bois-Dauphin and Marquis of Sablé. In the 1640s she had attended the principal Parisian *salons*. Through her late husband, Madame de Sablé had links to the House of Guise. That is, during the Religious Wars of the late sixteenth century her father-in-law, Urbain I de Laval, had supported the League and the Guises. Her son, Urbain II, had first married Marie (or Louise?) de Riants, ARMAND-JEAN DE RIANTS' sister; and after Marie's death he had wed his cousin's widow, generally known as "Madame de Bois-Dauphin." After Urbain II's death, Madame de Sablé welcomed her daughter-in-law, Madame de Bois-Dauphin, into the little *salon*-inspired court over which she reigned.

In 1656 that little court moved to the Parisian house of the ABBEY OF PORT-ROYAL, where Madame de Sablé had a small residence built for herself. As the nuns became increasingly fervent in their support of Jansenism, so did Madame de Sablé. When Noël Vallant entered her household in 1659, he was given a lodging at Port-Royal, the better to care for the hypochondriacal Marquise. Sympathizing with the Jansenists, if not an actual disciple, Vallant witnessed the traumatic events at the abbey during the mid-1660s.

When the two houses of Port-Royal were separated in 1669, it was to the Paris house that Vallant and Madame de Sablé gave their loyalties. There the Doctor almost certainly came into contact with MARIE CHARPENTIER THE CONVERSE, the composer's sister. Through Port-Royal, Vallant also became acquainted with the Pascal family and the Jansenist physician, Denis Dodart. And during the mid-1660s his friendship with PHILIPPE GOIBAUT DU BOIS began, a friendship that would deepen over the years and continue until Vallant's death.

Toward the end of her life, Madame de Sablé jotted down some thoughts about Doctor Vallant: "The [physician] I have been seeing for more than twenty years is a very fine man, very pious, very judicious, capable of forming a deep attachment and a great friendship."[4] As the years passed, Vallant became the Marquise's de facto intendant and secretary. This permitted him to make copies of her correspondence and to file away a few original documents.

So full of praise was the protectress for her protégé, that Vallant was soon being stopped in the street and asked what remedies he would propose for a cousin or an aunt in the provinces. He became the preferred physician in several of the female convents of the capital: the Great Carmel, the Parisian house of the ABBEY OF PORT-ROYAL, the ABBAYE-AUX-BOIS, and the ABBEY OF MONTMARTRE.[5] Among his patients at the Abbaye-aux-Bois was Madame de Sablé's widowed daughter-in-law, Madame de Bois-Dauphin, who had been left relatively penniless after her husband's death. Another patient was a certain "Madame de Saint-Aubin." It has not been determined whether this boarder at the abbey was Marthe Croyer, JACQUES HAVÉ DE SAINT-AUBIN's widow.[6]

In 1673 Vallant was offered the prestigious position of physician to MADEMOISELLE DE GUISE and her household. He therefore left Madame de Sablé's service, but he remained on good terms with the Marquise and cared for her during her final illness. The invitation to join the staff at the Hôtel de Guise was conveyed indirectly, through MADAME DE MONTMARTRE. Vallant's account of how he learned the exciting news reveals just the sort of ambiguous position—half-way between the House of Guise and the House of Orléans—that Marc-Antoine Charpentier had been experiencing for some three years:

> This Saturday, December 9, 1673, Madame de Montmartre paid me the honor of telling me that yesterday, the Feast of the Conception, Mademoiselle de Guise decided she wants to attach me to her person and put me on the list of her householders as of the new year; that she had stated this, and that Madame de Guise, who was present, said that since I was the physician of her two aunts [that is, her aunts by marriage, Mademoiselle de Guise and Madame de Montmartre], I could certainly go, on their behalf, to see Monsieur d'Alençon often, and her as well, and that she had very great trust in me, and that if her own physician should no longer be available, she would put me in his place.[7]

Vallant's summary of the terms of his employment contains important information about MADEMOISELLE DE GUISE's plans in early 1672, when she and MADAME DE GUISE were trying to patch things up after a dispute about the guardianship of the little Duke of Alençon. Having learned that Madame de Guise was being mentioned as a possible wife for her cousin, James Stuart, Duke of York, the future king of England, Mademoiselle de Guise declared herself ready to follow her grandnephew and his mother across the Channel:

> Madame de Montmartre had told me a year ago that Mademoiselle de Guise begged me not to accept any engagement, because she was saving me for Monsieur d'Alençon and for herself. At the time they thought that Madame de Guise might marry the Duke of York. I replied that Mademoiselle would be doing me a great honor, but that I did not want her to oblige me to leave the kingdom, because, by duty, I had engagements with people that would prevent [me] from leaving Paris, and that only an order from the King could oblige me to do so.[8]

Here Vallant provides additional evidence about the intricacies involved in selecting a householder. The invitation was proffered well in advance, with a request that the potential protégé reserve himself for Her Highness. (This way of proceeding strengthens the conjecture that Marc-Antoine Charpentier received this sort of invitation either prior to setting out for Rome, or during his stay there.) In addition, the new householder must be ready to follow his mistress, wherever she might go.

As of January 1, 1674, Noël Vallant was an official member of Mademoiselle de Guise's household. (That year he also began receiving wages from Madame de Guise: one hundred livres a month for the nine months she spent in Paris.[9]) He entered what has been described as a "sweet servitude."[10] Although the Doctor was permitted to see patients outside the Guise circle, he was now expected to ask permission to do so. Permission was not inevitably granted, especially if there was the slightest chance that the patient would attempt to steal Mademoiselle de Guise's treasured physician away from her.

For example, in 1679 MONSIEUR DU BOIS was informed that Mademoiselle de Guise was "creating difficulties" about lending her physician to a noble in the circle of the powerful Marquis of Louvois. The petitioner wrote:

> If you could make [the lending problem] go away, everyone in the household would be obliged to you, and in any event you would obtain what we hope for from that princess. I beg you humbly, Monsieur, to let me know, and to send us Doctor Vallant today between three and five.

Mademoiselle de Guise remained adamant. On the letter Vallant therefore jotted: "Mademoiselle de Guise cannot agree to it."[11] This example of Her Highness's possessiveness of course reinforces the probability that Marc-Antoine Charpentier not only was expected to obtain her approval before accepting any outside commissions, but that Mademoiselle de Guise reserved this privilege for a very select group.

After a little more than a year in the Guises' service, Vallant watched helplessly as the little Duke of Alençon sank into a coma and died. Throughout the night the two princesses kept a vigil at the child's bed, haunted by the ghost of the bleeding-versus-purging debate that had heaped such criticism upon them during LOUIS-JOSEPH DE LORRAINE's fatal smallpox back in 1671. (Vallant was a partisan of purges, because the Medical Faculty at Montpellier, where he was trained, was opposed to bleeding.) The Doctor's poignant description of the child's death reveals much about the interpersonal relations between the Guise princesses and their householders:

> Monsieur the Duke of Alençon, aged four years and six and one-half months, on Friday, March 15, 1675, at three in the afternoon, fell during an accident that left him almost breathless. I arrived at six o'clock and found him inert and breathing with difficulty and whistling, his pulse a bit irregular. Madame de Guise told me that they had given him an enema, and that he was incomparably better. I left him in the same condition at eight in the evening. Monsieur Bellay, the physician of Mademoiselle [de Montpensier] came shortly after that and found him very feverish, and he told Monsieur du Fresne that he thought they would have to bleed him in the

morning. But that was drastically changed, for at midnight, from Friday March 15 to Saturday March 16, he fell into such extreme oppression that they thought he was dead. I arrived at one-thirty in the morning. They told me that he was a bit better, that they had given him an enema [and some medicine]. I deemed him so sick that I bled him. ... I then made him drink, and he drank. Madame de Guise told me that before the bleeding, no one had been able to make him swallow. I made him drink again, and he drank half the cup without stopping. His fever was high and his pulse irregular, but less so. An hour later, noting that his chest was still laboring, I began to think that our efforts would be useless. I gave him a purging enema. ... Since I was alone, Madame [de Guise] and Mademoiselle [de Guise] told me they wanted only me in attendance, that I should do what I deemed appropriate, and that they were turning the child over to me. I insisted on having help. Monsieur Du Bois having arrived, I told him that things were going very badly. He replied that the previous evening Monsieur [Roquette] d'Autun had told him that I was not optimistic about this illness. It is true that on Friday evening I had told Monsieur d'Autun that I was very fearful about this illness, but that I did not dare reveal it to Their Highnesses, for fear of overwhelming them.

I ordered a second purging enema. ... Monsieur Belay arrived and told me he did not dare approach the bed [in case the illness was contagious], because of Mademoiselle [de Montpensier]. I told him there was no sign of redness. ... He did not approach, however, saying that the enemas should continue, and he left. Monsieur Brayer [another of Montpensier's doctors] arrived, said that the child was very ill, and that he should be bled, that his chest was full, and that was the only way to remedy it. Madame and Mademoiselle [de Guise] said that he was very weak, and I replied that we would take the blood that came out, by which we could judge his strength, and that we would stop the bleeding at once if necessary.

Monsieur Brayer asked the time when the night's bleeding had been done, and how long it had been since he had taken nourishment. When he learned that [he had drunk] recently, he said the bleeding should be in an hour, and that he would return to witness it. I went out with him and came back before Brayer did. I found that the child had sunk, and I told Madame, who was very moved. All the others who were there did not believe me. Monsieur Brayer came and said nothing after having taken his pulse, except that he should be bled. He came to the fireplace, where I was standing, and I told him the child was very low. He did not reply, returned to the bed, repeated about the bleeding, returned to the fireplace where I had remained. I told him that the [child's] face was greatly changed. I had pointed this out to Monsieur Du Bois at six in the morning, and an hour after that to Mademoiselle [de Guise], who was asking me if I had not noticed it.

Monsieur Brayer returned to the bed and looked at him. Madame de Guise cried out that her child was dying and asked Monsieur Brayer not to bleed him, because it would serve no purpose. Monsieur Brayer said, "That is true," and he left.

He continued to sink until eleven thirty, when he died. An hour before, Monsieur Belay had come and said that he was neither as weak nor as forsaken, and talked about an enema, and left. He came back a half-hour later and said, "*Actum est*," and as he left [he commented] that he had correctly stated on Friday that Monsieur d'Alençon was sicker than we thought. I replied that others besides him had said the same thing shortly before he died. He returned with Mademoiselle [de Montpensier] and said that nothing should be done, and that *remedia non erant infamanda*. I could not resist telling him that when one warns about a peril, ...[12]

With this bitter rejoinder, the account breaks off.

Vallant took notes during the autopsy conducted by three physicians and three surgeons. Although the child's spine was more or less normal, they commented on the "loosely articulated" knees and wrists that had kept him from standing unaided.[13] His head showed an anomaly: it revolved on his neck as if held only by skin, rather than vertebrae. When his skull was opened, the cause of death became evident. There was a large contusion that had invaded the bone:

Monsieur Belay whispered that the child had fallen, and someone replied that someone had bumped his head while he was lying on the table. Monsieur Belay persisted in his opinion, whispering to me that someone had dropped the child, and that was the cause of his death.

In the end, all but one of the physicians and surgeons agreed—and they made a pact to bury the fact in silence: "We agreed not to talk about it, because it would only double the princesses' anguish, and [would be] a great hurt to everyone around this young prince."[14]

Vallant's compassionate behavior did not go unnoticed. Madame de Guise was true to the word she had given him when he entered Mademoiselle de Guise's service. In April 1675 she made Vallant her "first physician" and provided him with lodgings at the Luxembourg.[15] The Doctor did not follow her to Alençon each summer, however; and if he left Paris, he was careful to ask Mademoiselle de Guise's permission. When Madame de Guise requested his presence in Alençon in July 1683,

to ward off the return of a fever, Vallant observed the formalities expected of a householder: "I first wrote to Mademoiselle de Guise," he
noted, "to receive her orders." Her Highness benevolently permitted him
to leave, but she imposed certain courtly obligations upon him: "She
commanded me to be careful of my person during the voyage, and that
I should share with Madame de Guise her concern over her health, and
that I should send news by every means possible." Only at that point did
the Doctor notify Monsieur Du Bois, "to ask him to send out notices of
his departure and the reason why."[16]

Vallant's tie to the Hôtel de Guise remained the stronger of the two
Guise links. With each year his friendship with PHILIPPE GOIBAUT DU BOIS
deepened. Du Bois named him as his sole heir in a will dated 1677; and
in his will dated 1685 he made his debt to Vallant very clear, referring to
a "close friendship that has existed between [us] for over twenty-five
years," and to the fact that Vallant had done many "helpful things, on
all sorts of occasions, as physician and personal friend." This generosity
had included

> advancing money from his own pocket, ... in the amount of thirteen
> thousand livres, to print the translation of Saint Augustine's letters,
> at his risk, peril, and chance, gaining no reward from the money
> that might come from selling the said publication.[17]

Actually, Vallant was supposed to receive one-third of any profits[18] on
this splendid edition that was dedicated to Mademoiselle de Guise and
that was ornamented with her engraved portrait by Mignard.

Quite a Latinist in his own right,[19] Vallant not only could appreciate
Du Bois' endeavors as a translator, he became an integral part of the neo-
Latinist circle in the capital. In fact, his files contain a letter from Du
Bois' witty and irreverent friend, neo-Latinist Jean Santeul.[20]

Vallant frequently stayed in the Du Bois apartment at the Hôtel de
Guise, and from there he kept abreast of MADEMOISELLE DE GUISE's and
MADAME DE GUISE's latest preoccupations. For example, when the princesses and their advisors were developing plans in 1675 for two educational institutions dedicated to the INFANT JESUS, Vallant copied out
materials about the pedagogy developed at a teacher-training institute
founded in Toulouse but suppressed by the Monarchy for its Jansenism.[21]
He wrote some "wise and gallant" poetry to compliment MADAME DE
TOSCANE.

He probably spent considerable time with ROGER DE GAIGNIÈRES,
which would explain the Doctor's increasing "curiosity" and his evident
feeling that he was living at a time and in a place where momentous
things were going on. That is to say, like Gaignières—and like Marc-

Antoine Charpentier—he carefully preserved his papers, and he sorted them according to a logic all his own. By the end of his life, his manuscripts included not only medical records but notes about the elephant in the Versailles zoo, the doctrine of the Immaculate Conception of the Virgin, Huyghens' vacuum pump, worms that somehow found their way into books, and recipes for purges intermingled with recipes for his favorite dishes at Montmartre and at the Hôtel de Guise. To prevent these papers from being destroyed or dispersed, Vallant gave them to the Abbey of Saint-Germain-des-Prés. (They are now part of the manuscript collection of the National Library in Paris.) Without this donation, many of the portraits in this gallery could not have been painted, or would have been still more sketchy than they are. For example, had Vallant not saved the letters that MADEMOISELLE DE GUISE sent him from Champagne in 1680, MONSIEUR DU BOIS' role as director of the GUISE MUSIC might still be a secret.

Over the years, a true friendship developed between MADEMOISELLE DE GUISE and her physician. During that trip through Champagne, Her Highness sent Vallant this warm commendation for his years of faithful, self-sacrificing service:

> One is very happy and very much at rest when one knows that you are visiting the sick [householders], for you do not think only of their bodies, your treatment extends to their souls, which is the principal [treatment]. ... I want to tell you that one cannot be more touched than I am by all your concern for keeping informed about me, and by the feelings you have for me, and that I so value them that I don't know how to tell you enough, and to say to what point I love and esteem you. *Guise*[22]

Doctor Vallant committed to paper some ironic thoughts about the servitude that shaped his days, and the medical profession in general. His observations could apply to a preceptor-governor such as MONSIEUR DU BOIS (were it not for the "plot" through which he received an impressive legacy from Mademoiselle de Guise), to a household equerry such as ROGER DE GAIGNIÈRES, or to a household composer such as Marc-Antoine Charpentier. One of the Doctor's ironic musings was prompted by the question of whether he should acquire a coach, as DU BOIS had:

> If I were married and had children, my wealth is so great that I would have a lot of trouble living. If I became infirm and my work brought in no money, I would not be too well off. If I had a vehicle, as you say I need for my work, I could pay for it. But if the persons who pay my pensions changed, or disappeared, I would have to get rid of the vehicle. It is more difficult to do without one, once one has

had one, than if one has never had one. The great lord's poverty is the worst of all.[23]

With an old friend, a provincial physician, he shared his thoughts about the profession he had fought so hard to enter many years before: "As for medicine, it appears to be a sure profession. One sees few physicians who die of hunger. ... But here [in Paris] one sees that most [physicians] who are close to the high nobles die with almost nothing."[24]

Doctor Noël Vallant breathed his last at the Luxembourg Palace on July 11, 1685.

VI

A close and very sincere friendship

LOULIÉ AND BROSSARD

Étienne Loulié, musician to Mademoiselle de Guise and theorist of sound;
and Sébastien de Brossard, collector, music theorist, and composer

The stories of Étienne Loulié, a Parisian lay musician, and Sébastien de Brossard, a cleric from Normandy, have been told elsewhere in considerable detail.[1] This joint portrait is therefore a quick sketch that emphasizes the role these two musicians played in preserving Marc-Antoine Charpentier's composition treatise, as well as some of his works that otherwise would have been lost.

Étienne Loulié

Étienne Loulié was born in Paris in 1654, into a dynasty of sword-polishers and sword-decorators who worked on the Left Bank. There is some evidence to suggest that his close relatives, the Croyers, were related to DAVID CROYER, Marc-Antoine Charpentier's cousin.[2] If that is the case, a family link through the Croyers may explain why Loulié became a member of the GUISE MUSIC in the fall of 1673.

Be that as it may, a determining consideration in his selection surely was Loulié's training at the SAINTE-CHAPELLE. For almost a decade he had received a solid musical education under Music Master René Ouvrard, a composer, pedagogue, theorist, and collector—that is, a "curious person," a *curieux*. Driven by a powerful curiosity about how music was related to mathematics and to geometric proportions, Ouvrard inculcated some of this curiosity in his pupil, Loulié:

> Since Ouvrard was as good a theorist as a practitioner, it apparently was from him that Loulié got this taste and inclination for musical theory that he kept until the end of his life. [He was] very different in that respect from almost all musicians, who, when they leave a choir school, being content with the practices, or to be more exact

508

the routine they learned there, do not even think of trying to understand why that routine is good. So that, of all the musicians of Paris, he was almost the only one with whom one could reason about music.[3]

Throughout his fifteen years at the Hôtel de Guise, Loulié's musical skills were in the foreground. He played recorder, viol, and harpsichord, but there is no evidence that he sang with the GUISE MUSIC. Since he was thoroughly grounded in the rules for composing by counterpoint, he probably composed music for the Guises as well; but if he did, nothing seems to have survived. Familiar as he was with the organ and with the different instruments played at the Sainte-Chapelle, he very likely advised Charpentier when the composer was ordered to write an instrumental mass for the MERCY, "instead of organs"[A]—a mass for transverse flutes, four sizes of recorders, a crumhorn, and strings. Concerts given at the Mercy by the GUISE MUSIC loomed so prominently in Loulié's memory that, years later, he worked the name of the church into a definition of "music": "*Music* signifies *concert*, and in this sense one says 'There is music today at the Mercy.' "[4] Any other contribution that Étienne Loulié may have made to Charpentier's artistry can only be conjectural.

In addition to his work with the Guise Music, Loulié seems to have participated in the development of a musical pedagogy for the Academy of the INFANT JESUS, drafting little manuscript method-books on how to teach the recorder and the viol, how to sight sing, how to compose music, and how to add vocal improvisations to a piece. Thus, by the mid-1680s he had acquired a solid reputation as a pedagogue.

Then, in 1689, shortly after MADEMOISELLE DE GUISE's death and the disbanding of the GUISE MUSIC, Loulié was engaged to teach the "elements" or "principles" of music to PHILIPPE III D'ORLÉANS, Duke of Chartres. To be precise, he led the prince through the intricacies of musical notation, and he probably taught him to play the recorder and the viol. Loulié carefully preserved his autograph copies of these teaching methods and of the other little theoretical treatises he would write during the 1690s.

One of these manuscripts involved the Duke of Chartres. By 1692 the prince was ready to study composition. Judging from Loulié's manuscripts, Chartres had already acquired the rudiments of counterpoint from him. However, for this task the pedagogues employed by PHILIPPE II D'ORLÉANS passed over Loulié and turned to Marc-Antoine Charpentier,

---

[A] Cahiers 7–8, H. 513.

who was now the music master at one or another of the THREE JESUIT HOUSES in Paris.

For a textbook, Charpentier used some manuscript "rules" that he had drawn up somewhat earlier and he had shared with Loulié, who had made a copy for himself.[5] Some two years later, Loulié had an opportunity to compare the copy in his personal files with a reworked version that Charpentier had given to Chartres. In the margins he noted the different "augmentations" that Charpentier had inserted into the prince's version. Without Loulié's copy of this composition treatise, and without its allusions to the Duke of Chartres, scholars would have been deprived of this insight into how Marc-Antoine Charpentier went about teaching composition.

The composition lessons were followed by a course on the physics of sound. This led to a project in which Loulié and several members of the Academy of Sciences attempted to fit acoustics into a "new" and universal "system" of musical intervals. There is no evidence that Marc-Antoine Charpentier contributed to this project.

Loulié was rewarded by his noble pupil. First he was granted the privilege to print some of these materials: *Les Éléments ou Principes de Musique* (1696), which he dedicated to the Duke of Chartres; *L'Abrégé des Prin-cipes* ... (1696), and *Le Nouveau Sistème* (1698). Then, in 1698, he was granted a half-share in revenues from the Ballard family's monopoly over printed and hand-ruled music. These very practical rewards corresponded to Loulié's own particular needs and preoccupations; but they are not all that different from PHILIPPE III D'ORLÉANS' generosity toward Charpentier, who owed his position as music master at the SAINTE-CHAPELLE to the Duke of Chartres and whose nephews, JACQUES ÉDOUARD and Jacques-François Mathas, were permitted to dedicate a volume of Charpentier's motets to the prince in 1709.

Loulié died on July 16, 1702, in the apartment from which he was supervising a music-copying business.

Sébastien de Brossard

During the crucial years when Loulié was setting out on his intellectual quest, he was being encouraged by Sébastien de Brossard. A Jesuit-trained Norman, Abbé Brossard had arrived in Paris in 1678 and had struck up a friendship with Loulié by 1680. Although no concrete facts prove that Brossard was personally acquainted with Marc-Antoine Charpentier—or any member of the GUISE MUSIC other than Loulié—scattered documents preserved in Brossard's collection of musical books and manuscripts indicate that the young Norman was closely following everything that went on at the Hôtel de Guise and at the Hôtel de

Condé, and that with surprising rapidity he had found his way into the little courts around the DUKE OF RICHELIEU and the DUKE OF CHAULNES.

That is to say, in 1684 Brossard tried to have himself appointed as almoner to music-loving Chaulnes; and he simultaneously had an entrée to the Richelieu household, via the Duke's intendant, who appears to have been a relative of CHARLES SEVIN, Marc-Antoine Charpentier's cousin. It is therefore not surprising that in 1685 Brossard was invited to write a little "opera," *Pyrame et Thisbé*, for RICHELIEU's cancelled fête at Rueil.[6] Charpentier had composed a pastorale[B] for the same fête.

By the time Brossard left Paris for Strasbourg in 1687, he was a very different person from the young man who had come to Paris a decade earlier. He had become a committed collector and theorist. The causes of this transformation are multiple. First, there was the intellectual awakening that took place during his conversations with an Englishman named Samuel Morland, who had come to France to help create a pump to bring water to the the fountains of Versailles. Brossard credited Morland with having "given him to such a degree the taste for music theory that since that time I have spared no reading, no time, no expenses, no troubles in order to perfect my knowledge."[7]

Then there was his fascination with Italian music. The sources of this enthusiasm are easy to deduce. Morland happened to be very close to Pietro Guerrini, the Florentine who so enthusiastically attended several concerts each week at the Hôtel de Guise during his visit to Paris in 1684.[8] Although there is no evidence that Brossard or Morland were admitted to one of MADEMOISELLE DE GUISE's "conversations," Loulié's descriptions of these musical events—where he performed with the GUISE MUSIC—would have sufficed to whet Brossard's curiosity about Italian music. Indeed, these were the years when Italian music is known to have been performed at the Hôtel de Guise.

Finally, there was Sébastien de Brossard's commitment to collecting. Like ROGER DE GAIGNIÈRES, the famous collector at the Hôtel de Guise who went to great lengths to obtain something rare, Brossard set about having copies made of manuscripts that could "only be found in the cabinets of a few collectors," and for which he often had to pay sizeable sums.[9] Thanks to copies made by or for Brossard, dozens of Marc-Antoine Charpentier's compositions that were not preserved in the *Mélanges* have survived.[10]

After Strasbourg, Brossard was named Music Master at the Cathedral of Meaux, where some of Marc-Antoine Charpentier's close relatives

[B] Cahiers XXVII–XXVIII, H. 485, H. 440.

still lived. In fact, in the course of his duties at the cathedral, Brossard could scarcely have avoided dealing with one of the composer's first cousins, Robert Charpentier, NICOLAS CHARPENTIER THE SERGEANT's son, who was a grand chaplain there.

Distance and years did not diminish the friendship that had begun circa 1680, when Étienne Loulié of the Hôtel de Guise met Sébastien de Brossard. Brossard had the highest regard for his friend: "Of all the musicians of Paris he was almost the only one with whom one could reason about music." This friendship changed Sébastien's life. He recalled out their conversations:

> [They] gave me the opportunity to form a friendship with him, a friendship that was very close and very sincere on both sides. For, each of us being free of that base and stupid jealousy that almost always drives people belonging to the same profession, we shared openly our discoveries with one another.[11]

Concerned that their papers might be dispersed after their deaths, the two theorists made a pact:

> We promised one another reciprocally that the first of us to die would leave his memoranda to the survivor. Which [Loulié] did not fail to do in his will. And the executor of the will ... gave me the packet of papers, ... which I have kept carefully ever since, especially since [the packet] contains a lot of very curious pieces, some of them by Loulié.[12]

Brossard probably did not know that Loulié did not actually mention these papers in his will but expressed this wish orally to his executor.

By the 1720s Brossard, now well into his seventies, began negotiating the transfer of his collection to a library, as GAIGNIÈRES and DOCTOR VALLANT had done. Having worked out an arrangement with the Royal Library, he began preparing a catalog. The information he included in it concerning Marc-Antoine Charpentier is perhaps secondhand, but it corroborates the statements of individuals who knew the composer personally, chiefly CORNEILLE and DONNEAU DE VISÉ. Better yet, Brossard added a few details that almost certainly came from Loulié, if not from Charpentier himself. There were also a few tidbits based on his own experience:

> Charpentier was, I believe, a Parisian. He lived in Rome for several years, where he was the disciple and very assiduous partisan of the famous Carissimi. I have been assured of something that is, however, difficult to believe: he had a prodigious memory, and once he had heard a piece of music, he could write down all the parts with exactitude, and this is how the motets *Vidi impium, Emendamus in*

melius, etc., and several of Carissimi's oratorios, which were not printed, reached France. At least that is what is claimed. After his return from Italy he worked for some time for the Comédie Française. ... He wrote a quantity of other works, both sacred and profane, that are of unusual excellence. ... It is owing to his contact with Italy in his youth that a few French purists, or to be more accurate, people jealous of the fineness of his music, have very inappropriately taken the opportunity to reproach his Italian tastes; for one can say, without flattering him, that he borrowed only the good, his works show it well enough.

Be that as it may, for true connoisseurs he has always passed for the most profound and savant of modern musicians. This doubtlessly is why the Jesuits of the rue Saint-Antoine chose him as music master for their church [Saint-Louis], one of the most brilliant positions of that time; and it is very noteworthy that the Duke of Chartres, subsequently Duke of Orléans and Regent of France, chose him to teach him the fundamentals of musical composition; and [I own a copy, Loulié's copy] of the manuscript he gave this great prince concerning the rules for composition.

In 1696 [read: 1698] the mastership of the Sainte-Chapelle of Paris became vacant, and Monsieur Fleuriau, who was Treasurer at the time, had one of his relatives write me in Strasbourg, where I then was living. It took a week to receive the letter and to come posthaste to Paris. During those eight days, Charpentier so effectively pressed the Duke of Chartres, his disciple, that Abbé Fleuriau was obliged to give him the position, which I found filled when I arrived; but I am easily consoled. ...

[As for] his opera Médée, it is undeniably the most savant and most exquisite of all printed operas, at least since Lully's death; and although, owing to the plots of envious and ignorant people, it was not as well-received by the public as it merited ... of all operas, without exception, it is the one from which one can learn the things most essential to good composition. That is why I wondered for some time whether I should categorize him as a theorist, that is to say, among the masters of the art of music, rather than put [Médée] among simple operas.[13]

Sébastien de Brossard died at Meaux on August 10, 1730. By selling his collection to the Royal Library in 1726,[14] he preserved for posterity a substantial number of pieces by Marc-Antoine Charpentier, and his composition treatise for PHILIPPE III D'ORLÉANS as well. In addition to the composition treatise, Brossard preserved Étienne Loulié's other manuscripts, which provide tantalizing insights into MADAME DE GUISE's pedagogical venture at the Academy of the INFANT JESUS, the education of princes, and the birth of the science of acoustics. It also seems that Brossard should be credited with saving Charpentier's *Mélanges* from dispersion, by encouraging the Royal Library to purchase the manuscripts from JACQUES ÉDOUARD.

The Portrait at the End
of the Gallery

At the far end of this imagined portrait gallery hangs the heavily restored portrait of a man in a dressing gown, painted in chiaroscuro.

Like so many of the portraits in this gallery, the man sits at his worktable. In this particular portrait the room is so full of shadows that the subject has ceased his labors and is staring out into the gallery, as if trying to communicate with visitors.

On the table beside him are stacked a dozen or so folio-sized music notebooks. A ray of sunlight rakes across several of the titles: *Salve Regina, In honorem Cæciliæ, Le Malade imaginaire, La Feste de Ruel.* In the shadowy background can be discerned a wall lined with shelves piled high with stacks of folio notebooks and smaller partbooks. Possessive gestures reveal that it is he who has composed the music on the table and on the shelves.

To one of the shelves someone tacked an Almanac for 1682, a large engraving that shows *Monsieur Charpentier* giving a menuet to a lady in courtly dress. In other words, this heavily restored portrait at the end of the gallery depicts Monsieur Charpentier.

In this portrait a window opens on a busy, sunlit cityscape. Churches and palaces stud the urban landscape, and in the distance the silhouette of a convent looms on Montmartre Butte. Through these city streets wander bourgeois and royal officials in their black or gray clothes, clerics in their cassocks, and religious in the distinctive habits of their orders.

515

Mounted noblemen in splendid suits salute ladies in sumptuous gowns as they pass by in their coaches or sedan chairs.

If the visitor to this imaginary portrait gallery puts his face right up to the canvas, he sees that the tiny figures of these promenaders have been painted by a miniaturist. The faces prove to be very familiar, for these same individuals are depicted in one or another of the portraits in this gallery.

By contrast, Monsieur Charpentier's features are obscure, blurred, lacking in detail. Here and there they border on the stereotypical, because centuries of neglect in some attic or cellar caused the lineaments to discolor or flake off. Referring to other portraits from the period, a restorer has retouched and in-painted the man's face, his hands, his clothes. Many of the objects depicted in the room suffered similar damage, and they too have been in-painted.

Thus the personal side of the "famous Monsieur Charpentier" remains blurred, dim, and often rather interpretive. Still, this restored painting has the merits of preserving the little we know or can reasonably conjecture about the private man, as contrasted with the public figure depicted in the Almanac.

1662

1684

1685

The most profound and savant of modern musicians

MARC-ANTOINE CHARPENTIER

Composer to the Guises, the Dauphin, the Jesuits,
and the Sainte-Chapelle

How does one write a "portrait," a biography, of a man who kept the private facet of his life so hidden? Two decades spent tracking him in the archives and libraries of several European nations produced only the blurred portrait that brings this imaginary portrait gallery to a close.

Marc-Antoine Charpentier the Man has eluded me. Yet his family, his family friends, his collaborators, and many of his patrons proved willing to share at least some of their secrets. I promptly passed many of these secrets on to the public.[1] As I think back, I am not certain that finding dozens of notarial documents and a few allusions to his activities would have made this portrait any more complete. As the celebration of the three-hundredth anniversary of the composer's death approaches, I therefore offer to "the famous *Monsieur Charpentier*" this imperfect portrait. He has remained a private person to the end.

The portrait has been created by assembling the evidence graciously provided by the other subjects in the gallery. After each research trip, new evidence was fitted into an emerging but highly fragmentary chronology that could be juxtaposed against events in the lives of the persons portrayed in this gallery, and against the chronological flow of Charpentier's manuscripts. In assembling these pieces, I was guided by the research of several *érudits* of the early twentieth century, and by the work of the leading historians of culture, mentalities, consumerism, patronage, religious history, and French musical history who flourished during the last half of that century. The result is less a biography of Monsieur Charpentier than the biography of a cultural moment.

517

1643–1661
PARIS

The childhood years

Marc-Antoine Charpentier was "born in the diocese of Paris" in 1643,[2] to Louis CHARPENTIER, MASTER SCRIVENER, and Anne Toutré. Louis had left Meaux as an adolescent, perhaps going first to Paris to complete an apprenticeship, and then to the Duchy of Nevers. Whether his bride came from Paris, from the region around Meaux, or from Nevers has not been determined.

By the early 1640s Louis and his wife were living in or near Paris and had produced three daughters who survived infancy: Étiennette, Élisabeth, and Marie. Then came Marc-Antoine and, two years later, Armand-Jean. The family seems to have settled down in the Latin Quarter, in the parish of Saint-Séverin, by 1645. They quickly gravitated into the orbit of the Jesuits at the Noviciate, one of THREE JESUIT HOUSES in Paris. There Étiennette was "instructed" by the fathers—a word that may have been synonymous with "catechized," but that just possibly may indicate that the Jesuits taught girls to read devotional tracts, write letters, and do basic arithmetic. That Élisabeth was "instructed" in this way is strong evidence that at some point all the Charpentier siblings were taken under the wing of the Society of Jesus, and that Marc-Antoine in particular received not only "instruction" but also, perhaps, some schooling on the level of the *collège*, the secondary school.

As the tumult of the Fronde subsided in the early 1650s, the Charpentiers began preparing their children to earn a living. What options were available to the children of a member of the scriveners' guild? Dowering three daughters was more or less out of the question, so the usual solution was to give one daughter to the Church, set up another daughter in a trade, and keep the third to help at home until she was twenty-five and had saved enough from odd jobs to accumulate the linens and household items that would constitute her modest dowry. An eldest son generally was privileged over his younger brothers. If he showed a commitment to his father's trade or profession, he would be trained from an early age to take over the family business. Since it was unlikely that the father's guild would admit more than one son as a master, younger sons tended to be given to the Church—especially if their father had taught them skills that would be useful in a parish church, a convent, a monastery.

Thus it was that, around 1660, Marie Charpentier (she is called MARIE THE CONVERSE in this gallery) took her vows as a converse nun at the ABBEY OF PORT-ROYAL, known for its willingness to accept undowered novices. For this reason, the Charpentier family's decision to create an affective and devotional link to Port-Royal, rather than to another convent in the Paris region, can be presumed to have involved more than financial expediency. For example, they may have looked favorably upon the Jansenist tendencies at this recently "reformed" abbey, a very strict and very devout establishment that would soon be accused of heretical leanings. Indeed, during the late 1650s and early 1660s the devotional outlook of the entire Charpentier family very probably was colored by the Jansenist view of human activities and devotions that is so palpable in the travel account of a Parisian priest and theologian named Charles Le Maistre, who like the Charpentiers was a friend and supporter of Port-Royal.[3]

Their father's assistants?

With financial help from the FERRAND FAMILY, Étiennette completed an apprenticeship as a linener and opened a shop. If it was not in Jesuit-sponsored classes, then it was at her parents' side that ÉTIENNETTE THE LINENER had learned to do sums, file her papers methodically, and read and write. The fact that her script never became polished, and that her spelling remained profoundly phonetic, suggests that she concentrated on acquiring the requisite business acumen. Her lifelong link to the Jesuits—who by the 1660s would become the archenemies of the Jansenists around Port-Royal—is no less revealing about the Charpentier family's devotions than was their choice of Port-Royal for Marie. Having lost two ancestors to the Saint Bartholomew's Day Massacre, Louis Charpentier took what he admired most from each religious group. In the Jansenists, the Charpentiers could admire the notable devoutness and uprightness; in the Jesuits, they could take advantage of the fathers' wondrous talent for educating the young and inculcating devotion by music, skits, and visual effects.

The handwriting of the other daughter, Élisabeth, was fine enough to make her a potential assistant, a copyist proudly contributing to the family business, as children of craftsmen and shopkeepers often did in the seventeenth century. It was more or less understood that she would remain single until she had reached the age of majority, helping at home and in the family business. The small sums she earned in this way—and perhaps by assisting Étiennette at her shop—would help her accumulate a small dowry.

At an early age Armand-Jean had likewise acquired a fine hand. So had Marc-Antoine, whose formal signature of 1685, written in so-called "round letters," reveals his mastery of the calligrapher's art and his fascination with the scripts and signatures of the late-sixteenth century.[4]

Which son would eventually succeed his father was a matter to be decided later. In the meantime, the boys were acquiring invaluable skills that would serve them in the guild, in the Church, or in the employ of a merchant, a royal official, or a noble. For example, Cousin CHARLES SEVIN had become quite well-to-do by working as an aide to Chancellor Pierre Séguier, and Cousin GILLES CHARPENTIER had been secretary to a marquis.

All the Charpentier children learned the importance of keeping records and filing them carefully,[5] making sure that documents and records drawn up for one client were kept separate from those belonging to another, to ensure that the Scrivener would never be accused of making off with papers, as Cousin Gilles had been. With the exception of Étiennette, the children almost certainly increased the family income by copying documents for their father.

What career for Marc-Antoine?

By the mid-1650s the Scrivener and his wife—if she was still alive, for the date of her death is unknown—must have realized that Marc-Antoine possessed a very special gift, the gift of song, of inventing melodies. Like MOLIÈRE, and like DOCTOR VALLANT, did adolescent Marc-Antoine express his distaste for his father's craft, by his face, his gestures, his angry words? Probably. So, what other options were open to the Scrivener's artistically gifted son?

The father surely would have opposed daydreams about eking out a living as a singer on the Pont-Neuf or at the Saint-Germain Fair. Sober, devout parents generally did everything possible to keep their children from being corrupted by street theater and ambulant musicians—art forms that tended to be lascivious and larded with sexual innuendo. In other words, unless he sneaked away like DASSOUCY, Marc-Antoine can be presumed to have had little contact with music in the vernacular, beyond popular songs and instrumental music played on violins and hurdy-gurdies at neighborhood fêtes. This conjecture is strengthened by DASSOUCY's assertion that, as late as 1672, Marc-Antoine had not mastered the art of setting vernacular words to music.

If Marc-Antoine did not want to be a scrivener, there were two other viable options.[6] He could become an ecclesiastic, for the Church looked favorably upon candidates with special skills—in his case, his skill at calligraphy, his high tenor voice, *haute-contre*, and his obvious talent for inventing tunes and harmonizing them. Ideally, this option was accompanied by both a strong religious calling and money for the pension that most religious houses expected from the family of a new monk or priest. Or else Marc-Antoine could, like his two cousins, enter the household of a nobleman or a royal official. People of that rank generally were overjoyed to hire a domestic who could add musical performance to his more routine duties. Although the individual who chose this option sometimes had amazing opportunities for advancement, threats hovered over him throughout his career. Wages often went unpaid; he might be disgraced on a whim; he might find himself on the street if his master died.

The first option was the preferred choice of modest families, because many a talented young man had demonstrated that a career in the Church not only posed few risks, it also offered the greatest opportunities for advancement and financial security. If the Charpentiers entertained any strategy along these lines, it clearly did not center upon a cloistered monastery. If it had, Marc-Antoine, almost nineteen, would have been living within convent walls in 1662 and probably would not have signed Élisabeth's wedding contract.

For Marc-Antoine Charpentier, a scenario constructed upon the typical decision to give a talented son to the Church would go more or less as follows. By the late 1650s, his parents would have been planning a career for him in the Church. In fact, one can conjecture that, as a young adolescent, Marc-Antoine was being wooed by one of the THREE JESUIT HOUSES—perhaps the Noviciate, with which the family is known to have been in contact since the mid-1640s, or perhaps their famed College of Clermont (later known as "Louis-le-Grand.") There were, of course, other religious establishments in Paris that were always eager to admit a talented adolescent, so the name of one or another convent or religious order might be inserted at will into this conjectural scheme. Continuing nonetheless to propose that the Jesuits were the order most likely to have appeared engaging to Marc-Antoine, one can imagine him being given access to the music master of the Church of Saint-Louis, whose mission it would be to supplement the youth's natural talents with a grounding in traditional counterpoint, and to hone his skills at setting Latin texts to music.

Someone clearly taught Marc-Antoine these skills during the late 1650s and early 1660s. Otherwise, why would his nephew, JACQUES ÉDOU-ARD—doubtlessly basing his assertion on family stories—tell Titon du Tillet that the composer had gone to Rome to "perfect his music"? In other words, prior to setting out for Rome in the mid-1660s, Marc-Antoine had acquired a solid grounding in the art of composing church music, and he presumably was already writing motets in the French style.

At some point in his education, Marc-Antoine acquired at least a modicum of Latin. Decades later, he would tuck Latin phrases into his personal copies of compositions.[7] His personal copy of a mass by

Francesco Beretta reveals a familiarity with the sort of Latin common-places acquired in a classroom. Expressing his frustration at a copying mistake, he jotted down a line from Horace's *Ars poetica: Aliquando bonus dormitat Homerus*, "Even good Homer sometimes dozes."[8] This familiarity with Latin suggests that, like MOLIÈRE, Marc-Antoine studied as an extern, if not an intern at the nearby College of Clermont during the late 1650s or early 1660s—a distinct possibility when one recalls the Charpentier family's links of friendship to MARIE TALON, the sister-in-law and niece-in-law of two of the FOUR JESUITS portrayed in this gallery.

The conjecture that a skilled music master had taught adolescent Marc-Antoine to put Latin words to music is strengthened by the fact that, in the very first works that he copied out into the two series of notebooks[A] that would become the *Mélanges*, the relationship between the musical meter and the Latin prosody is admirable. He clearly knew how to recite Latin with the prosodic rhythms that characterized the "vulgar" pronunciation espoused by learned French clergy.[9]

A decade later, in December 1671, just a year after his return from Rome, Marc-Antoine would be invited to write a plainsong setting of some Latin verse[B] by Father Commire, S.J., one of the most respected neo-Latinist poets of France. This commission would scarcely have been extended to a composer who was unable to appreciate the rhythms of Commire's poetry. When the Jesuits turned to Charpentier, were they turning to a former pupil who, they knew, possessed the requisite skills in Latin and the desired familiarity with poetics?

That Marc-Antoine had acquired this very special skill by 1671 means that he had acquired it by the mid-1660s—prior to setting off for Rome, where French-style pronunciation was viewed as an aberration. He therefore was either self-taught, going from church to church to steep himself in Latin motets and plainsong, and listening intently to the music sung at street altars during Corpus Christi processions; or else he was being brought along by clergy who knew how to give their Latin the long or short syllables that characterized the French manner of pronouncing that language. Indeed, it is difficult to imagine Marc-Antoine Charpentier seeking out CARISSIMI in Rome, if he did not already feel competent about his ability to set Latin texts to music. That said, he must have experienced a cultural shock when he heard Romans speak and sing Latin with Italian vowels and Italian prosody.

In 1661, as Louis the Scrivener's health began to fail, the family was

---

[A] That is, cahier1 and cahier I.
[B] Cahier IX, H. 55–57 (1671).

presumably going through a decisive moment that was scarcely unique: they were waiting for Marc-Antoine to decide whether he had been called to serve God in the Church. The end of their wait was fast approaching, for noviciates generally began at seventeen or eighteen years of age, and Marc-Antoine would soon turn eighteen.

1662–1669
PARIS AND ROME

Orphaned

Louis the Scrivener died in December 1661. In January 1662, after an unusually long delay, the CHÂTELET assigned Marc-Antoine and his younger brother a legal guardian, Nicolas Dupin, a procurator at the Parlement of Paris. Dupin was a friend or business associate of ÉLISABETH GRIMAUDET and her husband, both of whom would sign ÉLISABETH CHARPENTIER's wedding contract that summer, declaring themselves to be "friends" of the groom. Dupin promptly summoned a notary to draw up an inventory of the possessions of Louis Charpentier and his wife.

In his introductory paragraph the notary stated that he was going to list and summarize not only the "usual registers" but also the "letters and charters" that were locked up in an "expedition cabinet." But he never did. In fact, he apparently did not open the cabinet at all. Instead, he allowed Étiennette Charpentier and Dupin to go off with the key. Was this rather atypical behavior related to the Foucquet Affair? In January 1662 dozens of financiers were being arrested, prosecuted, fined, and even imprisoned. Among the accused were close relatives of several friends of the Charpentier family: Macé de La Bazinière, the stepfather of MARIE TALON's husband; and Claude Le Ragois de Bretonvilliers, Madame LOUIS DE BAILLEUL's father. All of which prompts a question that cannot be answered: Had Louis the Scrivener been keeping confidential records for one or more of these financiers? (By an irony of Fate, Marie Talon's husband, Daniel Voisin, and her brother, Denis Talon, would sit on the panel appointed to judge some of the accused.)

The Scrivener's inventory revealed that each son would inherit approximately 175 livres, an amount totally inadequate to provide for them until they reached twenty-five, the age of majority. Dupin and some of the Charpentiers' well-to-do friends would have to contribute to the boys' training and establishment, or Marc-Antoine and Armand-Jean could end up in the poorhouse or in the streets.

Perhaps more troubling still, Marc-Antoine, now several months into his nineteenth year, did not feel a calling in the Church. At any rate, when his sister Élisabeth wed a dancing-master that summer, Marc-

Antoine was not described as "living" at a noviciate or a seminary. In other words, his guardian was preparing him for a different career. The sources give absolutely no idea of what that career may have been, but one thing is quite clear: it was not the scrivener's craft. It had already been more or less decided that Armand-Jean would succeed his father.

Whatever career the Scrivener had been working out with his older son in 1658 and 1659, Marc-Antoine was distancing himself from his father's craft by 1662. For example, when he signed his sister's wedding contract that summer, he did not use his formal "round" signature, complete with the paraph that a scrivener, a notary, or a clerk added to his name. Instead, he opted for the "flowing letters" of his everyday signature, and signed M. Anthoine Charpentier[10]—thereby revealing that the family called him Antoine, rather than Marc, just as ARMAND-JEAN THE ENGINEER was known as Jean. Armand-Jean, who a few months earlier had been apprenticed to a master scrivener-engraver, signed this document with an immature version of the formal signature he would use for the rest of his life.

In addition to these scant facts, nothing is known about Marc-Antoine's activities between January 1662 and his departure for Rome in 1666 or 1667. He did not enter the Church, because as late as 1676 his sister, ÉTIENNETTE THE LINENER, had not ruled out the possibility that he would marry and beget children. In a will dictated that year, she provided for any children who might be born to him of a legitimate marriage. One can therefore only presume that Monsieur Dupin either continued an educational program on which Marc-Antoine had already embarked, or else he implemented one that the Scrivener had blocked out prior to his death. Or did Dupin find his own solution to the quandary, once it became clear that Marc-Antoine was rejecting both the Church and the scrivener's table?

Orphaned while still a legal minor, Marc-Antoine would be under Dupin's supervision until approximately the summer of 1668, when his twenty-fifth birthday had come and gone. Until that time, he could not marry, embark upon an apprenticeship or a noviciate, or conduct any financial transactions of consequence without the signed approval of his legal guardian. True, he could be "emancipated" prior to the age of majority, thereby gaining the right to decide such issues on his own; but no allusion to an "emancipation" for either Charpentier son has been found. In short, Marc-Antoine's future depended upon Dupin's good sense. Dupin would have to count on the generosity of prosperous Charpentier friends such as MARIE TALON, ÉLISABETH GRIMAUDET, and the FERRANDS, to contribute money or to vouch for Marc-Antoine's honesty, industry, and talent to a potential employer.

Let us suppose, for the sake of argument, that Marc-Antoine was determined to pursue a career in music, come what may. He could not rely on genius alone, for he lacked close relatives among the musicians of Paris. He would be harassed by the "minstrels' corporation," always ready to protect it own by controlling admission to the confraternity and claiming the right to regulate performance. Outsider that he was, being accepted into the guild would be extremely difficult. (Witness the shaky position his nephew, JACQUES ÉDOUARD, would find himself in three decades later, when his misguided mother attempted to set him up as a printer.) With the help of the Talons, the Voisins, the Bailleuls, or the Le Ragois, Marc-Antoine could perhaps find his way into the household of a powerful man or woman, just as Painter LE BRUN and Cousin SEVIN had found their way into Chancellor Séguier's entourage. A protector so powerful could perhaps quell the inevitable oppositions raised by the Parisian guilds. But dreaming about that sort of protector was tantamount to chasing after rainbows. If Marc-Antoine was determined to write music, that left only one reasonable option: composing for the Church without actually taking religious vows, with the Church as his protector.

Off to Rome

In 1666 or 1667 Marc-Antoine set off for Rome—presumably with Monsieur Dupin's approval, for a young man who had run away from home would scarcely have been deemed worthy of entering service to the House of Guise, as Marc-Antoine would do some three years later. Returning again to the Jesuit hypothesis to suggest how this voyage may have come to pass, one can conjecture that Marc-Antoine was the travel companion for a delegation sent to confer with the General of the Society of Jesus. And if not with the Jesuits, then he probably traveled with a group of clerics or laymen to whom he had been recommended. The return trip would have been made under similar circumstances.

Dupin would have worked out the financial arrangements—well in advance if time permitted, or after the fact if Marc-Antoine left precipitously, as was often the case when an individual was asked to join a traveling party.[11] This raises yet another unanswerable question about Marc-Antoine Charpentier's departure for Rome: Who agreed to pay his room and board so that he could pursue his musical studies there? It cannot be ruled out some of the family friends who had stepped forward to sign ÉLISABETH CHARPENTIER's wedding contract in 1662 committed themselves to send a stipend to Rome every quarter. Still, the fact that Marc-Antoine entered the Guises' service so soon after his return to Paris suggests that MARIE DE GUISE THE REGENT may have subsidized all or part of his trip, as a preliminary step to inviting him to join her nephew's household.

The mechanism by which this conjectural recommendation took place is not difficult to imagine, for the Guises had longtime affective ties to the Voisin–Verthamon–Versoris family, that is, to the in-laws of Élisabeth Charpentier's "friend," MARIE TALON. It therefore seems likely that these longtime servants of the House of Guise recommended Marc-Antoine to the princess in about 1665. If they did, it was because—having distant and close relatives in the Guise household, as they did—they knew that the youth met the three criteria that Her Highness observed when selecting a householder. First, the ideal candidate came from a family that already "belonged" to a prince or princess of the House of Lorraine. Marc-Antoine Charpentier met this requirement, for his relative, HAVÉ DE SAINT-AUBIN, had been gentleman in ordinary to the late husband of the DOWAGER DUCHESS OF ORLÉANS, Mademoiselle de Guise's Lorraine cousin. Second, a potential householder should be the friend of one of the Guises' friends, thereby enabling Her Highness to verify whether the candidate had been brought up by devout, honest, loyal parents. Marc-Antoine met this qualification too, for he was acquainted with MARIE TALON, whose husband came from a family that had served the House of Guise for a century. Finally, the ideal candidate possessed a unique talent that would be both useful and pleasing to Mademoiselle de Guise. Marc-Antoine qualified here too. His skills as a copyist could prove useful to Her Highness's secretary or intendant, and his skill at writing music would be perfect for her nephew's chapel—especially if young Charpentier were to become versed in the Italian style that she had come to love in Florence.

This scenario is less farfetched than it may seem. The years 1666 and 1667 were heady ones for MADEMOISELLE MARIE DE GUISE THE REGENT. Acting on behalf of her adolescent nephew, LOUIS-JOSEPH DE LORRAINE, who had just become Duke of Guise, she was in the process of putting together a household that would reflect his high rank and add luster to the somewhat tarnished glory of the House of Guise. In fact, roughly when Marc-Antoine Charpentier set off for Rome, Her Highness selected GOIBAUT DU BOIS to serve as her nephew's governor or preceptor, and to be the household chapel master as well. As DOCTOR VALLANT, the Guise physician, would soon learn, the princess planned such nominations well in advance, working through a third party to obtain a promise that the protégé would refuse all other offers until a new year dawned and a new household roster went into effect. In short, although no sources make it possible to move from conjecture to assertion, the House of Guise may well have been aware of Marc-Antoine's talents as early as 1665, and perhaps facilitated his studies in Rome.

Before Marc-Antoine started off for Rome, Nicolas Dupin would have provided him with letters of recommendation similar to the ones that Chancellor Séguier had given CHARLES LE BRUN when the young painter set off for Rome. The recipients of two of these letters about Marc-Antoine can be imagined. One would have been JACQUES II DALI-BERT, the impresario and secretary to Queen Christina of Sweden, whose father had been GASTON D'ORLÉANS' householder, just as ÉLISABETH GRIMAUDET's brother and Marc-Antoine's cousin, HAVÉ DE SAINT-AUBIN, had been. The other recipient would have been Pierre de Verthamon, who was then in Rome, serving as secretary to the General of the Society of Jesus. One of the FOUR JESUITS in the group portrait hanging in this gallery, Verthamon was MARIE TALON's uncle. Other likely recipients would have included one or more unidentified Roman contacts of Marc-Antoine's paternal cousins, the SEVINS, the one a bishop, the other a trusted aide to Chancellor Séguier. If MADEMOISELLE DE GUISE THE REGENT was involved in arranging the trip, the field would widen immeasurably, for in 1666 she was in constant contact with both the French Embassy in Rome and the French foreign ministry in Paris, concerning a lawsuit being decided by the Rota.

Marc-Antoine appears to have reached Rome by the fall of 1666. To what extent did his first impressions resemble those of his compatriot, Le Maistre, whose travel account has preserved in considerable detail the cultural shock this Jansenist priest experienced?[12] Little is known about Marc-Antoine's years in Rome, beyond the fact that he stayed for "three years," "several years," "a long time," and that he studied with CARISSIMI, the famed Jesuit chapel master. To be precise, Charpentier "saw Carissimi often."[13] While there, he is also known to have become acquainted with a poet and musician named DASSOUCY.

When did those "three years" begin and end? Although it was possible to cross the mountains in winter or brave the stormy Mediterranean, most travelers set out in the spring, in order to reach Rome before the summer heat.[14] In other words, Marc-Antoine can be presumed to have left Paris prior to Easter, and to have begun the return trip some three years later, in late August or September. Since the first compositions in his two series of notebooks date from approximately January 1670, he must have been back in Paris by the end of 1669. In order to have spent "three years" in Rome, he therefore either had to leave Paris early in 1666 and return to France in the fall of 1669 (for a stay of a full three years plus several months), or else his departure did not take place until the spring of 1667, and he spent considerably less than three full years in the Eternal City. If one assumes that he was minimizing the length of his stay, rather than exaggerating it, when he told THOMAS CORNEILLE and JEAN DONNEAU DE VISÉ, that he had spent "three years" in Rome, it becomes possible to date his residence in Rome with relative accuracy: May 1666 to September 1669.

Carissimi and Dassoucy

It may well have been a recommendation from Father Verthamon that gave Marc-Antoine access to the famed composer, CARISSIMI—who was so sought-after that the directors of the Jesuit college where he worked were discouraging the visits from admirers that kept him from fulfilling his duties. These visits with the great composer meant so much to Marc-Antoine that he subsequently recounted them to his Parisian collaborators, Corneille and Donneau de Visé, who mentioned Charpentier's link to Carissimi several times in their *Mercure galant*: "He lived a long time in Italy," they wrote on one occasion, "where he often saw Carissimi, who was the greatest music master that we have had for a long time."[15] "Often saw," *voyait souvent*, as one "sees" a physician today, that is, consults him.

And Dassoucy, the poet-composer-musician who had written theatrical music for Pierre Corneille back in the 1640s? When, and under what circumstances, did Marc-Antoine meet him? The latest possible date for this encounter is easy to determine, for Dassoucy was imprisoned by the Holy Office in late November or early December 1667 and remained incarcerated until the fall of 1668, when he was released and set off for Paris as fast as he could go. In other words, the two Frenchmen struck up a friendship—or, more likely, a working relationship—at some point between May 1666 and October 1667.

Where did they meet or work together? There are two possibilities. By mid-1666 Dassoucy had obtained entrées to Queen Christina's Riario Palace and to the French embassy at the Farnese Palace. At the Riario worked JACQUES II DALIBERT, a Parisian who almost certainly knew Marc-Antoine's cousin, HAVÉ DE SAINT-AUBIN, from the days when they had both been in GASTON D'ORLÉANS' service. Dalibert's duties as Christina's secretary took him from the Riario to the Farnese, and back, several times a week. In short, he was a bridge between the two palaces.

The French community in Rome being quite tightly knit, and the rules of politeness being rather rigid in the seventeenth century, Marc-Antoine presumably presented a letter of recommendation to Dalibert, and Dalibert subsequently introduced him to Dassoucy, who had made two unsuccessful attempts to be invited to join Queen Christina's Music, of which Dalibert was the impresario. The attempts came to nothing, for

Christina left Rome in May 1666, to see to her affairs in Hamburg. Under these circumstances, it is easy to imagine Marc-Antoine Charpentier, Dassoucy, and Dalibert—the latter's duties considerably lightened now that the Queen was away—meeting during the final months of 1666 and much of 1667, to gossip and talk about music. (Dalibert was famous for his irreverent tales about the foibles of the Romans.)

It was not long before Marc-Antoine discovered, to his chagrin—just as young CHARLES LE BRUN had learned two decades earlier—that letters of recommendation do not always reap the desired effect, and that letters of credit sometimes fail to materialize. A Roman protector might die or leave the city, and the patron back in Paris was not always punctual about sending the promised stipend. At some point prior to Dassoucy's incarceration in the fall of 1667, Marc-Antoine was forced to go begging to his compatriot: "Having needed, in Rome, my bread and my pity," as Dassoucy later put it.

Dassoucy's recollections of his encounter with Charpentier in Rome provide some insights into Marc-Antoine as a person, and about the context within which the encounter took place. Charpentier was, Dassoucy asserted:

> a lad who, although the ventricles of his brain are very damaged, is not however a madman who must be tied up, but a madman to be pitied; and who, having needed, in Rome, my bread and my pity, is scarcely more sensitive to my generosity than so many other vipers that I have nourished at my breast.[16]

The poet's suggestion that Charpentier was harmlessly mad, *fol*, should not be taken literally. Dassoucy uses the same word concerning a would-be poet who deluded himself about his talents and ended up as stage hand rather than playwright: "That is the destiny of madmen [*fous*] when they try to be poets, and the destiny of poets when they go mad." (When Dassoucy applied this word to Charpentier in 1672, he used it in a similar context: he was casting doubt on the young composer's ability to set French lyrics to music.)

"Nourished at my breast" is another of Dassoucy's favorite expressions. He uses it to talk about ungrateful young people to whom he has taught music. In other words, here he is stating unequivocally that—just as he had "nourished," that is, trained other musicians (among them several boy singers)—so had he nourished Marc-Antoine Charpentier's musical talents while in Rome. Specifically, he had "nourished" the poetical skills that could make one go "mad"—that is, he had showed Marc-Antoine how to match poetic rhythms and musical ones.

A third image that recurs in Dassoucy's writings is "bread," which is synonymous with "money" and the absence of "poverty." In short, although he very probably shared the contents of his larder with his young compatriot on one or more occasion, he was alluding here to money proffered in order to see Charpentier through a momentary crisis.

In short, for several months, and perhaps for a year or more, Charpentier was Dassoucy's apprentice of sorts; during that time he drank fully of everything his compatriot could teach him; and at one point the poet gave him some money, or perhaps took him in for a time.

By January 1667 Dassoucy was in the employ of French Ambassador CHAULNES, who was preparing a whole series of fêtes for the coming Mardi Gras season at the Farnese Palace: plays, songs in both French and Italian, and several entertainments in a genre that his French staff described as a *comédie en musique* and that the Italians at the Embassy called a *comedià in musicha*, a term more or less synonymous with "opera." The music for at least one of these "comedies" was written by a Roman composer, and the lyrics were primarily in Italian, although a prologue in French was eventually added to the opera. In other words, these entertainments were just the mix of the two cultures that would characterize the *Goûts réunis* of the eighteenth century. For example, the embassy staff arranged a torchlight parade during which a float carrying musicians and costumed members of the embassy staff, performed a "masquerade in French and Italian verse," the French poetry being Dassoucy's contribution.

"Carpentier" of the Farnese Palace

If Dassoucy "nourished" Charpentier, it almost certainly was at the Farnese, with the younger man serving as the older man's assistant—and perhaps working with costumers-tailors, as did a staff member whom the Italians called "Carpentier." Was it at the Farnese Palace that Marc-Antoine Charpentier was given an opportunity to set French lyrics and recitative to music, in an operatic-theatrical way, rather than in the manner of street ballads? Was it at the Farnese that Marc-Antoine tried his hand at Italian opera? When Dassoucy was arrested in November 1667, he upset the Ambassador's plans to entertain a guest, Abbé Le Tellier, with a "comedy." The entertainment was inexplicably delayed. Not until late January of 1668 were some "comedies" finally performed. Could these *"comédies en musique"*—that is, these operas, in the plural—have been Marc-Antoine's two lost Italian operas, *Dori e Oronte* and *Artaxerse*?[17] These were the last musical entertainments arranged by Ambassador Chaulnes, who turned the Farnese Palace over to a skeleton staff in July 1668 and returned to France.

What music did Marc-Antoine hear?

The entertainments at the Farnese prompt a broader question: In addition to the operas and plays performed at the Embassy, what other types of music could a young Frenchman hear during a visit to Rome in 1666, 1667, 1668, and 1669? Several works that Marc-Antoine wrote after returning to Paris, and a few of the manuscripts in his library, suggest that certain forms of Roman music stood out from the rest.

He of course became familiar with CARISSIMI's musical style. Not content to talk with the great man himself, he seems to have gained admission to the rather exclusive devotions at which Carissimi's oratorios were being performed. He allowed Carissimi's style to color and shape his own work. In fact, within his amazing musical memory Marc-Antoine literally stored away several of the compositions he had heard:

> He had a prodigious memory, and once he had heard a piece of music, he could write down all the parts with exactitude, and this is how the motets *Vidi impium, Emendamus in melius*, etc., and several of Carissimi's oratorios, which were not printed, reached France.[18]

Decades later, in the musical "Epitaph"[A] that Charpentier composed for himself, one of the protagonists was called *Marcellus*. Although, as we shall see, there is a learned explanation for the choice of this name, as a sort of double-entendre this could also be an allusion to the Lenten oratorios that renowned music masters (among them Carissimi) composed for the Confraternity of the Crucifix, which met in a small chapel just behind the Church of San Marcello, with which it was associated. Or was Marc-Antoine thinking of the Church of San Marcello itself, where Francesco Beretta was, or would soon be chapel master?

Marc-Antoine must also have attended some of the polychoral masses for which Rome was famed—for example, at the Church of Saint John Lateran where, for special devotions, there would be "four choirs of singers standing on four platforms in the middle of the choir, equidistant from one another"[19]—just the layout marked in a little sketch at the top of a mass for four choirs[B] that Charpentier would write in 1672. Polychoral music could also be heard at services sponsored by Ambassador CHAULNES at the French church, San Luigi dei Francesi. During one of the more splendid services sponsored by the Embassy, the music was sung by "six choirs consisting of the best voices in Rome."

He also became familiar enough with the musical genre known as "opera"—a genre that had not yet taken root in France—to write two

---

[A] Cahier "a," H. 474, a stray notebook that is difficult to date, but that is made of Jesuit paper.
[B] Cahiers XII–XIV, H. 4 (for the THEATINES, Aug. 1672?).

Italian-style operas of his own, *La Dori e Oronte* and *Artaxerse*. Where in Rome, besides the Farnese, could he have gained admission to an opera? The possible venue or venues can be reduced to a handful. The Pope would occasionally sponsor a devotional opera during the Mardi Gras season, as would princes such as the Colonna, but these were very exclusive events. Assisted by her French-born impresario, JACQUES II DALIBERT, Queen Christina of Sweden presented an opera for an audience made up primarily of cardinals during Mardi Gras of 1666, and again for Mardi Gras of 1669. Marc-Antoine probably reached Rome too late to attend the first event, but Dalibert may well have obtained authorization to admit him to the latter opera. All in all, the most plausible venue remains the Farnese Palace where, in one day alone, some "five or six hundred people" crowded into the vast, vaulted gallery. In sum, it probably was at the Farnese, in the spring of 1667, that Marc-Antoine Charpentier witnessed his first Italian opera.

Finally, if one supposes that the young composer was in fact benefitting from the benevolence of the Society of Jesus, he presumably had free access to the music masters of the different Jesuit houses of Rome, and to the religious services they organized. Is this why the second protagonist in Charpentier's musical epitaph was named *Ignatius*? (Here too, as we shall see, there may be a scholarly explanation for the choice of the name.) That is to say, are Marcellus and Ignatius allusions to the two types of Roman music that left the deepest imprint upon Marc-Antoine Charpentier: the oratorios sung for the miraculous crucifix of San Marcello and the music performed in the Jesuit Church of Sant'Ignazio, with its awesome trompe-l'œil dome?

Where did he live?

Marc-Antoine Charpentier's name was not found during a search of all the extant "books of the state of souls" compiled between 1665 and 1669 for each Roman parish.[20] DASSOUCY's name did not turn up either. Drawn up during Lent, these "books" list parishioners who had made their confession and were certified to take communion on Easter Sunday. In short, it is impossible to determine where the young Frenchman lived.

But we know where Marc-Antoine did *not* live. He was not rooming in one of the boarding houses near the Piazza del Popolo or the Piazza di Spagna, where many French visitors to the city rented rooms. He did not lodge near the Church of San Luigi dei Francesi, which, contrary to what one might imagine, was not situated in a quarter favored by the French. He was not renting a room from one of the Roman shopkeepers, artisans, and townspeople who lived in the more stable parishes of the city. Nor did he live with JACQUES II DALIBERT and his wife, who during Queen

Christina's absence were renting quarters on the via della Croce, in the parish of San Lorenzo in Lucina. Nor, it would seem, did he board with the Frenchmen who managed Dalibert's nearby tennis court.[21]

If Marc-Antoine's musical studies were being facilitated by the Society of Jesus, as proposed here, he could conceivably have lodged at one of their houses in Rome, as one of the "borders," *convittori*. (This would mean that the Jesuits were underwriting all or most of the young man's expenses.) However, the "souls" residing in the several Jesuit houses of Rome are never named: the records simply state the number of Jesuits, students, boarders, and domestics.[22] In short, it could not be determined whether Marc-Antoine boarded at one of these establishments.

It is equally impossible to say whether he lived near the Farnese Palace, for floods have destroyed most of the records for those years. Had these records survived, they almost certainly would have revealed little or nothing, because the French Embassy constituted a state-within-a-state; and, like the Riario, it certified the "state of the souls" residing there without naming the individuals. That said, just prior to Easter 1666 a "young Frenchman, age twenty-three," was living with the Vaccinaro family in the "Isola di Mandosi" not far from the Monte di Pietà and just a few streets from the Farnese. By Lent of 1667, he had left the Vaccinaro residence.[23] Marc-Antoine was, of course, twenty-three that spring, and he appears to have gone to Rome in 1666. But did he arrive in time for Easter? If he was the "young Frenchman," where had he gone by 1667?

In sum, Marc-Antoine's place of residence during those "three years" in Rome has not been determined, and perhaps never will be. We only know that prior to November 1667 he was short of money and had to approach DASSOUCY. Unless he had no head for budgeting, we can presume that someone who was not living in Rome was supposed to be sending him a stipend more or less regularly, and that the stipend did not arrive. Thus—like Charles Le Brun, who informed his protector that "I was forced to borrow from my friends"—Marc-Antoine had to turn to his compatriot. Beyond that, everything other than his acquaintance with Dassoucy and his conversations with Carissimi remains conjecture.

1670–1675
PARIS: THE HÔTEL DE GUISE

An apartment at the Hôtel de Guise
By the fall of 1669 Marc-Antoine was back in Paris. Somehow MARIE DE GUISE, THE REGENT had learned about him—supposing, that is, that she had not been instrumental in making his stay in Rome possible in the first place. When 1670 dawned, the twenty-seven-year-old composer was

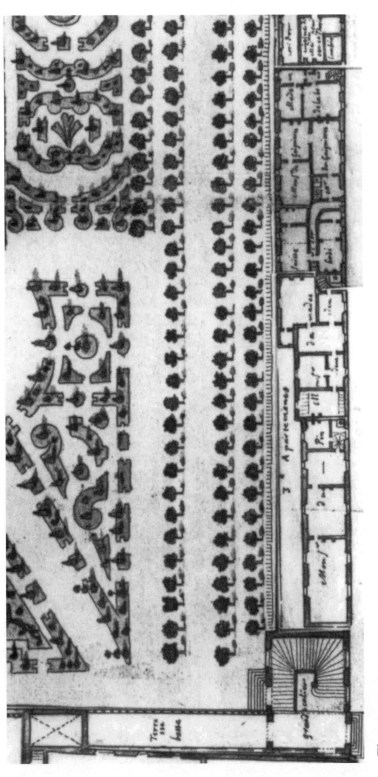

The apartments of Philippe Goibaut du Bois, Marc-Antoine Charpentier, and Roger de Gaignières.
Immediately to the right of the grand staircase of the Hôtel de Guise proper is the apartment occupied by Du Bois from 1667 to his death (occupied by "Monsieur du Pin" when this drawing was made). To its right is Charpentier's apartment, which was taken over by "Monsieur d'Amades" in 1687. The room with the shelves is situated just below the word *Apartemens*. To the right of the curved hallway, and slightly darker in this illustration, is Gaignières' apartment above the former indoor riding ring.

in the service of the House of Guise, whose annual household list went into effect each January 1. If the conjecture that Charpentier was being brought along by the Jesuits has any merit, this means that the reverend fathers placed on hold any plans involving the young man and allowed him to serve God in another way, as composer to the ultra-Catholic House of Guise, friends of the Society of Jesus.

On whose household roster did his name appear? The Duke's? The Duchess's? Marie the Regent's? No lists of Mademoiselle de Guise's household have survived for the period 1670 to 1687, but the absence of the composer's name on the roster of young MADAME DE GUISE's domestics for 1672 makes it possible to assert that Marc-Antoine Charpentier was not Her Royal Highness Isabelle d'Orléans' domestic. In other words, his room and board—and any stipend or gratifications he received—came either from Mademoiselle de Guise's household accounts, or from those of her nephew. If a roster of the aunt's or the nephew's household were found, it is unlikely that Charpentier's name would appear among the valets or other male domestics. Rather, he would be mentioned in a small group of protégés described as being "near," *auprès de*, the three Guises, as GOIBAUT DU BOIS was from the mid-1660s until 1688. Since that list would have called him "Monsieur Charpentier," that is what Marc-Antoine shall be called for the remainder of this portrait.

As a protégé living near Their Highnesses, Monsieur Charpentier was allocated a rather large "apartment" in the stable wing, rather than in the hôtel proper where salaried domestics—for example, Intendant CHRISTOPHLE ROQUETTE, Treasurer Jean-François Le Brun, Secretary Philippe Gourdon, and Comptroller Louis Martine—occupied quarters that usually consisted of a large living-and-sleeping chamber and an adjacent *cabinet*.

In the eighteenth century Marc-Antoine Charpentier's nephew, JACQUES ÉDOUARD, apparently told Titon du Tillet that, "having returned to Paris, Mademoiselle de Guise gave [Charpentier] an apartment in her hôtel."[24] The apartment in question was almost certainly the top-floor lodging situated in the newly renovated stable wing, between the apartments of PHILIPPE GOIBAUT DU BOIS and ROGER DE GAIGNIÈRES. There were six rooms in all. Having mounted the spiral staircase and passed through the antechamber, the occupant entered a large room with a window opening onto the narrow private "street" along which passed householders, horses, and coaches. From there he could move to one of three areas, each with a distinct function. If he turned right, he entered a large room with a fireplace and an adjacent *cabinet* overlooking the new Le Nôtre gardens. If he preferred not to eat at the householders' mess in the hôtel proper, he could warm his food here and sup privately. As a second option, from the antechamber he could go straight ahead to a second room, through which he could enter a small unheated room with a garden view. The latter room may have been a bedroom. Or else he could move all the way through the apartment, to a large room with a fireplace and a window opening onto the Le Nôtre garden.

A hasty glance at the plan of the apartment gives the impression that the side walls of this room were obstructed by wide stairways. Under closer scrutiny it becomes evident that these lines on the plan, running at right angles to the walls, do not remotely resemble the staircases shown elsewhere in the hôtel proper or in the stable wing. In fact, there is nothing like them in any other room of the entire Hôtel de Guise. These grids cannot represent stairs, which would have blocked the sole window in the room and occupied most of the principal room of the apartment below. They must represent shelves with large pigeonholes where flat items could be stored—deep shelves below and around the window, and somewhat shallower shelves on the other wall of the room. In other words, this large, warmable room appears to have been a workroom where the piles of notebooks that would one day be known as the *Mélanges* could be stacked flat, and where partbooks and scores could be copied and filed away.[25]

In this apartment Marc-Antoine would live and work for seventeen years—and, oh irony, would spend endless hours copying. He gradually became the esteemed "Monsieur Charpentier" whom a Parisian engraver of almanacs named Pierre Landry would depict at a court ball in 1682.

For the glory of the House of Guise

This "Monsieur Charpentier" of the 1680s emerges within the broader context of established notions about reciprocal duties between master or mistress and householder. The composer surely was aware from the outset that he would be toiling in anonymity, and that any glory reaped by his compositions would contribute to the luster of the House of Guise. His own personal, concealed glory would accrue to him in Heaven, for having faithfully expressed in music the prayers and devotions of the pious members of this great House.

It was the master's duty to be God's instrument on earth and to see to the well-being of each servant's body and soul. To this end, the conscientious master expected his householders to spend a part of each day in devotional activities—distributing alms, attending mass and vespers, and, in the case of the Charpentier and the members of the GUISE MUSIC, composing a motet, rehearsing it, and performing it. All householders were expected to work toward a common goal: "Those whom Providence has united, to serve in a single house, must all take up the same goal, to work together for the good of their master."[26]

At the Hôtel de Guise, this meant contributing to the glory of the House of Guise and the unity of the Church. Having alluded to the "glory of [Mademoiselle de Guise's] name and of her House," MONSIEUR DU BOIS would write: "I know that everything that can be of greater utility to the Church is always closest to Your Highness's heart."[27]

In striving toward this common goal, all householders had to avoid giving the impression that they knew more than someone higher up in the household hierarchy, especially the master or mistress:

> All superiority is odious, but that of a subject over his prince is
> always mad or fatal. ... Sovereigns want to [be superior] in
> everything that is the most conspicuous. Princes are willing to be
> aided, but not surpassed. Those who advise them must talk as if they
> were reminding them of something they have forgotten, and not as if
> they were teaching them something they do not know.[28]

Applied to the householders at the Hôtel de Guise, these precepts meant that Monsieur Charpentier had to be very careful not to give the impression that he knew more about music and musical genres than Monsieur Du Bois did. This deference permeated the entire household, from bottom to top.

Let us invent a scenario based on statements in handbooks on courtesy,[29] to suggest the route that Marc-Antoine Charpentier would have been likely to follow if he was longing to write an oratorio and did not want it to remain a purely intellectual exercise. Let us imagine the slow and subtle process by which he saw to it that one or the other princess would be willing to have an oratorio performed—as the first of a succession of oratorios would be in 1675.

The point of departure for this scenario is a statement in a handbook for domestics: "Householders should do most of their good deeds in the house where they serve, studying how to content their master, foresee his wishes, and please all the other householders."[30] This precept makes it very clear that Charpentier was expected to reserve most of his time for the Guises, although with their permission he could accept outside commissions. But more than that, he was supposed to "foresee" the sort of music the Guises might want. Suppose that he foresaw that the very thing they needed was an oratorio. He could not simply write one and present it to Their Highnesses as a fait accompli. To do so would be to appear "superior."

If he wanted see the oratorio he was dreaming about performed, he had to sow the seed well in advance, so that at some later date he could "remind" Monsieur Du Bois of an earlier discussion about that devotional genre. If the idea pleased him, Du Bois would proceed by a similar indirection and "remind" Mademoiselle de Guise about the oratorios she had so admired in Florence. The idea might well please her, but—she doubtlessly would conclude—hiring a large ensemble to perform something that ambitious was really impractical. Madame de Guise, on the other hand, had access to the King's Music. This consideration, plus the chance of finagling for herself a dress rehearsal performance by these royal musicians, would then determine Mademoiselle de Guise to plant the idea in the mind of her social superior, Madame de Guise. One day Her Highness would therefore think aloud, in Her Royal Highness's presence, about just how splendid that sort of music could be.

This great chain of deference could start at any level in the household hierarchy and would work its way inexorably to the top, at which point an order might, or might not, come down to the composer. That is to say, an idea might start with Charpentier, or it might start with Monsieur Du Bois, or it might even start with Mademoiselle de Guise. The approach was the same: one proceeded by indirection and by modesty—"which is nothing other than humility."[31]

Humility was expected of master as well as servant. The servant was, of course, the humbler of the two and could scarcely expect to be glorified for having faithfully served his master. The servant's finest deeds were usually concealed from the public, and the great noble received the glory in his stead. Born to rule, the highborn noble was theoretically born with "glory," *gloire*. Still, "glory depends on the person," that is, on an individual himself,

> and it is only conferred by virtue. ... This virtue consists not only of
> presuming nothing advantageous about oneself, but also of
> preferring, above all else, the satisfaction and the convenience of
> others, rather than one's own.[32]

Described by her contemporaries as virtuous, loveable, equitable, modest, and very polite, Mademoiselle de Guise exemplified just this blend of virtue and glory.

She and Madame de Guise expected to be the centers of the little courts that were their universes. That is, they expected to be praised in public—albeit discreetly and indirectly—for the achievements of their householders and protégés:

> The least actions of great nobles [*grands*] are celebrated, and with
> ordinary virtue they can acquire infinite glory. The finest deeds of
> little people are not talked about, and even with extraordinary virtue
> they can scarcely obtain great glory. Who is informed about the

valorous exploits of a soldier? Lost for him, they go to the profit and honor of his general.[33]

From the outset, Monsieur Charpentier presumably was aware that he could never be his own master as long as he lived in the house of a great noble. Nor could he expect to be praised for having gone about his ordinary responsibilities as conscientiously and as brilliantly as he could. His glory lay in enhancing the glory and virtue of the House of Guise.

Two stacks of notebooks

Having been taught by his father to keep orderly personal archives in chronological order, month after month and year after year, soon after his arrival at the Hôtel de Guise Monsieur Charpentier made two notebooks by folding in half six, seven, or eight large superimposed sheets of ruled paper, thereby creating what in French is called a *cahier*, a "notebook," a "signature." (When folded this way, the notebook was described as being of "in-folio" size.) Most of this paper was probably supplied by the Guises,[34] who every two years or so would purchase a ream of music paper, sometimes hand-ruled in a shop and sometimes with printed staves. The householder who made these purchases was far from consistent in his choice of paper. Each ream tended to be of a somewhat different quality, as shown by the watermark on one half of the sheet: "raisin," "coat of arms," "crowned L," "clock face," and so forth. More often than not, each ream was produced by a different paper mill that put its identifying watermark on the other half: "B ♡ C," "I ♡ B, "I ✿ C," "L ♡ B," and so forth. And so, for a year or two the composer used this paper for his notebooks—and presumably for his scores and partbooks as well. When a new supply of paper was delivered, more often than not the two watermarks would change—thereby making it possible for us to discern which notebooks are more or less contemporary with one another.[35]

It is not clear whether Charpentier dipped into this ream of paper for both his outside commissions and his in-house ones. All we can say is that for a year or two at a time, he tended to use the same paper for most of his notebooks. Now and then he would, however, employ a different paper for all or part of a notebook, apparently using sheets left over from paper supplied by an outside patron for the partbooks and performance score.[36] Doubtlessly recalling his late father's lectures about thrift, he was careful not to waste paper. For the next seventeen and one- half years, he lengthened most staves by hand, in order to squeeze an additional measure or two onto the pages of the personal archives now known as the *Mélanges*.

From the outset, the composer observed a very common secretarial practice. That is, he went to considerable length to ensure that his works for the Guises would not get mixed up with the outside commissions they permitted him to accept. Thus in January 1670, when he made his first two notebooks, he entitled one "Different Pieces." Into it he copied his first few works for the Guises—a collection of pieces that were not only about "different" subjects but that were written to please several "different" people. Concurrently with this notebook, he made a second one, which he labeled "Masses, psalms, and hymns." The works in this notebook were special commissions destined for at least two churches that either maintained large musical ensembles or could afford to hire the requisite musicians.

Starting with his very first notebooks, Charpentier separated in this way the "ordinary" work that he did in return for his room and board, from the "extraordinary" compositions the Guises permitted him to write for outsiders. (Yes, "permitted him," for a householder was expected to ask his master's permission to work for someone else; and, as DOCTOR VALLANT learned, there were times when "Mademoiselle de Guise could not agree to it."[37]) Although there was as yet no need to number these notebooks, he separated the two categories into two piles that eventually served as the point of departure for a numbering system.[38]

As he carefully stacked his notebooks in this way, two chronologically arranged piles of music took shape on the deep shelves of the workroom, the one containing his work for the Guises, and the other his outside jobs. He almost certainly resorted to another common practice of notaries and clerks: he protected small clusters of notebooks with a makeshift cover made from a spoiled sheet. On the outside of this cover he identified the contents, along with other information such as the venue, the event, the date, or the identity of the patron.[39] (Some if not all of these covers survived into the 1720s but were discarded after the manuscripts were purchased and bound by the Royal Library.) Like a notary or a clerk, he probably also kept a register book of the compositions that were flowing from his pen, to locate the specific bundle in which a given piece was to be found. If these registers did in fact exist, they have been lost.

We today can view these notebooks as a rare survivor of the practices inculcated into seventeenth-century clerks. What would become known as the *Mélanges* offers a happy and unique congruity of notarial-style recordkeeping and compositional practice. This congruity permitted Charpentier to be extremely honest with his attributions, as he separated one type of compensation and protection from another. His notebooks were both recordkeeping and bookkeeping. That the sums are missing suggests that the attribution was more important to him than amount earned. It was illegal for a notary or official to remove a document from its original chronological position. Even if modified or annotated at a later date, the document had to remain in chronological order. No one but he would know if he broke the rules of his attributional system. Yet *he* had to know. As a result of this recordkeeping, we are led to the heart of biography, if not autobiography—but a biography in which the things that interest us were not necessarily the things that Charpentier considered important. Whether his way of keeping records was unique—or simply a unique survivor—cannot be determined.

Not until the early 1680s—perhaps while recuperating from a serious illness during the summer of 1683—did Charpentier go back and number the individual notebooks in chronological order, giving the Guise notebooks arabic numbers and the outside commissions roman ones. The notebook labeled "Different Pieces" therefore became *cahier 1*, and the notebook called "Masses, psalms, and hymns" became *cahier I*.[40] Thus came into being the arabic-numbered series of notebooks (which the "Mémoire" drawn up for his nephew, JACQUES ÉDOUARD, in 1726 calls "French," *françois*) and the roman-numbered set (*romain*).

Over the years, Charpentier's handwriting changed somewhat, especially in one very noticeable detail: the shape of his treble clef. This particular change occurred in 1681, when the *S*-shaped treble clef that he had used almost exclusively since 1670 yielded to a clef that was a mirror-image *S*, similar to the modern treble clef but minus its vertical stroke. The presence of the latter clef in some of the first thirty notebooks of either series strongly suggests that minor modifications such as added preludes were made to a few notebooks, while others were recopied in their entirety after 1681. For Charpentier these modifications did not transform the compositions into new works: he put these materials back into their original chronological position.[41]

The two sets of notebooks survived relatively intact to our day. The things he wrote for himself, or on his own initiative, met a different fate. Most of these works have been lost. That is to say, we know that during the 1670s one of his vernacular songs, *Brillantes fleurs naissez*, could be found in "book G." In that book or in one of its companion volumes, he apparently kept personal copies of all his vernacular songs. A few dozen of these pieces have survived, having found their way into published songbooks or into the *Mercure galant*. We shall see that in the late 1680s Charpentier copied his "Epitaph,"[42] probably the most personal work he ever composed—as well as some pieces that may been personal gifts to

PORT-ROYAL—into an unnumbered "fat notebook," *gros cahier*[A] that he kept physically separate from the numbered notebooks. And then there was Charpentier's French and Italian music that President Louis-Denis Seguin owned in 1736.[43] Among that collector's treasured manuscripts were *Le Triomphe de Bacchus*, a "serenade"; at least seven volumes of French and Italian airs; *Flore*, a *divertissement*; *Le Sot suffisant*, a "*comédie* mixed with music"; a volume of "symphonies"; *David et Jonathas*; and two Italian operas, *La Dori e Oronte* and *Artaxerse*. With the possible exception of *David et Jonathas*, there is little reason to think that the missing notebooks of the *Mélanges* contained these works. Rather, the vernacular works, the epitaph, the pieces for Port-Royal, and the music owned by Seguin are things the composer wrote because he wanted to and that he kept physically separate from the work he did to earn his livelihood.

Ordinary and extraordinary

During his seventeen-plus years at the Hôtel de Guise, Marc-Antoine Charpentier would fill just over one hundred notebooks, almost equally distributed between the arabic-numbered series and the roman-numbered one. An average of six notebooks per year. Owing to the unpredictable demands of the princesses and of his outside patrons, his output was erratic. In a given year he could fill as few as four notebooks, or as many as twelve. (The relatively fallow years, and the desperately busy ones, will be evoked below, in the panoramic view of Charpentier's creative activity.)

These notebooks constitute a virtual double appointment book in which Marc-Antoine Charpentier's professional life unfurls month by month, year by year. A few basic principles make it easy to decipher this tableau of his career.

From 1670 to mid-1687 almost everything in the arabic-numbered notebooks was destined for one or another Lorraine, most of them members of the House of Guise: LOUIS-JOSEPH DE LORRAINE, DUKE OF GUISE; ISABELLE D'ORLÉANS OF ALENÇON, later known as "MADAME DE GUISE," his wife (and widow); the little Duke of Alençon, the child born of their brief union; Marguerite de Lorraine, DOWAGER DUCHESS OF ORLÉANS, Madame de Guise's mother; Marie de Lorraine, Demoiselle of Guise, known as "MADEMOISELLE DE GUISE"; and Françoise-Renée de Lorraine, Abbess of Montmartre, known as "MADAME DE MONTMARTRE." The content of these notebooks can be seen as representing Monsieur

---

[A] Now in cahier "a," H. 474 (on Jesuit paper).

Charpentier's "ordinary" obligations. Above all, they represent the less overtly public side of his creativity, the side for which his protectors received the glory.

Within these arabic-numbered notebooks one can also discern, across the years, the changing contours of the GUISE MUSIC. For example, it is possible to glimpse the moment when one singing chambermaid left and was replaced by another with a slightly different vocal range, or when newcomers came to swell the size of the existing group.

By contrast, during these same seventeen years, the public, "extraordinary" side of the composer's career parades by in the roman-numbered notebooks. Cassocked fathers from one or another of the THREE JESUIT HOUSES of Paris rub shoulders with MOLIÈRE and his successors in the theater, CORNEILLE and DONNEAU DE VISÉ. From the late 1670s and into the 1680s, nuns from the ABBAYE-AUX-BOIS, from PORT-ROYAL, and from the LITTLE CARMEL process modestly through the notebooks, as do the composer's lay patrons, MONSIEUR DE RIANTS, the DAUPHIN, CHARLES LE BRUN, the DUKE OF RICHELIEU. The circumstances under which some of these works were performed, and the individuals or institutions who commissioned them are presented in Panels 6, 7, 8, and 9 of this portrait gallery. Many of these compositions correspond to events mentioned in Corneille's and Donneau de Visé's *Mercure galant*, but the editors were not always free to name their composer friend.

The institutions and individuals for whom Charpentier composed between 1670 and 1688, and their very different priorities, shaped the content of the two series of notebooks. Yet the content of both series proves to have been shaped by the Guises, because the composer was expected to request the princesses' permission to work for outsiders, and the outside patron clearly had to be in the good graces of one or both patronesses.

The subject matter of the works in the arabic-numbered, Guise notebooks changed over the years, reflecting changed intentions or major events in the lives of these princes and princesses. To repeat these changing preoccupations here would be redundant, for they are recounted in the portraits in Panels 9 and 10. For the same reason, it would be redundant to talk here about the religious establishments and the generally highborn patrons who commissioned the works that Charpentier copied into his roman-numbered notebooks.

Thus this portrait of the composer simply alludes to the different people who came and went in the famous Monsieur Charpentier's rather circumscribed world. As we brush by them, the type of their names is changed into SMALL CAPITALS. The individual portraits of these protectors and outside patrons tell the story of the priorities to which Monsieur

Charpentier had to respond, just as the footnotes in each portrait (which evoke the twenty-eight blue-green volumes stacked on the gilded console in our imaginary portrait gallery) show how he responded. In addition, these footnotes make it possible to judge not only the extent to which Charpentier composed for a particular individual, but also the chronological point at which that individual disappeared from his notebooks, until only Mademoiselle de Guise and Madame de Guise remained.[44]

The composer within the hierarchy at the House of Guise
and in the world outside

The arabic-numbered series of notebooks paints the side of Charpentier's professional life that was not acknowledged publicly. Charpentier, MONSIEUR DU BOIS, and the members of the GUISE MUSIC were expected to keep their anonymity as they sent heavenward the prayerful thoughts of the Guise highnesses. Each member of this musical team had a specific function or functions. It was Du Bois who obtained Latin texts from one or another of his neo-Latinist acquaintances, pored over liturgical texts in order to piece together a libretto, or wrote original texts that would express the princesses' devotional thoughts. It was he who "made the Music sing." From time to time he probably joined the musicians on the viol.

To borrow terms from treatises of the day, Monsieur Charpentier's task was to "give a soul to the words"—or, to use another French expression of the time, to "animate the words," that is, give life to the text by a judicious and tasteful blending melody, rhythm, and harmony. All the while he had to keep in mind the strengths and the weaknesses of each individual musician, to avoid humiliating the ensemble by a bad public performance, thereby humiliating the princesses. He clearly was not a regular member of the Guise Music. Not until the first half of 1674 would music for a high tenor, *haute-contre*—who could it be if not Marc-Antoine Charpentier?—appear in the arabic-numbered notebooks, in works for the handful of musicians that typified the GUISE MUSIC of the mid-1670s. Over the next decade the participation of this high tenor would be sporadic, almost always in the context of Marian devotions.

As for the young women and men who were regular members of the Guise Music, they could not be content to give mere lip service to the devotional thoughts provided by Du Bois and given a musical soul by Charpentier. They were expected to express the kaleidoscope of emotions underlying these thoughts. Thus Chapel Master Du Bois, Composer Charpentier, and the Music worked together to give voice to what lay in the hearts of the nobles they served.

Many of these works were performed at venues outside the high walls surrounding these princely residences. For example, Mademoiselle de Guise probably envisaged having some of Monsieur Charpentier's works performed at the nearby parish church, Saint-Jean-en-Grève, where her late mother had founded a procession for the Holy Sacrament. And there was the ABBEY OF MONTMARTRE, a second home to Her Highness Marie.

Some of these compositions were, on the other hand, performed in one or another of the chapels at the Hôtel de Guise. The most famous chapel was the Renaissance one above the entrance gate, which had been decorated by Primaticcio. It appears to have been reserved for very special events. After around 1675, Mademoiselle de Guise had her private chapel, a small room near her bedchamber—so small that, with a bit of squeezing, the Core Trio of the GUISE MUSIC could just fit inside, behind Her Highness kneeling on a prayer stool. The third chapel was a large ground-floor gallery with an altar that could be concealed by moveable wooden panels. This room contained an organ that, judging by the fleurs-de-lis that decorated it, had been provided by Madame de Guise: "A large wooden armoire painted with fleurs-de-lis, in which is an organ with bellows."[45] Here the seventy-odd householders worshiped. And here, prior to public performance, Charpentier's music almost certainly was sung during daily devotions.

Owing to the restraints imposed by rank within the household hierarchy, it is quite unlikely that Charpentier selected the genre he preferred, nor chose the meditative thoughts he personally most enjoyed expressing in music. Decisions about genre and subject were the prorogative of Chapel Master Du Bois, perhaps after consultation with one or both princesses.

For his extraordinary commissions, as for the works he composed for the Guises, Charpentier can be presumed to have had little to do with selecting or writing the text he was expected to "animate," be that text in Latin or in the vernacular. Nor is it at all sure that he was permitted to use certain genres for outside patrons. For example, is the paucity of oratorios in the roman-numbered notebooks between 1670 and 1688 explained by the princesses' refusal to allow him to write in that genre for outsiders, in order to maintain an exclusivity—just as Mademoiselle de Guise refused to lend DOCTOR VALLANT to the ailing friend of a royal minister? If that be so, Her Highness appears to have been extremely generous toward a few outsiders, allowing them to commission an oratorio[A] and even lending them the Great Guise Music to perform the work. (It is, of course, entirely possible that few outsiders were captivated by this foreign devotional genre, and that they desired more traditional pieces based on familiar liturgical texts.)

During his years at the Hôtel de Guise, there were times when Charpentier must have worried about his future. For example, initially neither MONSIEUR DU BOIS nor the Guises appear to have had a clear idea of how to use his talents. His first pieces were settings for Tenebrae at MONTMARTRE.[B] Then he wrote a piece honoring Saint Bernard, founder of the Cistercian Order[C] to which PORT-ROYAL belonged, and another for Saint Augustine,[D] to whom Jansenists especially turned for guidance. There was also a work appropriate for Mademoiselle de Guise's birthday and patroness's day[E]; and so forth. Praising the composer publicly for his contributions to their devotions certainly was not a part of the Guise program. Indeed, one of the Tenebrae services at Montmartre was mentioned in the *Gazette de France*, but nothing was said about Marc-Antoine Charpentier.

The Duke of Guise's death in the summer of 1671, followed by the death of Madame de Guise's mother a few months later, propelled the composer to a new and unexpected trajectory. He was ordered to write a whole corpus of funeral music: a funeral mass, plus various texts from the vigils of the dead that would be appropriate for memorial services.[F] Here too, the funereal events were mentioned in the *Gazette*, but nothing was said about music.

1672: mourning, the theater, and some music-loving clerics

The quarrels between the two Guise women over the guardianship of the little Duke of Alençon during the spring and summer of 1672— followed by Mademoiselle de Guise's announced intention to follow the child anywhere that his mother might take him, even to England, and by Madame de Guise's move to the Luxembourg Palace in June 1673— brought home to the Guise householders just how precarious their livelihood could be. In Monsieur Charpentier's case, there were bursts of activity as he prepared music for a funeral or for an End of the Year Service. These hectic moments aside, he had little to do, because the

---

[A] Cahiers XLII–XLIII, H. 412 (for the consecration of the new Abbess of Montmartre?); and, prologue (commissioned by DU BOIS) added to an oratorio for Saint Cecilia, cahier XLIX, H. 162a.
[B] Cahier 1, H. 91–93.
[C] Cahiers 1–2, H. 306.
[D] Cahier 1, H. 307.
[E] Cahier 2, H. 426.
[F] Cahiers 3–5, H. 2, H. 234, H. 311, H. 156, H. 12.

princesses' deep mourning precluded music. In fact, save for the two and one-half notebooks that he filled with funeral music,[A] he wrote only four devotional pieces[B] for Mademoiselle de Guise's singing chambermaids during this entire time of mourning, August 1671 to June 1673.

Meanwhile, some music-loving clerics—presumably the Charpentiers' JESUIT FRIENDS—were giving him special commissions.[C] What institution in Paris, other than one or another of the THREE JESUIT HOUSES, could have requested all these masses and psalms for large ensembles, plus a variety of duos and trios appropriate for vespers and the Benediction of the Holy Sacrament, salut? This outside patronage could scarcely assure his livelihood in the long run. As deep mourning gave place to acrimony in mid-1672, and as the GUISE MUSIC's future became increasingly uncertain, the composer appears to have approached a family friend, the actor-playwright known as MOLIÈRE. Or was it the other way around? Did Molière seek out Charpentier, to replace Lully? Be that as it may, the Guise princesses permitted Monsieur Charpentier to show his wares in the revival of Le Mariage forcé and La Comtesse d'Escarbagnas that was scheduled for July 1672.

When this music for the theater was added to the compositions probably destined for the Jesuits, 1672 proved to be an extremely busy year. In fact, Charpentier filled twelve notebooks that year, not only composing the music and copying the work into his personal notebooks, but presumably preparing performing scores and partbooks as well—plus working with the singers and instrumentalists whom Molière had hired, and collaborating with Beauchamps, the dancer-choreographer. Each man received eleven livres per performance, and Charpentier's compositions were "recognized" with a payment of 110 livres.

Unfortunately for Charpentier, the commission for Molière's upcoming "machine play," Le Malade imaginaire, had been given to DASSOUCY, Charpentier's old acquaintance from Rome. That inconvenience was promptly remedied. Mademoiselle de Guise and Madame de Guise (whom contemporary sources repeatedly describe as "goddesses" and "heroines") swooped down upon Molière and convinced him to give the job to Charpentier. In an open letter to the playwright, Dassoucy gave vent to his negative thoughts about Charpentier's abilities:

[A] Cahiers 3, 4, and 5.
[B] Cahier 5, H. 18, H. 235; cahier 6, H. 157, H. 95.
[C] Cahier IX, especially H. 55-57 (to a text by Father Commire, S.J.); cahiers VI-VIII, especially H. 3, H. 236, h. 283, H. 524; and perhaps cahiers X-XI, H. 145, H. 162 (a Te Deum).

> They assured me that you were on the verge of giving your machine play to the incomparable Monsieur X– to write the music, although the relationship between his melodies and your lovely words is not totally accurate, and although this man, who doubtlessly is an original, is not however so original that a copy can't be found at the Incurables [madhouse]. Since great personages are needed for great designs, and since a simple pair of stilts will help this individual become the greatest man of the century, you are wrong to hesitate over such a fine choice.[46]

Why would two such pious princesses permit their protégé to collaborate with a company of excommunicated actors? And since the women were spatting during the summer of 1672, why would they cooperate in this way? The answer to both objections seems to be that things more momentous than profound piety and personal animosity were going on that year. Things so momentous that the women's rancor about Jean-Baptiste Lully's conduct overpowered any distaste their piety might cause them to feel for the theater, and effaced their anger at one another.

Lully—and his success at Louis XIV's court—was a flesh-and-blood challenge to the glory of the House of Guise and the House of Orléans. That is to say, Mademoiselle de Guise's brother Roger had brought young Giambattista Lulli to France in 1646, to teach Italian to their niece, MADEMOISELLE DE MONTPENSIER; but the ungrateful Florentine had dared to request his leave when Montpensier was exiled to her country estate late in 1652.[47] How it must have rankled Mademoiselle de Guise to recall how "Baptiste" had abandoned her niece from pure self-interest! (As her treatment of Intendant Lafitte in 1680 would demonstrate, Her Highness was always ready to do battle with anyone who did not show sufficient respect for the House of Guise.) And now Baptiste had snatched the opera privilege away Pierre Perrin, who had been GASTON D'ORLÉANS' introducer of ambassadors. MADAME DE GUISE was protecting Perrin in her late father's name. In fact, she had just paid Perrin's debts so that he could be released from prison.[48] In sum, both princesses had what a high noble would consider very compelling reasons to demonstrate to the world that Monsieur Charpentier was not only as good as Baptiste, but better.

After Molière's death in March 1673, Charpentier continued to work with the troop, collaborating with THOMAS CORNEILLE and JEAN DONNEAU DE VISÉ for the better part of a decade, until Lully managed to stifle the music that these three defiant artists were weaving into their plays. The very fact that Charpentier composed all that music means that Mademoiselle de Guise approved of the activity. Had she not authorized these worldly commissions, her composer would either have had to abandon the actors, or else beg Her Highness to release him from her service so that he could heed the sirens' call and work with the troop. The fact that Charpentier and the playwrights managed to flout Lully's monopoly for so long suggests that they had been given to understand that the Guise princesses were lending their weight to the venture. In sum, the Guises had reason to take special pleasure in the way Charpentier and his colleagues were thumbing their noses at the Florentine and employing more singers and instrumentalists than the number permitted.

Meanwhile, Monsieur Charpentier had resumed writing devotional pieces for the two princesses, although the armed truce between MADE-MOISELLE DE GUISE and MADAME DE GUISE caused his output to drop to what would become more or less the annual norm: two or three notebooks in the arab-numbered series and two or three in the roman-numbered one. Into the arabic-numbered notebooks he copied music for the street altar, reposoir,[A] that MADAME DE GUISE sponsored at the Luxem-bourg in June 1673; a few preludes for existing pieces in honor of the Virgin,[B] for whom both Guise women felt a devotion that had become especially intense since the Duke's death; and some instrumental music for Easter Sunday of 1674.[C] The Gazette de France mentioned the reposoir with its "excellent instrumental concert, and voices,"[49] but no reference was made to Monsieur Charpentier. After all, it was Madame de Guise who was being praised, not her protégé.

Then come three compositions that are extremely revealing about MADEMOISELLE DE GUISE's devotions during these years of mourning and animosity. The first is an instrumental mass[D] that imitated an organ that could not be delivered to the Church of Notre-Dame de la MERCY in time for canonization services scheduled for April 1674. The mass is followed in the notebooks by two pieces for high tenor (haute-contre), tenor, and bass—both for the Virgin.[E] The singers almost certainly were Charpentier and two members of the GUISE MUSIC: De Baussen, tenor, and Beaupuis, bass. The existence of these pieces suggests that Mademoiselle de Guise was already deeply involved in the Confraternity of Our Lady of the Scapulary, which met and worshiped at the Mercy, and that she had reached an understanding with the reverend fathers. The Mercedarians would be pleased to have Monsieur Charpentier write for devotions in

---

[A] Cahier 7, H. 508.
[B] Cahier 7, H. 509-10. H. 512.
[C] Cahier 7, H. 511.
[D] Cahiers 7-8, H. 513.
[E] Cahier 8, H. 159 (Little Office of the Virgin, Saturdays), H. 20 (complines of the Virgin).

their church. Female voices or mixed voices were quite appropriate at devotions organized by the confraternity, so her chambermaid-musicians would be most welcome at such services. However, since male voices alone were appropriate during masses chanted by the fathers, any music for these services would have to be performed by men. (The Mercy fathers themselves were technically forbidden to sing in harmony, although they are known to have sung "music" on at least one occasion. Or had they simply given that impression, thanks to lay singers discreetly concealed in a chapel?) Hence the small male ensemble—*haute-contre*, tenor, and bass—that would recur throughout Charpentier's arabic-numbered notebooks for the next decade, almost always singing the praises of the Virgin Mary, but occasionally talking about the God-Given King or his queen.

In sum, although he was not always named in the press, for much of 1673, 1674, and early 1675 "Monsieur Charpentier" was becoming known to theatergoers and to worshipers fortunate enough to attend devotional events sponsored by one or the other princess. In March 1675 the composer's name was again on the lips of theatergoers, who were eagerly awaiting the opening of the fabulous *Circé*. The special effects and the music of this "machine play"—which was neither an opera nor a tragedy, but a blend of both[50]—constituted a major challenge to Lully's monopoly.

1675: the Duke of Alençon's death

The day before the *Circé* opened, the little Duke of Alençon died in the Luxembourg Palace, a stone's throw away from the theater where final rehearsals were being held. The princesses immediately withdrew to MONTMARTRE, where the child was buried within a matter of days. Despite the frantic activity at the theater, Charpentier found enough time to write a *Languentibus*[A] for three voices, subsequently lost.[51] *Circé* opened on schedule. To delay the opening would have been tantamount to recognizing publicly the patron–servant link between the princesses and the composer.)

Once again the Guise Music was silenced; and once again the father at one or another of the THREE JESUIT HOUSES took up the slack, commissioning at least one work,[B] and probably more.[52] When Charpentier resumed composing for the Guises that fall, the content of the texts that he asked to put to music had changed markedly.

[A] Cahier 9, opening pages.
[B] Cahier XIX, H. 425a, a prelude to a setting of a text by Father Commire, S.J., that presumably was copied into the lost cahier XX.

1676–1688
COMPOSER FOR THE GUISE CHAPELS

New devotional programs

After this terrible blow, the princesses could not cope for several months; and when they did, they poured their energy into a broad devotional program. These new preoccupations led to the creation of a whole corpus of music made to measure for the two women. There was music in honor of the Virgin for Mademoiselle de Guise's devotions at the MERCY; and there were pieces for the Abbey of MONTMARTRE, where both princesses had lodgings. There was music to honor the INFANT JESUS, because each princess was sponsoring an educational institution named for the Holy Child. A succession of oratorios also poured forth, intended primarily, it would seem, for Madame de Guise's devotions at the THEATINES: oratorios for Saint Cecilia that rejoice at conversions of Protestants; and an oratorio in honor of Saint Charles Borromeo to celebrate the princesses' charitable activities. Lastly, there were scattered pieces in honor of the ROYAL HOUSE OF BOURBON, some of them devotional but others taking the form of courtly musical gifts in the vernacular.

The demands being placed upon Monsieur Charpentier by his protectresses opened the floodgates of his creativity. During 1677 alone, a particularly active year, he added seven[A] notebooks to the arab-numbered series: music for the Guise women's different devotions, prayers for the KING and the DAUPHIN, music for the Church of the MERCY, and two oratorios where virtuous women (Esther and Saint Cecilia) serve as God's instruments, as MADAME DE GUISE had recently declared herself to be.

Any anxieties about the future that may have tormented Charpentier during the gloom that descended on the Hôtel de Guise after Alençon's death, dissipated rapidly. His music was now a medium through which the two Guise women could express their devotion to the Virgin, the Christ Child, and Louis the God-Given. It was his duty to put to music their devotional thoughts, as expressed by liturgical texts and by devotional texts assembled or written by MONSIEUR DU BOIS and his neo-Latinist friends. In this way, via the youthful voices of the GUISE MUSIC, these thoughts would be songs rising to Heaven like prayers. If there is any merit to the conjecture that, as an adolescent, Marc-Antoine Charpentier had been considering service to God as his vocation, he was now beginning to understand why God had given him so many talents.

[A] Cahiers 13, 14, 15, 16, 17, 18, and 19.

Although the two Guise women no longer lived under a single roof, and although it was MADEMOISELLE DE GUISE who paid the musicians and housed and fed Monsieur Charpentier and MONSIEUR DU BOIS, MADAME DE GUISE could henceforth call upon the composer, the Chapel Master, and the GUISE MUSIC whenever she wished, just as she called upon DOCTOR VALLANT, Mademoiselle de Guise's official physician.

A corpus of works for the princesses' devotions

By the summer of 1675, Marc-Antoine Charpentier had composed eight Marian pieces[A] for two or three voices plus instruments, and had copied them into his arabic-numbered notebooks. At least two of these works appear to have been destined for performance at the Church of the MERCY in 1674. The completion of Mademoiselle de Guise's chapel in that church, in mid-1676, led to a corpus of Marian works that spanned the entire liturgical year: hymns to the Virgin, the Litany of Loreto, the *Magnificat*, and texts recited during the Little Office of the Virgin celebrated every Saturday. In all, nineteen works specifically identified as being for the Virgin[B] were created between early 1677 and the summer of 1685. (By contrast, for those same years, the roman-numbered notebooks contain only eight Marian works,[C] all but two of them for the DAUPHIN's Music.) Many of these compositions could be performed in a variety of devotional contexts and venues, but one of them—composed in 1679 for an *haute-contre* (presumably Charpentier) and a tenor[D]—was part of a newly approved liturgy for the the MERCY.

The Mercy proved to be Mademoiselle de Guise's preferred venue, although Charpentier's compositions surely graced the chapels of the Hôtel de Guise and echoed in the ancient abbey church at MONTMARTRE. Holding a service at the Mercy was tantamount to placing the event under the Virgin's widespread blue mantle. Thus, in late August or early September 1683, Mademoiselle de Guise placed the late QUEEN's soul in the hands of the Virgin of Mercy, by means of a solemn mass sung for her by the Mercedarians. That day, Marc-Antoine Charpentier, De

---

[A] Cahier 2, H. 426, H. 16, H. 309; cahier 5, H. 18, H. 19; cahier 7, H. 509 (a prelude, probably for H. 16); cahier 8, H. 159, H. 20.

[B] In 1677: cahier 16, H. 21, H. 22, H. 23, H. 59 (and H. 24 for a large ensemble); in 1678: cahiers 20–21, H. 60 (and H. 169 for a large ensemble); 1679: cahier 22, H. 25 (for the liturgy of Notre-Dame de la MERCY), H. 23a (a prelude); for 1680: cahier 25, H. 26; cahier 26, H. 27; cahiers 29–30, H. 400; 1681: cahiers 32–33, H. 63, H. 82 (and H. 180 for a large ensemble); 1682: cahiers 36–37, H. 330; 1684: cahier 41, H. 333, H. 75, H. 83; and 1685: cahier 47, H. 340.

[C] Cahier XXVII, H. 175; cahier XXVIII, H. 177; cahier XXX, H. 178; cahiers XXXII–XXXIII, H. 327, H. 328, and H. 181, are for the Dauphin's Music. Cahier XXXIII, H. 28, and cahier XLIII, H. 334, may be for nuns. Cahiers XX, XXI, XXII, and XL are missing.

[D] Cahier 22, H. 25.

Baussen and Beaupuis sang a diptych to honor the royal couple[A]: a *luctus* for the late Marie-Thérèse (set to words by Pierre Portes, a neo-Latin poet) and a motet for Saint Louis, the King's ancestral namesake, whose feast had just been, or would soon be celebrated. Not only did MADAME DE GUISE make a point of attending services at the Mercy whenever her responsibilities at court and at Alençon permitted, she also created her own chapel dedicated to the Virgin in the Church of Saint-Sulpice, her parish.

Another work invoking the Virgin—composed in 1685[B] and performed by an *haute-contre* (Charpentier?), a tenor, and a bass—almost certainly was intended for a confraternity of Domestics of the Virgin in which young boys participated beside men who had been entrusted with their care: "Receive us all in Her service, dissipate our hurtful behavior. ... Here we are, and the boys whom the Lord has given us." In all likelihood this work was written for the teachers and students at the Academy of the INFANT JESUS.

This devotion for the Christ Child—whose innocence had been exemplified in four-year-old Alençon—had become part of the princesses' worship in late 1675 or early 1676. Charpentier therefore composed four pieces for the Core Trio of the GUISE MUSIC in 1676 and 1677, to celebrate the principal feasts of this devotion: Christmas, Circumcision, Epiphany, and Purification.[C] These four works presumably were repeated year after year, because not until 1684[D] did the composer add to his arabic-numbered notebooks a new piece specifically for one of these feast days. (In the roman-numbered series the only works for the Infant Jesus copied out during that decade are vernacular Christmas pastorales[E] created for the Great Guise Music in 1684 and modified in 1685 and 1686.)

Both princesses were also firmly committed to a special devotion to Louis XIV the God-Given. Beginning in the spring of 1676 and continuing until 1687, Charpentier produced some very distinctive works to honor the royal family. Distinctive in that they were not routine *Te Deum*'s or *Domine salvum fac regem*'s, but instead echoed events in the lives of LOUIS XIV, the QUEEN, and the DAUPHIN. That Charpentier copied all these works into arabic-numbered notebooks strongly suggests that the compositions were requested by one or both Guises. After 1687,

---

[A] Cahier 38, H. 331, H. 332.
[B] Cahier 46, H. 340.
[C] Cahiers 13–14, H. 316, 317, 395, 318.
[D] Cahiers 42–43a, H. 414, for the Great Guise Music.
[E] Cahiers XLIV–XLV, H. 482, H. 483; cahiers XLVIII–XLIX, H. 495a; cahiers XLIX–L, H. 495b.

when the composer left their service, works honoring the Royal House of Bourbon disappear from the arabic-numbered notebooks. (Nothing remotely resembling them can be found among the outside commissions copied into the roman-numbered notebooks between 1675 and 1704.)

MADAME DE GUISE made a particular point of having Monsieur Charpentier write musical prayers for the royal family and for the success of the King's army; but on at least one occasion MADEMOISELLE DE GUISE commissioned such a work. From this corpus of works for the royal family it is possible to winnow out, with considerable certainty, the pieces for Mademoiselle de Guise: they were for small groups of musicians, and the texts were stated in an impersonal way. By contrast, the works destined for Madame de Guise tend to require a large ensemble, and they employ texts that are quite personal. Only a blood relative could have offered these musical gifts to the royal family.

The first of these gifts dates from the spring of 1676, when negotiations for a peace treaty with Holland began. This commission—for a large ensemble that was either hired by Her Royal Highness, loaned by the King, or provided by a religious establishment such as one or another of the THREE JESUIT HOUSES—consisted of a "song for peace" and a related *élévation*.[A] One of the earliest of the non-liturgical Latin texts that Charpentier set to music for the Guises, this song evokes the "King of France crowned with laurels," "our King," the "pacific King" over whom God is watching. The *élévation*—a type of prayer that ISABELLE D'ORLÉANS OF ALENÇON had become accustomed to using long before she became Madame de Guise—addresses Jesus directly, using the familiar "Thee" form, *Tu*. (That is how a member of the royal family spoke to the Lord.) Two years later, when Louis XIV led his troops toward the northern frontier, Charpentier set some lines of a psalm "for the King in time of war"[B]—once again for a large ensemble, and therefore almost certainly requested by Madame de Guise. An *Exaudiat*[C] written for a similar group in the fall of 1681 and performed "at Versailles"[53] to celebrate the official submission of Strasbourg, presumably was another gift from Madame de Guise.

By contrast, a cluster of pieces dating from 1677— they are almost the exact contemporaries of the "song for peace" just described—were almost certainly for Mademoiselle de Guise and the Core Trio of the GUISE MUSIC. In response to the prayers for Louis XIV that Archbishop Harlay had ordered that March, Charpentier set some lines from psalms to

[A] Cahiers 11-12, H. 392, H. 237.
[B] Cahier 20, H. 168.
[C] Cahier 33, H. 180.

create two prayers for the King and one for the Dauphin, who was visiting all the churches of Paris as part of a Jubilee.[A] (The final two of the three musical prayers probably were sung at the MERCY, on the day the QUEEN and the DAUPHIN performed their stations there.) Several months later, on Saint Louis' Day, August 25, it was at the MERCY that Mademoiselle de Guise honored the King with a motet[B] for an *haute-contre* (high tenor) and two instruments—apparently sung by Charpentier himself. Once again the text of this motet was impersonal: the "people" acclaim the saint.

Two years later, in August 1679, came yet another impersonal, that is, public piece for Saint Louis. Three singers and two instruments performed a "symphony"[C] and "song" in which the "people" hail the saint and his "militant faith." This piece almost certainly was performed during the mass sponsored by Royal Painter CHARLES LE BRUN near the royal Gobelins tapestry works. (Madame de Guise could scarcely have played a role in organizing this event, for she appears to have spent that entire summer at Alençon.) The performers were either the Core Trio of the GUISE MUSIC or—as a bouquet tossed to the DAUPHIN, for whom Monsieur Charpentier had recently begun working—the newly established Dauphin's Music. Irrespective of the performers' identities, Mademoiselle de Guise clearly was instrumental in Charpentier's collaboration with Le Brun. There is no way of knowing whether, as etiquette and deference demanded, Le Brun came personally to beg her to order Charpentier write for him; but the fact that the composer copied that work into an arabic-numbered notebook is strong evidence that Her Highness did in fact order her composer to write this piece, and that she offered it as a gift to Le Brun—doubtlessly savoring the prospect of seeing the son of a onetime Guise sculptor linked in the press to her current protégé, Charpentier.

During the fall of 1680, when the DAUPHIN kept suffering relapses after a particularly serious bout of malaria, Madame de Guise commissioned an extremely personal prayer of thanks.[D] In it, "I" speaks directly to the Lord and evokes the transmission of the crown from one generation to the next. Here the three singers of the Dauphin's Music performed with other royal musicians—almost certainly in late November, shortly after Her Royal Highness's return to the court from Alençon.

[A] Cahiers 14-16, H. 164, H. 165, H. 166.
[B] Cahier 17, H. 320, for Aug. 25, which forms a diptych with H. 321, also for an *haute-contre*, and based on a mass for Saint Laurence, Aug. 17 in the same missel of 1669. (Rodez, T 1043, p. 233).
[C] Cahier 22, H. 323.
[D] Cahiers 31–32, H. 326.

The Queen's sudden death in August 1683 prompted Mademoiselle de Guise to act. Monsieur Du Bois was ordered to write or find an appropriate text that Monsieur Charpentier could set to music. (Madame de Guise had nothing to do with planning this memorial service, for she was at Alençon. She did, however, come to Paris briefly on or about August 16, for the specific purpose of attending a service for the Queen.) At some point between August 16 and the Feast of Saint Louis, August 25, Mademoiselle de Guise's male musicians—among them an *haute-contre*, surely Monsieur Charpentier—performed a setting of neo-Latinist Pierre Portes' poem, *Luctus de morte* in memory of the Queen, and a companion piece for Saint Louis.[A] The poem for the Queen addresses "France" directly and refers to "princes and nobles who weep." Here again the first person is avoided, for this was a public service. It is significant, however, that a royal princess of the House of Orléans and a high noblewoman of the House of Lorraine attended this service at which "princes and nobles" wept.

The Guise princesses' devotions to honor the Royal House of Bourbon reached their apogee in January 1687, when Mademoiselle de Guise organized a splendid *Te Deum* at MONTMARTRE, to thank God for Louis XIV's recovery after life-threatening surgery. A "song of gratitude"[B] where "I" and "we" join in thanksgiving, was sung by the Pièches, that is, by the Dauphin's Music. Since Madame de Guise and PHILIPPE II D'ORLÉANS were among the guests of honor that day, it is difficult to determine precisely who the "I" was, and who the "we"; but it does seem that, for this special occasion, Mademoiselle de Guise herself employed the first person to speak to the Lord and addressed Him in the familiar form, "Thee." In short, the "we" who joined her were the King's cousins and the other great nobles present. An *élévation*[C] that appears to have been performed during this mass likewise employs the first person and "Thee." As far as can be discerned from the composer's notebooks, this is the first devotional event where Mademoiselle de Guise spoke to the Lord so intimately in public"[54] This also was the first time that the press not only credited her with having organized musical devotions but explicitly praised her for the "generosity" she had shown toward the King. (Some ten days later at the Luxembourg Palace, MADAME DE GUISE hosted a secular "Idyl"[D] to celebrate her first cousin's recovery.)

[A] Cahier 38, H. 331, H. 332.
[B] Cahier 50, H. 431.
[C] Cahier L, H. 259 (for either the Core Trio or the Dauphin's Music), which followed directly upon H. 195, a psalm of thanksgiving for the Great Guise Music.
[D] Cahiers 49–50, H. 489.

In the course of writing these devotions—devotions for the Virgin, devotions for the Infant Jesus, and devotions for Louis the God-Given and his family—Marc-Antoine Charpentier attained a new level of artistic achievement, as his horizons continually expanded. Challenges were being set before him, as he began putting non-liturgical Latin texts to music, worked with different combinations of voices and instruments, and saw his compositions performed at the royal court in 1679. To these experiences must be added, of course, his growing skill at writing for the vernacular theater—an expertise that he might never have acquired had those irritated "virgins" and "heroines" not swooped down on Molière back in 1672.

Oratorios

Starting in 1675 these three devotions—for the Virgin, for the Child, and for the Crown as personified in Louis XIV and his immediate family —served as the underpinnings of a succession of oratorios that flowed from Monsieur Charpentier's pen. In many respects, these oratorios were the splendid, more public side of the princesses' worship. For the composer, writing these oratorios was an exciting challenge: he was being allowed to work in an Italianate style and in the Italianate genre known as the *oratorio*—or, as he called it, the *canticum*, "song."

Most of these oratorios appear to be related to a "devotion" that MADAME DE GUISE was carrying on at the Church of Sainte-Anne-la-Royale, run by the Italian THEATINES. There a chapel had been made available to her in 1675. There is no evidence that Her Royal Highness had given much thought to Italian music prior to that date. Although she had studied Italian as a girl, and although her sister had married a Medici, her cultural perspective seems to have been very French—as French as that of her cousin the King, who had eschewed things Italian and was actively promoting a distinctive French style in all the arts.

By contrast, during her years at the Medici court, MADEMOISELLE MARIE DE GUISE had not lacked opportunities to hear oratorios. In fact, there is strong evidence that she had been caught up in Saint Philip Neri's "oratory" movement, a devotional approach that presumably was kept brightly burning in her heart over the decades, thanks to her continuing contacts with Florence. When Madame de Guise's sister, MADAME DE TOSCANE, announced that she would be returning to France in the late summer of 1675, the two Guise princesses apparently put their heads together and came up with a way of impressing and pleasing the Grand Duchess. Monsieur Charpentier would write an oratorio for performance in the most Italianate and theatrical religious setting in Paris, the Theatines; and Madame de Guise would ask the King to loan her the requisite number of musicians. The subject? Why not Judith, one of the "strong women," *femmes fortes*—"*Judith fortes*," goes the libretto—to whom Queen Anne of Austria (Mesdames de Guise and de Toscane's late aunt) had been likened in the "gallery of strong women" portrayed by Pierre Le Moyne, S.J. The subject was very timely, for Judith's decision to become Jehovah's instrument could be paralleled with a decision that Madame de Guise was just then making. For the well-being of her people, "upon the death of her husband" Judith had turned herself into God's instrument, thereby "demonstrating that, along with the blood of the patriarchs, her ancestors, she had inherited their faith and their constancy." Widowed Madame de Guise, who descended from a king, a patriarch, was preparing to vow that her life would henceforth be one of service to her cousin, Louis XIV: "The King is master of everything that lies within my control," she would inform him almost simultaneously with the performance of *Judith*,[A] which took place on or around September 28, 1675.[55]

The oratorio seems to have pleased Her Royal Highness greatly. At any rate, Monsieur Charpentier was ordered to write three more in 1676 alone. The first, a "song for peace"[B] for a large ensemble, was discussed above, in the context of Madame de Guise's devotion for Louis XIV the God-Given. The other two were for the Core Trio of the GUISE MUSIC, and each is related to one or another of the devotions that were dear to both Guise women. One was a "song" for Christmas,[C] the principal holy day of the devotion to the INFANT JESUS in which both Guise princesses were deeply engrossed. This oratorio—and the *élévation* and *Domine salvum fac regem* that follow it in Charpentier's arabic-numbered note-books—probably were performed at the THEATINES during a Christmas Eve service attended by PHILIPPE II D'ORLÉANS.[56] The other oratorio for the Core Trio honored Saint Cecilia,[D] the embodiment of the princesses' efforts to convert Huguenots by reason and gentleness. This work almost certainly was sung during the week of November 21, when MADAME DE GUISE attended the conversion of a Protestant woman at the Jesuit Noviciate, Louis XIV having asked her to win this Huguenot over to Catholicism. In other words, the oratorio for Saint Cecilia draws a parallel between the converting saint and Isabelle d'Orléans, Louis XIV's converting tool.

[A] Cahiers 9–11, H. 391.
[B] Cahier 11, H. 392.
[C] Cahier 12, H. 393.
[D] Cahier 13, H. 394.

Three oratorios were commissioned in 1677. The first—written for Epiphany and destined for the Core Trio of the GUISE MUSIC—again reflects the princesses' devotions for the INFANT JESUS. Next came *Esther*,[A] which, like *Judith*, used a text recited during the final week of September. Conceived for a large ensemble (like *Judith*), this oratorio extolls a strong woman who (again like *Judith*), served as God's instrument. It presumably was performed at the THEATINE church in late September of 1677. The final oratorio of 1677 was another work honoring Saint Cecilia,[B] this time for a large ensemble. Although the venue for this particular oratorio can only be guessed—the THEATINES?—the reasons prompting MADAME DE GUISE to commission a more splendid work for this saint are not hard to deduce. In November 1677 she was rejoicing over the dedication of her house for new converts at Alençon.

A hiatus of two years followed. Then, in 1680, came four more oratorios, three of them for large ensembles[C] and therefore presumably for MADAME DE GUISE. And indeed, the subject matter of the oratorio for Saint Charles Borromeo reflects the charitable activities to which Her Royal Highness was devoting much of her time, both in her parish of Saint-Sulpice and, it would seem, as a member of that saint's confraternity at the church of the THEATINES. The fourth oratorio, dedicated to the Virgin, was written for Mademoiselle de Guise's progress through Champagne with the GUISE MUSIC, which included visits to the Marian pilgrimage church of Notre-Dame de Liesse. (Monsieur Charpentier apparently was invited along, for the Music was joined by an *haute-contre*.)

The next two years brought two oratorios for large ensembles—works later[57] described as being "for the Jesuits."[D] The one recounting the story of Saul and Jonathan was composed for an unidentified event, probably held in July 1681 at one of the THREE JESUIT HOUSES of Paris. (The text that inspired the libretto was read every July.) The other oratorio, about Joshua, was copied into a notebook containing several sheets of Jesuit paper. Neither the date nor the circumstances of the performance have been determined.

The indication "for the Jesuits" should not be seen as evidence that the oratorios about Saul and Joshua were actually commissioned by the Jesuits. The composer's roman-numbered notebooks suggest the opposite. That is to say, there is little reason to believe that the Jesuits requested

---

[A] Cahiers 17–18, H. 396.
[B] Cahiers 19–20, H. 397.
[C] Cahiers 23–24, H. 398; cahier 29, H. 399; cahiers 30–31, H. 401.
[D] Cahier 32, H. 403; cahier 34, H. 404.

any of the oratorios for outsiders[A] that Charpentier wrote during the 1680s.[58] Indeed, throughout the composer's decade of service to the fathers during the 1690s, he wrote only one oratorio, a "dialogue" for Easter.[B] In short, the Jesuits of Paris do not appear to have been particularly enamored of this devotional genre, although they clearly were amenable to having oratorios performed in their churches, as gifts.

This general pattern—combined with the fact that these works "for the Jesuits" were copied into the arabic-numbered notebooks that Charpentier generally reserved for the Guises—suggests that the "Jesuit" compositions were a Guise initiative. That is to say, one of the princesses (it is not clear which one) commissioned these works for a special devotion at one of the Jesuit establishments, just as Madame de Guise had done for the conversion ceremony back in 1676. In all likelihood one or both princesses remunerated the opera singers and instrumentalists who had been hired to perform the work. (Does the presence of Jesuit paper suggest that the fathers graciously supplied the paper, in hopes that they would be permitted to keep the partbooks?)

By 1681 the number of oratorios being added to the arabic-numbered notebooks had fallen to one per year. After the two Biblical stories "for the Jesuits," 1683 brought a "dialogue" about communion for two *dessus* (sopranos) and a bass[C]—an unusual combination that may mark the maiden performance of one of the teenage sopranos who had recently joined the GUISE MUSIC. When the Great Guise Music began performing in 1684, several oratorios were written expressly for these musicians,[D] two of them extolling Cecilia, and another recounting the Christmas Story.

Monsieur Charpentier's final oratorio for the Guises was composed for the Feast of Saint Cecilia in November 1685. After that he stopped writing oratorios, although 1686 saw a revival of his final oratorio for Cecilia, with a new prelude almost certainly written and commissioned by MONSIEUR DU BOIS. The circumstances surrounding this abrupt abandonment of the genre appear related to recent events at the THEATINE church of Sainte-Anne-la-Royale. In June 1685 Paolo Lorenzani had been named official composer for a new "devotion" there. And that spring MADAME DE GUISE had shifted her devotional focus away from the pomp of the world, in favor of more intimate and apparently music-less devotions at the Great Carmel.

[A] For example, cahier XXX, H. 402; cahier XXXIX, H. 410; cahier XLI, H. 411 (all for large ensembles and contemporary with his association with the Dauphin's Music).
[B] Cahier LX, H. 417 (for 1691?).
[C] Cahier 37, H. 407 (surely associated with H. 187, which precedes it in the notebook).
[D] Cahier 42, H. 413; cahiers 42–42, H. 414; cahier 47, H. 415.

Having blazed the trail, was Marc-Antoine Charpentier disappointed when the Theatines hired Lorenzani? Or did he feel scant regret, being eager to try other things, other genres? No answers to these questions are, of course, possible. It is clear, however, that between 1675 and 1685 oratorios had not gained acceptance at the royal court, nor in the Jesuit churches of the capital. By contrast, the Theatines loved them. Having been bystanders at Madame de Guise's "devotions" for a decade, the Italian fathers realized the drawing power of this genre. It attracted the elite to the church, and with them, money—at least for awhile.

Irrespective of Monsieur Charpentier's personal feelings of relief or rejection, his decade of oratorio-writing had taught him how to convey musically the changing emotions expressed in a devotional text. He had sharpened his understanding of how the "energies" of each musical key affected worshipers. For example, in *Josué* he had made listeners hear trumpets where there were none; and in one of his oratorios honoring Saint Cecilia, he had used sound to suggest the presence of perfumed flowers, while in another he had created the "voracious flames" of her martyrdom. Without Madame de Guise's very special "devotions"— sometimes conducted at the Theatines, sometimes in one or another of the Jesuit houses of the capital—would CARISSIMI's French disciple have had an opportunity to work in this genre and hear his creations performed by skilled musicians?

A similar question can be asked about the operatic genre in which Marc-Antoine Charpentier would test his acumen in the early 1680s. He was, of course, free to write as many "operas" and "pastorales" as he wished, as an intellectual exercise; and he probably could have managed a discreet performance or two behind Jean-Baptiste Lully's back. But without Madame de Guise, would he have had an opportunity to see his operas performed at the royal court by the Dauphin's own musicians?

1679–1687
COMPOSER TO THE HOUSE OF BOURBON

The Dauphin

Without MADAME DE GUISE's recommendation, Charpentier almost certainly would never have had the exhilarating opportunity to compose for the DAUPHIN. To tempt her young cousin, Her Royal Highness appears to have taken the initiative in 1678, when she and the Grand Duchess of Tuscany went to court several times for lunch with the prince. Toward the end of that year, Madame de Guise ordered Charpentier to write a piece for the Dauphin,[A] who was so eager to have a musical ensemble all his own that he had agreed to pay for it from his *menus plaisirs*. During the next few years, Madame de Guise would give Monseigneur gifts[B] for his Music. For example, in June 1680 Charpentier provided music for a Corpus Christi procession at Versailles in which Her Royal Highness marched; and in the late autumn of that year he wrote a prayer for the ailing Dauphin in which she spoke to Jesus directly, as grandchildren of France were wont to do.

By March 1679 Monsieur Charpentier had been designated composer to Monseigneur, but on an ad hoc basis rather than an official one. The pieces were performed by a small group of musicians that came to be known as the "Dauphin's Music" despite the fact that, like Charpentier, they were not officially part of the royal musical establishment. The performers were the two teenage Pièche sisters, their instrumentalist brothers, and a bass vocalist named Frizon. Circumstantial evidence suggests that the composer played a crucial role in shaping the Dauphin's Music. In effect, Marc-Antoine Charpentier recreated the Guise Music at Versailles. (Save for the indication that two pieces written in 1678 and 1679 were "for the Demoiselles Pièche," his compositions for the Dauphin's Music would be more or less indistinguishable from the pieces he wrote for the Core Trio of the GUISE MUSIC.) Not only that, he ended up working with musicians whom he knew from the theater, where Frizon had sung in *Le Malade imaginaire*, and the little Pièche sisters had danced in at least one play. This suggests that he played a role in selecting the members of the Dauphin's Music.

In short, Charpentier appears to have shared his preferences, or at least his habits, with the heir to the French throne. The Dauphin apparently was willing to allow the Guise protégé to shape the esthetics of his Music. For example, he either asked Charpentier to compose oratorios for him, or else he agreed to let him do so at a time when the genre was more or less the preserve of the two Guise princesses. Irrespective of whose idea it was to perform oratorios at court, Charpentier wrote at least two for the Dauphin's little group of musicians. One was for Easter,[C] presumably for either the high mass or the vespers sung in the royal chapel of Saint-Germain-en-Laye on March 27, 1682, in the Dauphin's presence. The other was for the Feast of the Circumcision,[D] almost certainly for either the high mass or the musical vespers sung at

---

[A] Cahier 22, H. 170 ("Demoiselles Piesches").
[B] Cahier 23, H. 245, H. 246, and H. 247 (Corpus Christi); cahier 31, H. 326 (the ailing Dauphin).
[C] Cahier XXXIII, H. 405.
[D] Cahier XXXV, H. 406.

Versailles on January 1, 1683, in the presence of the Dauphin and the Dauphine.

Monsieur Charpentier's principal duty toward Monseigneur was, however, somewhat more mundane than writing music to be performed before the King. His principal task was to compose for the DAUPHIN's private low mass. (He copied these works into several consecutive notebooks dating from roughly 1679 to 1681.[A]) The content of Charpentier's roman-numbered notebooks for these years nonetheless suggests that he soon was being asked to compose for Corpus Christi processions and—a still greater honor—for the mass during which Monseigneur was inducted into the Order of the Holy Spirit, January 1, 1682. One of the motets performed that day appears to have been Charpentier's setting, for two women and a bass, of some lines from Psalm 75,[B] which ends: "He shall cut off the spirit of princes; He is terrible to the kings of the earth."[59]

There is evidence that Charpentier was spending quite a bit of time at court and had been granted access to the prince. For example, he is known to have been rehearsing the Dauphin's Music on December 29, 1681, for the coming milestone in their master's life. Hence, it would seem, Pierre Landry's decision to include an image of "Monsieur Charpentier" in the Almanac he engraved for 1682. Landry depicted the composer giving his Menuet de Strasbourg to Madame de Guise during a ball at the royal court, as Monseigneur, wearing his blue ribbon of the Order of the Holy Spirit, danced in the background. Behind Her Royal Highness stood a young woman in a modest coif, presumably Marguerite Pièche, the dessus for whom the Menuet was written. In other words, for every important event at court where one or more of his compositions was to be performed, Charpentier apparently went to Versailles or to Saint-Germain-en-Laye, to ensure that the musicians gave every word and every note just the right articulation and expressiveness.

Monseigneur was so supportive of his composer that he allowed his name to be linked publicly to Charpentier's in two consecutive descriptions of fêtes organized by his uncle, PHILIPPE II D'ORLÉANS. That is to say, Corneille and DONNEAU DE VISÉ, Charpentier's friends at the Mercure galant, were permitted to inform their readers that the King had furloughed his own Music, so that the Dauphin's Music—and Monsieur Charpentier's motets—could be the center of attention. Contrary to what we generally suggest when we quote a sentence or two out of their broader context, Charpentier's motets sung by the Pièches were not the

---

[A] Cahiers XXV, ("Piesches"), XXVI, XXVII, and XXVIII, plus Rés Vmc ms. 27 ("Pieche").
[B] Cahier XXXI, H. 179.

only music at these fêtes. Philippe II d'Orléans' Music played, as did Nicolas Lebègue, the royal organist. In addition, several comedies and tragedies were performed by theatrical troops from Paris.

Owing to the ad hoc nature of his position, Charpentier's future in Monseigneur's service was far from assured—this despite the fact that, as the paper of two of Charpentier's roman-numbered notebooks reveals,[60] Jean-Baptiste Colbert was supporting the composer's endeavors. First of all, Charpentier was not an official servant of one or another member of the royal family. Thus, unlike the King's "domestic officers and the persons who eat at his mess," he did not benefit from the usual "privileges, freedoms, liberties, immunities, exemptions from the *tailles*, and other such emancipations."[61] On the positive side of the coin, his marginal position exempted him from the hierarchical pressures and obligations encountered by royal householders. As a result, he presumably was able to come and go, and to compose in a genre he believed would please the Dauphin. It is, however, very unlikely that Monsieur Charpentier decided which texts would be set to music: Monseigneur's almoner or chaplain probably exerted his rights on that matter.

As the POISON AFFAIR began to stir terror in any circle with links to Italy, to drugs and medicines, or to one or more of the suspects with the surname *Charpentier* who were being investigated, Marc-Antoine Charpentier had every reason to worry about his future as composer to the heir to the French throne. The Dauphin's illness in late 1680 was especially worrisome, for it coincided with disclosures that a princess of the House of Lorraine had been trying to obtain a post in the Dauphin's household for a suspected poisoner, and with investigations into the suspicious activities of several individuals who were either named Charpentier or were related to someone with that name. One of these suspects had longtime links to the House of Guise, and another was employed by a close relative of the Bailleuls, friends of the composer's sister, ÉLISABETH CHARPENTIER. The King ordered the investigation closed and the files sealed in late 1682. Not long after the conclusion of the Affair, the composer became so ill that he had to withdraw from the competition for a sub-mastership in the royal chapel in April 1683. By June of that year, DONNEAU DE VISÉ's *Mercure galant* was using the past tense about his work for the Dauphin and announced that the King had rewarded Monsieur Charpentier with a pension.

Nothing is known about Marc-Antoine Charpentier's illness, beyond the fact that it was so severe that he composed nothing between April and mid-August 1683—at least nothing in the *Mélanges*. That is to say, the roman-numbered notebooks for that period include two compositions for January 1,[A] doubtlessly for the high mass or vespers sung at Versailles for the Feast of the Circumcision, in the presence of the Dauphin and Dauphine. These works are followed immediately by two pieces for a *reposoir* for Corpus Christi, June 17,[B] when the usual lavish procession was held at Versailles. The latter works presumably were written well in advance, say early April. After that, nothing—until the music for the memorial mass for the Queen sung at the LITTLE CARMEL on December 20, 1683.[C] There is a similar gap in the arabic-numbered series. After a *divertissement* for the Fête of the Apartments performed circa November 1682, come two works[D] that clearly were intended for a single religious service and that probably were performed in early January 1683. (These pieces, where two sopranos, *dessus*, sing with a bass, appear to have been written for Mademoiselle de Guise.[62]) After that, nothing—until two pieces for a service at the MERCY during the last half of August, in memory of the Queen.[E] In other words, Marc-Antoine Charpentier was not feigning illness in order to back out of a competition that he realized he could not win, Delalande being the Dauphine's clear choice.

Physical and mental exhaustion may have provoked the illness, for between 1679 (when he began working for the Dauphin) and the spring of 1683, the composer filled sixteen notebooks for the Guise women, plus eleven notebooks of outside commissions, plus two little booklets full of pieces for the Dauphin's Music. The equivalent of at least twenty-nine notebooks in the space of four years!

In many ways, composing for the Dauphin's Music was not all that different from writing for the Guise Core Trio; and Mademoiselle de Guise may well have permitted him to reuse for Monseigneur any of the works for her Music that seemed appropriate. Still, Charpentier was producing an average of more than seven notebooks a year, as contrasted with the mid-1670s, when he rarely filled five.

Averages can, of course, be deceptive. For example, 1680 had been especially busy: nine notebooks for the Guises, and four or five for outsiders, chiefly the Dauphin. The next year was relatively calm; but in 1682 he filled four notebooks for the princesses and five for outsiders. To the draining task of composing so many works, often on short notice, must be added the fatigue of copying out the requisite partbooks and journeying to and fro, from Paris to the court, for rehearsals. Thus it

---

[A] Cahier XXXV, H. 104 (a psalm for matins of the Feast of the Circumcision), H. 406.
[B] Cahier XXVI, H. 523; cahiers XXXV–XXXVI, H. 329.
[C] Cahiers XXXVI–XXXIX, H. 524, H. 408, H. 409, H. 189.
[D] Cahier 37, H. 187, H. 407.
[E] Cahier 38, H. 331, H. 332.

would not be surprising if the composer was suffering from mental and physical exhaustion. Still, profound depression that made any creative effort impossible cannot be ruled out—depression provoked by the tensions of the Poison Affair combined with the realization that he would not receive a court appointment, owing in part to favoritism but above all to the witch hunt that, while officially buried, was not forgotten.

Although Monsieur Charpentier's unofficial position as composer to the Dauphin had ended by early 1683, Monseigneur continued to call upon him for several more years. For example, in the spring of 1685 Charpentier wrote a psalm of jubilation[A] for what appears to be the Pièche trio. (The devotional event has not been identified.) For the Corpus Christi procession of June 13, 1686, he composed a "grand motet[B] for the *reposoir* of Versailles in the presence of the King."[63] The large ensemble that performed this work almost certainly was the King's Music. The Pièches sang the *Domine salvum fac regem*. The Dauphin and the King marched side by side that day. A year later, in June 1687, Charpentier again wrote music for the *reposoir*[C] at Versailles—this time a motet for the King's Music and a psalm for the Pièches and several of their colleagues. (Loyal to Charpentier, the DAUPHIN dashed back to court from the front, to attend the procession of June 5, 1687.) A few months earlier, on January 20, 1687, the Dauphin's musicians had gone to MONTMARTRE to sing[D] for Mademoiselle de Guise's lavish *Te Deum* celebrating Louis XIV's recovery. (The Dauphin did not attend.)

Several years later, when the composer was music master for one or more of the THREE JESUIT HOUSES of Paris, he called upon the Pièches one last time, setting to music a psalm[E] that was recited during matins on Monday. The devotional event has not been identified, but it seems to have been an "ordinary" one, that is, an annual holy day at Saint-Louis. At any rate, the composer copied the work into the arabic-numbered notebooks that represent his day-to-day obligations.[64]

Operas and pastorales

Although Monsieur Charpentier left the Dauphin's service early in 1683, thanks to MADAME DE GUISE he continued to write for court events. Without her protection it is extremely unlikely that any of his music, be it religious or be it secular, would have been performed at the royal court. Her hopes that her protégé would find a permanent post at court having

[A] Cahier XLVI, H. 194.
[B] Cahier XLIX, H. 344 (*reposoir*), H. 295 (*Domine salvum*).
[C] Cahier LI, H. 346, H. 196 ("Magd," "Marg," "Frizon").
[D] Cahier 50, H. 431 ("Magd," "Marg," "Frizon").
[E] Cahier 55, H. 201 ("Melle Magd," "Melle Marg," "Mr Bastaron," "Mr Frison").

been dashed, Her Royal Highness now proceeded to call attention to him by commissioning a series of "operas" and pastorales for performance at court. On several occasions Charpentier joined the performers and spoke indirectly to the Monarch.

In 1682 Madame de Guise hovered in the background as her composer and the Guise Music challenged Lully's operatic privilege on the Florentine's own turf, the royal court. This was not the first time that she had lent her support to this sort of challenge. Back in October 1676, she had offered her cousin and godfather, PHILIPPE II D'ORLÉANS, an "opera"[A] to be performed during the party that followed the baptisms of PHILIPPE III D'ORLÉANS, Duke of Chartres, and his baby sister.[65] That this entertainment was described in the press as an "opera" made it clear to every informed reader that the Duke of Orléans and the godparents (among them Madame de Guise) were in the camp of the unnamed composer and musicians who were opposing Lully's monopoly of the operatic genre. (Madame de Guise does not appear to have lent her support to the creation of another "opera" during Mardi Gras of 1678, performed at the elegant residence of ARMAND-JEAN DE RIANTS in the presence of a bevy of supporters and former protégés of the House of Guise.)

This twitting of Lully would continue into the mid-1680s. For example, the arabic-numbered notebooks for 1685 contain a dialogue between Angélique and Médor[B] to be inserted into Dancourt's *Angélique et Médor*. The fact that this piece was copied into the series of notebooks reserved for Guise commissions suggests that one or both of his protectresses had approved this satire of Lully's recent *Roland*—to the point that they apparently ordered their composer to set the dialogue to music.

In short, Madame de Guise enjoyed seeing Lully challenged in this way, just as she and Mademoiselle de Guise had been deriving pleasure from allowing Charpentier to challenge the Florentine's monopoly over theatrical music in general. Viewed in this context, the pastorales and the operas that stud the arabic-numbered notebooks of the *Mélanges* from November 1682 to January 1687 (and that inevitably evoke an event that took place while Her Royal Highness was in residence at the royal court) take on a new meaning.

If Monsieur Charpentier had not been serving the Dauphin in 1682, would the idea of writing opera-like entertainments for the royal court have arisen? For a decade his work in the vernacular had been limited to

[A] Cahier 13, H. 479.
[B] Cahier 45, H. 506.

the theater, primarily vocal airs and instrumental pieces. True, at Madame de Guise's request he had tried his hand at a sustained narrative for the princely baptism back in 1676; but after that, nothing in this genre had found its way into his notebooks. Yet he clearly wrote several such entertainments for his and his friends' enjoyment. That is to say, he composed a "serenade" entitled *Le Triomphe de Bacchus*, a work entitled *Les Amours tragiques d'Apollon*, and a "comedy mingled with music" entitled *Le Sot suffisant*[66]—apparently none of them copied into his numbered notebooks and all of them lost.

Now, in the fall of 1682—protégé of the Dauphin that he was, and exasperated with the constraints that Lully had been imposing upon him and his colleagues at the theater for the past decade—Monsieur Charpentier became a central figure in a covert assault against Lully by the disgruntled composers of the realm. With Madame de Guise's connivance, he began to write opera-like works for performance at the court of Louis XIV. Since these were gifts from the princess to her royal first cousin, Lully could scarcely protest. Within a year, the composer's colleagues, Corneille and DONNEAU DE VISÉ, would give voice to this opposition in their *Mercure galant*.[67] In an article brimming with irony, they would urge Lully to stop wearing himself out by insisting on writing every opera, and to let other composers try their hand at the genre.

The summer of 1682, and the revival of Pierre Corneille's *Andromède* by his brother, THOMAS CORNEILLE, had brought the usual opposition from Lully, followed by the requisite show of obedience by composer and troop. Not long after that, Charpentier attacked on a different front: the chamber opera, rather than the theatrical interlude. His "Piece for the King's Apartments"[A] was performed during the *Fête des Appartements* that Louis XIV invented late in 1682. Almost certainly written for the Pièches, joined by Charpentier himself, this entertainment served as a farewell of sorts, for the composer's service to the Dauphin would soon end. Not since the baptism party of 1676 had Charpentier sung before the King, addressing him indirectly. But now, as an afterthought—or yielding perhaps to pressure—he added a dozen measures where the "*haute-contre* in the first chorus of Pleasures" alluded to "Louis, the monarch of the lilies," and emphasized the importance of ensuring that the King would not be deprived of music: "Don't go," this high tenor urged the other characters, "or Louis will lack the pleasures that music provides." Did the audience see this as a veiled allusion to Lully, who—as the *Mercure galant* had pointed out—was depriving Louis XIV of the

---

[A] Cahier 37, H. 480.

pleasures that might come his way if other composers were permitted to write and perform operas?

The next opera-like challenge was made in the spring of 1685, perhaps for that year's *Fête des Appartements*, which continued into mid-April. The composition was a pastorale for the Great Guise Music. Using the flowers of spring [A] as an excuse, they praised "the glorious exploits of the famous conqueror," Louis XIV. Although Charpentier sang with the Guise Music, this time he did not address the King. Instead, Beaupuis —who two years earlier had obtained Mademoiselle de Guise's permission to perform in Lully's *Phaéton*—asserted that music is inadequate to praise the King, and that the only appropriate language is "silence." To the informed, this may have been understood as an allusion to Lully, to whom Charpentier was about to capitulate, that is, fall silent. (September of that year brought Charpentier's final collaboration with THOMAS CORNEILLE and his colleagues.)

A year later, the Great Guise Music performed an opera, almost certainly at court, probably in February 1686.[68] For this work, which tells of the descent of Orpheus into Hades,[B] the Guise musicians were joined by the Pièche brothers, members of the Dauphin's Music (and by the Pièche sisters in the chorus?). The Pièches' participation provides very strong evidence that Monseigneur was supporting Charpentier in this challenge to Lully's monopoly. The opera may well have been performed at an "entertainment" the Dauphin had arranged for his intimate circle: "Monseigneur gave a supper for the King, for the Dauphine, and for some ladies. There were only twenty at table. Afterwards there were very agreeable *divertissements*."[69]

That was Charpentier's final operatic performance with the Great Guise Music. In December 1686 he began marking François Anthoine's name beside the *haute-contre* line. (This gradual withdrawal from the Guise Music in the fall of 1686 seems related to the fact that earlier that year he had been named music master at the College of Louis-le-Grand, a post on which this portrait will soon train its attention.) For another year the composer nonetheless continued working for the two Guise highnesses, and he apparently did not vacate his apartment at the Hôtel de Guise until mid-1687.

In other words, he was still in Mademoiselle de Guise's service when he created an opera-like work for MADAME DE GUISE, an "Idyl"[C] to rejoice over the King's recovery. The performers were the Great Guise Music

---

[A] Cahiers 44–45, H. 486.
[B] Cahier "II" (probably the "missing" cahier 48 of early 1686), H. 488.
[C] Cahiers 49–50, H. 489.

(Charpentier did not sing). For a libretto he used a poem written a full year earlier by Madame Deshoulières and published in the *Mercure galant*.[70] Did Charpentier, on his own initiative, approach the poetess? It is highly unlikely. It cannot be ruled out, however, that Her Royal Highness ordered the composer—rather than Du Bois or Monsieur de Charmoy, her secretary—to inform Deshoulières of the honor she was about to be paid: her poem was being used for a splendid fête. Did Charpentier confer with Deshoulières about minor modifications in the text? It cannot be ruled out, but the excision of a few lines and of the final ode scarcely required such consultation; and the changes to several lines are the kind composers routinely made, to ensure that the lyrics would flow felicitously above the musical beat. Conveniently, the poem evoked many elements in the festivities being prepared at the Luxembourg Palace. For example, Deshoulières' allusion to gilded paneling suggested the famous gilded rooms of the palace; and her reference to fireworks and fountains of wine corresponded to public entertainments that the Guise princesses had sponsored in the past. The performance—which took place in Paris, not at the royal court—can be dated: January 30, 1687. After the King's visit to the Hôtel de Ville that day, all craftsmen were, predictably, given a holiday (just as the lyrics stated). Louis then left Paris; and that evening (just as the lyrics point out) fireworks were shot off throughout the city, and fountains of wine flowed in the streets. Madame de Guise—who had attended the banquet at the Hôtel de Ville earlier in the day—entertained friends at her palace.

During the early 1680s Charpentier wrote several opera-like works for the fortunate few whom the Guises authorized to approach their composer and who were willing to participate in this rebellion against Lully. Interestingly enough, in marked contrast to the works composed for Madame de Guise and the Dauphin, none of the operas or pastorales that Charpentier copied into his roman-numbered notebooks refers to Louis XIV. This strongly suggests that these particular works were not intended for performance at court, nor at a noble residence to which the King had been invited. (True, Louis XIV was expected at the Duke of RICHELIEU's fête at Rueil,[A] but the Duke carefully separated the pastorale, with its allusions to his granduncle the Cardinal, from the air honoring the Monarch whose statue would be inaugurated.)

In short, although some of these challenges to Lully's monopoly were mounted away from the royal palaces, they almost certainly were commissioned by great nobles or influential parlementaires. Although the

[A] Cahiers XLVII–XLVIII, H. 485, H. 440.

patron cannot always be identified, some of these people were not only sufficiently close to the Guises to receive their blessing, they were deemed so upright that Mademoiselle de Guise sent the Great Guise Music, with its teenage chambermaids, to perform for them. For example, during the early spring of 1685 a quite moralizing "dispute"[A] among shepherds was performed by the Great Guise Music, Charpentier included. (The libretto, which carefully avoids all mention of carnal "love," calls to mind the painting with a "very modest" subject that Gondi, off in Florence, was trying to obtain for MADEMOISELLE DE GUISE in 1684 and 1685.) Another composition was a hunting "opera" about Acteon,[B] punished by being turned into a stag. Commissioned for the early summer of 1684 by an unidentified patron who obtained permission for Geneviève De Brion of the GUISE MUSIC to sing in the chorus, it was reworked for the fall hunting season, when the role of Acteon was sung by a high soprano, *haut-dessus*—apparently a woman, hence the witty new title, "Acteon changed into a doe." The patron who commissioned a "pastorale" from Charpentier for September 1685 has been identified: the DUKE OF RICHE-LIEU, who was planning a lavish fête at Rueil.[C]

For the summer of 1685 Charpentier composed an "opera" about the arts,[D] for the Great Guise Music. Although the theme of this opera calls to mind the theme of the *Ballet des arts* that the students at the College of Louis-le-Grand were rehearsing that very summer, it is highly unlikely that Mademoiselle de Guise dispatched the Great Guise Music to the Jesuit school. Was this opera performed during the ceremony that ended the school year at the Academy of the INFANT JESUS? For Christmas of 1684, 1685, and 1686 Charpentier accepted a series of outside commissions for Christmas "pastorales"[E] in the vernacular. These Christmas entertainments, likewise performed by the Great Guise Music, probably were intended for the teachers' training institute known as the Daughters of the INFANT JESUS, created by Mademoiselle de Guise a decade earlier. These "pastorales," these "operas," infringed on Lully's monopoly.

Actually, from the moment in 1684 when it began performing in public, the Great Guise Music had been challenging Lully's privilege. That is, the Music exceeded the number of singers and instrumentalists that Lully's monopoly permitted for "all theatrical troops of French or foreign actors ... established in the city of Paris." In addition, although

[A] Cahiers XLV–XLVI, H. 484.
[B] Cahier XLI, H. 481, and cahier XLII, H. 481a.
[C] Cahier XLVII–XLVIII, H. 485, H. 440.
[D] Cahier 46, H. 497.
[E] Cahiers XLIV–XLV, H. 482, H. 483; cahiers XLVIII–XLIX, H. 483a; cahiers LXIX–L, H. 483b.

Lully's privilege stipulated that "no entire play can be performed to music either with French lyrics or foreign ones, without Lully's written permission," since 1675 the Guise Music had been performing dramatic narratives that were entirely sung—initially with lyrics in Latin, the "foreign" language used by diplomats and by the Church, and now in French as well. Finally, by destining quite a few of these works for performance before the Monarch and his son—an privilege that had officially been given to Lully—the Guise princesses were presuming to be similarly entitled to "perform these musical plays before Us [the King], when it pleases Us."[71]

The Guise Music was, of course, neither a theatrical troop nor an operatic academy. Still, the two princesses could scarcely have been unaware of what they were doing. Not only had they been abetting Charpentier at the theater, they were now, in their salons and in their chapels, busily ignoring Lully's claims to monopolize sung narratives. The issue became moot after Lully's death in early 1687, only a few weeks after the performance of Charpentier's last opera-like piece for Madame de Guise. With Lully gone, Corneille and DONNEAU DE VISÉ were free to praise, in the Mercure galant for March 1688, the "opera" that Monsieur Charpentier had written for the College of Louis-le-Grand, one of the THREE JESUIT HOUSES in Paris.

In sum, although some of these works of the early 1680s were called "operas," while others were "pastorales," the aim was clear. Joining hands with nobles such as the Duke of Richelieu, the Guise women had ordered Marc-Antoine Charpentier to prepare a succession of musical entertainments, each of them a barb aimed at Lully's monopoly. It is as if the two princesses were answering the challenge that Corneille and DONNEAU DE VISÉ had stated in the Mercure galant of May 1683, when they had urged composers to write operas, in order to lift from Lully's weary shoulders the burden of having to write them all himself.[72]

Italianism and courtly conversation

Marc-Antoine Charpentier was never really separated from Italy during the seventeen years he served the House of Guise. The Grand Duke of Tuscany's agents visited the Hôtel de Guise several times a month, delivering packages and letters and transmitting to Florence Mademoiselle de Guise's requests for Italian music, Italian medications, Italian plants, and chocolate.[73] Acting as middlemen, the Tuscans would assemble boxes from Rome, from Florence, and from other cities of the Peninsula, into one large shipment that they would send to their agent in Lyons, with instructions to forward the items to Paris.

It was probably through the Florentines that Charpentier obtained a copy of a psalm setting by Francesco Alessi, a chapel master at the cathedral of Pisa who is known to have worked for the Medici court in the 1670s.[74] The Medici agents may also have supplied him with an excerpt from *Marcello in Syracusa*, staged in Venice in 1670, shortly Marc-Antoine Charpentier's departure from Rome. Here again, a Florentine provenance is highly likely, for the librettist, Matteo Noris, had written plays for MADAME DE TOSCANE and her husband, and his operas were being performed in Florence during the 1670s. Still, the link is so strong between Venetian opera and Impresario JACQUES II DALIBERT, that this particular manuscript may well have reached the Hôtel de Guise via Rome. That is to say, not only was Dalibert's opera house, the Tordi-nona, in full activity during the early 1670s, but he is also known to have been in touch with the impresarios in Venice.

As for Charpentier's copy of a polychoral mass by the Roman composer Francesco Beretta, it was copied onto the French paper that Charpentier used in around 1680. Here again a link to Jacques II Dalibert can be discerned. Beretta was the chapel master for the parish where Madame Dalibert had been raised and where she wed. Irrespective of the sender, most if not all these works probably found their way to Charpentier's apartment in one of the many packages that the Tuscan agent delivered to the Hôtel de Guise.

Owing to these contacts with Florence, the Hôtel de Guise was one of the focal points of Italian music in Paris between 1676 and the mid-1680s, and this fascination for things Italian was strengthened by devotions at the THEATINES, the devotional venue preferred by the Italian colony in Paris. In 1683, and probably much earlier, Italian and Italianate music was also an important element in Mademoiselle de Guise's salon. If Charpentier's two lost operas with Italian lyrics, *Artaxerse*, and *La Dori e Oronte*,[75] were ever performed at the Hôtel de Guise, it doubtlessly was in 1685, when a homesick Florentine named Guerrini became a fixture at what he called Mademoiselle de Guise's "conversations"[76]—an expression the Italians used to denote an opera or a cantata-like work. Did Charpentier write his Italianate serenade[A] for Guerrini, perhaps honoring the foreign visitor by setting one of his poems to music? (Charpentier presumably sang the *haute-contre* line.) It was also in 1685 that he composed an *epitalamio* with Italian lyrics; but although the work may have been performed during one of the "conversations" at the Hôtel de Guise—assuming that the Guise Music could find a way to imitate

---

[A] Cahiers 43b–44, H. 472 (early 1685).

castrati and trumpets—it almost certainly was created to be MADAME DE GUISE's gift to the DAUPHINE's brother.

Italian music by a variety of composers clearly was a regular feature at Mademoiselle de Guise's concerts. Unless there was a shipping problem, the Florentine agents did not discuss the contents of the packages delivered to the Hôtel de Guise during the 1670s and 1680s. One such delay produced a flurry of letters in 1686, as Her Highness and DU BOIS kept prodding the Florentines about some Italian music books they had requested.[77] Judging from the tone of that correspondence, requests for music were far from unusual. Indeed, although it is not clear how much Italian music made its way into Du Bois' musical library, Marc-Antoine Charpentier owned song books printed in Italy, and other Italian works as well. In 1726 the papers preserved by his nephew, JACQUES ÉDOUARD, included "a packet of Italian music by the same author"—perhaps music written by Charpentier but more likely pieces copied out by him. His papers also included a *serenata*, several masses, and a "motet by CARISSIMI." In addition, he owned one sixty-page Italian publication (*ouvrage*) and "eight Italian books of airs containing both words and music."[78]

At some point in the early 1680s, the fondness for Italian music that was shaping Mademoiselle de Guise's entertainments spilled over to the parish of Saint-André-des-Arts, where Curate Mathieu began giving concerts of Italian music and works inspired by Italy.[79] Among the compositions he owned were manuscript copies of some of Charpentier's motets. It is easy to guess how these exclusive compositions escaped from the composer's workroom and made their way across Paris, to be performed at the Curate's residence. The composer's sister, ÉLISABETH CHARPENTIER, and her dancing master and instrumentalist husband, Jean Édouard, were Mathieu's parishioners, as was ARMAND-JEAN CHARPENTIER THE ENGINEER. What cannot be determined is any role the composer himself might have played in the creation of these concerts.

1678–1688
THE FINAL DECADE OF THE HOUSE OF GUISE

Although keeping up with the princesses' musical demands could be exhausting, life at the Hôtel de Guise was stimulating for anyone possessing curiosity, imagination, intelligence. Once mourning for the Duke of Alençon had ended, it became clear that MADEMOISELLE DE GUISE was not going to withdraw from the world and live like a nun at the ABBEY OF MONTMARTRE. In fact, she was determined to demonstrate to the Monarchy and to the elites of the realm that the famed "magnificence" of the House of Guise had not died with the last male. Since the magnificence, the glory of a great house (or of a great monarch) was the sum of the artists and writers protected, Mademoiselle de Guise encouraged her talented householders to expand their horizons by studying and by investigating new artistic genres.

Each in his own way, these householders strove to embody that magnificence. They realized that they were living at a special moment, that the great lady whom they served represented the end of an era. Thus GOIBAUT DU BOIS began the translations of Saint Augustine that would gain him admission to the French Academy. Equerry GAIGNIÈRES amassed a collection of "rare" and "curious" documents about the history of France. Emulating Gaignières, VALLANT, the household physician, carefully preserved his medical records and began saving documents about the arts and the sciences. LOULIÉ, the Guise musician, began writing the corpus of teaching methods and treatises on music theory that would make him one of the most learned musicians of his day. On the margins of this group stood Loulié's friend, BROSSARD, whose subsequent intellectual life was an amalgam of Gaignières' "curiosity," Charpentier's Italianism, and Loulié's passion for theory.

A savant composer

In the early 1680s MADEMOISELLE DE GUISE decided to create the GREAT GUISE MUSIC and embarked upon a search for talented young singers and instrumentalists. These were heady days when Italian music flourished in her palace. Above all, these were days when one householder began vying with another, each demonstrating his erudition. If they did so, it was owing to Her Highness's liberality, for which Du Bois would express his gratitude a few years later: "It is she who gave me the means to finish this work, through the sweetness of the repose that her goodness permits for all those who have the honor of belonging to her."[80]

Thanks to Mademoiselle de Guise's and Madame de Guise's devotions and courtly entertainments, Monsieur Charpentier had been expanding his horizons throughout the 1670s, working in a variety of genres. Having demonstrated his mastery of almost all the musical genres—intimate religious music, *grands motets*, oratorios, incidental music for the theater, and operas and pastorales—in the early 1680s he set about deepening his theoretical understanding of his art. He embarked on an intellectual quest that would consolidate his growing reputation as one of the most "savant" composers in the realm. Was he leading the way? Or was he responding to the example of LOULIÉ, a longtime member of the GUISE MUSIC?

During the 1680s Loulié worked on a series of extremely succinct and practical handbooks for music teachers, and he also began drafting a method on the art of composing. His approach and his preoccupations were primarily French in perspective. Charpentier, by contrast, scrutinized Italian music in detail, especially the mass by the Roman composer Beretta, which he copied out and commented upon at some point between the spring of 1680 and the spring of 1682.[81] One cannot, of course, rule out the possibility that the goal of this exercise was to produce a fresh copy of a now-shabby work he had brought back from Rome in 1669, a work that had inspired his Italianate four-choir mass[A] of the early 1670s.

The composer's annotations about this mass suggest something quite different. Irrespective of whether Beretta's mass was an old keepsake, or whether it was new to his library, Marc-Antoine Charpentier became so caught up in the intellectual ferment going on at the Hôtel de Guise that he began studying the anatomy of Italian polychoral music.[82] In the process, he moved from being a "person of erudition" (that is, "someone who knows things that depend principally upon the good taste that should regulate our judgement") to being a "savant" ("someone who has applied himself to things where the mind alone is involved," that is, the sciences).[83] In other words, he became something more than a merely "erudite" composer whose works showed consummate good taste and delicacy, plus an understanding of musical rhetoric. He became a "savant" composer who, in addition to his pleasing erudition, knew the intricacies of traditional counterpoint and the most recent advances toward tonal harmony. Charpentier soon drafted a little composition treatise that he discussed with Loulié—who made a copy for himself.

By 1690, partly as a result of his investigations of musical theory, Charpentier had become so "savant" that he would eventually be praised by SÉBASTIEN DE BROSSARD: "In the opinion of all true connoisseurs, he has always passed for the most profound and most savant of the modern musicians." Charpentier's Médée of 1693 was, Brossard would assert, "undisputably the most savant and most exquisitely worked-out opera of all those published ... after Lully's death." So savant was this opera that Brossard confessed that it had been difficult to decide whether to put Charpentier's Médée among the theoretical works in his library, "that is, among the masters of the musical art," or among the operas written by the rank and file of French composers.[84]

[A] Cahiers XII–XIV, H. 4.

Scarcely a sinecure

The post of household composer to the Guises was scarcely a sinecure, with Monsieur Charpentier lounging about until his muse inspired him to jot down a heaven-sent theme in the middle of the night. Rather, periods of intense activity alternated with calmer weeks or months. And, since it almost certainly was the princesses or MONSIEUR DU BOIS who determined whether something should or should not be written, the composer was scarcely more a master of his time than DASSOUCY had been at the court of Savoy. Dassoucy's description of his eagerness to please the Dowager Duchess of Savoy and her son—and the nervous distraction, exhaustion, and jealousies it produced—could well have been written by Charpentier during the months when his outside work for the DAUPHIN and his ordinary obligations to the Guises forced him to double his usual output. Ever burlesque and given to hyperbole, Dassoucy recounted how:

> I was the Boesset of this court where, ... appearing at all the fine events, they had to revere me. ... I worked day and night to make enemies in this court, where I could cause myself to be esteemed, but could not cause myself to be loved; because someone who undertakes so many things, and who succeeds in more than one art, cannot possibly avoid being exposed to the hatred and the jealousy of the multitude. In addition to that, I had no other aim but to please Their Royal Highnesses. ... Being agitated not only by the extreme contentment that my victories brought me, but also by my violent desire to add new laurels to my conquests, I found it easy to stay up all night thinking of the means by which I could obtain a permanent post. ... And so, during the fourteen months I remained at that court ... I lost no opportunity to make myself indispensable. ... This enthusiasm remained with me at table, and even in bed. All night long I did nothing but scrape my theorbo, tootle the recorder, sing, and revise. I bothered all my neighbors, and all the neighbors who were thus disturbed cursed me a hundredfold. My domestics, whom I kept from sleeping, cursed me a hundred times a day. ... But I was agitated by such a noble desire ... [that] the time I had to spend eating and sleeping seemed to me wasted time. Thus I could not remain at table, I could not stay in bed. ... My mind was so tense, and my imagination so filled with the fire of my thoughts, that ... I did not hear half of what was said to me; so that in replying, I almost always took the negative for the affirmative, and the affirmative for the negative. ... If my speech was extravagant, my actions were no less so. I can't say how many times, while writing my *errs* or my *airs*, instead of the pounce box, I grabbed the inkstand and spilled all the ink on my paper; how many times, dreaming over my dinner plate, I

brought to my eye the morsel intended for my mouth; or how many times, with my brain all stuffed with chromatic scales, instead of descending the steps from my apartment one after the other, I almost broke my neck by going down them four at a time. Such was the effect of my zeal, which was so great for these benign [highnesses] that if I had shown as much for God, I have no doubt that He would already have rewarded me with His Paradise.[85]

The Guise composer was not only expected to write whatever the whims of the princesses and DU BOIS might dictate, he also had to complete commissions from any outsiders whom Mademoiselle de Guise might order him to serve. We have seen that Charpentier went through two periods of especially great pressure, the first in 1680, when he was working simultaneously for the Dauphin and the Guises, and the second in 1685, when he was inundated with requests to compose operas, pastorales, and so forth, for the Guises and other patrons.

In 1680 he had every reason to feel as frantic as Dassoucy. He filled almost a dozen notebooks[A] that year, trying to content the princesses, trying (to borrow Dassoucy's words) to "think of the means by which I could obtain a permanent post" with the DAUPHIN, and "losing no opportunity to make myself indispensable." Several of the works he composed that year were quite lengthy, far too lengthy to be dashed off in desperation, as a brief motet or hymn for two or three singers could conceivably be. That year he wrote an oratorio in honor of the patron saint of MADAME DE GUISE's charitable Confraternity of Saint Charles Borromeo.[B] He also struggled to complete a corpus of Holy Week music for the ABBAYE-AUX-BOIS,[C] a project that may well have been imposed on him by DU BOIS and VALLANT, who had friends at the abbey. Working against time, he was given a reprieve when the diocese of Paris modified its breviary: "I didn't finish the other eighteen responsories because of the change in the breviary," the composer noted beside the ninth responsory. That year's output also included oratorios[D] about the Prodigal Son and about the Last Judgment that probably were part of Madame de Guise's devotions at the THEATINES. (The first oratorio was written prior to Her Royal Highness's departure for Alençon in July, and the second one more or less coincides with her return to the Paris area somewhat before November 15).

[A] Roughly, from the final sheets of cahier 23 to the opening ones of cahier 32, and some, if not all of cahiers XXV–XXIX.
[B] Cahiers 23–24, H. 398.
[C] Cahiers 26–28, H. 96–110, and cahiers 28–29, H. 111–19.
[D] Cahier 29, H. 399; cahiers 30–31, H. 401.

The second period of frantic activity, 1685, saw Charpentier filling six arabic-numbered notebooks and five roman-numbered ones.[A] His compositions that year ranged from incidental music for the theater, to devotional pieces and oratorios for the Great Guise Music, and on to several pastorales in the vernacular, including one commissioned by the Duke of RICHELIEU, to be offered to the King during a celebration at the Duke's country estate.

Monsieur Charpentier's role in these events was not mentioned in the press, although DONNEAU DE VISÉ, at the *Mercure galant*, did allude to the services at the Abbaye-aux-Bois, and to Charpentier's contribution to those devotions. In contrast to our modern priorities, the nature of the music performed at an event and the identity of the composer or the singers were of secondary importance. As the composer's future colleagues at the SAINTE-CHAPELLE were then asserting, music "is not the essence of the church service, it only adds decorum and solemnity."

In this context, one better understands the silence surrounding the activities of seventeenth-century French composers—among them Charpentier. In actual fact, the "decorum" and the "solemnity" that music contributed to a service were relatively inexpensive. Take, for example, Charpentier's commission for a service at the Academy of Painting in 1687. (It presumably was CHARLES LE BRUN himself, or someone acting on his behalf, who approached Mademoiselle de Guise and asked permission to engage Charpentier.) The composer received 350 livres, just fourteen percent of the total expenditure of 2,378 livres.[86]

Did this frantic schedule contribute to the composer's illness in April 1683? Charpentier was sick most of that summer. In fact, when his brother-in-law, Jean Édouard, was buried on May 19, Marc-Antoine was not present. ARMAND-JEAN THE ENGINEER tended to the formalities alone. Two years later, when guardians were selected for ÉLISABETH CHARPENTIER's minor children, "Sieur Marc-Antoine Charpentier, bourgeois of Paris, residing in the Great Hôtel de Guise,"[87] attended the meeting at the Châtelet. At the bottom of the official report he calligraphed his formal signature in "round letters." However, he either refused to accept these responsibilities, or he was deemed financially too insecure to assume the task. Indeed, his income probably was sporadic and unpredictable, his remunerations by pleased patrons sometimes consisting of a silver platter, a candlestick, or some other decorative object that he could sell, and sometimes a velvet purse containing a diamond or a gold coin or two. Charpentier continued to reside at the Hôtel de Guise and compose for

[A] Cahiers 43b, 44, 45, 46, 47, and "II"; and cahiers XLV–XLIX.

the princesses until mid-1687. He had, however, stopped singing with the Great Guise Music a year earlier.

Between 1670 and 1687 almost none of the events to which he contributed music—be they devotional or be they courtly—were mentioned in the press. Indeed, since the very outset, neither princess had wanted her name cited in tandem with that of any protégé or householder. This would have made public a master–servant relationship that both women wanted to keep private. They did their good deeds in private, and they rewarded their faithful servants in private. In 1684 MONSIEUR DU BOIS had broken the silence imposed on him by Mademoiselle de Guise: "For a long time I have yearned for the opportunity to give [you] some public mark of my respect and my gratitude," he confessed, because the princess "gave [him] the means to finish this work, through the sweetness of the repose that her kindness permits for all those who have the honor of belonging to her."[88] (Expressing himself in a similar vein, in a dedication to Madame de Guise in 1694, Du Bois dared refer only to "the protection and, if I dare say, the very special kindness with which Your Royal Highness has honored me for so many years."[89])

Monsieur Charpentier never broke the silence surrounding his service to Mademoiselle de Guise. It was his friends, DONNEAU DE VISÉ and Corneille, who finally informed the public in +March 1688 that Monsieur Charpentier had composed "some things" for the late princess. No allusion to the composer's crucial protection by Madame de Guise found its way into the pages of the Mercure galant.

1687–1698
MUSIC MASTER TO THE JESUITS

By mid-1687 seventy-two-year-old MADEMOISELLE DE GUISE was in failing health. Since her household would be officially "broken up" immediately after her funeral—that is, her principal officer would break his baton of authority and declare the household dissolved—it was her duty to find a position for the composer who had served her so faithfully for seventeen years. A chapel-mastership at one of the THREE JESUIT HOUSES of the capital was the ideal solution.

For this, Monsieur Charpentier needed her protection, because he could no longer call upon his family's powerful JESUIT FRIENDS at the profess house. Two of them had died and the third was teaching in the provinces. Her Highness appears to have turned to her own JESUIT, Father La Chaise. Before the end of the year the composer had moved out of the Hôtel de Guise, in all probability having been given the customary cash "gratification."

At this point, there is a brief gap in Monsieur Charpentier's musical archives. That is to say, the notebooks for the last half of 1687 and part or all of 1688 are missing in both series. When the series resume, both sets of notebooks are made of Jesuit paper. (Manufactured by a Jesuit-owned mill, this paper bears a watermark with Jesuit emblems.)[90] In short, the paper he used for his personal archives proclaims that Monsieur Charpentier was now in the pay of the Society of Jesus, a position deemed to be "one of the most brilliant positions [a composer could hold] at that time."[91] If there is any merit to the conjectures made earlier in this portrait, to the effect that the Jesuits had paid special attention to him and had nourished his talents ever since his youth, then the reverend fathers' expectations were fulfilled in 1687.

It has been conjectured that the works in what today is called notebook "d" were written during the last six months of 1687. If so, this stray notebook made of Jesuit paper represents a brief moment of freedom —mid-1687 to early 1688—when the composer's "ordinary" and "extraordinary" duties for the Society were not yet clear. He apparently took it upon himself to write several works for PORT-ROYAL,[A] where his sister, MARIE THE CONVERSE, was a nun, plus three antiphons for female voices to be sung during the vespers of the Assumption.[B] (The latter works almost certainly were not for Mademoiselle de Guise's name day, for there is no evidence that she employed violinists.) Since none of these works were connected to the Jesuits, he filed the notebook away in a bundle that later would be known as the "fat notebook," *gros cahier*.[92] (We shall see that this unnumbered notebook contained perhaps the most personal work he ever wrote, his "Epitaph.")

The composer was now free from the servitude that had shaped his days for seventeen years. When he informed his friends of his new position, did he, like the protégé of another duchess, rejoice at "presently being reduced to living in a furnished room, where I am experiencing with pleasure all the sweetness of freedom"?[93] Did his friends express their joy over the end of his "servitude," as one of GAIGNIÈRES' friends would a few months later, after Mademoiselle de Guise's death: "I see you are now delivered from a servitude to which your honor alone has long kept you committed."

Neither the sources nor Charpentier's notebooks reveal unequivocally the specific Jesuit houses for which he worked, and exactly when. That is to say, his nephew, JACQUES ÉDOUARD, told Titon du Tillet that

---

[A] Cahier "d," H. 226, H. 227, H. 81, and perhaps H. 419 (Saint Augustine).
[B] Cahier "d," H. 50, H. 51, H. 52.

the composer had first been music master for the College of Louis-le-Grand, and then master at the Church of Saint-Louis.[94] The nephew's assertions are corroborated by other evidence. In 1686 Charpentier wrote *Celse Martyr* for a program at Louis-le-Grand where students performed a Latin tragedy that was accompanied by a musical one. Two years later came a similar work for the College, a devotional "opera" entitled *David et Jonathas*. In addition, an autograph manuscript of his was sent off to Quebec with the inscription: "Music Master at our College in Paris in 1689."[95] This suggests that Charpentier was composing at least part time for Louis-le-Grand as early as the summer of 1686, and that he worked for the College well into 1689. The content of the two sets of notebooks for the Jesuit years[96] suggests, however, that he rather quickly left the College and its devotional operas, and began composing for Saint-Louis.

Henceforth an established liturgy would shape his creativity. First and foremost, this meant that he moved from holy day to holy day, from Sunday vespers to Sunday vespers, setting liturgical texts associated with specific devotions. In his notebooks of the 1690s, gone are the operas, pastorales, and divertissements in the vernacular. Gone too are settings of Italian verse. And with two exceptions,[A] there are no more oratorios. In their place are motet after motet—primarily settings of psalms, Marian texts, music for Tenebrae, a few motets for Jesuit saints, and a few circumstantial works such as a *Te Deum* or music for a Corpus Christi street altar, *reposoir*.

Owing to the liturgical constraints inherent in the established devotional patterns at one or another Jesuit church, the new music master no longer spent so much time testing his versatility by moving from one musical genre to another. Perhaps he felt no need to do so, having proved his mastery to himself and to the world. In fact, he was now in a position where innovations could bring criticism.

Yet Saint-Louis was not without its challenges. How could he add expressiveness and variety to a rather fixed devotional program, with its inflexible psalm texts, its inflexible hymns and litanies to the Virgin, its inflexible lessons for Holy Week? The notebooks he filled during his decade with the Jesuits offer the raw materials for an appraisal of how Charpentier achieved variety within stasis and expressiveness within predictability, and how this "savant" used harmony and tonal "energies" to stir emotion.[97] One example of his attention to the details of Latin recitation has been preserved in a piece for Corpus Christi, where the *Pange lingua* melody was to be repeated, with different words. "Adjust

---

[A] Cahier 58, H. 416 (for Christmas); cahier LX, H. 417 (for Easter).

something in order to make it match the syllable lengths,"[98] he instructed his copyist.

Constrained though it was, this new world brought a certain freedom, after nearly eighteen years at the Hôtel de Guise. For example, instead of having to keep in mind the inevitable interpersonal rivalries within the Great Guise Music, and the individual skills and weaknesses of its youthful members, he now wrote for the experienced opera singers whom the Jesuits hired for their splendid vespers. He was given access to copyists—witness the instructions for them that he added to the copies in his personal archives.[99] And so much paper was made available to him that he was less compulsive about extending the staves into the margins and filling every page from top to bottom.

The arabic-numbered notebooks that Charpentier filled during his decade at Saint-Louis contain works that clearly correspond to the "ordinary" obligations of the music master there; and the roman-numbered ones contain primarily "extraordinary" works that were not part of his weekly obligations and for which additional compensation could be expected. Most of these extraordinary pieces appear to have been written for one or another of the Jesuit houses.[100] In other words, when he left the Hôtel de Guise and began to work for the Jesuits, Charpentier maintained the old distinction between the two sets of notebooks. However, beyond the evidence presented in the portrait of the THREE JESUIT HOUSES, little is known about the specific services for which most of these compositions were intended.

The notebooks for these years contain unsolved mysteries. For example, about halfway through his tenure with the Jesuits, Charpentier wrote a mass "for Monsieur Mauroy" and copied it into an arabic-numbered notebook.[A] In other words, he seems to have considered this mass to be part of his ordinary duties. Yet he either was totally unfamiliar with the church where the mass would be performed, or else he expected the composition to be reused in several churches. He went to considerable length to give instructions that would meet every contingency:

> The organ plays the first *Kyrie*, and if there is no organ, the prelude that follows will suffice. ... The organ, if there is one, plays a short couplet, after which the symphony is played again, and the *Kyrie* as above. ... Here one sings any motet, or plays any symphony one wishes for the Offertory.

A Cahiers 60–61, H. 6.

... and so forth, to the end of the mass. Did he expect this mass to be made available to Jesuit churches throughout France? Or perhaps throughout the Jesuit world?

Although it is tempting to assume that his new position gave him more freedom than he had enjoyed at the Hôtel de Guise, such an assumption may be misleading. For example, the number of oratorios dropped sharply, presumably because the Jesuit fathers were not especially interested in that genre. This suggests that the music master of Saint-Louis could not impose his preferences upon the devotional style that had made services at the church so popular with the public.

A few of Charpentier's "extraordinary" commissions took him far afield. Some of these extraordinary pieces were for the KING[A] and his court; and MADAME DE GUISE may well have requested a funeral mass for her half-sister, MADEMOISELLE DE MONTPENSIER.[B] Monsieur Charpentier was by no means a prisoner of the Jesuits. As long as he fulfilled his obligations at Saint-Louis, he could carry on other activities. For example, it probably was during the Jesuit years that he gave private lessons to several high-born ladies:

> I used to see a woman of distinguished rank, possessed of a very fine mind, who learned composition from ... the late Charpentier. Charpentier had filled her with Italian maxims ... I imagine that Charpentier, who had other high-ranking pupils, spoiled others as well.[101]

(We shall see that one of the "high-ranking people he spoiled" during these years was PHILIPPE II D'ORLÉANS' son.)

One piece composed during his tenure at Saint-Louis provides insights into Charpentier the man. In fact, it may well be one of the few surviving pieces that he composed for his own pleasure. The work is his famous epitaph, *Epitaphium Carpentarii*,[C] where the composer himself presumably sang the role of the *Umbra Carpentarii*, "Charpentier's Shadow," his ghost. Since the piece was copied onto Jesuit paper, it almost certainly was written between 1688 and the spring of 1698; yet he did not store it in his ordinary–extraordinary filing system. Instead, the "Epitaph" is one of the remnants of an unnumbered "fat notebook," *gros cahier*, that belonged to neither series.

Although it is unlikely that the composer was a good enough Latinist to have written such a complex and learned libretto, he clearly knew

---

[A] Cahier LXIII, H. 364, H. 264, H. 365.
[B] Cahier LXIII, H. 7 (and a fragement in cahier "b").
[C] Cahier "a," H. 474 (once part of the "fat notebook, *gros cahier*).

enough Latin to appreciate the allusions and the poetic nuances.[102] In fact, the piece almost certainly was written for performance before a group of learned friends who were very good Latinists. Its ridicule of François Chaperon of the SAINTE-CHAPELLE, and any jealousy Charpentier may have felt about Chaperon's nomination to that prestigious post back in 1679 have attracted the attention of several scholars, as have the commonplaces that Charpentier's ghost makes about himself:

> I was a musician, considered to be good by the good, and an ignoramus by the ignoramuses. And since the number of those who scorned me was greater than the number of those who praised me, music was a scant honor for me, it was a heavy burden; and just as, when I was born, I brought nothing into this world, when dying I took nothing with me.

Commonplaces these may be, but reliable sources leave no doubt that the composer had fervent enemies and zealous partisans; and his sister's papers reveal that he died indebted. That said, what the *Epitaphium* reveals about the intellectual circle to which this "savant" composer belonged in the 1690s is far more telling than any of several possible interpretations of one or another commonplace. If one presumes that Marc-Antoine Charpentier was fully aware of the subtleties of the text, we know that he was a more than mediocre Latinist; he was familiar with the spiritual exercises promoted by the Counter Reformation, and particularly by the Jesuits; he had some understanding of the history of religious music in the Italian Peninsula; and he was so widely read that he was aware of the double readings that could be given to the names of the characters called *Marcellus* and *Ignatius*.[103]

Not much is known about Marc-Antoine Charpentier's relations with his family during the late 1680s and the 1690s. When his niece, MARIE-ANNE ÉDOUARD, married in November 1689, he did not sign the contract. That does not necessarily mean that he had broken with his brothers and sisters and had refused to attend the ceremony. To the contrary: in 1692 he and ARMAND-JEAN THE ENGINEER apparently were living together on the rue Dauphine.[104] His absence at the wedding may therefore be fictive. That seems to have been the Charpentiers' way of staying clear of financial responsibilities that could threaten their own financial stability. That said, at the time of the marriage, Marc-Antoine presumably was receiving more than adequate wages from the Jesuits.

The education of the Duke of Chartres

During the early 1690s Monsieur Charpentier became involved in an important experiment, the education of Louis XIV's nephew, PHILIPPE III

D'ORLÉANS, Duke of Chartres. The Charpentier family had been on the margins of the Orléans' network ever since the 1650s, when their cousin, HAVÉ DE SAINT-AUBIN, had been a gentleman in ordinary to GASTON D'ORLÉANS. Marc-Antoine himself had benefitted from that protection in 1670, when he entered the service of ISABELLE D'ORLÉANS OF ALENÇON, the young Duchess of Guise. He had been treated generously by PHILIPPE II D'ORLÉANS, who on several occasions had agreed to be linked to the composer in the *Mercure galant*. Perhaps owing to services that Marc-Antoine rendered by teaching Chartres, but perhaps on their own personal merits, the sons of another cousin, GILLES CHARPENTIER THE SECRETARY, found their way into the household of PHILIPPE II, DUKE OF ORLÉANS. Then, in the early 1690s—in what should be seen as a protective continuity—Charpentier was selected as Chartres' teacher.

In the course of this educational venture, Charpentier worked closely with ÉTIENNE LOULIÉ, a theorist and performer who had played with the GUISE MUSIC and subsequently taught Chartres the "elements" of musical notation and theory.[105] When JACQUES ÉDOUARD summarized for Titon du Tillet the role his uncle had played in Chartres' education, he seems to have blended truth and myth: "Monseigneur the Duke of Orléans [Philippe III, formerly Duke of Chartres], grandson of France, learned composition from him and made him intendant of his Music." Was it Édouard who used the word "intendant"? The term implies an official household post, but there is no evidence that Charpentier ever held such a position. In the same vein, perhaps it was Édouard who suggested that his uncle wrote most of a lost opera entitled *Philomèle*: Chartres "who had a hand in this work, wanted to keep it"[106]—that is, the prince refused to have it published, so that it would remain exclusive. As far as can be determined, these composition lessons began in November 1692 and continued until June 1693, when the prince went off to war. Chartres returned to Paris in late October, and *Philomèle* was performed three times at the Palais-Royal in 1694.[107]

Being engaged to teach the Duke of Chartres meant conforming to a model established by the prince's preceptors back in 1688. The very fact that Monsieur Charpentier was deemed capable of participating in this project provides precious insights into both his public persona and his principal character traits. These insights are especially valuable because they contradict DASSOUCY's bitter, negative remarks about him.

To teach this prince, one had to be an "honest person" who knew how to converse: "Surround [the prince] at all times with honest people who like him," the instructions read. "Be sure he avoids commoners who are dull." Above all, the prince was to have no contact with the "dregs" of society. In other words, Marc-Antoine Charpentier was perceived as being—and presumably was—upright and very courteous; he could express himself clearly and elegantly; and although he was a commoner, he was not "dull." In addition to these basic qualities, a teacher was expected to be either "erudite" or "savant." (A reminder: an erudite person knew the "things that depend principally upon the good taste that should regulate our judgement," while a savant "applied himself to things where the mind alone is involved," that is, the sciences. We saw earlier that Charpentier belonged to both categories.) As the educational program stated, "When not at war, a prince should attach himself to the conversation of honest people, which includes two sorts of persons: persons of erudition and persons who are savant."[108]

In addition, if Charpentier was selected for this mission, it was because the preceptors believed he could impose himself upon a high-spirited young noble, winning his respect while being simultaneously serious, inventive, humorous, and devout. (All the teachers were expected to teach the youth to respect the "great religious events.") Since "a prince always wants to be right," the composer would have to demonstrate his own strength of will. At the same time he must punish the prince for bad behavior, strike fear into him so that he would be willing to learn, keep him in good humor and entertain him so that he would not detest his studies, and teach him by examples, in order to catch the prince's attention and make him want to imitate each example. Without these skills, no teacher could hope to succeed, because the prince "ridicules complacent teachers." In preparation for the composition lessons, Charpentier revised the little manuscript method he had drafted a few years earlier.[109] For example, he added a list of the "energies" of the different *modes*, or keys. Under Charpentier's tutelage, the prince not only blossomed as a musician, he also developed a lasting respect and fondness for his teacher.

Médée

Now that Lully was dead, Monsieur Charpentier could try his hand at a full-length opera. The opportunity came in 1693. (Chartres' lessons may explain why Charpentier was selected to write an opera for the Royal Academy that year.) That summer he and his old collaborator, THOMAS CORNEILLE, joined forces for *Médée*, which opened on December 11, 1693. SÉBASTIEN DE BROSSARD viewed the opera as a demonstration of Charpentier's consummate skill, although a "plot" caused it to close after less than a dozen performances. (The run of a successful opera could last for months: for example Lully's *Bellerophon* was performed for nine months running.) The authors of *Médée* had the singular misfortune to present this opera just after the eruption of a "quarrel" about morality in the theater. Immediately after Lully's death a devout faction had begun booing and hissing each new opera, and tracts hostile to both theater and opera began stoking the fervor of the anti-theater faction. In 1693 the Sorbonne was consulted. It pointed out just how dangerous operas were to spectators' souls:

> Opera is all the more dangerous because, with the help of the music, all of whose notes are chosen and disposed specifically to move [the audience], the soul is made far more susceptible to passion.[110]

This was the "plot" to which the sources refer: it killed *Médée* in 1693— and Élisabeth Jacquet de La Guerre's *Céphale et Procris* in 1694.

Into his long article about *Médée* in the *Mercure galant*, DONNEAU DE VISÉ inserted a few consoling words for Corneille and Charpentier, whose masterpiece had fared so badly: "Its destiny was that of fine objects, against which envy speaks out first; but afterwards [these fine objects] shine all the more."

When 1693 dawned, Charpentier had been head over heels in work. His day-to-day obligations for the Jesuits alternated with his lessons for Chartres. The prince's departure in June had permitted the composer to concentrate on his opera. Chartres' return in late October, just as rehearsals were beginning, could hardly have come at a worse time— especially because the prince was proving so eager to emulate his teacher that he insisted on writing an opera all his own, the lost *Philomèle*.

Was it in 1693 that an overworked Charpentier went through his old notebooks and singled out some old Guise pieces that were now his property, instructing his copyists to adjust the vocal ranges?[111] Was it in 1693 that he recopied and perhaps revised some of his early compositions for the Jesuits?[112]

1698–1704
MUSIC MASTER AT THE SAINTE-CHAPELLE

In May 1698 news began to circulate that François Chaperon, the music master at the SAINTE-CHAPELLE, was gravely ill. Monsieur Charpentier promptly got in touch with his former pupil, PHILIPPE III D'ORLÉANS, and begged for his protection, thereby disappointing SÉBASTIEN DE BROSSARD, who was dashing to Paris to pose his own candidacy. Some months later ÉTIENNETTE CHARPENTIER loaned her brother the money to reimburse Chaperon's heirs, in what amounted to a purchase of the position. Monsieur Charpentier was now a paid servant of the Monarchy. The final six years of his life would almost certainly prove more constraining than anything he had known at the Hôtel de Guise or at the Church of Saint-Louis.

In order to be listed on the payroll of the chapel, as part of the living held by Abbé de Neuchelles, the new master was required to become a cleric "in ordinary." On June 18, 1698, during the high mass, he was therefore received as a cleric—that is, he was tonsured, took an oath in the sacristy, and was assigned a seat at the end of a row in the right-hand choir stalls. (If there are any merits to the conjecture that, as an adolescent, Marc-Antoine Charpentier had entertained the idea of becoming a religious, that vocation became a reality in 1698.)

The canonical hours henceforth determined his movements within the precincts of the Palais de Justice. Calling upon the pedagogical skills he had honed with Chartres, he instructed the eight choirboys, rehearsed them, worked with the grammar master to ensure that they pronounced Latin correctly, escorted the children to and fro between the chapel and their lodging, and supervised their vacations in the countryside. Although he occupied a private room in the vast apartment allocated to the master and the choirboys by the royal administration, the children were never out of earshot. All the while, he had to keep in mind the rivalries, the battles for precedence, the challenging acoustics in the Sainte-Chapelle, and the sometimes marginal vocal skills of the choristers.

Master Charpentier's compositions for the Sainte-Chapelle did not survive, for heirs customarily turned these manuscripts over to the royal officials immediately after a master's death. Owing to the degradations of time and political upheaval, the music collection from the chapel has been lost. Thus nothing remains of Charpentier's output for these six years but a few "extraordinary" works. Ironically, we know a great deal about the music master's position at the Sainte-Chapelle, and the conditions under which he worked; but we are totally ignorant of how he coped with wretched acoustics and, perhaps, his rather rigid and unimaginative colleagues.

Master Charpentier died in his lodging in the Palais de Justice at seven in the morning, February 24, 1704. His colleagues arranged a fine funeral—an occasion that broke the routine. When the bills began coming in, the Treasurer was so appalled that he drew up a list of prices that henceforth must not be exceeded. Why such large expenditures? An unusual gesture of affection on the part of bereaved colleagues? A gesture of respect for the man who had provided such lovely music? Or had the bills been padded by craftsman relatives to whom one or another of the chapel personnel had sent a bit of business?

Marc-Antoine Charpentier was buried in the little cemetery that encircled the apse of the Sainte-Chapelle. ÉTIENNETTE THE LINENER saw to his estate without consulting a notary. Having surrendered to the royal administration her late brother's compositions for the chapel—which by law belonged to the king—she kept the rest of his notebooks and eventually passed them on to her nephew, JACQUES ÉDOUARD. After several failed attempts to make money from the manuscripts, Édouard sold his inheritance, the Charpentier *Mélanges*, to the Royal Library in 1727.

NOTES

Panel 1, The Charpentiers of Meaux

I, Denis the Tawer, pp. 3–5

1. AN, ZZ^1 203, fol. 418, apprenticeship, Jan. 1, 1560.
2. The most revealing documents are: AD-77, 130 E 7, Aug. 6, 1561; 129 E 34, Dec. 31, 1592 (agreement with the Pasquiers); 79 E 11, Sept. 13, 1611, involving land at Coulommes and witnessed by SAMUEL THE WEAVER. See also Viel, pp. 2–14, to whom I am profoundly indebted for copies and transcriptions of most of the acts cited in his article.
3. Carro, pp. 184–324, and p. 520 for a list of those killed in 1572; Dom Toussaints Du Plessis, *Histoire de l'Eglise de Meaux* (Paris, 1731), I, pp. 379–416.
4. AD-77, 135 E 23, Jan. 15, 1606; 79 E 14, My. 4, 1614; 135 E 24, Jul. 8, 1609, where Nicolas the Sergeant is called the "uncle" of Pasquier's daughter Marie; GG 1, Oct. 6, 1590, Denis' son, LOUIS THE BAILIFF, stands godfather for Pasquier's son, JACQUES THE NOTARY.
5. AD-77, 79 E 14, My. 4, 1614.

II, Louis the Bailiff, pp. 6–9

1. Viel, pp. 2–14.
2. AD-77, 173 E 11, Jan. 16, 1609 (Louis is a witness); 135 E 24, Jul. 8, 1609 (he is the "uncle" of Pasquier Charpentier's daughter Marie); 135 E 25, Jul. 20, 1611 (a contract involving the Soudains).
3. AN, MC, V, 40, Je. 17, 1613, and V, 48, Jul. 2, 1617 (her relatives and those of her late brother, who had moved to Meaux in the 1590s).
4. AD-77, 146 E 3, Apr. 7, 1626.
5. AN, MC, V, 40, Je. 17, 1613; AD-77, 79 E 27, 1624.
6. AD-77, 112 E 31, Feb. 11, 1627; 146 E 3, Apr. 7, 1626.
7. AD-77, 129 E 45, Oct. 12, 1634.

III, Nicolas the Sergeant, pp. 10–13

1. AD-77, 80 E 13, Feb. 5, 1597.   2. AD-77, 135 E 23, Jan. 15, 1606.
3. AD-77, 151 E 25, Je. 6, 1660.   4. AD-77, 79 E 56, Je. 14, 1641.
5. AD-77, 135 E 24, Jul. 8, 1609.
6. AD-77, 2 Bp 1750, and 141 E 44, Aug. 5, 1614.   7. AD-77, 112 E 18, Apr. 29, 1618.
8. Among the revealing entries in the baptismal records are: AD-77, GG 1, Feb. 13, 1589: Marguerite Cosset, daughter of Roland Cosset, *élu*, is godmother for DAVID CROYER's daughter; GG 1, Jul. 28, 1589: Perrette Cosset, daughter of Nicolas Cosset, is godmother for the daughter of Marie Charpentier (daughter of PASQUIER THE MEASURER) and Nicolas Brion; GG 29, Mar. 5, 1600: Jean Cosset is godfather for the son of Pasquier the Measurer; GG 42, Oct. 13, 1588: Agnès Cosset, daughter of Roland Cosset, lieutenant general at Meaux, is godmother for the daughter of Marguerite Charpentier (Pasquier's sister) and Abraham Blanchet.
9. Acts involving family and inheritances for the Le Bers, Royers, and the rich officers named Charpentier: AD-77, 132, E 1, My. 10, 1572; 132 E 4, Nov. 23, 1576; 132 E 5, My. 15, 1579; 80 E 6, Apr. 16, 1580; 173 E 10, My. 19, 1602; 141 E 41, Je. 5, 1613 (Marie Charpentier, wife of Isaac Le Ber, councillor at Meaux); 112 E 26, Jul. 22, 1623 (Marie Charpentier, widow Le Ber; Nicolas Charpentier, councillor and *élu* at Meaux; and Marie Charpentier, wife of Jean Chabouillé); 80 E 77, Apr. 16, 1632 (Marie Charpentier, widow Le Ber; Nicolas Charpentier, councillor and *élu* at Meaux; Marie Charpentier, wife of Jean Chabouillé; Martin-Jean Chabouillé and Anne Royer, his wife; Louis Royer, second husband of Magdeleine de Vernon, whose first husband was Jean Charpentier, and whose children were Marie Charpentier–Chabouillé and Nicolas Charpentier, councillor and *élu*); 80 E 77, Dec. 27, 1632 (Nicolas Charpentier, councillor and *élu*, and Marie Chalmot, his wife); 112 E 54, Feb. 5, 1642 (Isaac Le Ber attends the wedding of Perrette Preudhomme, Marguerite Charpentier–Blanchet's granddaughter).

IV, Pierre the Chapelain and Étienne the Practitioner, pp. 14–16

1. For example, AD-77, 147 E 28, Je. 17, 1642; 112 E 66, Oct. 19, 1652; 151 E 24, Nov. 12, 1657 (Robert Charpentier is given three titles: "priest, sacristan, churchwarden," that is, *marguillier*. *Marguilliers* usually were laymen.)
2. AN, MC, XXIII, 308, Jan. 16, 1662.   3. AD-77, 129 E 57, Feb. 28, 1648.
4. AD-77, GG 32, baptismal records for Châge, Jul. 24, 1648; 79 E 161, Jan. 5, 1682.

V, Pasquier the Measurer, pp. 17–18

1. AD-77, 130 E 41, Oct. 5, 1579.
2. AD-77, 80 E 10, Jan 21, 1593 (the Oudots and Charpentiers of Chambry). See also AD-77, 141 E 28, Jan. 4, 1606, wedding contract of Antoine Charpentier, surgeon of Meaux, son of the late Médard Charpentier, signed by Pasquier Charpentier, one of his "relatives and friends."
3. AD-77, 135 E 24, Jul. 8, 1609; 2 Bp 1750; and 141 E 44, Aug. 5, 1614.
4. AD-77, 142 E 44, Sept. 27, 1645.
5. AD-77, 112 E 50, Aug. 1639, which mentions the loan made in 1628.
6. AD-77, 142 E 44, Sept. 27, 1645.

VI, Jacques the Notary, pp. 19–21

1. AD-77, 141 E 44, Aug. 5, 1614; and for the Chabouillés, AD-77, 80 E 43, My. 13, 1616; 143 E 23, Mar. 21, 1626.
2. AD-77, 2 Bp 1750, Aug. 6, 1614, witnessed by Jean Cosset.
3. AD-77, E 26, Jul. 30, 1623.   4. AD-77, 112 E 50, Jan. 21, 1639.
5. AD-77, 112 E 57, Dec. 28, 1643.   6. AD-77, 112 E 59, Jul. 4, 1645.
7. AD-77, 112 E 60, Feb. 7, 1646.
8. AN, MC, LIX, 112, Feb. 10, 1654 ("alderman," *échevin*).

VII, Samuel the Weaver, pp. 22–23

1. AD-77, 173 E 6, Jan. 10, 1595.   2. AD-77, 135 E 15, Apr. 21, 1596.
3. AD-77, 79 E 11, Sept. 13, 1611 (Samuel witnesses an act involving the Soudains and DENIS THE TAWER).
4. AD-77, 141 E 37, Je. 29, 1611. For more on the Samuel Charpentiers and the Boudets: AD-77, 141 E 48, Aug. 21, 1616; 80 E 51, Dec. 8, 1621; 129 E 50, Je. 14, 1640; 150 E 42, Oct. 27, 1656 (reference to André Boudet, upholsterer, living "beneath the pillars of the Halles"); Émile Magne, "Molière et la Maison des Pilliers des Halles," *XVIIᵉ Siècle* (1964), pp. 552–71: in 1672 Boudet gave Molière the income from renting this house.
5. AD-77, 79 E 18, Apr. 8, 1619.
6. AN, MC, LII, 9, Sept. 6, 1636 (Louis Croyer's inventory, document 54: a contract dated Jan. 31, 1634).
7. AD-77, 147 E 23, Feb. 10, 1637 (property at Neufmontiers that Samuel's son Louis had inherited from his father); 142 E 44, Sept. 27, 1645 (PASQUIER THE MEASURER's heirs settle his estate, which includes land at Neufmontiers worth 200 livres).
8. AD-77, 150 E 25, Oct. 11, 1649.

Panel 2, The Parisian Cousins

I, Monsieur and Madame David Croyer, pp. 27–30

1. AD-77, B 224, "Roole de ceulx qui ont juré la Saincte Union des Catholicques"; Carro.
2. AD-77, 130 E 6, Jan. 24, 1557/1558; 130 E 25, Oct. 23, 1572 (Quentin's sister was Marie Croyer, wife of a certain Charles Charpentier); 134 E 1, Nov. 14, 1573; AN, MC, III, 475, Oct. 13, 1604.
3. BN, ms. fr. 32588 (parish records for Saint-Jean-en-Grève); BN, PO, 868, "Cosset," fol. 10.
4. BN, PO, 644, "Chabouillé," fols. 23, 25.
5. Some typical acts: AN, MC, XXXV, 54, Je. 2, 1606; XXXV, 57, Apr. 14, 1608 (David was legal guardian of the children of Quentin Croyer, merchant at Mousseaux, near Meaux); LXXV, 60, Aug. 1 and Nov. 27, 1609.
6. AN, MC, XXXV, 70, Nov. 22, 1614.   7. AD-77, 112 E 34, Nov. 21, 1628.
8. AN, MC, XXXV, 71, Jan. 11, 1615.

9. Antoine Furetière, *Le Roman bourgeois*, 1666: "Histoire de Lucrèce la bourgeoise." The typical dowry of a merchant's daughter, he asserts, ranged from 6,000 to 12,000 livres.

10. AN, MC, XXXV, 74, Jan. 20, 1616.   11. AN, MC, LII, 4, Jan. 22, 1634.

12. AN, Y 165, fol. 430, Aug. 17, 1625.   13. AN, MC, LII, 9, Sept. 6, 1636.

II, Sevin the Aide, Sevin the Bishop, pp. 31–35

1. BN, DB, 614, "Sevin," no. 16181, especially fols. 1, 5; Léon Lecestre, ed., *Mémoires du chevalier de Quincy* (Paris, 1898), vol. I, pp. vi–viii.

2. AD-77, 142 E 2, My. 26, 1599; AN, MC, XXXV, 185, My. 5, 1607.

3. AN, MC, CXXII, 1584, Apr. 21, 1618.   4. BN, ms. fr. 20784, fols. 553–56.

5. BN, ms. fr. 17400, fol. 109.

6. Joseph Bergin, *The Making of the French Episcopate, 1589–1661* (New Haven, 1996); BN, ms. fr. 23508, fols. 52, 72 ff., 347–52 (his career and death).

7. BN, ms. fr. 17362, My. 5, 1654; and for other letters to Séguier from the Sevin brothers, BN, ms. fr. 17400 fols. 109–13, 185, and 187–88; ms. fr. 17407, Je. 22, 1666.

8. BN, ms. fr. 17362, Apr. 22, 1651, and My. 5, 1654; ms. fr. 17406, Dec. 16, 1665; ms. fr. 17407, Aug. 25, 1666 (correspondence with Séguier).

9. BN, ms. fr. 17406, Dec. 16, 1665.   10. BN, ms. fr. 17409, Jan. 5, 1667.

11. BN, DB, 614, "Sevin," no. 16182, fols. 3v–4.

III, Havé de Saint-Aubin the Gentleman, pp. 36–37

1. AD-77, 80 E 42, Je. 28, 1615; BN, PO, 1494, "Havé," fols. 10, 22.

2. AN, MC, XXXV, 74, Jan. 20, 1616.

3. AN, MC, LII, 9, Sept. 6, 1636 (inventory of Louis Croyer).

4. AD-77, 112 E 50, Aug. 26, 1639.   5. AN, Y 207, fol. 428v, Aug. 6, 1665.

6. AN, MC, XXXIX, 109, Mar. 15, 1664.

IV, Gilles the Secretary, pp. 38–43

1. AD-77, GG 6, Nov. 14, 1620.   2. AD-77, 112 E 50, Jan. 21, 1639.

3. *Cent ans*, p. 614. Removed from the archives of notary XXXVI in the nineteenth century, the document is currently in private hands. Thus it was impossible to verify the accuracy of the proposed reading: "H. Charpentier."

4. AD-77, 74 E 11, Sept. 13, 1611.

5. AN, MC, LVI, 578, wedding contracts of Jan. 27 and Jan. 29, 1658.

6. Ranum, "Lully."

7. Acts in which Gilles is described as Saint-Luc's secretary: AN, MC, LIX, 112, Feb. 10, 1654, and XVI, 117, Dec. 5, 1658; AD-77, 151 E 20, Nov. 21, 1655; 151 E 23, Dec. 17, 1658; 151 E 25, Je. 6, 1660.

8. AN, MC, XCIX, 214, Je. 14, 1663.   9. BN, ms. fr. 17406, fol. 127, My. 22, 1665.

10. AN, X²ᴬ 340, "arrêts tant d'audience que du Conseil," Apr. 4–Je. 30, 1665.

11. AD-77, 2 Bp 1750, Je. 1664.

12. AN, MC, XVIII, 93 and 94, Apr. 13, Je. 1, Je. 15, Jul. 13, 1680; XVIII, 384, Aug. 2 and 3, 1691 (Gilles receives 6,000 écus).

13. BN, Rés, Morel de Thoisy, 82, fols. 352–53; AN, MC, XI, 324, My. 18, 1691.

14. AN, MC, LVII, 187, My. 8, Je. 12, Je. 17, 1696.

15. AN, MC, LVII, 196, Apr. 25 and 29, 1698 (preamble of Justine Liger's inventory).

16. AN, Y 14062, affixing of seals in the residence of the late René Charpentier, Jan. 4, 1734, in the presence of his nephew.

Panel 3, The Composer's Family

I, Louis the Scrivener, pp. 47–52

1. On the *maître écrivain* see Lespinasse, *Histoire générale de Paris* (Paris, 1897), vol 3: *Métiers et corporations de la Ville de Paris*, pp. 665–70; AN, Y 9335, registers of the corporation, 1673–1729; B² 13, fols. 158v–64, instructions for a scrivener engaged by Colbert at Rochefort, 1671; BN, ms. fr. 11768, rules for the sworn master scriveners of Paris, fols. 361–73; ms. fr. 25047, p. 278: a

young man named Mazaudon came to Paris "to work for a procurator ... writing very perfectly, he became secretary to M. [Pierre] Séguier," who eventually gave him a venal office in the Chancellery.

2. For example, it could be *Toutre*, rather than *Toutré*. I wish to thank the archivist-paleographers of the Minutier Central who concluded that "Toutré" is the more likely reading.

3. AN, MC, XXIII, 308, Jan. 16, 1662.

4. BN, PO, 1359, "Gonzague," fols. 156, 189 (the Duke names a comptroller), 207, 213, 247 (in 1640 the princesses accept a resignation); AN, MC, LXXIII, 387 (acts dated 1647, signed by the late Duke's administrators); E. Gillois, *Les Comtes et les ducs de Nevers* (Nevers, 1863).

5. Brenet, p. 260 ("native of the diocese of Paris": since these registers usually say that a choirboy came "from Paris" and sometimes even name the parish, it cannot be ruled out that Charpentier was born elsewhere in the diocese); AN, MC, XXIII, 308, Jan. 16, 1662 ("aged eighteen or thereabouts," an expression that generally refers to the date of a baptismal certificate and that, in this case, suggests that the composer was born in 1643, probably during the summer or early fall).

6. AN, MC, XXIII, 308, Jan. 16, 1662 (postscript about "Mme. Guyot"; LXXII, 124, Apr. 10, 1690 (Jeanne Guyot's wedding, and her late mother's name).

7. A. Chéruel, *Mémoires sur la vie publique et privée de Fouquet* (Paris, 1862), vol. 2, pp. 132 (Mme. d'Huxelles, daughter of President Louis de Bailleul) and p. 351 (the dates of the arrests); BN, ms. 500 Colbert, 233, fol. 97 (Le Ragois), fol. 212–13 (JACQUES I DALIBERT), fol. 298 (Étienne Ferrand: it is not clear if he was related to the FERRANDS of the Châtelet); 500 Colbert, 234, fols. 212 (JACQUES I DALIBERT), fol. 620 (Olivier Picques, a future SEVIN in-law, per BN, DB, 614, "Sevin, no. 16182, fol. 3), and fol. 649 (the Le Ragois de Bretonvilliers, in-laws of the Bailleuls); 500 Colbert, 235, fol. 271–73 (Jacques Charpentier, *commissaire des guerres*); BN, n.a. fr. 9665, fol. 50 (the same Jacques Charpentier); AN, MC, 247, Jan. 2, 1674, and XC, 277, Jan 11, 1689 (acts involving Jacques Charpentier, *commissaire des guerres*, a straw man for Louis de Bailleul); D. Dessert, "Finances et société au XVIIᵉ siècle," *Annales, E. S. C.*, 29 (1974), with an appendix of financiers (among them Bailleul's in-law, Le Ragois de Bretonvilliers, and three of MARIE TALON's relatives: La Bazinière, Vanel, and Verthamon).

8. AN, MC, VI, 590, Nov. 13, 1689.

9. AN, Y 3948B, 3949A and 3949B. None of these files, many of them signed by "Ferrand" (Civil Lieutenant FERRAND, Étiennette Charpentier's friend) or "De Ryans" (ARMAND-JEAN DE RIANTS) contains a Charpentier guardianship.

II, Étiennette the Linener, pp. 53–62

1. On mistress lineners, see BN, ms. fr. 21796, "Lingères" (police papers); Daniel Roche, *La Culture des apparences* (Paris, 1989), pp. 279–312.

2. AN, LXVIII, 212, Jul. 8, 1672.

3. AN, MC, XCI, 398, Je. 27, 1676 (*rente*); and VIII, 881, Jul. 5, 1708 (rental of shop).

4. Comédie, Reg. 20, Dec. 10, 1687, and Dec. 17, 1687; Feb. 11, 1688.

5. AN, F³¹ 96 (her shop: plan of Ilot 22).

6. AN, XCI, 397, Jan. 30, 1676; and XXIII, 399, Mar. 22, Apr. 5 and 22, 1709 (second will, inventory and receipts).

7. "Mémoire" of 1726, fol. 15v.　　　　8. AN, Y 10830, Jan. 1, 1709.

9. AN, Y 10830, Mar. 22, 1709, the sealing of the rooms.

III, Élisabeth the Wife and Mother, pp. 63–68

1. Racine, II, pp. 628–29.　　　　　　2. AN, MC, XXIII, 309, Aug. 24, 1662.

3. AN, MC, XXIII, 275, Aug. 29 and Sept. 23, 1637 (obligation and wedding); BN, Factum, 4° Fm 988, no. 22522 (a family squabble).

4. Yolande de Brossard, *Musiciens de Paris* (Paris, 1965), p. 116.

5. AN, MC, LXVI, 148, Nov. 7, 1672.

6. AN, MC, XXIII, 399, Apr. 5, 1709, preamble of ÉTIENNETTE THE LINENER's inventory.

7. Michel Le Moël, "Un foyer d'Italianisme à la fin du XVIIᵉ siècle: Nicolas Mathieu, curé de Saint-André-des-Arts," *Recherches*, 3 (1963).

8. BN, Fichier Laborde, no. 10949, My. 19, 1683.

9. AN, Y 4003A, Feb. 1685, "avis des parents, tuition Édouard."

10. AN, MC, VI, 582, Feb. 20, 1685.

11. Comédie, Reg. 20, Dec. 10 and 17, 1687; Feb. 11, 1688.

12. AN, MC, XXIII, 399, Apr. 5, 1709 (doc. 6: loans).

IV, Marie the Converse, pp. 69–75

1. Her name appears on a list of professed converses drawn up in 1661, BN, ms. fr.17774, fol. 2v, and also in *Histoire des persécutions des religieuses de Port-Royal, écrite par elles-mêmes*, éd. Pierre Leclerc (Villefranche, 1753), p. xii; William Ritchey Newton, *Sociologie de la communauté de Port-Royal* (Paris, 1999), p. 61.

2. AN, MC, XXIII, 399, deposited Mar. 12, 1709.

3. *Constitutions du monastère de Port Royal du S. Sacrement*, by Agnès Arnauld (Mons, 1665), pp. 74–75.

4. *Constitutions*, p. 62.   5. *Constitutions*, pp. 98 ff.

6. Racine, II, p. 569.   7. *Constitutions*, pp. 91–93.

8. Racine, II, pp. 637–38, 639–40.   9. *Constitutions*, pp. 93–98.

10. AN, LL 1613, fol. 3 (Oct. 14, 1695).

11. Charles-Augustin Sainte-Beuve, *Port-Royal* (Paris, 1860), IV, p. 10.

12. *Vies édifiantes & intéressantes des Religieuses de Port Royal*, 1751, III, p. 280; Racine, II, pp. 160–63.

13. Racine, II, pp. 163–70 (departure of the nuns and separation of the two houses).

V, Armand-Jean the Engineer, pp. 76–78

1. AN, MC, XXIII, 308, Mar. 15, 1662.

2. On the *maître écrivain*, AN, Y 9335 (Register of masters); BN, ms. fr. 11768, fols. 361–73 (rules) and ms. fr. 21739, fol. 144 (rules); AN, Marine, B² 13, fols. 158v–64 (tasks of a scrivener working for the Navy, 1671).

3. BN, Fichier Laborde, no. 10949.

4. Vincennes, ms. in-fol. 208ᵇ, no. 1, pp. 23, 35 ff (1683); ms. in-fol. 206 VI, fols. 105, 106, 110 ff, 227–28 (1692); Anne Blanchard, *Les Ingénieurs du "Roy" de Louis XIV à Louis XVI: étude du corps des fortifications* (Montpellier, 1979).

5. AN, MC, VI, 582, Apr. 10, 1685.

6. AN, Y 4003A, Feb. 20, 1685, avis des parents, tuition Édouard.

7. AN, MC, CI, 58, Jan. 16 and Feb. 9, 1688; VI, 588, Oct. 7 and 12, 1688; Du Pradel, I, p. 213.

8. AN, MC, VI, 590, Nov. 13, 1689.

VI, Marie-Anne the Unfortunate, pp. 79–80

1. AN, MC, CI, 58, Jan. 16, Feb. 9, 1688; VI, 588, Oct. 7 and 12, 1688.

2. AN, MC, VI, 590, Nov. 13, 1689.

3. AN, MC, XI, 324, Je. 5 and 25, 1691; XI, 326, Dec. 30, 1691 (the Moreaus).

4. BN, Factum, f° F3, no. 1875.   5. AN, MC, XXIII, 399, Apr. 27, 1709.

VII, Jacques the Bookseller-Printer, pp. 81–88

1. BN, ms. fr. 21748, p. 6 (baptism date); AN, MC, LXXIII, 564, Je. 25, 1697; and BN, ms. fr. 21838, fol. 143v.

2. BN, ms. fr. 21856, fol. 209; ms. fr. 21748, pp.1, 3, 6, and fols. 95, 127.

3. BN, ms. fr. 21872, fols. 268, 271v (confraternity); ms. fr. 21871, fol. 17 (register of booksellers and printers); Béatrice Sarrazin, "La Librairie et l'imprimerie parisiennes à la fin du XVIIᵉ siècle," *Revue française d'histoire du livre*, no. 47, Apr.–Je. 1985, pp. 296–332. On the book trade in general, see Henri-Jean Martin, *Livre, pouvoirs et société au XVIIᵉ siècle (1598–1701)* (Geneva, 1969).

4. Lesclapart: BN, ms. fr. 21856, fol. 260, Oct. 20, 1713; AN, MC., LXXXII, 57, My. 4, 1698 (Le Page–Lesclapart marriage).

5. BN, ms. fr. 21949, p. 48: the title was *Remarques critiques sur la nouvelle édition du Dictionnaire historique de Morery donné en 1704*.

6. "Mémoire" of 1726, fols. 13v–14.

7. BN, ms. fr. 21949, p. 430.

8. Eight of the works in this publication cannot be dated, because they are not part of the *Mélanges*. Of the four datable pieces, three probably were unknown to the Duke: H. 22 and H. 243 were written for the Guises in 1677 and 1679, when he was a little boy; and H. 419 appears to have been written for PORT-ROYAL in 1687 or 1688, when the Duke was not yet an adolescent. The Duke could, on the other hand, have heard H. 268, which dates from the mid-1690s and probably was composed for one of the THREE JESUIT HOUSES. This somewhat explodes our notion that the printer was a musician and had talked with his late uncle about his works and the circumstances surrounding their creation. The facts he transmitted to Titon du Tillet appear to be more or less accurate, although they probably were based on family tradition rather than firsthand knowledge about his uncle's career.

9. Pierre Amand, *Nouvelles observations sur la pratique des accouchemens, avec la manière de se servir d'une nouvelle machine* (Paris, 1714).

10. Cessac, MAC, pp. 22–25 (the *Journal de Verdun*).

11. AN, MC, XIII, 186, Mar. 19, 1716; Philippe Vendrix et al., *L'Opéra-comique en France au XVIIIe siècle* (Liege, 1992), pp. 16, 34, 37, 48 (Saint-Edme).

12. This "memorandum," *mémoire*, has been attributed to Édouard; but the hand is not his, and there is no evidence to suggest that the bookseller-printer was capable of making the "reflections" it includes concerning matters of "taste" and connoisseurship, and the esthetic merits of Charpentier's music. Indeed, it is highly unlikely that the third-person allusion to "Sieur Édouard, the author's nephew" that concludes the memorandum came from the bookseller himself. See "Mémoire" of 1726.

13. Ranum, "Titon." 14. Ranum, "Entrée."

15. BN, ms. fr. 22107, Jan. 1, 1752.

16. BN, ms. fr. 22106, fols. 23v, 30v, 36, 45 (1762–66). She appears to have been his second wife, Marie-Jeanne Gueffier, a bookseller's sister.

Panel 4, Family Friends

I, The Châtelet, pp. 91–94

1. Charles Desmage, *Le Châtelet de Paris, son organisation, ses privilèges* (Paris, 1870); Marion, "Châtelet" and "Lieutenant."

2. BN, PO, 1128, "Ferrand," no. 25885, fol. 23 (rue Serpente, parish of Saint-Séverin).

3. AN, Y 130, fol. 19v, Oct. 6, 1587 (he is still an *élu* from Meaux); Y 141, fol. 173, My. 22, 1602; Y 169, fol. 21v, Jul. 9, 1625.

4. BN, ms. fr. 32588, p. 161. 5. AN, MC, XXXV, 71, Jan. 11, 1615.

6. AN, MC, XXIII, 275, Aug. 29 and Sept. 23, 1637.

II, Marie Talon, pp. 95–98

1. AN, MC, LXIV, 89, My. 31, 1650. 2. Montpensier, III, pp. 29–31.

3. AN, MC, CX, Dec. 1, 1657; CXII, 398, Jan. 15, 1688.

4. BN, Cabinet d'Hozier, 331, "Versoris," fol. 9.

5. BN, Cabinet d'Hozier, 331, "Versoris," fol. 7 (the Séguier estate); AN, MC, CX, 160, Mar. 15, 1666 (loan to Mlle. de Guise).

6. Daniel Dessert, *Argent, Pouvoir et Société au Grand Siècle* (Paris, 1984), p. 538; Tallemant, IV, pp. 297–313.

7. Plan of the city of Richelieu by Jean Barbet, 1633, *Richelieu, Art and Power*, ed. Hilliard Goldfarb (Montreal, 2002), p. 289.

8. René Kerviler, *Le Chancelier Pierre Séguier* (Paris, 1875), pp. 19–22; AN, MC, LXVI, 47, Feb. 21, 1623; LVII, 22, Feb. 26, 1612.

9. BN, PO, 2975, "Versoris," fol. 27; (Versoris–Chaillou); Cabinet d'Hozier, 331, "Versoris," fols. 10–11 (Versoris–Chaillou–Alesso, and Vanel, 1627); PO, 33, "Alesso," fols. 68v–69 (Versoris–Chaillou–Alesso–Vanel).

10. Montpensier, IV, pp. 278–9.

11. BN, Carrés d'Hozier, 15, "Alesso," fol. 230 (Jacques and Henry "Blacquevot," the father and uncle of Mme. Du Bois).

12. AN, MC, LXXV, 114, 17 Jan. 1662, to Nicolas Croyer, surely a relative of the three consecutive Baltasar Croyers who carried on the same trade from the 1620s to the 1650s.

13. AN, MC, CX, 160, 15 Mar. 1666 (reference to a loan dated Jan. 15, 1665).

III, Élisabeth-Marie Malier, pp. 99–102

1. AN, MC, CV, 424, Jan. 17, 1642, doc. 15.

2. BN, DB, 421, "Mallier," fols. 3, 10; PO, 1817, "Malier," fols 12, 25, 64.

3. AN, MC, XXXV, 28, Je. 24, 1608 (marriage to Louise de Fortia); CV, 341 Feb. 1621 (marriage to É-M. Malier, not consultable owing to humidity); XC, 90, Oct. 15, 1652 (his inventory); LXV, 126, Apr. 10, 1690 (her inventory).

4. AN, MC, V, 98, Jul. 16, 1644.

5. Séraphim was in her service by 1610 and handled Guise finances throughout their exile: BN, 4° Fm 14859, "intendant," Jan. 1640. He then helped her with her son's estate in 1654: BN, PO, 459, "Bourbon," fol. 56; AN, MC, LI, 165, Oct. 20, 1654.

6. AN, LL 1559, fol. 16v.   7. Arsenal, 8° S. 13744–13762.

8. AN, LL 797, fol. 94v.   9. AN, LL 1559, fol. 89.

10. AN, MC, LXV, 97, Jan. 31, 1678, inventory.

IV, Élisabeth Grimaudet, pp. 103–104

1. AN, MC, XXIII, 309, Aug. 24, 1662.

2. BN, Carrés d'Hozier, 314, "Grimaudet," fols. 100 (wedding contract); PO, 1410, "Grimaudet," fol. 6 (René, a "councillor" to Gaston, also 1648); AN, MC, XC, 229, Je. 23, 1665 (late Jacques Grimaudet).

3. BN, Carrés d'Hozier, 314, "Grimaudet," fols. 100, 104.

4. AN, MC, XC, 229, Je. 23, 1665.   5. AN, MC, XC, 229, My. 22, 1665.

6. "For executor of this will [Étiennette Charpentier] wishes to name and choose Messire Louis de Pâris, procurator at the Châtelet, whom she begs to take the trouble to do her this kindness, having full confidence in his faithfulness, begging him to accept as a present the sum of 500 livres ... along with her chiming clock in its case," AN, MC, 397, Jan. 30, 1676. Further research might discover parental (and devotional) links between Louis and the prominent Jansenist, François de Pâris.

V, Four Jesuits, pp. 105–109

1. BN, DB, 664, "Verthamon," fol. 3v; AG, Francia, 14, fol. 224.

2. AG, Francia, 14, fols. 224, 262.

3. AG, Francia, 14, fol. 262; Louis Blond, La Maison professe des Jésuites (Paris, 1956); Gustave Dupont-Ferrier, Du Collège de Clermont au Lycée Louis-le-Grand (Paris, 1921), III, p. 10.

4. AG, Francia, 14 and 15, triennial reports for 1672, 1675, 1678, 1681, 1685.

5. Ranum, "Jesuits."

6. AG, Francia 14 (François: born in Tours); François Aubert de La Chesnaye-Desbois, Dictionnaire de la Noblesse (Paris, 1980) "Fevre de la Faluère," (natives of Tours).

7. AG, Francia 14, fol. 224; Francia, 15 (1675, no. 11: "3 years in Rome"); BV, Barb. lat., 3525, fols. 460–61 (Jul. 1670).

8. AG, Francia, 14 and 15, triennial reports, 1665, 1669, 1672, 1675, 1678.

9. AN, MC, XCIX, 281, Sept. 30, 1679; and XCIX, 283, Dec. 30, 1679.

10. AG, Francia 16, 1675, no. 10; Georges Guitton, S.J., Le Père de la Chaize, Confesseur de Louis XIV (Paris, 1959), 2 vols., especially I, p. 37.

11. Le Gendre, p. 26; Spanheim, p. 411.   12. Spanheim, pp. 423–25.

13. BN, ms. fr. 17056, fol. 279, Oct. 15, 1682.   14. Mercure, Mar. 1688, pp. 242–53.

VI, The Ferrand Family, pp. 110–112

1. Antoine II's son had financial dealings with the Croyer–Faviers, AN, MC, XXIII, 277, Feb. 13, 1640, inventory, doc. 18.

2. AN, MC, CXV, 137, Apr. 30, 1657.   3. BN, PO, 1128, fols. 160, 161, 164.

4. AN, MC, XXIII, 277, Feb. 13, 1640, inventory, doc. 18; BN, DB, 265, "Ferrand," fol. 13, an excellent family tree.

5. AN, MC, LXIV, 89, My. 31, 1650.
6. AN, MC, XXIII, 399, will deposited Mar. 22, 1709.
7. Sévigné, III, pp. 179, 468, 478, 495–96, 523, 697.

Panel 5, Roman Contacts

I, Carissimi of the German College, pp. 115–118

1. For the school and church, see Thomas D. Cully, *Jesuits and Music*, Rome, 1970, especially chapter 3 on Carissimi.
2. Cully, p. 181.
3. Vicariato, "Anime," parish 4: San Apollinare.
4. Cully, p. 181.   5. Cessac, MAC, p. 23.
6. Cully, p. 178.
7. Cully, pp. 225, 233; AAE, Rome, 168, fol. 160.   8. Cully, pp. 203–05, 253.
9. *Mercure*, Jan. 1678, p. 231 ("il voyoit souvent le Carissimi"); and also: Feb. 1681, p. 249; Feb. 1687, p. 301; Mar. 1688, p. 321; Dec. 1693, pp. 333–34.
10. Cully, p. 195.

II, Dalibert of the Riario Palace, pp. 119–125

1. AN, MC, II, 130, Nov. 3, 1629.
2. Maurice Dumolin, *Études de Topographie parisienne* (Paris, 1929), II, pp. 124, 151–52, 180, 186, 330–31. Much of this land went into the dowry of Charpentier's daughter; but on August 22, 1631 (AN, MC, II, 137), shortly before Richelieu's project to build a palace in that area became official (Oct. 9, 1631), Jacques I Dalibert "ceded" the land back to Jean Charpentier in return for its cash value, 66,000 livres. Charpentier promptly began selling the property to the Cardinal's agents (Dec. 31, 1631). In other words, Charpentier was taking advantage of inside information, perhaps through Denis Charpentier, the Cardinal's secretary. Neither J.-F. Viel nor I have been able to discover parental ties linking Denis to Marc-Antoine Charpentier.
3. Arsenal, ms. 4213, fols. 84v–85.   4. Montpensier, III, pp. 84–85.
5. For some allusions to Dalibert's role in these negotiations, Montpensier, III, pp. 84–85, 216–17, 326; Ravisson-Mollien, *Archives de la Bastille*, I, pp. 227–45; Turin, 68, letter 38; Turin, "Dalibert," 35/2; Turin, Savoia, 79, *passim* (1659), Turin, Francia, 68, no. 38; and Turin, Firenze, 41 (marriage negotiations, 1660).
6. Turin, Francia, 70, no. 52. For other attempts: Turin, Roma, 76, no. 457; and Roma, 79, no. 312.
7. Turin, "Dalibert," 37/2 (Jul. 24, 1661); Alberto Cametti, "Giacomo d'Alibert costruttore del primo theatro pubblico di musica in Roma," *Nuova antologia, rivista di lettere, scienze et arti*, 7th series, February 1931, p. 342 (via dei Greci, Feb 12, 1662).
8. BN, ms. 500 Colbert, 233, fols. 212–13.
9. Arsenal, Archives de la Bastille, 10:332, "D'Alibert," 4.
10. AN, Z^{1}J 294 (Mar. and Apr. 1666).
11. Stockholm, K 402, Apr. 14, 1662; Bildt, p. 122.
12. Franckenstein, p. 153; Turin, Savoia, 84, fols. 24, 56v, 91v, 103; Turin, Roma, 82, no. 1127.
13. For a burlesque but reasonably accurate depiction of Christina and her household (the author clearly had access to oral and written sources inside the Riario, because many of his assertions are confirmed by irrefutable evidence), see Frankenstein, *passim*, especially pp. 153–66, 248–50, 272, and 297 for Dalibert.
14. Franckenstein, p. 154.
15. For the Roman Daliberts: Rome, Archivio di Stato, Secretari e concilliere della R.C.A., vol. 1285, fols. 219, 252, 266; Rome, 30 notai capitolini, officio 15, fols. 627–34, 634, 637, 642v, 678v, etc. (his estate), and officio 19, Apr. 28 and My. 1, 1661 (notarial documents).
16. Rome, Archivio di Stato, Camerale III, teatri, 2126, doc. 52.
17. Beretta was chapel master at Santo Spirito in Sassia, 1657–64, moved to San Marcello by 1677, and ended his career at the *Cappella Giulia*.
18. Franckenstein, p. 154.   19. Franckenstein, p. 157.
20. Franckenstein, p. 153.

21. AAE, Rome, 23, 174 (*Tartuffe*, 1666); Alberto Cametti, "Cristina di Svezia, l'Arte musicale e gli spettacoli teatrali in Roma," *Nuova Antologia di lettere, scienze ed arte*, ser. 5, vol. 155 (1911), pp. 344, 641-56, and 648-49 (Ciccolino).

22. Turin, Rome, 86, no. 179 (Aug. 1668), and nos. 295, 297, 299, 310, 317-18.

23. AAE, Rome, 176, fols. 150v, 252; Vicariato, "Anime," parish 13: San Lorenzo in Lucina 1668-71.

24. François de Salignac de la Mothe-Fénelon, *Correspondance*, ed. J. Orcibal (Paris, 1972-99), VI, p. 224, and VIII, pp. 203-04; Franckenstein, p. 165; plus divers letters in AAE, Rome.

25. Franckenstein, p. 159; Vicariato, "Anime," parish 13: San Lorenzo in Lucina, starting 1668 (vicolo del Carcioffolo, also called the "Orto di Napoli").

26. Franckenstein, p. 160; BN, ms. fr. 20746, fol. 42: "To the Jews who furnished my palace," noted Le Tellier.

27. Franckenstein, p. 159.

28. Alberto Cametti, *Il Teatro di Tordinona* ... (Tivoli, 1938), I, pp. 5-15, 16-22, 37 ff.; Filippo Clementi, *Il carnavale Romano nelle cronache* ... (Rome, 1939), I, pp. 551, 576-78, 582-87; Alessandro Ademollo, *I teatri di Roma* ... (Rome, 1888), pp. 129-33; Rome, Archivio di Stato, Camerale III, teatri, 2126, B2126.

29. Turin, Roma, 95, fols. 17, 23, 30, 31, etc. He had been proposing a move to Turin since 1670, Turin, Roma, 91, no. 286; Franckenstein, p. 161.

30. Franckenstein, pp. 166, 159-60.

III Dassoucy the Poet-Composer, pp. 126–131

1. For Dassoucy's life, see Henri Prunières, "Les singulières aventures de M. Dassoucy, musicien et poëte burlesque," *La Revue musicale*, 18-20 (1937-39); Scruggs; and Dassoucy, *Aventures*.

2. Marie-Thérèse Bouquet, *Musique et musiciens à Turin de 1648 à 1775* (Turin, 1968), p. 47: "Dasouci, musico."

3. Dassoucy, *Aventures*, p. 260.   4. Dassoucy, *Aventures*, p. 252.

5. Prunières (Apr., 1939), p. 202; Turin, "Dalibert," 35/2 and 37/2.

6. Dassoucy, *Rimes*, p. 125.   7. AAE, Rome, 181, fol. 91.

8. AAE, Rome, 181, fol. 91.   9. AAE, Rome, 181, fol. 270.

10. Dassoucy, *Rimes*, pp. 58-60, 62-63.   11. BN, ms. fr. 20746, fol. 42v.

12. Dassoucy, *Rimes*, p. 120.   13. Dassoucy, *Rimes*, pp. 42, 79, 100.

14. Dassoucy, *Rimes*, in *Aventures*, pp. 18-19.   15. Dassoucy, *Rimes*, p. 124.

16. Dassoucy, *Rimes*, in *Aventures*, pp. 18-19.   17. Dassoucy, *Rimes*, p. 124.

18. *Mercure*, Sept. 1678, p. 70: Mlle. de Guise: "a heroine"; Loret, II, Apr. 1657, p. 326: Mlle. de Guise's sister (Mme. de Montmartre): "of this heroic race ... demigods"; Loret's successors, I, cols. 840-41, nobles are "children of the Gods," and II, cols. 116, 851-52, the future Mme. de Guise is "the Divine Alençon," and she and her husband are "our dear divinities"; *Gazette*, 1656, pp. 1031, 1036, princesses are "divinities."

19. Dassoucy, *Rimes*, p. 119.

20. *L'Ombre de Molière et son epitaphe* (Paris, 1673), dedication.

IV, Chaulnes of the Farnese Palace, pp. 132–137

1. AAE, Rome, 168, fol. 160; 171, fols. 45-46, 323; 175, fol. 36v; 176, fol. 136v, 252; 177, fol. 111; 196, fol. 78.

2. AAE, Rome, 168, fols. 54, 61v, 147; 171, fol. 337v; 175, fols. 123-24v, 286, 287, 304; 176, fols. 191, 362

3. Saint-Simon, I, p. 164.

4. AAE, Rome, for the period 1665-70, especially 189, fol. 99; and BN, ms. fr. 20746, fol. 72-72v (Maffei lists some of the people at the Farnese).

5. Dassoucy, *Rimes*, pp. 148 ff.

6. AAE, Rome, 179, fol. 20 (Nov. 2, 1666); 186, fol. 235.

7. AAE, Rome, 177, fol. 404v; Loret's successors, II, cols. 315-18. For images of entertainments, see Per Bjurström, *Feast and Theatre in Queen Christina's Rome* (Stockholm, 1966).

8. BN, ms. fr. 20481, fol. 11, in a volume of letters from Condé's Roman contacts concerning Roquette's bulls.

9. AAE, Rome, 181, fol. 91.   10. AAE, Rome, 175, fols. 36, 120v.

11. AAE, Rome, 181, fol. 130.   12. AAE, Rome, 181, fol. 195.

13. AAE, Rome, 181, fol. 233v; Loret's successors, II, col. 745.

14. AAE, Rome, 181, fols. 270, 277v, 284–87; Loret's successors, II, cols. 738–40, 762–63.

15. AAE, Rome, 184, fol. 145v; 185, fols. 183, 227v.

16. BN, ms. fr. 20746, Abbé Le Tellier's notes, Dec. 29, 1667: "Pour les etoffes de mes livrées, aux correspondants de Carpentier, 62 p. d'Es., j'ay fait payer ... J'ay quittance." Having been assigned by Chaulnes to care for Le Tellier, Maffei was "constantly at his side" (ms. fr. 20746, fol. 53, and ms. n.a. fr. 6265, fol. 40v). Le Tellier made a point of speaking Italian whenever possible (so he would have heard "Carpentier," rather than "Charpentier"), n.a. fr. 6265, fols. 7v, 14v.

17. AAE, Rome, 187, fol. 157; 189, fol. 167; BN, n.a. fr., 6265, fols. 23v; BN, ms. fr. 20746, fols. 72–72v, 73v, 89, 103v, 119v; Dassoucy, Rimes, pp. 52, 62.

18. AAE, Rome, 189, fols. 123v, 130.

19. BN, ms. fr. 20746, fols. 108v, 120. For the dating of Dassoucy's arrest, Scruggs, pp. 49 ff.

20. Ranum, "Quelques ajouts."   21. AAE, 192, fols. 33–34, 40, 48.

22. Gazette, 1669, pp. 575, 715.

23. BN, ms. fr. 24986, fol. 379, Dec. 16, 1687: Mme. de Chaulnes "wants me to express her gratitude [to Mlle. de Guise] and tell her how impatient she is to thank her personally."

24. Ranum, "Brossard," pp. 297–98.   25. Saint-Simon, I, pp. 138–56, 163–64.

Panel 6, Charpentier's Collaborators

I, Molière, pp. 141–149

1. Moréri (1747), "Molière"; and, for a concise but reliable version of these events, Albert Pauphilet, Dictionnaire des Lettres françaises: le dix-septième siècle (Paris, 1954), "Molière."

2. For these years, and for Conti and Dassoucy, see Claude Alberge, Le Voyage de Molière en Languedoc (1647–1657) (Montpellier, 1988).

3. Cent ans, pp. 116, 319.

4. Comédie, Reg. Hubert, Je. 19 and Jul. 10, 1672.

5. Comédie, Reg. Hubert, Jul. 10–Aug. 7, 1672; La Grange, I, p. 126.

6. Ranum-Cessac.   7. Dassoucy, Rimes, in Aventures, pp. 18–19.

8. Georges Couthon, ed., Œuvres de Molière (Paris, 1971), I, p. lv: privilege to print his airs and the lyrics he had set to music.

9. Dassoucy, Rimes, p. 124.

10. Loret, II, Apr. 1657, p. 326; Robinet, Lettres en vers, Je. 7, 1665; Mercure, Sept. 1678, p. 70; Loret's successors, I, cols. 840–41; Gazette, 1656, pp. 1031, 1036.

11. AN, MC, CXV, 131, Dec. 9, 1655, doc. 15 (Louis Cressé); XCIX, 268, My. 2, 1676 quittance to J.-B. Cressé; obligation by Mlle. de Guise.

12. La Grange, p. 144; Nuitter and Thoinan, pp. 274–75.

13. Delamare, I, p. 474; and for details on the use of more musicians than allowed, Clarke, pp. 89–110; Powell, pp. 390–97.

14. La Grange, I, p. 147.   15. La Grange, I, p. 157.

16. Comédie, Reg. 17, fol. 244v.

II Du Bois the Chapel Master, pp. 150–169

1. Pelisson and d'Olivet, Histoire de l'Académie Française, ed. Ch.-L. Livet (Paris, 1858), II, pp. 284–88. See also Mesnard, passim, but especially pp. 654 and 656–57 (Poitou), 660, 672–73 (his marriage), 736–39 (education of the Dauphin), 872–78 (pre-Guise years), and 952–55 (his translations); and Thomas M. Carr, Jr., ed., Antoine Arnauld, ... and Philippe Goibaut Du Bois, Avertissement en tête de sa traduction des sermons de saint Augustin (1694), (Geneva, 1992), Introduction, pp. 11–44.

2. Mesnard, p. 669.   3. Mesnard, p. 672–73.

4. Mesnard, p. 650.   5. Le Maguet, p. 452.

6. MdP, 6186, Apr. 23 and My. 7, 1666; Mesnard, p. 875: Oct. 1666?

7. Abbé Testu de Mauroy, Discours prononcés dans l'Académie françoise ... à la réception de M' Du Bois (Paris, 1693), pp. 18–19.

8. BN, ms. fr. 17048, fols. 195–97, copied and preserved by DR. VALLANT, whose copyist wrote "Montagna". See also Mark Motley, *Becoming a French Aristocrat, The Education of the Court Nobility, 1580–1715* (Princeton, 1990).

9. Langlois, Gaignières' plan of 1697, when Du Bois' lodging was occupied by Condé's agent, "M. Dupin."; Ranum, "Feindre," especially p. 52, "y"; AN, MC, LXXV, 400, Jul. 13, 1694 (inventory of the Du Bois apartment).

10. MdP, 4815, Nov. 21 and 22, 1670.

11. Caietain's dedication, quoted by Jeanice Brooks, "Les Guises et l'air de cour," in Y. Bellenger, ed., *Le Mécénat et l'influence des Guises* (Paris, 1997), pp. 207–10; and Du Bois, *Lettres*, "Épître."

12. Quoted by Mesnard, pp. 665, 669.   13. Testu de Mauroy, *Discours*, pp. 18–19.

14. Du Bois, *Lettres*, "Épître."

15. AN, MC, LXXV, 400, Jul. 13, 1694 (memorandum dated Apr. 5, 1677, and inventory begun on Jul. 5, 1694).

16. MdP, 4791, Nov. 12, 1685: "[I am including] the discourse on the two letters of Saint Augustin that M. Du Bois, chapel master of Mlle. de Guise, translated at the request of the Archbishop of Paris."

17. Racine, II, p. 353; Pierre Blet, S.J., *Les Assemblées du Clergé et Louis XIV de 1670 1693* (Rome, 1972), pp. 445–85, especially pp. 475–76.

18. *Actes de l'Assemblée generale du Clergé de France ... concernant la Religion* (Paris, 1685), especially pp. 11, 35 (ROQUETTE: "you are our brothers"), but also pp. 60, 67.

19. MdP, 4792, Nov. 12, 1685.

20. Du Bois, *Conformité*, pp. i–xxxv.   21. BN, ms. fr. 17052, fol. 372.

22. BN, ms. fr. 17052, fol. 343.   23. *Mercure*, Aug. 1681, pp. 153–54.

24. Jean Duron, "Les 'paroles de musique' sous le règne de Louis XIV," in *Plain-chant et liturgie en France au XVIIᵉ siècle*, ed. Jean Duron (Paris, 1997), p. 169: by "M. Dubois de l'Hôtel de Guise," an attribution that suggests that Du Bois' setting was written prior to the mid-1680s, while he was still director of the GUISE MUSIC, although the book was not published for another decade. (This conjecture is strengthened by the fact that the volume contains a setting by Henri Du Mont, who died in 1684.)

25. Le Maguet, p. 540, Dec. 1, 1673, a friendly letter to Jean Santeul from DR. VALLANT, who became the Guises' official physician one week later and henceforth often lodged in Du Bois' apartment. For Claude Santeul, see Moréri, "Santeul"; and for Du Bois' link to this project directed by the monks of Saint-Maur, see the title page of Du Bois' translation of Augustine's letters (privilege, 1682).

26. BN, ms. fr. 17050, fol. 482, Je. 1, 1677.

27. The earliest recognizable piece for the Great Guise Music—which had not yet reached its maximum size—is H. 400, in cahier 30, composed for the progress through Champagne in the fall of 1680. Not until there were two singers for each vocal line did the composer begin to mark the designated performer's name in the margin.

28. Ranum, "Foyer."

29. AN, MC, LXXV, 400, Jul. 13, 1694, inventory (his music library).

30. BN, ms. fr. 17052, fol. 143 (Sept. 1677); and ms. fr. 17050, fols. 337, 343, 351, his coach and its gilded nailheads (Sept.–Oct. 1680).

31. Quoted by Mesnard, p. 665.   32. Quoted by Carr, p. 15.

33. BN, ms. Clairambault, 1204, fols. 681–90.   34. Quoted by Langlois, p. 97.

35. AN, MC, LXXV, 400, Jul. 13, 1694 (memo dated Apr. 5, 1677).

36. Du Bois, *Sermons*, "Épître."

III, Corneille the Younger, pp. 170–176

1. Georges Couthon, *La Vieillesse de Corneille* (Paris, 1949), p. 43.

2. Corneille, *Œuvres complètes*, ed. A. Stegman (Paris, 1963), p. 885.

3. John S. Powell, "Charpentier's Music for *Circé* (1675)," *Bulletin Charpentier*, no. 15 (1998).

4. Mélèse, p. 125; Cessac, *MAC*, p. 82; Clarke, pp. 89–110.

5. Cessac, *MAC*, p. 82; La Grange, I, p. 176.

6. Pierre Bayle, quoted by Cessac, *MAC*, p. 83.   7. Mélèse, p. 127.

8. La Grange, p. 184 (Jul. 7, 1676); Comédie, Reg. 8, fols. 94v, 96v.

9. Notably by Cessac, Clarke, Hitchcock ("Marc-Antoine Charpentier and the Comédie-Française," *JAMS*, 24 [1971], pp. 255–81); Powell.

10. Le Cerf, II, p. 215; De La Gorce, *Lully*, pp. 630–32.

11. Corneille, *Œuvres*, chronology, p. 19.

12. Comédie, Reg. 13, fols. 32v, 36v.

13. Quoted in La Grange, II, p. 131.

14. Comédie, Reg. 16, fol. 96v.

IV, Donneau and the Press, pp. 177–188

1. Mélèse, pp. 127–28.

2. Mélèse, pp. 163–64.

3. *Mercure*, Jan. 1678, p. 330.

4. Brossard, *Catalogue*, p. 275.

5. Cessac, *MAC*, p. 23.

6. *Mercure*, Jan. 1678, p. 231; Feb. 1681, p. 249; Feb. 1687, p. 301; Mar. 1688, p. 321; Dec. 1693, pp. 333–34.

7. Ranum, "Portrait."

8. *Mercure*, Aug. 1682, p. 159.

9. Cahier 36, which has lost its first pages, begins with a fragment, H. 428, then moves on to a *Domine salvum fac Regem*, H. 291.

10. *Mercure*, Oct. 1685, pp. 353–54.

11. *Mercure*, Dec. 1693, pp. 331–35.

12. BN, DB, 158, "Castille," fols. 27, 34. Marie-Henriette is the only *demoiselle* on the tree, which includes Mme. Nicolas Fouquet, whose orange trees were being safeguarded at the Hôtel de Guise in 1688.

13. Circa Oct 17, 1679, during this revival of *L'Inconnu*, the troop awarded Charpentier an "augmentation" of 16 livres 10 sous—presumably for the music he had written for RIANTS' fête and for which he apparently was never paid. Comédie, Reg. 9, fol. 103.

14. *Mercure*, Sept. 1679, pp. 55–56.

15. *Mercure*, Feb. 1687, 299–304; *Gazette*, 1687, p. 62.

16. *Mercure*, Apr. 1681, pp. 327–44, especially pp. 340–41.

17. *Mercure*, Jan. 1682, pp. 110–37, especially pp. 114–15.

18. *Mercure*, My. 1682, pp. 175–90, especially pp. 183–84.

19. *Mercure*, Apr. 1683, pp. 310–13.

20. *Mercure*, Je. 1683, p. 267.

21. *Mercure*, Je. 1683, pp. 252–68.

22. Turin, Archivio di Stato, mazzo 95: 29, 32, 36.

23. Copied into what today is called cahier "II," its paper suggests that it is the missing cahier 48. See MdP, 4784, Oct. 26, 1686.

24. *Mercure*, Dec. 1683, pp. 314–16.

25. It is difficult to explain this error. During their collaboration on *Bellérophon*, did Lully suggest something of the sort to Corneille?

26. *Mercure*, Mar. 1688, pp. 317–20.

27. *Mercure*, Oct. 1685, pp. 2–13.

28. *Mercure*, Jan. 1687, pp. 267–70.

29. *Mercure*, Jul. 1687, pp. 96–97.

30. *Mercure*, Apr. 1691, pp. 148–49.

31. Ranum, "Jesuits." It is extremely difficult to determine exactly what was "ordinary" and what was "extraordinary" for the Jesuit period. If this work is H. 418, which he copied into an arabic-numbered notebook, then music for the Feast of Saint Louis appears to have become part of the music master's "ordinary" duties at Saint-Louis.

32. *Mercure*, Aug. 1692, pp. 219–20.

33. *Mercure*, My. 1695, pp. 245, 251–52.

34. *Mercure*, My. 1695, pp. 225–26.

35. *Mercure*, Nov. 1698, pp. 233–34; Nov. 1699, pp. 184–85; Nov. 1700, p. 40.

V, The Guise Music, pp. 189–201

1. *Mercure*, Mar. 1688, pp. 305–06; Feb. 1688, p. 98. For this ensemble, see Ranum, "Servitude."

2. They are listed in the Guise estate papers at Chantilly (carton A 15), which state whether the individual has celebrated a twenty-fifth birthday. In Mlle. de Guise's will they are listed by seniority, as was customary.

3. *Mercure*, Oct. 1702, quoted by Mardal, p. 80.

4. *Mercure*, My. 1680, p. 138.

5. Marie Du Bois, pp. 37–38 (the Duchess of Chaulnes, 1647).

6. AN, MC, XCIX, 283, Dec. 28, 1679.

7. *Gazette*, 1670, p. 336.

8. AN, MC, XCIX, 251, Apr. 30, 1672.

9. That is how I interpret the personnel as Cessac, *MAC*, p. 484, lists it: the soloists were the two Pièche sisters (*haut-dessus* and *dessus*), Charpentier (*haute-contre*), Frizon (bass), a chorus made up mainly of the Guise Core Trio, and the Pièche brothers playing various instruments.

10. Thorin's notarial acts: AN, MC, X, 277, My. 3 and Dec. 19, 1689; X, 278, Jan. 9, 1690; LXXV, 338, Je. 19, 1687; XC, 277, My. 3, 1689; XC, 278, Jan. 9, 1690; XC, 284, Aug. 21, 1692. Jacquet: AN, Y 119, fol. 326; Y 120, fol. 135; Y 121, fol. 366v; Y 170, fol. 87v (re the same house); BN, Fichier Laborde, 35648, 35594.

11. Jacquet's notarial acts: AN, MC, LXII, 106, Aug. 31, 1644; XC, 277, My. 26 and Dec. 19, 1689; XC, 278, Jan. 9, 1690; Bernard Dorival, *Philippe de Champaigne* (Paris, 1976), I, pp. 198, 201, 205, 217; AN, MC, LXI, 174, Nov. 2, 1702. The Champaignes (who were relatives of the sixteenth-century householders of that name, to whom the Guises still owed money in the 1640s): BN, DB, 166, "Champaigne," especially fols. 198, 201, 205, 218, where Marguerite Jacquet, her relative, married a Claude Collin and had dealings with a De Brion.

12. Talon's notarial acts: AN, MC, V, 235, Jul. 20, 1695; XXXIX, 205, Feb. 22, 1698; XXXIX, 214, Dec. 21, 1699; XXXIX, 216, Feb. 16, 1700; BN, Fichier Laborde, 61726-29; BN, ms fr. 32839, fols. 175, 185. The Talon family tree was huge and included rather poor branches with artisans. Some of these Talons married Anthoines and Guyots: BN, DB, 624, "Talon," fols. 106, 109; PO, 2790, fol. 300; PO, 2791, fol. 679.

13. Guillebault's notarial acts: AN, MC, XIII, 181, Jul. 28, 1714. Angers: BN, PO, 1444, fol. 7. Duke Henri: AN, MC, XCVIII, 194, My. 3, 1657. The Loulié relatives named Guillebault and Croyer: AN, MC, XVIII, 151, fol. 618; XVIII, 242, fol. 209; XVIII, 245, fol. 142; LXXXVIII, 207, Mar. 24, 1668; XCIX, 269, Jul. 12, 1676; AN, Y 181, fol. 182.

14. Guyot's notarial acts: AN, MC, LXXII, 124, Apr. 10, 1690. Guise officers named Guyot: AN, MC, CXII, 393, Sept. 22, 1685; AN, 300 API, 922*, cahier 15.

15. AN, MC, XXIII, 308, Jan. 6, 1662, final added paragraph.

16. De Brion's notarial acts: AN, Y 256, fol. 487; AN, MC, L, 191, Nov. 17, 1686 (a cousin's wedding). Brions in the League: BN, DB, 136, fols. 6-8; PO, 520, fol. 157. The daughter of a Mlle. Claude Jacquet and a wine merchant named Jean De Brion became a nun at Montmartre in 1639: AN, MC, XX, 231, My. 31, 1639; XXXIV, 105, Mar. 14, 1633; LXXV, 95, Apr. 17, 1659. The Charpentiers of Meaux: AN, MC, XXXV, 60, Jul. 21, 1609; and numerous documents in AD-77.

17. Loulié: Ranum, "Loulié"; Baltasard Croyer: AN, Y 133, fol. 79v; Y 181, fol. 182 (Pierre Guillebault, his brother-in-law); Y 160, fol. 439 (rue Darnetal); AN, MC, XVIII, 245, Feb. 14, 1629; XVIII, 253, Sept. 19, 1638; LXXXIV, 270, My. 12, 1702 (rue Darnetal). David Croyer: AN, MC, XXXV, 61, Mar. 24, 1610 (rue Darnetal), and XXXV, 77, Mar. 15, 1618 (rue Darnetal).

18. Beaupuis' notarial acts: AN, MC, LXVII, Feb. 18, 1645; II, 187, Je. 17, 1648; LXVII, Mar. 14 and 26, 1659; XLIII, 359, Sept. 24, 1732.

19. Colin's notarial acts: AN, MC, LXXV, 329, Sept. 7 and 11, 1685. Ancerville: BN, PO, 815, "Colin," fols. 131-70; PO, 820, "Collin," fols. 29 ff. In Guise service: Chantilly, A 13, account no. 38, and register 33 (owed 25,304 livres by Guises), and carton 16; AN, MC, CXII, 395, Sept. 29, 1686. The relative of musician Anne Jacquet's relative, Marguerite Jacquet (d. ca. 1637) married a Claude Collin, Dorival, I, pp. 198, 201, 205.

20. Carlier's notarial acts: AN, MC, LXXXIV, 138, Aug. 7, 1650; XC, 280, Sept. 14, 1690; XC, 277, Mar. 3, 1689. The Mercy: AN, LL 1557, fol. 1v; LL 1560, fols. 68, 73. Guises: BN, PO, 598, "Carlier," fol. 36; AN, MC, LXXXVIII, 232, Apr. 9, 1674.

21. Joinville: AN, MC, CXV, 164, Feb. 21, 1664; AN, API, 922*, Oct. 24, 1682.

22. De Baussen's notarial acts: AN, MC, CXXI, 131, Je. 17, 1681; IX, 530, Nov. 19, 1696. He was raised in the Guise parish of Saint-Jean-en-Grève: BN, ms. fr. 32588, pp. 449, 668.

23. *Mercure*, Feb. 1688, p. 98.

Panel 7, Discreet Commissions

I, The Mercy, pp. 201-212

1. AN, L 1559, fols. 3v, 5v, 6v, 12, 16, 16v, 89; Loret, II, p. 327 (the window).
2. AN, MC, XXXIX, 109, Mar. 15, 1664; LIV, 614, Oct. 3, 1672 (Jeanne Pelloquin, the wife of MLLE. DE MONTPENSIER's equerry, used money from the estate of her late uncle, who happened to be the son of DAVID CROYER's Parisian relatives, Roland Croyer and Michelle Favier).

3. Loret, II, pp. 509–10.

4. Henri Quittard, *Un Musicien en France au XVIIe siècle, Henry Du Mont (1610–1684)* (Paris, 1906), p. 46.

5. "Ménagiana" in *Ana* (Amsterdam, 1799), III, p. 209.

6. Loret, III, p. 249 (at the Mercy), p. 254 (an encore at court); and *Gazette*, 1660, p. 826.

7. Loret, IV, p. 248.

8. J. Biroat, *Panégyriques des Saints* (Paris, 1668), p. 346.

9. AN, L 1559, fol. 85; *Institution de la Confrerie des Agonisans ... en l'Eglise du couvent ... de la Mercy* (Paris, 1673), Mazarine, 47181, pp. 161 ff.

10. *Gazette*, 1671, p. 737.   11. AN, L 1559, fol. 85v.

12. Ranum, "Mercy."

13. *Ceremoniale sacri ordinis Beatæ Mariæ de Mercede Redemptionis captivorum* (Valence, 1614), pp. 85–87, 130–31, 209; *Ritual sacri ... ordinis B.V. Mariæ de Mercede, Redemptionis captivorum* (Hispali/Seville, 1701), BN, B 29093; Mazarine, ms. 395, "Livre de Chœur," eighteenth century.

14. *Officium B. Virginis Mariæ de Mercede Redemptionis captivorum*, bound with an Augustinian breviary of 1684, Rodez Library, T 1019.

15. MdP, 4826, Aug. 16, 1683.   16. *Mercure*, Dec. 1683, pp. 314–16.

17. *Institution*, especially pp. 31–51; AN, S* 4291, pp. 14–15.

18. *Institution*, p. 59.

19. Biroat, III, pp. 816 ff.; Loret, III, pp. 355–56; *Gazette*, 1676, p. 816; BN, ms. fr. 23498, fol. 254v.

20. Biroat, III, pp. 836 ff.; *Reglemens des Confreries de la Charité ... et Confreries du grand S. Charles Borromée* (1676), Mazarine, A 16599, p. 31. The aims described in this pamphlet are almost identical to those of the Confraternity of the Dying.

21. *Mercure*, Aug. 1682, p. 159.

22. The first part of notebook 36 is missing and could conceivably have contained music for this event: for after the final few measures of a lost piece ("... et invocate sanctum nomen ejus," H. 428) comes a *Domine salvum fac regem*, H. 291.

23. Ranum, "Mercy."

24. *Office de la Semaine Sainte, ... à l'usage de Rome et de Paris* (Paris, 1701), Mazarine, Rés. Far 8°17, pp. 404–06: the mass, said at midday on Saturday, is shorter than usual, as are the vespers that come immediately after communion. Since the early 1660s the Mercedarians had hired guards to ensure that only the elite could enter, Loret, III, p. 249.

25. Based on BN, ms. fr. 22432, fols. 42 ff.

II, The Theatines, pp. 213–219

1. AN, LL 1587, fol. 10, Jul. 7, 1675.

2. For example, MdP, 6185, Apr. 17, 1663; 4672, Sept. 30, 1675.

3. Raymond Darricau, *Les Clercs réguliers Théatins à Paris, Sainte-Anne-la-Royale (1644–1793)* (Rome, 1961); Evelyne Picard, "Liturgie et musique à Sainte-Anne-la-Royale," *Recherches*, 20 (1981), pp. 249–54.

4. *Gazette*, 1660, p. 1249; 1661, p. 11; 1665, p. 1234; 1666, pp. 1591–92; 1667, pp. 1326, 1351; 1668, pp. 1351–52.

5. *Gazette*, 1669, p. 1236. In 1670, the Queen attended the opening service, *Gazette*, 1670, p. 1216; and in 1671 King Casimir and the Orléans were again singled out, *Gazette*, 1671, pp. 1212, 1242.

6. *Office de Saint Charles Borromée, latin-françois* (Paris, 1685), Mazarine, Rés. 34095, p. 16.

7. *Reglement des Confreries de Charité ... et Confreries du grand S. Charles Boromée* (1676), Mazarine, A 16599, piece 1: especially pp. 2, 5, 6, 15–16 (conversions), 31, 32 (Mme. de Guise), 34 (Infant Jesus and Virgin).

8. Mazarine, ms. 1217, final pages, and for MME. DE GUISE and Miramion's charitable group, Jan. 18 and Dec. 22, 1679; ms. 1216, Aug. 22, 1682 (on the Feast of Saint Louis, meditate about poverty), Dec. 2, 1688; ms. 1219, Oct. 22 and 28, 1691.

9. Ranum, "Foyer."

10. That is, at any rate, the implication behind Mme. de Guise's desire to imitate the chapel at Saint-Joseph-des-Carmes where Bernini's statue of the Virgin and Child stood.

11. "Mémoire" of 1726, fol. 3. The Confraternity of Saint Charles collaborated with the Jesuits to convert Huguenots, Mazarine, A 16599, piece 10, p. 17.

12. *Gazette*, Nov. 1676, p. 816 (a conversion in the presence of Mme. de Guise).

13. MdP, 4783, My. 7, 1682: she uses the word "we"; and *Mercure*, My. 1682, p. 110 (and again in Je.).

14. Brillon (born circa 1670), quoted by Picard, p. 252, n. 9.

15. *Gazette*, Aug. 1672, pp. 873–84.

16. BN, Morel de Thoisy, 420, fol. 17 (testament, Mar. 1, 1684).

17. MdP, 4791, Jul. 31 and Sept. 7, 1682; Apr. 5 and 14, 1683.

18. AN, LL 1587, fol. 57; MdP, 4791, Aug. 6, 1685.

19. *Mercure*, Oct. 1685, p. 272; MdP, 4677, Oct. 1, 1685: "great applause and a big attendance."

20. Quoted by Picard, p. 253 (Nov. 6, 1685); MdP, 4792, Jan. 6, 1686. The Theatines had long used Swiss guards to keep out ordinary people, Loret, III, pp. 444–45.

III, The Abbaye-aux-Bois and the Little Carmel, pp. 220–225

1. Mother Desnots: AN, MC, CXII, 365, Oct. 5, 1672; CXII, 393, Jul. 25, 1685. The musician's sister could not be identified among the nuns signing these two acts.

2. *Mercure*, Apr. 1680, pp. 323–24.

3. Pierre Clément, *Une abbesse de Fontevrault au XVIIe siècle: Gabrielle de Rochechouart de Mortemart* (Paris, 1869), letters 3, 31 (M. DU BOIS' health), 32 (greetings to DR. VALLANT, Aug. 1678), and 37 (letter to Vallant, Dec. 3, 1681, transmitting a letter to MME. DE GUISE and greeting Du Bois). Marthe Croyer-HAVÉ DE SAINT-AUBIN was born circa 1600, and her husband appears to have died in the late 1660s. It was common practice for childless widows to withdraw to a convent to be cared for by the nuns in return for an annuity.

4. For details, see Rodocanachi, pp. 322–23.   5. MdP, 4783, Jul. 3, 1682.

6. MdP, 4783, Thérèse de Remoncourt: Nov. 9, 1682; Sept. 5, 1683; Nov. 15, 1684; Feb. 14, 1685.

7. MdP, 4821, Jan. 17, My. 5, and My. 19, 1681.

8. Loret's successors, I, col. 189, Aug. 1665.   9. *Mercure*, Dec. 1683, pp. 314–16.

10. *Manuel des divers offices divins pour l'usage des religieuses de l'ordre de Nostre Dame du Mont Carmel* (Paris, 1628), pp. 332–33; and *Proprium Sanctorum et Festorum ad usum monalium ordinis Beatæ Mariæ de Monte Carmelo* (Paris, 1680), p. 244.

11. *Gazette*, 1675, p. 408.

12. Louise de la Vallière, *Reflexions sur la Misericorde de Dieu* (Paris, 1684), p. 12. For La Vallière as the Magdalene, see Conley, pp. 97–123.

13. J. B. Ériau, *L'Ancien Carmel du Faubourg Saint-Jacques* (Paris, 1929), p. 333.

IV, The Three Jesuit Houses, pp. 227–240

1. Based on the General's rulings about the college in Rome, AG, Busta 1, fol. 166, Jul. 1699. The payment to Paolo Lorenzani (discussed below) during Marc-Antoine Charpentier's tenure at Saint-Louis proves that outsiders were invited to compose for "extraordinary" events.

2. Pierre Delattre, *Les Établissements des Jésuites en France* (Enghein, 1956), III, "Paris, La Maison Professe," cols. 1281–82.

3. Nuitter and Thoinan, p. 221; Sévigné, Jan. 20, 1672.

4. Some of these works from the early 1670s are on paper produced by a Jesuit-owned mill. This Jesuit paper may, however, have found its way into the composer's manuscripts during the 1690s, when he recopied, and perhaps reworked some earlier pieces, perhaps repairing damaged sheets. A careful analysis of style and handwriting—especially noteheads, flags, and musical clefs—would make it possible to assert whether these compositions that Charpentier classed among his earliest works were in fact recopied in the 1690s. Even if these pages should turn out to date from the 1690s, since he replaced the works in their original chronological order, it appears that he was replacing an old Jesuit work with a somewhat revised and refreshed one.

5. So great was the Jesuits' devotion for Saint Nicaise at Rouen that they became associated with a new seminary with that name in 1680, Delattre, IV, col. 554.

6. Moréri, "Commire."

7. A central sheet of Jesuit paper tucked into the center of notebook 13 replaces a portion of the oratorio Charpentier wrote for this event (H. 394). The treble clefs on that sheet are the type he used during the 1680s and beyond. In other words, it seems that he went back and touched up or repaired this work performed at the Noviciate in 1676.

8. André Desautels,"Un manuscrit autographe de M.-A. Charpentier à Québec," *Recherches*, 21 (1983), p. 123. This attribution raises an intriguing question: If this autograph manuscript (H. 32a) was in fact copied out in 1689, why does it not appear in the *Mélanges* until cahier LVIII (H. 32), which—if one assumes that the notebooks from the Jesuit period are in strict chronological order—dates, at the earliest, from the spring of 1691? The most plausible answer is that H. 32a was written first.

9. Du Pradel, I, p. 213.

10. Ranum, "Jesuits," table 2.

11. Ranum, "Jesuits," table 2.

12. Brice, I, p. 183.

13. BN, ms fr. 23499, fol. 319v.

14. Racine, II, pp. 377–78 (Jan. 1659).

15. To these can be added descriptions of events with music organized by the Jesuits in provincial cities. There was a great homogeneity of Jesuit worship throughout France; thus many of the devotional entertainments recounted in BN, mss. fr. 23506, 23498, 23499, 23500, and 23502 appear to be imitations of the latest innovation in the three Parisian houses.

16. BN, ms. fr. 23500, fol. 39v (at Orléans, 1690).

17. BN, ms. fr. 23506, fol. 240v (at the Church of the Oratoire in Paris, 1677).

18. Its title supposedly was *Les exercices spirituels qui se font dans les assemblées particulieres et secretes de ceux qui sont de la Congregation de Notre Dame de Bonsecours dans la chapelle interieure du college de la Compagnie de Jesus, de la tres-fidèle ville de Perpignan...*, published at Perpignan by François Vigé of the Place neuve, 1688, BN, ms fr. 23500, fol. 235v.

19. See Ranum, "Jesuits," note, for how two of these commissions were combined by the eighteenth-century bookbinders.

20. AG, 631/A, "Livre de comptes de la procure de l'Assistance de France, 1680–1715," 1694.

21. Lecerf, II, p. 297.

22. The following manuscript volumes from Brossard's collection not only contain works by Charpentier but were copied onto Jesuit paper: BN, Vm^7 71; Vm^1 1175 bis; Vm^1 1175 ter; Vm^1 1269 (1); Vm^1 1478–80. In Vm^7 1110, which also has Jesuit paper, are works by Élisabeth Jacquet de La Guerre, the younger sister of a member of the GUISE MUSIC.

23. At any rate, the treble clef is the sort he used after 1681.

24. The "Mémoire" of 1726 mentions, fol. 13, in what today is called cahier "c," preludes for H. 226, H. 81, and H. 22. Cahier "c" is made of papers used in 1695 or 1696.

25. Lecerf, III, pp. 188–89.

V, The Sainte-Chapelle of the Palace of Justice, pp. 241–250

1. Nicolas Boileau, *Œuvres complètes*, edited by C.-H. Boudhors (Paris, 1939), pp. 312–18; Michel Brenet, *Les Musiciens de la Sainte-Chapelle du Palais* (Paris, 1910); BN, Morel de Thoisy, 78, "Usages de la Sainte-Chapelle" (1697), fols. 29 ff.; Henri Stein, *Le Palais de Justice et la Sainte-Chapelle* (Paris, 1927), especially pp. 130–60; M.A. Vidier, "Notes et documents ... sur la Sainte-Chapelle (XIIIe–XVe siècles)," *Mémoires de la Société de l'Histoire de Paris et de l'Île-de-France*, 28 (1902), pp. 213–383 (the rules differ little from those of the seventeenth century).

2. Brossard (Y. de), p. 30.

3. Brenet, pp. 260–61.

4. For the implications of the term *clerc*, see Marion, "Clerc," p. 91: "The title *clerc* is acquired by being tonsured, but a tonsure did not suffice for acquiring the privileges of the clergy. For that, according to the terms of article 38 of the Edict of Apr. 1695, men had to live clerically, that is, 'residing and serving during religious offices or [participating] in the ministry and holding livings [*bénéfices*] from the Church.'" The music master of the Sainte-Chapelle did not have a living, he was paid "wages"; and although he resided within the Palace of Justice and sat near the clergy in the choir stalls, this first vow and the tonsure that went with it did not make him a priest who could serve during a mass, nor did it bring him any of the fiscal privileges enjoyed by the clergy.

5. AN, MC, LXIX, 171, My. 12, 1698 (Chaperon's testament).

6. AN, MC, XXIII, 399, Apr. 5, 1709, doc. 13 (inventory).

7. AN, LL 609, fol. 66.

8. AN, LL 609, fols. 66v–67.

9. Brenet, p. 245.

10. AN, MC, LXIX, 171, My. 27, 1698 (inventory).   11. BN, Morel de Thoisy, 78, fol. 28.

12. AN, MC, LXIX, 171, My. 27, 1698 (inventory).

13. *Ceremoniale parisiense ... Ludovici Antoinii [de Noailles] ... archiepiscopi parisiense ...* (Paris, 1703), pp. 355–57, 363.

14. Brenet, pp. 242 ff.; *Mercure*, Apr. 1680, pp. 323–24. Lalouette was a personal friend, AN, MC, LXIX, My. 12, 1698 (will).

15. Brenet, p. 236, Jul. 12, 1681.   16. Brenet, pp. 257, 259, 261, 262.

17. Brenet, pp. 255–56 (and also Touzelin, My. 14, 1695).

18. Sauval, I, p. 445.

19. *Variétés historiques, physiques et littéraires* (Paris, 1752), III, pp. 46–50. Another "long Offertory" was performed in the Grande Salle of the Palace of Justice each December 6, when the procurators organized a vespers service for Saint Nicolas, with the participation of the musicians of the Sainte-Chapelle. The baton-carrier of the barristers would make "thirty-six bows, in imitation of the ones made by the First President in the Red Mass," p. 49.

20. Patin, III, p. 289.   21. Brenet, p. 252.

22. A possible sponsor is the Confraternity of Saint Michael and Our Lady of Tombelaine, which, like the Parlement, was independent of the chapter but called upon the musicians of the Sainte-Chapelle. The confraternity celebrated the principal feasts of the Virgin with masses that were "totally in music, as usual"; and on Saint Michael's Day the musicians of the Sainte-Chapelle customarily performed a "high mass and Benediction of the Holy Sacrament" and would then march with the members through the city streets. Anne Lombard-Jourdan, "La Confrérie de Saint Michel du Mont," *Bulletin de la Société de l'histoire de Paris et de l'Île-de-France* (1986–87), pp. 105–78.

23. Brenet, p. 268.   24. Mazarine, ms. 4404, fol. 23v.

25. Brenet, p. 268.

26. AN, MC, LXIX, 171, My. 27, 1698 (inventory).

27. "A bundle of five pieces concerning the estate of Master Marc-Antoine Charpentier, Music Master of the choirboys of the Sainte-Chapelle of the King in Paris, brother of the late [Mlle. Charpentier], among which are" her loans to him. AN, MC, XXIII, 399, Apr. 5, 1709.

Panel 8, Elite Patrons

I, Domestics of the Infant Jesus, pp. 253–261

1. AN, MC, CXII, 371, Sept. 20, 1675.   2. BN, DB, 554, "Ragois," fol. 2.

3. On Olier and Bretonvilliers, see Yves Poutet, *Le XVIIᵉ Siècle et les origines lasalliennes* (Rennes, 1970), pp. 317 ff.

4. Olier's sister married a Roger: AN, M.C., XXIV, 340, fol. 601; BN, DB, 576, "Roger," fol. 6. Neret: BN, DB, 485, "Neret," no. 12732, fols. 1–3. For Olier, see La Chesnay, "Olier"; and for Dalibert, see AN, MC, XX, 265, Oct. 1, 1647.

5. Joseph Grandet, *Mémoires: Histoire du Séminaire d'Angers* (Paris, 1893), II, p. 296. This statement is inaccurate. The school used the existing building and eventually enlarged it, but this expansion did not occur until some years after Bretonvilliers' death.

6. Joseph Grandet, *Les Saints prêtres français* (Angers, 1897), II, p. 297.

7. Grandet, *Histoire*, II, p. 296.   8. Grandet, *Histoire*, II, p. 560.

9. Grandet, *Les prêtres*, II, p. 297.   10. Grandet, *Histoire*, II, pp. 559–60.

11. Denis Amelote, *Le Petit Office du Saint Enfant Jésus*, by Sister Marguerite du Saint-Sacrement, Carmelite of Beaune (Paris, 1683), whose second edition, published in 1683, was dedicated to Mme. Pierre Séguier; Père Floeur, *Le Prince de la Paix, L'Enfant Jésus* (Brussels, 1662), BN, D 35203.

12. Yves Leskoutoff, *La Sainte et la Fée, Dévotion à l'Enfant Jésus* (Geneva, 1987), pp. 42–50; Bremond, III, pp. 511–81.

13. Leskoutoff, p. 55, who quotes Parisot.

14. AN, Y 2802, Mar. 29, 1732. In 1720 there were two paintings of Jesus in the chapel: "a large painting representing Our Lord in the Temple amidst the doctors" and "another painting ... representing Our Lord" (probably in the form of an Infant Jesus, that is to say, an infant-king surrounded by baby angels and nimbi), AN, MC, VIII, 937, Aug. 31, 1720.

15. G. Thiriot, "Les Carmélites de Metz," *Mémoires de l'Académie nationale de Metz* (1925), pp. 102 ff.

16. *L'Almanach du Palais*, bound with Louis de Bailleul's journal, Arsenal, 8° S 13762.

17. Doncourt, p. 106.

18. Doncourt, p. 102; Brice, III, pp. 450–51. The confraternity initially met at the convent of Notre-Dame-de-Liesse, near Franqueville's academy.

19. AN, R 4* 1056, item 876, quoted at length in Langlois, pp. 115–16.

20. René Thuillier, *Vie et Éloge du T.R.P. Nicolas Barré* (circa 1700), pp. 22–25.

21. *Sacra congregatio pro causis sanctorum officium historicum, 8, Parisien. Beatificationis et canonizationis servi dei Nicolai Barré* (Rome, 1970), doc. VII, p. 132, and doc. IX, which states that the institute opened its doors in "October 1675–January 1676." On Barré and the "Daughters of the Infant Jesus," see also Farcy, *Institut des Sœurs du Saint Enfant Jésus dites de la Providence de Rouen* (Rouen, 1939), and *Le Révérend Père Barré* (Paris, 1942); Charles Cordonnier, *Le R.P. Nicolas Barré* (Paris, 1938); Nicolas Barré (and Montigny-Servien), *Maximes Spirituelles* (Paris, 1694) and *Statuts et Reglements des Escoles chrestiennes et charitables du S. Enfant Jésus* (Paris, 1685); AN, S 7045, S 7048-7050 and M 57, the archives of the institute; and Poutet. The teachers were generally known as "Father Barré's girls," but the statutes published in 1685 give the official name: "The Christian and Charitable Schools of the Holy Infant Jesus."

22. AN, MC, XCIX, 270, Sept. 12, Dec. 10, and Dec. 11, 1676.

23. The inventory of this room in 1688 mentions a Virgin by Corneille, a "Descent from the Cross" and the "Infant Jesus by Nocret," AN, R 4* 1056, nos. 658-62.

24. AN, S 7045, "Abrégé de l'histoire de l'Institution."

25. Madame de Maintenon, *Lettres* (Paris, 1935), III, no. 419; *Mémoires de Manseau, intendant de la Maison royale de Saint-Cyr* (Paris, 1902), p. 63; Poutet, p. 322.

26. Archives of Saint-Sulpice, "Journal des actions de Monsieur Tronson," ms. 96, item 82.

27. AN, MC, 68, Jul. 16, 1685; Nicolas Le Jeune de Franqueville, *La grammaire abrégée et méthodique*, (Paris, 1686) 4th ed.

28. BN, Rés. Yf 434, "subject book" for *Le Ballet des Arts*, which was performed with a Latin tragedy, *Clisson*.

II, Riants the Procurator, pp. 262–267

1. AN, MC, XI, 227, Sept. 3, 1670 ("Armand-Jean"); XI, 282, My. 4, 1681 ("Jean-Armand"); VII, 150, Sept. 12 and Oct. 25, 1694, his testament and inventory ("Armand-Jean").

2. BN, PO, 33, "Alesso," fol. 2; *Mercure*, Oct. 1694, pp. 283–87 (genealogy of the Riants family, back to Denis and his wife).

3. BN, Cabinet d'Hozier, 7, "Alesso," fol. 1; DBF, "Alesso, Jean d'."

4. BN, Carrés d'Hozier, 15, "Alesso," fol. 230.

5. *Mercure*, Feb. 1678, pp. 215–18.

6. Chantilly, A, 13, debt no. 33.

7. AN, MC, XX, 265, Oct. 1, 1647.

8. La Fontaine, II, p. 407.

9. For these texts, see La Fontaine, II, pp. 612–20, 956–65.

10. BN, DB, 564, "Riants," fol. 37v.

11. *Gazette*, 1684, p. 768.

III, Le Brun the Painter, pp. 268–272

1. For all un-footnoted facts in this portrait, see the chronology that introduces *Charles Le Brun, 1619-1690, peintre et dessinateur*, catalog for the exhibit at Versailles, 1963; and AD-77, 112 E 27, Oct. 20, 1624, for the Broquoys of Bellé.

2. J.-P. Babelon, "Nouveaux Documents pour la restauration de l'Hôtel de Guise," *La Vie urbaine*, Jul.–Sept. 1965, p. 5.

3. Charles Le Brun, *L'Expression des Passions et autres conférences; Correspondance*, ed. Julien Philippe (Maisonneuve and Larose, 1994), pp. 203–04.

4. Le Brun, pp. 206–07.

5. Perhaps Séguier's papers in the Dubrowski collection in Russia could answer this question. The ones in the Manuscript Department of the Bibliothèque nationale de France have not.

6. *Mercure*, Sept. 1679, pp. 55–56, 63.

7. The earliest piece for the "demoiselles Pieches," cahier 22, H. 170, a psalm text appropriate for Thursday vespers, was probably performed while Mme. de Guise was at court, Mar. 3–Apr. 7, 1679. It is more difficult to date the first piece for the "Piesches" in the roman-numbered series: H. 74 of cahier XXV, a psalm for Thursday matins or for Corpus Christi. If H. 74 was in fact for Corpus Christi, it postdates the piece in cahier 22 by a month or so. Corneille and DONNEAU DE

VISÉ corroborate this date. In the *Mercure*, Apr. 1681, pp. 340–41, they imply that Charpentier began working for the Dauphin during the first half of 1679.

8. BN, ms. fr. 10265, Feb. 7, 1687.

9. *Gazette*, 1687, p. 110; *Mercure*, Feb. 1687, pp. 299–304.

10. Library of the École des Beaux Arts, ms. 556, carton II.

IV, Harlay the Archbishop and Madame Harlay of Port-Royal, pp. 273–279

1. Montpensier, III, p. 384.

2. BN, DB, 349, "Harlay," fol. 99 (in d'Hozier's own hand); Moréri, "Harlay," "Lorraine."

3. *Gazette*, 1671, p. 131.

4. That particular notebook, cahier VI, may have been recopied at a later date, for it is made of Jesuit paper and the names of two Jesuit singers are marked in the margins. If by chance the initial commission did come from Harlay, this means that Charpentier became owner of the work after the Archbishop's death in August 1695 and was free to rework and reuse the composition.

5. Bussy Rabutin, IV, p. 157 (*re* Mme. de Guise), and III, 377, 421, 427; IV, pp. 51, 158, 169; Choisy, p. 599 (on how La Chaise pushed Harlay into the background).

6. Daguesseau, quoted in Sainte-Beuve, *Port-Royal* (Paris, 1955), III, pp. 154–55.

7. *Mercure*, Jan. 1685, p. 247; Feb. 1685, pp. 309–11.

8. Sauval, p. 425.

9. *Mercure*, Je. 1687, p. 27; Aug. 1687, pp. 96–97.

10. The troublesome *gros cahier* was broken up by the royal librarians. Remnants are: cahier "a" (the "Epitaph"), now in vol. 13; cahier "d" ("for Port-Royal"), now in vol. 28, and a motet for Saint Anne, now at the start of cahier 9—all made of Jesuit paper. In 1709 Jacques Édouard inserted into this *gros cahier* the copies made for his edition of Charpentier's motets. The librarians discarded these copies. "Augustine dying" is not listed as part of the *gros cahier*, and may have been misplaced and tucked at the end of cahier 9 (which contains *Judith*, which Charpentier recopied onto the same Jesuit paper used for "Augustine dying"). "Mémoire" of 1726, fols. 13–14.

11. Racine, II, pp. 167–68.

12. Racine, II, p. 1037 ("p. 166, n. 1").   13. Saint-Simon, I, pp. 255–57.

V, Richelieu of Rueil, pp. 280–283

1. For the Duke's finances, see Joseph Bergin, *Richelieu: Power and the Pursuit of Wealth* (New Haven, 1985), chap. VIII.

2. Dangeau, Aug. 29, 1684, I, pp. 48–49.   3. Ranum, "Ruel."

4. Ranum, "Brossard," p. 298; MdP, 4768, Jan. 3, 1676 (newly appointed).

5. Ranum, "Brossard," pp. 297–98.   6. Ranum, "Brossard," pp. 297–98, 300.

7. Dangeau, I, p. 211, Aug. 26, 1685.   8. *Mercure*, Oct. 1685, pp. 2–9.

9. Ranum, "Brossard.", p. 300.

10. Tessin, quoted by D. Helot-Lécroart, *Le Domaine de Richelieu à Ruel* (Rueil, 1985), p. 68.

Panel 9, The Royal Houses of Bourbon and Orléans

I, Monsieur and Madame of the House of Orléans, pp. 287–299

1. Dethan, *passim*.

2. Dethan, pp. 121–24; and on the notion of a noble's "duty" to rebel, see Arlette Jouanna, *Le Devoir de révolte*, (Paris, 1989), especially pp. 65–90, for clientage networks.

3. Tallemant, II, p. 176.   4. Motteville, p. 109.

5. Montpensier, I, pp. 108, 141.   6. Saint-Simon, I, p. 278.

7. Montpensier, II, p. 453.   8. AN, MC, XXX, 216, Aug. 27, 1672.

9. Arsenal, ms. 4212, fols. 44 ff. (Pinette de Charmoy, 1660); ms. 4213, fol. 74 (Pinette de Charmoy, "intendant of His Royal Highness's household," 1662); ms. 4214, fol. 34 (Pinette de Charmoy, intendant of Madame, 1672); ms. 6525, fol. 55 (J. Pinette de Charmoy, "secretary of the commandments" of the late Mme. de Guise, 1696); ms. 6526, fol. 25 (N. Pinette de Charmoy, "general treasurer of the household and the finances" of the late Gaston, 1661); ms. 6533, fol. 12 (Pinette de Charmoy, Gaston's "general treasurer," 1644), fol. 43 (Macé Bertrand de la Bazinière, 1646), fol. 111 (Dalibert, Gaston's "general comptroller of finances," 1646), fol. 449v ("Dalibert,

nephew, secretary of finances," 1658); ms. 6535, fol. 5 (Malier, Bishop of Tarbes, "first almoner" of Mme. d'Orléans, 1668), fol. 31v (Pinette de Charmoy, "secretary of the commandments" of Mme. de Guise, 1672); ms. 6636 (Pinette papers); ms. 6637, fol. 28 (Montrésor, 1637), fol. 241 ("Charmoy, secretary of our finances," 1648), fols 380–90 (Dalibert, 1652); and so forth. For the Maliers' links to Monsieur and Madame, see the MALIER portrait; for the Doujats, MARIE TALON's portrait; for the Grimaudets of Blois, the portrait of ÉLISABETH GRIMAUDET; and the HAVÉ DE SAINT-AUBIN portrait. These papers also suggest that several of the Charpentiers' SEVIN relatives were in Gaston's service during the 1640s, but I have been unable to prove a cousinship between Jean Croyer and Mme. Sevin; between "Picques, gentleman in ordinary" and Anne Picques, who wed a Sevin in 1669; and between the composer and several other householders named Charpentier who served Gaston and Mme. de Guise over the decades. See also Mesnard, pp. 746–47, for links between the householders of the Guises and those of the Orléans.

10. Motteville, p. 179. 11. Montpensier, III, p. 376.

12. Armand de Bourbon, Prince of Conti, quoted by Tournoüer, p. 79.

13. Rombault, p. 501.

14. Montpensier, III, p. 496; Choisy, pp. 582–83. 15. Montpensier, II, p. 323.

16. Motteville, p. 486. 17. Montpensier, II, pp. 281–82.

18. BN, ms. fr. 10277, p. 32; Montpensier, III, p. 276.

19. Montpensier, III, pp. 425, 428.

20. Tournoüer, p. 83; Arsenal, ms. 4212, fols. 2, 8v; BN, ms. Clairambault, 491, fol. 31.

21. Montpensier, III, pp. 431–33. 22. MdP, 4891, Oct. 5, 1663.

23. For the financial aspects of the settlement, see BN, ms. Clairambault, 491, fol. 31v.

24. BN, ms. n.a. fr. 22951, fol. 95, July 30, 1660. 25. Montpensier, III, p. 423.

26. BN, ms. n.a. fr. 22951, fols. 86, 89, 91, 93.

27. Loret, III, pp. 335–36; Gazette, 1661, p. 284; and Montpensier, III, pp. 498–500, for another (?) service for Gaston.

28. Montpensier, III, p. 497.

29. Montpensier, III, pp. 391–92; MdP, 4661, Mar. 1, 1660.

30. BN, ms. Clairambault, 491, fol. 31. 31. Gazette, 1671, Dec. 27, 1670.

32. Psalm 112 (H. 149) was recited during Sunday vespers and on the Feast of the Circumcision, Jan. 1; psalm 126 (H. 150) during Wednesday vespers and the Feast of the Circumcision; Magnificat (H. 72) daily vespers; psalm 116 (H. 152) during Monday vespers and on Christmas. This week of services, reconstructed, with Charpentier's pieces and mass marked on the appropriate day: Sat., Dec. 27: mass and associated pieces; Sun., Dec. 28: Ps. 112; Mon. Dec. 29: Ps. 116; Tues., Dec. 30: nothing; Wed., Dec. 31: Ps. 126; Thurs., Jan. 1 (Circumcision), Ps. 112 or Ps. 126 (this would mean a reuse); Fri., Jan. 2: nothing; Sat. Jan. 3: Magnificat during Little Office of Virgin. With no reuse of a given piece, Charpentier provided a composition for five of the seven days.

33. Gazette, 1671, p. 604. 34. BV, Barb. lat., 3525, fol. 604.

35. Ranum, "Quenouille"; BN, ms. Clairambault, 1204, fol. 213.

36. La Fontaine, II, pp. 597–99. 37. Mazarine, ms. 2740, fol. 13v.

38. Gazette, April 1672, p. 360. 39. Mazarine, ms. 2740, fol. 15v.

40. Gazette, April 1672, p. 370. 41. Mazarine, ms. 2740, fols. 18–20v.

42. Mazarine, ms. 2740, fol. 18; BN, ms. fr. 16663, fols. 181v, 188v.

43. For adult burials: Brevarium romanum (Paris, 1669), hivernalis, p. clxv. For vespers: "cujus loco ad Laudes dicitur psalmus De Profundis, qui psalmi non dicitur in die omnium fidelium Defunct."; and Breviarium romanum (Paris, 1682), concerning the same service: "A laudes on dit le psaume De Profundis, lesquels psaumes ne se disent point au jour des Trepassez."

44. MdP, 4670, Sept. 23 and Dec. 2, 1672. 45. Mazarine, ms. 2740, fol. 20v.

46. Gazette, My. 1672, p. 492; MdP, 4670, My. 20, 1672.

47. Musical masses for Madame at Charonne: MdP, 4768, file 1, Apr. 5, 1677; 4769, Apr. 2, 1678. For Gaston at Charonne: MdP, 4769, Mar. 3, 1678; Gazette, 1673, p. 436.

II, The King, the Queen, and the Dauphin, pp. 300–317

1. Charles Robinet, Lettres en vers à Madame, Mar. 22, 1670.

2. Loret's successors, I, cols. 426–27. 3. Loret's successors, I, col. 715.

4. Chabod, I, pp. 300, 303. 5. Robinet, Jan. 5, 1669, Apr. 27, 1669.

6. *Gazette*, 1672, p. 551.

7. Mazarine, ms. "Lettres autographes," 1857, 83ᵉ pièce, Jul. 1, 1675.

8. Marie Du Bois, pp. 433, 442–44, 467. His library included all of Lully's operas and miscellaneous motets and airs. He also owned Laffilard's *Les principes de la musique*. BN, ms. n.a. fr. 10687, pp. 126–28.

9. *Gazette*, 1677, pp. 76, 176, 192, 219, 251, 252; MdP, 4674, Je. 27, 1678 (studies in his apartment).

10. MdP, 4768, file 1, Mar. 12, 1677.

11. MdP, 6265, Feb. 26 and Mar. 18, 1678 (Saint-Mesme).

12. *Gazette*, 1679, p. 86.   13. MdP, 4674, Mar. 28, 1678.

14. MdP, 4674, Je. 27 and Oct. 6, 1678 (he will study German); 4675, Oct. 6, 1679 (German was delayed a full year).

15. MdP, 4820, Dec. 16, 1678. D'Estival's post as "singer of the Music of the Chapel" initially went to Jean Gaye, "singer in ordinary to the Chapel," in consideration of both his musical abilities and the services he has been rendering for several years; but by Apr. 29, 1680, the post had been transferred to another singer, Jean Jouilhac, Marcelle Benoit, *Musiques de cour: chapelle, chambre, écurie, 1661–1733* (Paris, 1971), pp. 58, 71.

16. The piece that immediately precedes the psalm for the Pièche sisters cannot be dated to the month or week; but the text that immediately follows the psalm was approved by Rome on Mar. 17, 1679, and the notebook ends with the music CHARLES LE BRUN used for the Feast of Saint Louis, Aug. 25, 1679.

17. Ranum, "Colbert." This is paper "6": it appears in the middle of cahier XXVI (1680) and in cahier XXVIII (1679?–80?), Ranum, *Chronologie*.

18. *Mercure*, Apr. 1681, p. 341: Charpentier had been composing for the Dauphin for "two years."

19. Quoted by Maral, p. 72.

20. MdP, 4676, Feb. 2, 1680; Sévigné, Feb. 21 and 23, 1680.

21. *Mercure*, Mar. 1688, p. 320.

22. Maral, pp. 19–32, and figures 2, 3, 6, 7, 12, 14, 15.

23. *Mercure*, May, 1680, pp. 102–03.   24. *Gazette*, 1680, p. 239.

25. Sourches, I, p. 11.   26. *Mercure*, Apr. 1681, pp. 340–41.

27. *Mercure*, Je. 1681, pp. 4–10.

28. When not absent (Strasbourg and the northern frontier, Sept. 30 to mid-Nov.), the court spent most of its time that fall at Saint-Germain-en-Laye rather than Versailles; yet, apparently relying on a cover or slip of paper that subsequently was discarded, probably during the binding process, the author of the "Mémoire" of 1726, fol. 3, noted that H. 180 was an *Exaudiat* for Versailles."

29. Ranum, "Portrait."   30. Comédie, Reg. 13, fol. 243.

31. *Mercure*, Jan. 1682, pp. 114–18; *Gazette*, 1682, pp. 14, 17.

32. *Gazette*, 1682, p. 213.

33. *Mercure*, My. 1682, pp. 175–90; BN, ms. Clairambault, 816, fols. 217 ff.: Pierre and Antoine Pièche, the instrumentalists, were "bailiffs" of the Dauphine's "hall," 1683. Charpentier's name is not on the list.

34. *Gazette*, 1682, p. 468.

35. *Mercure*, Aug. 1682, p. 159; *Gazette*, 1682, p. 474.

36. *Mercure*, Dec. 1682, pp. 3–56. Note the similarities between the vocabulary of this article and the libretto of Charpentier's *Les Plaisirs de Versailles*: "His fatiguing work did not prevent the King from giving orders for the convenience of his court. He did more than that: he provided Pleasures, and specified what they would be each day" (*Mercure*, Nov. 1682, p. 355).

37. *Mercure*, Jan. 1683, p. 320.   38. *Gazette*, Jan. 1683, p. 24.

39. In the arabic-numbered series of notebooks, cahier 37 contains the piece for the Apartments, which clearly was written prior to Jan. 1683. Two works follow for an unusual trio (two *dessus* and a bass), written for an unidentifiable event (H. 187 and H. 407), perhaps in late Dec. or early Jan. 1683 since one of the texts is recited on Dec. 8, Jan. 1, and Jan. 6. The next work, copied into cahier 38, is music for the late Queen, probably performed in mid-Sept. In the roman-number series, cahier XXXV contains a work for Jan. 1, 1683 and two pieces for the Corpus Christi procession of Je. 17, the latter surely written prior to Charpentier's illness. Then there is a gap until the music for the late Queen, performed on Dec. 20. In other words, Charpentier composed nothing between early May and mid-September.

40. In the 1680s the musicians at the electoral court in Munich included Bombarda, Moradelli, Orlandi, Gianetti, Cagliardi, Steffani, Barberio, and Cattini, Archives, Munich, Furstensachen 677e. In 1667 the future Dauphine had gone to Italy. She and her brother spoke Italian, P. C. Hartman, "Die Dauphine Marie Anna Christine von Bayern und ihr Hofstaat," *Oberbayerishces Archiv für Vaterlandische Geschichte*, 93 (1971), p. 21; *Kurfürst Max Emanuel Bayern und Europa um 1700* (Munich, 1976), catalog of exhibit at Schloss Schleissheim, II, pp. 230–43.

41. Sourches, I, p. 267.

42. "Mémoire" of 1726, fol. 10.

43. Dangeau, I, pp. 349–356; *Gazette*, 1686, p. 290.

44. BN, ms. fr. 10265, fol. 105v.

45. Dangeau, I, p. 194; MdP, 4784, Oct. 28, 1686.

46. Dangeau, II, pp. 42 ff.

47. Ranum, "Jesuits."

48. *Mercure*, Dec. 1693, p. 335.

III, Two Philippes of the House of Orléans, pp. 318–327

1. For Philippe II, see Nancy Barker, *Brother to the Sun King, Philippe, Duke of Orléans* (Baltimore, 1989); and for Philippe III, see Jean Meyer, *Le Régent, 1674–1723* (Paris, 1985).

2. Ranum, "Lully."

3. Loret's successors, cols. 58, 83, 230–31, 235–36.

4. Chabod, I, p. 273; see also Robinet, Jan. 5, 1669.   5. *Pourtraicts*, p. 30.

6. Émile Magne, *Le Château de Saint-Cloud* (Paris, 1932), p. 59.

7. Sieur Combes, *Explication historique* ... (Paris, 1684), pp. 2–4.

8. *Gazette*, 1672, p. 817: "so many pleasures prepared in a single day by Sieur Guichard, gentleman in ordinary to Monsieur." For Guichard, see Ranum, "Lully."

9. Magne, p. 160; Nuitter and Thoinan, pp. 163, 202.

10. *Gazette*, 1670, p. 336; 1676, p. 264; 1677, p. 396; MdP, 469, Apr. 11, 1678.

11. *Gazette*, 1675, p. 984; 1677, p. 16; 1683, p. 12. This was not an innovation, however: they attended services there Dec. 23, 1671, for a Benediction of the Holy Sacrament, *Gazette*, 1671, p. 1242.

12. Comédie, Reg. 1, Hubert.

13. Quoted by Magne, p. 119

14. *Gazette*, 1676, p. 718.

15. Magne, pp. 124–40.

16. *Gazette*, 1680, p. 228; 1686, p. 240. *Mercure*, Apr. 1681, pp. 340–41; My., 1682, pp. 175–90.

17. *Mercure*, My. 1680, pp. 295–309.

18. *Mercure*, Apr. 1681, pp. 327–44.

19. *Mercure*, My. 1682, pp. 175–90.

20. *Mercure*, Dec. 1693, p. 335.

21. Spanheim, p. 157.

22. Sourches, I, pp. 395–97.

23. *Mercure*, Mar. 1688, pp. 28–29.

24. Ranum, "Loulié," 1987, pp. 67–75.

25. AN, MC, LXXXV, 213, Mar. 2, 1678.

26. BN, DB, 614, "Sevin," fols. 2, 3 (Claude Sevin, gentleman in ordinary to the Duke of Orléans, 1669, was married in the presence of BISHOP NICOLAS SEVIN, his "cousin." He was still Monsieur's gentleman when he remarried in 1684); and *Gazette*, 1676, p. 220, where he conducts body of Monsieur's son to Saint-Denis); Ranum, "Lully," pp. 18–19 (Guichard and GILLES CHARPENTIER THE SECRETARY).

27. AN, Y 14062, Jan. 4, 1734, estate of René Charpentier.

28. BN, ms. fr. 17050, fol. 279: Père La Chaise asks Mme. de Guise to accept the dedication of a book so that it could be published.

29. Cessac, MAC, pp. 22–23.

IV, Madame de Toscane, pp. 328–335

1. Rodocanachi, *passim* (he draws heavily on MdP), especially pp. 20–21 (portrait) and pp. 205–13 (her life at Montmartre).

2. BN, ms. fr. 10277, p. 133; Montpensier, III, pp. 371–72.

3. Montpensier, III, p. 451.

4. Rodocanachi, pp. 20–21.

5. Choisy, p. 582.

6. Choisy, p. 582.

7. Weavers, pp. 130–42.

8. MdP, 4815, Nov. 21 and 22, 1670.

9. MdP, 4815, Mar. 6, 1671; 4818, Oct. 12, 1674.

10. Montpensier, IV, pp. 353–55.

11. MdP, 4818, Mar. 19, 1675.

12. MdP, 6265, Dec. 1674.

13. Montpensier, IV, pp. 529–30.

14. *Mercure Hollandois*, Jul. 1675, pp. 402–03 (supplied by J. de La Gorce).

15. Sévigné, Je. 14, Jul. ∥10, and Aug. 19, 1675; MdP, 4791, Mar. 20, 1685 ("*prigione alta di Monmartre*").

16. Montpensier, IV, pp. 376–78, 520–23.   17. MdP, 4767, file 2, Aug. 23, 1675.

18. MdP, 4768, file 3, Feb. 10, 1676.

19. MdP, 4769, file 1, Nov. 13, 1677, and Feb. 4, 1678.

20. MdP, 4767, file 3, Feb. 13, 1674.   21. MdP, 6265, Je. 1676.

22. MdP, 4768, file 3, Jan. 31, 1676.   23. MdP, 4768, file 3, Feb. 24, 1676.

24. MdP, 4768, file 3, Je. 12 and 15, 1676.

25. MdP, 4768, file 1, Aug. 2, 1677 (*converzatione di musica*); she once went to Strasbourg's lodgings for a musical "*divertissement*": MdP, 4769, file 2, Jan. 5, 1679.

26. MdP, 4769, Jan. 2, 1678.

27. The similarities between the titles of his lost *La Dori e Oronte* and Cesti's *La Dori ovvero La Schiava Fedele* (composed in honor of Mme. de Toscane in 1670) raises the possibility that Charpentier's *La Dori*—and perhaps his *Artaxerse* as well—was written for the Grand Duchess during the late 1670s. Ranum, "Quelques ajouts."

28. MdP, 4767, file 2, Oct. 28, 1675.

29. *Gazette*, 1676, p. 718₁; MdP, 4768, file 3, Oct. 9, 1676 ("*converzatione di musica*," the term the Florentines used to denote an opera).

30. MdP, 4768, file 3, Nov. 27 and Dec. 11, 1676.   31. Montpensier, IV, p. 527.

32. MdP, 4768, file 1, Mar. 12, 1677.   33. MdP, 4769, Mar. 11, 1678.

34. MdP, 6265, Feb. 26, 1678.

V, Isabelle d'Orléans of Alençon, pp. 336–343

1. For her life, see Rombault, *passim*; Tournoüer.

2. BN, ms. fr. 23162, fol. 120; Antoine Oudin, *Dictionnaire Italien et Français* (Paris, 1663), revised by "Laurens Ferreti, Romain, secretary, interpreter, and language teacher of Their Royal Highnesses Mlles. d'Alençon and Valois," dedicated to the two princesses.

3. Arsenal, ms. 6533, fols. 290v, 344 (1656, 1657).

4. For Isabelle at thirteen: MdP, 4661, "portrait" of Mlle. d'Alençon.

5. Rombault, p. 478; Montpensier, II, pp. 281–82; *Gallia Christiana*, XIII: Marguerite de Lorraine is number LI (became coadjutrix in 1625), and Isabelle d'Alençon is number LIII (received bull in 1648 and was succeeded by a Lorraine relative in 1657).

6. Rombault, p. 480.

7. Bourgoing, quoted in Bremond, III, pp. 117–18 (and *passim* for Bérulle and Saint-Sulpice, but especially pp. 117–154, 458–507). A careful reading of Bremond, to situate Isabelle d'Orléans in the Oratorian and Sulpician devotional model, is essential for an understanding of the compositions that Marc-Antoine Charpentier copied into his arabic-numbered notebooks from 1671 to 1687.

8. MdP, 4661, Aug. 4, 1659; Sept. 6, 1659; Feb. 24, 1660.

9. Mareschaulx, canon of Chartres, "Oraison funèbre d'Élisabeth d'Orléans," BN, ms. Clairambault, 1100, fols. 157 ff. (pp. 9–10).

10. Rombault, p. 481.   11. MdP, 4661, Feb. 24, 1660.

12. Saint-Simon, I, pp. 279–80.

13. Montpensier, III, p. 467; Mesnard, pp. 744–47 (on Sainte-Mesme).

14. Montpensier, IV, pp. 33–35.   15. Loret's successors, I, cols. 18, 426–27.

16. Tournoüer, pp. 87–88.   17. Loret, III, p. 257.

18. Saint-Simon, I, p. 278; and Loret's successors, I, cols. 785, 913 (part of her mother's court).

19. MdP, 4666, My. 13, 1667.

20. Loret's successors, II, cols. 851–52; *Gazette*, 1667, p. 488, and p. 132 for the usual sort of festivities at the wedding of a noble: a snack, a supper, a concert, a play, and finally the marriage at midnight or later.

21. Saint-Simon, I, p. 279.   22. Montpensier, IV, p. 183.

23. Saint-Simon, I, pp. 278–79.

24. Montpensier, IV, p. 75. The domestics have been identified: Marie de Fioravanty, already in Mlle. d'Alençon's service in 1656 (Arsenal, ms. 6533, fol. 288; ms. 4213, fols. 6v, 64v; 6525, fol. 55) and indemnified by Mlle. de Guise (AN, MC, XCIX, 246, Mar. 19, 1671); and Charles

Fioravanty, her secretary, indemnified by Mlle. de Guise for the loss of his position (AN, MC, LXXV, 138, Nov. 15, 1667). They appear to have the relatives of Fioravanti, "a Tuscan-born gentleman who had long worked in Rome for the late Monsieur [Gaston]," ASV, Principi, 92, Jan. 13, 1668 (letter by Princess Isabelle recommending Fioravanti to the Pope).

25. MdP, 4818, Mar. 18, 1675; Arsenal, ms. 6631, file II, household lists, Jan. 1673 (and 1674, where his name no longer appears). Marc-Antoine Charpentier's name is not on either of these lists, which suggests that he was paid by Mlle. de Guise.

26. Montpensier, IV, p. 535.   27. MdP, 4669, Sept. 19, 1671.

Panel 10, The House of Guise

I, Mademoiselle Marie de Guise and her Family, pp. 347–358

1. BN, ms. fr. 32588, p. 271; BN, PO, 2804, "Tellier," fol. 31.
2. BN, ms. fr. 5800, Oudin's "Histoire de la Maison de Guise," fol 221; 5801, fol. 45v.
3. *Discours véritable de la délivrance de Monseigneur le Duc de Guyse, nagueres captif au Chasteau de Tours* (Paris, 1591), pp. 10, 17.
4. Ulysse Chevalier, *Notre-Dame de Lorette* (Paris, 1906), p. 365.
5. Caillières, *Le Courtisan predestiné, ou le duc de Joyeuse Capucin* (Paris, 1662), p. 151; BN, ms. fr. 10277, p. 37.
6. *Bulletin de la Société de l'Histoire de Paris et de l'Île-de-France*, 21 (1894), pp. 35–36: the heirs, who lived in the short same street as Philippe de Champagne, surely were the painter's relatives. In other words, the Guise officer of the sixteenth century, like the painter, was a relative of Anne Jacquet, a member of the GUISE MUSIC.
7. Caillières, pp. 170–73; note the similarities with the devout master depicted in Fleury.
8. In 1629 the General of the Society of Jesus commended Henriette-Catherine de Joyeuse for her "benevolence toward the Order," BN, ms. fr. 22443, fol. 31.
9. "Today there is [in France] no house more miraculous than that of Liesse. ... Marchais is not so much an inheritance of the House of Guise as a mark of its devotion. This Cardinal of Lorraine ... having a very strong devotion for the Queen of Heaven, bought this land for the convenience of Charles IX, who sometimes came to visit this Holy Chapel," R. de Cerisiers, S.J., *Image de Notre Dame de Liesse ou son histoire authentique* (Reims, 1632), pp. 493, 495. Mlle. de Guise's official title was "Dame of Marchais and of Liesse."
10. Tallemant, I, p. 225.
11. Jean Orcibal, *Jean Duvergier de Haurannes, abbé de Saint-Cyran et son temps* (Paris, 1948), II, p. 239, who quotes Lancelot.
12. Tallemant, I, p. 227.   13. Tallemant, I, pp. 226–27.
14. Loret, II, p. 166.   15. Tallemant, I, p. 228.
16. *Pourtraicts*, pp. 58–59.   17. Tallement, I, p. 55.
18. BN, ms. fr. 24986, fol. 42, Bouton de Chamilly to GAIGNIÈRES, Je. 26, 1679.
19. BN, ms. fr. 24985, fol. 421, letter from the Bishop of Boulogne to GAIGNIÈRES, Mar. 7, 1688.
20. Tallemant, I, p. 55.
21. BN, ms. fr. 24987, fol. 300, letter from Procurator General Harlay.
22. Motteville, I, p. 27.
23. Pierre Bayle, *Dictionnaire* (Rotterdam, 1697), "Guise, Charles de Lorraine, duc de," p. 1352.
24. Grillon, ed., *Les Papiers de Richelieu* (Paris, 1975), I, p. 384.
25. Montpensier, IV, p. 212.   26. BN, ms. Clairambault, 1130, fol. 35v.
27. BN, ms. Clairambault, 381, fol. 245.
28. BN, ms. Clairambault, 1204, fol. 163 (Genoa, Feb. 9, 1635).
29. AN, MC, CXV, 81, inventory, Apr. 23, 1641.
30. Langlois, p. 51.   31. Tallemant, V, p. 131.
32. From the 1650s on, the various Florentine agents in Paris regularly sought reimbursement for the costs of shipping *scatole* and *cassette* for Mlle. de Guise. See, for example, MdP, 6185, Nov. 9, 1663: "La scatola delle galanterie che la Serenissima Gran Duchessa invia a Mademoiselle de Guisa mi è stato dall'ordinario ...."
33. Florence, Archivio di Stato, ms. 135 (the *Settimana*); and Miscellanea Medicea, 11 (the *Diario Tinghi*).

34. Warren Kirkendale, *The Court Musicians during the Principate of the Medici* (Florence, 1993), pp. 367, 377, 381.

35. Weavers, pp. 113, 115; Kirkendale, pp. 337, 344.

36. François de Bassompierre, *Journal de ma vie*, ed. Chantérac (Paris, 1870-77), IV, p. 341; BN, ms. Clairambault, 1204, fol. 163.

37. BN, ms. Clairambault, 1204, fol. 165, Oct. 24, 1640.

38. Bassompierre, IV, p. 341. For Henri, see Joseph Bergin, "The Decline and Fall of the House of Guise as an Ecclesiastical Dynasty," *The Historical Journal*, 25 (1982), pp. 781-803.

39. Oudard Coquault, *Mémoires (1649-1668)*, ed. Ch. Loriquet (Rheims, 1875), p. 442.

40. BN, ms. Clairambault, 384, fols. 386-89.

41. Montpensier, I, p. 283; II, p. 444; Coquault, p. 443; BN, ms. fr. 10276, pp. 320-22, 408, 603.

42. Motteville, I, p. 160.   43. BN, ms. fr. 18431, fol. 528.

44. BN, ms. fr. 20475. fol. 165, Mar. 14, 1641.   45. Langlois, pp. 70-71 (Feb. 1642).

46. BN, ms. fr. 18431, fol. 534.

47. AN, MC, CXV, 94, Aug. 19, 1647; XCV, 99, Je. 27, 1650, redemption of a *rente* created in 1634. For Le Ragois, her intendant in the 1640s, see "Abrégé du plaidoyer," BN, factums, 4° Fm 14859, p. 28.

48. BN, ms. fr. 20475, fol. 165 (Mar.14, 1641); ms. Clairambault, 1204, fol. 166.

49. BN, ms. n.a. fr. 4293, p. 119.   50. BN, ms. fr. 14661, fols. 35v-43.

51. BN, ms. Clairambault, 384, fols. 211, 256, 285, 294; 385, fols. 7, 26, 55, 98, 100-05.

52. BN, ms. Clairambault, 1204, fol. 166.

II, Mademoiselle Marie the Regent, pp. 359-378

1. Motteville, I, p. 33.

2. BN, ms. fr. 11424, fols. 188-89, Aug. 17, 1611.

3. J. Loiseleur, *L'Expédition du Duc de Guise à Naples* (Paris, 1875).

4. BN, ms. fr. 20475, fol. 181.

5. BN, Factums, 4° Fm 14859, "Abrégé du plaidoyer de Mlle. de Guise," p. 29.

6. Motteville, I, p. 91; Fontenay-Mareuil, quoted by Langlois, p. 61.

7. See the doggerel verse quoted by Michaud and Poujoulat, Claude de Bourdeille, Count of Montrésor, *Mémoires*, ed. Petitot and Monmerque (Paris, 1826), p. 178; MdP, 4891, Mar. 3, 1656 (proposed marriage to the Duke of Beaufort).

8. Michel de Marolles, *Mémoires* (Amsterdam, 1755), II, p. 191.

9. Dethan, pp. 155-56; Montrésor, pp. 175-81.

10. Montrésor, p. 180.

11. BN, ms. fr. 20547, fols. 42-43v (unsigned), and fol. 45; BN, ms. fr. 20480, fol. 105: "Letter of lament to M. de Montrésor, by Mlle. de G" (reproduced in Montrésor, p. 178). It bears Marie de Lorraine's seal.

12. BN, ms. fr. 10265, fol. 14, circa My. 1682; BN, ms. Clairambault, 1205, fol. 701; AN, MC, XCIX, 283, Dec. 28, 1679, to "Sister of the Holy Martyrs, named in the world Marie Naudot, profess in the royal abbey of Montmartre five or six years ago, and who formerly was in her service." Since nuns generally took their final vows at approximately eighteen years of age, this would mean that Marie (or Marguerite) Nodot was born circa 1655, when Mlle. de Guise was forty; BN, DB, 403," fols. 24v and 60; Roger de Bussy Rabutin, *Carte géographique de la Cour et autres galanteries* (Cologne, 1668), p. 19; *Mercure historique et politique* (1688), Mazarine, 33891, IV, p. 279.

13. AN, MC, LXXXVII, 152, Jul. 16 and Aug. 26, 1653; XCIX, 249, Nov. 20, 1671; XCIX, 297, Apr. 12, 1684 ("Countess of Montrésor").

14. Moréri, "Bourdeilles."

15. Marolles, II, p. 191; *Lettres du Cardinal Mazarin*, ed. Ravenel, Société de l'Histoire de France (1836), II, p. 20; AN, MC, CXV, 142, Jul. 16, 1658.

16. Tallemant, V, p. 227; Langlois, p. 77 (Sept. 1646); René-Renaud de Sévigné, *Correspondance du Chevalier de Sévigné et de Christine de France Duchesse de Savoie*, ed. J. Lemoine and F. Saulnier (Paris, 1911), pp. 193, 198 (Oct. 1652); Henri d'Orléans d'Aumale, *Histoire des princes de Condé ...*, (Paris, 1863-96), VI, pp. 581-82.

17. Montpensier, II, pp. 442-43.

18. Montrésor gave as address the rue neuve Saint-Louis, Jul. 9, 1650, Chantilly, séries H, carton 9, "Bourdeilles"; AN, MC, LXXXVII, 152, Aug. 26 1653; CX, 136, Nov. 30, 1658. After her mother's death (CXV, 132, Mar. 6, 1656) and My. 1657, when she bought the Volière (CXV, 137, My. 3, 1657), Mlle. de Guise resided in "her hôtel" on the rue d'Orléans, parish of Saint-Jean-en-Grève.

19. Gazette, 1666, p. 484.

20. Claude-François Ménestrier, Des Représentations en musique anciennes et modernes (Paris, 1681), p. 191.

21. AN, MC, CXV, 132, Mar. 6, 1656.

22. AN, MC, CXV, 92, Aug. 17, 1646; and the public version in Gazette, 1646, p. 760.

23. AN, MC, CXV, 131, Nov. 20 and 22, 1655.

24. BN, ms. Clairambault, 1204, fol. 167; Loret, II, p. 165.

25. Patin, II, p. 240 (information provided by Jérôme de La Gorce.)

26. Montpensier, II, p. 382.   27. Loret, II, p. 166.

28. For this will: Loret, II, p. 166; BN, Factums, f° Fm 11621, "premier cahier."

29. BN, Factums, f° Fm 11621, "premier cahier."

30. BN, ms. fr. 20547, fol. 31: Mlle. de Montpensier congratulates him on his nomination, Mar. 5, 1656.

31. BN, ms. fr. 10277, pp. 167–68.

32. Nicolas Lescaloppier, Relation de ce qui s'est passé à l'arrivée de la Reine Christine de Suède à Essaune en la Maison de Monsieur Hesselin (Paris, 1656); Montpensier, II, pp. 455 ff.

33. Archenholz, I, pp. 530–31. This historian of Christina of Sweden had at his disposal a great number of sources that are no longer extant. He seems to be citing either Montpensier or Motteville here, but neither memorialist refers to Mlle. de Guise.

34. Gazette, 1656, p. 1000; Nicolas Lescaloppier, Sur l'entrée de la Reine de Suède Christine à Paris (Paris, 1656); Patin, Lettres, II, pp. 249–50.

35. Gazette, 1656, pp. 1031, 1036.   36. Archenholz, I, p. 255.

37. For Gilbert, the play, and Charpentier's music, see Charles Whitfield, "Une tragédie-pastorale de Gabriel Gilbert et Marc-Antoine Charpentier, Les Amours de Diane et d'Endimion (1681)," Littératures classiques: Théâtre et musique au XVIIᵉ siècle, no. 21 (1994), pp. 125–37. Although his "key to the allegory" of Gilbert's play seems based less upon a consultation of the Queen's papers at Montpellier and Stockholm than upon Greta Garbo's Queen Christina and a superficial reading of Bildt, for example, pp. 70, 90–93, the possibility of an allegory cannot be excluded. If the work is indeed allegorical, that makes the revival of 1681 especially intriguing.

38. BN, ms. fr. 10277, pp. 158–59.

39. On Quinault and Duke Henri, see, N. M. Bernardin, Tristan L'Hermite (Paris, 1895), pp. 304–05; and Étienne Gros, Philippe Quinault, sa vie et son oeuvre (Paris, 1926).

40. MdP, 4891, Feb. 6 and 16, 1657. Jérôme de La Gorce, "Les Plaisirs troublez de Louis de Mollier, Revue internationale d'études musicale, 8/9 (1996/1997), pp. 157–74.

41. Loret, II, p. 301.

42. Quoted by Henri Prunières, L'Opéra italien en France avant Lully (Paris, 1913), p. 205.

43. Quoted by Langlois, p. 84.   44. Motteville, I, p. 403.

45. Marolles, Mémoires, III, p. 209; Montpensier, III, p. 583.

46. AN, MC, IX, 425, Mar. 11, 1660.   47. Loret, II, p. 327.

48. Montpensier, II, p. 443.

49. AN, MC, CX, 136, Nov. 30 and Dec. 8, 1658.

50. MdP, 6161, Apr. 12, 1670 (autograph letter).

51. The girl's stay in Paris is scattered throughout MdP, 6185 and 6186, Feb. 1663–Mar. 1665.

52. MdP, 6186, Apr. 23, 1666.

53. BN, ms. Clairambault, 718, fol. 399, an undated autograph letter; and, on the Guises and the precedence due them, Saint-Simon's notes, Dangeau, II, pp. 245 and 248.

54. Saint-Simon, II, pp. 843–44; BN, ms. Clairambault, 1160, fol. 48.

55. Loret, III, p. 205.   56. MdP, 4891, newsletter, My. 27, 1664.

57. Gazette, 1664, pp. 555–56; Loret, IV, pp. 206–07.

58. Gazette, 1664, pp. 627–28.

59. BN, DB, 403, "Lorraine," fols. 462v–63v (Sept. 16, 1665).

60. For example, see AAE, Rome, 175, fols. 123–24, 286, 287, 304.

61. Ranum, "Feindre."

62. On the duties of a preceptor: "Preceptors take the place of fathers and mothers. For the same reason, ... they should not be viewed as the absolute masters of the children, nor claim to govern them according to their taste and their caprice, without any dependence upon the parents. ... Among the virtues of a good master, vigilance and assiduousness occupy the first rank," Charles Rollin, *De la Manière d'enseigner et d'Etudier les belles lettres* (Avignon, 1768), IV, pp. 569, 571.

63. Mesnard, pp. 876–77.

64. BN, ms. Clairambault, 1204, fols. 198, 212. Le Brun was already at work in Apr. 1668 (AN, MC, XCIX, 234, Apr. 28, 1668). His father had been captain at Mlle. de Guise's château of Marchais, AN, MC, LII, 128, Apr. 30, 1691, doc. 17.

65. MdP, 4666, My. 20, 1667.   66. Montpensier, IV, pp. 78, 80.

67. The "de Voisins" were not related to the TALON–Voisins who were friends of the Charpentiers. However, in 1674 Alzeau married Paule "d'Alibert" who, like JACQUES I DALIBERT had relatives in Toulouse. Like the Daliberts, Alzeau's father had served GASTON D'ORLÉANS back in the 1640s. BN, Carrés d'Hozier, 642, "Voisins," fols. 351-53. Jacques I Dalibert's mother, née Poussoy, came from Toulouse, AD-31, 3E 11855, no. 8180, Je. 12, 1640 (information provided by Gayle Brunelle); AN, MC, II, 130, Nov. 3, 1629 (Jacques I's marriage to Étiennette Charpentier).

68. Montpensier, III, p. 490. For noblewomen, protection, and patronage, see Sharon Kettering, "The Patronage Power of Early Modern French Noblewomen," *The Historical Journal*, 32 (1989), pp. 817–41; and Kettering, "The Household Service of Early Modern French Noblewomen," *French Historical Studies*, 20 (1997), pp. 55–85.

69. BN, ms. fr. 17052, fol. 343.

III, The Abbess of Montmartre pp. 379–389

1. Biver, pp. 478–95; Maurice Dumolin, "Notes sur l'abbaye de Montmartre," *Bulletin de la Société de l'histoire de Paris et de l'Île-de-France*, 58 (1931), pp. 145–238; André Maillard, *Les origines du vieux Montmartre* (Paris, 1983).

2. BN, ms. Clairambault, 1204, fol. 166.

3. Blémur, pp. 17, 28-29, 39, 45–46; *Les devoirs funèbres ... [pour la] coadjutrice de Madame l'abbesse de Montmartre* (1634), Mazarine, 21804, a life of Françoise-Renée's predecessor.

4. *Propre des saincts de la royale Abbaye de Montmartre* (Paris, 1638), BN, B 16297, especially p. 15 (text of H. 347, for Illation of Saint Benedict) and p. 41 (complete text of H. 29, for Feast of Saint Genevieve, Jan 3). In another copy of this *Propre*, BN, B 16296, one of the nuns marked circumflexes over the Latin syllables to be accentuated. *Proprium sanctorum regalis abbatiae et inclyti Monasterii Montis-Martyrum ...* (Paris, 1635), which lists all the feast days at the abbey and, p. 4, shows text of Charpentier's H. 347. *Processionel monastique de l'Abbaye royale de Montmartre, ordre de Saint Benoist* (Paris, 1675), Mazarine, 23853, pp. 220–21, the text of H. 29; p xxviii, "Veni sponsa Christi" (cahier 2, H. 17); and pp. liii-lvi, and lxiii for *salut* services that specify singing of "Ecce Panis angelorum" (cahier 22, H. 242), "O salutaris hostia" (cahier XXXI, H. 249?), "Panis angelicus" (H. 243) and "O sacramentum pietatis" (cahier "d," H. 274?). Dom Pierre de Sainte-Catherine, *Cérémonial monastique des religieuses de l'abbaye royale de Montmartre lez Paris* (Paris, 1669), whose section on organs is reproduced in Cl. Noisette de Crauzat, "Le rôle de l'orgue à ... Montmartre au XVIIᵉ siècle," *L'Orgue*, no. 231 (Jan.–Mar. 1997), pp. 21–25. *Rituel Monastique pour l'abbaye royale de Montmartre* (Paris, 1664), BN, B 16801. *Les Tenebres de la Semaine Sainte pour les religieuses ... de Montmartre* (Paris, 1647), BN, B 2889; *Ceremonial des religieuses de l'ordre de S. Benoist* (Paris, 1626), for the nuns of Monstervilliers, near Rouen, BN, B. 5221. And several almost identical *procès-verbaux* of the procession of Saint Denis: AN, MC, XX, 339 (My. 1, 1672), 353 (My. 1, 1679), and XX, 413, (My. 1, 1700).

5. Blémur, pp. 17, 41.   6. Mazarine, ms. 4404 (c. 1653), fol. 171.

7. Sauval, I, p. 353.

8. University Library of Utrecht, BPL 286/IV/41: André Pineau, Jul. 10, 1648 (transcribed by Jean-Luc Tulot, whom I thank for this information).

9. BN, ms. fr. 22431, fols. 109-15.   10. Loret, II, p. 337.

11. Loret, III, p. 267.

12. MdP, 4768, Mar. 9, 1676. PHILIPPE I D'ORLÉANS and his wife attended Tenebrae there, Apr. 3, but there is no mention of Louis XIV, *Gazette*, 1676, p. 264.

13. AN, MC, XX, 339 (Je. 25, 1672), a summary of donations and the creation of several masses for the dead; XCIX, 267, (Mar. 6, 1676), apartment for Mlle. de Guise; XCIX, 273 (Aug. 12, 1677), 279 (Jan. 26, 1679), 282 (Dec. 28, 1679), and 289 (Sept. 27, 1681), pensions to nuns; XCIX, 292 (Aug. 3, 1682), chapel for Holy Family of Jesus.

14. MdP, 4768, file 1, Apr. 5, 1677; 4769, Apr. 2, 1678; 4769, Mar. 3, 1678; 4817, Nov. 3, 1678 (his heart at Montmartre).

15. *Gazette*, 1673, p. 388.

16. Marie-Ange Duvignacq-Glessgen, *L'ordre de la Visitation à Paris au XVIIe et XVIIIe siècles* (Paris, 1994), pp. 230–31.

17. From an *Épître au bénédictines du Calvaire*, quoted by Dom Y. Chaussy, J. Dupaquier *et al.*, *L'Abbaye Royale Notre-Dame de Jouarre* (Paris, 1961), I, p. 196, n. 29.

18. MdP, 4767, file 2, May 17, 1675; and Duvignacq-Glessgen, pp. 229–38.

19. MdP, 6525, Feb. 26 and Mar. 18, 1678.

20. MdP, Prin., 4767, file 2, Nov. 8, 1675.   21. MdP, 4767, file 3, Feb. 13, 1674.

22. MdP, 4677, Dec. 11, 1687; BN, ms. fr. 23498, fol. 254v.

23. MdP, 4802, Mar. 7, 1688.

24. Marie du Bois, p. 28 (about Gaston d'Orléans' Music during the 1640s).

25. BN, ms. fr. 17052, fols. 337–72.   26. BN, ms. fr. 17048, fol. 191.

27. MdP, 4822, Nov.–Dec. 1682; 4823, early Jan. and Apr. 23, 1683; and BN, ms. fr. 17048, fol. 191.

28. MdP, 4791, Mar. 7, 1683.

29. MdP, 4783, in a cluster of autograph letters from Mlle. de Guise.

30. *Gazette*, 1687, p. 39, and *Mercure*, Jan. 1687, pp. 267–70; and, for comparable decorations at the Visitandines, Duvignacq-Glessgen, pp. 221–22.

31. MdP, 4891, Jan. 30, 1662.

IV, Louis-Joseph, the Last Duke of Guise, pp. 391–403

1. BN, DB, 403, "Lorraine," fol. 25.

2. Montpensier, II, p. 323; BN, ms. fr. 10276, p. 217; AN, MC, LI, 165, Oct. 20, 1654 (his inventory).

3. BN, ms. fr. 10276, p. 296 (his father's estate); AN, MC, CXV, 126, My. 25, 1654 (gifts to him from his grandmother, including the "tapestry of the ages" that had decorated his late father's bedroom).

4. BN, ms. fr. 20547, fol. 31.   5. Loret, IV, p. 51.

6. Jules Fériel, *Notes historiques sur la ville et les seigneurs de Joinville* (Paris, 1835), pp. 145–49, 162.

7. Paul Fréart de Chantelou, *Le Journal de voyage du Cavalier Bernin en France*, ed. Milovan Stanić (Paris, 2001), pp. 210–11, 254.

8. Loret's continuers, I, cols. 840–41, 844; and cols. 882, 889 (she entertains the Queen).

9. *Gazette*, 1666, p. 556.   10. BN, ms. Mélanges Colbert, 15, fol. 454.

11. Stockholm, Royal Archives, Gallica, 24, My. 27, 1667; MdP, 4666, My. 13 and 20, 1667.

12. Montpensier, IV, p. 183.   13. Saint-Simon, I, p. 279.

14. Montpensier, IV, pp. 45–46.   15. Montpensier, IV, pp. 74–75.

16. AN, MC, IX, 425, Mar. 11, 1660 (Duke Henri); AN, AP I, 106, will (Mlle. de Guise); Arsenal, ms. 6535, fol. 31, and ms. 6631, file II (Mme. de Guise).

17. ASV, Barb. lat. 3525, fol. 19.   18. AN, MC, XCIX, 234, 236, and 240.

19. BN, ms. fr. 20475, fol. 375.   20. Chabod, I, pp. 263, 273, 281, 320.

21. Bussy Rabutin, I, p. 180.   22. Montpensier, IV, pp. 75, 80.

23. *Gazette*, 1668, p. 767.

24. Sévigné, Feb. 9, 1671; MdP, 4815, Mar. 6 and My. 15, 1671.

25. Mayolas, *Lettres en vers*, BN, Rés. Lc² 29, "tenth day of Lent 1671."

26. *Gazette*, 1664, p. 812; MdP, 4668, Mar. 27, 1669 and Aug. 9, 1669; 2661, Jul. 1–22, 1667 (Minerbetti); 6388, fols. 67 ff., and 6389, fols. 99v–104 (Cosimo); 2662, Oct. and Dec. 1670 (Mattias Bartolomei's visit: "hopes one day to go to Italy"); 4669, Oct. 17, 1670 (son of Marchese Pucci), Jan. 9, 1671 (two *cavallieri* accompany Florentine resident), Je. 4, 1671 (more Italian visitors).

27. La Fontaine, II, pp. 597–98.   28. La Fontaine, II, pp. 581–82, 583, 930.

29. *Gazette de France*, 1671, pp. 630–33.   30. Montpensier, IV, pp. 278–79.

31. Patin, III, pp. 782–83; Sévigné, Aug. 5, 1671; MdP, 4669, Jul. 30, 1671.

32. ASV, Barb. lat., 3525, fols. 604–05.
33. MdP, 4817, Nov. 3, 1673.
34. *Gazette*, 1671, pp. 737, 781, 830–31, 854–55.
35. *Gazette*, p. 1672, p. 792.
36. Loret, II, p. 248.

V, Madame de Guise, pp. 405–425

1. MdP, 4669, July 31, 1671; 6161, Aug. 7, 1671; Montpensier, IV, p. 302.
2. AN, MC, LXXV, 163, Dec. 20, 1672.
3. Ranum, "Quenouille," p. 223–24.
4. BN, ms. Clairambault, 1204, fol. 190.
5. BN, ms. Clairambault, 1204, fols. 179–219.
6. MdP, 4669, Sept. 11, 1671.
7. AN, MC, LXXV, 161, My. 19, 1672, and LXXV, 163, Dec. 20, 1672; Tournoüer, p. 89.
8. Chabod, II, p. 160; Crussaire, p. 121.
9. *Gazette*, 1672, p. 551.
10. Arsenal, 6631, File V, "*mémoire*" by Boullet, 1674.
11. Simon de Doncourt, *Remarques historiques sur l'église et la paroisse de S. Sulpice* (Paris, 1783), p. 106; Mazarine, Rés. 19170, inventory of her furniture.
12. Ranum, "Feindre," pp. 12–13.
13. Gazette, 1673, p. 532; compare with *Gazette*, 1665, p. 1066 (DOWAGER OF ORLÉANS and MLLE. D'ALENÇON).
14. *Mercure*, Feb. 1693, p. 313.
15. Montpensier, IV, p. 370.
16. *Gazette*, 1675, p. 195. See *Gazette*, 1663, pp. 23–24, for the death of a royal child.
17. "Mémoire" of 1726, fol. 13. Copied into notebook 9, just before *Judith sive Bethulia*, the piece subsequently was lost along with the outside sheets of the notebook. This lost work—which used a text for the "faithful dead," recited after the office for the dead that was celebrated on the first Sunday of each month—was an integral part of the Office of the Virgin and probably was used many times in subsequent years at one Guise venue or another.
18. Montpensier, IV, p. 371.
19. AN, MC, LXXV, 175, Apr. 10, 1675, and LXXV, 163, Dec. 20, 1672; BN, ms. Clairambault, 732, fol. 50.
20. MdP, 4818, Mar. 18, 1675 (M. d'Alzau); Montpensier, IV, p. 78; Arsenal, ms. 6535, fols. 31v, 73 (Mme. du Deffand).
21. AN, MC, XXIX, 216, Aug. 27, 1672 (pays a debt for Pierre Perrin); AN, O^1 1687 B, a list of people living in Mme. de Guise's half of the Luxembourg in 1696: no. 703 (the widow of the DOWAGER's valet still lived at the Luxembourg and Mme. de Guise "gave her alms every month"), and no. 705 (several widows and aged domestics were lodged there); O^1 1684 B, no. 718 (Girardin the sculptor got his apartment there "because he was the son of an officer of the late Dowager").
22. Arsenal, ms. 6631, undated memorandum in a file about expenditures for 1674–76.
23. Charles Robinet, *Lettres en vers à Madame*, Aug. 30, 1670; the relics were kept at Saint-Germain-des-Prés, Maarten Ultee, *The Abbey of St. Germain des Prés in the Seventeenth Century* (New Haven, 1981), pp. 185–86.
24. Montpensier, IV, pp. 372–75, 530–35.
25. Tournoüer, p. 95.
26. MdP, 4767, file 2, Oct. 25, 1675, and Nov. 25, 1677; 6265, Sept. 20, 1675, and Feb. 26, 1678 (Saint-Mesme).
27. Rombault, p. 483.
28. MdP, 4819, My. 31, 1677.
29. MdP, 4783, Nov. 20, 1682 (M. de Saint-Frique).
30. H. 168, in cahier 20, was given a prelude, copied into cahier XXIII, which dates from mid-1679. That the prelude is in a roman-numbered notebook suggests reuse at court while Charpentier was composing for the DAUPHIN.
31. "Mémoire" of 1726, fol. 3.
32. *Gazette*, 1663, p. 1148.
33. *Gazette*, 1676, p. 816; Rombault, p. 490; Mazarine, A 16599, *Reglemens des Confreries de la Charité ... et Confreries du grand S. Charles Boromée ...* (Paris, 1676), p. 51: for the year 1676, the "missions" at Alençon included confraternities directed by Mme. de Guise that cared for the sick as well as for "new converts." See also BN, n.a. fr. 23162, fol. 119, for her position about the children of new converts (1687).
34. B. Robert, "Les Maisons des Nouveaux et des Nouvelles Catholiques à Alençon avant la Révocation," *Bulletin de la Société de l'histoire du protestantisme français*, 88 (1939), pp. 273–75; Odile Martin, *La Conversion protestante à Lyon* (Geneva, 1986), especially pp. 79–96, 110.
35. BN, ms. fr. 10265, fol. 89v.
36. AN, MC, LXXV, 182, Aug. 11, 1676 (Alençon); BN, ms. fr. 5989, fols. 96–97, 99.

37. MdP, 4769, Jan. 14, Mar. 11, Mar. 25, Apr. 21, Apr. 22, 1678; 4783, Feb. 16, 1686 (Mme. de Toscane), Je. 5 and Jul. 26, 1684, and Feb. 16, 1686 (M. de Saint-Frique). Abbé de Choisy, *La Vie de Madame de Miramion* (Paris, 1706), pp. 163 ff. (Mme. de Guise and MARIE TALON each contributed 6,000 livres).

38. MdP, 4769, Jul. 22, 1678.

39. MdP, 4820, Mar. 14 (and Apr. 2, Apr. 29, and Jul. 10, 1679; 4816, Oct. 17, 1672.

40. Du Bois, *Sermons*, "Épître."

41. Mazarine, Rés, 19170, fragment of her inventory. It would be interesting to compare her library with the large and quite scholarly library of Élisabeth-Charlotte, the German Protestant-born wife of PHILIPPE II D'ORLÉANS.

42. Ranum, "Portrait."

43. *Gazette*, 1682, p. 66.

44. Berton.

45. MdP, 4783, Aug. 18, 1683.

46. Sourches, I, p. 267 (Bellefonds did not leave until October, pp. 311–12).

47. MdP, 4821, Oct. 17, 1680.

48. MdP, 4819: narrative of Toscane's return; Rombault, p. 495; MdP, 6390, fol. 550, Nov. 8, 1684.

49. A. J. Krailsheimer, *Armand-Jean de Rancé, Abbot of La Trappe* (Oxford, 1974), pp. 298–303; Mazarine, ms. Rés. 19170 (inventory of the chapel).

50. Spanheim, p. 172.

51. Mazarine, Rés. 19170.

52. Tournoüer, pp. 99–101.

53. BN, Morel de Thoisy, 240, fol. 21.

54. Saint-Simon, I, p. 280.

55. Arsenal, ms. 6525, fols. 82v–83, 89v; 6634, doc. 10.

56. BN, Morel de Thoisy, 240, fol. 21.

VI, Marie de Lorraine, the Last Guise, pp. 426–454

1. MdP, 4669, Sept. 19, 1671.

2. BN, ms. Clairambault, 1204, fol. 213.

3. BN, ms. Clairambault, 1204, fols. 214, 219.

4. MdP, 4669, Sept. 11, 1671 (her threat); AD-Aisne, B. 2531, Oct. 7, 1671 (letters patent).

5. Crussaire, p. 121.

6. This hypothesis is based on the fact that two of the works in cahier IX were for a large ensemble similar to the one for which Charpentier wrote while at Saint-Louis. The hypothesis is strengthened by the fact that he apparently recopied the works onto Jesuit paper during his tenure as music master of Saint-Louis.

7. The Cardinal de Joyeuse founded a seminary at Rouen in 1615, to be directed by the Jesuits. H.-C. de Joyeuse, his niece, had carried out his request, and after her death in 1656 Mlle. de Guise tended to the problems that continually cropped up. See for example AN, MC, 283, Sept. 30 and Dec. 30, 1679 (where MARIE TALON's brother-in-law, Louis Voisin, the JESUIT, is rector.)

8. MdP, 4670, Nov. 16, Dec. 25, 1671.

9. AN, MC, XCIX, 249, Nov. 20, 1671.

10. AN, MC, XCIX, 250, Feb. 20, 1672; *Compte des bâtiments du Roi sous le règne de Louis XIV*, ed. J. Guiffrey (Paris, 1881), cols. 630, 644, 1185.

11. *Reglemens avec Instructions et prieres pour l'Association de l'Adoration perpetuelle du tres-saint Sacrement de l'Autel dans la Paroisse de saint Jean en Greve*, "under the authority" of Archbishop HARLAY (Paris, 1673), Mazarine, 42809, piece 2.

12. *Reglemens*, p. 56.

13. AN, LL 805, p. 114.

14. See Bremond, III, pp. 117–27.

15. *Mercure*, Mar. 1688, pp. 317–20.

16. MdP, 4672, My. 31, 1675.

17. MdP, 4672, Apr. 12, 1675

18. For the "regulated" life, see *La Vie réglée des dames qui veulent se sanctifier dans le monde* (Paris, 1693); *Exercice spirituel*, dedicated to Mme. Séguier (1664), Mazarine, Rés. 910.

19. AN, MC, LXXV, 176, Jul. 8, 1675; XCIX, 267, Mar. 6, 1676.

20. AN, LL 1557, fol. 13, Jul. 4, 1675; AN, MC, XCIX, 268, Apr. 29, 1676 (the decorations "she is having made in the Mercy Church").

21. Nicolas Barré, *Maximes spirituelles* (Paris, 1694), ed. Montigny-Servien, pp. 174, 204, 205.

22. AN, MC, XC, 269, Aug. 7, 1676 (hospital at Guise, which was founded only a few days before Mme. de Guise's hospital at Alençon, LXXV, 182, Aug. 11, 1676).

23. MdP, 4767, file 2, Jul. 5, 15, and 29, 1675; 4769, My. 3, 1678.

24. AN, R4* 1056, inventory of Mar. 1688, items 175 ff., 651 ff., 771 ff.

25. MdP, 4767, file 2, Dec. 6, 1675; 4768, file 3, Jan. 31, 1676, and file 1, Feb. 8 and 19, 1677. The Tuscan agents ceased describing these luncheons in 1677, but they presumably continued on into the 1680s.

26. MdP, 6265, Feb. 26, 1678. 27. Brice, I, pp. 141–42.

28. BN, ms. fr. 24987, fol. 290.

29. AN, R4* 1056, inventory of Mar. 1688, items 908 ff.

30. *Mercure*, Feb. 1688, p. 98.

31. MdP, 6390, fols. 492–663, especially fol. 609.

32. The adjective *galante* suggests that the talk was gracious and that men and women participated, while *studiosa* conjures up the studious and philosophical discussions that characterized some literary *salons*. For Mme. de Sablé's philosophical salon, see Conley, pp. 20–44, 167–74. An idea of what Guerrini, JACQUES II DALIBERT, the agents of AMBASSADOR CHAULNES, and the Florentine agents who reported on MME. DE TOSCANE's musical activities meant when they talked about "*conversazione*" is suggested in the article by Lorenzo Bianconi, "Teatro, musica, tradizione dei classici," in *Letteratura Italiana*, (Turin, 1986), VI, especially pp. 344, 354, 367. Bianconi investigates the struggle for supremacy between words and music, as Italian music moved from madrigals performed by small groups in small rooms to operas performed by large groups in large halls. Among nobles and prelates, the *cantata da camera* developed in the seventeenth century and was ideal for performance in the large rooms of their residences. In the late seventeenth and early eighteenth century the *feste musicale* developed—a genre that included *accademie, cantate, serenate*, and so forth. In 1702 the cantata was described as being a "conversation": "la leggiadrissima cosa, e il piú bello, et gentil divertimento che mai possa prendersi in qualunque onorata et nobile conversazione" (G. M. Crescimbeni, *Comentarii [...] intorno alla sua Istoria della volgar poesia*, I, Rome, 1702, book IV, p. 240.

33. Ranum, "Foyer"; and Ranum "Ajouts": were Charpentier's two "Italian operas," *Artaxerse* and *La Dori e Oronte*, written during the early 1680s, the heyday of these "conversations" at the Hôtel de Guise?

34. Ranum, "Foyer."

35. *Mercure*, Aug. 23, 1682, p. 159; *Gazette*, 1682, p. 474.

36. For Portes, see Jean Duron, "Les 'Paroles de musique' sous le règne de Louis XIV," *Plain-chant et liturgie en France au XVIIe siècle*, ed. Jean Duron (Paris, 1997), pp. 125–84, especially pp. 142–44. In 1685 Portes—who was part of the circle of neo-Latinists that included the Santeul brothers and GOIBAUT DU BOIS—was living near the Halles. Portes' poem was also set to music by Daniélis for a service at the cathedral of Vannes.

37. *Gazette*, 1683, p. 576.

38. De Saint-Peres, *Le Vray Tresor de l'histoire saincte ... de Nostre-Dame de Liesse* (Paris, 1647), pp. 28–29, 44–45.

38. Clairambault, 1205, fols 1–609, especially fols. 2, 3, 5, 6, 11, 17, 101, 108v, 121, 355, 473–73v. Minus their coats of arms, the new benches survived the Revolution.

39. MdP, 4783, Dec. 28, 1686. (Other letters: Aug. 15, Dec. 15, 1684, and Jan. 12, 1685, and an undated letter, circa Je. 1683. See also 4792, Je. 6, 1687.)

40. MdP, 4783, in a cluster of autograph letters from Mlle. de Guise to Gondi.

41. AN, MC, CXII, 393, Aug. 29, 1685 (agreement with a Lorraine d'Harcourt); BN, ms. Clairambault, 781, fols. 371–78v, 384v (donation to Stainville de Couvonge, 1686); Montpensier, IV, p. 489.

42. AN, MC, XCI, 297, Jul. 6, 1684.

43. Chantilly, A, carton 13: *rentes* still due in Dec. 1687.

44. MdP, 4791, Jul. 9, 1685; 4820, Jul. 19, 1679.

45. MdP, 4791, Dec. 13, 1683: her observations were so highly valued that they were summarized in code.

46. MdP, 4791, Mar. 27, 1684. 47. Du Bois, *Lettres*, "Epitre."

48. MdP, 4793, Mar. 1, 1688.

49. MdP, 4793, Feb. 16, 1688; 4785, Mother Renville, prioress of the LITTLE CARMEL, Mar. 8, 1688.

50. AN, R4*,1056, inventory of Mar. 1688, items 2–32.

51. Marc-Antoine Charpentier was not among the domestics receiving bequests. The Charpentier who received 2,000 livres was Guillaume Charpentier, a "kitchen boy." AN, MC, CXII, 398, for her autograph will and its codicils; and AN, 300 API, 106 (and MC, LXXV, 370), act of union

signed by recipients, July 19, 1690: "Guillaume Charpentier, living at the Hôtel de Guise, *garçon d'office*." There are numerous printed versions of the will, among them Harlay's copy, BN, ms. fr. 16214, fols. 110 ff., with evaluations of her total worth.

52. BN, ms. Clairambault, 1130, fols. 109v–11.

53. MdP, 4802, Apr. 12, 1688.   54. MdP, 4802, Mar. 7, 15, 1688.

55. MdP, 4677, Mar. 15, 1688; 4793, "nouvelles"; Chantilly, ms. 1218, fol. 85.

Panel 11, They Too Bear Witness

I, Mademoiselle de Montpensier, pp. 457–465

1. See Vincent J. Pitts, *La Grande Mademoiselle at the Court of France, 1627–1693* (Baltimore, 2000); Michel Le Moël, *La Grande Mademoiselle* (Paris, 1994).

2. Montpensier, I, pp. 2–3.

3. Typical are Montpensier, IV, pp. 278–79, 305–06, 325.

4. Montpensier, I, p. 6.   5. Montpensier, I, pp. 71–72.

6. Montpensier, I, pp. 90, 108–09, 116–17; II, pp. 431–33.

7. Montpensier, II, p. 22.   8. Montpensier, II, pp. 366, 395–96.

9. Montpensier, II, p. 296.

10. Montpensier, II, 345–46; Pitts, pp. 119–20, 296 (n. 90).

11. Montpensier, II, p. 349.   12. Montpensier, II, p. 381.

13. For the conditions of the will and the lengthy lawsuit and the sums involved, see BN, factums, f° Fm 11621; BN, Thoisy, 82 Fol 70; BN, 4° Fm 14858–59; and Montpensier II, pp. 65–66 (the diamond); Mazarine, Rés., 19170, Je. 2, 1693 (inventory of her papers involving the inheritance).

14. AN, MC, CX, 136, Dec. 8, 1658 (Dec. 1657–Dec. 1658).

15. Montpensier, III, pp. 243–47 (for the positions taken by both sides in 1658).

16. MdP 4676, Apr. 4, 1681.

17. Bussy Rabutin, V, pp. 251–52, Apr. 1, 1681; MdP 4676, Jan. 17, 1681, Apr. 4, 1681.

18. MdP, 4783, Mother Thérèse, Carmelite, Mar. 24, 1683.

19. BN, ms. fr. 22432, fol. 144.   20. BN, ms. fr. 15517, fols. 219v, 230.

21. Chantilly, ms. 1218, fol. 85.   22. Choisy, pp. 671–72.

23. Montpensier IV, pp. 219, 235.

24. Sévigné, Feb. 9, 1671; Montpensier, IV, pp. 278–79, 302.

25. Montpensier, IV, p. 325.   26. *Pourtraicts*, pp. 48–50.

27. MdP, 6265, Feb. 26, 1678.

28. MdP, 4783, Mother Thérèse: Mar. 24, 1683, Nov. 15, 1684; My. 1685; and Mother Reville: Nov. 10, 1686; 4821, My. 5, 9, and 19, 1681 (the donation); 4785, Aug. 29, 1687 (Montpensier will like the garden in their new convent).

29. Pitts, p. 231.

II, The Poison Investigators, pp. 466–474

1. Although the relationship is not specified, Pierre clearly was the nephew of Jacques I Dalibert. AN, MC, XX, 289, Feb. 12, 1658 (Jacques I Dalibert sells an office at Montauban to Pierre Dalibert); XLIII, 235, Je. 21, 1698 (Pierre's heirs settle with Pennautier). At the time of the sale, Pierre was financial secretary to GASTON D'ORLÉANS. (For corroboration, see Arsenal, ms. 6533, fol. 449v: "Sieur Dalibert the nephew," who was Gaston's financial secretary in 1656.) For more on Pierre and his role in returning Descartes' bones to France, see Descartes, *Œuvres*, ed. Ch. Adams (Paris, 1897–1910), XII, pp. xvi, 470, 554, 559, 597–98; and Adrien Baillet's *Vie de Monsieur Descartes* of 1691 (Paris, 1946), p. 270.

2. BN, ms. fr. Cinq Cents Colbert 234, fol. 212: papers of the Foucquet Affair, where his name rubs shoulders with that of Louis de Bailleul's mysterious strawman, Jacques Charpentier (fol. 134), and with Bailleul's in-law, Claude Le Ragois de Bretonvilliers (fol. 649).

3. Jean-Christian Petitfils, *L'Affaire des Poisons* (Paris, 1977), p. 21. See also Georges Mongrédien, *Madame de Montespan et l'Affaire des Poisons* (Paris, 1953); Frantz Funck-Brentano, *Le Drame des poisons* (Paris, 1936).

4. Nicolas Boileau's First Satire, 1660.   5. Bastille, IV, pp. 293–97.

6. Bastille, IV, pp. 112, 134–36; V, pp. 15, 40, 55.   7. Bastille, V, pp. 13–41.

8. Daniel Dessert, "Finances et société au XVIIᵉ siècle: à propos de la Chambre de Justice de 1661," *Annales, E.S.C.*, 29 (1974), annexe 1.

9. BN, ms. Clairambault, 986, p. 237.

10. BN, ms. Cinq Cents Colbert, 235, pp. 270-73; AN, MC, XC, 244, Jul. 13, 1672; XC, 247, Jan. 2, 1674; XC, 251, Je. 10, 1676 (two acts).

11. Bastille, V, p. 282, Mar. 20, 1679.

12. Bastille, V, pp. 298-300; BN, ms. Clairambault, 986, p 210; Petitfils, p. 65. Jacques I Dalibert had had business dealings (quarry rental) with a Jacques Belot, AN, MC, XX, 257, Nov. 24, 1645.

13. For example, MdP, 4819, Jul. 19, 1677 ("eau de fleur d'oranger," and pure chocolate, with no perfume or musk or amber added); 4820, Apr. 29, 1678 (*manne*, a purgative made from the ash tree); 4676, Dec. 31, 1679 (a box of "remedies"); and 4820, Mar. 14, 1678 (her request to Cosimo III for free medications).

14. Bussy Rabutin, IV, p. 353 (Apr. 28, 1679).   15. Bastille, V, pp. 388, 478, 484-85.

16. Bastille, V, p. 399.

17. Bastille, V, p. 484 (La Charpentier and the rue des Vieux-Augustins) and IV, p. 293 (Pierre Dalibert and the rue des Vieux-Augustins); AN, MC, 257, Nov. 24, 1645 (Jacques I Dalibert lived on the rue des Vieux-Augustins); II, 130, Nov. 3, 1629 (Jacques I's marriage to Étiennette Charpentier); XX, 259, My. 6, 1646 (a document listing all Charpentier–Daliberts); AN, Z¹J 294, Mar. 30-31 and Apr. 2, 1666 (confiscation of Jacques I Dalibert's house on the rue des Vieux-Augustins).

18. BN, ms. Clairambault, 986, pp. 223 ff.   19. BN, ms. Clairambault, 986, p. 234.

20. Sévigné, Feb. 7, 1680.

21. Quoted by Camille Rousset, *Histoire de Louvois* (Paris, 1862), II, p. 568.

22. Bussy Rabutin, IV, pp. 173, 178 (Oct. and Nov. 1680).

23. Petitfils, p. 73.   24. Sévigné, Nov. 8, 1680.

25. Bastille, VII, pp. 17-18, 84.

26. BN, PO, 1928, "Mérault," fols. 351, 375-37v, 376; AN, MC, XXXVI, 163, My. 31, 1639 (inventory of Catherine Charpentier-Mérault). Catherine Charpentier's first cousin was Madeleine Dreux, whose son, Louis Charpentier, married Jeanne Pinon, BN, DB, 170, "Charpentier," fol. 15. Like Jacques I Dalibert, one of their descendents, Pierre Mérault, was fined in the Foucquet Affair, BN, Cinq Cents Colbert, 234, fol. 515.

27. Bastille, VII, p. 78.   28. Bastille, VII, pp. 108, 182-83.

29. Bastille, VII, pp. 114, 117.

III, Gaignières the "Curieux," pp. 475–484

1. Charles de Grandmaison, "Gaignières, ses correspondants et ses collections de portraits," *Bibliothèque de l'École des Chartes* (1890), pp. 573-617; Henri Bouchot, *Inventaire des dessins exécutés pour Roger de Gaignières* (Paris, 1891); and for collectors, Antoine Schnapper, *Collections et collectionneurs dans la France du XVIIᵉ siècle* (Paris, 1988, 1994).

2. Salomon de la Broue, *La Cavallerie françoise* (Paris, 1620), pp. 2-7.

3. BN, ms. fr. 24987, fol. 12.   4. BN, ms. fr. 25691, fol. 7.

5. BN, ms. fr. 24986, fol. 104, Aug. 9, 1671.

6. BN, ms. fr. 24986, fols 114-15 (Sept. 1675), 371 (ca. 1675), fol. 41v (Je. 1679).

7. MdP, 4783, Oct. 18, 1682.   8. MdP, 4783, Jan 23, 1683.

9. Bussy Rabutin, III, pp. 377, 421, 427; IV, pp. 51, 157, 158, 169 (Nov. 1677-Jul. 1688); Spanheim, pp. 423-24.

10. BN, ms. fr. 24986, fol. 361.   11. BN, ms. fr. 24986, fol. 124.

12. BN, ms. fr. 24987, fol. 290, My. 1679.

13. BN, ms. Clairambault, 1205, fols. 681-89, removed from Gaignières' papers by Clairambault circa 1711.

14. BN, ms. fr. 24987, fol. 192.

15. BN, ms. fr. 24985, fols. 242, 399, 421; ms. fr. 24986, fol. 59.

16. BN, ms. fr. 24986, fols 166-67.   17. Sévigné, Mar. 9, 1688.

18. BN, ms fr. 24985, fols. 61-62.

19. BN, ms. fr. 24985, fol. 106, Mar. 30, 1688.   20. Sévigné, Oct. 18, 1688.

21. BN, ms. fr. 24991, Apr. 11, 1688.

22. *Collections de Louis XIV* (Paris, 1977), p. 238.

IV, The Four Roquettes, pp. 485–498

1. Pierre Poussoy, merchant and banker at Toulouse, was Jacques I Dalibert's maternal uncle. Poussoy divided his time between Paris and Toulouse from the 1620s until his death in 1640. AN, MC, II, 130, Nov. 3, 1629; CVII, 104, *quittance*; AD-Haute-Garonne, 3E 11855, no. 8180, Je. 12, 1640.
2. Quoted by Vicomte de Noailles, *La Mère du Grand Condé* (Paris, 1924), p. 343.
3. *Gazette*, 1646, p. 1136 (Nov. 25, 1646).
4. BN, mss. fr. 23203-04, contain Loménie's papers, with many minutes by Roquette; and also ms. fr. 20481, fols. 27, 28, which show Roquette working with Épernon; and Mélanges Colbert, 156 bis, fols. 456, 470, 535, 537, 553, 609, 623, 629..
5. AN, MC, XCI, 301, Apr. 29, 1654.   6. BN, DB, 581, "Roquette," fol. 2.
7. BN, ms. fr. 20481, from the 1660s and 1670s. Some of the papers were preserved by GAIGNIÈRES, probably after Christophle de Roquette's death.
8. Louis André, *Michel Le Tellier et Louvois* (Paris, 1942), pp. 234, 430-31.
9. AN, MC, XCIX, 229, Mar. 3, 1667; 234, Apr. 28, 1668; 238, Apr. 25, 1669. BN, DB, 581, "Roquette," fol. 2, which asserts that Christophle de Roquette came to the Hôtel de Guise in 1674, is therefore incorrect.
10. *Gazette*, 1667, p. 968.   11. BN, ms. fr. 20481, fols. 1-34, 36, 44-50.
12. Anatole de Charmasse, *Etat de l'instruction primaire dans l'ancien diocèse d'Autun* (Paris, 1873), pp. 27-109; Jean de Viguerie, *Une Œuvre d'éducation sous l'Ancien Régime* (Paris, 1974).
13. Mazarine, ms. 2741, fol. 20.   14. *Gazette*, 1672, p. 792.
15. *Gazette*, 1672, p. 119.   16. Montpensier, IV, p. 371.
17. Montpensier, IV, 372-75.
18. The "Infancy of Toulouse," a training school for female teachers, had been suppressed in 1662 for heresy. To learn more about this suspect but highly effective school, DR. VALLANT acquired a copy of the "Mémoire touchant les filles establies à Toulouse," BN, ms. fr. 17049, fols. 88-90.
19. BN, ms. Clairambault, 1205, "Première requête of Mlle. de Guise," fol.1 (p. 4).
20. BN, ms. Clairambault, 1130, fol. 122v: "On croit que l'Evesque d'Autun a pieusement fait mettre *in pacé* un fils."
21. AN, MC, XCIX, 268, Mar. 14, 1671; Vicomte de Grouchy, "Everhard Jabach, collectionneur parisien," *Mémoires de la Société de l'Histoire de Paris et de l'Île-de-France*, 21 (1894), pp. 226-27.
22. AN, MC, XCIX, 281, Sept. 19, 1679; 300 API 922*, "Premier cahier de mon voyage, 1682," with comments added by Mademoiselle de Guise: Joinville, Oct. 14; Ancerville, Nov. 22; Châlons, Dec. 3.
23. *Mercure*, My. 1681, p. 265.   24. AN, Y 246, fol. 128, Jul. 1, 1684.
25. AN, R*4 1056, item 1075, and the foldout version of Gaignières' plan in Langlois.
26. Abbé Deslions, quoted by Jean Serroy, ed., *Le Tartuffe* (Paris, 1997), pp. 171-72.
27. Choisy, pp. 625-26.   28. Saint-Simon, II, pp. 867-68.
29. Sévigné, Apr. 24, 1672; Apr. 12, 1680.
30. BN, DB, 581, "Roquette," fol. 2; BN, ms. fr. 12618, IV, 285.
31. Comédie, Reg. 20, Dec. 10, 1687. (They also attended "*Jaloux*" on Dec. 17, 1687, and paid for more tickets on Feb. 11, 1688).
32. BN, ms. Clairambault, 781, fol. 386v.
33. Bussy Rabutin, IV, pp. 216, 223, 249 (My. 13, 1689).
34. Le Gendre, p. 107.   35. *Les Caractères*, "Des Grands," ¶ 15.
36. *Les Caractères*, "De la Mode," ¶ 24. For Onuphre, Roquette, and the *dévot*, see Michael S. Koppisch, *The Dissolution of Character, Changing Perspectives in La Bruyère's* Caractères (Lexington, Ky., 1981).
37. Saint-Simon, II, pp. 867-68. See also La Bruyère, *Les Caractères*, "De la Chaire," ¶ 13, for an anecdote about the Abbé.

V, Vallant the Physician, pp. 499–507

1. Crussaire, p. 16, who apparently bases this assertion on Jean Astruc's history of the Faculty of Medicine of Montpellier published in Paris in 1767. The records of the Faculty state, however, that Vallant was born at Bourg-Saint-Andéol, a town on the Rhône, just south of Montélimar. Louis Dulieu, *La Medicine à Montpellier* (Avignon, 1983), I, p. 1105.

2. Dulieu, I, p. 1105. For Vallant's life and career, see Crussaire, *passim*; Le Maguet, pp. 441-553; and Mesnard, especially pp. 727-28, 878, 953.

3. Crussaire, p. 71.

4. Crussaire, pp. 73-74, 94, 116, 117-18; 121.

5. For Mme. de Sablé, see Conley, pp. 20-44, 167-74.

6. Crussaire, pp. 118-19. 7. Crussaire, pp. 120-21.

8. Crussaire, p. 121, transcribed that line: "des engagements de devoir pour des personnes qui n'empecheroient de sortir de Paris ...." The sentence does not make sense, unless the *n* is changed to an *m*: "qui m'empescheroient."

9. Arsenal, ms. 6631, household list for 1674.

10. Ranum, "Sweet Servitude." 11. Crussaire, p. 125.

12. BN, ms. fr. 17047, fols. 229-230v; quoted by Le Maguet, pp. 510-13.

13. Montpensier, IV, p. 370. 14. Le Maguet, pp. 514-15.

15. Le Maguet, p. 454 (appointment); BN, ms. fr. 17048, fol. 139 (lodging).

16. BN, ms. fr. 17054, fols. 272, 275.

17. AN, MC, LXXV, 400, Jul. 13, 1694, (M. Du Bois' wills).

18. Mesnard, p. 953. 19. Crussaire, p. 135.

20. Le Maguet, p. 540. 21. BN, ms. fr. 17049, fol. 88.

22. Crussaire, p. 124. 23. Crussaire, p. 137.

24. Crussaire, p. 135.

VI, Loulié and Brossard, pp. 508-514

1. Ranum, "Loulié," and Ranum, "Brossard"; Brossard (Y. de); *Sébastien de Brossard, Musicien*, ed. Jean Duron (Paris-Versailles, 1998); Brossard, *Catalogue*; Jean Duron, *L'Œuvre de Sébastien de Brossard (1655-1730)* (Paris-Versailles, 1995).

2. The strongest piece of evidence is several acts involving Croyers living on the rue Darnetal in Paris. Loulié's relative: AN, Y 160, fol. 439, Nov. 30, 1619; David Croyer: AN, MC, XXXV, 61, Mar. 24, 1610, and XXXV, 77, Mar. 15, 1618.

3. Brossard, *Catalogue*, p. 384.

4. BN, n.a. fr., 6355, Ms. XVIII, fol. 148. 5. Cessac, MAC, 346-61.

6. Duron, p. 105. 7. Brossard (Y. de), p. 15.

8. Brossard (Y. de), p. 14; MdP, 4823, Sept. 20, Oct. 8, 1683; 6390, fols. 492 (Sept. 12, 1684, Guerrini first mentions Morland), 550v, 554, 576, 603, 608v, 609 (Mlle. de Guise's "conversations"), 615, 637, 646, 663.

9. Brossard (Y. de), p. 24.

10. Among others, the pieces in BN, Vm^1 1175 bis, I and II; Vm^1 1478, IV; Vm^1 1269, II; Vm^1 1175 ter, I; Vm^7 71, some of which are not only in another hand than Brossard's but are on Jesuit paper and can therefore presumed to be the work of copyists working for Charpentier during the 1690s.

11. Ranum, "Loulié," (1987), p. 47. 12. Brossard, *Catalogue*, p. 384.

13. Brossard, *Catalogue*, pp. 275-76.

14. Élisabeth Lebeau, "L'entrée de la collection musicale de Sébastien de Brossard à la Bibliothèque du roi d'après des documents inédits," *Revue de Musicologie*, 95-96 (1950-51); and Ranum, "Entrée."

The Portrait at the End of the Gallery

Marc-Antoine Charpentier, pp. 517-590

1. For my principal articles on Charpentier and the people around him, see *Abbreviations*, "Ranum ...," pp. 633-34, *infra*.

2. Brenet, p. 260 ("native of the diocese of Paris." Since these registers usually say that a choirboy came "from Paris" and sometimes even name the parish, it cannot be ruled out that Charpentier was born elsewhere in the diocese); AN, MC, XXIII, 308, Jan. 16, 1662 ("aged eighteen or thereabouts," an expression that generally refers to the anniversary of a baptism rather than the date of birth. In this case, it suggests that the composer was born during the last half of 1643).

3. Charles Le Maistre, *Voyage en Allemagne, Hongrie et Italie, 1664-1665*, ed. Patricia and Orest Ranum (Paris, 2003), *passim*.

4. AN, Y 4003A, avis des parents, Tuition Édouard, Feb. 20, 1685. The most archaic aspects of this "round" script are the C, the r, and the e. For the different hands learned by calligraphers, see plates IX–XII of Diderot's *Encyclopédie*. Another bit of evidence that Charpentier was a trained calligrapher: in cahier XXV, fol. 3, he incorporated into the word "Pieches" the dotted lines that calligraphers made by allowing the quill to jump lightly over the surface of the paper.

5. Étiennette's inventory describes her carefully kept account books; and Marc-Antoine's chronologically numbered classification of the *Mélanges* surely was inspired by his father's practices.

6. Having written the following paragraphs about the indecision that conceivably plagued Marc-Antoine Charpentier during his late teens and early twenties, I read André Blanc, *Racine* (Paris, 2003) and was struck by the similarities between the early years of the future composer and the future poet. Details differ, but pp. 56–58 of Le Blanc's portrait of Jean Racine (the orphaned son of a rather impecunious family whose provincial forebears call to mind the Charpentiers of Meaux, with their successes and their failures) sketch the young man's aspirations and hesitations. As Le Blanc wrote, Racine "had a dream, literary fame. To be a poet: ... in the seventeenth-century this meant first and foremost writing poetry, very good poetry, comparable to the verse of Horace or Virgil. ... This required an enormous amount of work; and it brought in very little money, and until one is recognized, none at all." (Please replace "poetry" by "music.")

7. For example, in an *élévation* composed in 1678 (H. 241), he wrote "Ut supra usque ad *Sed prius*" (As above, up to the words *Sed prius*); and, a bit later, "Sicut in principio usque ad *Sed prius*" (Just as at the beginning, up to the words *Sed prius*), cahier 21, fols. 80–80v.

8. See Jean-Charles Léon, "La rature et l'erreur: l'exemple des messes à quatre chœurs chez Charpentier," *Bulletin Charpentier*, no. 19 (2002), p. 12; and also the sometimes elaborate Latin titles and personages he used in his compositions, among them H. 391, H. 400, H. 415, H. 422.

9. Patricia M. Ranum, "Le Chant doit perfectionner la prononciation & non pas la corrompre: l'accentuation du chant grégorien ...," *Plein-chant et liturgie en France au XVIIᵉ siècle*, ed. J. Duron (Versailles, 1997), pp. 58–83; Trévoux, quoted by Cessac, MAC, p. 23 ("It is true that Charpentier, who was not surpassed in Latin music, was not equally successful with French music"). Note also that the Music Master of the SAINTE-CHAPELLE was expected to help the grammar master instruct the choirboys in the proper pronunciation of Latin.

10. AN, MC, XXIII, 309, Aug. 24, 1662.

11. Le Maistre, pp. 47–49. Save for personal purchases, his expenses were paid by the Duke of Brissac.

12. Le Maistre, pp. 336–66, 433–80.

13. Allusions to his work with Carissimi: *Mercure*, Jan. 1678, p. 231; Feb. 1681, p. 249; Feb. 1687, p. 301; Mar. 1688, p. 321; Dec. 1693, pp. 333–34; Brossard, *Catalogue*, p. 275.

14. For the dangers of winter travel, see Le Maistre, pp. 514–71.

15. *Mercure*, Jan. 1678, p. 231; Feb. 1681, p. 249; Feb. 1687, p. 301; Mar. 1688, p. 321; Dec. 1693, pp. 333–34. It is understandable that this reiterated assertion would be repeated by Titon du Tillet: Ranum, "Titon."

16. Dassoucy, *Rimes*, BN, Rés. R 1936, p. 119. See Dassoucy, *Aventures*, p. 285, for the meaning of *fou*. His remark about Charpentier's mental state is so cryptic that it is impossible to interpret. For a study of the perceived links between creative genius and madness, as understood in Rome at the time, see Rudolf and Margot Wittkower, *Born under Saturn* (New York, 1963). For other uses of the image of the "serpent in his bosom," see Scruggs, p. 194 (*re* his protégé Pierrotin: "Having noted that this little serpent that I was nourishing at my breast ... had kept some of the money..."), p. 205 ("In this distant country, I could not expect bread from the hand of my assassin [Pierrotin], and that to get this bread, I had to give him some at a time when I had none for myself"), and pp. 210–11 (the full text about Charpentier).

17. Ranum, "Quelques ajouts."

18. Brossard, *Catalogue*, p. 275. For the prodigy and memory, see Françoise Waquet, "L'histoire merveilleuse d'un enfant précocement savant: Jean-Philippe Baratier," *Revue de la Bibliothèque nationale*, 47 (1993), pp. 2–7.

19. Le Maistre, p. 451 (Dec. 1664). For more on the music Charpentier could have heard in Rome, see Jean Lionnet, "Charpentier à Rome," *Bulletin Charpentier*, no. 10 (1994).

20. Vicariato, "Anime." There were 81 parishes in the 1660s. Of them, 27 have no records for 1664–67, 4 have incomplete records, and 48 have complete records.

21. Vicariato, "Anime," parish 13: San Lorenzo in Lucina: starting in 1667, via del Carcciofilo (tennis court). For Dalibert: 1665, p. 37 ("Sig. Giuseppe Alberti"; 1668, fol. 32 ("Marchese d'Aliberto" was "renting" from Giovanni Salutati: Dalibert had left that street by 1671 and the lodging was occupied by Jean Tessier, a Frenchman, and "four heretics," that is, Protestants.)

22. Vicariato, "Anime," parish 79: San Stefano del Cacco (Collegio Romano); parish 4: San Apollinare (the *Germanicum*); parish 13: San Marco (*Il Gesù*).

23. Vicariato, "Anime," parish 52: Santa Marie in Monticelli, 1666, fol. 206v, and 1667, fol. 232.

24. For Édouard as the source of Titon's assertions, see Ranum, "Titon."

25. This apartment was vacated in mid- or late-1687 and was promptly occupied by ROQUETTE D'AMADES.

26. Fleury, p. 124.   27. Du Bois, *Lettres*, "Épitre."

28. Baltasar Gracian, *L'Homme de Cour*, trans. by Amelot de la Houssaye (Paris, 1702), Maxim VII, p. 7.

29. Fleury, which is a priceless source for master–servant relationships and obligations; Gracian, which depicts courtly manners and conversation; *Nouveau traité de la civilité qui se pratique en France* (Paris, 1750), p. 20, which discusses in detail the politeness to be observed within a noble household; and Louis de Sacy, *Traité de la Gloire* (Paris, 1715), a depiction of glory, virtue and modesty for nobles and commoners alike.

30. Fleury, p. 145.   31. *Nouveau traité de la civilité*, p. 20.

32. *Nouveau traité de la civilité*, p. 21.   33. De Sacy, p. 225.

34. A glance at Table 1 in Ranum, *Chronologie*, pp. 30–33, shows how the "French" (arabic-numbered) series of notebooks tends to move through the capitalized alphabet. (Each capital letter indicates a brand of paper that appears in both series of notebooks.) There are, of course, a few scattered brands (shown in lowercase) that appear only in that series. By contrast, in the "Roman" (roman-numbered) series of notebooks, whole blocks of paper are indicated by numbers because they appear only in that series. Many of these papers can be linked to an outside patron. When I wrote *Chronologie*, I as yet had no proof that the paper I call "*similijésuite*" (and that I indicate by a †) was produced by a Jesuit-owned mill (Ranum, "Colbert") and that the extremely opaque paper 6 actually shows Colbert's snake rather than a dolphin (Ranum, "Colbert"). As a result of these discoveries I therefore would like to modify my statement on pp. 11–12 of *Chronologie*: It clearly was not "the person who wants to copy his commission onto a paper ... to its very fibers," who hunted for a paper with a watermark that would suggest the patron. Rather, it was the Jesuits themselves, it was Colbert himself who supplied paper bearing their watermark.

35. This is the approach used in Ranum, *Chronologie*.

36. In the main the papers in the arabic-numbered series appear to have been supplied or paid for by the Guises, while the paper used for outside patrons such as MOLIÈRE and the DAUPHIN was perhaps supplied to Charpentier by the patron. (This would explain why, for several consecutive notebooks, a given paper appears in one series, but not the other.) Or perhaps he bought special lots of papers and used leftover sheets for his personal copies of these outside commissions? To see how these papers are distributed, see pp. 30–32 of Ranum, *Chronologie*.

37. Crussaire, p. 125.

38. He seems to have inverted the order of two notebooks in the roman-numbered series: cahier XXIII contains preludes for works composed between June 1679 and early 1680, and cahier XXIV contains preludes for pieces composed in 1677 and the first half of 1678.

39. Among the information that the anonymous compiler of the "Mémoire" of 1726 added to the title, but that he was unlikely to have known without doing archival or liturgical research: H. 180, (which Charpentier called *Exaudiat pour le Roi*) is listed as "Exaudiat pour Versailles" (fol. 3); H. 404, (*Josue*) is listed as "Josué, historia pour les Jésuites" (fol. 3); H. 403, *Mors Saülis et Jonathæ*, is listed as "Mors Saülis et Jonathæ, grandmotet ou dialogue, pièce pour les Jésuites en tragédie" (fol. 3); H. 345 (*Canticum Zachariae*) has a strange allusion to "extraordinary" music (as contrasted with "ordinary"? or as being "extraordinary in conception"?) appended to it: "Motet de Zacharie avec symphonie; cette pièce est extraordinaire" (fol. 4v); and H. 422 (*Judicium Salomonis*) is listed as "Judicium Salomonis, Messe rouge pour l'ouverture du Parlement de Paris à quatre voix et instrumens" (fol. 12v). Anyone who has worked extensively in the Minutier Central of the AN is familiar with this type of makeshift cover.

40. He inverted the order of two notebooks of instrumental music (cahiers XXIII and XXIV, 1677–79), so the notebooks clearly were not yet numbered in 1679. In 1680 he was still using

verbal clues to indicate the move from one notebook to the next. For example, at the bottom of the last page of cahier 24 he indicated "*Miserere*"; the actual piece begins on the first sheet of notebook 25. This was a device used by printers to indicate the next signature in a book. That numbers had not yet been marked on the notebooks is confirmed by the fact that he grouped several notebooks containing music for the Dauphin's Music (cahiers XXV–XXVIII), and inserted them, *en bloc*, in front of cahier XXIX, which begins with music written for Nov. 1680 (H. 500). By 1685 (cahier 43b) he could, however, instruct a copyist to go back to notebook XVII, to find *Nott'e dì* from *Le Malade imaginaire*. In other words, the numbering of both series (and the references to preludes in other notebooks, up to approximately cahiers 35 and XXXV) was done after Nov. 1680 and before the end of 1685. For the first time since his return from Rome, Charpentier composed nothing for several months in 1683. As he recuperated from a serious illness that summer, he apparently numbered the two growing piles of notebooks.

41. Notebook 5, which contains music written for the funerals of LOUIS-JOSEPH, DUKE OF GUISE, and the DOWAGER OF ORLÉANS, was recopied onto a paper that appears nowhere else. The center sheet is Jesuit paper. This suggests that the H. 12 was used for MADEMOISELLE DE GUISE's funeral in Mar. 1688, when Charpentier was music master for the Jesuits. (It cannot be ruled out that H. 12 was also used for Madame de Guise's funeral, although she had requested no pomp.)

42. "Mémoire" of 1726, fols. 13v–14 (the *gros cahier* that contained his "Epitaph"); and notation in H. 479: for *Brilliantes fleurs naissez*, "it is in book G, page 182."

43. Ranum, "Ajouts."

44. This of course presupposes access to H. W. Hitchcock's *Les Œuvres de/ The Works of Marc-Antoine Charpentier, catalogue raisonné* (Paris, 1982); Cessac, *MAC*, especially the tables, pp. 476–525; and Ranum, *Chronologie*.

45. AN, R4 1056*, items 70–76.   46. Dassoucy, *Rimes*, pp. 121–22.

47. For Lully, the Guises, and Mlle. de Montpensier, see La Gorce, pp. 22–56.

48. AN, MC, XXX, 216, Aug. 27, 1672.

49. *Gazette*, 1673, p. 532; compare with *Gazette*, 1665, p. 1066 (DOWAGER OF ORLÉANS and MLLE. ISABELLE D'ALENÇON).

50. John S. Powell, "Charpentier's Music for *Circé* (1675)," *Bulletin Charpentier*, no. 15 (1998).

51. "Mémoire" of 1726, fol. 13. Copied into notebook 9, just before *Judith sive Bethulia*, the piece subsequently was lost along with the outside sheets of the notebook. It is also possible that the *Dies irae* (H. 12) written for Alençon's father, was revived in early 1675. Cahier XVII originally contained a prelude for H. 12.

52. For example, H. 167 is a psalm for a large ensemble and follows immediately after *Circé* in cahier XIX. Thus the motet presumably was composed during the first half of 1675. It is followed by three instrumental preludes, the first two of which were copied out with a finer quill and a lighter ink. The third prelude was for a setting of a text by Father Commire, S.J., apparently lost along with cahier XX. The ink used for this prelude is considerably darker, and the quill was quite stubby. In other words, the devotional music in cahier XIX appears to have been composed for three separate events, all of them perhaps sponsored by one of the THREE JESUIT HOUSES of Paris.

53. "Mémoire" of 1726, fol. 3.

54. A few months later, in H. 258—an *élévation* that seems to be Charpentier's final work for an ailing Mademoiselle de Guise—"I" talks to "Thee," Jesus.

55. Tournoüer, p. 95, who suggests that she made this vow shortly before Oct. 1675. *Judith* relies on a Biblical text that was only read when Sept. had five Sundays, as it did that year. To be exact, in 1675 this specific text was supposed to be recited on Saturday, Sept. 28. It can scarcely be a coincidence that the Florentine agent attended a service at the THEATINES on that very day, MdP, 4672, Sept. 30, 1675. For the "strong woman, see Pierre Le Moyne, *La Gallerie des femmes fortes* (Paris, 1661), especially the "Épitre panégyrique" and pp. 54–67.

56. *Gazette*, 1677, p. 16.

57. "Mémoire" of 1726, fol. 3. *Mors Saülis* (H. 403) ends with a text for the fifth or sixth Sunday after Pentecost, that is, roughly Jul. 1681. *Josué* (H. 404) does indeed seem to be linked to the Jesuits, for the cover of cahier 34, with folio 22 left blank, is made of Jesuit paper, and some of the inner sheets are also Jesuit.

58. Judging from the musicians required, H. 405, and H. 406 were for the Dauphin's Music.

59. This psalm was recited during matins on Thursday; Jan. 1, 1682, fell on a Thursday.

60. Colbert's watermark is found on some of the sheets of paper in cahiers XXVII and XXVIII, which contains pieces written in about 1680 for the Dauphin's Music. Since Charpentier's was a somewhat ad hoc appointment and he was being paid from the Dauphin's own *menus plaisirs*, did Colbert supply his personal paper to Charpentier? See Ranum, "Colbert."

61. Maral, pp. 69–70.

62. The text of H. 187 was recited on the Feast of the Circumcision (Jan. 1) and for Epiphany (Jan. 6). Since these two days were especially dear to devotees of the INFANT JESUS, H. 187 and H. 407, both for two *dessus* (sopranos) and a bass, were probably intended for Mlle. de Guise's devotions of early Jan. 1683.

63. "Mémoire" of 1726, fol. 10.   64. Ranum, "Jesuits."

65. *Gazette*, 1676, p. 718. Charpentier called his work both a "pastorale" and an "eclogue" (*Petite Pastorale, Églogue des bergers*). And he called *Les Arts florissants* (H. 487) both an "opera" and a "pastorale." It is therefore difficult to determine whether Charpentier's pastorale-eclogue was the "opera" the followed the baptism, or whether it served as the prologue to an opera prepared by the impresario to PHILIPPE II D'ORLÉANS.

66. Ranum, "Ajouts."   67. *Mercure*, Je. 1683, pp. 252–68.

68. *La descente d'Orphée aux Enfers*, H. 488, fills the "problematic"cahier that Hitchcock calls "II." Judging from the paper, cahier "II" is the missing cahier 48 and therefore dates from early 1686.

69. BN, ms. fr. 10265, fol. 105v.

70. Berton. Some lines were excised: the assertion that Louis XIV did not cease working, which may have been accurate in early 1686 but certainly did not apply to the days after his surgery; and the final "Ode," a prayer where "I" (the King) speaks to the Lord ("Thee") about his "medications" and his "torments"—material that scarcely lent itself to a courtly entertainment.

71. Nuitter et Thoinan, pp. 239–40 (Mar. 1672); Delamare, I, p. 474, Apr. 30, 1673.

72. *Mercure*, Je. 1683, pp. 252–68.   73. Ranum, "Foyer."

74. For his Italian music, see "Mémoire" of 1726, fols. 14v–15.

75. Ranum, "Ajouts."

76. *Conversazzione* can also be translated as "social intercourse," that is, the sort of polite conversation that characterized the seventeenth-century *salon*.

77. Ranum, "Foyer."   78. "Mémoire" of 1726, fols. 14v–15.

79. Michel Le Moël, "Un foyer d'italianisme ... Nicolas Mathieu, curé de Saint-André-des-Arts," *Recherches*, 3 (1963), pp. 43–48.

80. Du Bois, *Lettres*, "Épître."

81. Charpentier copied this mass onto paper F, which he used for cahiers 27–28 (spring 1680) and cahier XXXIII (spring 1683), Ranum, *Chronologie*, pp. 31–32.

82. Cessac, MAC, pp. 433–36.

83. V. de Seilhac, *L'Abbé Dubois, premier ministre de Louis XV* (Paris, 1862), I, pp. 189–90. These distinctions between "savant" and "erudite" were at the foundation of Chartres' education.

84. Brossard, pp. 275–76. For Lecerf de la Viéville, the "savant" aspect of Charpentier's music was intolerable: see Cessac, MAC, pp. 48–49, for a summary of Lecerf's position.

85. Dassoucy, *Aventures*, pp. 251–53.

86. Library of the School of the Beaux-Arts, ms. 556, carton II (my appreciation to J. de La Gorce for this reference).

87. AN, Y 4003A, avis des parents, Tuition Édouard, Feb. 20, 1685.

88. Du Bois, *Lettres*, "Épître."   89. Du Bois, *Sermons*, "Épître."

90. In Ranum, *Chronologie*, paper "✝," pp. 12, 57.   91. Brossard, *Catalogue*, pp. 275–76.

92. "Mémoire" of 1726, fol. 13v, for the contents of the *gros cahier*.

93. Univ. of Leyden, Library, BPL 286/IV/41 (André Pineau, a protégé and factotum of the Duchess of La Trémouille, Jul. 10, 1648, transcribed and shared with me by Jean-Luc Tulot).

94. Ranum, "Titon."

95. Quebec, Archives of the Hôtel Dieu, T 11, C 925.

96. Ranum, "Jesuits."

97. For an overview of these "energies" and their relationship to Expression, see Ranum, *Orator*, pp. 326–42.

98. Cahier LIV, H. 64: "In supremæ comme *pange lingua*, en ajustant quelque chose pour accorder la quantité des syllabes."

99. Cahier LV, H. 120, instructions for both the copyist and the person directing this special commission for Easter, fol. 2v, for example: "Il faut escrire ce couplet separé du precedent" (This couplet must be written separately from the preceding one); cahier LVIII "Icy quelqu'un chantera le troisieme couplet, auquel le chœur repondra *alleluya*,..." (Here someone will sing the third couplet, and the choir will reply *Alleluia*:; cahier LXVIII, H. 269, "Il faut mettre dans toutes les parties *Pie Jesu tacet, hormis celles qui les chantent*" (Into every voice one must put '*Pie Jesu, tacet*, except for the people who are singing those words' "); and at the end of the *Agnus Dei*, he noted: "Icy il faut recoppier dans toutes les parties le 1er *Agnus* et ajouter à la fin le *sempiternam* suivant" (Here one must recopy all the parts of the first *Agnus*, and add at the end the following *sempiternam*).

100. Ranum, "Jesuits"; and C. Jane Lowe, "Charpentier and the Jesuits at St. Louis," *Seventeenth-Century French Studies*, 15 (1993), pp. 297–314.

101. Lecerf, II, p. 297.

102. "Mémoire" of 1726, fols. 13v–14. See Cessac, MAC, pp. 12–15, 364–65, 425–27, for the text and comments; and Françoise Waquet, "*L'Epitaphium Carpentarii*, Étude littéraire," *Bulletin Charpentier*, no. 8 (Jan. 1993), pp. 2–7.

103. Pope Marcellus II had attempted to keep partsong out of churches, which would have made it impossible for oratorios, among them CARISSIMI's, to be performed in the little chapel behind San Marcello in seventeenth century Rome. In a vision Saint Ignatius of Antioch had seen angels singing, and at the Jesuit Church of Saint Ignatius in Rome, singers performed polychoral masses beneath a vault in *trompe-l'œil* where singing angels hover around Ignatius Loyola as he is carried to Heaven.

104. Du Pradel, p. 214; AN, MC, VI, 588, Oct. 7, 1688 (Armand-Jean: rue Dauphine).

105. For the lessons and their chronology, including Charpentier's participation, see Ranum, "Loulié," 1987, pp. 67–75.

106. Ranum, "Titon."   107. Ranum, "Loulié," 1987, p. 71.

108. Seilhac, p. 189 (4).

109. In the margin of his copy Loulié marked the differences between his personal copy and the one used by Chartres. Ranum, "Loulié" (1987), p. 72. For the model teacher and the educational program, Seilhac, pp. 185–205.

110. Jules Écorcheville, *De Lulli à Rameau 1690–1730, l'Esthetique musicale* (Paris, 1906), pp. 55 ff.

111. For example, H. 18, H. 21, H. 23, H. 244, H. 246, H. 247, H. 253, H. 258, and H. 333. "Of the Jesuits" was added to H. 27, H. 193.

112. Cahiers VI–XI are on Jesuit paper. In addition to numerous short devotional pieces, these notebooks contain a mass and a *Te Deum* for large ensembles, and a plainsong setting of Father Commire's poem about Saint Nicaise. References to Dun and Beaupuis, opera singers who performed at Saint-Louis, are scattered throughout. This recopying appears to slightly postdate cahier 63, which contains works for Aug. 1692 and early 1693. (That is to say, cahier IX, H. 160, contains an allusion to a prelude in cahier 63 that was suitable for this psalm.)

ABBREVIATED CITATIONS
of materials cited in more than one portrait

AAE—Archives des Affaires Étrangères.

AD—Archives départementales.

AD-77—Archives départementales, Seine-et-Marne.

AG—Archives of the Jesuits, Rome.

Archenholz—Johann Archenholz, *Mémoires concernant Christine* ... (Amsterdam, 1751–60).

ASV—Archivio Segreto Vaticano, Rome.

Bastille—*Archives de la Bastille*, ed. François Ravaisson-Mollien (Paris, 1866–1904).

Berton—Nathalie Berton, "L'*Idyle sur le retour de la santé du roy* (H. 489), livret de Madame Deshoulières," *Bulletin Charpentier*, no. 17 (2000).

Bildt—Baron de Bildt, *Christine de Suède et le Cardinal Azzolino* (Paris, 1899).

Biver—Paul and Marie-Louise Biver, *Abbayes, monastères, couvents de femmes* (Paris, 1975).

Blémur—Marie-Jacqueline Boüette de Blémur, *L'Année bénédictine, ou les vies des saints de l'ordre de St Benoist* ... (Paris, 1667).

BN—Bibliothèque nationale de France, Paris.

Bremond—Henri Bremond, *Histoire littéraire du Sentiment religieux en France depuis la fin des guerres de religion jusqu'à nos jours* (Paris, 1935).

Brice—Germain Brice, *Description nouvelle ... de la ville de Paris* (Paris, 1684).

Brossard, *Catalogue*—Sébastien de Brossard, *Catalogue des livres de musique*, published as *La Collection Sébastien de Brossard, 1655–1730*, ed. Yolande de Brossard (Paris, 1994).

Brossard (Y. de)—Yolande de Brossard, *Sébastien de Brossard, théoricien et compositeur (1655–1730)* (Paris, 1987).

Bussy Rabutin—Roger de Rabutin, *Correspondance de Roger de Rabutin, comte de Bussy (1666–1693)*, ed. L. Lalanne (Paris, 1858).

BV—Biblioteca Vaticana: Library of the Vatican, Rome.

Carro—A. Carro, *Histoire de Meaux* (Paris: 1989, facsimile of 1865 edition).

Cent ans—Madeleine Jurgens and Elizabeth Maxwell-Miller, *Cent ans de recherches sur Molière* (Paris, 1963).

Cessac, MAC—Catherine Cessac, *Marc-Antoine Charpentier* (Paris, 1988).

Chabod—Thomas-François Chabod, Marquis of Saint-Maurice, *Lettres sur la Cour de Louis XIV*, ed. Jean Lemoine (Paris, 1910).

Choisy—François-Timoléon de Choisy, *Mémoires*, ed. Champollion, Mémoires relatifs à l'histoire de France, directed by Michaud and Poujoulat (Paris, 1881).

Clarke—Janet Clarke, "Music at the Guénégaud Theatre, 1673–1680," *Seventeenth-century French Studies*, 12 (1990).

Comédie, Reg.— Archives de la Comédie Française, registers.

Conley—John J. Conley, S.J., *The Suspicion of Virtue, Women Philosophers in Neoclassical France* (Ithaca, 2002).

Crussaire—André Crussaire, *Un Médecin au XVIIᵉ siècle, le Docteur Vallant* (Paris, 1910).

DB—Dossiers Bleus, Manuscript Department, Bibliothèque nationale de France, Paris.

DBF—*Dictionnaire de biographie française*....directed by J. Balteau *et al.* (Paris, 1933–).

Dangeau—Philippe de Courcillon, Marquis de Dangeau, ed. Soulié *et al.* (Paris, 1854–1860).

Dassoucy, *Aventures*—Charles Coypeau d'Assoucy, *Les Aventures burlesques de Das-soucy*, ed. Émile Colombey (Paris, 1858).

Dassoucy, *Rimes*—Charles Coypeau d'Assoucy, *Les rimes redoublées de M. Dassoucy* (Paris 1671), BN, Rés. Ye 3489 and Rés. R 1936. (R. 1936 includes materials about Charpentier that are missing from Ye 3489.)

De La Gorce, *Lully*—Jérôme de La Gorce, *Jean-Baptiste Lully* (Paris, 2002).

Delamare,—Nicolas Delamare, *Traité de Police* (Paris, 1722–38).

Dethan—Georges Dethan, *La vie de Gaston d'Orléans* (Paris, 1992).

Doncourt—Simon de Doncourt, *Remarques historiques sur l'Eglise et la Paroisse de Saint-Sulpice* (Paris, 1773).

Du Bois, *Conformité*—Philippe Goibaut du Bois, *Conformité de la Conduite de l'église de France, pour ramener les protestants, avec celle de l'église d'Afrique, pour ramener les donatistes à l'église catholique* (Paris, 1685).

Du Bois, *Lettres*, "Épître"—Philippe Goibaut du Bois, *Les Lettres de saint Augustin* (Paris, 1684), "Épître" to Mlle. de Guise.

Du Bois, *Sermons*, "Épître"—Philippe Goibaut du Bois, *Les Sermons de saint Augustin* (Paris, 1694), "Épître" to Mme. de Guise.

Du Pradel—Abraham du Pradel (Nicolas de Blegny), *Le Livre commode des adresses de Paris pour 1692*, ed. E. Fournier (Paris, 1878).

Fleury—Claude Fleury, *Les Devoirs des maîtres et des domestiques* (Paris, 1688).

Franckenstein—C. G. Franckenstein, *Histoire des intrigues galantes de la Reine Christine de Suède et de sa cour pendant son séjour à Rome* (Amsterdam, 1697).

Gazette—*Gazette de France*.

La Fontaine—Jean de La Fontaine, *Œuvres complètes*, ed. Pierre Clarac (Paris, 1958).

La Grange—B. E. Young and G. P. Young, *Le Registre de La Grange, 1659–1685* (Paris, 1947).

Langlois—Ch.-V. Langlois, *Les Hôtels de Clisson, de Guise et de Rohan-Soubise au Marais* (Paris, 1922).

Lecerf—Jean-Laurent Lecerf de la Viéville de Fresneuse, *Comparaison de la Musique italienne et de la Musique françoise* (Brussels, 1705–06).

Le Gendre—Louis Le Gendre, *Mémoires*, ed. M. Roux (Paris, 1863).

Le Maguet—Paul-Émile Le Maguet, *Le Monde médicale parisien sous le Grand Roi* (Paris, 1899).

Loret—Jean Loret, *La Muze historique*, ed. Ch.-L. Livet (Paris, 1857–78).

Loret's successors—*Les continuateurs de Loret, Lettres en vers de Mayolas, Robinet, Boursault, Perdou de Subligny, Laurent et autres (1665–1689)*, ed. J. de Rothschild (Paris, 1881–82).

Maral—Alexandre Maral, *La Chapelle Royale de Versailles sous Louis XIV* (Sprimont, 2002).

Marie du Bois—Marie Du Bois, *Mémoires de Marie Du Bois, sieur de Lestourmière ... 1647–1676*, ed. L. Grandmaison (Vendôme, 1936).

Marion—Marcel Marion, *Dictionnaire des institutions de la France* (Paris, 1976).

MdP—Florence, Archivio di Stato, Mediceo del Principate.

Mélèse—Pierre Mélèse, *Un homme de lettres au temps du grand roi, Donneau de Visé, fondateur du Mercure* (Paris, 1936).

"Mémoire" of 1726—"Mémoire des ouvrages de … Mr Charpentier," BN, Rés., Vmb. ms. 71. (This was summarized by H. W. Hitchcock, "Marc-Antoine Charpentier, Mémoire and Index," *Recherches*, 23 (1985), pp. 5–44).

Mercure—*Mercure galant*.

Mesnard—Jean Mesnard, *Pascal et les Roannez* (Paris, 1965).

Montpensier—Anne-Marie-Louise d'Orléans, Duchess of Montpensier, *Mémoire*, ed. A. Chéruel (Paris, 1858).

Moréri—Louis Moréri, *Grand Dictionnaire historique*, which went through numerous editions. Most eighteenth-century editions contain the articles cited in this book.

Motteville—Françoise Bertaut de Motteville, *Mémoires de Madame de Motteville sur Anne d'Autriche et sa cour*, ed. M. F. Riaux (Paris, 1886).

Nuitter and Thoinan—Charles Nuitter and Ernest Thoman, *Les Origines de l'opéra français* (Paris, 1886).

Patin—Gui Patin, *Lettres*, ed. J. H. Reveillé-Parise (Paris, 1846).

PO—Pièces Originales, Manuscript Department, Bibliothèque nationale de France.

Pourtraicts—*Pourtraicts de la Cour* (Cologne, 1667).

Powell—John S. Powell, *Music and Theatre in France, 1600–1680* (Oxford, 2000).

Racine—Jean Racine, *Œuvres complètes*, ed. R. Picard (Paris, 1952).

Ranum, "Brossard,"—Patricia M. Ranum, "À la recherche de son avenir: Sébastien de Brossard à Paris, 1678 à 1687," *Sébastien de Brossard Musicien*, ed. Jean Duron (Paris, 1998), pp. 283–306.

Ranum, *Chronologie*—Patricia M. Ranum, *Vers une chronologie des œuvres de Marc-Antoine Charpentier* (Baltimore, 1994).

Ranum, "Colbert"—Patricia M. Ranum, "Jean-Baptiste Colbert: un protecteur de Marc-Antoine Charpentier?," *Bulletin Charpentier*, no. 14 (1997).

Ranum, "Entrée"—Patricia Ranum, "L'Entrée des manuscrits de Marc-Antoine Charpentier à la Bibliothèque du Roi," *Bulletin Charpentier*, no. 9 (1993).

Ranum, "Feindre"—Patricia M. Ranum, "'Feindre des poutres pour faire simmetrie aux vrayes': la rénovation de l'Hôtel de Guise, 1666–1667," *Histoire et Archives*, no. 10 (2001), pp. 6–60.

Ranum, "Foyer"—Patricia R. Ranum, "Un foyer d'italianisme chez les Guises: quelques réflexions sur les *oratorios* de Charpentier," *Bulletin Charpentier*, no. 12 (1995).

Ranum, "Jesuits"—Patricia M. Ranum, "Marc-Antoine Charpentier compositeur pour les Jésuites, 1687–1698: quelques considérations programmatiques," *Bulletin Charpentier*, no. 18 (2001).

Ranum, "Loulié"—"Étienne Loulié (1654–1702), Musicien de Mademoiselle de Guise, Pédagogue et Théoricien," *Recherches*, 25 (1987), pp. 27–76; 26 (1988–90), pp. 5–49.

Ranum, "Lully"—Patricia M. Ranum, "Lully Plays Deaf: rereading the evidence on his privilege, *Lully Studies*, ed. John Hajdu Heyer (Cambridge, U.K., 2000), pp. 15–31.

Ranum, "Mercy"—Patricia M. Ranum, "'Il y a aujourd'hui Musique à la Mercy,' Mademoiselle de Guise et les Mercédaires de la rue du Chaume," *Bulletin Charpentier*, no. 13 (1996).

Ranum, *Orator*—Patricia M. Ranum, *The Harmonic Orator* (Hillsdale, N.Y., 2001).

Ranum, "Portrait"—Patricia M. Ranum, "Un portrait présumé de Marc-Antoine Charpentier," *Bulletin Charpentier*, no. 4 (1991).

Ranum, "Quelques ajouts"—Patricia M. Ranum, "Quelques ajouts au Corpus Charpentier, *Bulletin Charpentier*, no. 9 (1993).

Ranum, "Quenouille"—Patricia M. Ranum, "Mademoiselle de Guise, ou les défis de la quenouille," *XVIIe Siècle*, 36 (1984).

Ranum, "Ruel"—Patricia M. Ranum, "Marc-Antoine Charpentier et la 'Feste de Ruel,' (1685)," *XVIIe Siècle*, 40 (1988).

Ranum, "Servitude"—Patricia M. Ranum, "A Sweet Servitude: a Musician's Life at the Court of Mademoiselle de Guise," *Early Music*, 15 (1987).

Ranum, "Titon"—Patricia Ranum, "Titon du Tillet: le premier 'biographe' de Marc-Antoine Charpentier," *Bulletin Charpentier*, no. 6 (1992).

Ranum–Cessac—Patricia M. Ranum and Catherine Cessac, "'Trois favoirs d'ut ré mi fa sol la': les Comédiens français taquinent leurs confrères italiens, *Bulletin Charpentier*, no. 15 (1998).

Rodocanachi—E. Rodocanachi, *Les Infortunes d'une Petite-Fille de France, Marguerite d'Orléans, Grande Duchesse de Toscane* (Paris, n.d.).

Rombault—Abbé Rombault, "Élisabeth d'Orléans, Duchesse de Guise et d'Alençon, (1646–1696)," *Bulletin de l'Orme*, 12 (1893).

Rome, Stati d'Anime—Rome, Archives of the Vicariato, Stati d'Anime for the different parishes of Rome.

Tournoüer—H. Tournoüer, "Élisabeth d'Orléans, Duchesse de Guise et d'Alençon," *Bulletin de l'Orne*, 61 (1942).

Saint-Simon—Louis de Rouvoy, duc de Saint-Simon, *Mémoires*, ed. Yves Coirault (Paris, 1983–).

Sauval—Henri Sauval, *Histoire et recherches des Antiquités de la ville de Paris* (Paris, 1724).

Scruggs—Charles E. Scruggs, *Charles Dassoucy: Adventures in the Age of Louis XIV* (Lanham, Md., 1984).

Sévigné—Marie de Rabutin-Chantal de, *Lettres*. Since several editions exist, the date of the letter is given, rather than the volume and page.

Spanheim—Ezekiel Spanheim, *Relation de la Cour de France en 1690*, ed. E. Bourgeois (Paris, 1900).

Stockholm—Royal Archives, Stockholm, Azzolino collection.

Tallemant—Gédéon Tallement des Réaux, *Historiettes*, ed. G. Mongrédien (Paris, 1932?–34?).

Turin—Turin, Archivio di Stato.

Vicariato, "Anime"—Archivio Storico Diocesano del Vicariato di Roma, "Anime."

Viel—Jean-François Viel, "Les Charpentier avant Charpentier," *Bulletin Charpentier*, no. 7 (1992).

Weavers—R. L. and N. W. Weaver, *A Chronology of Music in the Florentine Theater, 1590–1750* (Detroit, 1978).

INDEX

None of the subjects of portraits are listed in this index: the SMALL CAPITALS in which their name is set throughout the book permit easy recognition of passages about them.

Several individuals with the same first name are grouped (indicated by *diverse*) and members of a family who pass rapidly through this gallery are grouped under "family," because the family usually counts more than the individual. Names in the notes have not been indexed.